WHEN WORLDS BEGIN

A COLLECTION OF FOUR FANTASY NOVELS

MEGAN O'RUSSELL

Ink Worlds Press

Visit our website at www.MeganORussell.com

This book is a work of fiction. Names, characters, places, and incidents either are products of the author's imagination or are used fictitiously. Any resemblance to actual persons, living or dead, events, or locales is entirely coincidental.

WHEN WORLDS BEGIN

Ember and Stone
Ena of Ilbrea, Book One

Girl of Glass
Girl of Glass, Book One

The Tethering
The Tethering, Book One

The Girl Without Magic
The Chronicles of Maggie Trent, Book One

EMBER AND STONE

ENA OF ILBREA, BOOK ONE

Courage to topple kingdoms.

1

The crack of the whip sent the birds scattering into the sky. They cawed their displeasure at the violence of the men below as they flew over the village and to the mountains beyond.

The whip cracked again.

Aaron did well. He didn't start to moan until the fourth lash. By the seventh, he screamed in earnest.

No one had given him a belt to bite down on. There hadn't been time when the soldiers hauled him from his house and tied him to the post in the square.

I clutched the little wooden box of salve hidden in my pocket, letting the corners bite deep into my palm.

The soldier passed forty lashes, not caring that Aaron's back had already turned to pulp.

I squeezed my way to the back of the crowd, unwilling to watch Aaron's blood stain the packed dirt.

Behind the rest of the villagers, children cowered in their mother's skirts, hiding from the horrors the Guilds' soldiers brought with them.

I didn't know how many strokes Aaron had been sentenced to. I didn't want to know. I made myself stop counting how many times the whip sliced his back.

Bida, Aaron's wife, wept on the edge of the crowd. When his screams stopped, hers grew louder.

The women around Bida held her back, keeping her out of reach of the soldiers.

My stomach stung with the urge to offer comfort as she watched her husband being beaten by the men in black uniforms. But, with the salve tucked in my pocket, hiding in the back was safest.

I couldn't give Bida the box unless Aaron survived. Spring hadn't fully arrived, and the plants Lily needed to make more salves still hadn't bloomed. The tiny portion of the stuff hidden in my pocket was worth more than someone's life, especially if that person wasn't going to survive even with Lily's help.

Lily's orders had been clear—wait and see if Aaron made it through. Give Bida the salve if he did. If he didn't, come back home and hide the wooden box under the floorboards for the next poor soul who might need it.

Aaron fell to the ground. Blood leaked from a gash under his arm.

The soldier raised his whip again.

I sank farther into the shadows, trying to comfort myself with the beautiful lie that I could never be tied to the post in the village square, though I knew the salve clutched in my hand would see me whipped at the post as quickly as whatever offense the soldiers had decided Aaron had committed.

When my fingers had gone numb from gripping the box, the soldier stopped brandishing his whip and turned to face the crowd.

"We did not come here to torment you," the soldier said. "We came here to protect Ilbrea. We came here to protect the Guilds. We are here to provide peace to all the people of this great country. This man committed a crime, and he has been punished. Do not think me cruel for upholding the law." He wrapped the bloody whip around his hand and led the other nine soldiers out of the square.

Ten soldiers. It had only taken ten of them to walk into our village and drag Aaron from his home. Ten men to tie him to the post and leave us all helpless as they beat a man who'd lived among us all his life.

The soldiers disappeared, and the crowd shifted in toward Aaron. I couldn't hear him crying or moaning over the angry mutters of the crowd.

His wife knelt by his side, wailing.

I wound my way forward, ignoring the stench of fear that surrounded the villagers.

Aaron lay on the ground, his hands still tied around the post. His back had been flayed open by the whip. His flesh looked more like something for a butcher to deal with than an illegal healer like me.

I knelt by his side, pressing my fingers to his neck to feel for a pulse.

Nothing.

I wiped my fingers on the cleanest part of Aaron's shirt I could find and weaved my way back out of the crowd, still clutching the box of salve in my hand.

Carrion birds gathered on the rooftops near the square, scenting the fresh blood in the air. They didn't know Aaron wouldn't be food for them. The villagers of Harane had yet to fall so low as to leave our own out as a feast for the birds.

There was no joy in the spring sun as I walked toward Lily's house on the eastern edge of the village.

I passed by the tavern, which had already filled with men who didn't mind we hadn't reached midday. I didn't blame them for hiding in there. If they could find somewhere away from the torment of the soldiers, better on them for seizing it. I only hoped there weren't any soldiers laughing inside the tavern's walls.

I followed the familiar path home. Along our one, wide dirt road, past the few shops Harane had to offer, to the edge of the village where only fields and pastures stood between us and the forest that reached up the eastern mountains' slopes.

It didn't take long to reach the worn wooden house with the one giant tree towering out front. It didn't take long to reach anywhere in the tiny village of Harane.

Part of me hated knowing every person who lived nearby. Part of me wished the village were smaller. Then maybe we'd fall off the Guilds' maps entirely.

As it was, the Guilds only came when they wanted to collect our taxes, to steal our men to fight their wars, or to find some other sick pleasure in inflicting agony on people who wanted nothing more than to survive. Or if their business brought them far enough south on the mountain road they had to pass through our home on their way to torment someone else.

I allowed myself a moment to breathe before facing Lily. I blinked away the images of Aaron covered in blood and shoved them into a dark corner with the rest of the wretched things it was better not to ponder.

Lily barely glanced up as I swung open the gate and stepped into the back garden. Dirt covered her hands and skirt. Her shoulders were hunched from the hours spent planting our summer garden. She never allowed me to help with the task. Everything had to be carefully planned, keeping the vegetables toward the outermost edges. Hiding the plants she could be hanged for in the center, where soldiers were less likely to spot the things she grew to protect the people of our village. The people the soldiers were so eager to hurt.

"Did he make it?" Lily stretched her shoulders back and brushed the dirt off her weathered hands.

I held the wooden box out as my response. Blood stained the corners. It wasn't Aaron's blood. It was mine. Cuts marked my hand where I'd squeezed the box too tightly.

Lily glared at my palm. "You'd better go in and wrap your hand. If you let it get infected, I'll have to treat you with the salve, and you know we're running out."

I tucked the box back into my pocket and went inside, not bothering to argue that I could heal from a tiny cut. I didn't want to look into Lily's wrinkled face and see the glimmer of pity in her eyes.

The inside of the house smelled of herbs and dried flowers. Their familiar scent did nothing to drive the stench of blood and fear from my nose.

A pot hung over the stove, waiting with whatever Lily had made for breakfast.

My stomach churned at the thought of eating. I needed to get out. Out of the village, away from the soldiers.

I pulled up the loose floorboard by the stove and tucked the salve in between the other boxes, tins, and vials. I grabbed my bag off the long, wooden table and shoved a piece of bread and a waterskin into it for later. I didn't bother grabbing a coat or shawl. I didn't care about getting cold.

I have to get out.

I was back through the door and in the garden a minute later. Lily didn't even look up from her work. "If you're running into the forest, you had better come back with something good."

"I will," I said. "I'll bring you back all sorts of wonderful things. Just make sure you save some dinner for me."

I didn't need to ask her to save me food. In all the years I'd lived with her, Lily had never let me go hungry. But she was afraid I would run away into the forest and never return. Or maybe it was me that feared I might disappear into the trees and never come back. Either way, I felt myself relax as I stepped out of the garden and turned my feet toward the forest.

The mountains rose up beyond the edge of the trees, fierce towers I could never hope to climb. No one else from the village would ever even dream of trying such a thing.

The soldiers wouldn't enter the woods. The villagers rarely dared to go near them. The forest was where darkness and solitude lay. A quiet place where the violence of the village couldn't follow me.

I skirted farmers' fields and picked my way through the pastures. No one bothered me as I climbed over the fences they built to keep in their scarce amounts of sheep and cows.

No one kept much livestock. They couldn't afford it in the first place. And besides, if the soldiers saw that one farmer had too many animals, they would take the beasts as taxes. Safer to be poor. Better for your belly to go empty than for the soldiers to think you had something to give.

I moved faster as I got past the last of the farmhouses and beyond the reach of the stench of animal dung.

When I was a very little girl, my brother had told me that the woods were ruled by ghosts. That none of the villagers dared to cut down the trees or venture into their shelter for fear of being taken by the dead and given a worse fate than even the Guilds could provide.

I'd never been afraid of ghosts, and I'd wandered through the woods often enough to be certain that no spirits roamed the eastern mountains.

When I first started going into the forest, I convinced myself I was braver than everyone else in Harane. I was an adventurer, and they were cowards.

Maybe I just knew better. Maybe I knew that no matter what ghosts did, they could never match the horrors men inflict on each other. What I'd seen them do to each other.

By the time I was a hundred feet into the trees, I could no longer see the village behind me. I couldn't smell anything but the fresh scent of damp earth as the little plants fought for survival in the fertile spring ground. I knew my way through the woods well enough I didn't need to bother worrying about which direction to go. It was more a question of which direction I wanted to chase the gentle wind.

I could go and find fungi for Lily to make into something useful, or I could climb. If I went quickly, I would have time to climb and still be able to find something worth Lily getting herself hanged for.

Smiling to myself, I headed due east toward the steepest part of the mountains near our village. Dirt soon covered the hem of my skirt, and mud squelched beneath my shoes, creeping in through the cracked leather of the soles. I didn't mind so much. What the cold could do to me was nothing more than a refreshing chance to prove I was still alive. Life existed outside the village, and there was beauty beyond our battered walls.

Bits of green peeked through the brown of the trees as new buds forced their way out of the branches.

I stopped, staring up at the sky, marveling at the beauty hidden within our woods.

Birds chirped overhead. Not the angry cawing of birds of death, but the beautiful songs of lovebirds who had nothing more to worry about than tipping their wings up toward the sky.

A gray and blue bird burst from a tree, carrying his song deeper into the forest.

A stream gurgled to one side of me. The snap of breaking branches came from the other. I didn't change my pace as the crackling came closer.

I headed south to a steeper slope where I had to use my hands to pull myself up the rocks.

I moved faster, outpacing the one who lumbered through the trees behind me. A rock face cut through the forest, blocking my path. I dug my fingers into the cracks in the stone, pulling myself up. Careful to keep my legs from being tangled in my skirt, I found purchase on the rock with the soft toes of my boots. In a few quick movements, I pushed myself up over the top of the ledge. I leapt to my feet and ran to the nearest tree, climbing up to the highest thick branch.

I sat silently on my perch, waiting to see what sounds would come from below.

A rustle came from the base of the rock, followed by a long string of inventive curses.

I bit my lips together, not allowing myself to call out.

The cursing came again.

"Of all the slitching, vile—" the voice from below growled.

I leaned back against the tree, closing my eyes, reveling in my last few moments of solitude. Those hints of freedom were what I loved most about being able to climb. Going up a tree, out of reach of the things that would catch me.

"Ena," the voice called. "Ena."

I didn't answer.

"Ena, are you going to leave me down here?"

My lips curved into a smile as I bit back my laughter. "I didn't ask you to follow me. You can just go back the way you came."

"I don't want to go back," he said. "Let me come up. At least show me how you did it."

"If you want to chase me, you'd better learn to climb."

I let him struggle for a few more minutes until he threatened to find a pick and crack through the rock wall. I glanced down to find him three feet off the ground, his face bright red as he tried to climb.

"Jump down," I said, not wanting him to fall and break something. I could have hauled him back to the village, but I didn't fancy the effort.

"Help me get up," he said.

"Go south a bit. You'll find an easier path."

I listened to the sounds of him stomping off through the trees, enjoying the bark against my skin as I waited for him to find the way up.

It only took him a few minutes to loop back around to stand under my perch.

Looking at Cal stole my will to flee. His blond hair glistened in the sun. He shaded his bright blue eyes as he gazed up at me.

"Are you happy now?" he said. "I'm covered in dirt."

"If you wanted to be clean, you shouldn't have come into the woods. I never ask you to follow me."

"It would have been wrong of me not to. You shouldn't be coming out here by yourself."

I didn't let it bother me that he thought it was too dangerous for me to be alone in the woods. It was nice to have someone worry about me. Even if he was worried about ghosts that didn't exist.

"What do you think you'd be able to do to help me anyway?" I said.

He stared up at me, hurt twisting his perfect brow.

Cal looked like a god, or something made at the will of the Guilds themselves. His chiseled jaw held an allure to it, the rough stubble on his cheeks luring my fingers to touch its texture.

I twisted around on my seat and dropped down to the ground, reveling in his gasp as I fell.

"You really need to get more used to the woods," I said. "It's a good place to hide."

"What would I have to hide from?" Cal's eyes twinkled, offering a hint of teasing that drew me toward him.

I touched the stubble on his chin, tracing the line of his jaw.

"There are plenty of things to hide from, fool." I turned to tramp farther into the woods.

"Ena," he called after me, "you shouldn't be going so far from home."

"Then don't follow me. Go back." I knew he would follow.

I had known when I passed by his window in the tavern on my way through the village. He always wanted to be near me. That was the beauty of Cal.

I veered closer to the stream.

Cal kept up, though he despised getting his boots muddy.

I always chose the more difficult path to make sure he knew I could outpace him. It was part of our game on those trips into the forest.

I leapt across the stream to a patch of fresh moss just beginning to take advantage of spring.

"Ena." Cal jumped the water and sank down onto the moss I had sought.

I shoved him off of the green and into the dirt.

He growled.

I didn't bother trying to hide my smile. I pulled out tufts of the green moss, tucking them into my bag for Lily.

"If you don't want me to follow you," Cal said, "you can tell me not to whenever you like."

"The forest doesn't belong to me, Cal. You can go where you choose."

He grabbed both my hands and tugged me toward him. I tipped onto him and he shifted, letting me fall onto my back. I caught a glimpse of the sun peering down through the new buds of emerald leaves, and then he was kissing me.

His taste of honey and something a bit deeper filled me. And I forgot about whips and Lily and men bleeding and soldiers coming to kill us.

There was nothing but Cal and me. And the day became beautiful.

3

I let Cal follow me up and down the mountain for hours. Cal filled the silence with news of everyone in the village. His family owned the tavern, so all news, both the happy and the terrible, passed through the walls of his home. He didn't know what the people were saying about Aaron yet. He'd followed me before anyone had grown drunk enough to loose their tongue.

"Les had better be careful, or he's going to be on the hunt for a new wife," Cal laughed.

I forced a chuckle. I hadn't been paying close enough attention to hear what Les had done this time.

I cut through a dense patch of bushes, trying to find where treasures would grow when summer neared. I didn't mind the twigs clawing at me or the mud clinging to my clothes.

Cal didn't mention his displeasure at being dirty. He was too content being with me.

I let him hold my hand, savoring the feel of his skin against mine. His warmth burned away the rest of the fear the soldiers had left lodged near my lungs.

Cal pulled me close to his side, winding his arm around my waist.

"I can't go home without proper goodies for Lily." I wriggled free from Cal's grasp.

I followed a game trail farther up the mountain, searching for evergreens whose new buds could help cure the stomach ills that always floated around the village in the spring. By the time the peak of the afternoon passed, I had enough in my bag to please Lily and had spent enough time climbing to give myself a hope of sleeping that night. I turned west, beginning the long trek home.

"We don't have to go back." Cal laced his fingers through mine.

"You think you'd survive in the woods?"

"With you by my side?" His hands moved to my waist. He held me close, swaying in time to music neither of us could hear. He pressed his lips to my forehead. "I think we could stay out here forever." He kissed my nose and cheeks before his lips finally found mine.

My heart raced as he pulled me closer, pressing my body against his.

"Cal"—I pulled an inch away, letting the cool air blow between us—"we have to get back. Lily won't be happy if I'm out too long."

"What'll she do? Scowl at you?"

"Kick me out, more like." I started back down the mountainside. "I don't fancy sleeping in the mud."

I'd lived with Lily for more than half my life, but that didn't make the old healer obligated to keep me a day longer than she wanted to.

Cal caught me in his arms, twisted me toward him, and held me tighter. He brushed his lips against mine. His tongue teased my mouth, luring me deeper into the kiss.

I sank into his arms, reveling in the feel of his hard muscles against me.

He ran his fingers along my sides, sending shivers up my spine.

I sighed as his lips found my neck and trailed out to my shoulder.

"We have to go," I murmured.

Cal wound his fingers through mine. "Let's hide in the wood forever."

"Cal—"

"I love you, Ena." A glimmer of pure bliss lit his eyes.

"I'm going," I said. "Come with me or find your own way back."

Cal pressed his lips to my forehead. "Lead the way."

If I hadn't known him so well, I might not have heard the hint of hurt in his voice.

I didn't want to hurt Cal, but I didn't have anything of myself to offer him. It was easy for Cal to declare his love. He had a solid roof, a business to inherit, a family who cared for him. I was nothing but an orphan inker kept from sleeping in the mud by the goodwill of an ornery old woman.

Cal followed me silently down the slope of the mountain.

I stopped by a fallen tree. The stench of its rot cut through the scent of spring.

"You're the best part of the village." The words tumbled out of my mouth before I'd thought through them.

"I guess that's something. Better than anyone else has gotten out of you."

"Better than they ever will."

His boots thumped on the ground as he ran a few steps to catch up to me. I didn't fight him as he laced his fingers through mine and pressed his lips to my temple. I didn't slow my pace as I started walking again either.

I hadn't been lying—we needed to be heading back to the village. As much as I loved the woods, I didn't fancy being in the trees at night.

The villagers and soldiers might have avoided the forest and mountains because of ghost stories, but their foolishness didn't make the woods entirely safe. I could hear the howls of the wolves at night from Lily's loft where I slept. And farm animals had been lost to creatures far larger than wolves. I didn't fancy having to hide up a tree, shivering as I waited for the dawn. I didn't know if Cal would be able to make it high enough in a tree to be safe.

I let my mind wander as we reached the gentler slopes toward the base of the mountain, wondering over all the terrifying animals that could be hiding just out of sight. Dug into a den that reached below our feet. Hiding in the brush where I couldn't spot them.

A shiver of something ran up my spine.

"You should have brought something warmer." Cal let go of my hand to take off his coat.

"I'm fine." I searched the shadows, trying to find whatever trick of the forest had set my nerves on edge.

Trees rustled to the south, the sound too large to be a bird and too gentle to be death speeding toward us.

I stopped, tugging on Cal's hand to keep him beside me, and reached for the thin knife I kept tucked in my bag.

Cal stepped in front of me as the rustling came closer.

My breath hitched in my chest. I wanted to climb the nearest tree but couldn't leave Cal alone on the ground. My hand trembled as I gripped the hilt of my blade tighter.

"Are you going to try and stab me?" a voice called out. "I don't think it would do you much good."

I would have known that voice after a hundred years.

I gripped my knife tighter, fighting the urge to throw it at my brother's face as he stepped out from between the trees.

"Emmet." Cal stretched a hand toward my brother as a man with black hair and dark eyes stepped out of the shadows beside Emmet.

I took Cal's arm, keeping him close to me.

"Ena"—my brother gave a nod—"Cal."

"What are you doing here?" I asked before Cal could say something more polite.

My brother shrugged. His shoulders were wide from his work as a blacksmith. The familiarity of his face—his bright blue eyes, deep brown hair, and pale skin—tugged at my heart. He looked so much like my mother had. She'd given the same coloring to both of us.

But the hard line of his jaw, which became more defined as he turned to the other man, that Emmet had inherited from our father.

The black-haired man gave my brother a nod.

"I found out you'd gone to the woods, and I decided to check on you," Emmet said.

"How did you find me?" I asked at the same moment Cal said, "We were just heading back."

"You should go then," Emmet said. "I can make sure Ena gets home safe."

"I'd rather—" Cal began.

"I think you've spent enough time in the woods with my little sister." Emmet pointed down the slope. "Keep heading that way, you'll find the village soon enough."

The man next to my brother bit back a smile.

Pink crept up Cal's neck.

"It's fine." I laid a hand on his arm. "Go."

Cal turned to me, locking eyes with me for a moment before kissing the back of my hand. "I'll see you tomorrow." He didn't look back at my brother before striding away.

I glared at Emmet as Cal's footsteps faded.

A new scar marred Emmet's left cheek. His hands had taken more damage since the last time I'd seen him as well.

"You shouldn't be alone with him in the woods," Emmet said when the sounds of Cal's footsteps had vanished.

"And you shouldn't be following me."

"I wanted to be sure you were safe," Emmet said. "A man was killed in the village today, did you not hear?"

"I saw it." I tucked my knife into my bag. "I watched the soldiers whip Aaron to death. But I don't see any soldiers around here, so I think I'll be just fine."

The man gave a low laugh.

"Who are you?" I asked.

"A friend," he said. He looked to be the same as age as my brother, only a couple of years older than Cal and me. If I hadn't been so angry, I might have thought him handsome, but there was something in the way he stood so still while I glared daggers at him that made me wish I hadn't put my knife back into my bag.

"You should get back to the village," Emmet said. "The mountains aren't a safe place to wander."

I turned and climbed farther up the mountain, not caring that he was right.

"Ena." Emmet's footfalls thundered up behind me. "You should get back to Lily." He grabbed my arm, whipping me around.

"Don't tell me where I should be." I wrenched my arm free.

"Then don't be a fool. Get yourself home. You don't belong out here."

"I had Cal with me."

"Being alone with him in the woods is a fool of a choice, too. You've got to think, Ena."

"Don't pretend you care!"

A bird screeched his anger at my shout.

"Ena—"

"You don't get to show up here, follow me into the woods, and try to tell me what to do." My voice shook as I fought to keep from scratching my brother's damned eyes out. "Once a year—once a gods' forsaken year—you show up in Harane. You don't get to pretend to care where I go or who I'm with."

Emmet's brow creased. "I do care. I make it back as often as I'm allowed."

"Liar." The word rumbled in my throat. "The only reason you haven't come back is because you don't want to."

A stick cracked as the black-haired man stepped closer.

"Where have you been, brother?" I'd been saving the question for nearly a year. Holding it in, saying it over and over again in my head as I imagined myself screaming it at Emmet. In all the times I'd thought through it, I'd never pictured him drawing his shoulders defiantly back.

"I've got to work for the blacksmith," Emmet said. "I've finished my apprenticeship, but I've got to pay—"

"You're a damned chivving liar."

"What would I be lying about?" Emmet asked.

"I went to Nantic," I said, "caught a ride in a cart to get to you."

"What?" Emmet said.

"Found the smith where you were supposed to be." I stepped forward, shoving Emmet in the chest. "Two years? Two years since you ran from the blacksmith's, and you've been lying to me."

Emmet's face paled.

"I went to find you, and you weren't there! I was lucky Lily even took me back after I left like that."

Emmet caught my hands. "Why did you go looking for me?"

"You don't get to care. You don't get to lie to me and pretend to care."

Emmet's stone face faltered for the first time. "I do care, Ena. I've come to visit because I care."

"Stopping in once a year doesn't make you a decent brother." I tore my hands free, feeling the bruises growing where he'd gripped my fingers. "You left me here. I didn't even know how to find you. I didn't know if you'd ever come back."

"I had to. I'm sorry, but what I'm doing is more important than being a blacksmith."

"How?"

Emmet looked up to the sky. "It is. You just have to believe that it is."

"And it's more important than I am?" I stared at my brother, waiting for him to crack and tell me there was nothing in all of Ilbrea more important than his only living blood relation.

"It's more important than all of us," Emmet said. "I'm sorry if I can't be the brother you need me to be, but my work has to be done."

"Why?"

"Because there has to be more to this chivving mess of a world than waiting for the Guilds to kill us." Wrinkles creased Emmet's brow. "I can't spend my life waiting to die."

The black-haired man placed a hand on my brother's shoulder. "She should get back to the village."

"Right." Emmet nodded.

I stared at the dark-haired man, wishing he would fade back into the shadows and disappear.

"Then let me help you," I said.

"What?"

"If you have work that's so important, let me help you. I'm not the little girl you left behind in Harane. Wherever it is you've been hiding, take me with you. We're blood, Emmet. I should be with you."

"No." Emmet shook his head. His hair flung around his face. "You belong here."

"I belong with the only family I have." I stepped forward, tipping my chin up to meet his gaze. "I'm not a child. I can help. Let me come with you."

"You can't." Emmet stepped away from me. "You've got to stay with Lily. You're safer here, Ena."

"You're a chivving fool if you believe that."

"It's true. You have to stay in Harane. I have to keep you safe."

"See you next year, brother." I stormed past him and back down the mountain.

He didn't follow.

4

I've never believed in peaceful lives and beautiful tales. Those are no truer than ghost stories. Both are lies we tell ourselves to make the pain we suffer a little less real.

Happiness doesn't swoop in and save us when everything turns dark and bloody. And men do far worse to each other than monsters could ever manage.

Even the men who aren't demons, the ones you should be able to trust when the worst storm comes, they'll hurt you as well.

At the end of the tale, there is nothing left but pain and forcing yourself to survive.

5

The ink stained my fingers, leaving them a bright blue. The color was pretty, I'd done my job well, but against the dull brown of the workshop, the hue seemed obscene. There was nothing in Harane to match the pigment's brightness.

But Lily had asked me to make the color, preparing for the merchants who would come all the way down from the capital, Ilara, seeking inks as summer neared.

It should have been Lily inside grinding up leaves and berries to make the inks that were her living, but she was too busy with her other work. Work that would see her hanged by the soldiers.

A cough had swept through the village, and no one in Harane could afford the gold demanded by the Guilds' healer. It was left to Lily to see to the children so far gone with fever they couldn't hold their heads up anymore.

She'd sneak her herbs into the houses of the desperate, treating the ill with whatever she could grow in her garden and the things I could forage in the woods. Lily rarely brought me with her when she tended to the sick and wounded. Only when there was something she wanted me to learn, or too many desperate people for her to handle on her own. I don't know if she kept me away out of fear or mercy, but either way, it ended up the same.

Lily would leave a written list of inks for me to blend and give spoken orders of what tonics and salves she needed made. I'd sit in the house, letting it fill with enough steam to clog my lungs as I made vials of ink in one set of bowls and healing things in another, all on the one worn, wooden table. I think Lily believed any Guilded soldier sent to her home wouldn't have the sense to know which flowers had been chosen for their ability to fight fever and which had been selected for their pigment. She was probably right.

Whatever her reasoning might have been, the rains hadn't stopped in the three days since I'd left my brother in the forest, and I was trapped with a mortar and pestle, grinding sweet smelling leaves until I couldn't move my fingers anymore as the storm finally drifted east over the mountains.

I left the pulpy mixture of the ink to sit. It would be hours before the stuff would be ready to be carefully strained and then poured into a glass jar to be sold.

Sun peeked in through the windows as I moved on to grinding roots for Lily's remedies. The pungent smell tickled my nose as I worked my way through one knot and then another.

A tap on the door, so light I almost thought the rain had come back, pulled me out of the monotonous motion. I froze with the pestle still in my hand, listening for sounds outside.

The tapping came again.

I gave a quiet curse before calling, "Lily's out, but I'll be with you in one moment," as I pulled down the tray that hid under the tabletop. I set the roots, leaves, mortar and pestle, and vial of oil on the tray and fixed it back under the table as quickly as I could without risking any noise.

I untied the top of my bodice, shaking the laces loose and grabbing both strings in one hand as I opened the door.

"So sorry." I tied my bodice closed over my shift. "I must have drifted off."

I looked up to find, not a soldier come to drag me out for whipping, but Karin, who gave me a scathing look as she slipped past into the workshop.

"Fell asleep?" Karin circled the long table where I'd hidden the tray before peeping through the curtain that blocked off the bit of the first floor where Lily slept.

"The storm made me sleepy." I ran my fingers through my hair, leaving smudges of blue behind that would drive me mad trying to wash out later.

"And there's no one else here?" Karin's eyes twinkled as she stopped at the ladder that led to the loft where I slept. "No one who might make you forget to work?"

If I hadn't known Karin since before either of us could walk, I would have grabbed her skirts and torn her from the ladder as she climbed up like she owned the chivving shop. But Karin meant no harm, and stopping her search would only make the rumors that I'd had a man in the house keeping me from answering the door fly through the village faster.

I could have told her the truth. I had been busy working on illegal remedies for Lily and was afraid a soldier had come to the door. And I'd rather be accused of sleeping on the job than hanged for helping an unguilded healer offer remedies. But then Karin would be obligated to turn me in or risk punishment from the soldiers herself.

I leaned against the table, tracing the outline of a purple ink stain, listening to the sounds of Karin checking under my cot and opening my trunk that wouldn't have been large enough to hide Cal anyway.

"You really are the most boring person who's ever lived." Karin carefully lifted her skirts to come back down the ladder.

"I'm sure I am." I took a box of charcoal and dumped a few bits into a fresh mortar. "So you might as well scoot back to more interesting company and leave me to my work."

"Don't you dare start on something that's going to make so much of a mess." Karin snatched the charcoal-filled mortar out of my reach. She stared at me, a glimmer of delight playing in the corners of her eyes.

I knew she wanted me to ask why she'd come and what I'd need clean hands for. The bit of obstinance that curled in my stomach wasn't as strong as the part of me that wanted something interesting to be happening after all the rain. Even if it was only Handor and Shilv fighting over whose sheep were harassing whose again.

"What is it, you fairy of a biddy?"

"Only the best, most delightful news." Karin took my shoulders, steering me to the pump sink in the corner. She worked the handle while she spoke. "Well, after word came south on the road that the map makers with a load of their soldiers were coming our way—"

"What?" I froze, a brick of harsh soap clutched in my hand.

"There's a whole pack of Guilded heading our way. How have you not heard?"

"I've been inside working." I scrubbed at the blue and black on my hands. "Some of us have things we actually have to get done."

"You should admit the real problem is you never bothering to talk to people besides Cal and Lily. You should try making friends, Ena. It would be good for you."

"Yes, fine." I snatched the pot of oily cream from the shelf. "What about the soldiers?"

"Right." Karin leaned in. "So, word comes down the road that there's a whole caravan of paun Guilded headed our way. Cal's parents are head over heels planning to have all the fancy folks at the tavern, the farmers have started trying to hide their stock so it can't be counted, and"—she paused, near shuddering with glee—"Henry Tilly took his horse and disappeared for two days."

"What?" I wiped the cream and the rest of the color from my fingers with a rag. "Did the soldiers get him?"

"No." Karin laughed. "He rode north, all the way to Nantic."

"Toward the paun caravan? Who in their right mind would do such a thing?"

Karin took my elbow and led me to a seat at the table. She pushed aside the curtain to Lily's room and snatched up Lily's hairbrush.

"Nantic is a much bigger place than Harane." Karin shook my hair free from its braid. "So many things to offer that we don't have in our tiny little village."

"Like people who tell stories that actually make sense?"

Karin dragged the brush roughly through my hair in retaliation. "Like a scribe."

"What?"

"A Guilded scribe. One who can offer all the official forms the Guilds force us to use for every little thing we do. Like buying land, being buried...getting married."

"Henry is getting married?" I spun around wide-eyed. "To you?"

"Oh gods no, not me!" Karin screwed up her face. "I'd never marry him. His left eye's bigger than his right."

"Who is he marrying then?" I knelt on the chair, gripping the back.

"Malda!" Karin clapped a hand over her mouth.

"What?"

"Henry found out the soldiers, and map makers, and entire fleet of paun were on their way and raced through the night all thirty miles up to Nantic to get marriage papers from the Guilds' scribe." Karin twirled the brush through the air. "And do you know why?"

"Love, I suppose."

"She's pregnant. That little mouse Malda is pregnant and more than just a little. Gods, now that I know, it's impossible not to see how her belly's grown."

"Henry's a slitching fool." I dragged my fingers through my hair.

Karin grabbed my shoulders, making me face front in the chair again.

"A fool he is," Karin said, "but at least he cares for Malda enough not to risk the paun catching her pregnant without a husband. If those soldiers found her out, she'd be taken and sent to give birth on Ian Ayres in the middle of the sea. No one ever comes back from that place."

A chill shook my spine, but Karin kept talking.

"Henry brought coin to Nantic to pay the scribe, but the scribe told him he'd have to wait seven months for marriage papers."

"Seven months?" I tried to turn again, but Karin whacked me on the head with the brush.

"By which time there will be a new little screaming Henry or Malda in this world. Henry had to give the scribe his horse to get the papers and spent the last two days trudging back through the rain."

"Is he all right?" My eyes darted toward the tray hidden under the table. That long in the cold rain, and it was only a matter of time before Lily had to darken his door.

"He's in the tavern right now having a warm frie to cheer him for his wedding this afternoon." Karin twisted my hair. "They're laying hay out in the square to make a space for it. The whole thing will be done long before the sun sets, so Malda will be a married woman before the Guilds can set eyes on her ever-expanding belly."

"This afternoon? Today?" I asked.

"Yes, Ena. That is how days usually go. The whole village will be turning up for this wedding, so you need to look like a proper lady, and I need just a little bit of your magic to give me a wonderful spring blush." Karin scraped my scalp with pins.

"What for? Even if they put down enough hay to feed the horses for a season, we'll all still end up covered in mud."

"Because," Karin said, stepping in front of me and pointing a finger at my nose, "nothing makes a man consider the fact that marriage is inevitable more than a wedding. Henry panicking could be our chance to snatch a prize worth having."

Heat shot up to my cheeks.

"No." I stood, not meeting Karin's eyes as I stalked to the corner where the few small tubs of powders and paints for women's faces were kept. "You dab as much pink on your cheeks as you like, but I'll have none of it on me. I'm too young to be worrying about marriage."

"But is Cal?" That awful twinkle sprang back into Karin's eyes.

"Paint your face, you wretch." I tossed her a tin.

6

It took more than an hour for Karin to paint her face to a marriageable hue, riffle through the few clothes I owned to choose what she wanted me to wear, and give up on the idea of her painting my cheeks as well.

She'd just finished tightening the laces on my bodice to display enough of my breasts to be considered obscene, when Lily stepped in through the garden door, basket over her arm and mud clinging to her boots.

Lily stared from Karin to me. "So, you've already heard the joyous news."

"I told her." Karin gave my bodice laces one more tug. "Had to get her ready for the wedding, didn't I?"

"What's to be gotten ready for?" Lily set her basket on the table. "Put your breasts away, Ena. You're pretty enough to get into plenty of trouble without two beacons poking out the front of your dress."

"They're not poking out." I glanced down, making sure there wasn't more showing than I'd thought.

Lily unloaded the goods from her basket. "There is a fine line between the kind of beauty gods bless you with, and the kind given by the shadows to bring trouble into your life. You, Ena Ryeland, are balancing on the edge of beauty becoming a curse. So, tuck your tits back in your top before someone you don't fancy decides they have a right to the body you were born with."

"Yes, Lily." My face burned red.

Karin slapped my hands away as I tried to loosen my bodice. She grabbed the pale blue fabric of my shift instead, giving it a tug to cover more of my chest.

"Help me get these things put away so we don't miss the wedding." Lily went to her bedroom, leaving a trail of muddy boot prints behind. "We need to bring something for the bride and groom. I would say they should be gifted a lick of common sense, but it seems they threw that away five months ago when a roll in the hay seemed worth risking a life for."

Karin turned to me, her eyebrows creeping up her forehead. "I'll see you there," she mouthed before dodging out the door.

"Is that girl gone?" Lily asked.

"Yes, Lily." I examined the goods Lily had brought home with her. A fair number of eggs, two loaves of seed bread, a bottle of chamb, and a skein of thick spun wool. "You saw that many today?"

"Bad stomach, an awful cough, and had to stitch up the side of Les's head."

"What happened to Les's head?" I tucked the eggs into the shallow basket by the iron stove and wrapped the bread in a cloth.

"If you ask Les, he knocked his head in the barn." Lily stalked back out of her bedroom, a clean dress on, mud still clinging to her boots. "If you look at the manic glint in his wife's eyes, she finally got sick of the slitch and smacked him upside the head hard enough to draw blood."

"What did Les do to make her so mad?"

"Damned if I know what he's done this time." Lily pumped the sink to scrub her hands. "That boy was born stupid, and he didn't get much better once he learned to talk."

"Fair enough." I took over pumping the giant metal handle.

Lily methodically washed the skin around her nails in the cold water. "The map maker's party is coming through. Should be here tomorrow from the sounds of it."

"Karin said as much."

"Map makers always come with a pack of soldiers. Who knows how big the company will be?"

"Either way, they should be through pretty quick." I passed Lily a cloth to dry her hands on. "They aren't coming to Harane on purpose. They're only taking the mountain road to get someplace else."

Lily nodded silently for a moment. "I don't want you in the village tomorrow. Head out to the mountains in the morning."

"It's been raining for days. There won't be anything for me to bring back but mud."

"Then bring back some mud." Lily took my face in her hands. "I don't want you around when the paun come through. I won't have it on my head when that pretty face of yours becomes a curse."

A knot of something like dread closed around my stomach. "I'll just stay inside and out of sight."

"You'll get to the mountains and thank me for it." She squeezed my face tighter.

I stared into her steel gray eyes.

"Do you hear me, girl?"

"Yes, ma'am."

"Good." She let go of my face. "Now, what in this chivving mess should we give the idiots getting married this afternoon?"

"Something for a chest rattle." I pulled up the loose floorboard that housed all of Lily's illegal goods. "If Karin is right, Henry will need it in a few days if he doesn't already."

"Fine. Give it to his mother so the fool doesn't go losing it."

"Yes, Lily." I pulled out one of the little wooden boxes that held the thick paste.

"Out you get then." Lily grabbed the broom from near the woodstove. "Go celebrate the panic caused by young lust."

I managed to pull my coat on before she spoke again.

"And let this be a lesson to you, Ena. Give yourself to a man with no sense, and you'll end up getting married on a godsforsaken muddy day to a fool who no longer owns a horse."

I darted out the door before Lily could say anything else. I cared for the old lady, even if she was harsh and a little strange. She swore worse than a Guilded sailor just as easily as she whispered comfort to the dying.

No one in Harane could blame Lily for her rough edges. Nigh on all of us owed our lives to her for something or other, and the few who'd been lucky enough never to need Lily's help would have been awfully lonely living at the foot of the mountains with the rest of us dead.

Mud soaked my boots before I'd made it through the garden and to the road. I lifted my hem as I leapt over the worst of the puddles, though I knew there was no hope of my skirt making it through the day unscathed.

The air in the village tasted different than it had a few days ago, and not just from the rain. The stink of despair had fled, replaced by a dancing breeze of hope.

It was true enough that Henry and Malda were only getting married to escape the wrath of the Guilds. If the lords far away in Ilara hadn't passed a law banning children being born outside marriage, then Shilv wouldn't have been carrying hay to the square.

Malda wouldn't have had to fear being snatched up by soldiers, loaded onto a ship, and sent out to the isle of Ian Ayres to give birth. Henry wouldn't have had to give up his horse. I wouldn't have been dodging puddles with salve in my coat pocket. And the whole village would have had endless hours of entertainment for the next few months wondering if Malda was carrying a child or had only taken too strongly to sweet summer cakes.

But the Guilds ruled Ilbrea with their shining, golden fist. If they said women carrying babies out of wedlock were to be taken, there was nothing we could do to fight the paun. Just like we couldn't stop them from whipping Aaron to death. In the whole land of Ilbrea, there was nothing unguilded rotta like us could do but try and avoid the Guilds' notice and hope they weren't bored enough to come after us anyway.

I'd gotten so lost in wondering what would have happened to Malda and her baby if Henry hadn't had a horse to offer, I walked right past the tavern.

"Ena!" Cal called out the kitchen window, waving a flour-covered rag, which left a puff of white floating in the air.

"Don't hang out the window," Cal's father shouted. "If you want to talk to the girl, bring her inside like a civilized man."

Cal bit back his smile. "Miss Ryeland, would you grace us with your presence in our humble kitchen."

"Why thank you." I gave as deep a curtsy as I could manage without sinking my hem deep into the mud and headed back up the street to the tavern door.

Harane didn't have many businesses that would interest travelers, and everything that might appeal, aside from Lily's ink shop, had been packed into the very center of the village. The tavern, cobbler, stables, tannery, and smith had all been built close together with narrow alleys running between them, as though whoever had laid the foundations had thought Harane would become a town or even a city someday.

That person had been wrong.

Harane was nothing but a tract of fertile farmland situated thirty miles south of Nantic and twenty-nine miles north of Hareford on the Guild-approved road that ran as close to the mountains as travelers dared to get. The only reason the tavern managed to fill its aged, wooden tables every night was the travelers who needed a place to stop between Nantic and Hareford, and the village men, like Les, who were too afraid of their wives to go home.

The tables in the tavern only had a smattering of people since the travelers hadn't arrived for the night and the village folk were getting ready for the surprise wedding.

"Ena." Cal waved me in through the kitchen door.

The scent of baking pastries, roasting meat, and fresh poured frie warmed my face before I even neared the wide fireplace and big iron oven.

"I take it you heard?" Cal raised an eyebrow at my hair.

I ran my fingers along the delicate twists Karin promised would win me a husband, blushing to the roots of my hair as I met Cal's gaze. "Karin insisted."

"Careful of the hot." Cal's mother pulled a tray of sweet rolls from the oven. The tops had been crusted to a shining brown.

"Those are beautiful." I leaned in to sniff. "I didn't think you'd spend the time on a last minute wedding."

Cal's mother tsked. "I'm making three loaves of bread for the wedding. One for each of them."

I coughed a laugh.

"The rolls are for the Guilded coming through," she said. "I only hope it's true they're coming tomorrow. If not, the lot will go stale. But if I wait to start until they arrive, I won't be able to make enough to sell." She worried her wrinkled lips together. "I've already had the rooms upstairs cleaned, and Cal's pulled fresh barrels of frie and chamb. I only hope it's enough."

"Does it matter?" I leaned against the edge of the table. "It's a caravan of paun. If you don't have enough for them, they'll just have to stay in their camp where they belong and move on south all the faster."

"We need their business," Cal's father said. "A day with the caravan will be more coin than we'll see for the rest of the summer. The gods smiled on us when they sent the map makers down the mountain road."

"Right." I felt my mouth curve into a smile even as a horrible cold tingled down my neck and surrounded the dread in my stomach. "I'm very happy for you."

"Is there anything else you need me for?" Cal asked.

"Go." Cal's mother shooed him toward the door. "But if anyone dares say something snide about your father and me not coming to the square, tell them not to darken the tavern door for a month. I don't care how thirsty they are for frie."

"Yes, mother." Cal kissed his mother's cheek and took a basket from near the stove.

"Someday soon, there will be a wedding worth leaving work undone for," Cal's mother said. "This is not that day."

I bit my lips together and let Cal put a hand on my waist, guiding me back out into the main room of the tavern.

"Honestly," Cal said in a low voice as soon as the kitchen door shut behind us, "it's probably better my parents not come."

"Why?" I whispered.

"Poor Henry has to stand in front of everyone, with the whole village knowing full well what a slitch he was to let Malda hang for so long. Imagine adding my mother's glare to that weight."

I laughed, and the cold and dread around my stomach vanished with a tiny pop of joy.

7

I'll never know how they managed to find enough hay to coat the mud in the square. Not that the square was large, or even properly a square.

On the northern end of the village, someone, a very long time ago, had surrounded a square of land with heavy stones. No one had moved the stones or stolen them to build for fear of angering some unknown spirit. So, the rocks as big as my torso lay undisturbed, and the people of Harane gathered within them whenever the need arose.

Most often, the need came from the soldiers issuing Guild decrees or doling out punishment. But we used the square for things like weddings and summer celebrations as well. I don't know if people thought there was some good to be gained from gathering within the stones, or if it was pure stubbornness in not letting the Guilds steal the square and make it an awful place where none of the villagers dared tread.

Either way ended with Henry and Malda standing side by side in front of a horde of people.

Tomin had become the eldest in the village after a lung infection took a few of the older folks during the winter, so it was his place to stand with Henry and Malda to perform the wedding.

"And in the bonds of marriage, do you swear to protect your other half?" Tomin said. "Through winter and drought? Through flood and famine?"

"I do," Henry and Malda said together.

Henry's face was pale, whether from fright of being married or exhaustion from walking back from Nantic, I couldn't tell.

Tomin reached into his pocket and pulled out a filthy rag. "Hands please."

Malda and Henry both held up their right palms.

Tomin unfolded the rag and patted the clump of dirt within it flat. "Hard to find anything dry."

The villagers chuckled, and Tomin gave a gap-toothed grin.

"From the dirt we all have come." Tomin sprinkled dirt onto Malda's palm. "And to the dirt we all must go." He sprinkled dirt onto Henry's palm. "May your journey in between be sweeter for standing by each other's side."

Together, Henry and Malda tipped their hands, letting the dirt tumble onto the muddy hay at their feet.

"Your lives are one," Tomin said. "Live them well!"

The crowd cheered.

Malda threw her arms around Henry's neck and kissed him.

The children winced and whined—the rest of us clapped and hollered.

Before Malda had stopped kissing Henry, someone began playing a fiddle. A drum joined a moment later, and Henry took Malda's hands, dragging her to the center of the square to dance.

I laughed at the look of pure horror on Malda's face. An arm snaked around my waist.

"Are you going to look as petrified when I make you dance?" Cal whispered in my ear.

"I don't think you could make me do anything." I twisted out of his grip and darted toward the center of the square where everyone had picked up on the dance.

Cal raced to my side, taking me in his arms before anyone else could have the chance. We spun and bounced in time with the music as the hay beneath our feet was eaten entirely by the mud.

Cal lifted me and twirled me under his arm until my heart beat so fast I thought it might race out of my chest. His laughter rang in my ears. The bright joy that lit his eyes sent my soul soaring up high above the clouds.

Then Henry's father wheeled out a barrel of frie. The crowd shifted toward the drink.

And the whipping post was there, waiting at the back of the celebration.

There was no blood on the ground, the rain had washed it all away, but dark stains mottled the post. The wood had been worn down in places where the soldiers' victims had strained against their bonds.

My feet lost the feel of the dance, and I swayed, staring at the bloody monument to all the damage the Guilds had done.

"Ena?" Cal took my waist in his hands. "Are you all right?"

"Tired." I nodded. "I'm just tired."

"Come on." He led me to the side of the square where Henry's father doled out frie in borrowed cups. I stood on the edge of the crowd while Cal dove between people to snatch each of us a drink. He emerged a moment later, his hair rumpled, but clasping a cup in each hand. "Here."

I took the cup and sipped the frie. The drink burned a path down my throat, past my lungs, and into my stomach, but didn't make me feel any better.

Cal laced his fingers through mine and led me to the south side of the square. We sat on one of the largest of the boundary stones, watching the dancers spin round and round.

"It's a nice wedding," Cal said. "And Henry's family seems happy to be getting Malda."

"They do." I took another sip of frie, trying to burn away the taste of sick in my mouth.

"Malda grew up on a farm, so she won't have trouble getting used to the labor Henry's land will require."

"She's a strong girl," I said. "They'll do well together."

"We'd do well together." Cal leaned in close. "Better than them. I could provide for you better than Henry ever—"

"I have my own work." I tightened my grip on my cup.

"And you could work with Lily if you wanted," Cal said. "But you wouldn't have to. I'm going to inherit the tavern. It's a good income, Ena."

"Don't, Cal. Please don't."

"I know we're young." Cal knelt in the mud front of me, making it impossible for me to look away from his beautiful eyes. "And I'm not saying we should get married soon. We could wait until next summer, give Lily some time to get used to the idea of you moving to the tavern."

"I couldn't." The truth of the words tore at my chest. "I can't."

"She'll make do on her own."

"I can't live in the tavern. I can't be married to a man who makes his coin from soldiers."

"Ena—"

"The soldiers coming is good for your family, but to me it only means death. I couldn't smile at them and serve them. They are monsters. Your family makes their living feeding the monsters who slaughter us."

The glimmer of light in Cal's eyes faded. I could still see the post over his shoulder, coming in and out of view as the people danced where they had stood to watch Aaron murdered only a few days before.

"You are everything bright and wonderful, Cal. But I could never be your wife."

I stood up, set my cup down on the rock, and walked out of the square. I didn't look back. Cal didn't follow.

8

The night is pitch black, and I am racing down the road.

The thundering of the horse's hooves doesn't cover the pounding of my heart. I search for a glimmer of light up ahead, but there's nothing.

Only endless night.

I keep riding until fear finally wakes me.

9

I left for the woods at dawn the next morning. I'd heard Lily come in after the wedding but stayed silently huddled under my blankets. I didn't want to talk to her. Didn't want her to stare at me with her steel gray eyes and know she felt sorry for me—even though she'd never say it.

After a night spent trapped in a horrible dream, I still didn't want to see her. I slipped out of the house when the sun finally rose and fled for the safety of the forest.

The trees didn't ask what kind of a foolish girl would turn down the best marriage Harane had to offer. The birds didn't call me a hypocrite for making inks to be sent to Ilara where only the gods knew if Guilded paun would be using them. The rotting leaves squishing under my feet didn't say there could be no hope of joy for an orphan girl incapable of loving anyone.

I made it higher in the mountains that day than I ever had before. I stuffed every chivving leaf and lichen into my bag that had a chance of making Lily happy and took pleasure in the pain its growing weight caused me.

Better now than later. I tried to comfort myself. *Better for Cal to know you could never live in his tavern now, before Karin chooses a husband.*

The thought of Karin lying in Cal's arms made me scream loud enough to send a flock of birds scattering to the sky. But it didn't change anything. Cal belonged in the tavern with his family. I could never live with being glad the Guilds were coming.

Simple as that.

When I'd finally gotten tired enough that climbing back down the mountain would be painful, I turned around and headed home.

By the time I made it out of the forest, my legs shook so badly I wasn't sure I would be able to climb over the fences to get back to Lily's. I took a deep breath to steady myself. There was something more in the wind than the usual scent of animal dung and trees.

I took another breath, trying to find what the stench might be. My gaze caught on something on the horizon, a pillar of smoke rising from the northern side of the village.

Taking off at a run, I headed toward the flames, ignoring the trembling in my legs that threatened to send me face first into the dirt.

The smoke wasn't from the very northern edge of the village, and it was back from the main road, off toward the farms on the western side of Harane. I scrambled over fences, dodging around terrified livestock that had scented the fire and knew they had no chance of escaping their pens.

I didn't hear the screams until I neared the road.

A man crying out in agony.

I stopped behind Shilv's house, teetering between running to get Lily to help whoever had been hurt badly enough to make that sort of noise, and being afraid of leaving someone to die alone.

The man screamed again, and I ran forward, toward the sound.

"What..." My question faded away as I saw why Shilv had been screaming.

Five Guilded soldiers in black uniforms stood in a line, staring down at Shilv who clutched the bloody stump of his arm to his chest. Shilv's wife Ester knelt ten feet away, sobbing as she stared at her husband.

I stood frozen for a moment before instinct took over.

And I ran.

Around the side of the house, leaping over the fence and tearing through the pasture without looking to see if any of the soldiers had followed me.

My breath hitched in my chest as I ran. Shilv had been toying with the Guilds for years, hiding his livestock when the scribes came to do their tax accounting.

A hand for the money Shilv owed. If Lily could take care of the wound and make sure no infection set in, Shilv wouldn't be too bad off. His wife was strong. They'd find a way to make do.

I looped back out to the road, heading toward the fire. I pressed my back to a house to peer down the road before venturing into the open.

Shilv's screams had faded, and there was no blood here. But there were soldiers. A pack of soldiers moving down the road with some purpose I didn't understand. They kicked in the door of a house. I ran across the street while they weren't looking and dove into the shadows of a stable.

The horse kicked against the wall, fighting to break free. The banging shook my ears as I ran to the western end of the stable.

I didn't have to go farther than that.

Flames shot up from the Tillys' house. The whole place had been eaten by the inferno. Two figures lay bloody and bare across the walkway. Henry's unmoving back bore the marks of a terrible whipping. His father's chest had been cut open by something sharper. Both of them were dead.

I bit my lips together until they bled as I swallowed my scream.

I didn't know where Malda was. If they'd left her in the house, there was nothing I could do for her. Nothing even Lily could do for her.

"Lily."

A fear like I hadn't known in nine years seized my lungs, choking the air out of me. I ran south, along the backs of the houses, racing toward home.

Lily was smart. She hid the things the Guilds had banned. She only treated people she knew she could trust. The villagers loved her. They would sooner let themselves be whipped than turn Lily in to the Guilds.

Soldiers had gathered behind Les's house. I ducked between buildings and toward the main road before I could see what might have become of Les and his angry wife.

I made it all the way to the side of the tannery.

If I cut between the tavern and the public stables, then looped behind the houses, I'd reach home in a few minutes. I had to warn Lily, make sure she had everything hidden.

I leaned out to check up and down the street. Pain cut through my head as someone grabbed my hair and tossed me to the ground.

The dirt flying into my mouth cut off my scream.

"Who is this sneaking around?" a man said.

I pushed myself to my knees. A kick to the ribs sent me back to the ground.

"Get her up," a second voice said.

A hand grabbed the back of my coat, hauling me to my feet.

Screams came from the south end of the village as a new pillar of smoke drifted toward the sky.

"What's your name?" A soldier leaned close to my face.

I wanted to scratch his leering eyes out, but another soldier had pinned my arms behind my back.

"Your name." The soldier took my chin in his hand.

"Ena." I spat the dirt out of my mouth, letting it land on his fingers. "Ena Ryeland."

"Ryeland isn't a land owner here." A man in white scribes robes stepped forward.

"I don't own land," I said. "I'm a worker, that's all. Now let me go."

Laughter came from behind me.

I glanced back. There were six other men in black uniforms. I tried to yank my arms free.

"What kind of work would a pretty little thing like you be doing?" The soldier trailed a finger down my neck.

"Don't touch me." I kicked back, catching the man who held me in the shin.

The soldier stepped closer to me, pinning me between him and the one I'd kicked.

"You have attacked a soldier of the Guilds of Ilbrea." He wrapped a hand around my throat, cutting off my air. "You just made a terrible mistake."

"Gentlemen!" Cal's voice shouted from across the road. "Come have a drink!"

"We're busy here." The man behind me pressed his hips to my back.

I coughed as I tried to pull in air past the pain squeezing my throat.

"I can promise each of you, you'd rather have some frie and roasted lamb than mess with that." Cal laughed. "Come in. Drinks are on the house, and you can forget that little street scum ever bothered you."

None of the soldiers moved.

"You're here to uphold the laws of our great country." Cal beckoned them toward the door. "You are doing all of us a service by clearing the law breakers out of our village. Come, let me give you a good meal as a token of thanks. I promise the frie we have is the best you'll find south of Ilara."

The soldier in front of me stepped away. He let go of my throat, and the world swayed as I gulped down air. "One this pretty must be diseased anyway. Let's go, lads."

The man holding my arms threw me back down into the dirt.

"I have chamb, too, if any of you prefer," Cal said. "Six years old. I'm told the grape harvest was perfect that season."

Cal led the soldiers into the tavern.

I pushed myself to my feet before the last of them disappeared and ran back between the buildings. I'd made it past the smith's when footsteps pounded up behind me and a hand slammed me into the rough clapboard.

"Do you think I'm that much of an idiot, girl?" The man's breath touched my neck. He leaned into me, pressing his stiffness against my back. "I will not be disrespected by a filthy little rotta."

"Please don't." I tried to reach into my bag, for the knife tucked under the layers of foraged things.

He grabbed my wrist, twisting my arm with one hand and snaking my skirt up my leg with the other.

"Don't do this." I wanted to scream for help, but helping me would be a death sentence.

"Rotta need to learn their—"

A grunt, a rasp, and a gurgle cut through the man's words.

I turned in time to see a spray of red fly from the soldier's throat as he toppled to the ground.

"We need to go." A hand seized mine, dragging me away from the dying soldier.

I looked to the one who had saved me. Black curling hair and deep brown eyes—the man who'd been with my brother in the woods dragged me away.

10

"Emmet." That was the first word I managed to say. "Where's Emmet?"

"South. Far away from here." The black-haired man kept my hand held tightly in his.

His skin was clean. His hand hadn't been covered in the blood that had sprayed the dirt alley.

"Why are you here?" I asked.

"Are you angry I saved you?" He pressed me into the shadows as he peered around the side of Handor's shed.

"No."

"Then it should be enough that I'm here. We need to get to the woods."

"I can't." I yanked my hand from his grasp.

"If you stay here, they'll kill you. The soldiers watched that man follow you, and now that man is dead."

"I can't just leave. I have to get to Lily. If the soldiers are going after people, I have to warn her."

The man closed his eyes for a moment. "Where's her home?"

"Southeast end of the village," I said. "I can get there on my own."

"You're not leaving my sight." He grabbed my elbow, steering me to the trees between homes. "Is Lily fit enough to travel?"

"She's old but she's not decrepit."

"It'll be easier for us to stay alive if I don't have to carry anyone." He didn't offer any explanation as he took off running behind the houses.

I didn't ask for one.

"It's across from the next house," I said as the towering tree that stood in front of Lily's worn, wooden home came into view. Smoke rose from behind the barren branches.

I ran faster, outpacing the black-haired man.

My heart thundered in my ears. The pounding of faraway hooves rattled away all reasonable thought.

The man caught me around the waist, keeping me in the cover of the shadows. I didn't need to go any closer.

The soldiers had displayed her out front by the road. Her gray hair drifted with the breeze as the rope around her neck twisted. Flames cut through the roof of Lily's home, their brightness outlining her shape, as though her death would set the whole world to blazing.

11

The man kept his grip around my waist as we ran away from Lily's house. He darted between buildings and sprinted for long stretches. I made it up and over the fences on my own. I don't know how. I couldn't feel anything. Not the pain in my limbs. Not the terrible, silent scream that echoed in my chest.

I had gone numb. Completely and totally numb.

The man spoke words. Instructions for when to run, and when to lie down in the grass and hide.

I must've done as he said. We made it to the cover of the trees alive.

The stench of the smoke had broken through the scent of the forest. Or maybe it only clung to me.

"We need to keep moving." He grabbed my arm again, steering me farther into the woods.

"Moving?" The word felt heavy in my mouth.

"I can't be sure the soldiers didn't see us coming this way," he said. "The farther we get from Harane, the better off we'll be."

"But I can't just leave." I shook free of his grip. "I'll hide here until they all move on."

"And then what?" He had a cut on his forehead. I didn't know how he had gotten it. "You can't go back there. I killed that soldier—the soldier who left his friends to follow you. They'll blame his murder on you. Harane isn't safe for you, not now, not ever again. We have to keep moving."

"But I can't just leave. The soldiers might not"—a sharp pain pummeled my chest—"the soldiers can't have killed everyone."

"Probably not." He grabbed my arm, dragging me into the forest.

"What does that mean?"

"If people cooperated and didn't fight back, they might still be alive." He stopped at a thick patch of brambles.

"Karin might need help," I said. "Cal is still back there."

He dug a heavy pack out of the brambles, swinging it onto his back before turning to me. "Cal is the boy from the woods?"

I nodded.

He looked up into the trees. "Will he follow you?"

"What?"

"If we wait until dark, I can try to go back for him. If I tell him you're waiting in the woods, will he come?"

"I..." I wasn't sure if Cal would come. If he would hear I had lost the little shred of a life I had been clinging to for so long and come running to my side, ready to abandon everything he had ever known. "I don't want him to. He has a family and a home in the village."

A wrinkle formed between the man's dark eyebrows. "Then there's nothing for us to do but leave. You can't go back to Harane. I'm sorry."

"But where am I supposed to go?" I said. "I could go to Nantic or Hareford, but I don't have any coin. I can work—"

"You can't go anywhere along the mountain road." He reached toward me. "It'll be the same soldiers patrolling."

The trees twisted and swayed around me.

He took my hand, and somehow I managed to make my feet move.

To get farther away than Nantic or Hareford would take days. To get anywhere off the mountain road I would need a map, and food, and money.

"Where am I supposed to go?" A hollow, childish fear settled in my chest.

"I'll take you to your brother."

"South?"

"No." He paused for a moment, staring up at the steep mountain ahead of us. "I'll take you where he's supposed to meet me. You'll be safe there until you can figure out where you want to go."

The light faded from the sky, but he kept moving farther up the mountain. My legs screamed their protest at being asked to climb even more. Part of me wanted to lie down and wait for the forest to eat me whole. More of me wanted to run as far away as the land reached, beyond even the power of the Guilds.

"Why?" I asked when I couldn't bear to swallow the question any longer.

It took a moment for the man to speak. "Why what?"

"Why Harane? Why did the soldiers decide to come after our village? Weren't they satisfied with the damage they'd already done?"

"I don't know if a Guilded soldier is capable of feeling satisfied until a town and all its people are nothing more than ash." He stopped next to a wide boulder. Moss covered the stone, hiding most of its rough texture. He trailed his fingers along the bare patches of rock. "The whisper I heard on the wind said some fool traded a horse for marriage papers. No reason but hiding a baby to be that desperate for a scribe's help. Even the paun scum from Ilara were smart enough to know that. Made them wonder who else might be breaking the laws in Harane."

"Henry." I dug my fingers into my hair. The grit of dirt and soot covered my scalp. "All of this happened because of Henry."

"That's not true." He patted the boulder and started climbing again. "He might have been wrong not to take better care of the girl carrying his child, he might have been a slitching fool for trading his horse and thinking the scribe wouldn't know why, but the death, the blood—that's on the Guilds. They're the ones who are determined to destroy us. Everything else is just reasons the Guilds tell themselves they have a right to slaughter the tilk."

Tilk.

I hadn't even thought the word in forever. The Guilded never used the kind term for common folk. They called us rotta instead. I'd started thinking it, too. Like I believed we were disposable rodents who deserved to be exterminated for contaminating the Guilds' perfect kingdom.

"Do you think they'll leave any of the village standing?" I asked.

"Maybe. It would be a long ride from Nantic to Hareford otherwise."

I had more questions, but I couldn't bring myself to ask them. My soul had grown too heavy to bear another word of pain.

The twilight chill tickled the back of my neck. The sounds of the forest waking up for the night carried through the shadows.

I wanted to say we needed to stop, climb high in a tree and hope we made it until morning. But he kept walking, and I didn't know if letting the animals kill me would be the kinder fate.

He took my hand as he cut sideways along the edge of a rise, as though he were afraid I would tumble off the slope or run back to the village if given the chance.

I ducked my head as bats chittered above us. A gaping darkness grew from the mountainside, blocking our path.

I took a quick step to walk nearer to him. My free hand fumbled, digging into my bag for my knife.

"It's all right." He let go of my hand and stepped into the darkness in the mountain.

I held my breath, waiting for the sounds of some animal tearing him apart.

A tiny spark broke through the black. Then a deep blue light glowed in the cave.

He stood in the middle of the hollow, holding a blue light in his hand, searching each of the stone corners.

"Nothing's been sleeping here for a while." He waved me toward him. "We'll be safe here for the night."

Giving one last glance to the woods behind me, I stepped into the shelter of the cave.

It wasn't large—it only cut about ten feet back—and wasn't wide enough for me to spread my arms out. There were no loose stones on the ground, though aging sticks had been piled in the back where something had once made its bed.

He set the blue light down in the center of the cave before shrugging out of his pack. "You should eat something before you sleep."

"I'm not hungry." I knelt next to the blue light.

It wasn't a lantern with colored glass as I'd thought, but a stone formed of bright blue crystals that seemed to have trapped the spark of a fire deep within itself.

"What is this?" I reached out to poke the stone, expecting him to tell me to stop. But he only watched as my finger grazed the cool surface of the rock.

"A lae stone." He pulled a set of six black rocks from his bag.

"Won't the soldiers be able to see all that light?" I trailed my fingers over the sharp ridges of the lae stone.

"These don't light up." He laid the six stones out along the mouth of the cave.

"Then what are they for?"

"Protecting us." He eyed the line of stones before turning back to his pack.

"What do you mean?"

He didn't speak until he'd unfastened the bedroll from his bag, pulled out a packet of dried meat, and forced a piece into my hand.

"Do you know the ghost stories that keep people out of the mountains?" He leaned against the wall of the cave.

"Sure." I shivered. The cold of the night seeped into my bones now that the heat of the climb had left me. "Everyone knows the stories, even the paun."

"Well, the ghosts that haunt these mountains aren't dead," he said. "I should know. I'm one of them."

I sat against the cave wall opposite him, pressing my back to the cold, damp rock.

"There's magic in these mountains, Ena." He pointed to the stones. "These hold a tiny piece of it."

"You're mad."

"No. I'm a Black Blood."

"No." I shook head. "No. Black Bloods are a legend. Magic doesn't exist outside the Guilds' control. The sorcerers in Ilara hoard all the magic in Ilbrea."

"Your brother said almost exactly the same thing." A hint of a smile caught in the corners of his eyes.

"My brother does not have a speck of magic in him."

"He doesn't. But he saved my life, and he's joined my family. Which makes you my family as well."

"I don't understand." I looked toward the night beyond the opening of the cave. I had trapped myself in the forest with a madman.

I have nowhere else to go.

"You don't have to understand," he said. "I owe your brother a debt. I heard the Guilds had decided to raid Harane and there was no way Emmet could have gotten to you in time. So I came for you myself."

"You came to the village for me?" The weight of his words sank into my stomach, pulling my gaze back from the open air.

"I promised your brother you would be protected." A hint of worry flitted through his dark eyes. A wrinkle that had no place on the face of one so young creased his brow. "I'm sorry I made it so you can't go back. It wasn't my intention."

"You saved me. I can't be anything but grateful for that." I wrapped my arms around myself, trying to stop my shivering.

"Here." He untied the bedroll, laying the thin pad and heavy wool blanket out on the ground. "You should get some sleep."

"You've just said there's magic outside the Guilds' control and you want me to sleep? With a fancy, glowing, blue stone and six rocks as protection?"

"We've got a long journey ahead of us. You'll have plenty of time to figure out if you think the Black Bloods are real."

I didn't move. "Where are we going to meet my brother?"

"Farther into the mountains. No point in telling you where, you'd never be able to find it."

"Right." I crawled over to the bedroll. The cold ached in my hands. "Can we start a fire?"

"Not safe." He leaned his head back against the stone wall. "Not with the chance of soldiers trying to find us."

"Are you keeping watch?" I untied my dirt-caked boots.

"No need. The stones will protect us."

"Do you have another set of blankets?" I crawled under the heavy wool, grateful for the weight of it even though the air had left the material chilled.

"I was supposed to be traveling alone."

"You should share with me." I pulled the blanket up to my chin.

"I'll be fine."

"If you die of cold, I won't be able to find my brother."

He gave a smile that only moved one corner of his mouth. "I'm not sure which Emmet will do first," he said as he untied his boots, "thank me for saving you, or murder me for dragging you through the mountains."

"I've no idea. I don't really know him."

I turned away as he crawled under the blanket. Even through my coat, I could feel the heat of him. It made the cave seem less like a tomb.

The blue light blinked out, leaving us in darkness.

I took a shuddering breath. "I don't know your name."

"Liam." His breath whispered on the back of my neck.

"I have nightmares, Liam. I'm sorry if they wake you."

12

The night stretched in front of me. Endless blackness I would never be strong enough to defeat. The pounding of hooves battered my ears, but there was a new sound.

Screaming.

A terrible, painful shriek.

I knew someone was dying. I could hear it. The awful resigned fear of a horrible end to a tortured life. I strained my eyes, trying to see into the darkness, searching for the one whose life would soon end. I couldn't let them die alone. I couldn't let their legacy be nothing more than ashes and blood.

But the blackness surrounded me, and the racing horse carried me onward, deeper into the dark.

The screams fell silent.

"Ena," a voice called. "Ena, wake up."

I opened my eyes to a darkness that was not pitch black. Faint hints of the moon and stars peered into the cave.

"Ena?" Liam had a hand on my shoulder. He'd shaken me awake. "Are you all right?"

I blinked up at him, needing to be sure this wasn't just a horrible new trick the years old nightmare had learned. I took a deep breath. The blanket that covered me stank of damp and dirt.

"I'm fine," I said. "I told you I have nightmares."

"You did." Liam laid his head down on his arm. "You're safe here. I won't let anyone hurt you."

I turned back toward the stone wall and stared at the cracks, trying to memorize as much of the pattern as the dim light would allow me to see. I dug my nails into my palms, trying to keep myself awake.

But the world had asked too much of me that day, and sleep swallowed me.

The nightmare didn't come again.

13

We woke at the first hint of dawn. I rolled the blankets back up while Liam packed his stones away. In the early morning sun, there was nothing remarkable about the rocks. They were all dark stone, so black they almost looked like the obsidian I'd seen in some of the fancy traders' carts. There were no markings on their surfaces, no spark glowing within like the lae stone.

When the few things were packed up, Liam stood outside the cave, staring east toward Harane for a long time.

I followed his gaze.

Even as high as we'd climbed, the trees still blocked our view of the land beyond the forest.

I knew Harane was down there somewhere. Whether it was still on fire, already reduced to ash, or if the ones who had survived the soldiers' terror were waking up to another day as though nothing had happened, I didn't know. I would never know.

I hoped some of them were still alive. I hoped someone would be kind to Lily and give her a proper funeral in thanks for all she had done for the villagers. But they were a part of a life I could never return to.

I said a silent thanks and farewell to Lily, who had scooped a crying child out of the mud and given her a home.

I sent a wish to Karin that she would survive and find a husband who would protect her.

I asked for forgiveness from Cal. The boy who made me laugh and forget the darkness. The boy I'd very nearly loved. The boy who would grieve for me.

I held them all close to my heart and tossed their memories into the wind, where they could fly free and far away from whatever journey lay ahead of me.

Liam turned and started up the mountain.

I followed him without looking back.

We climbed in silence for a long while. Liam would stop every so often and look back as though wanting to be sure I could keep up. I'd stare back at him, munching on the dried meat I was finally hungry enough to eat, then he'd climb again.

I picked through my bag as we went, tossing the things I'd gathered for Lily away from our trail.

"What are you doing?" Liam asked after a root clump I'd pitched hit the ground hard enough to make a sound.

"Lightening my bag." I tossed another root ball onto a mound of rocks that had slid down the mountainside. "I don't think the soldiers will follow our trail because of it, do you?"

"I don't think any of them would be brave enough to climb this far into the eastern mountains, no matter whose throat I slit."

"Then keep going." I shooed him onward. "If this journey is going to take as long as you said, it's best for us to make good time."

I pitched a clump of lichen aside.

"You use that in ink making?" Liam crossed his arms, decidedly not climbing the mountain.

"No, for Lily's other business."

He stared at me for a moment.

"Healing," I said.

"Healing?" Liam wrinkled his brow. "Emmet never mentioned Lily being a healer."

"I'm not sure he knew. Since he only showed up once a year, it was hard to be sure I told him all the good stories about learning how to stitch skin back together, being vomited on by half the village, and hoping I didn't get hanged by the Guilds for it." I clenched my jaw, refusing to let my mind slip back to seeing Lily hanging from the tree. "Lily helped everyone in Harane who couldn't afford to pay the Guilded healer or was too sick to make it all the way to Nantic. I gathered this lot for her from the woods, but"—I pulled a handful of moss from my bag and tossed it aside—"no point in lugging all this through the mountains."

Liam started up the slope again, moving more slowly, as though inviting me to walk by his side.

I kept my pace even, not catching up to him until we'd reached a new twist in the rise.

"She shouldn't have gotten you involved in healing," Liam said without looking at me.

"I lived in her house. If a soldier had lifted the wrong floorboard, they would have executed me whether I had ever been useful or not. If the Guilds are going to murder me, I'd rather have it be for something worth dying for."

It took me a few minutes' walking to notice Liam had shortened his steps to match my own, smaller stride. I wanted to run up the mountain out of spite, but my muscles ached with every step.

"You should have told him," Liam said. "If Emmet had known Lily was getting you involved in something dangerous—"

"He'd have found another place to abandon me?" I took a deep breath, willing the scent of the forest to bring the comfort it always had. "Lily was closer to family than my brother. I wouldn't have left her to go to some stranger's house if he'd bothered to try and make me."

A stranger's house was where I'd have to go. If I could find someone to take me. An inker or a healer who needed an extra hand. I could clean, too, cook a bit, though nothing wonderful. I'd have to find work, find something useful to do. If I couldn't, I'd have to find a man to marry who could pay my way. I was young, but I'd seen girls wed well before my age. It was either that or end up a whore.

"Emmet will find a place for you," Liam said, like he'd read the fears in my mind. For all I knew, he could have. "He's been to plenty of places off the mountain road. He'll help get you settled someplace safe."

"I don't want my brother's help. I don't need him."

"I never said you did." Liam looked sideways at me, a hint of pity playing in his dark eyes.

"And I don't feel bad for not telling him about Lily." A fist of anger wrapped around my gut. "It's none of his business to begin with. And if we're worrying about keeping secrets, my brother running around with a man who keeps magic rocks in his pack is a bit worse than me shoving lichen in some wounds."

Liam's face turned to stone. For a moment I thought he'd shout. I wanted him to.

"Of course, maybe my brother's plain lost his mind. He ran from a fine life as a smith to follow a madman with a bag full of rocks through the mountains." I untied my rag of evergreen buds and scattered them across our path.

"You're following the same man through the mountains," Liam said.

"I didn't have much of a choice."

"And the *rocks* in my bag protected us last night."

"Because of your magic?" I tossed a mushroom at his boot. "Magic the Guilds haven't claimed?"

The muscles on the sides of his neck finally started to tense. "The Guilds can't use the kind of magic that runs in my blood."

"I really have followed a madman."

"Worse, you've followed a Black Blood." He stopped and turned to face me.

"A children's story." I stepped nearer to him, tipping my chin up so I could glare into his eyes.

"Tilk whisper of my people, but that doesn't make us any less real."

"Ghosts of bandits rampaging through the mountains, slaughtering anyone fool enough to cross them? We have enough monsters in Ilbrea without scary stories coming true."

"I'm not a monster. And my people are not bandits." He stepped forward, leaving only enough space between us for my bag on my hip. "There is plenty of blood on my hands. I've killed more men than I care to count, but it's either that or hide in the woods and wait for the Guilds to slaughter every last tilk. If fighting for an Ilbrea free from the Guilds makes you think I'm a monster, so be it."

"Fighting against the Guilds." All the air had left the mountainside. The echo of his words muffled the birdcalls in my ears. "That's where my brother has been? Not whoring his way through the countryside or being a back alley thief?"

"He found out what the Black Bloods are working toward. He chose to join our cause."

"Cause?" Sound and air popped back into existence as I shouted at him. "Like you think you could do any good? Like you're actually going to rebel against the Guilds."

"We are. We are standing at the dawn of a new age of freedom. Our rebellion—"

"Rebellion is not possible!" I paced in angry circles between the trees. "Fighting the Guilds isn't possible. How many thousands of soldiers do they have? How many sorcerers? All standing against the Guilds does is make you a volunteer for execution."

"Freedom is only impossible until someone has won it."

"So you and my brother are just going to march into Ilara and demand the Guilds stop tormenting us?"

"Eventually, yes." Blazing determination shone in his eyes.

He meant it.

It was the most terrifying thing I'd ever seen. Not because I was afraid of him. It was the idea of hope that scared me down to my very soul.

I laughed loudly, dimming the fierceness in his eyes.

"I suppose that's what you've been using my brother for, making you swords for your battle." I clapped a hand to my chest. "My apologies, Lord Black Blood, you don't need a sword. You've got magic rocks to guard you."

He stayed silent for a moment, then picked up the mushroom I'd chucked at his feet. "We do have stones to guard us. We have people and plans, weapons, and the will to bring down the Guilds forever. You don't have to believe me, not about the Black Bloods, or the magic, or the end of Ilbrea as we know it.

"But I'd have thought better of you, Ena. A girl who climbs into mountains known to kill and comes out alive with the means to save others—if she can't believe in the hope for a better tomorrow, then maybe we are all damned to burn." He tucked the mushroom back into my bag. "You should hold onto that. People outside of Harane get sick. Someone might need this where we're going."

"And where would that be?" I ran to catch up to him as he strode up the mountain. "Further into your fairytale?"

"We're going to a place guarded by stone, where the people who fight against the Guilds have made their home."

"What if I say no?" I dodged in front of him, blocking his path. "What if I refuse to indulge a lunatic in his madness?"

Liam stared at me. I waited for him to shout. He pointed behind me. "The mountain road is that way. If you want to avoid soldiers who might recognize you, I'd head north, away from the map makers' party. Get as close to the coast as you can, and hope fate favors you and allows you to stay hidden. Having to explain to your brother that you walked away from me in the woods won't be pleasant, but I won't force you to come with me."

Part of me wanted to turn and head west. Forge out into the mountains, and if an animal decided to eat me, so be it.

Part of me still wishes I'd turned and walked away.

But I didn't.

Liam nodded and started climbing the damned mountain again.

I followed him.

I tied the flap of my bag shut to keep the rest of the things I'd collected for Lily safe.

I stared at the mound of lumps in the bottom of his pack where he'd stowed the stones. I pictured myself slitting the bag open, stealing the stones, and pelting Liam's head with them. Safer to imagine that than to even begin to let myself think he could be telling the truth.

The top of the rise peeked through the trees with a wonderful glimmer of sunlight promising my legs flat ground to walk on. Gritting my teeth against the pain, I sprinted up the last bit of the mountain. Rocks took over the very edge of the slope, marking the end of the forest's reign. I burst out of the trees and into the sunshine.

There was no glorious meadow waiting for us at the top of the mountain. Only more mountains reaching as far as the land would allow me to see.

The beast we'd climbed was nothing more than a foothill to its fearsome brothers, who soared so high, trees stopped growing far before their summits. I thought I knew how deep the mountains ran, but I had never seen a full view of them, never once understood the terrifying vastness of the land.

Liam stopped next to me, scanned the mountains, took a deep breath, and headed north.

Toward a place the Guilds' map makers had never laid out for the world to know.

I stepped forward as far as I could on the eastern edge of the rise. The ground crackled beneath my feet like it might give way and toss me over the side of the mountain. I leapt back from the rocks, onto the ground softened by the dirt of the forest.

Liam stood a hundred feet away, waiting at the curve where one ridge descended to the next. He watched me as I looked back out over the mountains I'd never seen on any map. The enormity of it threatened to swallow me whole.

For a moment, I was a little girl staring into the endless black, terrified she'd be lost forever.

I felt Liam staring at me.

I turned away from the cliff to follow him.

He waited while I caught up to him, gave me a nod, and kept walking.

A long time ago, before the Guilds came to power in Ilbrea, there was a mother and a baby and a terrible storm.

The wind raged and howled. The rain came down so hard, no man could see the path in front of him. But the mother had been gifted with magic. She could form her own lightning, burn with her own fire—she had no reason to fear what the ungifted hid from. She ventured out into the storm with her baby, refusing to let the skies dictate her path.

The gods saw the mother and knew she thought herself stronger than the might of their storm. So they brought more rain, flooding valleys and upending forests until the mother's magic began to wane.

Exhausted and afraid, she lost her way, and had no hope of finding a safe haven from the storm. She clutched her baby in her arms, and begged the gods for forgiveness.

The gods do not forgive, and the storm raged on.

She scaled the summit at the heart of the mountains, climbing ever upward as strength abandoned her limbs, searching for a place she could shelter her child. A wide boulder was the slim hope the mountain granted, offering relief from the wind but not the pounding rain.

Lightning split the sky, and her baby wailed in her arms. The gods would not grant her child mercy, so the mother begged the mountain itself. Offered everything she had, everything she was, if the mountain would shield her child from the wrath of the gods.

She lay her hand on the great boulder, and poured out every ounce of magic she had, filling the black rocks far below with a power never meant to live in stone.

The eastern mountains are one, and separate. A vast range ruled over by one mighty summit no mortal could conquer. But the magic stirred the great one, and she bade the smaller peaks obey her. The mountain opened, granting the child shelter, as the mother was washed away by the gods' storm.

The child grew within the mountain, raised by the magic its mother had infused into the stone.

The child became a part of the mountain, and the mountain a part of the child. The mountain had bargained for the safety of the babe to gain magic. The mountain didn't know the mother's magic would change the shape of its stones, and make the mountain feel. For the heart of the mountain, where the baby found shelter, grew to love the child. To cherish each beat of its heart that echoed through the caverns and rocks.

But even young raised by magic grow up.

When the child was grown, the mountain opened its gates and let the person it loved walk out into world. But the mountain gave the one it had raised a promise—those who shared the child's blood would be marked as beloved of the mountain, and would always find safety in its embrace.

The child found a partner and had children. And those children had children. And each of those children carried the mark of the mountain in their blood.

And then the child raised in stone died.

The mountain mourned, and feared it would never again have anyone to love.

So the mountain sent a cry out on the wind, calling all the children who carried its mark in their blood home.

The generations of children felt the cry, felt the black stone in their blood calling them back to the heart of the mountain. So they ventured deep into the mountains where no one else dared go.

The mountain sheltered them from the outside world, killing all who would threaten the ones who carry the black stone in their blood. And the beloved children only left their sanctuary to slaughter those who dared to threaten the mountains they'd claimed as their own.

15

The day after the Guilds murdered Lily, I followed the madman Liam through the mountains, heading toward a place where impossible people believed in impossible things.

We didn't speak much the rest of that day, only an offer of food, and a warning of slippery ground. He found another cave for us to sleep in and surrounded the opening with his black stones. He crawled under the blanket beside me without protest.

The nightmare came. The endless black and the pounding of hooves. A gentle voice pulled me from the dream before the screaming began.

I woke to the weight of Liam's arm draped over me. I fell back asleep before I could wonder if he was awake.

16

My legs had never been so sore in my life.

We started the morning climbing up and over the ridge of a mountain. I looked at the long downhill waiting for us and felt a foolish sense of relief. Then I started down and realized what an idiot I'd been.

Liam kept to a pace I could match. I tried to tell myself his legs were dying, too, but I knew he was probably trying to be kind.

I had things I wanted to know—how exactly my brother had saved Liam and gotten involved in this fool's rebellion, what the hell kind of good he thought he was going to be able to do throwing stones against a giant like the Guilds, how much longer we'd have to walk—but I was too stubborn to break the silence. I didn't know if he was too stubborn to speak or just enjoyed hearing only our footsteps for hours on end.

It didn't matter much either way. I just kept tromping up and down mountains, refusing to hint at the pain that made my legs tremble.

The sun had moved past midday when Liam finally spoke more than five words at a time.

"We should get some more water." He didn't actually address me, or look at me. For all it mattered, he could have been speaking to the stones in his pack.

"We need water and more food," I said. "Unless you've got more dried meat stashed in your pack, or we'll be getting wherever we're going soon."

"I'll get us some fish."

"Fish from…" The sounds of flowing water stole my will to speak.

We rounded the corner, and a wide, shallow river blocked our path.

I opened my mouth to ask how he'd known we were close to water, before swallowing the question.

Liam shrugged out of his pack by the side of the river.

I fished the empty waterskin from my bag and knelt by the bank. I hadn't realized how thirsty I was until water was within reach. I uncorked the skin and dipped it into the wonderfully cold river.

The chill of it raised goose bumps on my flesh. I downed half the skin before sitting and unlacing my boots.

"We're not crossing through," Liam said as I set my boots aside.

"I didn't say we were." I stripped off my stockings. Deep purple bruises marked my feet and legs. I laid my stockings out next to my boots.

"Then what are you doing?"

"Catching fish between my toes."

His brow furrowed as I rolled my skirt up past my knees.

I dipped my feet into the freezing water and didn't bother biting back my moan of joy as the cold dulled my pain. A fish twice the size of my hand swam past my ankles.

"Hmm, too big for my toes. I guess you'll have to use your magic on the fish."

Liam pulled out each of his three waterskins and began filling them one by one.

"I don't know much about magic. We've never had a sorcerer visit Harane." I kicked my feet through the river. "Maybe you could form a spear of water to skewer us a meal. Or make the river solid and trap the fish where they swim."

He splashed water on his face.

"You could tell them about your rebellion and see if they'll jump up on land," I offered. "See if they're willing to sacrifice themselves to a worthy cause."

He crouched down next to the stream, running his fingers through the dirt as though searching for something.

"If you can't catch a fish, I'll find us something to eat." I scanned the plants around us—some trees, a few low-lying bushes, plenty of scrub and grass growing along the ground. "I can't promise it'll taste very nice, but—"

A sharp buzz cut through my words as a stone streaked out of Liam's hand and shot into the water. A moment later, a fish bobbed to the surface.

Liam leaned over the river and snatched the fish out of the current. He held the lifeless fish up, flipping it one way and then the other before laying it on the ground.

"What was that?" I dug my fingers into the dirt.

"Fishing." He shot another stone toward the river.

I pulled my feet from the water and dragged my stockings back on, not caring that my feet weren't dry.

Liam lifted another slain fish from the river.

"How did you do that?" I yanked on my boots.

He gave a half smile and laid the second fish next to the first.

"Was that magic?" I asked.

"Of course not." Liam pulled the knife from his belt. "I have it on good authority that magic only exists under the control of the Sorcerers Guild."

"Well, clearly I was wrong." I stood and inched my way toward him. "Unless you are from the Sorcerers Guild and are wasting a massive amount of effort tormenting me."

He started to clean the fish, like he hadn't done anything strange.

"You can't clean them with magic?" I asked.

"Some could. But that's not the sort of gift I was given."

He didn't look up. I desperately wanted him to. I wanted to look into his dark eyes and search for something I hadn't noticed before, any hint that he belonged to a world so different from the one in which I'd lived my life.

"What sort of gift were you given?" I asked.

"I'm a trueborn Black Blood."

"So you've said."

"That is my gift." With a flick of his finger, the killing stones flew out of both the fish and landed in the water with a plop, plop.

"What does *trueborn Black Blood* mean?" I knelt beside him.

"I'm a keeper of the pact." He looked up at the mountains. "I work with stone magic."

"So flying stones and the rocks that guard us?"

"Close enough."

"And that's all?"

His gaze met mine. There was no hint of magic in his dark eyes, just a touch of laughter. "I wasn't given the sort of gifts the Sorcerers Guild prizes."

"It doesn't matter. They'd still take you, lock you in their tower in Ilara and make you move stones for them."

"I know." He started cleaning the second fish. "They've taken some of the Black Bloods before, tried to take even more. The beasts hoard magic, and what's not under their control, they'll stop at nothing to destroy. We save as many as we can, get them out of reach of the Guilds."

"Aren't we already out of reach of the Guilds? All of Ilbrea could have fallen into the sea and we'd have no way of knowing."

"We keep the Black Blood children with strong magic hidden from the

Guilds," Liam said. "It's the tilk children we have to rescue. Show one hint of magic, and the Guilds will snatch a child from their mother's arms to lock them in the Sorcerers Tower in Ilara."

A shiver shot up my spine.

"Some want to go," Liam said. "Safety, prestige—the Guilds paint a beautiful picture of what they offer. We don't fight that. They can go if they like. But the children who see joining the Sorcerers Guild for what it really is—captivity, being forced to fight against your own people if the order comes down from the Guilds. The ones who would rather die than be taken to the stone tower, we get as many of them out as we can find."

"How?"

"Carefully." He rinsed his hands in the water. "I'll go get some wood for a fire."

He walked off into the trees, leaving me sitting next to the two dead fish.

"Magic," I whispered to the river. I'd seen it. I couldn't deny it. "I'm following a madman with magic."

I dug into the very bottom of my bag, pulled out the bits of moss that were left behind, and made a little bundle by the riverbank. I searched the ground near the fish for twigs and sticks to start a fire.

"Magic." I leaned the twigs against the moss. "What has my chivving slitch of a brother gotten himself into?"

I waited until I heard his footsteps coming back to strike the flint and light the fire.

"Hungry?" Liam laid his armful of wood by the flames.

"I've been tromping up and down mountains. Yes, I'm hungry."

A laugh rumbled in Liam's chest. Not a bursting laugh, or a true cough of joy, but I liked the sound. It was good to know someone could laugh after slitting a monster's throat.

I built the fire up while he skewered the fish. Birds I didn't recognize circled overhead as we ate our meal. They were larger than the kinds that searched for carrion on the western edge of the mountains. I ate my fish as quickly as I could without risking swallowing bones.

"We'll have to find shelter earlier tonight," Liam said.

I rinsed my hands in the river, and took one last, long drink.

"I can walk as far as you can," I said.

"It's not that." Liam pointed northeast along the edge of the river. "Shelter is hard to find in some parts of the mountains, and there are things I'll not risk meeting after dark."

"But you're a Black Blood." I slung my bag across my shoulder. "The mountains will protect you."

"Some myths really are myths." He reached down and took my hand, helping me to my feet. "And some myths are too real for my liking."

"What's that supposed to mean?" I stayed close to his side as he headed north, suddenly afraid one of the birds high above would swoop down and try to carry me away in its great talons.

"Nothing. It doesn't mean anything at all." The tension in his shoulders told a different tale.

"Did you grow up here?" I asked. "In the mountains?"

He didn't answer until we'd cut around a bow in the river. "I was raised like a Black Blood."

"I don't know what that means."

"Does it matter?" He climbed to the top of a mound of rocks and reached down to help me follow.

I ignored his hand as I climbed. "It matters to me."

"Why?"

"Because if a fool like you managed to survive childhood in these mountains, I'd be less afraid of birds swooping down to carry me off." I jumped down on the far side of the rocks. My legs screamed their hatred of me.

"I grew up in the mountains farther east than where we're going." He stood on top of the rocks, gazing east. "There are beasts that will carry off children if you give them the chance, but it's still safer than being near the soldiers."

"So"—I looked up to the birds still circling above us—"you're saying one of those beasts could come down and snatch me?"

"If they got hungry enough." He jumped down from the rocks and landed next to me with a thump that shook my nerves. "But they prefer their food to be decaying before they taste it. Don't die and they'll probably leave you well enough alone."

He gave me another of his half smiles and strode off up the river.

"I hope he knows he's not funny," I muttered to myself.

One of the great birds cawed overhead, and I ran to catch up to Liam, hating myself for acting like such a coward.

We followed the stream for hours. I gathered berries and edible sprouts, tucking them into my bag for later. There were plants I'd never seen before. I wanted to stop and examine them, see what use they could be, but Liam's constant plodding forward kept me from pausing. The way he moved, the way his gaze darted between the peaks on either side of us, made me afraid to linger.

When the sun had started to drop toward the west, the path ahead of us opened up into a wide valley. Scrub bushes and grass covered the flat terrain. The mountains to the east and west of the valley were formed of steep rock with no hint of plants clinging to their sides.

I turned to the path behind us. There weren't the towering woods of the slopes near Harane, but there were proper trees. Then the valley began, and it was like the trees were too frightened to grow on the open ground.

"Where are the trees?"

Liam gnawed on the insides of his lips. "They don't grow in the Blood Valley."

"I can see that."

"We could wait here for the night," he said.

"And if we do?"

"We'll be stuck sleeping in the valley tomorrow night. It takes more than a day to cross. I hate taking you on this path."

"Probably could have avoided it if you hadn't come south to help me."

"There are easier paths to where we're going." Liam looked up to the graying sky.

The birds that had been following us for hours had abandoned their chase.

"Bit late to go back now." I walked past him, out into the valley. A chill nipped at the base of my neck, like a frozen noose ready to tighten.

I waited for him to pull me back or for the ground to swallow me whole.

"We should be able to get a mile or two in before we have to stop for the night." He stepped past me and into the scrubland.

1 7

The sharp snap of thin branches came with every step. The flatness of the valley was a relief, but I'd never been so glad to be wearing a long skirt in my life. At least the thick folds of the material offered a bit of protection from the twigs constantly jabbing at my legs. And at least the pain of the poking distracted me from the valley.

There was nothing truly frightening about the valley. The ground held firm, the wind smelled of new spring growth. But I couldn't get rid of the chill on my neck.

As the sun crept farther down, Liam began gathering wood as we walked, picking up the thickest of the branches that had fallen from the low bushes.

"Does this mean we'll get to have a fire tonight?" I gathered a handful of twigs and tucked them into my bag.

"We'll need one." He pointed east to a boulder that stuck out of the mountainside. "Ena, you're very brave."

"Am I?" I snatched up every twig I could find as we headed toward the boulder.

"You know you are. If you weren't, you wouldn't still be alive." He shook his head.

I wanted so badly to know what thoughts were rattling around in his head hard enough he had to shake them into order, to hold his face in my hands and stare into his eyes until I'd gotten one complete truth out of him.

"What's coming tonight," he said, "I'm sorry you have to witness it, and I swear I will keep you safe."

"Safe from what?"

He stopped in front of the boulder. The brush had been pulled up along the face of the rock, as though some other travelers had sought the same, poor refuge.

"The Blood Valley isn't a pleasant place." Liam laid down his firewood and took off his pack.

"I figured as much from the name." I added my wood to his pile.

He pulled out the stones and surrounded us, making a wide circle with the boulder at our backs.

"Are monsters going to come for us when night falls?" I forced out a laugh.

Liam looked up toward me. There was no smile playing on the corner of his lips. "The monsters don't come until well after dark."

"Huh." I knelt beside the firewood. "We've got some time then."

"Most don't mean any harm." Liam sat beside me, sorting through the wood as though rationing our supply. "I'm not even sure they can think."

"Does it matter if they can think if they're trying to kill us?" I pulled the flint from my bag.

"Don't light the fire yet. Better to save the wood."

"For when the monsters come." I set the stones down next to the frame of twigs he'd built.

He leaned against the boulder, staring out over the valley. "If you believe the legends, this place used to be the most beautiful land in the eastern mountains. A valley of flowers and trees, some even say a stream ran through the center."

"What happened?" I sat by his side, watching the light around us fade.

"People settled here."

"And they tore up the trees and trampled the flowers?"

"No. They lived peacefully, until they were attacked. One dark night, strangers came into the valley from the north and the south, trapping the valley folk."

"The Guilds?"

"I don't think so, but I can't say for certain. The invaders brought true monsters, things I don't think exist outside the mountains."

I pulled my coat closer around me.

"The valley folk were penned in. They had no chance of escaping," Liam said. "When morning came, the valley floor had been stained red with blood. They say the trees and flowers died before the next sunset."

"That's a terrible story."

"It's not a story," Liam said. "All of it's true."

"How do you know?"

"I've seen it." He untied the bedroll from his bag, shook the blanket free, and handed it to me. "I need you to trust me, Ena. Whatever you see, whatever comes for us, you have to stay here."

"Is this meant to be a joke?" I knew it wasn't, but I couldn't give up that last sliver of hope.

Liam touched my cheek. His fingers were warm against my chill skin. And despite their calluses, and the blood he'd spilt, there was tenderness as he brushed back the hair that had fallen free from my braid. "I won't let them hurt you. I need you to believe that."

My heart thundered in my chest, but I only nodded.

He stayed looking into my eyes for one more breath before turning away and picking up my flint to start the fire.

A tiny pang sliced through my lungs, and the chill of the night tripled without his touch.

As the last of the sun faded from the valley, our fire crackled to life.

A shiver shook me to my teeth.

"You should wrap up," Liam said.

I tucked half the blanket around me, and held up the rest for him.

"I'll be fine," he said.

I didn't move.

He poked at the fire, keeping the wood from tumbling apart, then sat beside me and took his half of the blanket.

We sat in silence as the darkness came in full. I hadn't realized how much comfort the caves had offered. Sitting with the boulder at our backs and the stones in front of us seemed like a fool's way of begging to die.

The first sound that carried on the night wind was laughter, a cheerful chorus of it, as though someone had just told an excellent joke on their way out of a tavern.

I would have wondered what the joke was if Liam hadn't tensed beside me.

The hum of distant music filled the air as a fiddler struck up a fresh tune.

I leaned close to Liam's ear to whisper, "Are there people out there?"

"Not anymore."

Voices spoke not twenty feet away.

I squinted, peering into the darkness toward the noise, but I couldn't see anyone.

"Mama, mama!" The child's voice traveled in front of us as though he were running to his mother's arms.

I glanced to Liam. Pained lines creased his brow.

"How often have you come through the Blood Valley?" I asked.

"Twice," Liam said, "but I sheltered farther on. I've never heard these echoes before."

"I'll not stay in the dark with you," a female giggled. "I don't care if you're handsome. That only makes you more of a rogue."

"If you don't want to sneak away with me, I'll find someone who does," a man said.

"You wouldn't dare." The laughter left the woman's voice. "How could you even threaten such a thing?"

A wisp of a shadow fluttered through the darkness.

"Tamin," the woman shouted. "Don't you dare walk away from me. Tamin!"

The music changed, and voices joined the tune. The happy song settled a stone of dread in the pit of my stomach.

I gasped as a figure appeared in the distance, walking briskly as though following a long lost road. The man wore a light shirt with no coat to protect him against the night chill. The feeble light of the lantern he held in front of him flickered with a wind I could not feel.

"What is he?" I whispered.

"A ghost," Liam said, "or maybe he's only the valley remembering."

The man weaved across the valley and faded from view.

More voices came from distant wisps of shadow, patches of the night that seemed to solidify, swirling around a life that was meant to be led. They moved about in a group near where the music seemed to play. The way they shifted in the night changed with each new song, as though the darkness danced to the long dead tune.

It wasn't until my hands began to cramp from clutching the blanket that another solid form appeared—a girl my age leading a boy away from the other shadows.

They ran silently through the night until he caught her around the middle and pressed his lips to her neck. She twisted in his arms and kissed him, twining her fingers through his dark hair.

It seemed like an intrusion to stay so near them as his fingers found the edge of her blouse and traveled up the bare skin of her back.

A crack cut through the air.

The sound wasn't loud or terrifying, no worse than a branch breaking off a tree, but Liam sat up straight as though preparing to run.

"They're coming."

My breath hitched in my chest. The young pair were still kissing, unaware of the danger preparing to end their lives.

"They need to run," my words came out as a strangled whisper. "We have to tell them to run."

I let go of the blanket, but Liam took my hand before I could try to stand.

"It's too late," Liam said.

Another, louder crack cut through the night.

The young couple finally noticed something was wrong. The boy stepped in front of the girl as though trying to shield her, but there was no way for him to know from which direction the danger came.

A scream carried from the southern side of the valley.

Before I could try to see if the one screaming had taken form, a wail sounded from the north.

"We have to get inside." The boy grabbed the girl's hand, dragging her toward the center of the valley to some safety I couldn't see.

A third crack shook the ground beneath us. I held tightly to Liam's hand.

"I won't let them hurt you." Liam spoke over the terrible screams that rent the night.

A great blackness tore up from the ground, sweeping through the fleeing wisps, seizing them and dragging them below the earth.

"What kind of a monster lives below the ground?" I asked.

"I don't know."

A band of solid figures charged into view, their shining weapons raised. For a moment, I thought they had come to slay the beasts that attacked from below. Then one of the men buried his blade in a shadow. The shadow screamed and became a woman with blood dripping down her chest.

My muscles tensed, ready to run out into the darkness to help the woman. The man stabbed again, and she fell to the ground and lay still as deep red stained the dirt around her.

"Please no!" a man shouted. He ran not thirty feet in front of us, fleeing from two men chasing after him, swords ready to kill.

A tentacle of darkness writhed up from the ground and seized the fleeing man around the stomach. His cry of pain and terror echoed in my ears.

"Run! Everyone run!" a fool called into the night.

Dozens of people took shape, fleeing from their attackers. An arrow caught an old man in the back before he had taken two steps.

"Run," I whispered. "Please run."

Liam laced his fingers through mine, offering the only comfort he could.

The boy and girl who had cared for nothing but each other's flesh such a short while before were both slain by swords. He was stabbed through the chest. Her head was taken clean off.

Bile shot up into my throat.

A shriek carried from high overhead, and the pitch of the terror on the valley floor changed. A great bird soared through the darkness, picking up people and tossing them aside, grabbing a woman in its sharp beak and cracking through her spine before swallowing her whole.

The high scream of a child cut through the ringing in my ears.

The bird heard the noise as well and dove toward the sound.

"No!" I leapt to my feet, desperate to save the child from the vicious beast. "Ena!"

I stepped forward, and the night around me changed. The stench of blood and fear filled the air. There weren't dozens of shapes running through the slaughter, but hundreds.

"Leave them alone!"

The attackers turned toward my shout.

Liam seized me around the waist, dragging me back.

"No." I fought against his grip as the scent of blood disappeared. "I have to help them!"

"It's too late, Ena." He kept his arms wrapped tightly around me. "They're already dead."

A tendril of darkness lashed up from the earth, snaking closer, swaying back and forth as though scenting the air.

"Can it see us?" I asked.

"You stepped outside the stones," Liam said. "They all can."

The great bird spiraled through the sky and dove straight toward us.

A scream tore from my throat as the bird opened its talons, reaching for us. But the shouts of the attackers and the shriek of the bird drowned out the sound.

I tried to think of a way to escape, but Liam kept me pinned to his side, one arm wrapped around my waist, the other shielding my head as the talons stretched toward us.

A hum that shook my bones and a blazing blue light burst from the six stones Liam had laid on the ground. The bird's talons scraped against the glow but could not reach our flesh.

The men attacked our sanctuary, but the stones blocked their swords. The tendrils of shadow whipped through the darkness, cracking up from the ground as though determined to swallow our barrier.

"I'm sorry," I said. I don't know if Liam heard me.

A scream in the distance dragged the bird's attention from us. It soared up and over the valley. Cries of terror echoed in the monster's wake.

The men turned their backs on us, ready to slaughter the innocents who didn't have magic to protect them.

Liam didn't let me go. I think he was afraid I would run toward the ones screaming in pain. I wanted to. Every bit of me ached to. But he held me tight, and what chance did I have fighting against a giant beast?

The screams of the dying valley folk dimmed as time wore on. There were fewer of them left to cry, and their defiance had abandoned them.

The fire at our feet flickered feebly.

I looked to our pile of unburnt wood. I didn't want the fire to die, but I didn't know if I could keep from running if Liam loosened his grip on me.

"Let me in," a voice whispered from the darkness. A little girl crouched in front of the rocks. Tears and blood stained her face. "Please let me in before they find me."

"We can't," Liam said.

"We can't leave her out there." I broke free of his grip.

"Ena, she's not real. She hasn't been for a very long time."

I knelt next to the stones, inches from the girl.

"Please," the girl said, staring into my eyes, "I don't want to be alone."

"You can't go out there." Liam knelt beside me, locking his arm around my waist. "The monsters would add you to the tally of their dead, but you won't be able to save her."

A ball of grief pressed into my throat. "It's all right, littleling. You're not alone, I'm right here with you."

"They're coming." A sob shook the child's chest.

"I know," I said, "but you are brave, and you are strong."

"Don't let them find me."

"I…" I had no words of comfort to offer.

The clang of swords came closer.

"I'm right here," I said. "I will not leave you."

Liam took my hand, anchoring me to a world away from ghosts as the men found the child.

"No!" She tried to run, but the men were too quick.

One caught her by the arm and spun her around, shoving his blade into her stomach as though her death meant nothing.

The world tilted.

He dragged her back and dropped her next to the safety of our stones. He laughed as he walked away.

The child lay gasping on the ground, fighting for air that would only prolong her pain.

"It's all right," I said. "Just close your eyes and everything will be better. No one can hurt you, not anymore."

My whole body shook as I watched the little girl take her last few breaths.

Her eyes fluttered closed, and she faded into darkness.

Liam lifted me away from the stones, back to the boulder. He laid more wood on the embers of our fire.

"When will it end?" I asked.

"Not for a while." He draped the blanket over me and sat next to me.

A fresh wave of screams came from farther north in the valley.

He wrapped his arms around me, and I leaned into his warmth, waiting for the battle to end.

I don't know how long it took for the valley to finally fall silent. The human screams stopped first, then the bird vanished, and then the ground stopped shaking. Sometime before dawn, I drifted to sleep.

The sun on my face woke me the next morning. I kept my eyes shut.

If Liam had been wrong, if it wasn't ghosts we had been forced to witness being murdered, but real, living people, then I'd sat in safety and let them all be killed. If hundreds of people had been slaughtered right in front of us, then the valley floor would be coated in blood.

The weight of Liam's arm around my shoulder changed. I could tell from the pace of his breathing that he was awake.

This is the world, Ena. Bloody or not, it's all there is.

I took a deep breath and opened my eyes.

A vast valley of low scrubland shone gold and green in the dawn light. I gave a shaky exhale, burying the fear and grief down far enough they couldn't break me.

"Are you all right?" Liam asked.

"Yes." I pulled the string from the bottom of my braid and shook my hair free. "We'll be out of here before dark?"

"Unless disaster hits." Liam's gaze kept darting back to me as he rolled up the blanket. "I'm sorry you had to see that. I didn't—"

"I'm fine." I ran my fingers through my hair and wove it into a fresh braid. "I just don't understand why. Of all the terrible things that have happened in this world, why does this keep coming back? Why should these people continue to suffer in death?"

"The mountains have magic all their own. Some even say the mountains have a heart that feels and loves." Liam picked up the stones that had protected us from the monsters, both men and beasts. "Maybe the mountains don't want us to forget how evil the world can be."

"I didn't know that was a thing people forgot."

"Ena, I..." His voice trailed away. He slung his pack onto his back. "I only wanted to help you. I'm sorry if any of this makes your nightmares worse."

I stomped out the last embers of our fire. "Don't worry. The nightmare came long before I met you."

He waited while I draped my bag over my shoulder. Then we walked to the center of the valley and headed north.

There wasn't a trace of blood on the ground.

19

We found shelter under an outcropping of rocks that night. I was so tired I fell asleep before Liam climbed under the blanket behind me.

I slept through the whole night without a single dream. I woke in the morning to find I'd turned in my sleep. My cheek rested on Liam's chest, and he held me tight, as though even in sleep he wanted to protect me from the ghosts of long ago torment.

20

"This place we're going," I said as I trailed my fingers along the bark of the trees, "what sort of place is it?"

"What do you mean?" There was a hint of a smile in Liam's voice.

I wanted to dash in front of him to see if the smile had actually made it all the way to his face. Instead, I tipped my head back to stare at the treetops. We'd left the scrublands behind, and trees had taken over the mountainside again.

The forest we'd spent the afternoon trudging through wasn't made of the harsh sort of trees that had clung to the other slopes we'd traveled. These trunks were thick and healthy, with hordes of bright green buds waiting to burst through. The soil beneath our boots held a strong scent of fertility, as though the mountain herself bade the plants to grow.

"Are we going to a village?" I asked. "Is that where we're meeting my brother?"

"There aren't villages in the mountains. Villages need roads for people to reach them."

"A settlement then?" I stopped beside a low patch of berries, kneeling down to touch the waxy leaves.

"I suppose?" Liam leaned against a tree. "It's our encampment for the warm months."

"Encampment?" I picked one of the nubs that would become a berry, crushing the hard knot between my fingers. "Right."

"What were you hoping for? A grand set of caves?"

I heard the smile again and glanced up to find a beautiful glimmer in his dark eyes.

"If you want to know the truth, I was hoping for someplace I might be able to take a bath and wash my clothes." I wiped the sour-scented pulp from my fingers onto a tree. "There's enough mud on my skirts to plant a thriving garden."

Liam stepped forward, raising his hand.

I froze, not even remembering how to breathe, as he wiped his thumb across my cheek. "I'll make sure you get the chance to wash your face, too."

Heat rose up my neck and flared into my cheeks. Days in the mountains, of course I looked like a child come in from playing in the mud.

He brushed something away from my other cheek and stepped back.

I missed the warmth of his hand on my skin. An odd knot twisted the place where my lungs and stomach met.

"We'll find you a new pair of boots as well," Liam said. "A dozen more miles in yours and you might as well be barefoot."

I swallowed the sound I had meant to be a laugh.

"You'll be comfortable enough. I promise." He turned and started weaving through the trees again, heading east.

You're a filthy little waif he saved because he made your brother a promise, Ena Ryeland.

Yelling at myself in my mind didn't lessen my want for him to turn around and touch me again.

Don't be a chivving fool.

I ripped the knot from between my lungs and stomach, and packed it away with all the other things I refused to feel.

The dark space where I shoved the things I didn't want to face was bottomless. Like the sacks of the demons who come to steal naughty children in the dead of winter. A massive void that could fit all the horrors I wished to shove inside it. The seams never tore. The fabric never protested the weight.

So I shoved more and more darkness inside, hiding from the danger, one cast away thought at a time.

"Will my brother be there already?" I quickened my pace to catch up.

"I doubt it. Even with our having to take the long way, and even if his work had gone better than we'd hoped, I can't imagine he'll have beat us back."

"Long way? Did you say *long way?*"

Liam stopped and rubbed his hands over the dark scruff that had grown on his chin. "I couldn't keep you close to the mountain road. Not with the chance of Guilded soldiers wanting to see you in a noose. We had to go into the mountains, and once you dive that deep into the range, there are few paths men can survive."

"But you're a trueborn Black Blood. You can use stone magic."

"How do you think I know which ways a man can survive? We'll be to the encampment soon, and once Emmet arrives and we figure out where the best place for you is, I'll do what I can to make sure the journey out of the mountains is an easier one."

I bit my lips together for a moment, letting the things I wanted to say fade away.

"I needed new boots anyway," I said.

Liam shook his head. When he started to walk, he didn't move as quickly as before. Not like he wanted to be sure I could catch up, more as though he were searching for something.

I scanned the forest around us, trying to spot whatever it was he might be looking for.

Birds filled the trees in greater numbers than we'd seen farther east in the mountains. Small animals scurried through the woods as well, rustling the decay of last autumn's leaves in their wake. Moss clung to the northern side of the trees, though none that I saw would be useful in healing. Lichen grew in a patch by the side of a great boulder made of dark stone.

It struck me as strange that the moss and such hadn't seen fit to grow on the stone's surface.

The base of the boulder dug into the ground, hiding its edge from view. I pictured the stone reaching all the way down to the root of the mountains, touching the heart that had cared for the ill-fated woman and her stone-raised babe.

"Ena"—Liam stepped back to walk by my side—"I think you should take my arm."

"What for?" I asked even as I rested my hand on his elbow. "You think after our days of climbing, this gentle stroll will drop me?"

"No." Liam slowed his pace again. "But the first time feeling it can be shocking to some."

I didn't have the chance to open my mouth to ask what under the sky he was talking about.

It started like a bright flash of heat in the front of my ribs and tip of my nose. I flinched, shying away from the unnatural warmth, but Liam placed his hand on mine, guiding me forward.

"Trust me, Ena."

I let my body lean farther into the heat and found the warmth didn't burn.

The feeling was less like a fire trying to sear my skin away and more like the bright burning of wanting something with my whole being. The utter joy and pain of longing filling my entire soul, and knowing that desire might burn away everything I was, and not having enough thought left beyond the wanting to care.

Liam led me forward, and the feeling ate me whole. I gasped and swayed on the spot.

"Just a little farther and you're through." Liam wrapped his arm around my waist, holding me close to his side.

We took two more steps, and the feeling faded, leaving me bereft and empty.

"Are you all right?" A hint of worry wrinkled Liam's brow.

"What was that?" I said, thankful my voice came out strong and not as hollow as I felt.

"A much larger version of the stones that protected us on our journey." He pointed back over my shoulder.

A second black boulder, free of moss and lichen, hid between the trees. If I squinted through the forest, I could see another stone poking up in the distance.

"Liam?" a voice called.

The shock of it sent me reaching for the knife in my bag.

"It's all right," Liam said softly before raising his voice. "It's me."

The branches of a tree to our left rustled and groaned as a man climbed down from a perch high above.

"You're late." The man beamed at Liam, striding over to give him a clap on the back before even bothering to look toward me. "And you've found a stray."

I tipped my chin up and met the man's laughing gaze without a hint of mirth.

"This is Ena Ryeland." Liam stepped away from me, giving a little nod in my direction. "Emmet's sister."

The man looked from Liam to me as though trying to see what part of the joke he'd missed out on. "She's not." He shook his head, sending his sandy brown hair flying around his face. "She can't be."

"I am." I shot the man a glare. He wasn't much taller than me, and though I'm sure he was cleaner than I was, the only reasons I could see for being the slightest bit polite to the man were the two long knives dangling from his belt. I crossed my arms and stepped toward him. "Is my brother here?"

"No," the man said, "haven't heard a chirp of him. Oh, Emmet's not going to like this."

"There weren't any other options," Liam said. "Sal, run on to camp and have them toss up a tent for Ena. Get Cati on finding her some fresh clothes and a bath."

Sal nodded, narrowing his eyes at me. "Emmet is not going to like this." He turned and ran into the trees.

"Sal," Liam called after him.

Sal turned, his face brightening as though Liam might tell him my existence had actually been a joke.

"Put her tent next to mine."

Sal shook his head, flattening his mouth into one long line. "Whatever you say, Liam."

"I'll make sure you get a good meal, too." Liam gave me a nod.

"Right, thanks."

I followed him through the trees in the direction Sal had fled.

The air beyond the stones tasted different than it had on the outside of whatever magic the boulders created.

It was something beyond the scent of smoking meat that drifted through the trees. More like a tang of vibrancy. Like the flavor of that one precious day when spring is done with its hard labor and decides to flourish into full summer bloom had been bottled, and the perfume of it had been misted through the trees.

Voices carried through the woods, more than just Sal and Cati. Dozens of voices.

My shoulders tensed as a cluster of tents came into view. All of the tents were large, big enough to fit an entire shop. Behind a cook fire, one wide tent had the flaps tied open, so the five people sitting inside laboring over food at a long table could stare at me as Liam led me past.

The number of actual living people in the camp sent my heart skipping at an irregular beat, ricocheting against my ribs, though I wasn't sure why.

Liam nodded and waved to the people we passed, but he didn't stop to answer their questions.

Where had he been, had he been attacked...who was I?

No one seemed angry their questions weren't being answered. They just turned back to their business while staring at me out of the corners of their eyes.

"Are you in charge?" I whispered as Liam led me past the last tent.

"How do you mean?" Liam turned down a worn path toward a clearing in the trees.

"You know damn well what I mean."

"Then yes."

The dirt in the clearing had been packed down as though trampled by hundreds of angry feet. Halved logs and carved stumps surrounded the space, as though spectators had enjoyed whatever sport had driven even the slightest hint of growth from the ground.

We passed by a chair wide enough to fit two, with a soaring bird carved into the back. I wondered for a moment how they had found a tree large enough to create such a thing.

Magic.

Prickles tingled the back of my neck.

On the far side of the clearing waited another batch of tents, larger than the first. A path cut through the center of them, with smaller trails leading off to the back rows where the tents seemed barely large enough to fit a cot.

A few men and women poked their heads out to gape at me as we passed.

I tucked the hair that had pulled free from my braid behind my ears and kept my head held high. I couldn't stop them from worrying that Emmet's sister had been brought to the camp, but I wouldn't have them murmuring that she had shown up looking like a filthy, chivving coward.

We stopped in front of the largest tent in this area.

A girl waited next to it, her arms crossed as she stared between Liam and me. Her hair was cut short so it rested above her shoulders. She wore a shirt and bodice, and pants like a man. The hilt of a knife poked out of the top of her boot. But it was the way she watched us, like she wasn't staring at the filth on my clothes but instead thinking of how best to gut me, that made me like the girl.

"Cati." Liam nodded.

"You've been gone a while." Cati tipped her head as she examined me. "She does look like him."

"Makes sense, I suppose," I said.

"Speaks like him, too," Cati said.

I started to say she was wrong before swallowing the words for fear my speaking might prove her right.

"I'll get her cleaned up," Cati said. "Rothford wants to meet with you, and I'm sure there's a dozen other things need doing. If you get started now, you might get to sleep tonight."

Liam shut his eyes for a moment before nodding and shrugging out of his pack. "Thanks, Cati."

"This way." Cati started down another path, leading me away from the tents. I followed her, not giving in to the temptation to look back at Liam. "We'll get you washed and work on some decent clothes for you."

"Thanks."

"Glad to," Cati said. "What kind of terrible would we be if we weren't kind to someone who came up the mountain road to get to us?"

"We didn't come up the road," I said. "We cut east and came north through the mountains."

"What?" Cati whipped around and studied me again, taking in everything from my worn boots to my filthy face.

"It's a bit of a story." I shrugged. "Liam thinks the soldiers might want me hanged."

Cati stayed silent for a moment before tipping her head back and laughing. "I think I might like you."

She beckoned me on through the trees to a mound of rocks sticking out of a cliff.

"Honestly," Cati said, "I've told Emmet he should bring you here more than once. Gods, he'll be furious. I can't wait till he gets back."

She stepped between the stones and out of sight. I took a deep breath before following her, expecting the burning to flare in my chest again, but a humid warmth and the sound of flowing water greeted me instead.

Two lae stones hung from the ceiling of the cave, casting their glow on the pool beneath. A crack in the rock wall fed water into the bath. The overflow from the current surged over the edge and into the darkness on the far side.

Cati fished in one of the dozen alcoves carved into the wall and pulled out a basket of soap that smelled as fresh as summer flowers. "Give yourself a good scrub, and I'll be back with some clean clothes."

She pressed the soap into my hand and left me alone in the cave.

21

I lay in the pool, trying not to wonder at how the water had been heated. It might have come from a fire burning far beneath the ground. Or, there was the far more terrifying option—I was sitting in a bath warmed by magic. In a camp protected by magic. After following a man whose blood held magic.

I scrubbed my hair with the sweet-smelling soap, digging my fingers into my scalp hard enough to hurt.

If Karin had been here, she'd have been positively giddy at being surrounded by magic.

Karin wouldn't have made it through the mountains.

It wasn't a pretty thought, but I couldn't come up with a way to tell myself it wasn't true.

My eyes stung with missing Harane and all the people there. Or who had once been there.

I ducked beneath the water, rinsing the suds out of my hair. I stayed under for a moment, letting the faint rumble of the water entering and leaving the pool drown out the thoughts of wounds I couldn't mend.

Warmed by magic or not, I couldn't help but be grateful for the bath. I scrubbed my face hard before coming up for air.

"You all right?" Cati stood at the edge of the pool, looking down at me.

I brushed aside the instinct to cover my nakedness and met her gaze. "I'm halfway to clean, so things are looking up."

"Good." She stared at me for another moment before moving to a pile of clothes set at the side of the cave. "We don't usually get unexpected guests in the camp, so we don't keep many extra clothes on hand. Lucky for you, when I said I needed things for Emmet's sister, a few of the women volunteered their wardrobe."

"Is Emmet that well liked?" I scrubbed my arms, getting rid of the last layer of mountain dirt.

"I don't know how many people like him, but we all owe him, and that's worth even more." Cati knelt by the clothes. "We've got three choices for boots, so we'll see which fits best. All of them are worn, but they're in better shape than the tatters you climbed here in." She rummaged through the pile and pulled out a slightly worn, deep blue skirt. "It'll be a bit short at the ankles on you, but honestly that's for the best up here."

"It doesn't matter to me. If it's clean, I'll take it."

Cati flashed me a quick smile. "Good. I truly don't know how the southern runners manage to get clothes onto all the sorcis they save."

"Sorcis?" I climbed out of the pool, wrapping myself in the cloth she'd laid out for me.

"Sorcerers we save from being trapped by the Guilds." Cati held a shift up to the light of the lae stones. "We don't bring the sorcis here, though. We funnel them south as quick as we can. The farther from Ilara they are, the safer they are."

"Is that what my brother is doing? Bringing children with magic south to keep them away from the Guilds?"

"No." Cati held a bodice up to my torso, tossed it aside and picked up another, which would fit tighter than Lily would have ever allowed. She scowled at it for a moment, then pressed it into my hands. "That'll look nice."

"What is Emmet doing?" I held out my arms for her to drape the shift and skirt across.

"Things that are better not spoken about."

I didn't like the sound of that.

I didn't know Emmet, not as he was. My understanding of my brother was a strange mix of what I remembered of him from when I was little and we still lived together in our parents' home, and the Emmet I'd created in my head over the years of him being gone.

For so long, the Emmet in my mind had been brave and strong, a warrior I could depend on if the Guilds ever came for my blood. When I found out he'd abandoned Nantic and me, I'd decided he was a chivving coward who didn't care for anyone but himself. Now, with Cati holding boots up to the bottom of my foot, I realized I didn't know Emmet at all. I probably never had.

I'd been a little girl when Emmet and I had shared the loft in our parents' home. I'd still thought the fairy stories he'd told me to get me to go to sleep were real.

Then I learned that nothing as beautiful as a happily ever after existed in this world, but he was already gone. Taken far away where I could pretend I still knew my brother.

"This should work for now." Cati left a pair of brown boots by my feet. "Get dressed, and we'll find you something to eat."

She walked out of the cave, leaving me alone.

I tried not to think of who the clothes actually belonged to as I pulled them on. Liam had already saved my life. I didn't like the idea of being beholden to so many people at once. But the feeling of being genuinely clean was enough of a comfort to make me forget how many times I might have to say thank you to strangers.

I picked up my old clothes to take them with me. The dull stink of them sent heat to my cheeks. I'd shared blankets with Liam in these mud-packed clothes.

My face flushed even hotter at the idea of him thinking of me as the filthy little sister of the great Emmet Ryeland. Then I realized he had probably already stopped thinking of me at all, and hurt nibbled at the edges of my stomach.

After days spent with only Liam, it seemed strange to be without him.

But he'd trudged back to his home, a place where he was in charge and had tasks to tend to and decisions to make. I'd left the ruins of my home behind. I had no ink to blend, no chores from Lily to accomplish. I was wearing other girls' clothes in a strange place where the only certainty about my future was how livid my brother would be to find me here.

"Ena?" Cati called in.

"Coming." I stepped out into the late afternoon sun. The wind chilled my neck under my wet hair.

"That's better." Cati gave a nod. "There'll be a comb waiting in your tent. At least there will be if Marta did as I asked."

"Thanks," I said, "for the clothes and all of it."

"Think nothing of it. You just came through the mountains to get here. The fact that you survived the journey makes you worthy of clean clothes and a comb in my book."

"Right." I followed her back toward the cluster of little tents. "Thanks though."

"Sure." She stopped next to the largest tent at the head of the path. A small tent had been set up right beside it. "This'll be for you."

She pulled aside the flap of the small tent and bowed me in. A cot, a stump for a chair, and a taller one for a table had been set up inside. A carved wooden comb lay on top of the thick blankets on the bed.

"It's not much," Cati said, "but this is about all we have to offer here."

"It's all I need." I pushed a little smile onto my face, hoping I looked thankful without having to say it again.

"I'll have someone bring food in a bit." Cati gave a nod, let go of the tent's flap, and I was alone.

For the first time since I'd smelled the smoke in the woods near Harane, there was nothing for me to do. No one for me to try and save, no soldiers to flee from, no mountains to climb.

I stood in the tent for a long while. The chatter of voices cut through the fabric, but the stillness in my little shelter smothered me. I lay down on the bed and shut my eyes, wishing there were something familiar left in the world.

Music dragged me from the blackness of my dream. I woke to find myself still surrounded by darkness.

For one terrible moment, I thought the nightmare had learned another new trick, a way to keep me pinned in its grasp by not letting me know if I was awake.

Then I saw the glimmers of light fighting through the fabric of my tent and remembered where I was. I lay on top of my blankets for a few minutes, listening.

Someone plucked at an instrument. A few voices sang along, though not all of them very well. Chatter weaved in and out of the music. Laughter, too. The steady thumping of feet striking the ground kept time with the tune.

Dancing.

Old stories of ghosts reveling in the woods, luring in living men and making them dance until they died, shot a shiver through my shoulders.

"You ran into the mountains with a Black Blood, Ena. You can't afford to become a coward now."

I sat up on my cot and combed my hair. The normality of the motion soothed my nerves. I didn't have a string to tie the end of a braid with, so I let my hair lie loose around my shoulders in a way that would have driven Lily mad.

Remembering her scowling face carved another tiny hole in my chest.

One day, there might be nothing left of me but a vast emptiness.

I pressed my hands to my chest and took a deep breath. My heart beat within my ribs, thumping against my hands. That had to be enough. Breathing and living had to be enough. It was all I could manage.

I ran the comb through my hair one last time and stepped out of my tent.

Lae stones hung along the wide path between the tents, making a trail of blue light to the clearing beyond. Squaring my shoulders, I walked toward the music, determined that, if I was going to walk into the middle of a ghost's revel and be made to dance until I died, I would do it with my head held high and not a hint of cowardice about me.

People filled the clearing—sitting on the halved logs and stumps, clustered around a barrel and small fire on the far side, dancing on the packed earth in the center. Two women stood on one of the benches, playing their instruments, switching between songs with barely a nod or word spoken between them.

Lae stones hung from the trees, casting their light on the whole joyous mess.

I stood at the far edge, watching, searching for the reason for the celebration. I didn't see a pair acting like a new bride and groom, or spot anyone preening like the party was being held in their honor.

But they were all smiling and laughing.

"Ena?" A girl my age with hair so blond it was almost white stepped in front of me.

"Yes." I didn't know what else to say.

The girl smiled, and dimples punctured her rosy cheeks. "I was wondering if you were going to wake up hungry. I tried to bring you some dinner earlier, but you were asleep, and Cati said you'd been through the mountains so I didn't think it would be right to wake you."

I dug my nails into my palms, praying to whatever god could listen so far into the mountains that if this blond girl had seen me sleeping, she at least hadn't found me in the middle of the nightmare.

"Well"—the girl took my hand like we'd been friends since childhood and led me into the clearing—"you're awake now, and you've got to be starving. Bless the stars for Liam, but I'm sure he didn't feed you nearly as well as he should have." The girl gave a bright laugh.

"We managed."

The sounds and movement in the clearing changed as the revelers began to notice me. The whispers started lapping from the far end. One of the women stopped playing, only starting again when the other stomped on her toe.

"Come on." The girl tugged me through the center of the pack.

I kept my face front and my breathing even, refusing to let any hint of pink creep into my cheeks.

"We've got a bit of stew over here," the girl said. "Neil doesn't usually take well to people ferreting for food once he's done feeding the camp for the day, but if you want something more than that, I think he might make an exception for you."

A cluster of men just older than me stopped their whispering as we drew level with them.

"Because I'm Emmet's sister?" I said loud enough for the men to hear.

Three of the four had the good sense to turn their faces from me. One with bright red hair met my gaze and gave me a nod.

"That and you managed to survive being alone with Liam for days." The girl laughed again.

"What's your name?" I asked.

"Oh, sorry." The girl wrinkled her nose as she stopped next to the barrel. "I hardly ever meet new people, so I suppose I forget how it's meant to be done. I'm Marta."

"Nice to meet you," I said, but Marta had stopped listening to me.

"Can I get a stew and ale?" she spoke to the older man who seemed to be in charge of minding the barrel and the fire with the stewpot hanging over it.

The man looked at me with narrowed eyes before nodding.

"We eat pretty well here," Marta said, "at least as far as being in the camp goes. It's not anything compared to what we get in the winter, but I suppose that's the price we pay."

She kept chattering as the older man pressed a wooden bowl of stew into one of my hands and a mug of brown ale into the other. He gave me a nod, and what might have been a smile, as Marta led me away.

"Honestly," Marta said, patting the bench for me to sit next to her, "I think you'll be happy here once you've settled in a bit. Life isn't fancy, but we're safe here, and we're helping, and that makes it all worthwhile. And I am glad to have another girl near my age here. There aren't very many of us, you know, and to have a new person come in, it really is exciting."

"I'm glad." I took a bite of my stew, risking burning my mouth in exchange for a reason not to have to say more.

"I've been telling Emmet he should bring you here for two years now," Marta said. "The look on his face when he finds out you're here will be brilliant. I hope I get to see it. And I hope we get to keep you. Maybe we'll work on convincing him together. Between the two of us, I think we could do quite the job of it."

"Maybe."

Marta kept talking while I ate the thick stew and drank the ale that tasted of pressed flowers. I didn't say much, I just tried to ignore the people pretending not to stare at me, and watched the ones dancing.

There wasn't a hint of fear clouding their joy. People laughed and sang in a way I'd never witnessed in Harane. I hadn't even known enough about what being safe was supposed to mean to realize how much fear had tainted every part of life in the village.

I blinked away images of a dark-stained post, and tamped down the anger even thinking the word *safe* boiled within me.

23

"If you would only let me do something to help," I said for the fifth time that hour as I followed Marta through the camp.

"You need to rest," Marta said. "Don't worry about helping."

"Marta, if—"

She ignored me and ducked into the open kitchen tent, leaving a sheet of paper under a stone on the table and giving Neil a wave before hurrying on toward the makeshift stables near the western side of the camp.

"I could be useful." I spoke through my teeth as I chased Marta through the trees.

I'm not proud of the three days I spent following Marta through the camp.

The first full day I had with the Black Bloods I mostly just slept. The climb through the mountains had taken more out of me than I cared to admit.

After that, the horrible itching ache to be doing something set in. I didn't care if it was climbing through another mountain range, digging for roots, or mucking up after the horses. The idea of sitting still and waiting for my brother to come back set my every nerve on edge.

Marta paused at the fence of the horse paddock. There were only six horses roaming between the trees. Truth be told, I wasn't exactly sure how they'd gotten the horses up the mountain. They certainly wouldn't have made it on the path Liam and I had climbed.

Even thinking his name set a chill on my neck and a stone in my stomach. I hadn't seen him since he'd left me in Cati's care when we'd arrived. From the little people were willing to tell me, he wasn't even in the camp anymore.

"It'll only leave us with four horses for now." Marta chewed the tip of her thumb. "I don't like it at all, but I suppose we haven't got a choice, have we?"

"Are you actually asking me?" I stepped in front of her. "Because if you'd tell me what the horses were for or where they were going, maybe I could help you work it out."

"It's nothing for you to worry about." Marta gave me a smile just large enough to display her dimples. "We have plenty of supplies here. There's no reason for you to fret."

"I'm not fretting."

"Good." Marta dodged past me and spoke a few whispered words to the woman who minded the horses.

The woman's tan brow furrowed. She pursed her lips, glaring at Marta for a moment before shrugging and going to the tent where the saddles were kept.

"I could help her with the horses, you know," I said as Marta hurried through the trees back up to the main body of the camp.

"She'll have it done in no time," Marta said. "Tirra's quite used to working on her own."

"It's not Tirra I'm fussed about. It's me losing my chivving mind."

"You're not going to lose your mind from a few days' rest." Marta waved a hand in the air as though batting away the foolish notion that the lack of work could be rapidly stripping me of my sanity.

We passed through the clearing where the camp gathered every night—dancing, laughing, talking, perfectly secure in their home far up in the mountains.

I wanted to stand in the middle of the packed dirt and scream. Shout to the entire camp that if they didn't give me something to occupy my time, I might catch fire from the inside out and burn the whole mountain down.

Sleeping brought nightmares. Sitting idle allowed thinking, which brought memories I couldn't bear. I had been reduced to chasing after Marta as she bustled through camp, organizing things in whispers, just so being angry at her would give me something to do.

"If you won't let me help with the horses, food, laundry—"

"There are already people doing all those things," Marta said.

"Then I'll leave camp and gather some plants for healing. You can never have too many supplies if an illness comes."

Marta turned back toward me, chewing on the tip of her chivving thumb again. "I can't let you do that. Liam said you weren't to be allowed out of camp under any circumstances."

A flash of white hot anger burned away the little self-control I'd managed to retain. "Liam says I'm not allowed out of camp? And the chivving slitch didn't see fit to tell me himself?"

"Ena." Marta blushed.

"And why am I not to be allowed out of camp? Am I a prisoner now? Is he afraid there will be soldiers hunting me this high in the mountains?"

"He only wants to keep you safe."

"Don't you even—"

A slow clapping cut me off. I turned to find Cati leaning against a tree in the shadows.

"She's finally cracked." Cati pushed away from the tree, a tiny smile playing on her lips. "I thought it would have happened sooner."

"Cati," Marta warned.

"I bet you were going to explode yesterday." Cati ignored Marta. "Rothford won the bet. I'm out a copper."

"You bet on me losing my mind from sitting still?" I asked.

"That wasn't a very welcoming thing to do," Marta said.

Cati shrugged. "So what's wrong then?"

"I can't just sit around here waiting for precious Emmet to show up," I said. "And I won't be told I'm not allowed to leave camp."

"But Liam—"

"I'm not a child who needs to be kept in the garden." I spoke over Marta. "I'm not useless, and I won't be treated like I am."

"Well, Marta?" Cati crossed her arms, still smiling.

"I suppose," Marta said, looking up to the treetops as though seeking answers from the gods, "there is always a use for more people in the kitchen tent. Neil tells wonderful stories—"

"I don't—"

"Sounds like you don't need Ena's help." Cati stepped between us and looped her arm through mine. "Come with me, Ena. I've got something to keep you busy."

She led me off through the trees, not bothering with a path.

"Wait." Marta chased after us. "Where are you going?"

"To train," Cati said.

"No," Marta said. "Absolutely not. She is not going to train with you. She is to be kept safe until Emmet returns."

"I'm not going to stab her," Cati said.

"She is not a fighter," Marta said.

Cati let go of my arm and rounded on Marta. "I don't care what Liam said. I don't care what Emmet will think. Whatever ends up happening, wherever Ena ends up going, she'll be better off if she knows which end of a knife to shove into someone's eye. Consider her training an investment in her future survival, whether or not she ends up staying with the Black Bloods."

Marta bit her lips together as her face turned bright red.

"Go tally supplies and save Ilbrea." Cati shooed her away.

"If this goes badly, you're taking the blame." Marta gave one final and decisive shake of her head before striding away.

Cati didn't speak again until Marta had disappeared through the trees. "Ready then?"

I wanted to ask what I was supposed to be ready for, but I was too afraid Cati might change her mind and leave me to sit on a stump.

I followed her deep into the trees toward the largest clearing in the camp.

I don't know why they had set the training field so far back from the tents. Maybe it was to keep the clanging swords from making it seem as though the Guilds had come to rip through their canvas homes and kill them all. Maybe it was because there was so little flat space in the mountain refuge, it had to be used where it could be found.

It was a ten minute walk to the open space where the trees had been cut down and the stumps cleared away. The first time I had wandered through the camp, I had wondered at the size of it all. How had so many massive stones been laid to be able to protect a place so large?

But the idea of the mountain shooting talons of stone up around us, as though the rocks themselves held us in their grip, had been frightening enough I'd decided not to worry about how the camp had been formed. If it had that much to do with magic, it was probably best I not know.

The clangs of swords and twangs of bows carried through the trees.

"I meant it, you know," Cati said. "You do need to learn to fight, whatever ends up happening when Emmet gets back. A girl like you needs to know how to protect herself."

"What's that supposed to mean?" I watched as the young man with the flaming red hair hoisted his sword and charged at another man.

"The Guild paun who attacked you—" Cati began.

"Liam told you?"

"Of course, and the sad part is, I wasn't surprised." Cati turned to me, looking at my bodice that showed my curves a bit too well, before staring into my eyes. "You do know you're very beautiful?"

"So men will decide they want to come after me whether I want them to or not?"

"They can try it. But once you know how to fight, you'll be able to slit the throat of the next chivving bastard who tries to touch you." She pulled a knife from her boot and pressed the hilt into my hand. "Sound good?"

I gripped the heavy blade. The weight of it absorbed the hopeless, helpless worry that had been stinging my chest. "All right."

Every muscle in my body hurt. Bruises had formed on my arms and stomach from Cati's blows. We'd both used wooden knives for practice, thank the gods, otherwise I would have been sliced to ribbons.

I'd never seen someone fight the way Cati did. It was as though someone had taught her a fancy dance that just so happened to involve killing people. When the men on the field watched her, their faces filled with a beautiful mix of admiration and fear.

She showed me no pity as she taught me how to block an attack, and I was grateful for it. Even as I sat in the clearing, too sore to join in the evening's dancing, I was grateful for every blow.

She'd let me keep her knife and had given me a sheath so I could tuck the blade into my boot as she had. Having a weapon pressed against me felt like the most powerful secret I could ever hold. I was not helpless, and someday, I would be dangerous.

When the dancers had begun to slow for the evening, Liam walked into the clearing, his pack on his back and dirt covering his boots.

He gave a wave to the ones still frolicking but didn't slow as he crossed through his people and toward his tent. No one stopped him to speak to him.

His footfalls were heavy and his shoulders rounded. He looked exhausted.

We'd climbed through the mountains for days, and even in the worst of it, he'd never looked like that.

I waited until he'd disappeared up the wide row of tents before following him. I gave a nod to Marta, who'd been avoiding me since I'd gone off with Cati, and blushed a bit as the redheaded boy smiled at me.

The music followed me up the lae stone-lined path. Shadows flickered around me as though the night wanted to take over for the tiring dancers.

The flaps on Liam's tent were still swaying when I reached them. I raised my hand to knock, but the canvas wasn't a door. A foolish, nervous fear pressed on the front of my chest. I shook it away and settled for knocking on the tent post.

"What do you need?" There was an unfamiliar, harsh edge to Liam's words.

"Wanted to make sure you were all right," I said. "But if you're bent on being in a sour mood, I won't offer to bring you a mug of ale."

My heart thumped against my ribs as I waited for him to reply.

He didn't.

"Night then." I turned toward my own tent.

Liam pushed the flap of his open.

He stared at me for a long moment, then held out a small waterskin.

I took it, not even needing to get the skin close to my nose to smell the frie. "So you don't want ale then?" I took a sip, letting the fire of the liquor burn away the bit of me that was embarrassed for following him.

"I find the two don't mix well," Liam said.

"Depends on the person, I think." I took another sip from the skin. "A few of the fellows back in Harane took combining the two to a near masterful level. It was rather impressive."

A smile lifted one corner of Liam's mouth.

"So you're all right then?" I asked.

"Fine," Liam said, "nothing you need to worry about."

"So you're worried?"

"That's not what I said."

"As good as. Did it go badly? Whatever it was you disappeared to do?"

He looked at me for a long moment. It felt like he was judging the weight I could bear. Like I was a bridge he wasn't sure was steady enough to be crossed.

"It didn't go as well as I'd hoped," Liam said.

"Want to tell me about it?" I held the frie out to him.

"There are some things it's better for you not to know." He took a long drink.

"Because when my brother decides where I'm to be placed for safekeeping I might go running to the nearest paun soldier and tell them all about your plans to free Ilbrea of the Guilds?" I took the skin and had another drink.

"You wouldn't betray us." Liam leaned against the pole of his tent. "It wouldn't even matter if you felt any loyalty to the Black Bloods—you hate the Guilds too much to offer them help."

"Well then." I ducked under his arm and into his tent.

A bed, a table with two chairs, and a trunk left most of the space in the tent empty.

"Tell me what's wrong." I took a seat at the table before he could argue with me.

Liam stared at me for a long moment, as though warring with himself as to whether or not to toss me out.

I waved the frie at him and nudged the other chair at the table with my toe. "Come on."

My brashness started a steady thrumming in my chest. I don't know if it was the knife tucked in my boot, the frie in my belly, or the simple fact that I didn't care if he got mad at me as long as I got to speak to him.

Liam sighed and let go of the tent flap, shutting out the rest of the camp. "We need more."

"More what?"

"More fighters, more resources." He sat opposite me with a soul-cracking sigh. "We need more everything."

"And you can't get it?"

"I thought I had a chance," Liam said. "I went to speak to one of the other clans—"

"Other clans?" I leaned in.

"There are five clans in the Black Bloods. Unfortunately, none of the others seem to care as much about Ilbrea as we do. I thought telling them what the Guilds had done to Emmet's home would make them see how bad things have gotten. I thought it had worked." He reached into his pocket and pulled out a bird carved of black stone.

He ran his finger along the bird's spine, and its wings shivered as the stone came to life. The bird hopped around the table, its stone-making the only thing giving away that it wasn't a natural creature. Liam held out his palm, and the bird lifted its chin.

A short, tightly wound scroll grew out of the bird's throat. Liam unrolled the paper and read it aloud.

Trueborn Duwead,

Your bravery is the pride of all Black Bloods, but we can see no path forward to a free Ilbrea that will not bring suffering to all the mountain's people. We will continue to protect the magic you bring us and ferry the power safely away from the Guilds' control. If the chance for freedom comes, we will stand with you. Until then, we must protect our own.

Blood Leader Brien

Liam crumpled the paper. "And he didn't even bother to tell me to my face. It sounded like he'd help us. Then I get this when I'm halfway back here."

"Sounds like he's a chivving coward." I held out my hand and the stone bird hopped toward me. "Would you really want someone like that helping you?" The bird leaned into my fingers as I pet its cold head.

"I don't have anyone else." Liam took another drink, watching as the bird nibbled at my fingers. "We do well enough rescuing the ones who want to hide from the Sorcerers Guild. And I'm not saying it isn't important work."

"Freedom for them and one less trained sorcerer ready to kill any common folk who cross the Guilds."

Liam nodded, rubbing his hand across the scruff on his chin. "But it's not enough. How can the other clans not see it? After what the soldiers did to Harane, after what that bastard tried to do to you." He froze, staring at me.

He thinks I'll shatter.

I took a deep breath, testing myself for cracks. "The Guilds torment us. It's how it's always been."

"That doesn't make it right."

"No, it doesn't. Not even a little. But up here"—I let the bird hop up onto my palm as I tried to fit the words into the right order—"I can understand how the other clans ignore it. Up here, the mountains block out the entire world. They swallow everything beyond. All of Ibrea could be on fire, and we wouldn't know. We might not even get a hint of smoke on the wind.

"If I hadn't lived it, if I hadn't watched so many people bleed because of the Guilds, I don't know if I'd be willing to leave the mountains to try and fight the most powerful people in the world either."

Liam passed the skin of frie back to me. The bird hopped up onto my shoulder while I drank.

"There are people dying down there every day," Liam said.

"I know."

"What kind of monsters would we be to ignore that?"

"The kind that stay alive."

"Only until the Sorcerers Guild gets strong enough to conquer the mountains." Liam looked up to the canvas above him. "It'll happen. Maybe not for another generation, but Ilbrea won't leave the mountains free forever. If we just hide and let them slaughter and gain power, then how will we be able to say the Black Bloods deserve aid or freedom when the Guilds come for us?"

"Did you explain it to the Blood Leader like that?"

"I tried. But he's so caught up in this year's rations, he can't think of the people starving outside his control."

"Then find another way to get more people," I said.

"If the Brien won't fight with us, none of the other clans will."

"Who says you have to have Black Bloods? You recruited my brother. Haven't you gotten more out of Ilbrea?"

"Some."

"Then you'll find some more." I nudged his chair with my toe. "You've got magical rocks on your side. You'll find a way."

Liam held out his hand. The bird soared over to him, landed on his palm, and became lifeless. He tucked the bird back into his pocket.

"I—" I began, but Liam met my gaze. Fatigue bordering on defeat filled his dark eyes.

"What happened to Emmet and me when we were young, we're not unique. We're not the only children the Guilds stole everything from. What the soldiers did to Harane, how they killed Lily—she expected it. She knew they'd murder her for helping people eventually."

Liam took my hand in his. His callused palm pressed against mine, the warmth of his touch giving me courage.

"And what that man tried to do to me. No one would be shocked at that either."

"It's not right." Liam squeezed my hand. "People shouldn't have to live like that."

"No, they shouldn't." I leaned closer to him. "And you and I, and the rest of the Black Bloods in this camp, aren't the only ones who see that. There are people who will want to help you. You just have to find them."

"I thought you didn't believe we could overthrow the Guilds."

"I don't. But I don't think you're capable of sitting idly by while the world burns either. And if you're going to fight against the flames, there are a lot of other people incapable of doing nothing who will fight with you. And who knows? Perhaps, if you get enough fools together, you can save us all."

"Maybe." His gaze fixed on my hand clasped in his. He moved his thumb toward my wrist, his skin just barely grazing mine.

The edge of my sleeve shifted, falling up my arm. A flock of bruises darkened my skin. I moved to pull my sleeve down, but he'd already taken my arm in both his hands.

"Who did this to you?" His face turned to stone, even harder than the bird's wings.

"No one."

"Did someone in this camp hurt you?" I could hear death in his voice. He'd already slit one throat to protect me—he wouldn't hesitate to do it again.

I didn't say anything.

"Ena, I brought you here to keep you safe, and if one of my own people—"

"It's not like that." I lifted my arm from his grip.

"It's not hurting you to leave you covered in bruises?"

"She did hurt me, but not like you think."

Liam opened his mouth to speak, but I pressed a hand over his lips.

"It's Cati. She's teaching me to fight. Which does involve hitting me quite a bit, but not in a way for you to get fussed over."

Liam lifted my hand away from his mouth. "Why is she teaching you to fight?" He kept my fingers locked with his.

"Because I can't count on there always being someone around to save me. I have to know how to protect myself."

"You shouldn't have to." He held my hand tighter.

"But I do, and learning something is better than sitting around waiting for Emmet. Besides, since the Brien won't help you, shouldn't you be grateful for anyone who's willing to fight on your side?"

He let go of my hand. "I'm glad Cati is teaching you. She's one of our best."

"She is."

"You should get some rest." Liam stood and opened his tent flap. "I'm sure she'll want to leave more bruises on you in the morning."

"Right." I pushed away from the table and stood, refusing to let the chill night air make me shiver. "Rest well, trueborn Duwead."

I lifted the flap from his hand and let it fall shut behind me.

I closed my eyes, warring with myself as to whether to go into my tent, knowing I wouldn't be able to sleep, or to go back to the clearing, knowing someone might notice I wanted nothing more than to tear a tree up by its roots.

A prickle that had nothing to do with the cold touched the back of my neck. I opened my eyes, searching for whatever had set my senses on edge.

A head of bright blond hair glinted in the moonlight. Marta stood in the trees far off the main path, an over-large mug of ale in one hand, a bowl of stew in the other.

Our eyes met for a moment before she spun on her heel and stalked off into the darkness.

I turned the other way and ducked into my tent. I didn't bother lighting the lae stone. I pulled the knife from my boot and set it under the thin thing I pretended was a pillow. I yanked off my shoes and let the cold bite at my skin as I undressed.

I could hear him through the canvas. He couldn't have been more than fifteen feet away from where I stood. From the soft thumping of his feet, he was pacing in the open space of his tent.

I tried not to picture it. Him pacing and drinking frie. Him plotting to find more people to help save Ilbrea. Him worrying about saving villages and stopping the violence of the Guilds. Him thinking of how to get me away from the mountains and the Black Bloods and him as soon as my brother returned.

I crawled under the heavy layers of my blankets and stared into the darkness at where Liam paced, listening to the sound of his footsteps as I faded to sleep.

25

When I was a very little girl, my mother swore I would be the death of her. I loved to run and climb and tear down the road on our horse, even though my legs weren't long enough to reach the stirrups.

When I was six, my mother found me sitting on the roof of our house.

She screamed and screamed. My father bolted out of the barn to find my mother wailing like I'd already fallen to my death and me giggling at the spectacle of it all. Soon, the neighbors came to see what the fuss was all about.

The Ryelands' girl had gotten herself into trouble again. No one was shocked, and everyone but my parents seemed to enjoy the afternoon diversion.

While the villagers offered suggestions of how to get me safely down, no one noticed Emmet climbing up the far side of the house to join me. He hated heights, but he thought I was in danger. So he braved falling to come collect me. He took my hand and led me to the side of the house where the boards had cracked wide enough to create handholds for child-sized fingers, and matched me step for step the whole way down.

The adults had been so busy arguing as to whether it would be safe to have me jump and if my father was strong enough to catch me, they didn't notice I'd disappeared from the roof until Emmet led me over to make me apologize to the crowd for causing a fuss and to my mother for making her worry.

26

"How long did it take you to learn to fight?" I asked, shaking my wrist out, trying to get feeling back into my fingers after Cati's latest blow.

"Does it matter?" Cati tossed her wooden blade from one hand to the other.

"Yes. If you've only been training for a while, then I'm a hopeless slitch who will never get any of this right. If you've been fighting for a long time, then I should resign myself to years of bruises and pain while I try and learn how to not get stabbed."

Cati's laugh rang out over the clanging of the swords next to us.

"And when will I get to use bigger weapons?" I pointed to the blades glinting in the light.

The ginger boy dove under his opponent's sword, leaping back to his feet with a wide grin on his freckled face.

"You won't. I'm teaching you to defend yourself, and keeping a sword tucked under your skirt isn't very practical now is it?" Cati winked at me and mouthed something that looked like *soon.*

She hadn't said anything, but I was fairly certain Liam had laid out what Cati was allowed to teach me in no uncertain terms.

It really was the most practical course—teaching me how to throw a proper punch, kick someone who grabbed me from behind, and the simplest way to gut someone who tried to hurt me. And, though I was improving day by day, it was still far too easy for Cati to disarm me.

But the idea that Liam had forbidden me from learning the weapons that would be used in a real fight grated against every fiber of my being.

"Let's go again." Cati took her place opposite me, her legs set apart, her wooden blade resting in her hand. She didn't even look like she was trying to hold onto the hilt.

I wiped the sweat off my palms and prepared myself for her inevitable attack.

She waited until I was ready, then began shifting her weight ever so slightly from side to side.

I watched her movements, trying to predict where her attack would come from. Just when I was certain she would lunge at me from the left, she leapt straight for my center and knocked my feet out from under me.

I hit the ground hard, coughing all the air from my lungs, but I managed to hold onto my wooden knife. She planted one foot on my chest. I tapped the back of her knee with my blade before she managed to swipe hers across my throat.

"Well done!" She gripped my hand and hoisted me to my feet.

I sucked air into my lungs as casually as I could while pretending the trees weren't swaying from how hard I'd hit my head on the ground.

"We really should get you a pair of pants to practice in." Cati pursed her lips at my skirt. "Liam might not like it, but that will only make it more fun."

"Right." I blinked at the trees, trying to get them to stop drifting around.

"I'll find you something for tomorrow then."

Cati took her place opposite me again, but I still couldn't look away from the trees. The shadows of them had become familiar in the days I'd spent learning from Cati, but a figure that didn't belong lurked under the branches, staring at me.

I took a step toward the trees and felt the world tilt, as though I'd been knocked to the ground again, as Emmet walked out into the open.

He favored his left leg as though he'd been hurt, but that didn't slow his pace as he stormed toward me.

No, not toward me. Toward Cati.

"What do you think you're playing at?" Emmet pointed to the wooden blade in Cati's hand.

"I thought it was better than using the real thing and risking your sister's life." Cati crossed her arms and glared at Emmet.

"She has no business on the training field," Emmet said.

"Don't even start with me, Ryeland." Cati tapped her blade against his chest.

"Your job is to train warriors," Emmet growled. "She will not become one of your minions. She is not going to fight."

The rest of the people on the field had given up on their own training to watch.

I wanted to say something, but everything inside me had gone viciously cold. I couldn't remember how words were meant to work.

"I am training her to defend herself," Cati spat. "Your sister was nearly murdered. I am trying to make sure that doesn't happen again. She should be able to protect herself."

"It's my job to protect her," Emmet said. "It's my job to keep her safe."

"Grand chivving job you've done of it so far," Cati said.

"She is not yours to train." Emmet stepped in front of me like he was shielding me from Cati. Like of all the things in Ilbrea, Cati was the true danger.

Through the chilling numbness I felt my feet move as I walked around to stand in front of Emmet. I felt the blade fall from my hand and my fingers curl into a fist. My weight shifted as I drew my arm back and punched my brother straight in the jaw.

He stumbled, blinking at me like he couldn't quite make sense of why his face suddenly hurt so badly.

"You do not speak for me." The words scratched like stones in my throat.

"Ena, I—"

"You have no right to say what I'm allowed to do."

"You don't understand—"

"What?" I shouted, letting my voice ring over the field. "What don't I understand, dear brother? That you abandoned me? That you left me with a woman who defied the Guilds every day? Let me grow up in the house the soldiers burned to the ground with Lily swinging out front?"

"I didn't know." Emmet's face paled. "I didn't know Lily was a healer."

"How could you have? You weren't there. You never showed up for long enough for me to tell you the sort of danger that hid beneath the floor in Lily's house. You weren't there when the soldiers murdered her."

"I'm sorry." Emmet reached toward me. "I never wanted anything like this to happen. I only wanted you to be safe."

"Safe." I spat the word. "Safe in a village where the soldiers whip people to death? You're right, that's so much better than being here where my dearest chivving brother has been hiding. The gods would hate you for bringing your sister into this dangerous place where there are no people being hanged from trees."

"Ena, you don't understand. The work I'm doing—"

"Has worse consequences than being executed by the Guilds? Than watching the only thing close to family you have swing? Than having a chivving stranger save you from being raped in the streets?"

Emmet just stared at me, pain creasing the corners of his eyes.

"Well, you needn't bother yourself with me ever again. You abandoned me a long time ago. As far as I'm concerned, I don't have a brother."

I turned and strode away into the woods.

I forced myself to breathe. To pull air into my lungs like somehow that might make the shattering in my chest stop. I pressed my palms to my stomach, trying to keep my hands from trembling. But all of me had started shaking like I might crack apart at the seams.

The trees began to sway again as my breath stopped filling my lungs and a sob broke free from my chest. I swiped the tears from my cheeks, but more took their place.

My sobs banged against my ribs, threatening to split me in two, but I couldn't make them stop.

I had lost Lily. She was gone, killed, and I hadn't been there to help her. My home had been burned, the life I'd known ripped away, and there was no hope of ever getting it back.

For the second time in my life, I'd been stripped of everything I was and everyone I'd cared for.

I had run from the flames of Harane, but I couldn't escape what had happened. Emmet pretending he cared had fractured the dark place where I'd hidden the reality of what I'd lost.

I wanted the tears to stop. I tried to shove everything back into the void where it couldn't hurt me. But the pain had broken past its boundary, and I didn't know how to shut it away.

A hand touched my shoulder, the weight of it familiar even through the haze of grief.

"Ena," Liam whispered my name.

A deeper crack cut through my chest. Nine years' worth of grief and fear refused to be tucked away any longer.

Liam wrapped his arms around me. I lay my cheek against his chest.

The harder I cried, the tighter he held me. Like somehow he could hold together the shattered pieces of my soul, keep them safe in his grip and make sure no part of me tumbled away and was lost forever.

I don't remember him lifting me, but somehow he was sitting with me cradled in his lap. His cheek pressed to my hair, his body arching around mine.

Sense started to come back as the tears slowed, and part of me wanted to explain. To offer some excuse for why I had shattered into so many pieces. But he had seen the nightmare torment me, and I didn't know if I was strong enough to start the story from its true beginning.

Liam held me without question until the tears finally stopped.

"I'm sorry," were the first words I managed to say without sobbing.

"For what?" He kept his arms tight around me.

I closed my eyes, trying to memorize the way my body nestled into his. "All of it."

"You've nothing to be sorry for."

I coughed out a laugh that made my ribs ache.

"I mean it, Ena. You've nothing to be sorry for."

"I'm not going." I listened to the wind whisper through the branches while I waited for him to speak.

"What do you mean?"

"I don't care what Emmet wants. He is not in control of my life, and I'm not going to let him choose a place to send me."

Liam leaned away and tipped my chin up so he could look into my eyes. "Then where do you want to go? Pick a place, and I'll do everything I can to see you safely there."

"I'm staying here. I want to help you."

"No. Ena, no. You can't stay here. You can't be a part of this."

"Why not?" I wiped the tears from my cheeks, trying not to think of how swollen my face might be. "You need people, and I can help."

"No, you can't." Liam lifted me off his lap and stood me up.

"I'm useful, and I'm not afraid."

"It doesn't matter." Liam stood.

I didn't back away. "I don't know how to fight, but I can learn. I know enough about healing to be of good use. You should be grateful I want to stay."

"You can't."

"Give me one good reason why not." I laid my hands on his chest. His heartbeat thundered under my palms. "And it better not have anything to do with helping you being too dangerous. Life in Ilbrea is dangerous. If the Guilds are going to kill me, let it be because I was doing something worthwhile. Lily taught me that. It's all I have to hang on to. Do not try to take that from me, Liam."

He looked down at my hands. "This isn't an easy life, Ena."

"I'm not fool enough to think it is."

"If you want to join the Black Bloods, I won't stand in your way."

"Thank you." I took his face in my hands. The rough feel of his stubble beneath my skin sent fire flying up my fingers. "You won't regret this."

He shook his head, and creases wrinkled his brow. "We'll talk to Marta about getting you work to do."

"Good." A tiny shard of something a bit like hope broke through the shattered bits of my chest.

Liam held my gaze for a long moment. "I'll see you back at camp then."

"Right." I watched him walk away, disappearing into the maze of trees.

I sank onto the rock where he'd sat as he cradled me in his arms. One by one, I tucked each of the bits of my life I didn't want to remember back into the shattered void. But the hollow blackness wasn't there to swallow them anymore.

So, I folded the horrors beneath layers of fierce fire. If I was to be a Black Blood, then maybe I didn't need a vast nothing to protect me. Perhaps it was time to use fire to burn the pain away.

"I'm happy to help," I said, careful to keep the smile on my face as Neil squinted at me.

The entire camp seemed to have heard about my punching Emmet in the face. Some seemed offended, others impressed. From the whispers floating on the wind, most of the camp had also heard Emmet shouting at Liam when he was told I would be staying.

I wished I had been there to hear Emmet shout and to hear Liam's defense of my joining the Black Bloods. But the whole thing had been over before I'd trusted my face to look normal enough for people not to know I'd been crying.

As far as I knew, Liam hadn't told anyone what had happened in the woods. I was grateful. If this was to be my new home, I didn't want everyone to know I'd won my place with tears on my cheeks.

Neil pursed his wrinkled lips and leaned closer to me. I don't think his eyesight was that bad. It just seemed to be how he always looked at people.

"Go foraging if you like," Neil said. "I've plenty to keep our people fed, but only a fool says no to extra food in their larder."

"Good." I hurried out of the food tent before Neil could change his mind.

I trusted Liam to tell Marta I needed work, but I didn't want to wait. Crying had left me a kind of tired I hated. But climbing around, foraging for useful things, would leave me the kind of tired that might allow me to sleep.

As much as I longed to run, I kept my pace steady as I walked to my tent to get my bag. I didn't want to risk looking like I was misbehaving as soon as my older brother returned to camp.

I had no reason to think myself unworthy of staying, but knowing how everyone spoke of Emmet made me afraid. Like the Black Bloods might decide they didn't want me, even if Liam himself had said I could stay.

I grabbed my bag and headed east of the camp, to the slopes that cut steeply up the mountain. I searched the ground for berries, or places where some might grow later in the season. If the camp would even still be in the same place when the peak of summer came.

I didn't know where the Black Bloods stayed when they weren't in that camp, or how long they would be there for. I didn't know how they traveled from place to place. I didn't know much of anything. I pressed my forehead to the rough bark of a tree.

The deep scent of the sap calmed me.

Liam was in charge of the camp and of his people, and I trusted him.

I remembered the feel of his arms around me. The warmth of his face beneath my fingers.

I shook my head, flinging aside thoughts of Liam's hand touching mine, and climbed farther up the slope.

I found a patch of mushrooms that were safe to eat, and a bit of sour grass to help season food.

I was so busy searching the ground for edibles, I almost strolled past the boulders that surrounded the camp.

The stones were just like the ones Liam and I had passed between when he brought me into the camp, formed of black rock with the bottoms swallowed by the earth and not a bit of moss daring to mar their surface.

Glancing around to be sure no one had followed, I laid my palms on the boulder. I waited, trying to see if I could feel some pulse or spark of the magic the mountains had granted the stones. I leaned my weight against the boulder as though I were trying to merge my body with the rock.

A laugh at my own foolishness bubbled in my throat before a tingle of something tickled my skin. Not like fire or a bee's sting, because it didn't bring pain. I pressed my hands against the boulder as hard as I could.

A pull.

That was the feeling. Like something inside the stone called to the blood in my veins. My blood answered with a hunger and a wanting that crackled and sparked.

I lifted my hands away, severing the pull of the magic.

A longing tugged at my heart as I turned west and foraged my way back to camp.

I kept looping up and down the slope until my body was tired enough to make sleep a possibility, then headed back to the kitchen tent.

The line for dinner stretched out along the path, so I cut through the back way. I caught a glare from the woman stirring the pot, but I gave her a nod and started unloading my bounty onto the table.

"I know it's the same meal as yesterday," Neil shouted down the line of hungry Black Bloods, "but if the hunters keep bringing back deer, then you'll keep eating deer."

"Couldn't you make something other than stew with it?" a voice called.

I bit my lips together and dumped the mushrooms out of my bag.

"If you don't like the food I'm offering, you can feel free to eat some hard-tack," Neil said. "And anyone who takes the hardtack won't be needing any ale to wash it down."

Swallowing my laugh, I snagged a bit of seed bread and a bowl of stew from the table before ducking back out the far side of the tent.

The woman stirring the pot tsked after me, but I didn't stop.

I felt like I'd been wrung out. Every bit of my being was exhausted.

By the time I reached my tent, I'd finished my dinner. I set the empty bowl on the stump that served as my table and lay down on top of my cot, boots and all.

I didn't remember falling asleep or the start of the dream. The pounding of the hooves had been dulled since I'd arrived in the camp, and the terror of the unending darkness unable to consume me. I waited through the nightmare, clinging to the hope that morning would come and wake me, but angry whispers carrying through my tent dragged me from sleep long before dawn.

"We can't." Liam's words drifted through the canvas.

I blinked at the darkness, trying to reassure myself I really was awake.

"It doesn't matter how much it needs to be done," Liam said. "We just can't."

"Why not?" Emmet said in a low, measured tone. Even when we were children, he spoke like that when he was angry. It used to make our mother laugh.

A pain shot through the newly sealed armor of flames in my chest.

"It's too dangerous," Liam said.

"He knew the risks when he agreed to the assignment," Emmet said. "Gabe is willing to sacrifice himself for the cause."

"But it's more than just Gabe we'd be losing."

"You've got to take a chance like this when it comes," Emmet said. "How many people are you prepared to let die?"

There was a thump like a fist pounding a table.

I sat up and ran my hands over my braid, trying to coax the stray strands into submission.

"We aren't going to get many chances like this," Emmet said.

I stepped out of my tent and walked the few feet to the front of Liam's.

"We would be setting ourselves back," Liam said.

Without giving myself time to wonder what the consequences might be, I knocked on the pole of Liam's tent.

Liam and Emmet fell silent.

I had time to look up at the stars in the moonless sky before Liam opened the flap of his tent.

"Ena, are you all right?"

I ducked under his arm and into the tent. "Oh, I'm just fine." I smiled at Emmet, taking a tiny bit of pleasure at the new bruise on his cheek. "I was actually sleeping fairly well until you two started worrying about Gabe's fate. I hope the poor fellow is all right. From the way you talk, he might as well be a sheep lined up for slaughter."

"This has nothing to do with you," Emmet said.

"Then maybe you should be careful talking about poor Gabe ten feet away from my bed." I sat in one of the chairs.

"I'm sorry, Ena," Liam said, not lowering the tent flap, "we should have been quieter."

"It's fine," I said. "What's a little lost sleep compared to the sacrifices Gabe is willing to make?"

Emmet looked from Liam to me as though waiting for Liam to kick me out. When Liam said nothing, Emmet leaned across the table toward me. "Ena, we're discussing important things here. Matters of life and death."

"Sounds like it." I crossed my arms and leaned back in my chair. "Of course, when you're dealing with the Guilds, sneezing at the wrong moment can be a matter of life and death. So, what makes Gabe's impending doom so important to the Black Bloods?"

"It's not your concern," Emmet said.

"Ena"—Liam let go of the tent flap—"I know you want to stay here."

"And you agreed that I can." I swallowed my glee as the veins on the sides of Emmet's neck bulged through his skin.

"But there are some things it's best if fewer people know," Liam said. "The work we're trying to do is dangerous. We may not have the forces to fight on a grand scale, but if we keep the small things we do hidden, the people we have are safer."

"Sound reasoning," I said. "But, as I already know about Gabe's death wish, since you failed to take into account that fabric is easy to hear through, is there anything I can do to help?"

"Yes," Emmet said. "Go back to bed."

"Because you think I'm a useless child or because you just don't like me?" I asked.

"Because you don't belong here," Emmet said. "You're not a Black Blood. You're not a fighter or an assassin. You've no experience killing people. You can't help."

"How many lives have you ended?" I looked to Emmet's hands, foolishly expecting the blood of the people he'd killed to be staining his fingers.

"Enough," Emmet said.

"And what about Gabe?" I hid my shudder at Emmet's cold glare. "Is he an accomplished killer? Does Cati need to go and make the kill for him?"

Emmet glanced to Liam.

"We couldn't risk losing Cati either." Liam pressed his knuckles to his temples.

"Sounds like whoever you want dead isn't worth very much trouble," I said.

"He is." Liam paced the open space in the tent. "That's the problem. We have a chance to rid Ilbrea of a monster."

"But you don't want to sacrifice one of your own?" I asked.

"Ena, you should go," Emmet said.

Liam stopped. He looked at Emmet and me both staring at him.

"I would be losing more than just one good man," Liam said.

Emmet gripped the edge of the table.

"We would be losing a spy we spent a long time putting in place," Liam said.

"Because if the spy kills the monster, he'll have outed himself and most likely be hanged?" I said.

"It has to be done," Emmet said.

"But how many lives will be lost if we don't know what's happening in their ranks?" Liam began pacing again.

I watched him tramp back and forth across the tent, treading the dirt path his boots had worn.

"Gabe can't slay the monster without anyone knowing?" I asked.

"I don't want to shock you, but it's usually pretty easy to tell when someone's been killed," Emmet said.

"I'm aware," I said. "I've seen more than my share of killing and corpses."

Emmet looked up at me.

I turned my back on him, focusing my gaze on Liam. "But does he have to stab the monster in front of a crowd?"

"No," Liam said, "but trying to make a death look like an accident would take more resources and men than we have."

"It doesn't need to look like an accident," I said. "Just poison the monster, and people will think he died of an illness."

"What?" Emmet said.

"It wouldn't even be that hard. A few years ago, Han decided she hated her husband, baked him a pie filled with shadow berry pulp. He died, and no one thought anything of it until Han went mad from the guilt and tore about town half-naked, confessing her crimes. If Lily didn't know Han had poisoned her rat of a husband, no one else would have guessed at it either. Lily had to treat shadow sickness all the time."

"Shadow sickness?" Liam asked.

"In children, mostly." I nodded. "Shadow berries smell sweet, and they grow in the shade of other berry bushes. The little ones eat them without knowing they've done anything wrong. By the time their parents notice they're sick, they're most of the way to dead.

"You can save them if they haven't started coughing blood yet, but that's the first symptom most people show. Got so bad last summer, parents started rushing their children to Lily if they found a trace of berry stains on the little ones' faces."

Liam sat down on his bed.

"You can't be considering this," Emmet said.

"Does it look like a normal illness?" Liam asked.

"Close enough to a fever fit, you can't tell unless you know what they've been eating," I said.

"It could work." Liam looked to Emmet. "Gabe could poison the chivving bastard, and no one would need to know it was him."

"We are freedom fighters," Emmet said, "not murdering mad women."

"If you're trying to kill a monster, does it really matter how you do it?" I asked. "Have the Guilds ever once stopped to think about what the good way to murder us would be?"

Emmet shook his head, but didn't look at me.

"Could you make the poison?" Liam asked.

"No," Emmet said.

"I'm not asking her to deliver it," Liam said, "only to make it. Could you do it, Ena?"

I bit my lips together, trying to sort through the realities of making a tonic not to save, but to kill. "Theoretically, yes, but I've never tried making a poison before. My work with Lily was always on the lifesaving end of herbs."

"Then we'll come up with another plan." Emmet stood.

"If I can get my hands on some shadow berries, it shouldn't too hard to mix them down into something subtler than a deadly pie." I stood up as well, looping around the table to stand closer to Liam. "I'd have to test it to be sure it was strong enough, and we'd have to choose the right way to mask it to be sure poor Gabe isn't caught serving something that tastes like poison."

"Who are you going to try the poison on?" Emmet asked.

"You could volunteer," I said.

"Where can you find shadow berries?" Liam asked.

"They grow all over around Harane, anywhere people haven't found them to rip them up," I said. "I've heard tell of children dying of shadow berries in other places, too, so they've got to be spread out along the mountain road."

"You haven't seen any in the mountains?" Liam looked up to the peak of the tent.

"No." I followed his gaze, though I didn't see anything but plain canvas above us. "The soil isn't right, I suppose."

"She can't go near the mountain road," Emmet whispered. "Liam, please."

Liam met my gaze, a battle warring behind his eyes.

I couldn't tell which side I should be fighting for.

"She'll only have to go far enough out of the mountains to find the berries," Liam said. "After that, you can stay with her in the woods while I take the poison on to Gabe."

"Congratulations, Ena. You've just agreed to kill a man." Emmet stormed out of the tent.

"I should be going with you." Cati shoved stockings into my bag. "I should be going instead of you. What does Liam think he's playing at?"

"I'm happy to help." I passed her the few fresh rolls I'd been granted, along with the packet of hardtack and dried meat Marta had given me for the journey.

Marta hadn't said a word to me as she passed off the food, turned on her heel, and hurried away.

"If he needs a woman, it should be one who hasn't just arrived here," Cati said. "I don't want to hurt your feelings, Ena, but it's not as though you're ready for a fight."

"I know that," I said.

Liam had warned me not to tell anyone of our plans to mix poison. I didn't know why it mattered if Cati knew or not, but I'd only just been allowed to join the Black Bloods and had actually wheedled my way into being given something important to do, so I only shrugged under Cati's glare. "Maybe he thinks they'll need a healer. I don't want to brag, but I've a fine hand for stitching flesh together."

"That is a valuable skill." Cati tied the top of my pack closed. "Just try not to forget everything I've taught you while you travel. And if anyone tries to hurt you—"

"Gut them?" I laughed.

"Be careful." Cati squeezed my hand. "That's all I ask."

I let her lead me out into the bright morning. She gave my hand one final squeeze and headed off toward the training field to torment some other student.

It seemed strange to be leaving camp. I'd never packed to leave a place with the intention of returning.

A few people gave me curious looks as I walked toward the paddock. I held my head high and my shoulders back, ignoring the weight of my pack. I'd salvaged a few small things from the kitchen tent when Neil hadn't been looking. I didn't know if the weight of the items felt heavier because they'd been pilfered or because of what they were meant to help me do.

Marta waited by the side of the paddock, watching as Tirra checked the saddles on four horses.

"Who's the fourth?" I looked to Marta. "Are you coming with us?"

"Me?" Marta gave a low laugh. "Not me. I, unlike some people, remember the promises I've made and intend to keep them."

"What?" I dodged around Marta. Dark circles stained the pale skin under her eyes. "Are you all right?"

"Why wouldn't I be?" She gave a smile that didn't show her dimples.

The tromping of boots came up the path to the paddock.

"Safe journey." Marta turned on her heel and strode away, barely bothering to give a nod to Liam, Emmet, and the red-haired boy.

A stone weighed heavy in my stomach. I wanted to chase after her and ask what I'd done to make her mad. But Liam had reached the rail around the paddock, Emmet was glaring at me, and I was too afraid I might already know why Marta no longer liked me. So I watched Tirra minister to the horses instead.

"Are you a comfortable rider?" Liam asked.

"She loves to ride," Emmet said.

"I can answer for myself," I said. "And if I was a slitch who couldn't ride a horse, wouldn't now be a bit late to be worrying about it?"

The red-haired boy chuckled.

I waited patiently while Tirra glared at each of us before passing over the reins of a horse. I was given a beautiful brown mare who didn't fuss as I strapped my pack of pilfered goods to her back. She wasn't the sort of horse one would dream of riding through fields, but she didn't look like she was going to drop down dead either.

No one spoke as we rode out past the edge of the camp. Liam led, then the ginger boy, then me, with Emmet riding in back as though making sure I didn't run away.

As we passed beyond the boulders that protected the Black Bloods, the pull of the magic within the stones sparked in my veins. I took a breath, letting the scent of the forest dissolve the heat in my blood.

The branches on the trees left patches of shadow scattered across the ground. I kept myself busy, scanning every plant in view, trying to find the treasure we sought. Trying to ignore the growing whispers of Lily's voice creeping into the back of my mind.

You fool of a girl. Leaping right out of the only safety you've ever known.

The day slipped past as Liam led us on a winding trail down the mountains. The slopes on this side were far kinder than the ones we'd climbed farther east. The horses didn't seem to mind them at all. Though, I suppose the paths through the mountains were what they were used to traveling.

We rode until dusk neared.

Liam stopped beside a stream and hopped off his horse. "We should rest here. There won't be another chance for a while."

"You know the path that well?" I climbed down from my horse, gritting my teeth to hide how sore my legs already were from riding.

"He's a trueborn," the ginger said. "Even the Guilds' fancy map makers couldn't know the mountains as well as Liam."

"There are some places in the mountains I'm sure I'll never know," Liam said. "But I have learned this is the best path for the horses to reach the mountain road."

"And the fancy map makers of the Guilds are too coward to do much exploring in the mountains anyway." The ginger began tending to the horses, removing their saddles and tying them close to the stream.

"What's your name?" I knelt by the edge of the bank and splashed chill water on my face.

"Finn," ginger Finn said. "Nice to meet you, Ena."

"You as well." I took a long drink of the water, feeling its cold trickle all the way down past my lungs. "How soon do you think we'll reach the base of the mountains?"

"Tomorrow," Liam said.

"We really did take the long way then," I said.

Liam caught my eye and held my gaze for a moment. "The paths in and out of the mountains aren't the same."

"And there are only a few men can survive?" I dried my hands on my skirt. "I'm thankful I've had such a fine guide."

Liam chose a spot and laid out the black stones around it. Emmet gathered wood for a fire while I pulled the few bits of almost fresh food from our packs.

The dread didn't trickle into my stomach until the sun began to fade from the sky. I had been so excited to be doing something that might hold a bit of meaning, I hadn't really thought through the actual journey.

Finn said cheerful things every few minutes when the silence seemed to become too dull for him, but the rest of us didn't speak much. Once Finn had finished eating, he untied his bedroll from his pack and laid it on the ground.

My heart raced as though the nightmare had already begun. I had to warn Finn that terror would come for me while I slept, but I couldn't warn Finn without Emmet hearing.

No one in the camp had mentioned me screaming in my sleep, but the four of us were packed in together. There was no god I could think of to silently beg for mercy, and whatever thin veil of safety had comforted me in my tent had vanished.

Emmet would know about the nightmare soon enough. As soon as I started screaming, he would know something was wrong. But Emmet hadn't been there on the night the terrible dream had been born. Even he wouldn't understand the darkness that trapped me.

Liam unrolled his blankets, leaving a space between him and Finn large enough to fit my bedding. "You should get some sleep."

"I'm not tired." I met Liam's dark eyes, trusting the fading firelight to hide my fear.

"We'll need you rested when we reach the valley." Liam unrolled my bedding and laid it out beside his. "Don't worry, Ena, I promise to keep you safe."

"We've got magic stones," I said. "Why would I be worried?"

Finn laughed from his bed.

I took a long time untying my boots and retying my pack. The others had all lain down by the time I crawled under my thick blankets.

I lay, staring up the branches crisscrossing in front of the sky, wondering if I should find a sharp rock to put under my back to make sure I didn't fall asleep.

I was a chivving coward. I would have to sleep eventually, but the idea of Emmet knowing the monsters that still stalked me…

Liam's fingers grazed the back of my wrist. The panic in my chest ebbed. He laced his fingers through mine and squeezed my hand. He didn't let go.

When I woke in the morning, our hands were still locked together.

"It's not that I mind berry picking. It's just not what I pictured when we left camp." Finn popped a handful of blackberries into his mouth. "Definitely worse ways to spend an afternoon."

"Thanks, Finn." I weaved between the trees, searching for a briar patch that might hide our quarry. "Just be careful not to eat anything you shouldn't."

Finn's eyes widened.

"Don't worry. You can eat blackberries. I'll tell you when we find the poison kind," I laughed, trying to shake off my fear.

We were searching for berries to murder a monster. As much as I hated the Guilds, as often as vengeance for the horrible things they'd done had flitted through my mind, I'd never actually thought through the process of killing a person.

"They are much sweeter than hardtack," Finn said. "I really doubt hardtack should be eaten."

"Better than starving, I suppose." I moved on to the next patch of trees. A few low plants grew in the shadows, but nothing like what I was searching for.

"Maybe." Finn sounded unconvinced.

Liam and Emmet walked close behind, leading the horses and keeping an eye out for anyone who might want us dead. At least, that's what it felt like with Emmet keeping one hand resting on the hilt of his sword and Liam holding a fistful of rocks.

We'd reached the edge of the forest before midday, and Liam had turned our path north, keeping us within the safety of the trees and out of view of the mountain road.

"Supposing we don't find the death berries," Finn said.

"We will," I said with as much determination as I could after hours of fruitless searching.

"But if we don't," Finn said, "you could find something else that would work, couldn't you?"

I pinched my nose between my hands. "I don't know. There are plenty of plants that could kill a man, but I don't know how we'd drop flower petals into a paun's stew."

"We'll keep looking then," Finn said.

The low rumble of Emmet muttering carried from behind, but I couldn't make out the words.

"What?" I rounded on him.

He stared stone faced at me.

"What were you saying?" I asked.

"We might be too far north," Emmet said. "We're more than fifty miles above Harane. Shadow berries might not grow here."

"We've got horses," Finn said. "We can ride south."

"They should grow up here," I said. "We just have to find them."

"Or maybe we should accept this as a sign from the sky and go back," Emmet said.

I tipped my face to the sky and laughed. "You would rather let a monster torment people than let me help. Well, I am not a coward, and I am not helpless, Emmet Ryeland. I'm not going back up that chivving mountain until we've found the chivving berries."

I turned and stalked toward the edge of the forest.

"Ena," Liam called after me. "Ena, where are you going?"

"I've always seen shadow berries in the open, so I'm going out into the open," I said.

There was a muttering of curses before boots pounded after me.

"Ena, you can't." Liam took my elbow.

The sun peered through the trees just ahead of us, unobstructed by the shade of branches.

"Soldiers could be hunting for you," Liam said. "We're fifty miles north of Harane, but we're only fifty miles. If you had stuck to the mountain road, you could have easily walked this far."

"So you want to give up?" I yanked my arm from his grip.

"I want to keep searching the forest," Liam said.

"Just keep walking north in the trees and hope we get lucky?"

"We need to keep heading north anyway. And this is already the easiest path for us to safely travel. We're only looking along our way."

"Way to where? Is Gabe in the north?" I waited for a moment, but he didn't answer. "Because if he's not, we're wasting our time. I'll dodge out of the trees and do a quick search around. It's not as though soldiers are quiet when they travel. If I hear any trace of a great host of murderers coming my way, I'll run straight back into the forest."

"We need to head north," Liam said. "We have a friend there. We'll need to see her before I can go to Gabe."

I seized that one tiny seed of information he'd been willing to give since we'd left the camp, setting it aside to think about later.

"Will we need the poison for when we meet her?" I asked.

"Yes," Liam said. "There would be no point otherwise."

"Then I suppose when we get to her, you'll finally have to let me out of the woods to search."

"Do these look poisonous to you?" Finn held a bright red berry in the air.

I peered at the low weeds Finn had been digging into. "They won't kill you, but they'll make you wish you were dead."

Finn let his handful of berries tumble to the ground. "Good to know."

"Don't they have bird bushes in the mountains where the Black Bloods live?" I asked.

"Not really." Liam bowed me north. "We've got plants in the mountains near Lygan Hall, but none like this."

"What's Lygan Hall?" I marched north, carefully searching for any sign of shadow berries, though I knew full well I wouldn't find a chivving thing.

"It's our home," Liam said.

"The camp's called Lygan Hall?" I asked. "It's a nice name, but a bit fancy for the tents, don't you think?"

"Can you imagine those tents being Lygan Hall?" Finn tossed a tiny green thing to me. "Can you imagine living in those tents year round?"

I looked at the thing he'd tossed me before scowling and tossing it back. "Can you imagine mistaking a tree tip for a berry?"

"At least I'm trying to help." Finn winked.

"You can eat that if you want," I said. "Might not taste the best unless you're brewing ale."

"Hmm." Finn popped the bright green bud in his mouth and chewed. "I've definitely tasted worse when Neil's in charge of the kitchen."

"Is he not in charge of the kitchen in Lygan Hall?" I asked.

"Things don't work the same way there," Liam said. "People have homes. Most cook for themselves."

A wide patch of fallen trees blocked the path in front of us. The ground beneath them had collapsed, leaving a dark crater under the tangle of trunks.

"If people have homes at Lygan Hall," I said, climbing up onto the trunk of one of the wider downed trees, "why are you living in tents?"

"Camp is closer to the mountain road," Liam said. "It makes it easier to do our work. We can't stay year round—we'd freeze to death come winter—but for the warmer months, it helps to get more done."

"And helps us protect the people we care about at home in the Hall." There was an edge to Emmet's voice.

I walked across the trunk, heading toward the center of the sunken-in earth.

"Careful, Ena," Liam said.

"How does it keep them safe?" I took a long leap onto another tree, picturing Emmet's terrified face as I jumped.

"The mountains protect us," Liam said, "but going back and forth as much as we do, we'd risk someone managing to follow us home."

"There's not a Black Blood in the camp who wouldn't die before giving up the path to Lygan Hall," Emmet said.

"Not that the Guilds would be able to follow the path," Finn said.

I climbed down close to the cracked earth.

"Ena, what are you doing?" Emmet said.

"Looking for berries. Didn't you know?"

There was nothing in the darkness beneath the tangled branches but a dug out lair where some great beast had made its home. From the scratches in the dirt, the animal would have had no trouble tearing out Emmet's intestines.

Or mine, for that matter.

My heart battered against my ribs as I scrambled onto the highest of the downed trees' trunks and ran to safety on the other side. I leapt down onto solid ground, not sure if I should be grateful the animal hadn't been home or terrified it was out in the woods.

"Is Lygan Hall beautiful?" I resisted the urge to glance behind to make sure the others hadn't been eaten alive.

"I think so," Liam said. "Not like the grand halls the Guilds have built with gold and blood. But the Hall is beautiful in its own way."

"I'd like to see it someday," I said.

"You're one of us now, Ena." Liam gave a small smile that actually reached his eyes. "I don't know where else you'd go come winter."

We spent the next ten miles walking and searching. Finn ate everything I knew wouldn't kill him, while I got more eager to go search out in the open as the sun drifted down. Emmet stayed silent and angry through it all.

The forest we trekked through was the same as the one that bordered Harane. The mountains that blocked us to the east were the same range I'd seen my whole life, but somehow it felt as though no one had bothered to tell the trees.

The air in the woods had a different taste than it did near Harane. The ground had a spring to it, too, like there was something alive hidden right beneath our feet. I tried not to wonder what magic might lurk in the forest floor. If the legends of the stones in the mountains holding magic were true, what other wonders had been hiding from the Guilds?

Liam switched with Finn, taking his place at the front of the group. Between searching for berries, I watched Liam's shoulders growing tighter and higher.

We're almost there.

I thought the words a dozen times, but didn't dare say them.

When the light had begun to slant through the trees, Liam stopped, rolling around the stones in his hand before turning to look over my shoulder.

I glanced behind to find Emmet staring back at Liam.

"No." Emmet gripped the hilt of his sword. "Absolutely not."

"Absolutely not what?" I looked back to Liam.

"We can't," Emmet said.

"Can't what?" I asked Emmet.

"I'll go out," Emmet said. "I know what the berries look like. You make camp in the forest, and I'll meet you here tomorrow. I'll bring the shadow berries with me."

"You want to go tromping out of the woods and leave us here?" I asked.

No one bothered to respond.

"It's better this way, and you know it," Emmet said after a long moment.

"No." I rounded on Emmet. "I don't know it, because you're a chivving slitch who doesn't say anything when he speaks. I need to find the shadow berries, not you. I have to make the poison, not you. Because I'm the only one among us who has even the faintest notion of how poisoning a person should work. So once again, me, not you."

Finn let out a low whistle.

"I am going out of these trees to find what I need to make this whole chivving trip worthwhile," I said. "Now, either you can come with me, or you can hide in here and wait for me to come back. But if any of you so much as mentions it being too dangerous for me to be out where the soldiers might spot me, so please the gods I'll poison the lot of you."

"You're a fool," Emmet said.

"Don't." Liam stepped forward. "We'll head into the city and search along the way. If we can't find anything, we can come back out and look again tomorrow."

"You think she'll be pleased to have four of us knocking on her door?" Emmet asked. "And that's if we can get through the city without trouble."

"Why would there be trouble?" I said.

Emmet scowled at me with one eyebrow raised.

"Fine." I stomped over to the horses and pulled my bedroll free. I draped my blanket around my shoulders and shook my hair from its braid, letting it hang limp over my face. I gave a cough that would have made Lily cringe.

"Ena?" Finn said.

"No one is going to get close enough to a sickly girl to see if she might have been around when a soldier got his throat slit." I glared at Emmet. "Besides, of the four of us, aren't I the one who's done the least to anger the Guilds?"

"Shockingly, I think she might be right." Finn shrugged.

"But we've all been careful to keep our faces away from soldiers," Liam said.

"I'm a girl. I'm certain the last thing those soldiers were staring at was my face."

Emmet gripped the hilt of his sword so hard, if it had been wood, I'm sure it would have broken.

"Unless you want to tie me to a tree, I'm walking out of these woods." I looked to Liam. "Would you like to travel together, or should I just be on my way alone?"

Liam stared at me for a long moment before speaking. "We stay together. We'll go straight to Mave's and wait there until tomorrow."

"She won't like it," Emmet said.

"I don't like it." Liam headed to the edge of the woods, still clutching his fistful of stones.

I kept close on his heels, not letting myself look back at Emmet for fear he might come up with some better argument for keeping me hidden.

It only took a few minutes for us to reach the tree line. The sunset glimmered over the valley beyond.

A city built of stone and spires sat nestled in the bend of a roaring river. I'd never before seen a river so wide, with a current so fast, I'd have no hope of swimming across it.

On the far side, a second river flowed between two rocky cliffs, racing toward the city and down behind the silhouettes of the buildings. The mountain road stretched from north to south in front of us, but a smaller road by the big river was where dozens of wagons had gathered.

There were more buildings than I'd ever seen in one place, and no trace of the hint of Harane my heart had been longing for.

As Liam led us toward the city, the weight of how little I knew of the world sank in my gut.

The stench of sweaty men and horse dung tainted the scent of the river and the tang of spices coming from the carts.

Young boys lifted crates larger than themselves off the boats bobbing in the river, hauling them up the dock and into the waiting wagons. The wagon men leaned against the sides of their carts, chatting while the children did the work.

"Are those men Guilded?" I asked, keeping a close eye on the river dock as my horse followed Liam toward the city.

Liam's neck tensed before he looked at the wagons. He studied the people there for a moment before speaking. "No, just laxe."

"What?" I guided my horse to ride beside Liam.

"I thought you were supposed to be ill," Emmet said.

I gave a great cough in his direction. "Better?"

"Do you not call your merchants *laxe* in Harane?" Finn asked. "Or are they not filthy enough to have earned that title?"

"There isn't a merchant class in Harane," Emmet said. "The village isn't big enough."

Finn gave a low whistle.

"Everyone in Harane works to survive," Emmet said.

Doesn't everyone everywhere work to survive?

The question crept toward my lips, but I swallowed it, too afraid they might decide I was ill-prepared to meet the frightening world of a proper city and send me back to hide in the woods with whatever clawed beasts lurked there.

"So the laxe make the children work for them?" I asked.

"They pay whoever needs coin," Liam said. "Sometimes children, sometimes adults, whatever tilk they can find."

"And the Guilds allow it?" I watched as the sun reached the tops of the low mountains to the west, casting the great city into golden shadows.

"The Guilds encourage it," Liam said. "They have to get their fancy robes, wine—"

"Jewels, shoes, houses," Finn added in.

"The Guilds only do their own work," Emmet said, "and they aren't going to go bargaining with the tanner to have a saddle made. The merchants sell to the Guilds. Profit off the Guilds abusing the common folk in Ilbrea. The lot of them are nothing but filthy collaborators."

"Ink for the scribes, blood for the healers, steel for the soldiers, wind for the sailors—land for the makers of maps to behold, and for sorcerers, magic, to defend royals' gold." Finn spoke in a sing song voice. His cheerful verse sent a shiver down my spine. "No bankers, traders, or builders in the Guilds. Those low positions are filled by merchants."

"Traitors," Emmet said.

"I think you've made your opinion clear," I said. "Though I can't say I remember anyone asking you to speak."

Finn chuckled.

"It takes all types to keep Ilbrea running." Liam looked back at Emmet. "We have to remember who the real enemy is."

Emmet's face hardened, but he nodded.

"If we make good time to Mave's, we might even be able to get a decent meal," Liam said. "The streets shouldn't be too crowded tonight."

I tried to picture streets crowded with people. Enough people in my path that it would change my time going from one place to another. I couldn't imagine it.

The walls surrounding the city rose up thirty feet, with turrets sticking up at steady intervals. Tall, thin windows had been built into the stone. I peered into the shadows of each, trying to spot a person staring back at me.

High gates stood open at the end of the road, and a line of wagons, horses, and people waited to be let into the city.

"Twelve soldiers," Emmet said, his fingers twitching as he reached toward the sword he'd tied under his pack.

Men in black uniforms flanked the gates.

My heart leapt into my throat, and I pulled the blanket higher around my head.

"We'll be fine," Liam said, either to Emmet or me—I don't really know.

The scent on the wind changed as we reached the back of the line of people waiting to enter the city. Hints of baking bread, strong frie, and too many people packed together wafted through the gates.

"It shouldn't be taking this long to get through." A woman perched on a fine horse spoke to the young girl tending the horse's reins.

"I'm sorry, ma'am," the young girl said.

The woman glared down as though expecting the girl to have something more than an apology to offer.

I gave a rattling cough that grated my throat.

The woman shifted her glare toward me, horror filling her face as she lifted her sleeve to her nose and turned back to the gates.

My horse fidgeted beneath me as we made our way closer to the soldiers. I watched as a farmer was let in with his giant containers of milk, and a merchant with wooden crates slipped a few coins into a soldier's hand before being allowed through. A young man entered the city, his arms wrapped tightly around the waist of a giggling girl.

We never would have survived in Harane if the Guilds had guarded who went in and out of the village. If they had been able to see who had snuck off with a giggling girl and had the chance of checking any goods that came down the road to us, half the town would have been whipped on a weekly basis.

But we hadn't survived anyway. They hadn't lurked over us every day, only come to kill us when the fancy struck them.

"What is your business here?" A soldier glared between the four of us when our turn came. He wasn't as soft as I would have expected from someone told to guard a gate. His chiseled jaw, narrowed eyes, and firm grip on the sword at his hip made it seem as though he expected an attack rather than a pair of young fools back from rolling around in the forest.

"We're traveling north on the mountain road and seek a warm place to stay for the night," Finn said.

I glanced over to Liam, but he was looking daftly up at the wall as though he'd never seen something so big in his life.

"What's your business in the north?" the soldier asked.

"I've got a friend in Marten who might be willing to marry my sister," Finn said.

The soldier glared at me.

I gave another rattling cough.

"We want to get her rested and well before we get there." Finn gave a hopeful smile. "We've money to pay for a good room."

"Is she catching?" the soldier asked.

"No," Finn said, "her lungs have always been a chivving wreck. But if we get her rested, she'll look well enough he might take her."

Anger rolled in my stomach, and I gripped my reins to keep from punching Finn in the back of his chivving head.

The soldier eyed me for another moment before giving a low laugh. "May the gods help you in getting that one married." He stepped out of our way.

"Thank you, sir." Finn gave a little bow and led us in through the gates.

The wall was thicker than I'd imagined it to be when we were looking at it from the outside. We traveled under twelve feet of stone, which loomed over our heads as though waiting to drop and murder us, before riding out onto the cobblestone streets of the city.

The people didn't spare a glance for the soldiers waiting by the inside gate. Women in fancy silk dresses strode past on the arms of men in finely made coats. Children ran by, giggling as though the soldiers weren't even a threat to be feared.

"This way," Liam said when I'd fallen too far behind our party. "We have to get the horses settled."

Finn stopped in front of a wide stable with a giant white horse painted across the front.

"What is this place?" I stared at the entrance of a pub that had a sparkling silver sign above the door, which read *River of Frie.*

"Frason's Glenn." Liam took my hand, helping me down from my horse. "It's a trading port. Ships stop on the northern coast by Ilara. Some of the goods stay there. Some get loaded onto smaller river boats and brought down here. Then the laxe load them onto wagons and haul them south to be sold."

"So"—I pulled my pack free from my horse, dodging out of the way of a cart selling sweet bread and honey—"this whole town only exists because people earn coins off the goods from the river."

"The whole of Ilbrea only exists because someone is making coin. The only thing that changes from place to place is whose pockets get heavy and whose back gets whipped." Finn took the reins of my horse and tried to hand them to a gangly boy who stared open mouthed at me. "Take the chivving horses." Finn flapped the reins at the boy. "I promise you haven't a chance with the girl."

Finn waited until the blushing boy had gotten all four horses inside before leading us down the street.

I stayed close to Liam, taking his arm as we passed a towering building made of white stone. People in red, blue, white, and purple robes lingered by the glittering metal doors.

I had heard of Guilded folk beyond the normal soldiers, scribes, and healers we dealt with in Harane. I'd seen the black, white, and red robes marking each of their Guilds. I'd even seen a sorcerer in purple robes once. But to see a pack of Guilded paun, chatting on the stone steps that some poor fool had carved swirls and leaves into, sent a cold sweat on the back of my neck.

A lady healer tipped her head back and laughed to the twilit sky. Joy filled her face like there was no duty that called for her time besides standing with her fellow paun enjoying the late spring evening. Like there were no common folk in need of her aid.

Good folk who went hungry to pay their taxes to the Guilds so they could have the right to a Guilded healer's aid. Good people who would die because the lady in the red robes was standing on the steps instead of saving lives.

My stomach twisted so hard I thought I might be sick on the stone street.

Liam took my hand, holding it tight as we passed shops with sparkling glass windows. Dresses, lace, boots, sugar cakes, books—everything I could imagine anyone wanting to spend coin on was displayed in the shops. Lamps burned brightly, inviting customers in, even though the sun had faded from view.

Emmet took the lead, veering off the main street and onto a narrow road lit by lamps that hung from the sides of the stone buildings.

There were fewer people on this street, and most of the businesses had already closed for the day, though the colorful signs describing their trades still hung in the shadows.

There was beauty in the details of the signs, almost as though someone had made up a competition for the most intricate plaque. I didn't know which would win—the cut out of a platter of sweets that had been carved so deep in places, it looked like I might actually be able to pry a slice of cake free, or the woman with long hair, where each strand seemed to have been painted on individually.

My shoulders relaxed as houses took the place of shops, and lamps only hung on the corners of the cross streets. The darkness and quiet might have been frightening if I were alone, but with the others, the isolation seemed safer. Fewer prying eyes and less of a chance someone might spot the girl from Harane who had run from a dead soldier.

Just as I began to wonder how big the city was and how much longer it would take to reach Mave, laughter floated up the dark street. A quick melody of a cheerful tune came a moment later.

Emmet picked up his pace, leading us around the corner and closer to the music.

"Where is that coming from?" I asked.

EMBER AND STONE | 135

"Mave's," Liam said.

We reached a set of tall stone buildings that blocked the street we had been traveling down. There were no windows on the first floor of the buildings, but on the second, third, and fourth stories, bright light shone out of the windows. Swirls and flowers of twisted iron surrounded the small balconies that dotted the buildings.

A few of the balconies had been taken by couples enjoying the darkness. Others sat vacant, as though inviting people to come and fill them.

The song ended, and a cheer rose from beyond the buildings.

Emmet shook his head and cut through an alley toward the music.

The dazzling light of a hundred lanterns bathed the square beyond. Five buildings surrounded the open space, all facing each other like old men gathering to gossip. A fiddler, a drummer, and a woman with a tin whistle stood on a high platform at the center of it all.

Around the sides of the stage, young men in matching orange shirts minded great barrels of drink. People stood in line, waiting for their chance at the barrels.

The players began another song, and the crowd hollered their joy.

A man darted out of the barrel line, sweeping a girl into his arms and leading her into a dance. In a few moments, the whole square had filled with couples dancing.

I smiled under the cover of my blanket. I didn't recognize the song, but it was nice to see that even people who lived with soldiers at their gate could find a moment of joy in music.

Emmet led us around the edge of the dancers to one of the buildings on the far side. On the front of the building, the windows started on the ground floor, peering out over a wide porch packed with tables. Men and women filled the seats, some sitting on each other's laps when there were no extra chairs to be had. Plates of food and glasses of chamb had been set out on every surface. Smoke drifted from pipes, laying a haze over the whole scene.

"Fresh ones!" a girl called to no one in particular as she peeled herself off a man's lap and sauntered toward us.

Her blond hair had been pinned up, leaving only a few curls to drip around her long neck. The laces of her bodice had been pulled so tight, she was one quick move away from her breasts falling out and making her having worn anything on top utterly pointless. Her painted red lips curled into a smile as her gaze drifted from Finn to Liam then finally landed on Emmet. "This is turning out to be a lovely night."

"We're here for Mave." Emmet stepped in front of our group.

"Why?" The girl narrowed her kohl-lined eyes.

"Mave and I are old friends," Emmet said.

"Pity." The girl shrugged and headed toward the pale blue painted door. She didn't bother shutting it behind her.

I peered through the doorway to find more tables. Girls dressed to please the men around them, and handsome young men with their shirts unbuttoned prowled through the crowd.

"What is this place?" I whispered to Liam.

"Mave's brothel," Liam said.

"Why are we standing on the steps of a brothel?" I asked.

A pair of red-haired girls led a man inside. One of them had already begun unlacing her bodice.

"Mave's a good friend," Liam said.

A woman stepped into the doorway, blocking out the room beyond. I don't know if it was the mass of dark curls surrounding her face, her perfect features and dark complexion, or the way she held herself that made me forget to breathe. She tipped her head to the side, and a slow smile spread across her face.

"I didn't think I would see you here again," the woman said.

"Hello, Mave," Emmet said. "It's good to see you, too."

"Should I be returning the compliment or kicking you out of my square?" Mave stepped forward. The lantern light caught her dress, glistening off the tiny beads that had been sewn into the maroon fabric.

"You should be pulling down your best bottle of chamb and bringing us in." Emmet stepped forward, reaching for Mave's hand. "Have I ever brought anything you haven't wanted to your door?"

Mave crooked an eyebrow. "More than once. And I don't like having filthy girls dragged to my home. You know my thoughts on men who do such things."

"She's my sister," Emmet said. "The blanket's just to make her feel safe on her first trip into Frason's Glenn."

Mave looked to Liam for a long moment before nodding. "Then welcome, weary travelers. May you find rest and the best of life's comforts within my walls."

The music from the square carried up to the second floor window, drifting into the parlor where Mave had left us.

A painting of the seven-pointed star of Ilbrea hung over the mantle, though no fire burned in the stone hearth beneath. Blue fabric woven into a flower pattern covered the walls and the furniture that took up the center of the space. Three chairs and one, long fainting couch surrounded a table made of rich, cherry-stained wood.

I sat on the very edge of the seat I'd been given, too afraid of tainting the fabric with my forest filth to get comfortable.

"Not like Harane then?" Finn winked at me.

"Careful." Liam nodded to the open window.

Finn shrugged and leaned back in his chair.

"You can take the blanket off," Liam said.

"Right." I lifted the blanket over my head, folding it up before laying it at my feet. I ran my fingers through my hair, weighing how awful it must look against how much the others would laugh at me for digging in my pack to find my wooden comb. For all the world, it felt like I'd been brought in front of the Queen herself.

"Not everywhere outside Harane is like this," Emmet said. "Most places are closer to the village. But Frason's Glenn has a lot of money—"

"And coin buys fancy things," I cut across him. "I am smart enough to have figured that out for myself."

"Just be kind to Mave and she'll like you," Emmet said.

"Of the two of us, which usually has trouble with being kind?" I asked.

"Enough," Liam said. "We made it into the city without any fuss. Let's not go feeding the shadows ourselves."

A knock on the door kept me from answering.

A man in a bright orange, silk vest stepped into the room without waiting for us to answer. He carried a tray of food with a bottle of chamb sitting right in the middle.

"Compliments of Mave." The man set the feast on the table, took a moment to look at each of the men, and went back out into the hall.

"By the gods, I'm hungry." Finn dove toward the table, grabbing a roll and a slice of meat before the rest of us even stood.

"Are you always hungry?" I examined the bowl of berries, plate of cheese, pile of fresh baked rolls, slices of meat, and bottle of chamb.

"I was born starving, and it hasn't stopped since." Finn spoke as soon as he'd swallowed. "Honestly, when my mother found out I'd chosen to travel outside the Hall, she openly wept. The neighbors all said it was because she loved me so much, but I'm smart enough to know they were tears of joy that she wouldn't have to worry about feeding me any longer."

"Smart woman." Liam smiled. A bright, comfortable smile without any trace of the hardened Black Blood I had followed through the mountains.

The door swung back open.

"Now that I've fed you"—Mave sauntered into the room, closing the door behind her with a sharp click—"tell me why I should let you stay here. Unless, of course, you've come to enjoy an evening of the flesh, in which case eat up and go choose a partner before all the good ones have been claimed. Don't worry"—Mave looked to me—"I can find someone for you as well."

Heat flooded my face.

Liam walked to the window and pulled it closed. The glass dampened the music but didn't block it out. He looked toward the door.

"We're safe." Mave sat on the fainting couch, fluffing the folds of her skirt around her.

"We need a favor, Mave," Liam said.

"I thought as much," Mave said. "Why else would I find a trueborn Black Blood in my home?"

I glanced toward the door, waiting for everyone from the square to come storming in to murder us.

"Do you have any prisoners?" Liam asked.

Mave smiled. "As far as you're concerned, no."

"We need one, Mave," Emmet said.

"Why?" Mave asked. "Who of yours was foolish enough to be caught and important enough to be traded for?"

"No one," Emmet said. "We're not looking for a trade."

"We're looking for a victim," Liam said.

Mave stood, poured herself a glass of chamb, and sat back on the couch. She watched the bubbles rising in her fluted glass for a moment before speaking. "Victim for what?"

"Poison," Emmet said.

Sour rose in my mouth.

"We're planning something," Liam said. "I've got to know everything will work as needed."

"So you want someone to poison?" Mave said. "Should I just haul a victim in here? I'm sure there's plenty of filth in the square who deserve a bit of death."

"We aren't murderers," Emmet said. "But your prisoners are already going to be executed for crimes against the people of Frason's Glenn. They might as well do a bit of good on their way out."

Mave sipped her chamb.

I looked to Liam who gave the slightest shake of his head. I nodded and stayed silent.

"I like you Emmet Ryeland," Mave said. "I'd go nearly so far as to consider you a friend."

"Thank you, Mave." Emmet knelt in front of her and kissed her outstretched hand.

"But there are some risks I can't take, even for friends," Mave said. "I won't put my family in that kind of danger."

"There is no danger," Emmet said.

"Having Black Bloods in my home is a danger," Mave said. "Bringing you to my dungeon is too much to ask."

"We wouldn't need to go." I waited for Emmet to glare at me for speaking, but he kept his gaze fixed on Mave. "I could give you the poison, and you could just…" I swallowed, wishing I had my own glass of chamb. "Tell me how it worked. How long it took for the symptoms to show, and how quickly your prisoner died."

"We're trying to make a difference," Liam said. "This is how we save lives."

Mave studied my face for a long moment. "Fine. I'll let your brew be the end of one of my prisoners. It's not how things are usually done, but I can make an exception. Though, a debt like this will need to be repaid."

I gripped the edge of my seat, no longer caring about the dirt on my fingers contaminating the fancy fabric.

Emmet looked to Liam.

"Our aim is worth owing a friend a debt," Liam said. "I will see you repaid for the prisoner and for sheltering us while we are in Frason's Glenn."

"The shelter I give freely out of friendship," Mave said. "The prisoner is what comes with a price."

"Thank you, Mave." Emmet kissed her hand again.

"Do you have the poison?" Mave asked. "I have a paun fit for the task."

"Not yet," I said. "But I will soon. Tomorrow night, after I've had time to search outside the city walls."

"I'll search," Emmet said. "We can't risk you being seen."

"Why would that be?" Mave sipped her chamb.

I stood and poured myself a glass. "I was a bit too near a soldier who ended up dead."

I heard the rustle of her skirt before she took my chin in her hand. "You're pretty."

"I know." I met her dark eyes, willing myself not to flinch.

Her gaze swept down to my breasts and back up to my face. She took a bit of my hair and rubbed it between her fingers before tracing the line of my jaw.

"Mave," Emmet said.

"Do you want to hide in a filthy blanket?" Mave asked.

"No," I said.

"Would you like to roam free, not worry about who spots you?"

"Yes."

The right corner of Mave's mouth twisted into a smile. She leaned in and kissed my cheek. "Good girl."

The scent coming off her skin sent my head swimming, like she had somehow bottled sunshine, firelight, and longing and had found a way to bathe in their perfume.

"You boys go get washed up before the stink of you taints my parlor forever. You, girl—"

"Her name is Ena," Liam said.

"Ena, come with me," Mave said. "By morning, I'll have you fit to catch the eye of every soldier at the gates."

"We don't want her to be seen." Finn froze with a slice of cheese halfway to his mouth. "Unless I've missed something."

"No one questions the feathers of a beautiful bird. They only marvel at her beauty and let her fly away. Come." Mave reached for my hand.

I downed the rest of my chamb, letting the bubbles tickle my throat as I took Mave's hand and followed her out of the parlor.

The sound of voices carried up the stairs from the floor below. A man gave a booming laugh. A chorus of female titters answered.

"Mave." The man in the orange vest bowed as we passed.

"You're free to go." Mave gave him a nod.

The man slipped back down the stairs to the first floor.

"This way." She led me down a long hall with doors on either side.

I bit my lips together, trying to focus on the sounds of Mave's rustling skirt instead of the noises coming from the rooms around us.

We stopped at a narrow door at the end of the hall. Mave pulled a key from the folds of her skirt and slipped it into the lock. "Don't go wandering while you're here. I like your brother, but that doesn't mean I'm willing to trust you with a key."

"Yes, ma'am."

A staircase waited for us through the door. There were no fancy fabrics covering the walls here, only bright, unstained paint. Voice drifted down the stairs, but they weren't the same as the raucous crowd below.

"Charge her double and make her buy you a bottle of frie next time," a girl said.

"Double wouldn't cover it," another girl laughed. "She's as sweet as a lamb, but there's only so much a girl can take."

We stepped up into a brightly lit room, and everyone around us froze.

"Mave." A girl in a pink robe was the first to spring to her feet.

The other four were up a moment later, nodding to Mave while keeping their eyes locked on me.

Mave looked at each of the girls in turn, though what she was searching for I had no idea.

"Is everything all right, Mave?" a girl with bright blond hair asked after a long moment.

"I have a project for you, Nora." Mave put a hand on my back, guiding me toward the blond. "This little bird angered the wolves. Give her a new pair of wings."

"Of course, Mave." Nora bowed her head, then narrowed her eyes as she studied me. "She'll be beautiful."

"Good girl." Mave swept back toward the stairs. "Now I've got to manage her brother."

I watched Mave disappear down the steps, feeling the stares of the five women prickling the back of my neck.

"Who's your brother?" the girl in the pink robe asked.

"I…" I felt as though I were withering under their gazes. "I'm not sure you'd know him."

The girl in pink raised an eyebrow.

"Emmet Ryeland," I said.

"Emmet's here?" A girl with chestnut curls started toward the stairs. "*The* Emmet?"

"Leave it, Lolli." Nora caught her arm. "I don't think Mave would like you storming in."

"How do you know my brother?" I asked.

A chorus of laughter rang from the girls.

Nora fluttered a hand for the others to stop. "The poor thing is covered in mud. At least show an ounce of compassion." She bit her red painted lips to stop her own giggle. "Now come with me, little bird. Stories of Emmet Ryeland are best told in the daylight."

"What's that supposed to mean?"

Nora didn't answer my question, but I followed her anyway.

This floor hadn't been built on the same pattern as the one beneath. The stairs had brought Mave and me up into the large room where the girls had been sitting. There was space in the room for twenty more to have seats at the table, near the fireplace, or by the bookshelf. I blushed as I tried not to think of where the others who normally sat in the room might be.

Nora led me down a brightly painted, narrow corridor. The rooms lining either side were quiet. Some of the doors had been left open. I slowed my steps enough to peek into one of the rooms. A plain, wooden-framed bed stood next to a rack of beautiful gowns.

"We never leave this floor without our paint on," Nora said. "It's safer that way."

"Safer?" I ran a few steps to catch up.

"Soldiers wear armor to protect themselves. We wear paints, powders, and silk. We step into battle every time we leave the safety of the haven Mave has built for us. I, for one, would never be foolish enough to go into battle unarmed." She stopped in front of an open door.

A set of four brass tubs took up the center of the room, with shelves and mirrors lining the walls. Two of the tubs had women in them.

"Fresh blood?" One of the girls sat up out of her tub.

I averted my gaze from her naked breasts.

"Oh, she won't make it long," the girl said.

"Ha!" the other bathing girl laughed. "When you first came here, you couldn't look at a naked man without vomiting."

"Oy." The first girl splashed the second, sending a wave of water onto the floor.

"Hush, both of you." Nora held up a hand, and the two fell silent. "Either mind your baths or get out."

The first girl ducked sheepishly under the water, while the second picked up a sponge and dabbed at her arms while staring at me.

Nora sighed. "I will never understand these girls. Ah well. Get your clothes off. We've got to get you clean before we start on the real work."

"Right." I reached for the laces on my bodice but couldn't manage to make my fingers work. "A proper bath would be nice."

"By the Guilds." Nora swatted my hands away and untied the knot herself. "We sell pleasure to people at an exorbitant rate. We aren't perverted, and we won't eat you alive."

"Unless you've got the coin to pay for that sort of thing," the sponge girl said.

"I don't think we could convince Mave to agree to host such a horror." Nora wriggled my dirt-covered bodice over my head. "I've seen some strange things in Mave's halls, but there are limits to everything." She unbuttoned my skirt, and it fell to the floor. "Get your shoes off, and I'll find a comb."

I untied my boots, tucking my knife into the bottom where the hilt wouldn't show, and tried to ignore the dark smears of dirt I'd left on the tile floor.

"What sort of new feathers are you hoping for?" Nora pulled a basket down from the shelf.

"I don't know," I said. "I mean, I haven't thought about it."

"You should cut her hair short," the sponge girl said. "A bunch of the Guilded have been asking about short-haired girls. I think it might be a fashion in Ilara."

My stomach rolled at the idea of a Guilded paun touching me. Pain ached in my throat where the soldier had tried to squeeze the air out of me.

"Hush now." Nora petted my cheek. "Breathe, little bird. Just breathe."

"Who hurt you so badly?" the sponge girl said. Or maybe it was the other one. The room had started to go blurry around the edges.

"Out, both of you," Nora ordered. She didn't look away from me or take her hand from my cheek. "No one here is going to hurt you. No one in Mave's home will make you do anything you don't want to do."

The baths sloshed as the girls got up and scampered out of the room.

"We'll get you in a warm bath and give you a fresh set of armor." She took my hand, leading me to the tub on the far right side of the room. "You share Emmet's blood. Whatever wrong the world has done to you, you're strong enough to survive."

"I am." I pulled off my shift, let it fall to the floor, and stepped into the hot bath.

"It's really not frightening here." Nora pressed a brick of soap into my hand and knelt behind me, lifting my hair away from the water. "We're lucky. You're lucky Mave let you up here. Outsiders aren't permitted above the second floor. I don't think she would have allowed it if you weren't Emmet's sister."

"The most amazing luck." I scrubbed at my hands with the sweet-smelling soap. I'd only been away from the camp for two days, but it had already begun to feel as though I might never be properly clean again.

"Are you staying with us?" Nora ran a thick-bristled brush through my hair.

"I'm only here for a day, maybe two, I suppose. Not that there would be anything wrong with staying." The last part tumbled out.

Nora laughed softly. It was the gentlest laugh I'd ever heard. If the wind could laugh as it swept through a summer field, I think it would have made the same sound.

"Our way of life isn't for everyone," Nora said. "There are times I wish I hadn't chosen it."

"Why did you?" I scrubbed at my arms. "If you don't mind my asking."

"My father drank away any money that would have seen me into a decent marriage. Duck down."

I dunked my head below the water, reveling in the silence for a moment before coming back up into the world.

"I had a few men who wanted me anyway." Nora ran her fingers along the teeth of a carved comb. "But I didn't want any of them. To marry a man I didn't love, to spend the rest of my life rolling on my back for him, and then popping out his screaming children, I couldn't stomach it.

"I could have found work as a domestic for a Guilded or a merchant, but then I would have spent the rest of my life toiling in someone else's home only to die old and lonely, owning nothing of my own. With all those years of drab misery laid out in front of me, I couldn't turn down what being a part of Mave's family provides."

"What do you mean?"

Nora started working through the ends of my hair with her comb. "By the time I'm not fit to work the downstairs anymore, I'll have enough coin for ship passage south to the kingless territories with plenty left over to live comfortably for the rest of my life. I'll be done working before I'm thirty."

I tried to imagine that sort of riches, but I couldn't. Cal's family had more income than anyone I'd ever met, but even they couldn't survive if they stopped working.

"It can't be said for the poor souls who whore on the streets." Nora stood and went to the shelves on the right hand wall. "If they aren't beaten to death and manage to stay healthy, they still barely make enough to eat and have a solid roof. The Guilds forget our profession existed long before they took control of Ilbrea, but Mave never forgets. She's built a family, and strength. I wouldn't be surprised if she's the richest woman in Ilbrea outside the Guilds."

"And when you're done, you'll sail away from the Guilds forever?"

"Exactly." Nora held out a thick, black cloth.

I stood and let her wrap me in the soft fabric.

"I'll gladly pay the price for my freedom," Nora said. "I won't ask what brought you to Mave's door, but is what you came here for worth the cost the stars will demand?"

I touched my neck, where the remembered pain had pounded. "Yes."

"Good." Nora kissed my cheek. "In case Mave didn't warn you, beauty is not a pleasant process."

I ignored the pain in my neck and shoulders that having my head tugged at strange angles all night had brought, but I couldn't get my fists to unclench as Nora flitted around me, dabbing pink on my cheeks.

"I'll leave your hair down," Nora said. "The color brings a nice contrast to your fair complexion."

I didn't bother trying to answer. After protesting her using the kohl pencil on my eyelids, I learned Nora didn't actually care what I thought of the manner in which she preened me. It had been two hours since she'd finished with my hair and dragged me into her room. She dressed me and painted me like I was nothing more than her doll. A doll she preferred to remain mute at that.

Nora dabbed a bit of tingling cream on my lips. "It really is a pity." She looked at me as though waiting for me to speak.

"What's a pity?" I asked, careful not to let any of the cream get into my mouth.

"That you were born so pretty," Nora said. "It's a waste. Do you know how many girls come crawling to Mave's door who would give their left tit to be half so beautiful as you?"

"No."

"Well, it's a lot." Nora pulled the blanket from around my shoulders. "I'll have to make you a box of treasures when you leave us. It would be wrong to dress you in armor and leave you helpless when it washes off."

"Thank you."

"Come take a look." Nora waved me toward a floor to ceiling mirror in the corner of her room.

Let there be something left of me.

I stepped in front of the glass, examining myself from my toes up.

The boots were the same pair Cati had found for me back at the camp. The long, deep green skirt had more material to it than I was used to. The fabric was finely woven, soft with a hint of texture that pleased my fingers as I trailed them into my pockets.

The black bodice cut low in front and left no need for imagining the curves of my body. Nora had pulled the neck of my shift down to meet the bodice, displaying enough of my chest to send heat to my cheeks.

"Don't blush, you'll ruin the look." Nora squeezed my hand.

The deep brown of my hair had been swallowed by black dye.

Like a raven's feathers.

I took a deep breath, straining against the laces of my bodice, and looked up to my face.

I still looked like me, but the girl in the mirror was different. Fierce and powerful in her beauty. A more romantic version of me, one meant for moonlight and love. The Ena Ryeland that would exist if I had been created in a daring story.

Is this how Cal saw me?

"No one will suspect you've ever even passed through Harane. You are a true girl of the city now." Nora furrowed her brow. "Do you hate it? I could go a bit further with your face, but you've said you aren't staying here—and that much paint would be suspicious on the road."

"You've done wonderfully." I managed to make my voice cheerful. "It's just very different. I'm not used to it."

"That's the point." Nora leaned her head on my shoulder. "If you don't feel like you, what chance does the rest of the world have of picking you out in a crowd?"

"None." A blissful sense of freedom tamped down my trepidation.

If the soldiers who had been in Harane saw me on the streets of Frason's Glenn, they'd never guess I was the girl they'd attacked a few short weeks ago. I shifted my weight, letting the sheath of the knife hidden in my boot press into my skin. If the soldiers came after me again, I would not be helpless. I wouldn't allow myself to be.

"We should get you down to your brother." Nora took my hand, drawing me away from the mirror. "I'm excited to see what the great Emmet Ryeland thinks of my work."

"Why do people here know Emmet?" I followed Nora out into the corridor that ran between the sleeping quarters of Mave's girls.

Nora laughed, then whispered, "I'm not sure I'm the best one to tell that tale."

"You said it was best told in daylight, and the sun has risen." I slowed my steps as we reached the big room that led to the stairs.

A girl in a deep blue dress slept in a chair next to the bookshelves. Another girl sat at a table, sipping out of a steaming mug.

"By the Guilds, last night flew," Nora said.

The girl with the mug looked up. "Maybe for you."

"Oh hush." Nora wrinkled her nose at the girl and dragged me toward the stairs.

"Just tell me," I said.

"I wasn't even there," Nora said, "so I couldn't do a proper job."

"But—"

"Ask one of the kitchen folk about the time a naked boy caught the square on fire." Nora pulled a key from her pocket and unlocked the door at the bottom of the stairs. "You'll get a far more accurate and thrilling rendition than I can provide."

We stepped out into the hall, and Nora locked the door behind us.

Women in plain dresses bustled between the rooms on the second floor, hauling buckets, baskets, and rags. They nodded to Nora and me but kept buzzing about their work, moving in a manner that seemed to imply they'd performed these very same tasks a hundred times before.

There was no music pouring in from the square and no laughter drifting up from below. The sound of the floorboards creaking beneath my feet felt like an intrusion on the quiet of the women's morning work.

"Do you know where the others I arrived with are?" I whispered to Nora as we passed a room where the bed had been turned on end. "Liam and Finn?"

"They might be on the fourth floor, sleeping in the men's rooms," Nora said, her voice barely above mine. "If not, they'll be in the kitchens."

"Are the men not fed where they sleep?"

"They are, but Mave eats in the kitchen. If your friends came to see her, that's where they'll be." Nora let her hand glide along the banister as we climbed down to the ground floor.

The great room that had been packed with people the night before sat empty—all the chairs carefully tucked around the tables with not a rogue chamb glass lying around to ruin the perfection. The faint sounds of voices and pots clunking together carried from the far back of the dining room.

The temptation to sit down at one of the tables and revel in the shining solitude grew in my stomach, but a low rumbling voice kept me at Nora's heels.

"I'm not sure it's worth the risk," Mave said as Nora swung open the door to the kitchen, "but if anyone has a manifest, it's him."

I opened my mouth to ask what sort of manifest was worth any sort of risk but lost my question in marveling at the sheer size of the kitchen. The space was bigger than any of the houses in Harane. Larger even than the tavern. Five iron stoves sat along one wall, with a fireplace large enough to burn a bed at one end, and a sink the size of a bath at the other.

"There she is." Mave's words drew my gaze to a long table in the center of the room. She'd changed out of her maroon gown and into a finely made day dress of the same color.

Liam and Emmet sat opposite her.

Liam turned toward me, freezing with his mug halfway to his mouth, while Emmet stood, glowering at me.

"Emmet"—Nora stepped forward, extending her hand—"how lovely to see you with your pants on."

"What have you done to her?" Emmet looked from Nora to me.

"Exactly what I was told to do." Nora planted her hands on her hips. "I created a new and glorious creature and spent the whole night working on it. Some gratitude would be in order."

"Say thank you to Nora, Emmet," Mave said.

Emmet clenched his jaw for a moment before speaking. "Thank you, Nora. No one would suspect this girl is my sister."

"I would." Liam lowered his mug.

Nora turned to me, tapping her lips with one, well-manicured finger. "I could take her back up and change the color of her hair."

"No." I stepped away. "Getting my hair to black was bad enough."

"I don't think the soldiers will know it's her." Liam stood, his chair scraping against the stone floor. "But she looks the same to me."

My heart flipped in my chest so hard I was certain everyone could see its movement through the fabric of my bodice. "Then I'll be going out of the city today?"

"I still don't think—"

"I wasn't speaking to you," I cut across Emmet.

Liam studied me, the line of his jaw set like stone. "We can ride out together. Hopefully, we won't have to go too far."

"I should fetch Finn, then." Emmet started toward the door. "If we're going to go, the sooner the better."

"You and Finn have other things to attend to," Liam said.

"They can wait." Emmet stood in the doorway, glaring at Liam as though he could change his mind through sheer force of loathing me.

Liam didn't flinch. "I'll keep my word, Emmet. I hope I can trust you to keep yours."

Emmet looked at me, his eyes resembling our father's more than I remembered.

"We won't go far," I said.

Emmet looked back to Liam and nodded.

The entire kitchen stayed frozen as Emmet's footsteps thumped away.

"Must be an exciting outing you have planned," Nora said when the only sound left was the girl in the corner scrubbing out a stove.

"Get yourself to bed, Nora," Mave said. "You need your rest."

"Yes, ma'am." Nora bowed her head and floated out of the kitchen.

"Feed the girl." Mave seemed to speak to no one in particular, but a man in an orange coat appeared before I could think to look for him, bearing a tray of pastries the likes of which even Cal's mother could never have dreamt of.

The man bowed and extended the tray toward me. My fingers hovered over the confections as I tried to choose between the shiny one with the chopped nuts on top, the thing filled with jam, and a roll that looked so fluffy I wasn't sure it counted as food.

"We should go," Liam said.

"Let the girl pick something to eat," Mave said. "Beauty is a tiring process, and she's had a hard night."

I picked the nut-covered thing.

The man winked and kept his tray toward me. I grabbed a fluffy roll as Liam waited by the door.

"Thank you," I said. "Thank you, Mave."

"Get out before Liam has a fit." Mave shook her head, her curls bobbling around like a living crown.

I slipped out the kitchen door behind Liam, barely able to believe I'd not only gained two cakes for breakfast, but was also going to be riding out of the city without Emmet.

Bright morning sun bathed the square outside Mave's house. The men sweeping away the debris of the revelry paused as Liam and I passed, holding their brooms steady as though wanting to be sure they didn't kick a stray bit of dirt onto my skirt.

I waited until we were out of view of the workers to bite into my breakfast.

The sticky sweetness of the nut-covered pastry made me feel like a little girl who had stolen a bit of pie.

"Are you all right?" Liam glanced sideways at me.

"Fine." I held the roll up to him. "Want some?"

He shook his head. "Mave's already stuffed me full."

Liam weaved a different path through the streets than the one we'd followed Emmet on the night before. He turned down an alley so narrow it looked like people shouldn't be allowed to cross through. Before I could ask where he was taking me, we'd stepped out into a square packed with market stalls.

"How often do you come here?" I asked over a vendor's shout of, "Morning remedies! Take a swig and clear your head."

"It depends." Liam took my arm, guiding me past a man selling vegetables and eggs and a woman offering slabs of meat. "I only make my way to Frason's Glenn when I've no other choice."

A pack of children ran by. The girls had ribbons in their hair. The boys had bright rosy cheeks. This wasn't the Frason's Glenn I'd seen the night before when only the laxe and the night workers had been out. In the fresh morning air, normal people filled the city.

Buying milk, trading gossip, looking for a new packet of needles. Doing normal things like Black Bloods and monsters were no more than myths. I studied the people as I passed, wanting to memorize the beautiful blandness of it all.

The more I watched the people, the more I realized they were watching me as well. I ate the fluffy roll as quickly as I could, just waiting for someone to come charging after us.

We passed out of the square and onto a wide road. No one chased us, but the man with the candle cart and the little girl selling flowers both stared at me.

"Liam," I whispered, "I think people might recognize me."

I felt his arm tense beneath my touch, but he didn't change his pace. "Who?"

I swallowed hard, trying to rid myself of the urge to be sick on the cobblestones. "All of them. They keep looking at me."

Liam scanned the street. I stepped closer to him, holding his arm tight.

He didn't speak until the gate came into view. A line of people had already gathered to exit the city. "They don't recognize you. They just want to look at you."

A prickle sprang up on the back of my neck. The feeling of being watched by a horde drained the warmth of the sunlight from my shoulders.

Liam's tone held no trace of fear as he chatted with the gangly stable boy, asking for our horses.

I steeled my courage and looked at the people around me, searching for the eyes of a monster that sought to destroy me.

Instead, I found a tiny boy with his fist in his mouth as he stared up at me, and an older woman who smiled gently as she looked at me like she was remembering someone else. A boy my age blushed scarlet when I met his gaze.

They all watched me like I was a curiosity. A beautiful bird who had landed in a garden and would soon fly away and be forgotten.

I am wearing my armor, and they don't even see it.

The stable boy brought me my brown mare, and Liam and I rode through the gate, past the soldiers and the river docks, and to the open fields beyond.

35

I know my memory of that day isn't right.

I remember the sun kissing my face and the wind lifting my hair as I rode through the fields beyond the reaches of Frason's Glenn.

I remember laughing with abandon.

And Liam laughing with me, the deep tambour of his joy burning in my soul with a fire I didn't understand.

I remember the sun glinting off my darkened hair in a new way, and somehow not being frightened by the change.

If the perfection in my mind were somehow true, the first blooms of spring had begun to appear, and white flower petals clung to the green fabric of my skirt as I wandered, searching for treasure. The sweet perfume of the blooms tickled my nose, and I tucked a pink flower in my hair.

We rode for miles, searching and knowing the city waited for us, but somehow still wanting to ride a bit farther. To find another meadow to wander through, Liam by my side, a solid pillar of a man that somehow made the sun burn brighter.

The way his eyes burned brighter when we found the shadow berries and piled them into a black pouch. The way he kissed the back of my hand and thanked me for helping him while in the same breath telling me he would find a way to see the rest of our work through without me. I didn't have to do anymore.

But I did.

Walking away from him, from what had begun the moment I'd decided to follow a Black Blood into the mountains, was impossible. So I touched his cheek, the warmth of his skin calling to every bit of my being, and told him I would do the work that needed to be done.

I remember the ride back to Frason's Glenn being too short.

I remember desperately wishing my time by his side would never end.

I remember the smoke hovering over the western edge of the city and drifting out over the river, like morning mist gone mad. Trying not to breathe in the smoke because I didn't want to lose the scent of sunshine and spring the day had left etched in my soul.

But I know not all of the perfect sunshine can be true. Such wonderful days do not exist in a world ruled by the Guilds. Their torment taints even the brightest joy.

I will never know how much of that day was truly how I remember it. I rode out of the city an innocent girl who had never done anything a decent man would judge as wrong.

I returned to the gates a Black Blood with the power to murder hidden in her pocket.

The Guilds had stolen so much from me. My innocence I gave willingly to destroy them.

There were more people trying to exit the gates than enter when Liam and I joined the end of the line. The sun had begun to sink, and the smoke left an ominous haze over the city.

I wished I had a cloth or something to hold over my face, but the clothes Nora had dressed me in left lifting my skirt to my nose as my only choice. I might have been tempted to try it, but the black pouch of berries burned in my pocket, and I was too afraid of calling attention to myself to do anything more than wrinkle my nose at the stench and wait patiently in line.

Liam kept his horse next to mine as we moved slowly forward.

I glanced around before leaning toward him. "Are they searching people?"

The thought brought me no fear. I doubted the soldiers were smart enough to know the berries in my pocket were deadly. And, even if they did, it would be easy enough to pretend I was a fool bringing bounty home to be made into a tart.

Liam didn't answer right away. He sat up straight, staring at the gate, looking angry at being kept from his supper. "They're searching the people leaving, not entering."

"Leaving?" My brown mare shifted as I stood in my stirrups, trying to see past the gate.

One by one, the people entering crept past a pack of soldiers searching every person exiting the city. The soldiers had pulled down all the crates from a man's cart, leaving the merchant with bolts of fabric lying in the dirt.

Another man had been stripped of his pack and stood pale-faced as a young soldier dug through his possessions.

Why? Why should they care what leaves their protected city?

I opened my mouth to ask, but a different question came out. "Will you promise me they're safe?"

Liam kept his gaze fixed on the gate.

"Liam?" I gripped my horse's reins.

"We should be able to make good time once we get through the gate." Liam gave me a smile that didn't reach his eyes.

All the joy from the day's sunshine drained from my chest.

"Keep moving in." A soldier climbed up onto a stack of crates so he towered over the crowd. "If you don't want us to shut the gates and keep you all out for the night, keep moving in."

"We're trying," an older man in a fine coat shouted up at the soldier. "Don't blame us for your soldiers blocking our path."

I flinched, hunching my shoulders out of instinct. There were people in line behind us, but not so many I couldn't turn my horse and ride away.

A scuffling came from the front of the crowd, inside the gate where I couldn't quite see.

"Stay, Ena," Liam said.

"I am a soldier of the Guilds," the man on the crates spoke above the growing voices by the gate. "Any citizen of Ilbrea who questions my authority will be taken to the prison and dealt the Guilds' justice."

Prison.

I rolled the word around in my head, trying to reason through the Guilds locking up the man who had spoken rudely to the soldier instead of just whipping him on the street.

"I'm sorry," a woman wailed from the front of the crowd. She was inside the gates, hidden from view by five soldiers. "I've done nothing wrong. Please!"

"Stay, Ena," Liam said again, as though he could scent my desire to run.

But as the woman wordlessly screeched, I wasn't sure which way I wanted to run. To the forest, or toward her? I had a knife in my boot and berries in my pocket, but neither would have done much good against so many paun.

The soldiers parted as two of them grabbed the woman. She screamed as they dragged her down the street.

"Help her," I whispered.

Liam looked to me, pain filling his eyes. "I can't."

I reached across the distance between us, needing to feel his skin against mine to assure myself I hadn't fallen into some new nightmare.

The line started moving forward more quickly. The people exiting the city plastered themselves to their side of the road, keeping their heads bowed and staying silent as the soldiers searched them.

Liam moved to ride behind me as we passed under the stone wall and into the city. Ruined skeins of yarn, trampled food, scattered papers, and a shattered doll lay on the ground. Parts of people's lives the soldiers had cast into the dirt without care.

The stable boy stood in front of the white painted horse, his hands behind his back and chin tucked as he watched the soldiers search a fresh batch of tilk.

"Do you still have space?" Liam hopped down from his horse and reached up to help me.

I didn't argue that I could chivving well climb down from a horse without his help. The soldier outside the gate had started shouting again, and Liam's hands on my hips soothed my desire to flee.

"I do." The boy didn't look away from the gate.

"What happened?" I asked.

Liam wrapped an arm around my waist, keeping me close to his side.

"Not sure," the boy said. "Bells rang across the city. There was a bit of a panic about a fire spreading and burning all of Frason's Glenn. Then people said we wouldn't burn, but there were bandits out to steal all our gold. Then the soldiers came.

"Truth be told, I doubt any of what I heard is even true. I can't think of a sane reason any bandit would break into the sailors' offices. There are plenty of places with more gold in them. And if they wanted to break in, why do it during the day?"

"I can't see any sane purpose for it," I said.

The stable boy smiled at me. "I'm glad I've not lost my reason." He stepped forward, taking charge of our horses. He glanced to the gate before leaning in close to Liam and me. "If you want to know what I really think, some Guilded slitch got drunk off their knob and set their office on fire. Now the whole city's stuck paying for the fool's mistake."

Liam gave a laugh that might have sounded real if I hadn't known him. "You just be careful not to down too much frie and light the stable on fire."

"I care for these horses as if they were my own." The boy gave a nod. "Most of them are good as babes, and even the chivving bastards among them deserve a safe stall and fine hay."

"Thank you for taking care of them," I said.

The boy bowed. "I am at your service." He blushed and led our horses away.

Liam gave a laugh that came closer to real. "We should have you fetch the horses when we leave. He might not charge you for their keep."

I aimed an elbow at Liam's stomach. He dodged away, but kept his hand on my back as he guided me through the city. He walked just behind me, as though terrified someone might sneak up and try to steal me away.

We cut back through the square where the common folk had been doing their morning shopping. The vendors were still out finding buyers for their wares, but the cheerful note the scene had held earlier had vanished. Shoppers moved quickly from one stall to the next, taking the goods they wanted and handing over coins with barely a word exchanged. The children had disappeared altogether.

"What did you send them to do?" I asked.

Liam led me into the tight alley without answering.

"What did you ask them to do that's affected a whole city? Liam"—I stepped away from his hand and turned to face him—"what have they done?"

Liam ran his hands over his face. "Nothing that should have caused this. If everything went as I'd asked, there shouldn't be any fuss or fire. Maybe it's not them at all."

"Do you really have any hope of that?"

"I'm not one to give up hope." Liam laid his hand on my shoulder, his fingers touching my bare skin. "But I'd like to get to Mave's and find out what's happened."

"If Emmet's gone and mucked everything up with Mave—"

"Come on." Liam skirted around me and took my hand, leading me out onto the street.

We heard the music coming from Mave's long before the backs of the buildings that surrounded her square came into view.

While the market had gone quiet, Mave's folk seemed to have taken the smoke in the air as a sign from the stars that the revelry needed to be bolder than before. Seven musicians stood on the platform, playing for a packed crowd who whooped and hollered along with the tune.

The girls on Mave's porch swept from man to man, flirting and teasing as easily as butterflies flitting from bloom to bloom.

Nora perched on the edge of a table filled with men who gazed at her like she was a goddess fallen from the sky.

She wore her armor well.

I recognized her face, her hair, the way she smiled in a pitying way at the men who fawned over her. But there was a façade covering the Nora who had spoken gently to me as she dyed my hair and painted my face.

She'd become a knight, going into battle against all mankind.

She is a beautiful warrior.

A man leaned back in his chair to look at me as we crossed the porch. Liam tucked me close to his side, wrapping his arm around me. The man raised an eyebrow and turned back to his drink.

The dining room had filled with patrons as well. The scent of roasted meat and fresh baked cakes wafted from the kitchen. Men in green, chest-baring vests roamed the room as the girls had on the porch. Men in orange carried silver trays heavy with glasses of chamb.

"Can I help you, love?" A girl stepped in front of the stairs, blocking our path, and eyeing Liam.

"I'm Emmet's sister." I tipped my chin up, meeting her gaze.

Her face paled, and she fumbled for the pocket in her skirt. "You should come with me."

"Why?" I followed her up the stairs. "Is he all right? What happened to him?"

The girl spun on the steps and glared at me. "Don't ask such questions in front of the guests."

"Sorry." I stayed close on her heels as we cut through the long corridor of rooms.

Some of the doors were still open. The beds had been made and the lamps lit.

If something were horribly wrong upstairs, life below wouldn't be continuing uninterrupted. But Mave kept her business going while holding prisoners and planning executions. If she could do a thing like that, there was no way to know she wouldn't have my brother's corpse upstairs while her family plied their trade in the long line of rooms.

The girl unlocked the door and stepped aside. "They're on the top floor."

"Thank you." I ran up the steps to the girls' floor.

The big room was empty. I climbed the stairs to the floor above. Another large room, built like the one below but painted a calmer hue, waited at the top of the steps.

Two men stood from their seats at the table.

"Where are they?" Liam asked.

"In the back." One of the men eyed me. "It might be best if she waits out here. It's not a pretty thing."

I ran down the hall without bothering to reply.

"Ena." Liam chased after me. "Ena." He grabbed my arm. "Let me go in. Let me see what's happened."

"Don't be a chivving slitch." I didn't have to ask what door I was looking for. Both Finn's voice and the smear of fresh blood on the handle gave it away.

Gritting my teeth against the feel of blood-covered metal, I opened the door.

The room was small, like Nora's. But instead of beautiful gowns, this room had been taken over by the spilled contents of Finn's pack, a pile of bloody clothes and bandages, and a bowl of red-stained water.

"What under the stars have you done?" I glanced between my brother sitting in a chair, looking pale as a corpse, and Finn kneeling beside him, trying to tie on something they seemed to think was a proper bandage.

"Evening, Ena." Finn gave me a fleeting smile. "Your new hair looks lovely."

"Thank you, Finn." I lifted my skirt over the blood-stained shirt on the floor. "Emmet, what have you done to yourself?"

Emmet glared at me, wincing as Finn tugged on his bandage. "I didn't do anything to myself. Things didn't go as planned, and I had a bit of a run in with a sword."

"If I didn't know better, I'd think you were trying to be funny." I shooed Finn away.

"We got the papers." Finn leaned against the wall.

"What chivving papers?" I knelt beside Emmet.

Liam shut the door and leaned against the frame. "Cargo orders for the river boats."

"That's what you're bleeding for?" I untied Emmet's bandage. "Did you start the fire in the city, too?"

"We didn't have much of a choice." Emmet hissed through his teeth as I began unwrapping the thin cloth they'd used to bind his arm. "We got into the sailor's office saying we had a shipment coming in and needed to know where they'd want it."

"Paun bought it, too," Finn said. "Went searching through the records for where we should deliver our grain. Got him out of the room, got everything we wanted from his desk. Then a soldier walked in from the street, shouting about needing supplies before we could fade into the distance."

"And the soldier carved you up on your way out the door?" I asked.

"More or less," Emmet said.

"How long ago?" I peered at the cut. It was longer than my hand and deep enough to need stitches, though the edges were clean and not too swollen.

"A couple of hours," Emmet said.

"It should have stopped bleeding by now," I said. "Could Mave not find a healer?"

"I won't have trouble brought on Mave's head over my bloody arm," Emmet said.

"You're a fool, Emmet Ryeland." I sat back on my heels. "Your arm needs to be cleaned and stitched if you don't want a nasty infection."

"I'll be fine." Emmet pulled his arm away from me, sending a fresh trickle of blood sliding down his skin.

"How many men have said that only to end up armless or dead?" I looked toward my pack, hoping against hope Lily's basket would appear. "Liam, I need a sturdy needle, thread, strong liquor, clean water, soap, and a bandage these fools haven't made a mess of."

"No," Emmet said, "absolutely not."

"Don't fuss like a baby. It won't take long."

"You're going to stitch him up?" Finn said.

"Of course I am."

"She's not," Emmet said.

"Liam, go fetch the supplies to stitch up this fool." I glared at Emmet as I spoke.

The door clicked closed behind Liam.

"We don't have time for this," Emmet said. "Mave is going to her dungeon tonight. You have to make her the poison."

"Did you even find the mythical berries?" Finn asked.

I pulled the pouch from my pocket and tossed it to him.

"Work on the berries, Ena," Emmet said. "I'll be fine."

"Stop arguing with me and be grateful I'm here." I dug in my pack, pulling out the things I'd pilfered from Neil. A tiny pot and a tight-knit sieve were all I'd brought with me. It didn't seem like enough now that it was actually time to brew something to kill a man.

"Finn, empty the berries into the sieve," I said.

"All right." Finn took the pot and sieve from me.

Footsteps thumped toward the door.

"I've got everything but the soap and water." Liam came back, a bottle of frie in one hand and a needle, thread, and bandages in the other.

"I'm coming," a voice called from down the hall. A boy my age stepped into the room, carrying a bowl of steaming water and a brick of soap. He wore only a thin green wrap around his waist that hid absolutely nothing.

"Get out of here dressed like that," Emmet said.

"You"—I nodded toward the boy—"get me a spoon and two empty vials."

"Yes, ma'am." The boy ran out of the room.

"Press the berries through the sieve." I looked to Finn while I washed my hands in the near burning water.

"With my fingers?" Finn asked.

"Sure," I said. "Just don't lick them afterward."

I took the bottle of frie from Liam, pulling out the stopper with a pop.

"Ena, you're being ridiculous," Emmet said.

I lifted his arm, twisting the gash toward the ceiling. "This is going to hurt." I poured frie into his wound.

Emmet gave another satisfying hiss through his teeth.

"I've got the berries pressed through." Finn held up his deep-violet stained fingers.

"Find a bit of thin cloth." I took the needle and thread from Liam's outstretched hand.

"Can we send the naked boy to get that, too?" Finn asked.

"Just use a bit of the bandage you ruined." I held the needle in the lantern's flame.

"But it's all been bled on," Finn said.

"You only need a bit, and there are some clean patches." I threaded the needle and knelt back down beside Emmet. "Besides, I think the man we're making it for will have bigger things to be fussed over than how cleanly we strained the juice."

Emmet laughed.

I looked up to find a faint glimmer of true mirth playing in the corners of his eyes.

"This is going to hurt, but I honestly don't feel too badly about it." I stuck the needle into my brother's flesh.

I'd washed the blood and berries off my hands before I'd even left the men's floor. Mave had come to take a vial of the dark liquid. I'd tucked the other vial into my pocket as she led me downstairs to a room at the very end of the row on the third floor.

The bed was made and the lantern lit. I'm sure Mave told someone to make the room up for me, but it didn't seem like it at the time.

With the music still playing and laughter rumbling up from below, it felt as though the house itself were a living creature. And the animal made of stone and wood had created a room for me. A little cave where I could rest huddled in its embrace.

I hadn't slept in more than a day. I should have been able to topple down onto the clean bed and drift instantly away. But I couldn't. I scrubbed my face and hands in the washbasin, and stared out the window at the dark street instead.

Had I been facing the square, I could have watched the dancers and musicians. But my window gave me a view of the sleeping city away from the revelry.

A boy passed beneath my window, moving like he was hurrying somewhere. I wondered if maybe Mave had given him the poison.

No one had told me who would be feeding the man the berries I'd mixed. All I'd been offered was a promise of a full report as to how it had worked once the thing was finished.

If I'd done my job well, a man would be dead by morning. A man whose face I would never see, whose name I would never know. If it was even a man at all.

The air in my room pressed against me, too heavy for me to breathe properly. I unlatched my window, swung the tall panes inside, and stepped onto the small balcony beyond. The chill night air kissed my bare neck, easing my nerves.

"Don't be a fool, Ena," I whispered to the darkness. "You begged to be here. The choice has already been made."

"That doesn't mean you have to be happy about it," Liam said.

I looked up, half-expecting him to be floating in the air, hovering on his stones.

Instead, he leaned over his railing, watching me from the balcony above mine.

"What we're doing is right," Liam said. "It's for the good of all tilk. That doesn't make it any easier."

"No. It doesn't."

Liam looked up toward the sky. The sliver of moon cast shadows on his face.

I wanted to be closer, to gaze into his eyes and see what had truly kept him awake to this horrible hour of the morning. I wiped my palms on my skirt and stepped up onto the metal railing that bordered my balcony.

"What are you doing?" Liam looked down as the rail clanged beneath my boots.

"Climbing." I stood perched on the metal rail for a moment, testing my balance and reveling in the wind blowing around my ankles.

"Ena, get down from—"

I jumped, catching a spiral loop on his balcony in each of my hands. My arms burned as I pulled myself up. I enjoyed the pain of it, the way my muscles remembered how I wanted them to work. I got myself high enough to sneak my toe onto his balcony, and pushed the rest of the way up with my legs. Keeping my back to the open air and my hands on the iron, I looked down at the ground far below.

There was nothing between me and falling but my own strength and calm head. Such a simple path to death with no tricks, plotting, or malice to be found.

"Can you climb over to this side now?" Liam said. "Before the wind gusts and you fall?"

"Wind wouldn't knock me over." I kicked a leg up and over the railing, careful to keep my skirts low enough to not give the sort of show the people downstairs sought. "Maybe if there were a horrible storm, but not a normal wind."

"I'd still rather you stay on this side of falling." Liam leaned against the rail opposite me.

We stood together in silence for a moment. The crowd on the other side of the building cheered as a new song began.

"I suppose it's good thing I didn't have my heart set on sleeping," I laughed.

"You should try anyway," Liam said. "We've a long ride ahead of us tomorrow."

"Even if the berries don't work?" I gripped the rail behind me. The edges of a metal flower cut into my palms.

"They will."

"I hope." I sat on the ground, bending my knees to fit in the small space that was no wider than the window. "It's an awful thing to hope for."

"Maybe." Liam sank down, scooting toward the edge so both of us could fit. "But Ilbrea will be a better place without him."

"Are you sure?" A knot I hadn't noticed before squeezed my stomach tighter.

"I asked Mave who the prisoner was. I thought you might want to know eventually, even if not for a long time. Questions about things like this tend to linger."

I looked up to the stars fighting to shine against the lamps on the streets below.

"Who is he?" The question caught in my throat.

"A Guilded scribe."

I let out a long breath.

"He embezzled tilk taxes," Liam said. "Made it look like some of the farmers north of here hadn't paid."

"Were the farmers killed?" My hands shook.

Liam reached forward, taking my hands in his. "One. Two others were whipped and stripped of their land."

"That scribe is a murderer."

"And the Guilds would never have given him true justice. They'd have kicked him out of the Scribes Guild at worst—sent him to a lesser post more likely."

"Where he could destroy more people's lives for his own selfish greed."

"He'll never harm anyone again." Liam held my hands tighter. "The people he hurt may never know justice was given, but at least they're safe from the monster who placed his desires above common folks' lives."

"Then I'm glad I had a hand in his end. Does that make me awful?"

"Not to me." Liam gave a tired smile. "Not to any of the Black Bloods in the camp. This is the only scale we can fight the Guilds on right now. We do the best we can to stop one monster at a time."

"And tomorrow we ride to Gabe? Help him slay a beast?"

Liam leaned forward, looking straight into my eyes. "We ride to rid Ilbrea of a man who has harmed hundreds of innocents."

"Good."

He let go of my hands and leaned back against the railing. "You should get some sleep. It'll be a long day tomorrow."

"Sleep isn't something I'm very good at." I nudged his leg with my foot. "You've seen it. Better not to disturb the people below my room."

"You shouldn't have to carry such a burden."

I shrugged. I hated myself for not having anything brave to say.

"The nightmare"—Liam pulled something from his pocket and held it up to the sky—"what happens?"

"Does it matter?" I leaned in, examining the thing he held between his fingers. A small black stone, like the ones he'd protected us with in the forest, glinted in the hint of moonlight.

"Perhaps." Liam rolled the stone between his fingers. "Maybe it's only the way the Black Bloods live, but I was always taught you can't fight a monster you can't name."

"There is no monster in the dream." I looked up at the moon, holding on to its faint light so the darkness of the nightmare couldn't surround me. "I honestly don't know if it would make sense."

"Just try."

"Has Emmet told you," I began, fighting to keep my voice steady with every word, "has he told you how our parents died?"

"Fever took them both."

I looked to Liam, searching his face for a lie. But I could see it in his eyes. He honestly believed that was what had happened to them both.

"Emmet's a liar." I laced my fingers together, tucking them under my chin. "Or maybe he doesn't remember. He was so sick when it happened, maybe no one told him."

I waited for Liam to ask a question, or to defend Emmet, but he just sat watching me.

"I was the first to catch the fever. It wasn't that bad for me. I felt chivving awful, but I got better in a few days. Then Emmet and our mother took ill. They didn't get better."

The long-forgotten scent of sweat and sick brought bile to my throat. "Emmet could barely breathe. Mother got so bad she started having seizures. Lily came. She did everything she could, but they were beyond her help. We needed a proper healer. But there's never been a Guilded healer assigned to Harane. The nearest is in Nantic, thirty miles north of the village."

"That's too big a territory." Liam clasped the stone between his hands.

"The villagers in Harane have been asking for a healer since before I was born. But the answer is always *just ride to Nantic*. Father had started to get the fever by the time Lily said she couldn't help us any further. I was well enough, and I loved to ride, so he told me to race for Nantic. Set me up on the horse and told me not to stop for anyone. My mother and brother would die if I didn't find the healer before sunrise."

Tears pooled in the corners of my eyes, but I couldn't reach up to brush them away. My body had frozen, trapped in the memory of that terrible ride.

"The sun had set, but I knew the way. There's only one road between Harane and Nantic. All I had to do was follow it. I rode and rode, crying, begging the horse to go faster, but the night stretched on, and there was nothing but darkness and the pounding of the horse's hooves.

"The poor creature collapsed before we'd even reached the city. So I ran. I ran and ran, until there were finally buildings along the road. I didn't know where to find the healer, so I just kept screaming for help. An old woman came out of her house. She was kind. She led me to the healer's door. But there was a note pinned up. A soldier had broken his leg on the crossroad, and he'd gone to tend to the wound.

"The woman begged me to come into her house. Promised me food and a bed, but I had to find the healer. If I didn't, Mother and Emmet would die. I found the crossroad and ran west. There was blood in my shoes, and the road swam in waves as I tried to keep going. I found the camp just after sunrise. I begged the soldiers to help me, to take me to the healer. I told them my family would die.

"They just laughed. Their own healer had gotten too drunk to help anyone, so they had called for the one from Nantic. I told them I'd raced all the way from Harane for help, I sobbed and pleaded. They spit on me, and hit me, and tossed me out of their camp. By the time I could stand again, the sun was already high."

"Ena." Liam took my hands, guiding them away from my chin. "I'm so sorry."

"It took me two days to walk home." The heat of my tears tortured my face. "By the time I got there, Mother was dead. Those soldiers arrived a few hours after me. They'd come to collect spring taxes. Father didn't have the money. He'd sent it to the scribe in Nantic to get the papers so mother could be buried. The soldiers threatened to take our fields. Father argued.

"He stood there, screaming at a silver-haired soldier holding a shining sword. When the soldier got tired of it, he ran father through. My father bled to death in the cold mud. The soldiers left me weeping next to his corpse. They rode away like nothing had happened."

Liam pressed my hands to his lips. "You survived, Ena. I'm sorry for what those bastards did to your father, but the horrors of the nightmare, you survived those soldiers in the real world. You're strong enough to survive them in the dream, too."

A horrible laugh cut through my throat. "The nightmare never gets that far. I'm trapped on the ride to Nantic, knowing I won't make it. Knowing my parents will die because I failed."

"That's not true." Liam touched my cheek, brushing away my tears. "Your mother died because she was ill, because the Guilds didn't see fit to make sure there was a healer to help her. Your father died—"

"Because the greed of the Guilds murdered him? I know. Lily told me that for years. I can repeat her whole speech if you want me to. None of it changes the nightmare."

Liam leaned away from me and took his hand from my cheek. I thought he'd given up, realized there was nothing to be done to help a girl who'd let her parents die because she couldn't ride fast enough.

But a deep blue light glimmered in his hand, emanating from the stone. He breathed onto his palm and the light grew brighter.

"I wish I could take away what happened to you." He pressed his finger onto the stone, bending the light. "I wish I could change the past so your father never placed that responsibility on your shoulders. I wish I could make the healer be in his home and force a shred of compassion into the soldiers' hearts." He pinched the stone between his fingers. "None of those things are within my power, but at least the nightmare can stop."

The stone faded to a shining black oval with a hole pinched through near the center. He pulled his purse of coins from his pocket, untied the leather cord that held the bag shut, and tucked the loose coins away.

"I wish I could protect you from more, but at least I can let you sleep." He strung the leather through the stone. "May I?"

I leaned forward, holding my breath as he lifted my hair to tie the cord.

"It won't protect you from monsters, but it will keep you safe from your own mind."

His face was so near, only a breath between his lips and mine.

A pull began at the center of my chest where the stone touched my skin. A burning that reached deep into my veins as though my blood itself had discovered longing.

He brushed the rest of my tears from my cheeks with his thumb.

"Liam..."

He pressed his lips to my forehead. "You should rest now."

Our gaze met, and the whole world froze. There was no sound from the square, no wind chasing in the coming storm—nothing had ever existed but Liam and me.

His fingers touched my lips, and I leaned into his warmth.

His lips grazed mine, and I forgot to breathe. A hunger like I'd never known ached inside me.

Before I could memorize his taste, he stood, letting the cold night air reclaim me.

"Mave will be looking for us at sunrise." He pushed his window open. "You should get some sleep."

A wave of laughter carried up from the dining room below.

"Right." I stood, sliding my fingers over the smooth pendant at my neck.

"You can cut through here and take the stairs down."

"I'd rather climb."

"Be careful." Liam stepped inside.

"Emmet and Finn," I said before the window closed, "they were seen by the soldier at the sailor's office. They can't be given new feathers like me. They won't be able to travel with us."

"They didn't leave any witnesses behind." He closed the window, and I was alone in the night.

I climbed down to my bed and lay on top of the covers, waiting for the world to come crashing down on me, or for the Guilds to come burn me alive. But the flames that singed me didn't come from the torches of evil men.

I stared at the ceiling above, wishing I could close the short distance between us. Wanting to taste his lips again if only for a moment, just long enough to be sure I would remember the feel of his hand on my cheek.

But sleep came instead, and there was peace in the darkness.

Tap, tap, tap.

I opened my eyes, blinking at the early morning light spilling in through my window.

Tap, tap, tap.

It took me a moment to remember how I had ended up on a soft bed in a fancy, painted room.

"Yes," I called.

"It's Nora. I've been sent to collect you."

"Come in." I sat up, running my hands over my face. My fingers grazed my lips and heat burned in my chest.

Nora stepped into my room carrying a small leather box. "By the Guilds, your hair."

"What?" I leapt to my feet. "What's happened to it?" I ran to the mirror, afraid it had somehow become orange or purple or some other outlandish color.

The black had stayed in place while I'd slept, but the mass of my hair had tangled in an almost impressive way.

"You can give a mouse peacock feathers, but it takes them more than a day to learn to fly." Nora set the leather box on the windowsill and pulled out a brush. "You're going back through the gate today, and you can't do it looking like a gutter snipe."

"Are the others up?" I wondered if Liam had slept, if he'd had even a moment to remember kissing me.

"They're all locked in Mave's parlor."

"Without me?" I started for the door.

"Come back here."

"There are things they could be talking about that I need to know."

Nora dodged around me and planted herself in front of the door. "The man died. He was a fat, old slitch, and it took an hour for him to go. It wasn't pretty either. Whoever you have in mind for that potion, I hope they deserve a painful death."

"They do."

Nora hugged me tight. "Then I'm glad the Black Bloods have found someone like you." She gave a shaking sigh and stepped away. "Now, let's get you ready to go."

"I didn't know you knew." I let her lead me to the mirror without a fight.

"I've been helping Mave for years." Nora combed roughly through the knots in my hair. "I have private clients around the city. It makes my coming and going at odd hours an easy thing to explain."

"What else is Mave talking to them about?"

"One thing at a time, little bird. You haven't earned Mave's secrets, only Liam's."

Heat rushed to my cheeks at the sound of his name.

Nora looked at me in the mirror, one eyebrow raised. "Guard your heart with that one."

"I don't know what you—"

"Liam loves his cause. I don't how much affection he has left for anything else." She pulled a tin of powder from the leather box. "I hope this will all fit in your pack. I cut it down to the bare minimum of what a girl really needs to survive."

I glanced into the kit of weapons Nora had chosen for me. She'd packed more powders and pigments than Karin could have thought up in her wildest daydreams.

"I've already tucked a few clean clothes into your pack. Eyes shut."

I closed my eyes, careful to keep still as she drew the kohl across my lids.

"Thank you, for all of this," I said, "but you really don't have to."

She bopped me on the nose. "Of course I do. Eyes open. The world may be cold and cruel, but that doesn't mean we shouldn't help where we can."

"Thank you." I hugged Nora again.

"Promise to take care of yourself in your travels, and that will be thanks enough for me." She dug back into the box and pulled out the cream. "Lips."

It only took her a few minutes to primp me back into a well-groomed bird.

We walked arm-in-arm down through the empty dining room and into the kitchen. The boys stood around the table with Mave, their coats on and all our packs ready.

"She's fit to travel." Nora presented me to the group.

Emmet tossed a warm roll to me and turned to dig in his pack. Liam didn't look my way at all.

"Thank you, Nora," Mave said.

"It's been my pleasure." Nora tucked the box into my pack.

"Can you even ride in a top that tight?" Finn asked.

I swatted him on the arm. "Faster than you can."

"We should be on our way." Liam hoisted his pack onto his back. "We've a long road ahead, and the sooner we're out of your hair, the better."

"Are you sure you wouldn't rather take my path out of the city?" Mave asked.

"We need our horses." Emmet kissed Mave's hand. "Thank you, Mave, for all you've done."

Mave took Emmet's face in her hands. "Be safe, and come back again someday."

Emmet nodded and headed for the door.

I tucked my roll into my pocket. My stomach had started to squirm too much to consider eating.

"Pleasure meeting you both." Finn gave a nod and followed Emmet.

"Trueborn," Mave said, "don't forget what we're fighting for."

"Never." Liam picked up my pack, balancing it on his shoulder.

"I can take that." I reached for my bag.

"A girl dressed like you wouldn't be carrying a pack in the city." Liam held the door open for me.

"Take this and be well." Mave lifted a bundle of black fabric from the table and pressed it into my arms.

"May we meet again in a land of freedom." Nora kissed my cheek.

"Thank you." I gave them both a brief smile and walked out into the dining room.

Finn and Emmet stood on the porch out front, watching the men cleaning the square.

"Do you think the soldiers will be searching people at the gate?" My voice echoed strangely in the empty room.

"Probably." Liam didn't say anything else as he ushered me out of Mave's house.

I clutched the black fabric tight and touched the pendant at my neck. The smooth stone held the warmth of my body, it had no imperfection in its making, and it was very much real.

What have I done to anger you?

I wanted to ask Liam, but as we weaved through the streets, more pressing questions had to come first.

"Do we have anything we can't let them find?" I asked.

"Not that you need to worry about," Emmet said.

"We're traveling together," I said. "We'll be searched together."

"You and Finn will go through first," Liam said. "He knows which way to ride. We'll catch up to you."

"We should stay together." I clutched the fabric closer as panic crept into my chest.

"You don't trust me, Ena?" Finn clapped a hand to his heart. "You have wounded me beyond healing."

"It's not that."

We entered the market square. The children were back out, running and laughing as though the soldiers weren't a thing to fear.

The noise of the shoppers made speaking softly impossible. The man selling milk joked merrily, and a drunk woman laughed above the rest of the chatter.

We reached the far side and stepped out onto the main road. I slowed my pace to walk beside Liam.

"What if something goes wrong at the gate?" I asked. "How will we know? What if you can't find us? It makes more sense to stay together."

"Ride with Finn, we'll catch up," Liam said. "Emmet."

Emmet stopped, waiting for Liam and me to reach him.

"Let them get their horses before we do," Liam said. "I don't want the soldiers guarding the gate to see us at the stable together."

Finn took my pack from Liam's shoulder. The bulk seemed absurd on his smaller frame. "See you on the road."

I looked at Emmet and Liam but couldn't come up with a thing to say that would let us all stay together.

I tried to think of an argument to make as the stable boy blushed and passed me the reins of my horse. But the poison lay tucked in my pocket, and the papers Liam had wanted badly enough to warrant theft were with him.

Liam's decision made sense.

I mounted my horse and draped the black fabric over the saddle in front of me. A carved wooden clasp caught my eye. A little bird to fasten the neck of a thick black cloak. I smiled, sending a silent thank you to Mave and Nora.

The soldiers gave a quick search through our packs and sent us on our way.

"All we've got to do is ride," Finn said. "They'll find us."

He headed north to the glenn that bordered the city. I followed him, hoping to soon hear hooves pounding behind me.

39

For the first hour, it was easy to make excuses for why Liam and Emmet hadn't caught up to us. I made Finn stop in the trees by the glenn so I could scavenge for a few more supplies. They hadn't come by the time I ran out of reasons to linger.

I looked behind as we took the road that headed west, but they still weren't there.

When the storm came and lightning split the sky, I took comfort in the downpour. With the rain whipping across us, blurring the road and the towering trees surrounding us, they could have been riding just behind and we wouldn't have seen them.

It wasn't until the lights of the town came into view that I gave in to the dread that had threatened for hours.

I was soaked through. Mave's cloak had protected me from the storm for a while, but the protection wasn't meant to last forever.

The rain finally slowed to a manageable pace as Finn led me into the town of Marten.

I clutched my reins with half-frozen hands, studying the stone buildings around me.

The place looked more like Harane than Frason's Glenn. No great wall surrounded the houses that had been built close together like those at the center of Harane. But, if whatever fool had placed the businesses in Harane had also been charged with the planning of Marten, here their gamble paid off.

Shops, a tanner, two taverns, and a proper inn had all been packed together on the main road with more businesses on the two streets that cut through it like a cross. The buildings were taller than the ones in Harane, built three and four stories high to make up for not being able to expand from side to side.

The houses were all made of sturdy stone, and most had their shutters closed tight. I couldn't remember which houses in Harane had even bothered with shutters.

Finn turned down a smaller road and stopped at a tavern that looked a bit sadder than the others we'd passed.

There was no music pouring through the windows. The front door had been solidly shut against the storm, and the paint on the sign out front, which read *The Downy Loft*, had been worn away in places so I had to squint to make out the words.

"They've a stable back here," Finn said. "You stay with the horses, and I'll run in and get us a room. I think..." He scrunched up his face. "I think it would be better if we shared, told them we were together. I don't fancy the idea of leaving you alone in a room here."

I gripped the stone pendant. "Whatever you think is best."

He passed me his horse's reins and dashed inside.

I held my breath, playing out a beautiful scene in my head.

Liam and Emmet would appear behind me. Liam would be cross that Finn had left me alone in the dark. Emmet would say something rude about my needing to be more careful.

We would all go inside and have a hot meal and cup of frie to warm us up. Emmet and Finn would fall dead asleep, and Liam and I would be alone.

I would tell him I'd been worried about him. That I was sorry if I'd somehow tricked him into kissing me, but if he wanted to, I would be happy to kiss him until all the stars fell from the sky.

"They've had a hard ride." Finn came back out of the tavern, leading a sour-looking girl behind him. "If you could give them a bit of extra attention, I'd be very grateful."

"I love gratitude," the girl said. "It does so well when buying food at the market."

"Too right you are." Finn untied my pack from the back of my saddle. "Just see that you care for them as you'd like me to care for you."

I slid off of my saddle, not bothering to hide my wince as my legs protested being asked to straighten.

"I've gotten us a nice room, my love." Finn took my hand, awkwardly shouldering open the door as he balanced both our packs. "I'm told there's already a fire burning in the grate, and the kind lady who owns the place has promised to send up frie and soup."

The murmurs in the dining room, not that a place like that deserved such a fancy name, stopped as everyone turned to look at me.

I resisted the urge to wipe my face in case any of Nora's paint had dripped all the way down my nose. Keeping my chin high, I followed Finn through the crowd of men. Two older women sat in the booths tucked up along the walls. I tried to give them the same sort of smile I'd have given Nora, but both just stared at me.

The wooden stairs had filth lodged in the corners and creaked as we climbed them.

"Second floor, third room down, my love." Finn let go of my hand to fish a key out of his pocket. "We'll get you dry and settled in no time."

"I doubt I'll ever be dry again."

Finn stopped at the third room down and fitted the key in the lock, which gave a heavy thunk as it turned.

The woman who'd rented us the room hadn't lied about the fire in the hearth. The flames crackled mercifully in the grate, the bed had been laid with thick blankets, and before we could close the door, a little boy thumped up behind us with a tray of soup and frie.

"Thank you, sir." Finn set our bags aside and took the tray from the child. "Would you be a fine gentleman and fetch us a pitcher of hot water to wash up with?"

The boy grinned and ran down the hall.

I closed the door behind him.

"It could be worse." Finn set the tray down on the shaky table beside the bed. "It could definitely be better, but it could be worse."

"They'll know to find us here?" I unfastened my cloak and hung the soaked fabric on a nail beside the fireplace.

"It's the choice Liam would make." Finn kicked off his boots. "Can't say I agree with him, but such is life."

I sat in one of the two spindly chairs in front of the fire, letting the flames warm my fingers before I even bothered trying to untie my boots.

"Here." Finn pressed a cup of frie into my hands. "Drink up before you lose a finger."

"I'm not in much danger of that." I sipped the frie, wrinkling my nose as the liquor burned its way down my throat.

"Can't be too careful with those types of things. We can always have the boy bring more up."

"Will Liam and Emmet find us tonight?" I took another sip of frie. "Will they ask what room we're in?"

"Not unless there's a reason for us to run." Finn sniffed his soup before daring to sip from the bowl.

"What if they've already arrived and decided to stay somewhere else?"

"They haven't."

"What if they got lost along the road?"

"They didn't."

"What if they were stopped at the gate and are trapped in Frason's Glenn?"

"Eat your soup." Finn nodded toward the bowl on the table.

"When are we supposed to meet Gabe?" The bowl nearly burned my fingers, but I drank anyway, grateful for the distraction as panic welled in my stomach.

"It's not so much a set time," Finn said. "His regiment is stationed just north of Marten. As far as I know, they aren't set to move anytime soon."

"So we just sit here and wait?"

"No. We wait for the lad to come back with some water to wash up, order some more frie and something other than week old soup to eat, then go to sleep and dream of better food for breakfast."

"You really do think only of food, don't you?" I downed the rest of my soup.

"Food, freedom, and love, sweet Ena. Those three things occupy all the space my mind has to offer."

40

I slept on the bed while Finn curled up near the fire. Lying under the heavy blankets, I clutched the stone pendent, trying to promise myself I was brave enough to sleep. As the storm's wrath began again, I finally drifted off.

When I woke in the morning, the storm hadn't changed. So little sun peered through the thickness of the rain, it was nearly impossible to tell day had come at all. The floor creaking as Finn paced was the only thing that dragged me from my dreamless slumber.

"What's happened?" I asked as soon as I managed to remember where I was and what we'd come for.

"Nothing." Finn stopped midstride. "Just lots of rain and a bit of thunder, but now that you're awake, we might as well go and eat."

I rubbed my hand over my face. "Why don't you go down and order us some food while I try and make myself presentable."

"If that's what you want." Finn flipped the lock on the door. "I just didn't want to have you wake up alone." He stepped out into the hall. "See you down there then."

"Squeaked the floor to wake me up and ran for food," I said after the door had closed behind him.

I took my time brushing my hair and painting on my armor, checking the vial I'd hidden in my bag to be sure it was safe, making sure the other plants I'd gathered in the glenn hadn't been ruined by the rain. I dawdled for as long as I could.

There were only two possibilities I could think of. Either Liam and Emmet were downstairs, in which case they would still be there watching Finn eat an extraordinary amount of food even if I lingered in my room.

Or they weren't downstairs. The soldiers had caught them with the papers they'd taken from the sailors. They'd been trapped somewhere awful and needed Finn and me to rescue them. They could already be dead.

I didn't know if I was brave enough to face that possibility.

I tore the brush through my hair one last time and headed downstairs.

The scent coming from the kitchen promised a better meal than the soup we'd had the night before. Voices carried from below, though I didn't recognize any of them.

Holding my breath, I stepped down into the dining room.

The same two women sat in the booths along the wall. Another woman stood behind the bar, polishing metal mugs with a rag browner than my boots. A pack of men waiting for drinks from the woman leaned against the bar, and a few others sat at the tables dotted around the room.

The young boy shuffled from the kitchen, carrying a tray laden with food, heading toward a table near the door where Finn sat, his red hair as bright as a beacon against the dull brown surrounding him.

There was no one else sitting at his table.

My nails bit into my palms as I walked toward him, keeping my face calm so no one would see my panic.

"There you are, my love." Finn stood and pulled out a chair for me. "I'm afraid I've already eaten my breakfast, but I didn't want you to eat alone, so I ordered another round."

I stared down at the roast pig, vegetables, and porridge on the little boy's tray, wanting nothing more than to throw the food against the wall.

"I'm not very hungry." I sank down into the seat opposite Finn.

"Well, eat what you like and I'll finish the rest." Finn set a plate in front of me.

I stared at him.

"Perhaps some tea for my love, young sir." Finn smiled at the boy. "It seems she needs a bit of perking up."

The boy bowed deeply and backed into the kitchen as though Finn and I were the King and Queen of Ilbrea.

"We don't have time to eat." I spoke through clenched teeth as Finn skewered a roasted potato.

"Of course we do."

"They aren't here."

"I figured that out for myself, shockingly enough." Finn popped the potato into his mouth, closing his eyes at the ecstasy of food.

"Finn," I said, gripping the edge of the table to keep myself from tossing the tray aside, "they could have been captured, they could be dead. We have to ride back to Frason's Glenn and find them."

"That's the part where you're wrong." Finn ate another chivving potato. "What we have to do is wait right here and make sure no one notices us lingering. So we eat."

"We can't just—"

"Hush now, my love." Finn held his potato laden fork to my mouth. "You've got to eat, darling. I know you're exhausted from the trip, but I promise we can rest here for a few days."

I bit the potato from his fork as the little boy shoved a tea tray onto our table.

"Thank you, young sir," Finn said.

The boy backed away again, giving an even larger bow, his face split in a wide grin.

"They might not have stuck to the road," Finn said in a much softer voice. "If something went wrong at the gate, then they're probably keeping to the wilds. Which would mean, if we headed toward Frason's Glenn on the road, we'd miss them. They'd arrive here. We'd be nowhere to be found. Liam and your brother would think we'd gotten ourselves killed, and that is a type of wrath I don't care to see."

"We can't just sit here forever." I shoved another chunk of potato into my mouth to keep from screaming.

"Not forever." Finn took my hand. "We wait a few days. Get our gift to our friend on our own if we have to. If they still haven't come, we head home."

"Without them?"

"To find them there." Finn looked up to the spiderweb-strung ceiling. "That's why Liam split us the way he did."

"What do you mean?" I leaned across the table.

"There are paths through the mountains that are open to Liam and me that you and Emmet wouldn't be able to travel alone."

"You're a trueborn?" I whispered.

"No." Finn laughed. "Thank the gods I'm not. I'd never want to carry that sort of responsibility. But the mountain runs through my veins. As loyal as you and Emmet may be, the mountain cares for those born of her child."

I buried my face in my hands, picturing the mountain swallowing Liam and Emmet whole.

"I've seen Liam get out of scrapes that would have killed the best paun," Finn said. "And, to be honest, I've seen Emmet get out of a lot worse. They are fine. We have to focus on getting our own work done, or there will have been no point in leaving camp. Except escaping Neil's cooking for a while. That is quite the welcome change."

I poured myself a cup of tea, letting the steadiness of my own hands give me courage. "So, where do we find our friend?"

"We can look for him tonight." Finn held his cup up for me to pour for him. "If you want no part in it—"

"Tonight will be fine. I have a few more things to do before we meet him anyway."

I spent the day in our room, working on things that would have horrified Lily.

Or maybe she would have been proud. Maybe she would have smiled, glad the skills she had taught me would have a hand in saving lives, even if one man had to die to do it.

I looked up every time a floorboard squeaked in the corridor, hoping it would be Liam and Emmet, terrified it would be a soldier come to hang me. The day passed without either happening.

When night came, I hid three packages in my pocket and polished my armor.

The rain had turned to a fine mist by the time I walked out of The Downy Loft, arm-in-arm with Finn. He hadn't said exactly where we were going, only that I should look my best. He had put on a clean shirt and run my brush through his hair.

We wandered up the side street where we'd been staying. I studied each building we passed, better able to see them now than when we'd come into town in the rain. The buildings were a bit sadder than I'd thought, with the mortar between the stones crumbling. The paint on the doors peeled away in places, and the shutters all had heavy hooks on the inside, as though ready to be locked against a terrible storm at a moment's notice.

"Are most towns this sad?" I leaned in close to whisper in Finn's ear.

"Only the ones who have an army camped on their doorstep," Finn said. "If a demon were lurking in the garden waiting to steal your child the moment they showed a lick of magic, you'd stop caring about everything but keeping your doors locked tight, too."

"What?" I tugged on Finn's arm, stopping him midstride.

"Didn't Liam tell you why we were coming to kill Drason?"

"No." A heavy weight pressed down on my chest. "I never even asked for his name."

"The Sorcerers Guild noticed a strange number of sorci children being born in Marten." Finn drew me into his arms and spoke close to my ear. "They sent Drason and his men to investigate. He's been stalking the city for more than a

184 I MEGAN O'RUSSELL

year, trapping the children born with magic, then taking their mothers, too. The children are shipped to the Sorcerers Tower in Ilara. We haven't been able to figure out where the women are taken."

A heavy weight sagged in my stomach as I looked at the hooks on the windows. Locks could keep out a storm but not the Guilds.

"This is why we slay the beast." Finn squeezed my hand and led me onto the main road.

Light and music poured through the taverns' windows. Soldiers in uniforms roamed the streets, but not as though they were patrolling. A fair handful of them seemed to be very drunk for the sun having just gone down, and the rest seemed intent on joining the stumblers soon enough. They strode through the town without a hint of guilt for the pain they'd caused.

Finn stopped in front of a common man carrying a sack on his back. "Sorry, sir." Finn gave a little bow. "I'm looking for a recommendation for a lively tavern."

The man wrinkled his brow. "They're all right behind me."

"Yes, I can see them." Finn gave a smile that would have looked foolish on anyone else. "But I wanted to know which you'd say was best."

"Fiddler's Mark." The man nodded. "Good barkeep, good ale, good music, and I've seen them wash the glasses once or twice before. There are soldiers in there, but..." The man shrugged and shook his head.

"Thank you very much, sir." Finn bowed and stepped around the man as though to lead me to the tavern.

But when the man had turned a corner and was out of sight, Finn veered away from Fiddler's Mark and back out to the center of the street to step in front of a young man with a lady on each arm.

"Excuse me, folks," Finn asked. "Which tavern would you recommend?"

"Fiddler's Mark," the girl to the left of the boy said. "We're going. You can come if you like." She gave Finn a wink as the boy led her away.

"What are you doing?" I asked as Finn stopped to stare into the window of a bookshop before looping back out to walk down the street.

"Whenever the soldiers camp close to a town, they always flock to find a drink away from their commanders," Finn said. "Gabe will be at the most popular tavern, not recommended by the soldiers, but the locals. That's how we find him."

Finn asked three more people which tavern would be best. Only one answered anything but Fiddler's Mark.

"I think it's time for a drink." Finn smiled as the elderly woman he'd spoken to toddled away.

"No food?" I asked.

"Of course food," Finn said. "But I was thinking we'd start with a drink and have food to celebrate a job well done after I've finished our work."

"No."

"Fine," Finn sighed. "Food first if you insist."

"I'll be doing the work. Not you."

Finn stopped ten feet in front of the door to Fiddler's Mark. He dragged me away from the cheerful music and into the narrow alley beside the tavern.

"What are you talking about?" Finn whispered.

"I'm giving it to him, not you."

"Don't be a chivving fool, Ena." Finn held out his hand. "Give me the vial and let's be done with it."

"There's more than just the one vial. Liam wanted to be sure Gabe wouldn't be found out."

"Which is why you've brewed the berries," Finn whispered.

"A single death from an illness, taking a commander no less, would still be suspicious."

"So we should just kill the whole regiment? I'm not opposed to it, but I think we should have spoken to Liam about this new idea."

"I'm not talking about killing." I leaned in as though moving to kiss Finn's cheek. "If a group of people take ill and one doesn't recover, they'll blame the food or the gods and not spare a thought for anyone plotting."

"By the stars, Ena."

"I have everything I need in my pocket. I just have to give it to him and be sure he knows how to use it."

Finn leaned against the tavern wall.

"I can do this, Finn. Trust me. I'm sure I'm right."

"Chivving cact of a god's head. Do you not understand, Ena? Liam and Emmet will both kill me if they ever catch wind of me letting you do this."

"They don't need to know." I took Finn's face in my hands. "But I do need to be sure Gabe understands what he's got to do, or the wrong person could die."

"You've literally cornered me." Finn kissed my cheek. "If you get yourself captured or killed, I will never forgive you. I may seem cheerful enough, but I've stone in my blood and fury in my heart."

"I'm terrified of you." I took his hand, leading him back out of the alley.

A chorus of whistles and laughter sprang up as a pack of soldiers spotted us stepping out onto the main street.

"Didn't know they had such beauty available in Marten." One of the soldiers gave a mocking bow.

Heat rushed to my cheeks.

"Oh, Emmet is going to murder me." Finn looped an arm around my waist and ushered me into Fiddler's Mark.

The place was packed with as many men in black uniforms as there were in common clothes. Women dotted the crowd, some huddled together at tables of their own, others mixed in with the men.

I wanted to tell the women to run away, to hide from the soldiers.

But Lily had told me to hide, and my world had been burned in my absence.

A long bar took up one side of the room. Three women poured for the customers, and a panicked-looking man ran food from the kitchen. A woman sang on a stage tucked into the far corner, surrounded by four men playing stringed instruments.

"I hate to say it, but the locals have decent taste." Finn weaved through the tavern, searching for an empty table. "If I could smell anything from the kitchen over the liquor in the air, I might even be excited about dinner."

"How do they do it?" I watched a pair of tilk men laughing as though the soldiers at the table beside them weren't their enemies.

"Allowing your hate for the Guilds to show only gives them reason to suspect you and your family." Finn pressed his lips to my forehead. "Better to drink with a demon than to have him look too closely at your children."

A sick feeling rolled through my stomach.

Finn tipped my chin up and spoke loudly enough for the people around us to hear. "Give me a laugh, girl. If I'm going to pay for our drinks, that's the least you can do."

I hovered on the edge of telling him I owed no man my smile before coming to my senses and giggling as the woman onstage pulled out a pipe to play.

"There we are." Finn darted to the back of the room where a table had yet to be claimed.

We were far from the front door, nestled against the wall, with a flock of drunken soldiers between us and the way out.

"Are you sure we want this table?" I asked. "We could wait for another."

"This is perfect." Finn pulled out a seat for me. "You wait here, and I'll grab us a round of drinks."

He walked away before I could tell him the nerves in my stomach might make drinking anything a disaster.

I unbuttoned the carved bird fastening at the neck of my cloak and let my fingers graze my stone pendant to be sure it was still there. Even after wandering in the chill mist, the stone still held a blissful warmth to it. I draped my cloak over the back of my chair, sat, and began watching the people around me.

Gabe had been placed as a spy among the soldiers, so he would be wearing a black uniform. But beyond that, I couldn't guess what he might look like. Of the Black Bloods I'd met, there didn't seem to be one trait that ran amongst all of them. Between Finn's red hair and Liam's dark eyes, any man in the room could say they had been born a Black Blood and I'd have no way of knowing if they were lying.

"Here we are." Finn set a mug down in front of me. "The woman who owns this place swears by her ale. It may be awful, but honestly I was too afraid to order anything else."

I laughed and took a sip of the bitter brew that tasted like dried flowers.

Finn leaned in to whisper in my ear. "He's here."

"Where?" I started searching the crowd for Liam and Emmet before realizing who Finn was talking about.

"Table on the far side of the bar, facing the door to the street."

"Are you sure?"

"Of course I'm sure, I've met the fellow before." Finn tucked my hair behind my ear. "He's got two others at the table with him. Gabe will stay late. We'll wait and hope his friends leave."

"Do they call him Gabe?" I trailed my finger along Finn's cheek.

"Gabe Louers is his name registered with the Guilds."

A big man in a soldier's uniform came in from outside, giving a booming laugh as though making sure everyone in the room would notice his entrance.

"This"—the man raised his arms toward the sky—"this is an evening to celebrate."

A roar of approval shot up from all the soldiers.

"This, this could be a long night." Finn sighed as the big man lumbered his way to the bar.

Other soldiers followed him, buying drinks for everyone in sight.

I shuddered even thinking of reasons a paun soldier would want to celebrate.

"Maybe we should try again tomorrow night." Finn took a long drink of his ale.

I sipped from my own cup. "No. We should get it done tonight."

"We'll be here till morning."

"What does Gabe look like?" I ran my fingers through my hair, making sure it hadn't been matted by the mist.

"It doesn't matter until the place clears out." Finn took my wrist.

"It does if I want to do a little flirting." I glared at him. "Just tell me what he looks like, and I'll go see if I can spot a way to talk to him."

"You do realize if anything happens to you, I'll be killed. By the Guilds' hand or Emmet's, I will die."

"I'm well aware. Now tell me before I start shouting *Gabe* to see who answers."

Finn froze for a moment as though thinking through his chances of getting me out of the tavern quietly.

"Blond, curly hair, devilishly green eyes, and a scar on his lip that makes him look like a rogue."

"Sounds fascinating." I yanked my arm from Finn's grip and stood. "Try not to panic while I'm gone."

"Thanks."

Pressing my shoulders back, I started through the tables. I didn't know if it was taking off my cloak or not being held close by Finn, but more men eyed me as I worked my way toward the front of the room.

I can be Nora. I have the armor she's given me. I can have her strength as well.

I scanned the tables I passed, offering little smiles to the handsomer men.

"A fine evening." A man in common clothes nodded to me as I passed.

"I don't fancy the mist." I turned away from him.

His friends' laughter followed me as I made my way toward Gabe's table.

I spotted him without trouble. While Finn's description of Gabe's eyes and scar had been accurate, he had understated the color of Gabe's hair. Flaxen ringlets topped the head of the soldier who sat laughing with his friends.

My gut told me to hate him. Laughing with a pack of soldiers, probably telling stories of the tilk lives they had destroyed.

He is one of us.

I fixed a coy smile on my lips and walked up to his table.

The men stopped laughing as they spotted me.

"Good evening." One of the soldiers nodded, his gaze drifting none too subtly to my breasts.

"Not really," I said.

You are brave. You are a warrior.

"The man I came in with is a horrible bore. You"—I pointed to Gabe—"come buy me a drink. I've asked all the locals and they promised this is the best place to find decent ale."

I ignored the simmering disappointment on the other men's faces.

Gabe stood, downing the rest of his frie. "If a man was fool enough to bore you, then please allow me to be the one to regain the dignity of my sex."

"What a kind man." I held out my hand for him, taking his elbow as he stepped away from his table. "Is Fiddler's Mark ale really wonderful?"

"It's not to be missed."

I kept my gaze fixed on Gabe's face as we waited at the bar, carefully ignoring the stares of the other men.

"Two ales please," Gabe called when he caught a barkeep's eye. "It's not usually this hard to get a drink around here. I suppose everyone's come out now that the storm's passed."

"Pity it's so crowded." I leaned closer to him. "I was hoping we might be able to get a table to ourselves."

Gabe unhooked his arm from mine and laid his hand on the back of my waist. "I don't care the size of the crowd. I'm sure I can find us a private table."

"Here you are, Gabe." The barkeep shoved two mugs our way with a smile for Gabe and a glare at me.

"This way." He wrapped his arm around my waist and led me closer to the musicians.

The woman had begun singing.

"As the stars gleam above, so our love shall survive,
As the moon falls from the sky, our children will thrive."

"Fellows," Gabe said, stopping at a table filled with boys who didn't seem old enough to be wearing soldiers black, "do us a favor and find other seats."

Two of the boys leapt to their feet. The third stared at me wide-eyed until his friends hauled him away.

"That wasn't too hard." Gabe pulled out a chair for me.

I sat and he moved to sit across from me.

"Sit here." I patted the chair beside me. "No point in putting a whole table between us."

Gabe smiled and sat.

I took a deep breath, trying to think of how to say who I was.

The players started a new, faster song.

"So where is he?" Gabe asked.

"Who?" I twisted in my chair, leaning close to him.

Gabe trailed a finger from the top of my bodice, up my chest, and to the pendant at my throat. "The one who made this. Where's Liam?"

4 2

"I don't know." I leaned closer, pressing my lips to his ear. "But I have a gift he's sent for you."

"A gift?" Gabe tipped my chin so my lips brushed against his. He tasted of ale. "What sort of gift would I be sent?"

"Poison to slay a monster."

"That doesn't sound like Liam." He traced his nose across my cheek and nibbled the bottom of my ear.

"It was my idea. A way to keep you in place while getting rid of the beast."

"I've no experience in poison." He kissed the side of my neck.

I tipped my head to the side, offering more skin for him to explore. "That's why I'm here. All you have to do is exactly as I say." I shifted to sit on his lap, draping one arm around his neck.

Gabe's eyes widened.

I whispered in his ear. "There are three things in my pocket." I took his hand, guiding it down my hip to where my treasures hid in the folds of my skirt.

The song ended, and everyone in the tavern cheered.

I tipped my head back, laughing at the racket of the drunken men.

Gabe pulled me closer to him, slipping his hand deep into my pocket.

"Gabe's having a good night," a burly man hollered through the crowd.

I winked at the man as Gabe kissed the skin just below my pendant as though there were no one watching us.

The musicians struck up a fresh tune. Men began stomping in time with the song. The sound of their thumping rattled into my chest, shaking my lungs.

I tipped Gabe's chin up, kissing him, then guiding his lips to the side of my neck.

"The little vial is for the beast. It'll have a taste of berries. Slip it into his drink."

Gabe ran one hand up the side of my ribs, while the other stayed in my pocket.

"Dump the powder into a small food pot, there's enough to make ten men ill. Make sure it's not too diluted, or it won't work."

"What will it do?" He lifted me, shifting my weight so my torso pressed against his.

"Nothing they won't survive." I twined my fingers through his ringlets. "The pouch of berries is for you. Eat them as soon as the others show signs of illness."

"Why?" The ridges of his muscles tensed.

"To be sure you look like one of the fallen." I kissed him as fear flitted through his eyes.

"What will it do to me?" His lips teased mine as he spoke.

"You'll wish the gods would take you for a few hours and be fine by the next day." I rested my forehead against his. "Compared to being hanged, whipped, or burned alive by the paun, your suffering won't be much."

"When should it be done?"

I hadn't thought about the when, hadn't thought about setting a time to end a man's life.

I looked toward the ceiling, wishing the room were quiet and I could have one moment to think through the best time for murder.

Gabe kissed the top of my breasts, his tongue grazing the skin just above my bodice.

I gripped his ringlets, tipped his head back, and kissed him, trying to tell him I was sorry for giving him such a terrible task and for the pain my plan would cause.

Forgive me. May we meet again in a land of freedom.

I whispered in his ear, "The first chance you get. Let it be done."

I kissed him on the cheek and stood. His hands trailed along my waist until he couldn't reach me anymore.

I walked toward Finn, to our table in the back of the room.

A man took my hand as I passed him. "Did he not have enough to please you? I can promise I do."

I didn't look down to see the man's face. I couldn't see anyone in the tavern but Liam, standing at the back of the room. His jaw set and eyes dark.

"That's not what I brought you here for." A hand pinched my arm, dragging me away from Liam.

"What?" I blinked, trying to get my eyes to focus on anything besides Liam's face.

Someone shook my arm. "I pay to bring you here, pay for our drinks, and this is how you thank me?"

My gaze found a head of red hair and a livid face.

Men sniggered as Finn dragged me through the tables toward the front door.

"I have never met such an ungrateful, wretched whore in all my days." A light shone in Finn's eyes, a glint of something between triumph and warning.

I pulled my free hand back and slapped him hard across the face. "If you'd like me to pay attention to you, perhaps you should try being more interested in me than ale."

Finn pulled me to him and kissed me. I wrapped my arms around his neck, and leaned my weight against his body.

He scooped me up and carried me to the door. "This night is for me, and I'll not be sharing you." He kicked the door open and strode out into the misty night, still cradling me in his arms.

A round of hoots and cheers to lift the roof of the tavern followed us toward The Downy Loft.

"Tell me you got him everything he needed," Finn whispered as he turned onto the side street.

"He has everything, and I gave him as clear instructions as I could."

"May the gods bless you, Ena." He kissed my temple. "That was a damn fine performance."

"Did Liam see?"

"Liam and Emmet came in about when I thought Gabe was going to tear your bodice off with his teeth." Finn set me down in front of The Downy Loft. "I'm not sure what your brother thought of Gabe nigh on rolling his sister in the middle of a bar, but I don't think anyone could suspect anything but sex came of that meeting."

He opened the door, and the scent of stale soup greeted us.

Finn wrinkled his nose. "I wish we could've eaten elsewhere, but it seemed best to make a dramatic exit before more fiends came looking for a taste of you."

The little boy ran out of the kitchen, his face bright as he beamed up at Finn.

"Young sir"—Finn bowed—"I'd like any breakfast leftovers you have brought straight up to my room, along with a bit of frie."

The boy bowed so low it looked like he might tip over.

"And a pitcher of hot water for washing up," I said.

I could still taste Gabe and Finn. My neck burned where Gabe had kissed my skin. I wished I was back at Mave's where I could soak in a bath and wash Gabe's scent from my skin.

"Come on, my love." Finn took my hand, dragging me toward the stairs. "The night is young, and we mustn't waste it."

The two women hunched in the booths furrowed their brows at me as we passed.

"A bit of food and a nice night's sleep," Finn whispered as he closed the door to our room behind me. "Liam and Emmet are here, we've done our work, and tomorrow we can turn our attention toward getting home."

"Right." I untied my boots.

"Unless Liam wants to linger until the thing is done." Finn paused halfway through unbuttoning his jacket. "I'd rather be well away, but Liam is the one in charge."

"We'll see what he says."

Tap, tap, bang.

Finn opened the door and ushered in the little boy. I took the pitcher from the tray and went straight to the wash stand in the corner.

"That will be all for the evening, young sir."

I poured water on the cloth and scrubbed at my neck. Liam had seen. Had been standing there watching as Gabe…

I moved the cloth to wipe the kohl lining from my eyes, but I wasn't ready to remove my armor.

"Eat." Finn held out a plate of food. "It's cold but still better than the gray soup."

"Thanks." I sat by the fire and ate cold potatoes, listening for boots in the hall. "Do you think he'll be caught?"

"Gabe's smart. He'll find a way to do as you instructed."

"I hope so."

Boots thumped up the stairs.

I held my breath.

Knock, knock, knock.

Finn was on his feet before I could decide if I thought it was soldiers or Liam and Emmet, and which possibility was more terrifying.

Finn opened the door, and Liam and Emmet stepped through. Neither spoke as Emmet closed the door behind them.

"I'm glad you've made it here safely," Finn said. "Was it trouble at the gate?"

"What under the chivving sky were you thinking?" Emmet tossed my black cloak down at my feet. "What sort of madness has taken your mind?"

"It worked," Finn said. "We've done what we set out to do."

"You put my sister into a pack of men." Emmet stepped toward Finn, seeming to tower over him as anger pulsed from his skin.

"It was my idea." I set my plate down. "And truth be told, I didn't give him much of a choice."

"What?" Emmet rounded on me.

"I needed to speak to Gabe myself, to be sure he understood how to use everything I gave him." I brushed my skirt off and stood. "I made Finn tell me who Gabe was and went after him myself."

Emmet's jaw tightened.

"And if you're looking for an apology, you won't get one from me." I tipped my chin up. "Frankly, I think I did a wonderful job. No one will think anything of Gabe having a bit of fun with a girl, so if you're searching for any words to say to me, you'd best start with *thank you.*"

"Thank you for playing the whore to aid our cause," Emmet said. "I'm glad you take such pride in placing yourself in danger."

"Would you say such a thing to your beloved Mave's girls?" I growled.

"I don't like them putting themselves in danger either, but they aren't my chivving sister." Emmet stormed out of the room, slamming the door behind him.

"That went about how I expected." Finn dug his fingers into his hair. "Shall I make sure he doesn't tear apart the town stone by stone, or would someone else like to claim that pleasure?"

I stared at the door. There were things I wanted to scream at Emmet but had nothing to say that would make him any less angry.

"I'll do it then." Finn grabbed the bread from his plate and his coat from by the fire and slipped out the door.

I couldn't bring myself to look at Liam. I didn't want to see the same anger in his face I'd gotten from Emmet.

"What did you give Gabe?" Liam said.

I picked my cloak up off the ground and hung it on the nail by the fire.

"You said *everything*," Liam said. "What did you give him besides the shadow berries?"

"A powered root to cause a fever for some of the other soldiers, bird berries for Gabe to eat to get a bit sick as well."

"You asked him to poison himself?"

"He'll be fine. He may wish he'd never heard of food, but it'll keep him out of the way while people are worrying about the beast's death."

Liam paced the room.

"Tell me I wasn't right," I said. "Tell me I didn't protect Gabe."

Liam kept pacing.

"It's done." I spread my arms wide. "I got the work done. And if you don't like—"

"You could have been killed." Liam's boots thumped against the floor in a maddening rhythm. "If you had been caught carrying poison, you'd have been hanged."

"Any of us would have been. I knew this was dangerous going into it. Didn't you?"

"You walked into a room packed with foul paun men, teasing them, luring them—"

"That's what Mave's primping made me fit to do."

"I saved you from that soldier in Harane. I didn't do it so you could throw yourself straight back into a den of beasts. Letting Gabe paw you like that, do you have any idea what sort of ideas that puts in evil men's—"

"Stop chivving pacing."

Liam stopped, still staring at the wall in front of him.

"Look at me."

He didn't move.

"I said look at me." I took his face in my hands.

He met my gaze, his eyes dark and unreadable.

"I had Finn," I said. "I was safe enough."

"You think Finn could protect you from a whole tavern of paun soldiers?"

"You sent me away with him. If you trust him with my safety, shouldn't I?"

He hadn't shaved since the balcony. The stubble on his cheeks had lost its coarseness.

"If Finn had been caught, we both would have hanged anyway. The ending was the same if either of us failed."

Liam stepped away from me, rubbing his hands over the place where my fingers had touched his cheeks only a moment before.

"I said that I wanted to be a Black Blood, that I wanted to help."

"By letting Gabe kiss you with a room full of men leering at you?"

"It had to be done."

"Not by you!"

I stepped forward, close enough that I had to tip my chin up to look into Liam's eyes. "What are you mad about? That I got it done, that I let Gabe touch me, or that you ever kissed me in the first place?"

Liam's gaze drifted down to my mouth. I remembered the feel of his lips against mine, and the burning of wanting flared in my chest. I leaned closer, begging the stars for him to take me in his arms and kiss me.

"Ena." He brushed his thumb over my lips and trailed his fingers down the side of my neck.

"Do you want me or not?"

Our eyes met, and then he was kissing me.

He wrapped his arms around my waist, drawing me toward him. He tasted of fire and honey and sweet winds and freedom. I parted my lips, wanting to savor more of him.

He held me closer. His heartbeat thundered in his chest, keeping time with mine.

I laced my fingers through his hair as my hunger for him burned as bright as a star destined to consume worlds. Every bit of my being knew nothing but wanting Liam.

His hand moved up my ribs, his thumb grazing the side of my breast.

I gasped as heat seared through me. I pressed myself to him, feeling every ridge of his body against mine.

"No." He stepped back.

My head spun at the absence of his touch.

"No." He stared past me, through the window to the night beyond.

"Liam." I reached for his hand.

He shook his head, turned, and walked out the door, leaving me frozen in place.

44

I have never believed in true love or happy endings. They are not things that have ever existed in my world.

I have always believed in pain. In agony that cuts so deep, you fear your very soul will pour out of the wound and be lost to you forever.

That torment I know well. It is as familiar to me as the scent of the air after a storm.

But my soul has never poured out of me. Somehow, I have always woken up the next morning.

Mine is not a happy love story. But there is a monster to be slain, a multitude of demons that torment our land. As long they steal innocent souls, at least I have a beast to battle.

That fight must be enough to keep me breathing.

45

Finn had slept on top of the covers next to me. He'd tried to sleep on the floor beside the fire, but given the bruise growing on his cheek, I'd insisted he rest somewhere soft.

I woke before he did in the morning and lay in bed, fingers wrapped around the pendant on my neck.

Part of me cherished it, a bit of Liam that was mine even if I couldn't have him. Part of me wanted to throw it out the window as a first step in shedding all thoughts of how badly I wished he were lying in bed beside me.

But I'd slept through the night, and that was a gift even the horrible mixture of shame, hurt, and longing that buried me couldn't convince me to toss aside.

The sounds of movement on the street below began just after dawn. The rattle of cart wheels fighting through mud and mumble of sleepy voices made the morning seem so peaceful for a town that had a regiment of soldiers camped nearby.

The scent of burned food drifted up the stairs. I forced myself to grin as I imagined the little boy telling Finn there was nothing for breakfast as every edible scrap in the place had been turned to ash.

Finn woke, sniffing the air. "It that breakfast?"

"You are a mockery of yourself." I tossed my pillow at his back.

"That implies a consistency of character that is difficult to find." Finn sat up. "So, I will take it as a compliment."

He gave me a lopsided grin, wincing as his swollen cheek moved. The bruise on his face took up most of the left side of his jaw. The right side, where I'd slapped him, had only been left a bit pink.

"Emmet should be walloped for hitting you." I crawled over him and out of bed. "What was the slitch thinking?"

"He didn't hit me." Finn gingerly touched his cheek.

"Did you fall and smack your face on something fist-shaped?" I tore my brush through my hair a bit harder than was wise.

"No." Finn grabbed his boots and tugged them on. "He got into a fight with some local boys, and I got punched trying to get the poor slitches out of Emmet's way before he pummeled them into the dirt."

"Why would he do that?"

"I imagine he pictured each of them as the men from the tavern who were quite openly fantasizing about shoving themselves inside his sister."

"Finn!" I tossed my hairbrush at him.

He caught it and began brushing his own hair. "I did manage to ensure no one sustained life-threatening injuries in your brother's rampage. I should be given quite a bit of credit for that feat."

"Credit to you and an earful for Emmet. How has such a chivving fool managed to keep himself alive?" I picked up the box Nora had given me.

"You've never seen him fight, have you?"

My fingers hovered over the tins of powder. Part of me wanted to throw it all away, like somehow I could blame the paint for luring Liam close enough that I thought I could have him. But there were soldiers all around, and I couldn't go back to being the girl from Harane, even if that was what a very large part of me wanted.

"Do you think we'll ride out today?" I brushed pink onto my cheeks.

"I doubt it. Liam and Emmet don't have horses."

"What?" I froze with a brush of pigment halfway to my eye.

"I haven't heard the full story, what with the neck kissing and fighting, but they made their way here on foot."

"No wonder it took them so long." I tamped down the tiny bit of sympathy that rose in my chest at the idea of the two of them traveling through that storm on foot.

"I'm sure it will be a delightful story." Finn inched closer to the door. "Once we get some food in them, and make sure Emmet's gotten past his rage at having a beauty for a sister, we can ask them to tell us the whole thrilling tale."

He stopped with his hand on the doorknob.

"You can go." I trailed the kohl along my eyelid.

"I'll wait." Finn shrugged. "Wouldn't want to leave you alone."

He gazed longingly at the crack in the door as though the scent of burned food were somehow appealing.

"Are you afraid of facing them without me?" I laughed. The feel of it grated against the wound in my chest.

"Not afraid, just wise enough to better my chances with your presence."

I finished drawing on the face of someone who cherished their beauty and let Finn lead me from our room.

"Well, my love," Finn said as we stepped down into the dining room, "a bit of breakfast, and I'm sure we'll both feel better about last night."

A hint of smoke drifted out of the kitchen and lingered on the dining room ceiling, swirling through the spiderwebs. The woman behind the bar had red in her cheeks. I couldn't tell if the hue had been born of anger or tears.

Emmet sat alone at a table, facing the front door.

"We could ask the boy to bring food to our room," I whispered to Finn.

"I hear the kingless territories are beautiful this time of year," Finn said. "We could hop a boat and leave Ilbrea behind forever."

I nudged him in the ribs. "Do not tempt me, Finn, or you'll find yourself on a ship sailing south."

"We all must have dreams." Finn laughed.

Emmet turned toward the sound, glowering as though his glare could burn the world.

"You woke up cheery." I set my face in a pleasant grin, delighting as Emmet balled his hands into fists on the table. Cuts and bruises marked his knuckles. "A good night's sleep can fix the worst of woes. Though those"—I pointed to the fresh wounds—"could use a bit of care. Have you even bothered to wash them properly?"

"I'll order some food." Finn darted toward the bar.

"Of course, in a place like this, who knows how clean the water is?" I said. "We could find some strong liquor to pour on them. I'll have to check your stitches, too. I'm sure not all of them are still in place after you ran around like a chivving fool last night."

I waited for Emmet to say something. I wanted so badly for him to scream and rage so fresh anger could drown out the hurt in my chest.

"Do you want to die of infection?" I sat opposite Emmet, blocking his view of the door. "It's a terrible way to go, but I suppose it's your choice to make."

He inched his chair to the side to see around me.

I stood, leaning in toward him. "Answer me, Emmet."

"I've lived through far worse than this with no one to tend my wounds. I'm not concerned about scrapes and pulled stitches. A few more scars won't damage me. Now sit down and pretend to be a proper girl."

"A proper girl?" I perched on the edge of the table. "What makes a proper girl? Should I find myself a nice man to marry, stay out of the way while the men do the work?"

"I'm not fool enough to expect such a thing of my sister." Emmet laid his hands flat on the table. "But as you played whore and assassin last night and we still need to get back to the mountains alive, a smart girl would sit nicely and eat her chivving breakfast. The best we can hope for is no one taking notice of us."

I slid into the chair to Emmet's right, clearing his view of the door. "Is that what you were doing when you went out to pick a fight last night? Was that you not being noticed?"

"At least I kept my clothes in place."

Finn froze beside our table.

"I wish you hadn't waited so long to tell me shifting my skirts upsets you," I said. "From now on, I'll have to make a point of being naked as often as possible."

"Perhaps I will eat in the room." Finn backed away.

"Of course not." I pushed the chair opposite me out with my toe. "*Proper* people eat breakfast in the dining room, and we must appear *proper*."

"Right." Finn sank down into his chair, his ears turning pink as he glanced between Emmet and me. "I asked about breakfast. It might be a minute as there was an incident, which we can all smell, of course, but I've been promised there will be edible food available soon."

"Good," I said, "we can't have you going hungry after you so bravely helped Emmet last night. As a matter of fact, I think Emmet should thank you for saving him from himself."

"That's not necessary." Finn widened his eyes at me.

"Of course it is," I said. "You got hit in the face for him."

"You're the one who slapped him," Emmet growled.

"Oh, Finn didn't mind that," I laughed. "Matter of fact, I think he liked it. The kissing wasn't bad either."

"Ena!" Finn said at the same moment Emmet leapt to his feet and a bell rang outside.

Everyone in the tavern froze.

The ringing came closer, like whoever held the bell was running along the street.

"What does the bell mean?" I whispered.

Emmet glared at the front door, and Finn shook his head.

I crept toward the bar as the ringing came closer still. "What does the bell mean?" I whispered to the barkeep.

"Someone is searching town for the healer," the woman said. "They ring the bell to call her if she's not at home."

A sense of dread trickled into my stomach. If the healer were being called, then the time had come for the beast to die.

But soldiers traveled with their own healers.

That didn't make a difference nine years ago.

I dug my nails into my palms to keep my hands from shaking as the ringing moved past us.

Nantic's healer had been helping the soldiers when my mother died because their own healer had been drunk. Maybe this healer was drunk as well. Maybe the soldiers' healer had been confounded by the poison and wanted help. Maybe it wasn't a soldier who needed help but a woman gone into labor.

Movement in the dining room resumed as the ringing faded away.

I walked silently back to the table and took my seat. "Where's Liam?"

"Finding new horses," Emmet said.

"Probably best you didn't go with him. Who knows if you punched the stable boy last night?" My joy in needling Emmet had vanished.

We sat at the table, waiting for food, as the bell rang again, traveling back in the opposite direction.

I buried my hands in my pockets to hide their shaking. If the healer had been called to the camp and a tilk was looking for the healer as well, then it would be my fault their call for aid was going unanswered.

I could help. If someone was ill or bleeding, I should help. But offering my skills to strangers could too easily end in my being hanged.

The bell had long since faded away by the time the little boy brought us a tray of food.

"Thank you, kind sir." Finn's bow lacked it usual playful joy.

The boy didn't seem to notice.

We ate half-cooked potatoes and some sort of meat. The three of us kept glancing toward the door, searching for Liam.

"Does he have enough money for two horses?" I asked after a long while.

Emmet nodded.

A sound began in the distance, not the ringing, but a different noise. A steady booming like the beating of a massive drum.

I stood and crept toward the bar again. "What does that mean?"

"I've no idea." The woman furrowed her brow.

There was something in the booming that made me afraid, though I wasn't sure why.

"I'm going to look for Liam." Finn stood as I returned to the table.

"No, you're not," Emmet said.

"We need to leave," Finn said.

"And if he shows up a minute after you walk out?" I took Finn's arm. "You're the one who said we couldn't risk missing each other in the wild."

"Fine." Finn pinched his nose between his hands. "You get our packs, I'll make sure the horses are ready."

I shoved one more cold, crunchy potato into my mouth and headed for the stairs. Emmet's boots thumped against the wooden floor as he followed me.

"You don't think I can get my pack without a man toying with my breasts?" I asked as I hurried up the stairs.

"I have my own bags to gather."

We split ways as he ran two stairs at a time to the floor above. I shoved the few things Finn and I had used back into our packs, hoisted them onto my shoulders, and draped my cloak over my arm. The tightness of my bodice made it hard to breathe while bearing the extra weight.

The door to my room flung open before I could reach it.

"Ena." Liam stood in the doorway, sweat slicking his brow, worry marring his eyes.

"What's wrong?"

He lifted Finn's pack from my shoulder. "We have to go."

"Why?" I followed him down the stairs, lifting my skirt so I could run. "Liam, why?"

A dozen horrible possibilities raced through my mind.

Emmet ran down into the dining room the moment after we'd arrived.

The booming had grown louder in the few minutes we'd been gone.

Boom. Boom.

The women who had been in the booths were gone. The barkeep had disappeared as well.

"Where's Finn?" Liam asked.

"Getting our horses," I said as Liam shoved me out the door.

Two new horses waited for us, tied up outside The Downy Loft.

The booming carried from the main street, and voices sounded over its resonance.

"Emmet, take Ena. Ride to the edge of the woods." Liam yanked my pack from my shoulder, tying it onto the back of his horse.

"You take her," Emmet said. "I'll go with Finn."

"He's in the stable. He's right behind us," I said as Liam grabbed me around the waist, lifting me toward the horse. "We should—"

A familiar clink of metal carried from the north, a sound I had only heard a few times before and would grow to know too well by the end of my life.

I broke free from Liam's grip.

"It's not too late." Emmet met Liam's eyes.

Finn tore around the corner, the reins of our horses in his hands.

The main street fell silent.

"We are not mud!" a voice shouted. "We are not filth to be abused. Our women do not give birth for the pleasure of the Guilds. Our children are not born to be hoarded by the Sorcerers. Our lives are worth more than waiting to die at the hands of the golden demons."

I walked toward the shouted words. I had never heard such things spoken of in the open, let alone shouted for an entire town to hear.

The clinking came faster, surrounding us from the south and the west as well.

"We have spent years convincing ourselves we deserve to be punished, to have our children stolen by the Guilds. If we have suffered for so long, then the stars must have ordained our punishment."

A hand took mine, but didn't try to hold me back as I continued toward the voice.

"But the gods have seen fit to teach us how wrong we have been. Drason is dead. The monster who tormented us has been killed by the gods. They have brought illness among his men. The gods themselves have smiled upon us. They have set us free."

I reached the corner and looked down the main street.

A hundred people surrounded a wagon.

A man stood on top of the wagon, a club in one hand, a wide-stretched drum in the other. He tipped his face up to the sky. "What will you do with that freedom?"

The world seemed to slow as the man on the wagon looked back toward the crowd. The clinking stopped, and an arm wrapped around my waist, pulling me toward the side of a building.

"You have not been granted permission to gather," a voice shouted.

A sea of black had closed off both ends of the main street and come up behind us to block our path back to The Downy Loft.

"Disperse at once." A soldier stepped in front of his fellows. The golden star stitched onto the chest of his uniform glinted in the light.

"The gods have granted us freedom from you." The man on the wagon raised his arms toward the sky. "The beast Drason is dead. Leave our home."

"This town, all land in Ilbrea, is the property of the Guilds," the soldier said. "You dwell here at their pleasure."

"My family's been on our land for five generations," a woman shouted. "How can that not give us a claim to it?"

"There is no claim but the Guilds'." The soldier took another step forward.

The men behind him matched his movement.

"They claim our land, our blood, our children." The man on the wagon struck his drum with a boom that shook my ears. "The gods have freed us from the monster, and we will not lose that freedom."

"The Guilds will send a new commander," the soldier began. "Commander Drason's death—"

"Is a miracle," a young man shouted. "Chivving bastard got what he deserved."

A roar of approval rose from the tilk.

"Get out of our town!" a woman shouted.

"He deserved to die twenty times for what he stole from us." A girl reached down and picked up a clump of mud.

I watched her gather the dirt in her hand. Watched her throw the filth at the soldiers. I strained against the arm that held me, as though I could somehow outpace the flying mud and catch it before it struck its mark.

The scraping of swords clearing sheaths cut through the shouts of the mob.

"We will not allow you to steal the freedom the gods have granted us!" The man banged his drum. An arrow tipped with black feathers struck his chest before the boom had died.

A moment of calm, quicker than a heartbeat, stilled the street.

With a roar, the tilk charged toward the soldiers, carrying no weapons but their rage.

"No!" I fought against the arm that held me. "Stop them. You have to stop them!"

A clang of metal close by drew my gaze from the bloodshed on the street.

A pack of soldiers surged toward us, their weapons raised. Finn met them head on, parrying the blows of the pauns' weapons with his sword.

Bellowing, Emmet leapt into the fray, unsheathing the daggers at his hips.

"Stay here." Liam let go of me and ran toward the others, both hands raised.

Emmet ducked beneath a slicing sword, driving his blade into the throat of a soldier as Finn slashed through the belly of another.

"Get down!" Liam shouted.

Emmet and Finn dove, rolling away from the soldiers.

Liam opened his hands. A horde of stones hovered above his palms then shot toward the soldiers, striking a dozen of the beasts in the chest. But as the men fell, ten more stepped up behind them.

Emmet and Finn were already on their feet, diving back into the fight. Liam ran forward, drawing his own blade.

"Help me!" a voice shouted from the main street.

The soldiers had surrounded the tilk, cutting them down like they were no more than weeds. A boy broke free of the soldiers, clutching a wound in his side.

I started toward him, desperate to help stop the bleeding. An arrow struck him in the back of the neck. He didn't even scream as he fell toward the ground.

A hand grabbed my arm, whipping me around. A soldier with blood on his face seized my hair, flinging me into the mud as though I were no more than a doll. The fall knocked the air from my lungs, and mud blurred my vision.

He raised his sword, its point aimed at my gut.

"Please don't," I begged, my fingers fumbling as I reached for the blade hidden in my boot. "I'll do anything you want, just don't kill me."

The man smiled.

I closed my fingers around the hilt of my knife and yanked it free. It glinted in the sunlight for a split second before I drove the blade into the soldier's thigh.

He screamed, whether from pain or anger, I didn't know.

I pulled my knife free and aimed higher, stabbing just above his hip as his sword slashed for my neck.

I rolled to the side, wrenching my blade from his gut. Pain sliced through my back as I scrambled to my feet, my skirt heavy with mud.

A roar of rage came from behind me.

I set my teeth, determined not to scream as the soldier killed me. I spun to face him, but he was already dead with Emmet's dagger sticking out of his chest.

"Get up." Finn rode toward me, my horse beside him.

"But—"

"Now." Emmet shoved me toward my horse.

I fought against the weight of my mud-laden skirt, trying to get my foot into the stirrup.

Emmet lifted me, setting me stomach-first on the saddle as he had done when I was too little to climb up by myself.

By the time I had gotten astride, Liam and Finn were mounted on their horses beside me, facing the soldiers on the main street.

"We have to help them." The words tore at my throat.

"There's no one to help." Finn kicked his horse and rode away from the Massacre of Marten.

47

I wished for a storm during that horrible ride back to the mountains. I wished the sky would open and rain would wash away the blood and dirt that covered me. But the sky seemed as determined as I not to shed a tear.

I didn't speak in the hours it took to reach the forest, or stop to tend to the others' wounds or let them look after mine. Our injuries were not as dangerous as being out in the open.

Dusk had come by the time we reached the canopy of trees. The forest smelled of new life. No one had told the woods of the death that surrounded us.

"It's my fault." My voice crackled as I spoke. "It wasn't the gods who killed the beast, it was me. I started it, and now those people are dead."

A heavy burden beyond grief weighed on my entire being.

"It's not your fault." Emmet guided his horse to ride next to mine. "The soldiers didn't come to town seeking vengeance for a murder. They came to stop a man from spreading hope. Hope is more dangerous to the Guilds than we could ever be."

"It started with me," I said.

Finn passed me a waterskin. "Don't think like that. Unarmed men who run against swords—they're already dead. We saw them choose the end of their torment. They had a moment of freedom, one choice that was theirs alone. Many would be willing to die for that."

"More will before the end of it." Liam didn't look back. He kept riding in front of us, guiding us to safety in the mountains. "But we have to keep fighting. If we stop, there won't be any hope left at all."

48

Hope and freedom. The words pounded in my head for weeks, burning themselves into my memories of the Massacre at Marten. The blood washed away, the wounds healed, but hope and freedom—they carried me into the darkness that lay ahead.

Ena's journey continues in Mountain and Ash. *Read on for a sneak preview.*

THE GUILDS ARE NOT HER ONLY ENEMY.

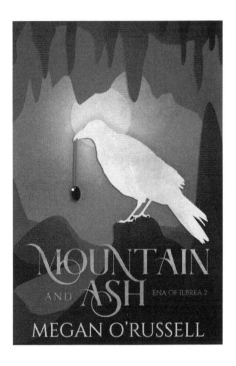

Continue reading for a sneak peek of *Mountain and Ash*.

1

"Look at me." I took the child's face in my hands, blocking her view of everything but my eyes. "Look at me, love. Don't look at anything but me."

Her tear-filled gaze found my face.

"Good girl." I smiled.

A banging echoed from the street, but I couldn't tell the distance. The next house over, maybe the one beside that—my heart raced too fast for me to be sure.

"You are the bravest little girl in the world," I said. "Did you know that?"

She took a shuddering breath but didn't answer.

"You are so brave, you can do anything. I promise you can." I picked the child up. She weighed nothing in my arms. "Do you know what we do when we're brave?"

The girl looked over my shoulder toward the corner of the room.

"No, look at me." I balanced her on one hip, using my free hand to block the side of her vision. "When we are very brave, we look into the darkness, and we say, *I am not afraid.*"

A woman screamed in the distance.

The child gripped the front of my bodice in her little hands.

"We do not scream, we do not cry." I moved closer to the window. "We stare into the shadows and whisper, *I am not afraid.* Say it. Say, *I am not afraid.*"

Her lips wobbled as a fresh batch of tears glistened on her cheeks.

"Say, *I am not afraid.*" I slid the window open.

The crash of splintering wood carried from the street.

The child didn't look away from my eyes.

"Say, *I am not afraid*. Come on." I wiped the tears from her cheeks. "*I am not afraid*."

"I am not afraid." Her voice cracked as she spoke with me. "I am not afraid."

"You are the bravest girl in the whole world," I whispered in her ear. "You will not scream when you're scared. Only whisper, *I am not afraid*."

"I'm not afraid."

"Good girl." I held her out the window and let go.

She didn't scream as she fell, but a gasp came from the corner of the room.

"What have you done?" The woman cowering deep in the shadows shook with quiet sobs.

"What's best for your daughter," I said.

A bang came from close by, but the floor didn't rattle. The soldiers hadn't reached this house.

"Do you want to join her or not?" I said. "We're out of time. You have to choose."

"I..." The woman stepped toward the window. "I have five children. I have a home and a shop."

"May you find peace with the choice you've made." I lifted my skirt and climbed onto the windowsill.

"Please"—the woman grabbed my arm—"she's my baby."

"Not anymore. You have four children. Your baby does not exist."

"She needs me."

I took the mother's face in my hands as I had done with the child's. "She will never know fear again. She will not know pain or darkness. For the rest of your days, think of her in sunlit fields, running through bright spring flowers. You have given her endless peace, and she will always be thankful."

The woman fell to her knees, coughing through the sobs that wracked her chest.

"Remember her laugh and her smell." I turned toward the starless night. "Remember that it is still your duty to protect her." I stepped from the window ledge and plummeted into the darkness.

The warm wind lifted my hair from my neck as I fell. I exhaled all the breath in my body, bending my knees as I landed in the wide bed of hay.

"Ena?" Finn leapt up onto the front seat of the wagon. "Are you hurt?"

"Go." I scrambled through the hay, fighting my way to the front of the cart. "Is she under?"

"Didn't make a peep." Finn clicked the horse to walk. "I've seen grown men crumble at what that five-year-old faced silently."

"She's strong." I climbed into the seat beside Finn, brushing the hay from my skirt. "She'll make it."

"Of course she will. She's got us looking out for her." Finn steered the cart out of the alley behind the houses and onto the rut-covered thoroughfare of the tiny chivving town called Wilton.

"Halt." A soldier stepped in front of our cart.

"Whoa." Finn reined in the horse. "Happy to stop for you, sir. Is there something I can help you with?"

I clung to Finn, sliding my hand beneath his to coat to grip the hilt of his knife.

"We're searching for a sorcerer hidden in this village," the soldier said.

Four men in black uniforms stepped out of the shadows to surround our wagon.

"Sorcerer?" Finn said.

"Like magic?" I asked. "By the Guilds, you've got to find them. Are we safe? Is the sorcerer going to try to kill us?"

Two of the soldiers climbed into the back of our wagon.

"Do you really need to search our wagon?" Finn asked.

"Who cares about where they're searching?" I swatted Finn on the arm with my free hand. "We've got to get out of here. Unless the sorcerer is on the road. Oh, by the Guilds, do you know which way the sorcerer ran?"

The soldiers dug through the hay in our cart, tossing it out onto the dirt road.

"Hush, my love." Finn wrapped an arm around my waist.

"What if they're waiting in the dark?" Fat tears slid down my cheeks. "What if they're lurking by the road, waiting to attack? I told you I didn't want to leave home. My mother warned me of all the horrors that wait in the world."

"You're fine, my love." Finn wiped the tears from my cheeks. "I promise, I will not let any harm come to you." He brushed his lips against mine.

I pulled myself closer to him, letting my chest press against his as I parted his lips with my tongue.

"Hey." A soldier smacked his hand against our wagon.

"Sorry," Finn said.

"Sorry." I pulled away from him, tucking his blade under my skirt.

"The wagon's empty." A soldier hopped down from the back of the cart.

"Move on then."

The men stepped aside to let us pass.

"Thank you." Finn bowed his head. "Thank you for reminding me there are some things in Ilbrea that are worth protecting." He laid his hand on my thigh.

"You are such a wonderful man." I leaned in to kiss Finn again.

"Get out of here before we have to take you in for indecency." The soldier had a smirk on his face as he waved us on.

"Sorry about that." Finn clicked for the horse to walk. "Have a lovely evening."

I clung tightly to his arm as the wagon rattled forward, smiling at the soldiers and listening for the sniffles of a small child coming from below.

It was well into the night by the time we'd gotten far enough away from Wilton to risk sleep.

Finn stopped by a stand of trees, cooing lovingly to our horse as he unhooked her from the cart.

"You are such a good girl." Finn patted the horse. "Such a pretty, kind girl."

"Should I be jealous of the horse, my love?" I hopped down from my seat, taking one last look around before heading to the back of the wagon.

"Never," Finn said. "There is nothing in this world that comes close to my adoration of you."

"Careful, you might make a girl blush." I ran my fingers along the back of the cart, searching for the latch to our hidey hole.

I slipped the metal aside and lifted the three long boards that made up the center of the cart. The compartment below was wide enough to fit two adults if they lay side by side, and just deep enough to leave a few inches of space above a person's nose.

I held my breath as I squinted into the shadows. I'd come up with a hundred different things to say to comfort the child and a dozen apologies for having locked her in the dark.

The child lay in the corner, clinging to a folded up blanket.

"You're all right now," I whispered as I climbed into the compartment. "Let's get you someplace more comfortable to sleep."

The child didn't move.

"You can come out now." I knelt beside her.

She didn't stir.

My heart skittered against my ribs as I laid my fingers on the child's throat. She gave a shuddering sigh and nestled her face into the blanket.

"Oh, thank the gods." I ran my hands over my face.

"She all right?" Finn peered in from the back of the wagon.

"Sleeping." I lifted her, cradling her to my chest. "I wonder how long it took her to drift off."

"Hopefully not too long." Finn reached for the child.

Part of me didn't want to hand her over. I'd taken the girl from her mother. I should be the one clutching her in my arms until we could leave her someplace where she wasn't in any danger. But her safe haven was still very far away.

She would be passed from hand to hand a dozen times before she'd truly be free of the Guilds. Finn and I were just one tiny cog in the massive clockwork that would ferry her south to a place where she would never need to be afraid again.

"Come on." Finn held his arms higher. "The sooner we get to sleep, the happier I'll be."

"Try not to wake her."

It didn't take long for us to get the tent up, a circle of stones placed around us, and the bedrolls down. I tucked the child in, and she still didn't fuss. Finn and I slept on either side of her, each with a weapon tucked beneath our heads. I stared at the canvas of the tent for a long while, waiting for sleep to come. I drifted into darkness, clutching the stone pendant around my neck.

Order your copy of Mountain and Ash *to continue the story.*

GIRL OF GLASS

GIRL OF GLASS, BOOK ONE

Hope at the end of the world.

1

Nola dug her fingers into the warm dirt. Around her, the greenhouse smelled of damp earth, mist, and fresh, clean air.

Carefully, she took the tiny seed and placed it at the bottom of the hole her finger had made.

Thump.

Soon the seed would take root. A sprout would break through to the surface.

Thump, bang.

Then the green stem would grow until bean pods sprouted.

Bang, thump!

The food would be harvested and brought to their tables. All of the families would be fed.

"Ahhhhh!" the voice came from the other side of the glass. Nola knew she shouldn't look, but she couldn't ignore the sounds any longer.

It was a woman this time, her skin gray with angry, red patches dotting her face. She slammed her fists into the glass, leaving smears of red behind. The woman didn't seem to care as she banged her bloody hands into the glass over and over.

"Magnolia."

Nola jumped as Mrs. Pearson placed a hand on her shoulder.

"Don't pay her any mind," Mrs. Pearson said. "She can't get through the glass."

"But she's bleeding." Nola pushed the words past the knot in her throat.

The woman bashed her head against the glass.

"She needs help," Nola said. The woman stared right at her.

Mrs. Pearson took Nola's shoulders and turned her back to her plant tray. "That woman is beyond your help, Magnolia. Paying her any attention will only make it worse. There is nothing you can do."

Nola felt eyes staring at her. Not just the woman on the other side of the glass. The rest of the class was staring at her now, too.

Bang. Thump.

Families. The food she planted would feed the families.

Bang.

Pop.

Nola spun back to the glass. Two guards were outside now. One held his gun high. A thin spike protruded from the woman's neck. Her eyelids fluttered for a moment before she slid down the glass, leaving a streak of blood behind her.

"See," Mrs. Pearson said, smoothing Nola's hair, "they'll take her where she can't hurt herself or any of us ever again."

Nola nodded, turning back to the tray of dirt. Make a hole, plant the seed, grow the food. But the streaks of blood were burned into her mind.

The setting sun gave the greenhouse an orange-red gleam when the chime finally sounded.

"Students," Mrs. Pearson called over the sounds of her class packing up for the evening, "remember, tomorrow is Charity Day. Please dress and prepare accordingly. Anyone who doesn't come ready to leave the domes will be sent home, and their grades will be docked."

"Thank you, Mrs. Pearson," the students chorused as they drifted down into the hall.

"Magnolia."

Nola pretended she hadn't heard Mrs. Pearson call her name as she slipped in front of the group leaving the greenhouse. She didn't want to be asked if she was all right or told the sick woman would be cared for. And she didn't want to see if the glass had already been wiped clean.

Lights flickered on, sensing the group heading down the steps. Hooks lined the hallway, awaiting the gardening uniforms. Nola pulled off her rubber boots and unzipped her brown and green jumpsuit, straightening her sweater before shrugging out of the dirt-covered uniform. The rest of the class chatted as they changed—plans for the evening, talk of tomorrow's trip into the city. Nola beat the rest of them to the sink to scrub her hands. The harsh smell of the soap stung her nose, and the steaming water turned her hands red. But in a minute, the only sign of her time in the greenhouses that remained was a bit of dirt on the long brown braid that hung over her shoulder.

"Nola." Jeremy Ridgeway took his place next to Nola at the sinks, shaking the dirt from his light brown hair like a dog. It would have been funny if Nola had been in the mood to laugh. "Are you ready for tomorrow?"

"Sure. It's our duty to help the less fortunate." She sounded like a parrot, repeating what their teachers said every time Charity Day came around. Nola turned to walk away.

Jeremy stopped her, taking her hand.

"Are you okay?" Wrinkles formed on his forehead, and concern filled his deep brown eyes.

"Of course." Nola forced herself to smile.

"Do you want to come over tonight?" Jeremy asked, still holding her hand. "I mean"—his cheeks flushed—"my sister and my dad are off-duty tonight, and she hasn't seen you in a while."

"I've got to get home. My mom leaves tomorrow. But tell your dad and Gentry I said hi." Nola pulled her hand away and half-ran down the hall. More lights flickered on as she sped down the corridor. She made herself breathe, fighting her guilt at running away from Jeremy. She liked being in the greenhouses better than the tunnels that dug down into the earth. There might only be a few feet of dirt on top of her, but knowing it was there pressed an impossible weight on her lungs.

The hum of the air-filtration system calmly buzzed overhead. The solar panels aboveground generated power so she could breathe down here. She pictured the schematics in her head. Lots of vents. Great big vents. The air would be filtered, cleaned and purified, and the big vents would bring oxygen down to her.

Blue paint on the wall read *Bright Dome* above an arrow pointing to a corridor on the left. Nola ran faster, knowing soon she would be aboveground. In a minute she was sprinting up the steps. She took a deep, gulping breath. The air in the tunnels might be the same as the air in the domes, but it felt so different.

The sun had set, leaving only the bright lights of the city across the river and the faint twinkle of the other domes to peer through the glass. Nola squinted at the far side of Bright Dome. The other homestead domes glowed gently, but if she tried, she could almost make out a few stars. At least that's what she told herself. It might only have been wishful thinking.

Tall trees reached almost to the roof of Bright Dome. Grass and wildflowers coated the ground around the stone footpaths that led from house to house.

Nola followed the path through the buildings to the far side of the dome. Twelve families shared Bright Dome, each of them lucky enough to have been granted independent housing units.

The trees in the dome hung heavy with crisp, green leaves. The flowers had begun to close their petals for the night. A squirrel darted past Nola's feet.

"A little late getting home, buddy." Nola's pulse slowed with each step closer to home.

The birds were all flying back to their nests. Bright Dome had been assigned robins and blue jays this cycle. The birds and the squirrels shared their home to be kept safe from contamination. The domes provided them all protection from the toxic air and tainted water.

The lights were on in Nola's house as she swung open the door.

"Hey, Mom," Nola called.

"Mmmmhmmm." The sound came from her mother's office in the back of the kitchen.

"How was your day?" Nola pulled the pot of steaming vegetables from the stove, knowing they would be overdone without having to lift the lid.

"Fine," her mother said, running her fingers through her shoulder-length, chestnut hair, which had been graying quickly of late. "We've been running samples in the lab all day."

"You'll figure it out." Nola didn't ask what the problem in the lab was. Her mother, Lenora Kent, was one of the heads of the botanical preservation group. It was their job to decide what plants from the outside needed to be preserved and how to take care of those plants once they were safely inside the domes. Whatever her mother was working on was for the good of them all. Beyond that it was all vague answers about classified projects.

Nola pulled bowls down from the cabinet, dishing out steamed beans and broccoli, adding spices to make the food taste like something real.

Nola pushed the bowl in front of her mother. Only when she put the spoon in Lenora's hand did her mother seem to notice Nola was still in the room.

"How was your day, sweetie?" Lenora looked up at her daughter.

Nola's mind flashed to the woman. Pounding on the glass, shattering the serenity of the greenhouse.

"It was fine." Nola smiled. "Don't forget to pack for the conference. It'll be colder at Green Leaf, so pack your sweaters."

"Of course." Lenora nodded, but she was already looking back at the charts on her computer screen.

Nola carried her dinner up the narrow stairs to the second floor. She crept into her mother's room and found the duffel bag under her bed. Nola pulled clothes out of the tiny closet. They were lucky. The residents of the domes hadn't been forced into uniforms outside of work and school. Yet. That would come when there was no one left on the outside to work in manufacturing.

When she had counted out enough blouses and slacks for her mother's week-long trip, Nola moved the suitcase to the head of the bed, where her mother would have to see it if she went to sleep that night. A picture in a carved wood frame sat on the nightstand. Six faces beamed out of the photo. A ten-year-old version of herself sat in a tree above her mother and father. Kieran sat on the branch next to her, and below him were his parents.

Nola touched her father's face, wishing the photo was larger so she could properly see his bright blue eyes that had matched her own. But her father was dead, killed in the same riot as Kieran's mother. And now Kieran and his father had been banished from the domes. The photo blurred as tears pooled in Nola's eyes.

She slid the picture into the top of her mother's bag. Lenora would need a bit of home during the Green Leaf Conference—even if their family had broken.

Nola snuck across the tiny landing at the top of the stairs and into her room. She climbed straight into bed, leaving her dinner forgotten on her desk. She pushed her face into her pillow, hoping sleep would come before the face of the woman desperate to get through the glass.

The scent of stale vegetables filled Nola's room when her lights flickered on the next morning. A faint beeping came before the computerized voice that said, "Reminder: today is Charity Day. Please dress in uniform, remember sun protection, pack I-Vent…"

"Yeah, yeah." Nola rubbed her eyes.

"Remember," the computer continued, "charity must be done to ease the suffering of those on the outside, but protecting yourself means the salvation of mankind."

"I said, I got it!" Nola tossed her shoe at the wall.

Her mother's bedroom door was open, and the kitchen was empty. "Have fun at your conference, Mom," Nola muttered to the empty house as she ran out the door.

It was easier to go through the tunnels in the morning, when she knew sunlight filled the domes above, but still, Nola walked as quickly as she could without being glared at by the people she passed.

The bus into the city would leave from the atrium, the only place in the domes with an exit to the outside world. Five-minute walk underground, then in the outside for four hours, then class, then to the greenhouses. Nola made the list in her mind.

Not too bad. I can get through today.

"Nola!" a voice called from behind her.

Nola slowed her step without looking back.

A moment later, Jeremy walked at her side.

"You ready for this?" Jeremy's voice bounced with excitement.

"Yep." Nola held up her wide brim hat and gloves before patting the I-Vent in her back pocket. "Ready for a trip into the dangerous world. How could I not be with PAM's help this morning?"

"So, your computer got a little snarky with you, too?" Jeremy smiled. "I love how it gives us the 'greater good' speech before we go out and try to help people."

Nola shrugged. She wanted to say, *How much good do you think doling out one meal a month to the people we deem worthy of our assistance really does?* But Jeremy looked so hopeful she couldn't bear to disillusion him before they had to look the outsiders in the face.

"If we get on the bus soon enough, we can call the good jobs." Jeremy took her hand and pulled her, running down the corridor.

Nola laughed as she tried to keep up, her voice echoing through the hall. People turned to stare at them, but that only made Jeremy run faster.

Nola's step faltered as she tried to keep up with Jeremy's much longer stride. She laughed through her panting breath as they rounded a corner and darted past a group of their classmates.

"Last one to the bus scrubs the pans!" Jeremy shouted.

The green bus waited for them in the atrium. Mr. Pillion shook his head but didn't bother hiding his smile as they skidded to a stop in front of the bus.

"Morning." Nola pinched the stitch in her side.

"Good morning, Magnolia. Jeremy." Mr. Pillion's puffy white hair bounced as he nodded.

Nola bit her lip. He always reminded her of one of the snowy white sheep from the Farm Dome. Images of the farm workers sheering Mr. Pillion's hair floated through her mind.

"I'd like to take ladle duty." Jeremy turned to Nola.

Nola didn't really care what job she had. Being out there and seeing the outsiders was terrible. Did it really matter if she scrubbed pans, too? But Jeremy stared at her, eyebrows raised.

"Ladle for me, too, please," Nola said.

Jeremy smiled and moved to pull Nola onto the bus.

"Wait," Mr. Pillion said, holding out a hand. "One dose each from the I-Vent before we get on the bus."

"But we don't use them till we're on the road," Nola said.

The I-Vents cleared their lungs of the smog that hung heavy over the city. There was no reason to use them in the pure air of the domes.

"There was a riot last night." Mr Pillion's usually cheerful face darkened. "There's still smoke in the air, so we need to be more cautious."

Nola pulled the I-Vent from her back pocket. Holding the metal cylinder to her lips, she took one deep breath, letting the vapor pour over her tongue. The medicine tasted metallic and foul. She shivered as the mist chilled her throat. Nola pictured the drugs working. Finding all of the impurities in her lungs and rooting them out. Forming a protective layer to keep the toxins from seeping deep into the tissue.

"Good." Mr. Pillion nodded, lowering his arm and allowing them onto the bus.

A line of other students had formed behind them now.

"Everyone. One puff of the I-Vent before you can get on the bus," Mr. Pillion called to the crowd. "No, Nikki, you cannot get on the bus without your hat."

"That girl is going to fail again this year," Jeremy whispered as a girl with bright blond hair ran back to the tunnels.

A few of their classmates had beaten them onto the bus. Their class was for ages fifteen through eighteen. Some aged into the next group before others, but really they had been together since they were little, the younger ones rejoining the older ones when they moved to the next age level. They had all split into groups of friends years ago, and nothing had changed besides their heights. Until Kieran left.

"Nola," Jeremy said, offering Nola the seat next to his.

She should be sitting next to Kieran.

If he were still here.

Lilly, Nikki's best friend, raised an eyebrow and tilted her head toward the open seat next to her.

"Sure." Nola smiled at Jeremy.

Lilly winked, giving Nola a sly grin before turning back to her book.

Nola sat down next to Jeremy. He leaned casually against the wire-laced window, watching the other students loading onto the bus. Nola's chest hummed. She kept her gaze on her hands, afraid Jeremy would hear her heart racing. How could he look so calm and handsome when they were about to leave the domes?

"Everyone ready?" Mr. Pillion asked.

"Yes, sir," the class chorused.

"Good." Mr. Pillion took his seat. Eight guards in full riot gear loaded onto the bus, sitting up front by the door.

"Umm, Mr. Pillion," Lilly said, "are you sure we should be going out there if we need eight guards?"

They always had guards when they went out for Charity Day. But usually only four, and never in full riot gear.

"We cannot allow the unfortunate actions of a few to dissuade us from helping the many," Mr. Pillion said as the bus pulled up to the giant, metal bay doors. "We must show the population we are here to assist and protect them as long as they remain law-abiding citizens. I promise you we have done everything possible to ensure your safety."

A low rumble shook the bus roof as the atrium ventilation system prepared for the bay doors to open. Nola's ears popped as a *whoosh* flowed through the bus. She pinched her nose and pushed air into her ears along with the rest of the class.

The metal door scraped open, and unfiltered sunlight poured in. Guards in uniforms and masks stood at attention outside the dome doors, their gaze sweeping the horizon for unseen threats.

"What happened last night?" Nola whispered to Jeremy.

"A bunch of Vampers," Jeremy muttered. The people in the seats around them leaned in. "They're ridiculous. They take a bunch of drugs that make them crazy then cause trouble for the poor people who are just trying to survive."

"I've heard the Vampers are invincible," Rayland said, his pudgy face pale with fright.

"They aren't invincible." Jeremy shook his head. "My dad's Captain of the Outer Guard, so I've heard more about the Vampers than you could come up with in your nightmares. And my dad's people have taken them down before."

"But what about last night?" Lilly said.

"The Outer Guard went in to raid one of the Vamp labs," Jeremy said. "It got messy."

"I heard," Lilly said, shivering as she spoke, "Vampers actually drink blood. I don't think I could fight a person who drank blood. It would be like offering them a buffet of you."

"Vampers aren't people." Disgust twisted Jeremy's face.

"Why would they drink blood?" Nola swallowed the bile rising in her throat.

"Because they're a bunch of sickos," Jeremy spat. "And they're taking the city down with them. The rest of the neighborhood around the Vamp lab freaked out, like the guards were stealing food from orphans, and the riot started. They burned down a whole block before the guards could stop it."

"Were any of the guards hurt?" Nola's balled her hands into tight fists, hiding their trembling.

"No." Jeremy took her hands in his. "All of our people are fine."

"I get that life out there is a nightmare," Lilly said, sliding back to her own seat, "but why would they try to make it worse?"

Nola looked out the window, watching as they crossed the long bridge into the city. Children ran barefoot on the sidewalks, their heads exposed to the pounding sun. Garbage had been tossed along the curb, bringing insects and wild animals to feast on the refuse. Even with the ventilation system on the bus, the stench of stagnant water and the sickening sweetness of rotting fruit tainted the air.

Jeremy squeezed her hands tighter as he followed her gaze out the window.

It was easy to forget the world was ending when you lived in the safety of the domes.

3

When they were only a few blocks from the Charity Center, a video screen folded down from the ceiling at the front of the bus.

"Are you ready for this?" Jeremy snuck past Nola to kneel in the center of the aisle, facing the rest of the students.

Jeremy coughed as the screen blinked to life.

"Jeremy," Mr. Pillion said in a warning tone.

"I'm word-perfect, sir," Jeremy said. "They will receive all the dire warnings accurately."

A man appeared on the screen, and Jeremy turned back to the class, plastering a somber look on his face to match the man in the video.

"Good morning, students," Jeremy said with the man on the screen.

"Good morning, Jeremy," the class echoed.

Jeremy smiled and nodded in perfect sync with the man.

"As we near the Charity Center, please take a moment to utilize your I-Vents." The man lifted a shiny, silver tube to his mouth and took an exaggerated breath.

Sounds of squeaking seats and pockets unzipping floated through the bus as the students dug out their I-Vents to follow suit.

"Good," Jeremy said with the man on the screen. "Remember, it only takes one day of soiled air to begin contaminating the lungs." Jeremy faked a cough before continuing with the video. "Your work today is important. While we within the domes work hard to live a healthy life, the people in this city do not have the opportunities for safety and security that we do. Poverty is rampant, and sometimes even simple things like food are unattainable."

Jeremy dropped face-first onto the floor as the screen switched to a video of orphans, sitting at a long table, their young faces sad and drawn. Even as they ate, hunger filled their sunken eyes.

The screen changed back to the man, and Jeremy popped up to his knees.

"Poverty can induce desperation." Jeremy placed both pointer fingers on his chin, his hands clasped together. "To ensure your safety while helping the needy, here are a few simple rules to follow: First, do not leave the Charity Center or the perimeter secured by the guards."

The guards at the front of the bus waved, earning a laugh from the students.

"Second, do not partake in the food we are here to provide the less fortunate. The food provided is for them, not for the people of the domes. Third, an unfortunate side effect of living in the sad conditions of the city is an insurgence of drug use among the desperate." A new face appeared on the screen. The man's eyes were bloodshot almost to the point of his irises being red. Red splotches marked the pale skin of his cheeks. "Everyone who enters the Charity Center must submit to testing to ensure no drugs are present in their systems. However, should an addict—"

"Vamper!" the students shouted together, laughing at their own joke.

But the image of the woman beating on the glass flew unbidden into Nola's mind. She dug her nails into her palms as the man on the screen, and Jeremy, kept talking.

"—attempt to enter the Charity Center, approach the bus as you enter or exit the Charity Center, or in any way harass you, alert the guards immediately. Though a user may seem normal and calm, they could become violent at any moment. While helping those who live on the outside is important, above all, we must consider—"

"The safety of the domes!" the class chanted together as the bus rumbled to a stop outside an old stone building.

The doors opened, and the eight guards piled out. The students stood, all cramming into the aisle, ready to get off the bus.

"Did you like my dramatic interpretation?" Jeremy asked.

Nola nodded, pulling on her sunhat and trying to stay in step as everyone moved off the bus.

The Charity Center was dark gray, almost black stone. But in a few places the black had been worn away in long tear-like streaks, showing the rosy brown color the building had been before years of filth had built up on it. Iron bars strong enough to keep rioters away from the charity supplies crisscrossed the closed windows.

The class filed up the chipped stone steps. The guards flanked the stairs, their gaze sweeping the streets.

How terrible was the riot to make the best of us afraid?

Jeremy leaned into Nola and whispered, "Two more."

"What?" Nola said, trying not to gag as the smell of harsh cleaners and mass produced food flooded her nose.

"I turn eighteen in two months." Jeremy smiled as they filed into the changing room. Aprons and gloves had been laid out for each of the students. "Eighteen means I graduate and go to trade training. Eighteen means no more Charity Days. I only have to do this two more times."

Nola counted. Eleven months. Eleven more times she would have to look into the eyes of hungry people and know that, though she was feeding them today, tomorrow they would be hungry again. And while they suffered, she would be locked safely back in the domes. With fresh food and clean air.

Jeremy pulled on his gloves with a sharp *snap*. "Let's do this."

It took an hour to heat all the food in the giant kitchens. Old stoves and ovens lined one wall, their surfaces covered in years of built up grease and grime that refused to be cleaned. Shelves of chipped trays and bent utensils loomed over the giant sinks that hummed as the dome-made filters cleaned the water before the students were allowed to wash their hands.

Years of repetition had trained the class in how to get the work done as quickly as possible. One group prepped the giant pots and pans as another group pulled great sacks of flour and milled corn down from the shelves.

Nola and Lilly went into a hallway in the back.

Large cans of food lined the corridor. In the dim, flickering light, Nola had to squint to read the labels to find the cans they needed.

Stewed beets and black beans.

"Can you believe they think this is food?" Lilly shook her head, loading as many cans into her arms as she could carry. "How old is this stuff?"

Nola watched Lilly's silhouette waddle awkwardly down the hall before loading cans of processed fruit into her arms and following.

An iron-barred window bled light into the back of the kitchen. Nola peered through the soot-streaked glass. The line of people waiting to be fed wound around the block.

"What's out there?" Wrinkles formed between Mr. Pillion's white eyebrows as he squinted out the window.

"I've never seen that many people waiting before." Nola tightened her grip on the cans as they slipped.

"A good number of people lost their homes last night." Mr. Pillion shrugged before turning to the rest of the class and shouting, "We open the doors in five minutes!"

The trays and pots of food were moved to the serving room as the doors opened.

The first in line was a woman with two little boys behind her.

"Hand," the guard said, though the woman already had her hand held up as though she were carrying a tray.

The guard held a small black rectangle over the woman's palm. She winced as the needle pierced her skin. The device glowed green, and the woman lifted her older son, who bit his lip as the black box tested his blood, immediately flashing the green light. The smaller boy couldn't have been more than three. He buried his face in his mother's shoulder as the guard tested him for the drugs that ran rampant in the city. The little boy pulled his hand away and held it close to his chest as the guard waited for the light.

Nola hadn't realized she was holding her breath until the guard said, "Enjoy your meal," as the light flashed green, clearing the small boy.

The mother handed each of the boys a tray before picking one up for herself. Nola watched as they came down the line. Each of the ladle workers doled out portions of whatever was in their pot. Nola looked down at the green and brown slop as she scooped it onto the small boy's plate. She didn't even know exactly what she was serving him.

He paused in front of Nola. Purple rings marked his face under his big brown eyes. His lungs rattled as he took a breath to mutter, "Thank you."

A fist closed around Nola's heart. She wanted to stop the line. To find a way to help the poor boy with the bad lungs. But he had already walked away, pushed forward by his brother, and his mother, and the long line of other hungry people wanting food.

Nola worked mechanically, staring at the little boy until his mother took him out the heavy wooden door at the far end of the room, clearing seats so more could eat. But the line still hadn't stopped. Nola's ladle scraped the bottom of the pot.

She'd run out of food. And judging by the angry murmurs rising from the front of the line, she wasn't the only one.

"Go get more cans," Mr. Pillion whispered in Nola's ear. "I don't care what it is. Get cans, mix it together, and put it in a pot."

A man at the back of the line shoved people out of the way, trying to get to the food before it disappeared.

With a *hiss* and a *pop*, one of the guards shot the man in the neck with a tiny needle that disappeared into his flesh, leaving only a glint of silver at the top of a trickle of red.

The crowd screamed as more people began to push.

"Go. Now." Mr. Pillion scrambled up onto the counter. "Please remain calm! We are going to start making more food immediately. Everyone in line will be fed, but we must ask for your patience."

Nola slipped into the kitchen as the crowd began to shout over Mr. Pillion's voice.

4

The darkness of the storage hall had never bothered her before. But the echoing shouts from the dining room, from people who could have been a part of the riot, transformed each shadow she passed into a person waiting to attack.

"Get it together, Nola." She grabbed cans down from the shelves.

She stumbled under their weight as she ran back to the kitchen and shoved the armload of cans onto the counter. Shouts carried from the serving room. The angry voices of the crowd drowned out Mr. Pillion. Nola sprinted back into the storeroom, reached up to the top self, and pulled down giant cans of beans.

"Nola."

Pain shot up her leg as the heavy can dropped onto her foot.

"Careful now," the voice came again.

Nola spun around.

A pale boy with dark hair and green eyes flecked with gold smiled at her.

"Kieran," Nola gasped, running to him and throwing her arms around his neck, all thoughts of food and riots forgotten.

He had changed since the last time she had seen him nearly a year ago. Muscles had filled out his lanky frame, and his hair had grown longer, hanging over his ears.

"What are you doing here?" Nola stepped back, looking into his face.

"It's Charity Day." Kieran shrugged, his smile fading.

Nola's stomach dropped. "Are you here for food? Are things that bad?" She thought of Kieran's father, a man so brilliant simple things like eating had always seemed trivial to him.

A man like him shouldn't be on the streets.

Kieran shook his head. "Dad and I are fine. I know this may shock you, but getting kicked out of the domes didn't kill either of us."

"Kieran—"

"Dad's still working in medical research, but now instead of being told only to help the elite and getting thrown out for trying to help people who really need it—"

"That's not—"

"People out here love him," Kieran said, his voice suddenly crisp and hostile. "Out here, he saves people."

"He's brilliant," Nola said. "He's been saving people as long as I've known him."

A smile flickered across Kieran's face. "We're doing good." Kieran took Nola's hand. Calluses covered his cold palms.

"If you're doing well, then why are you here?" Nola asked. She had been in the storage room for too long. Someone would come looking for her soon.

Unless the dining room's turned into a riot.

"I came to see you." Kieran brushed a stray curl away from her cheek. "I don't need contaminated food dished out by Domers."

"The food isn't contaminated," Nola said, trying to ignore her racing heart and Kieran's tone when he said *Domers*.

"Then why aren't you allowed to eat it?" Kieran asked.

"Because it's for the poor."

"Someday you won't be able to believe that."

He reached across the few inches between them, sliding his hand from her shoulder to her cheek.

"I need your I-Vent," he whispered.

"You're sick?" The butterflies in her stomach disappeared, replaced by the sting of panic.

"I'm fine," Kieran said. "It's not for me."

"I can't give medicine out." Nola took a step back, shaking her head. "I'm not allowed to distribute resources."

"They have stores of medicine in the domes," Kieran said. "I only need one."

"If I give you medicine and they find out…" Kieran's father was important, a savior to the domes, and they cast him out for giving away the community's food.

I'd be banished before sundown.

"I can't do that."

"Tell them it was stolen." Kieran stepped forward, closing the distance between them. "Tell them I did it." He wrapped his arms around her, pulling her close.

Nola's heart pounded in her ears. His face was a breath from hers. His hands on her waist. The cold of his fingers cut through her sweater as he traced the line of her hips.

He pressed his lips to her forehead. "Thank you, Nola."

She raised her lips to meet his, but Kieran stepped back, holding out his hand. Her I-Vent rested in his palm.

"You're saving a life."

He turned and strode away, disappearing into the darkness before the tears formed in her eyes.

Nola stood alone in the dark.

She could scream. She *should* scream. She should shout to the guards that an outsider had stolen dome medicine. But would they be able to hear her over the chaos in the dining room? And what if they caught Kieran? Would they shoot a tiny, silver needle into his neck?

She grabbed a few cans without reading the contents and ran back to the kitchen. Her whole class stood in the back of the room, craning their necks to look out the window.

"I can't believe they thought they could get away with that," Jeremy growled. He was taller than most of the class and had a clear view of the street below.

"What happened?" Nola stood on her tiptoes, trying to see over the heads of her classmates.

"After they neutralized the first guy, people got crazy," Jeremy said. "More people started shouting. Then people were pushing to get to the food. Mr. Pillion got knocked off the counter. Then the guards took a few more people down, and everyone else just sort of ran away."

"It was terrible." Lilly's voice wavered. Marco wrapped an arm around her, and Lilly turned to cry into his shoulder.

Mr. Pillion burst through the doors to the kitchen. "Everyone back on the bus, now."

Nola turned to go back to the hall to put the cans away.

"Leave it, Magnolia!" Mr. Pillion said.

Jeremy grabbed the heavy cans from her and tossed them onto a table before grabbing Nola's hand and dragging her back through the door they had come in less than two hours before.

Only two guards joined them as the students scrambled to their seats. The door shut, and the bus jerked forward.

Nola stumbled and Jeremy caught her, holding her close as they drove away.

Groups of people lined the sidewalk. Whether they had been in the Charity Center or only come to see what the commotion was, Nola didn't know.

A terrible *crunch* sounded from the front of the bus as a brick hit the windshield, leaving a mark like a spider web in the glass. The bus accelerated as the shouts of the crowd grew.

They reached the outskirts of the city. The domes rose in the distance, shining across the river, high in the hills.

"Class," Mr. Pillion said, holding a hand over his heart as he spoke, "our world is falling apart. It has been for a long time. The greatest trial of those who survive is to watch the continuous decay that surrounds them. As the outside world grows worse, so too does the plight of the city dwellers. We witnessed the desperation that plight is causing today. Let us not dwell on the harm they might have done to us. Rather, let us be grateful for all we have. For if our roles were reversed, I promise you each of us would be as desperate as those we saw today." He took his I-Vent from his shirt pocket and held the silver tip to his lips, taking a deep breath. "We must be grateful for even the simplest of things."

Mr. Pillion sat, and the students dug through their pockets for their I-Vents. Jeremy took a deep breath from his before turning to Nola.

She stared down at her hands, willing Jeremy not to look at her. There were scratches on her fingers. How had she gotten them?

"You need to do your I-Vent." Jeremy nudged Nola.

"I lost mine," Nola whispered, "I—" Jeremy had known Kieran. They had been friends. But Kieran wasn't one of them anymore. "I think it fell out of my pocket when things got crazy."

"Use mine." Jeremy pressed the silver tube into her palm.

Nola stared down at it. Kieran had come to find her for a tiny tube.

To save a life.

"Look, don't be nervous about asking for a new one," Jeremy murmured into Nola's ear, wrapping his arm around her. "I'll go with you. And after what happened today, I don't think anyone is going to blame you for losing it."

"Right." Nola gave a smile she hoped looked real before holding the tube up to her lips and waiting for the metallic taste to fill her mouth.

5

Nola flopped down in bed.

It had taken hours to get a new I-Vent from the medical department. There were forms to fill out and questions to answer. Jeremy had wanted to stay with her to keep her company, but the doctor kicked him out. A quick "See you tomorrow!" was all he managed to say before the door *swooshed* shut in front of him.

They drew blood and performed a chest scan to be sure she hadn't been skipping her doses. Nola was too tired to argue that she hadn't been skipping anything. That she had used Jeremy's I-Vent on the way back from the Charity Center.

After a few hours, the doctor finally declared her lungs undamaged and gave her a new I-Vent. None of them seemed to suspect the old one had been stolen. And no one mentioned Kieran Wynne.

Nola lay on her back, staring at the new I-Vent in her hand. She held it up, watching the light reflect off its silver surface.

Such a simple thing.

Medicine in a tube. But Kieran needed it to save someone. Nola dug her fists into her eyes, trying to wipe away the thoughts of Dr. Wynne ill. Or Kieran himself.

It's just a little tube.

She had been carrying one in her back pocket every time she left the domes for as long as she could remember. Was that why Kieran had come to her, because he knew where she kept her I-Vent? Or had he simply been waiting in the darkness for one of the students to be alone?

Her skin tingled where he'd held her hips, pulling her close. All he had wanted was a chance to steal the I-Vent.

How had she not felt him take it? Was she that mesmerized by seeing him again?

Nola shoved her hand in her back pocket. Her fingers found something crisp. She pulled out a piece of yellowed, folded up paper.

Nola

Her name was written on the paper in Kieran's untidy scrawl. She recognized the careless way he swished his pen. Her hands shook as she unfolded the note.

Dear Nola,

I'm sorry I had to get you involved in all this. I needed the medicine, and I had a feeling you wouldn't turn me in. If you knew the girl who needed it, you wouldn't be angry at all. She's sick, Nola. Lots of people out here are. I know I can't save everyone right now, but I need to start with her.

I wish you could meet her. I only hope the I-Vent can buy her some more time. I wish I could repay you. If you ever need me, the folks at 5th and Nightland know how to find me.

I miss you, Nola.

Please forgive me,

Kieran

Nola buried her face in her pillow. He had planned to see her. He had written a note for her.

He came for me.

She couldn't breathe. The pure air of the domes crushed her lungs. Nola's heart raced. The energy pulsing through her veins begged her to run away or break through the glass. She opened her bedroom window and climbed up onto the sill. With a practiced motion, she grabbed the groove at the edge of the roofline and, using the wall for support, pulled herself up onto the soft moss that covered the roof. She lay down, taking deep, shuddering breaths. Her arms stung from pulling herself up, but she was grateful for the ache. The sting took her mind off her racing heart. And Kieran.

If you ever need me.

What would she need him for? He was an outsider. A city dweller. She had everything she needed in the domes.

Everything but him.

She dug her fingers into the moss. The thin layer of dirt beneath still held the heat of the day. Kieran had known her better than anyone. He had been her best friend. They had held hands, supporting each other at her father and his mother's funerals.

He was the only boy she'd ever kissed.

Three faint beeps echoed throughout the dome. Then there was a little *pop* and a *hiss* as the rain system turned on.

The cool water spattered her skin. Nola didn't move as it soaked her. If she lay there long enough, would she disappear into the soft moss of the roof?

The dome-made rain drenched Kieran's letter, washing the ink away. Nola tore the letter into sopping pieces and let them dissolve with the rain. No one could see that letter. No one could know she had seen him.

5th and Nightland. That was all she needed.

"One of the most elementary lessons farmers learned early on was crop rotation." Mrs. Pearson drew the words on the wall with her silver pen. "Why is crop rotation so important?"

Nikki's hand shot up in the air.

Mrs. Pearson's eyebrows arched high. "Yes, Nikki?"

"You have to change what crops you grow where so you don't exhaust the soil," Nikki said.

"Very good," Mrs. Pearson said.

The concept of crop rotation was something they covered every year. Just like studying the importance of the ozone when the summer heat scorched the city beyond the glass—an inescapable measure of the passing of another year.

Mrs. Pearson slid her hand on the wall, and the words she had written flew away. She began to scrawl out equations. Tapping the corner of the wall, pictures of plants and soil sprung up around the border of the screen.

Nola let her mind wander, staring out the tiny window in the corner. She knew the equations. She knew how to test the soil and how to make it fertile again. Her mother had been training her to join the Botanical Preservation Group for years. Some kids got to choose which branch of the domes they wanted to work in once they turned eighteen and finished school. Nola had known her path since she was a little girl.

Her eyelids grew heavy. She hadn't been able to sleep last night. Hadn't been able to keep thoughts of Kieran from racing through her mind. What if he needed her?

What if I need him?

The bell beeped softly in the corner. As one, the class stood, putting their tablets back into their bags.

"Nola," Mrs. Pearson called as Nola reached the door to the hall.

Nola gritted her teeth and turned around.

"I wanted you to know I spoke with your mother over the com system yesterday," Mrs. Pearson said, her tone serious as she folded her hands in front of her.

"My mother?" Nola asked. "What happened? Why did she call?"

"We were discussing the progress of the Green Leaf Conference, and the topic of the incident at the Charity Center came up," Mrs. Pearson continued. "You reacted so poorly to the unfortunate woman outside the Green Dome, and then to have another shock so near after…" Mrs. Pearson pursed her lips, giving Nola a pitying look, like she was ill. Like there was something wrong with her, Nola, for being upset.

"I'm fine." Nola pushed her face into a smile.

"After losing your father—"

"That was three years ago," Nola cut across. "I'm fine."

Nola turned and walked out of the room, ignoring Mrs. Pearson calling after her.

As she turned into the hall, a hand caught her arm. Nola gasped as Jeremy fell into step beside her. "Don't scare me like that."

"You all right?" he asked.

"Why does everyone think I'm not okay today?" Nola twisted her arm away from Jeremy.

"Maybe it's the full moon." Jeremy took Nola by the shoulders, turning her to face him. "Maybe you're a member of one of the new packs."

Nola caught herself smiling a little. "Pack of what? Did the wildlife department bring in coyotes?" Nola rubbed a hand over her face. "I mean, I get we're the new Ark and we're supposed to preserve living creatures in a dying world and all, but I still think the insect habitats are creepy. And now they want to bring in coyotes?"

"I never said anything about coyotes. It's the new big thing in the city. I was talking to my dad about it."

"So, pack of what then?" Nola asked.

Jeremy draped an arm around her shoulders and started walking slowly down the hall. He spoke in a low voice as though telling a frightening bedtime story. "Werewolves. It's the new drug craze. Lycan. Outsiders have started injecting it."

"Isn't Vamp bad enough?" Nola shuddered. "Exactly how many drugs do people need? And why would they risk taking something that dangerous?" The woman outside Green Dome flashed through Nola's mind. Fighting to get through the glass, seeking out flesh to tear with no thought left for anything else. A zombie.

Jeremy shrugged. "This one is different. It makes you stronger, faster. You heal more quickly."

"Just like Vamp," Nola murmured.

"But Lycan changes your pheromones. The riot two nights ago. The guards tried to arrest a man for prowling around during the raid on the Vamp lab. Turns out he was the alpha of one of the packs."

"Like wolves."

"Just like wolves," Jeremy said, his voice shifting from conspiratorial to angry. "And when the pack found out the guards had their Alpha, they attacked. They're the ones who lit that building on fire. It destroyed a whole block, and the guards had to kill a few of them just to get away."

Vampires, zombies, and now werewolves.

A thousand horrible images of blood and fear tumbled through Nola's mind.

"So, they're still out there?" Nola asked, wishing she were aboveground, not just so she didn't feel like she were being crushed by the earth, but to be able to see out the glass—to be able to see if the wolves were coming.

And to escape.

"For now," Jeremy said.

Nola stared at Jeremy's face, trying to see the color of his eyes instead of streets painted red with blood.

"How do you know any of this?" Nola asked.

"My father," Jeremy said.

"Why did he tell you?" Nola asked. "You're always complaining he doesn't tell you anything about what he does outside."

His father was the head of the Outer Guard who patrolled the city. What they did, most people didn't want to know about.

"Because"—Jeremy paused, stepping forward to face Nola—"I just found out that, as of my birthday, I'll be training to join the Outer Guard."

"What?"

"Dad told me." Jeremy beamed. "It's everything I want."

"That's amazing!" Nola stood on her toes and threw her arms around Jeremy's neck. He pulled her in close, his chest rumbling against hers as he laughed.

"He's been telling me things so I'll be up on all the business of the city when I start training," Jeremy said. "Just don't tell anyone. About the Outer Guard or the wolves. The 'guard' thing won't be announced until next month, and my dad doesn't want people freaking out about the werewolves."

"Why would they want to be called that?" Nola shivered.

"When I get one, I'll ask." Jeremy winked. "But don't worry about them." Jeremy took Nola's hand, pulling her more quickly down the hall, almost running in his excitement. "We're safe here. No one can get into the domes. There isn't a way in or out of this place not covered by guards."

Nola stumbled, but Jeremy didn't notice.

There is a way out.

---

*I*t had been pouring outside the domes that night. Dark sheets of rain that roared as they struck the glass. Nola's mother had gone to a conference at the domes on the far western side of the country. Dr. Wynne had been charged with watching Nola. Not that she needed it. She was fourteen. But it meant more time with Kieran. And Dr. Wynne had been too distracted to pay Nola or Kieran much mind anyway.

His research had been keeping him in the lab until all hours. His face had been growing paler and thinner for months.

"There has to be a way," he would mutter over and over as he wandered through the house. Kieran cleaned and made supper as he had done since his mother died. But there was something more to Dr. Wynne's ramblings now. More than his brilliance-bordering-on-madness, more than missing his wife. He had a secret.

Nola had spent many nights lying out on the roof of her house. She liked it up there. If she squinted, she could pretend there was no glass between her and the stars. More than once, she had seen a shadow coming out of the Wynne's house and disappearing into the night.

The last night Nola was to stay at the Wynne's, there had been a riot in the city. Nola had curled up on the couch, covering her ears, trying to block out the sounds that were too far away for her to hear. She watched as fire sprang up around the city. Flames danced on the glass. A fire so large, even the pounding rain couldn't douse it. The flames sent shadows swaying in the orange glow of the burning city.

"There won't be anything left if they keep burning sections of the city down," Kieran had said. "Don't they know they're destroying their own homes? Once the city is gone where will they live? Build huts and tents?"

"The rain will burn them like the fire," Nola had muttered, burying her face on Kieran's shoulder.

"Not tonight. The rain won't burn tonight. The clouds were white. There are still good days to bring hope. But they're hungry," Dr. Wynne spoke softly, the red glow of the city reflecting in his eyes, giving him the look of the mad scientist he had always threatened to become. "The rain didn't come this year. And the clean water that fell wasn't enough to feed the plants. If you were starving, if you were watching your child starve, your anger would outweigh your reason. Their homes have been on fire for years. Only tonight, we can see the flames."

Tears streamed down Nola's cheeks. There were guards out there trying to protect the city dwellers, but the outsiders wouldn't see that. They would only see attack… never help.

"It's okay, Nola." Kieran wiped the tears from her face with his sleeve. "We're safe here." He laced his fingers through hers. "There are guards at every entrance and exit. No one could get in here without the guards stopping them."

"No," Dr. Wynne snapped, lifting his son by the collar.

Kieran staggered, his eyes wide with shock.

"There is no such thing as safe when the world is descending into madness. When the people burn the city, the palace will fall, too." Dr. Wynne clung desperately to his son. "One day, the outsiders will have had enough, and they will find a way into our paradise."

"But we can't have them all here," Nola said. "We don't have the resources."

"They will not come to join us." Dr. Wynne grasped Nola's shoulders, forcing her to look into his face. "They will come to destroy us. You have to know the way out."

Dr. Wynne grabbed Kieran and Nola by the hands and ran from the house, dragging them both behind him. He ran down the stone walkway and under the great willow tree. When they were nearing the far corner of the dome, he pulled them onto the grass and into a stand of trees.

Nola wanted to shout at him to stop, to scream they were safe. But something in the doctor's madness swept through her, and she followed, running as quickly as her feet could carry her. Dr. Wynne stopped inches before hitting the glass of the dome. They stood, staring into the darkness for a moment. Watching the rain stream down the outside. Nola pressed her face to the glass, looking to the west, where the fire was slowly beginning to die.

"When the time comes, and the only chance for survival is to go into the dying world, you must take the only way out," Dr. Wynne murmured.

Terror filled Kieran's eyes as his father knelt in front of the glass. Slowly, Dr. Wynne dug his fingers into the top corner of the bottom pane. With the tiniest scraping noise, the pane inched forward enough for him to squeeze his fingers in, pushing the panel to the side. The second layer of glass was still there, blocking them from the rain, but Dr. Wynne didn't hesitate. Pulling a penknife from his pocket, he shoved the blade into the crack where the pane met the metal beam, and the glass fell silently into his waiting hands.

"This is the way to salvation." The gleam of victory dancing in Dr. Wynne's eyes frightened Nola more than fires and riots.

Dr. Wynne crawled out of the passage he had created and into the rain. Spreading his arms wide, he gazed up into the storm. Lightning split the sky, silhouetting the triumphant form of Dr. Wynne.

Nola hadn't spoken to anyone about that night or the way out through the glass. Not even to Jeremy. Not even when the guards couldn't figure out how Dr. Wynne had been smuggling food to the city.

This is the way to salvation. And the way to Kieran.

6

Nola sat alone at the kitchen table, poking at the food on her plate and trying to do her reading for school.

The medicinal applications of plants must be weighed equally with their nutritional value. Also included in the assessment must be other species that would be required to maintain a proper habitat, and their accessibility—

There was a tap on the kitchen door.

"Coming," Nola called. Her heart dropped when she saw a giant shadow through the window.

Captain Ridgeway stood outside her door, his face somber.

"What happened to my mom?" Nola asked before Captain Ridgeway could speak. "Is she sick? Did she get hurt?"

Green Leaf is too far away. I don't know how to get to her.

"You're mother's fine." Captain Ridgeway stepped into the kitchen. As tall as Jeremy, Captain Ridgeway's well-muscled frame overwhelmed the tiny kitchen, leaving Nola no room to breathe.

"Oh." Nola clasped her shaking hands together. "What happened? Is somebody dead? Is Jeremy okay?"

"There was an incident in the city last night," Captain Ridgeway said. "There was a fight between two groups that accelerated to the point where the Outer Guard had to become involved."

"But everyone's all right?"

"There were a few injuries," Captain Ridgeway's voice dropped.

"Gentry?" Nola knew she was right before Captain Ridgeway nodded.

He's not just an Outer Guard. He's Jeremy and Gentry's father.

"Is she going to be all right?" Nola pictured Gentry, tall and strong with short, blond hair framing her round face. Always laughing, but now she was hurt.

"She'll recover," Captain Ridgeway said. "But there were a few deaths. The packs that were attacking each other dragged in bystanders that shouldn't have been involved in their fight."

"Werewolves," Nola breathed.

"Nothing travels faster than rumors in the domes," Captain Ridgeway said without surprise. "When we searched the casualties for identification, we found dome medicine on one of the deceased."

The room swayed.

"You lost your I-Vent?" Captain Ridgeway continued.

Nola nodded, not trusting her voice.

"Is there anyone who stood out to you at the Charity Center? Anyone who tried to get close to you?"

Nola shook her head.

"If someone is stealing dome medicine, we need to know," Captain Ridgeway said, his eyes searching Nola's face.

"I just lost my I-Vent," Nola said, her voice shaking. "I think I..."

Kieran dead. Killed by werewolves.

"I dropped it. The person who had the medicine—"

"Is dead. But that doesn't mean there isn't someone out there trying to steal dome supplies. If a black market for our medicine is creeping into the city, it needs to be stopped immediately. Did you see anything suspicious? Anything at all?"

"I don't know," Nola said.

Captain Ridgeway nodded, his eyes still locked on Nola's face. "If you remember anything, please come to me immediately."

"But—" Nola stepped in front of the Captain as he turned toward the door. "No one we know, none of our people died?"

"No. All the guards will recover."

He stepped outside and shut the door behind him with a sharp *click*.

Nola slid down the wall, her head in her hands.

All the guards will recover.

But what about Kieran?

Had he been trapped between the wolf packs?

What if someone had stolen the I-Vent from him? What if he had lied, and he was the one who needed the medicine? What if he was the one they had found the medicine on?

He could be dying. He could be dead, and she would never know.

Nola pressed her palms together, trying to stop her hands from shaking. Her breath came in panicked gasps.

Kieran torn apart by wolves.

I have to know.

Nola sprang to her feet, willing herself to move quickly enough she wouldn't have time to change her mind.

There was only one way to know if Kieran was alive.

5th and Nightland.

7

The damp chill of the night air cut through Nola's coat. The wind had pushed the stench of the city all the way up to the domes. Nola crouched just outside the glass, like a child reaching for something dangerous with the certainty someone would snatch it away before she could get hurt.

A night bird soared overhead, cawing at the darkness. Nola jumped at the sound, flattening herself against the glass. The bird kept flying into the distance, not caring that Nola stood alone in the dark. She waited for a moment, counting each breath of outside air. She pulled out her I-Vent and took a deep breath of the medicine. But still, no guards came charging toward her.

I'm alone.

Carefully, she knelt and slid the outer glass so it was nearly in place. No one passing would see anything amiss, but there was enough space to squeeze her fingers in to push the pane aside.

She stood and turned toward the city. Lights glowed through the haze that hung over the buildings. She wanted to turn and crawl back into the dome and into her warm bed where she could pretend Captain Ridgeway had never come to the kitchen door.

Kieran.

She took a step forward. And then another. She would do this. She would find Kieran.

One road ran from the domes to the city. The only path with lights and guards. Nola stayed away from the road, cutting through the old forest.

She had seen pictures of what the forest had looked like before, when her mother had been young and the founders were still building the domes. The trees here had been thick and lush, their branches so dense the sunlight could barely peek through to the forest floor.

But the trees had begun to die a long time ago. A few still had leaves clinging to them. Most now stood like skeletons—dead and barren.

The moon peered through the clouds, and the naked branches cast strange shadows onto the ground.

Keep moving, Nola. Just keep moving.

One foot, then the other. A single step at a time. Moving deeper into the woods.

Did animals still live in these trees? Or worse, had people too poor to live in the slums of the city dared to make the dead forest their home?

Nola moved as quickly and quietly as she could. Every now and then, a rustle in the distance would send her sprinting for a few minutes, fleeing from the unseen danger.

Soon she neared the edge of the woods, and the city rose above her. She cut to the left toward the bridge that led into the city. The river roared beneath her. The foul stench of chemicals and rot sent bile into her throat. How many times had the bus taken them to the city, and she had never smelled the river like this. She had always been sheltered from the worst of it by the technology of the domes.

Shadows stalked across the bridge. Some in groups, some alone. Nola clenched her fists in her pockets, wishing she had thought to grab a heavy stick or rock from the woods. Anything to defend herself with.

She quickened her pace, trying not to walk so fast as to seem scared. The metal of the bridge gave a dull *thunk* every time she took a step. Nola kept her eyes forward, moving with purpose, pretending she belonged.

She was halfway over the bridge and could see the streets in front of her. The Outer Guard patrolled the city at night. If she had to call for help, would she be banished from the domes?

A group of people near Nola's age had bunched together at the city end of the bridge. Talking and laughing like the reek of the river and danger of the night meant nothing. Both the boys and girls wore torn up leather clothes. The girls' tops were ripped in deep Vs, letting their pale skin gleam in the night as they hung from the boys' arms. The pairs all stood under one man, bigger and older than the rest. He perched on the railing of the bridge, holding court over those beneath him.

Nola turned her gaze away from the group. She was almost off the bridge. She could see the seam where metal met concrete.

The man who stood on the railing turned to look at her. His cheeks sunk into his pale face, a scruffy beard covered his chin, and in the glow of the city lights, the man's eyes gleamed a deep, blood red. He smiled, and a sound like a wolf growling rumbled from his throat before he tipped his head to the sky. Flinging his arms to his sides, the man howled. The group around him threw their heads back, joining him.

Nola ran, not knowing if they would follow or where she was going. Her feet pounded on the concrete as the howling rent the night.

Werewolves.

Jeremy hadn't been lying. Lycan changed people. Wolves filled the city.

She turned a corner and pressed herself into the shadows of a building.

5ᵗʰ and Nightland. Just get to 5ᵗʰ and Nightland.

A sign on the corner that appeared to have been painted over and over again read *12ᵗʰ Street*, the other read *Rotland* in an untidy scrawl. Nola's hands trembled. She closed her eyes, picturing the maps of the city in her mind. The number was right, but the name was wrong. Who had renamed the streets of the city, and why had she never known?

North. Go north to find 5ᵗʰ.

Staying close to the buildings in the depths of the shadows, Nola walked, keeping her head down, trying to picture what the city would have looked like when it was still prosperous. When the river water was clean, and people rode in boats on its glittering surface.

11ᵗʰ Street. 10ᵗʰ.

What would it have been like to live in a city in the open air, with parks to play in and a whole world to explore?

Nola passed a dark stairway leading down to a basement.

A hand reached out, grabbing her leg.

"Please," a woman's voice came from the shadows, low and crackling. "Please, do you have any change?"

"No." Nola stumbled back, wrenching her leg from the woman's weak grasp. "I don't have any money."

It was true. They didn't use money in the domes. Currency had always been a vague concept—numbers on a screen, not something to be kept in a pocket.

"You're strong," the woman muttered, crawling up the stairs. "Vamp. Do you have Vamp?" The woman dragged herself into the light of the street lamps. Wrinkles covered her thin face. Cracks split her dried lips, and the skin under her eyes hung loose in horrible bags. "I'm dying!" the woman shrieked, trying to push herself up but crumpling to the ground. "You have Vamp. I know you do!"

"I don't." Nola shook her head, backing away from the woman. "I'm sorry. I can't help you."

"Lycan, ReVamp. Please!" the woman screamed after her as Nola ran down the street. "I'm dying. Murderer!"

Nola ran from the woman, not caring who saw her, her only thought to escape from the echo of the woman's voice.

Murderer!

In her haze of panic, she almost ran right past the sign that read *5th Street* and *Blood Way*.

Turning her back to the river, Nola walked west down 5th. There were lights in the windows here. And the farther she walked, the more people there were on the streets, some walking on the cracked pavement, some sitting in doorways. The scent of the river had disappeared, replaced by the stale smell of humans and animals living too close together.

The back of Nola's neck prickled with the feeling of a dozen people staring at her back.

"You," a voice called from behind her.

Nola quickened her pace.

"Don't bother trying to get away," the voice said. A moment later a hand had locked around her arm.

Nola clenched her fists, ready to punch whomever had grabbed her, but the man already had her by both wrists.

"Please, I don't have—" Nola began.

"Anything but a dome jacket?" the man said, eyebrows raised.

Nola glanced down at her coat. It was plain black, made for warmth, not protection from the sun or acid rain. But the man's coat was tattered and dirty, like everything else in the city. Nola's looked brand new.

"Why would a Domer be out on the streets this late at night?" the man asked, tightening his ice-cold grip on her wrists. "A little thing like you clearly isn't an Outer Guard."

"I'm looking for someone." Nola tipped her chin up, staring into the man's eyes.

His irises were black, leaving voids where color should have been.

"Who?"

"That's none of your business," Nola said, trying to sound confident the man wasn't going to kill her in the middle of the street.

"Look, sweetheart," the man whispered in her ear. His breath smelled of iron as it wafted over her. "I don't care if you're here to buy Vamp or get laid. But this is my territory. If a Domer gets killed here, we'll have the Outer Guard after our heads, and the last thing I want is a riot getting all my people killed. Believe it or not, I'm probably the only thing standing between you and getting your throat ripped open."

Nola gasped as the man squeezed her wrists so tight she thought they might break.

"Tell me who you want to see so I can make you somebody else's problem to clean up."

"Kieran," Nola said, "Kieran Wynne. I'm supposed to be able to find him at 5th and Nightland."

The man cursed under his breath. "I love it when the hero sends a pretty girl to die."

"He's my friend."

The man took her by the shoulders, steering her roughly down the street.

"Friends don't send friends into Vamp territory," the man said.

Fear shot through Nola's body, setting fire to every nerve.

"What, sweetheart?" the man hissed. "You didn't know you were being saved by a monster?"

He smiled, showing two long fangs in the front of his mouth.

Nola swallowed her scream.

The man gripped her tighter, shoving her down the street. "The better to eat you with, my dear."

"That's the wolf's line," Nola said. A Vamper was steering her through the dark. What would people think when she wasn't in the domes tomorrow? How long would it be before they noticed?

They'll never find me.

"Be glad a wolf didn't grab you," the Vamper laughed. "They like to fight and die. And if you think all this shit with vampires and werewolves is going to work out like a fairytale, this really is your first time in the city. Here"—the Vamper pushed her up onto the curb—"5th and Nightland. Have your friend get you out, if you make it that long. The next time you cross through my territory, I'll let them have you. They'll dump your dried up body into the river before the Domers know you're gone."

The man turned and strode away, leaving Nola alone under a flickering street lamp.

She looked up at the sign. 5th Street and Nightland. But there was no one in sight. No one waiting to give her help, no sign reading *find Kieran alive and healthy here.*

Where are you, Kieran?

Nola closed her eyes. A very small, very foolish part of her thought when she opened her eyes Kieran would be there. Or maybe if she called his name he would appear.

When she opened her eyes, there was nothing in front of her but an empty street. Maybe the Outer Guard had raided the area? Why would they need to raid a place where Kieran would be?

Muffled voices came from nearby, but Nola couldn't see anyone. No lights on in the houses, no people roaming the streets.

A thumping pounded from below her feet. A strong, steady rhythm. Like music. Nola studied the ground. Trash, dirt, and soot covered the cracked sidewalk.

Something white twenty feet away caught her eye. The thumping grew louder as she approached. Voices became distinct, and a melody broke through the noise. A metal trapdoor had been built into the sidewalk, a single word painted across its surface. *Nightland.*

Nola reached into the hole in the metal door just big enough for a hand and tried to lift. She gritted her teeth against the weight of the metal, but the door didn't budge.

She took a breath and tried again, pulling until pain shot through her shoulders. Panting, she let go of the door and staggered back a step.

Go to Nightland, find Kieran. I have to find Kieran.

"I have come too far to get turned back by a door."

Taking a deep breath, she stomped three times on the metal. The sound echoed through the empty street, and the noise from below changed.

The music still thumped on, but the voices were different. Their tones loud and urgent.

Nola jumped back as the metal door flew open with a *clang* that shook her ears. Four people leapt onto the sidewalk.

Each of them held a weapon in their hand—a pipe, a sword, a staff, and a knife. The four glared at Nola. She took another step back, missed the curb and fell into the street.

A woman with bright purple and scarlet-streaked hair stood over Nola, twirling a knife in her hand.

"Such a pretty little thing to be knocking on our door." The woman grinned.

A dark-skinned man with scars dotting his skin stepped up next to her, digging his staff into the pavement next to Nola's neck. "Did someone order dinner?" The man had fangs, like the one who had brought her here.

"Bring her inside," the man with the sword said.

"Not worth the risk," the man with the pipe said, staring at Nola with frightening hunger.

"Then we kill her out here." The woman raised her knife.

"Kieran!" Nola shouted, covering her face, waiting for the blade to strike. Even if he heard her scream she would already be dead.

"What did you say?" the woman said.

"Kieran," Nola said, uncovering her face. "I'm here to see Kieran Wynne."

"How do you know Kieran?" The woman lifted Nola to her feet by the collar of her coat.

"F-from the domes," Nola stammered.

"But how did you find out about Nightland?" The man with the pipe sneered, showing his frighteningly white teeth.

"He told me," Nola said.

The woman lifted her higher so her toes barely reached the ground.

"He came to the Charity Center. He stole my I-Vent and left a note in my pocket. It said to find him at 5th and Nightland."

The woman let go of Nola's collar, and she fell back onto the pavement, cracking her head against the stone.

"You're the one." The man with the staff tilted his head from side to side as he stared at Nola. "If the boy wants her..." He shrugged.

"Is Kieran alive?" Nola asked as the man with the sword lifted her to her feet and clamped a hand firmly around her arm.

"If you don't mind"—the man ignored Nola's question. His tone and accent sounded strange, like he wasn't from the city—"I would suggest you not try and run away. I'm sure it was quite a feat for you to make it here from the domes alone, but I promise, if you go off on your own, you won't survive Nightland."

The man with the staff struck the metal door four times, pausing for a moment before repeating the four beats. The sound echoed through the streets. The Outer Guard would hear.

They'll save me.

The door swung open, and the pounding rhythm of the music drifted up into the night. Kieran could be down there. Nola didn't know if she wanted to be rescued by the Outer Guard or not.

The man with the sword bowed, still keeping a grip on Nola's arm as he gestured down the steps. "Welcome to Nightland."

8

The metal stairs vibrated under Nola's feet, but the music ate the sound of her steps.

The woman with the scarlet and purple hair waited at the bottom, knife still drawn. Once all of them had descended below the street, two men appeared from the shadows and closed the door. It was thicker than Nola had realized. At least three inches of heavy metal, as thick as the doors to the outside in the atrium. But the two men lowered it back into place as if the weight were nothing and bolted the door shut.

Nola's heart raced.

There's no way out. I'm trapped underground.

Even if there weren't guards, she would never be able to lift that door.

"If you please," the sword man said, sliding his blade back into the sheath at his waist. The sword looked new, and its embossed leather sheath shone with fresh black polish.

Who makes new swords and sheaths?

The woman walked in front, leading them down another set of stairs. The music grew louder with each step, and flashing lights bounced across the landing below.

Nola's gasp was lost in the music as the room came into view. Hundreds of people in a seething mass, all moving to the same rhythm. Arches were carved into the walls of the room, some leading nowhere, some disappearing into darkness. The smell of sweat, metal, and dust permeated the air. It was different from the stench of the city. A scent as primal as the dancers, all swaying to the music, some alone, some wound tightly around their partners.

The woman walked into the crowd, and the dancers parted, leaving a path as though frightened of the woman. A few of them stared at Nola, speaking loudly to their fellows, but Nola could only make out one word over the music: *Domer.*

They drew near to the speakers, and the sound vibrated in Nola's chest, sending her heart sprinting. She balled her fists tightly, letting her nails bite into her skin, willing herself not to panic. She could hear now that there were words in the music, but she couldn't tell what they said.

The woman turned left, heading toward an arch that was blocked off by another heavy metal door.

A woman as tall as any man Nola had ever met stood beside the door, her arms crossed and her face set in a grimace. She nodded at the woman with the knife and opened the door. The scraping of the metal against the concrete floor cut through the music, slicing into Nola's ears.

As soon as they entered the dark passage, the door screeched shut behind them, dampening the music. Nola glanced back. Only the four who had been aboveground accompanied her now.

The woman led on, and the man with the sword didn't let go of her arm. Dim lights were set into the ceiling of the tunnel, leaving shadows for them to pass through every few steps.

"What is this place?" Nola asked, half-choking on the damp smell of the tunnel, panic squeezing her chest.

We're twenty feet underground. Maybe thirty. Far enough for the weight of the earth to crush us.

"Nightland," the woman said.

They walked in silence for a moment. The pounding of the music faded, and the walls muffled the sounds of their footsteps.

The ceiling here was short, barely above the sword man's head. The woman at the door to the tunnel would have needed to hunch to walk down it.

The walls swayed, closing in around them. Smothering Nola in dirt.

Nola blinked, willing the walls to hold still.

"You all right?" the sword man asked, raising a sculpted black eyebrow at Nola.

"She's fine," the man with the pipe said. "She's from the domes. If the air bothers her, she can just use her I-Vent."

"Not the air," Nola said. Her voice sounded faint even to her own ears. She took a deep breath and tried to sound stronger. "I don't like being underground."

The woman with the knife laughed, her voice bouncing down the tunnel. "And Kieran asked you to come here? And I thought you must be an old friend of his."

"I am," Nola said. "What is this place?"

"Nightla—"

"What is Nightland?" Nola cut the woman off.

It was the man with the staff's turn to laugh. "Nightland is exactly what it sounds like, Domer. It's the land of the night dwellers, and you just wandered into it."

Night dwellers. Impossibly heavy doors. People in the city who roamed the night. All of those people were dancing, not coughing, not sick. Dancing underground in the night.

Vampers. Kieran led me to a Vamper den.

Nola stopped walking and almost toppled over as the man continued. But his grip on her arm was so strong she couldn't fall to the floor. He held her up without seeming to notice.

She should run away or shout for help. But there was nowhere to go and no one to hear.

"What are your names?" Nola swallowed hard. "I'm Magnolia." Maybe if they thought of her as human, like them, not as a meal. But were they human? If a drug changed you that much....

"Raina," the woman said, looking back at Nola. The turning of her head sent her purple and scarlet hair dancing in the dim light.

"That's Julian."

The man with the sword and the dark shining hair bowed his head. "It's a pleasure."

"Desmond."

The dark-skinned man with hundreds of tiny scars gave a jerk of his head.

"And Bryant."

The man with the pipe didn't acknowledge Nola.

"Those are great names," Nola said.

"What were you expecting?" Desmond asked, his voice a low grumble.

"Something along the lines of Fang, Shade, Bloodlust, and Satan I expect," Julian said.

"I-I meant," Nola stammered, hoping accidentally being rude wasn't enough of a reason to eat a person, "that it is lovely to meet all of you. And thank you for bringing me safely to Kieran."

"Don't worry, Domer," Bryant said from behind. "We won't hurt you. Not before you get to see Kieran."

"So, he's alive?" Nola's heart leapt into her throat. "Kieran's fine?"

"I don't think our definitions of *fine* would match." Raina sneered, baring her teeth.

Nola tensed. Kieran was alive. He would protect her. Kieran wouldn't let them drink her blood. He had told her to come here.

He wouldn't lead me here to watch me die.

They walked in silence. Every once in a while, there would be a metal door in the wall, or another tunnel twisting away into the darkness.

Nola tried to remember each time they turned. But there were no arrows on the walls like in the domes. No signs pointing the way. And even if she could remember the path, there was no way she could get back the way she came. Not unless they wanted her to go.

"How big is this place?" Nola asked, more to break the endless pounding of their footfalls than because she actually wanted to know.

"No idea," Raina said. "I don't own a measuring tape."

"Then how much longer until we get there?" Nola asked. She didn't know how long it had taken her to find Nightland or how long she had been down here.

If I'm not back in the domes by sunrise . . .

"We'll be there soon," Julian said as the tunnel began to widen and slope downward.

"Where is *there*?" Nola's voice shook. How far underground were they now?

The tunnel widened even more, and the doors along the walls became more frequent. Soon they were passing people in the hall. Some nodded, others averted their eyes, but all of them gave the group a wide berth.

Brick and stone replaced the dirt of the walls. The lights were evenly spaced, giving the hall a more populated feel. The doors were still made of metal, but they didn't look as though they were meant to withstand a bomb blast.

Two boys a few years younger than Nola ran down the hall, laughing, only falling silent as they passed the group. Nola could hear their laughter begin again behind her.

A sudden jerk shot pain through Nola's arm. Raina had stopped in front of an antique-looking, intricately carved wooden door, and Julian held Nola in place.

Raina knocked, and the sound echoed through the hall. Shadows passed behind a small piece of glass set in the door.

Slowly, the door opened. Nola had hoped Kieran would come running through and tell Julian to let go of her arm where she could feel bruises forming. But instead, a tall man whom she had never seen before stood in front of her, his arms crossed as he stared at the group. Young and handsome, he had curling black hair down to his shoulders. His skin looked as though it should have been a deep olive but had grown pale without the sun. And the man's eyes were dark with black irises the same as the man who had led her to Nightland.

Nola glanced at Julian. His eyes were black as well.

"Emanuel." Raina bowed. "This Domer showed up at the gate. She said Kieran Wynne told her to find him here."

Emanuel examined Nola, starting from her feet and ending with her brown hair. "She looks like the right one. Nola?"

"Yes." Nola nodded. "How do you know my name?"

"Kieran told me about the girl who gives Eden breath." Emanuel smiled. "I'm glad you decided to brave the outside world. Bring her." Emanuel turned and walked away.

Julian steered Nola through the door, and Bryant closed it behind them. The inside of the door had been built of the same heavy metal as the door that led to the street. The intricate wood was only a façade.

Nola turned to Emanuel but gasped at the space around her. They were in a chamber larger than Nola's whole house. But instead of bare walls, beautiful art decorated this room.

Paintings, like the ones Nola had only ever seen on computer screens, adorned the tops of the walls. In the center of the ceiling hung three large crystal chandeliers, bathing all the paintings in their warm light. In one corner sat a piano and in another a harp. Below the paintings, the walls were covered with bookshelves, six feet tall and packed with books.

"Wow," Nola whispered.

"It's beautiful, isn't it?" Emanuel said. "These things would have been destroyed aboveground. Burned in the riots or for warmth, but we decided to protect them. You see, the Domers care about protecting the genetics of the human race. But down here, we want to protect what it is to be human. Sometimes, things have to change in order to survive. It all depends on which part of ourselves we're willing to give up. Some choose the body, others choose the soul."

Nola's mind raced, trying to take in everything in the room and understand what Emanuel was saying at the same time. She wanted to ask them to stop and let her look at the paintings or touch just one of the books, but they led her on and out through the far side of the room. They entered what appeared to be a home. Dark and, Nola shivered, underground, but a house nonetheless.

An older woman hovered over a stove, and a little girl clung to her skirt. She reached up to Emanuel as they walked by, but he shook his head at the child and kept walking. Hurt filled the little girl's big brown eyes as the group moved past the kitchen. Open doors to rooms filled with beds came next and then a steel door. Emanuel pushed the door open, and they all stepped through.

9

Nola caught a flash of scrubbed metal tables and brick walls draped in clear plastic before a voice shouted "Nola!" and Kieran's arms were around her.

"You're not dead," Nola breathed, burying her face in Kieran's jacket. "I thought you were dead."

"I'm fine," Kieran whispered. "I told you the medicine wasn't for me."

"But Captain Ridgeway found dome medicine on a dead body. After a riot." Tears streamed down Nola's face. "I thought it was you. I had to see if you were alright."

"I'm fine." Kieran pressed his lips to her forehead. "I'm fine. And you're safe here."

"Safe?" Nola half-shrieked. "There was a werewolf pack on the bridge. A sick woman was begging me for help, and I didn't have anything to give her. And then a Vamper almost killed me. He dragged me out of his territory and told me not to come back. I don't know how I'm going to get home, if I even have time before they find out I'm gone and decide they don't want me in the domes anymore."

"Are all Domer girls this hysterical?" Raina asked from her place by the door.

"Oh, no." Dr. Wynne appeared behind his son's shoulder. His hair stuck out at strange angles and had turned almost completely gray now, and his skin was nearly translucent in its pallor. "Nola is usually quite calm and reasonable. She is simply not used to our element, so you'll just have to be patient while she adjusts." He gave Nola a fatherly pat on the shoulder, muttering, "It is good to see you," before wandering back to his worktable.

"If it's good to see me"—Nola rounded on Kieran—"then why didn't you warn me what was at 5th and Nightland?"

"No one asked you to come here," Raina said. "I certainly didn't ask for a Domer to ruin my night."

"Raina," Emanuel said, silencing her. "How could we have known if you would turn us in?" Emanuel stared intently into Nola's eyes.

"Or that you weren't dumb enough to get yourself killed your first trip outside the domes." Raina shrugged as Emanuel turned his gaze to her.

"I'll make sure you get home before dawn." Kieran took Nola's hand. "I won't let them find out you're here. I won't let them banish you."

"I thought you were dead," Nola said to Kieran, keeping her voice low though she knew the rest of the room could hear. "You stole my I-Vent, left me a note telling me how to find you, and now I'm in a den full of Vampers."

"We prefer the proper name: *vampire*. Vamper is a rather nasty term. Rather like us calling you Domer. But I should give you some credit. At least you're smart enough to have figured that part out," Julian said in a genial tone. "Although Desmond's fangs do rather give it away."

"Kieran, why are you here?" Nola gripped Kieran's hand, hanging onto the one thing in the room that didn't terrify her.

"I think it's time we had a talk," Emanuel said, gesturing for Nola to sit at the large metal table.

The table looked like a slab for a corpse, not a place to sit for a pleasant chat.

"Emanuel—" Kieran began, but Emanuel silenced him with the wave of a hand.

"It is providence that you traveled to us tonight." Emanuel pointed again for Nola to sit.

Nola nodded and took a seat at the table. Kieran sat next to her, his smile disappearing as his brow furrowed.

"Raina, if you could—" Emanuel started.

"Get the Domer some refreshments?" Raina said, her tone barely polite. "Of course. The woman will go to the kitchen and get some snacks for the guest." She spun and walked out of the room.

Julian shut the door, leaving Bryant and Desmond standing on either side like guards, neither putting away his weapon.

"I must admit, Nola," Emanuel said, "we did have a courier that was caught up in the unfortunate incident last night. And he had an item with him. Something we need very badly. Where do we begin?" Emanuel took a seat across the shining metal table.

"With Fletcher," Dr. Wynne said. "If you want her to understand, you have to start with Fletcher."

Emanuel sat for a long moment. "Before you were born, before even Dr. Wynne was born, the Incorporation started building the domes. Forty-two sites around the world. To be filled with the best and the brightest. Not only to encourage research, but also to protect the gene pool. People were sick, dying. Cancer had become a plague. Clean water was scarce, and food supplies were in danger. But that wasn't what the people who created the domes feared.

"Fertility rates were dropping, and birth defects were becoming more common. The Incorporation had to protect the future of the human race by making sure it could breed. That's what the signs read, what was spouted at every conference. *To protect our children.*" Emanuel spat the last sentence. "But soon, the people realized it wasn't all the children the Incorporation were trying to protect, just the chosen few who lived in the domes. The rest of the population was left out here to watch their children suffer and die. The sicknesses became worse. But all of the researchers were in the domes. The brilliant minds were gone, and we were left with Fletcher."

"I've never heard of a researcher named Fletcher," Nola said.

"You wouldn't have," Kieran said. "They don't talk about him in the domes."

"People were in pain, and Fletcher came up with a new medicine. A drug that could stop tumors from growing. Make lungs impervious to the filth in the air. The medicine made people strong and slowed the natural aging process."

"That's amazing," Nola said.

"But the cure came at a price. Sensitivity to light. The inability to metabolize normal food, the reliance on blood for nutrition. Anger, violence, bloodlust. It changed you to the very core. But it was a way to survive. At first, the drug was only given to a few people. The ones who were very ill, on the brink of death. But soon, others outside Fletcher's control began to manufacture the drug, and it spread like wildfire."

"Vamp," Nola said, studying Emanuel's black eyes. "Vamp was made to be a medicine?"

"Not all vampires set out with the intent to wander the night. We were trying to survive. Vampires are what we had to become. There was no other choice," Emanuel said.

"But the wolves," Nola began.

"Someone tried to improve Vamp. To alter the way Vamp affects the ability to eat food."

"So, it is true." Nola swallowed the burning in her throat. "Vampires drink blood."

"Animal blood," Kieran said, reaching for Nola and pulling his hand away when she flinched.

"Nightland does not allow vampires who hunt for human blood," Emanuel said.

"But there are some who do?" Nola asked.

"You met one tonight," Julian said. "The man who showed you here, he was from a group who drink from humans. Almost all those who live aboveground do."

"Wolves are able to eat but suffer pheromone changes that alter the way they interact with each other," Emanuel said.

"Packs," Nola said. "It makes them run in packs."

"Yes," Kieran said, "which makes them more dangerous than any of the vampires."

"Ours is the only real community of vampires," Emanuel said. "Most prefer to roam and hunt on their own. There are turf lords, and territorial groups, but they would kill each other without hesitation for fresh blood. We have banded together in Nightland because we want something more. More than injecting Vamp and living to breathe another night. We want a chance for the children on the outside."

"And that is where I come in." Dr. Wynne spun his chair around and faced the group as though he had been waiting for his cue. "Vamp has a tendency to alter the user's moods. With the increase in strength comes increased aggression. With the need to drink blood comes a taste for violence."

"And the eyes, and the teeth," Nola said, her gaze darting to Emanuel's eyes.

"The eyes, yes," Emanuel said.

"The teeth are prosthetic," Desmond said from behind Nola. "If I'm going to be called a vampire, I might as well embrace it. Besides, it makes hunting easier."

"Desmond," Dr. Wynne said, flapping his hands as though fangs were trivial, "lived as a roamer for a long time and has no personal aversion to human blood." He paused, scratching his head for a moment. "But if there were a way to create a new formula of Vamp, one that would make people strong and healthy without subjecting them to the unfortunate side effects, we would have essentially found a cure. A way for people to live healthily on the outside without constant fear of contamination and death."

"That's what he's working on. ReVamp," Kieran said. "It would keep people healthy and keep the streets safe."

Nola ran through it in her mind. The woman who had begged her for help. The little boys at the Charity Center. All healthy.

"You could save everyone," she breathed.

"Not everyone," Emanuel said softly before looking to Desmond. "Fetch Eden."

"What's Eden?" Nola asked.

"Eden isn't a what," Emanuel said. "Eden is a who."

Emanuel nodded, and Desmond opened the door, disappearing into the hall.

"Before you meet her, I want to thank you," Emanuel said. "Without you, we would have lost her already."

Desmond returned, holding the small girl from the kitchen in his arms. As soon as the little girl's big brown eyes found Emanuel, she reached out, wanting him to hold her. Emanuel stood and took the child, kissing her gently on the cheek before kneeling next to Nola.

"This is Eden," Emanuel said. Eden hid her face on his chest. "She is my child."

"She's beautiful," Nola said.

"Eden," Emanuel said. The little girl turned her eyes back to her father. "Can you say thank you? This is the nice girl who gave you your medicine."

"Thank you," Eden said so softly her words could barely be heard.

"Good girl." Emanuel kissed her black curls that matched his own.

He handed Eden to Desmond, who slipped back out of the room.

"That's why I stole your I-Vent," Kieran whispered. "She needs the medicine."

"Eden has tumors in her lungs," Emanuel said. "They were getting bad enough she couldn't breathe. Your I-Vent bought her more time."

More time for a little girl with big brown eyes. Someone so small shouldn't be so sick.

"I'm so sorry. An I-Vent can't cure tumors," Nola said. "But when Dr. Wynne finishes ReVamp, he can cure her."

"Vamp, Lycan, ReVamp"—Emanuel gripped the table. The shining metal bent under his grasp—"they all have consequences."

"You just said—"

"If you're too sick or too young," Julian said, "all of the drugs can kill you. Or worse."

"What's worse?" Nola's heart raced as though she already knew the answer.

"Zombies." Julian glanced at Emanuel. "If the body rejects the drug, the body will start to decay. Beginning with the mind. All that's left is a craving for human flesh. Zombies would eat their own family without a thought. They know no pain. No fear. Only hunger. You've probably never seen such a thing."

"I have," Nola said, swallowing the bile that once again rose in her throat.

"The zombies come to the domes sometimes. The guards drug them and take them away for treatment."

"There is no treatment," Emanuel said, his voice breaking. "There is no medicine that can cure a zombie. There is no medicine in the outside world that can save Eden."

"But there is in the domes." Dr. Wynne placed a hand on Nola's shoulder.

"I had a contact from far outside the city," Emanuel said. "He had managed to procure the medicine Eden needs."

"But he didn't make it all the way to Nightland," Kieran said.

"And somehow," Emanuel said, his black eyes studying Nola's face, "you did. And you have brought hope with you."

"We would only need a vial," Kieran said, "and that little girl could live until she's old enough—"

"To become a vampire," Nola said.

"To live to see twenty," Emanuel said. He reached across the table and took Nola's hand. His fingers were colder than the metal surface. "It's such a small thing in the world of the domes, but it's my daughter's life out here."

"You want me to steal medicine from the domes?" Nola pulled her hand out of Emanuel's reach.

"I am asking you as a father to save my daughter's life. I'm not asking as an outsider, or as a vampire. I am asking as a human, a man who is terrified. I am no different from you."

"You are." Nola stood up. "And not because I'm from the domes and you're an outsider. You are a vampire. You're asking me to help vampires."

"We are all humans." Julian spread his arms as though reaching out to every person in the city. "We've done what we had to in order to survive. But we are still humans. Can't you try to see us that way?"

"If you want to be seen as human, why would you name yourselves after monsters?" Nola asked. "Why would you choose to be called something so evil?"

"We've been forced to live in the dark for years. Is it so strange we would name ourselves after children of the night?" Raina asked as she pushed open the door, carrying a tray of tea. "We are living the nightmare. But we didn't choose it. We were abandoned out here. We're just the ones that have become strong enough to survive."

"Nola," Dr. Wynne said, "that little girl will be dead within the month. We need one vial. One tiny tube to save her. And you're the only one who can get it."

"But you know how to get into the domes." Nola shook her head. "You're the one who showed me how to get out."

"The medicine is in medical storage. You have to get to the lower levels to get near the room," Dr. Wynne said.

"And your mom works right down the hall from medical storage," Kieran said, his voice low and steady as he took Nola's hand in his. "All you have to do is visit her and then take a detour. No one will ever know."

"And if I get caught?" Nola said. "If they banish me for stealing from the domes?"

Forced to live in Nightland, stuck in a living tomb for the rest of my life.

"Tell them I broke in," Dr. Wynne said. "Tell them I came to your room and threatened to kill you if you didn't do it. They already believe me insane. I'm sure they can believe I could become violent."

"They would send the Outer Guard after you." Nola's mouth went dry in her panic.

"A worthy risk to save a child's life." Dr. Wynne shrugged and went back to his work.

"You won't get caught." Kieran took both of Nola's hands. "I know how you can do it. All you have to do is trust me. Please, Nola. For me."

Nola found herself nodding before she knew she had made a choice.

1 0

Nola clutched her hot tea, afraid her trembling hands would give away her fear if she lifted the cup to her mouth.

Dr. Wynne spoke first, explaining to Nola exactly what medicine he needed. Then Julian appeared, bringing with him maps of the domes.

"How did you get this?" Nola reached for the map. Bright Dome was there with her house drawn in the far corner.

"All the domes were built the same," Julian said, "and the Wynnes aren't the only ones who have left."

Nola's shoulders tensed at the word *left*. *Left* didn't seem to describe it.

"Under the circumstances, I would think you would be grateful for the breach in dome security as it will make your job that much easier. Medical storage is here." Julian pointed to a small square space. "It's environmentally controlled."

"Cold storage," Dr. Wynne said. "It'll be in the back cage."

"Isn't medical storage locked?" Nola asked.

"It is," Dr. Wynne said, "but seed storage isn't. And they share a vent system."

"All you have to do is go see your mom," Kieran said. "You're still planning on going the botany route?"

"It's not like I have a choice," Nola said.

"Head into seed storage," Kieran said. "No one will question why you're there. Go through the vent."

"Go through?" Nola pushed away from the table, her heart racing at the mere thought of entering such a small, dark place. "You want me to climb into a vent!"

"Only for a minute," Kieran said. "And then once you have the vial, you walk out the door and back to your room. I'll come into the domes tomorrow night and get the medicine from you." He took Nola's face in his hands. "You can do this, Nola."

"You shouldn't risk coming back into the domes," Nola said. "If they catch you…"

"They won't," Kieran said.

"When your mother returns from Green Leaf tomorrow," Emanuel said, "will she be going back to her lab?"

"She will." Nola nodded. "She'll go straight to the lab to check on her samples before she comes home. She'll make a guard bring her bag to our house. It's what she always does."

Kieran nodded to Emanuel.

"Then go see your mother as soon as you can," Emanuel said. "Eden is depending on you."

The room fell silent for a moment. Nola wanted to say something brave, or hopeful, but her mind buzzed with fatigue.

"Your walking into Nightland was providence, Nola," Emanuel said. "Even in the darkest of places, hope can appear."

"We should get you home," Kieran said, standing up and laying his hand on Nola's shoulder.

"I won't make it back before dawn," Nola said. "How long have I been down here?"

I should have brought a watch.

Kieran looked at Emanuel who nodded to Desmond and Bryant. Both men stepped aside, and Raina opened the door.

"There's a shortcut to the domes," Kieran said. "I'll take you."

"Raina, Julian," Emanuel said, "make sure Nola gets home safe."

Kieran's hand tensed on Nola's shoulder.

"This way." Raina led them back past the kitchen, but Eden was nowhere to be seen. They went through the gallery and back into the halls, going in the opposite direction of where the people had been dancing.

"How long have you been here?" Nola asked Kieran softly, though she had no real hope Julian and Raina wouldn't hear.

"Since the night after we were banished from the domes." Kieran rubbed the back of his neck. "My father had a few friends in the city, the ones he'd been helping."

"The starving children he had been feeding with the overabundance of the domes," Raina said.

"We went to them," Kieran said, "but I suppose word travels fast out here. In the middle of the night, Emanuel showed up where we were hiding."

"It's not every day a brilliant medical researcher ends up on the streets," Julian said. "Emanuel has been looking for an alternative to Vamp for a very long time." He opened a door and bowed them into a narrower corridor that sloped farther down into the earth.

"He asked my dad to come down here. Promised food, shelter, protection, and all my dad had to do was try to find a way to help people."

"By giving them better drugs?" Nola said. "There has to be a way to make people healthy without making them vampires."

"And what's so wrong with being a vampire?" Raina rounded on Nola. "Is hiding behind glass really better than living underground?"

"Raina," Julian warned.

"If she's going to be around, she should learn how to not insult people who could break her in half." Raina's black eyes gleamed.

A low growl came from Julian.

Raina shrugged and continued down the tunnel.

"I'm not going to be around," Nola said. "One vial. I'm getting one vial to help a little girl, and then I'm done."

Kieran squeezed her hand. "Then you're done."

Raina had stopped walking again, and Nola, too busy looking at Kieran, almost ran into her. His dark hair had fallen over his eyes, but it didn't hide their hurt and fear.

"Kieran—" Nola began, but Julian stepped forward.

"No time for teenage angst, I'm afraid. Cinderella must get home." Julian took Nola by the shoulders, steering her out of the corridor and down a small tunnel with a dead end.

The air in the tunnel was thick and damp. Nola squeezed Kieran's hand, willing herself not to panic at the sheer wall of blackness.

Raina pulled out a heavy key attached to a long chain that had been hidden inside her black leather top. In the darkness of the tunnel, Nola didn't notice the door until Raina reached for the keyhole.

The lock gave a heavy *thunk* as Raina turned the key.

Where she had only been able to see shadowed wall before, cracks of moonlight now split the darkness. Cool, crisp air flooded the hall as the door opened.

"Up you go." Julian pointed to a set of metal stairs.

Nola glanced at Kieran who nodded, and began climbing the metal steps. She expected the stench of the river, or the haze of the city to greet her, but instead, the air smelled like wood and decaying leaves.

A pool of light bathed the top of the steps. Nola reached her hands out, expecting to feel metal or concrete, but her hands met wood. Light crept in through a crack large enough for her to climb through. She turned sideways and slid out into the forest. She looked behind to see Raina climbing out of the tree after her.

No leaves clung to the branches. There would be no reason to look at the tree twice. Kieran climbed out of the vertical slash in the trunk. It looked like the tree had been split by lightning or time. The gap in the bark didn't seem large enough for a person to fit through until Julian emerged from the opening.

"Onwards?" Julian asked.

Nola's gaze followed him as he started up the hill toward the glittering domes, rising just above them.

"What?" Nola said, her feet not moving as she glanced from the tree to her home.

"I know, I know," Julian said, shaking his head, laughter bouncing his voice. "It is a bit passé to have a secret entrance hidden in a tree. However, I find when one becomes the stuff of legend, one might as well embrace the whole fantastical existence. I prefer to write myself into an unlikely fairytale rather than accept my fate is a horror story."

"But it's right here. There's an entrance right here!" Nola shouted before clapping a hand over her mouth.

They stood silent for a moment.

Nola listened for the sounds of guards coming to search the night but couldn't hear anything beyond the pounding of her own heart.

"I was almost killed getting to Nightland tonight," Nola finally whispered. "And you mean to tell me I could have just climbed into a tree and found out Kieran wasn't dead in twenty minutes? Skipping entirely over nearly being killed three times?"

"We couldn't allow that." Raina grabbed Nola's arm, dragging her up the hill toward the domes.

"Why not?" Nola yanked her arm from Raina. "You want me to sneak around and steal things for you, but you couldn't let me use a short cut?"

"It may be hard for you to understand"—Raina tossed her hair, her fingers twitching as though aching to reach for her knife—"but it's just as hard for a vampire to trust a Domer as it is for a Domer to trust a vampire. We couldn't just let Kieran tell his little girlfriend all our secrets, even if he did think you had an actual soul."

Julian hissed, silencing Raina.

"Fine," Nola said. "But if I had died, how long would it have taken you to find someone else who could get you the medicine?"

"If we'd known you would be more useful than the I-Vent, perhaps we could have arranged a parade to escort you to Nightland." Raina took a step toward Nola, her hand draping over the hilt of her knife. "Then again, showing someone who is going to betray you the second they get inside their cozy little domes an easy way into the only safe place you have is a sure way to get all of Nightland slaughtered."

"Enough," Kieran said, stepping between Raina and Nola. "I'll take her the rest of the way."

Raina opened her mouth to argue, but Julian spoke first. "We'll wait for you here, Kieran. Shout if you need us."

Kieran put a hand on the back of Nola's waist, guiding her up the hill.

"This is crazy," Nola said.

"You can do it," Kieran said. "I know you, Nola. You'll be all right."

"No, not just the medicine." Nola ran her hands through her hair, her tangled curls snagged on her fingers. "Vampires, and werewolves, and zombies. This isn't how the world is supposed to be."

"The world is broken," Kieran said. "We broke the planet. Is it so hard to believe the planet broke us right back?"

"But it's all legends, story stuff." Nola tripped over a root.

Kieran wrapped his arm tightly around her waist, steadying her.

Nola looked away from the worry creased on his forehead, blinking in the darkness, trying to focus her tired eyes on the uneven ground. "All I wanted to know was if you were alive. And now…"

"I'm fine," Kieran said. "And now you have the chance to do some real good. Don't forget, Nola, people living in domes was once story stuff, too. We can't choose which stories come true and which stay stories. None of us are that strong."

They were almost to the domes now. The sun had barely begun to paint the night sky gray. Soon the workers would be up, and then the new shift of guards would take up their posts.

Kieran stopped at the last of the trees in the forest. "I don't think I should go any farther."

"They might catch you."

"I might not be strong enough to leave." He touched the ends of Nola's hair and then her cheek. "Be careful."

"I'll see you tomorrow." Nola nodded. She walked out into the field, forcing herself not to look back, knowing Kieran would be watching her.

She half-expected guards to be waiting by the loose pane of glass. Or an alarm to sound as she crawled inside. She crept through the trees and back out onto the stone path as the gray light from the sky turned orange.

She peered through the glass, down over the forest and thought she saw a flicker of movement, but there was no way to know. Back into the empty house and up to her bed. She pulled the I-Vent from her pocket and took a deep breath, letting the metallic taste fill her mouth as her eyes drifted shut and she tumbled into sleep.

11

The faint ringing of PAM's bells dragged Nola from sleep. Her head pounded as she tried to sort through everything that had happened the night before. The scent of the damp tunnels clung to her tangled hair. Her shoes were still on, and she clasped her I-Vent in her hand.

It wasn't a dream. There is a tunnel in the woods that leads to a den of vampires living under the city. Kieran is with them.

I've agreed to help them.

"Good Morning," PAM's voice said as soon as Nola climbed out of bed. "Reminder: Today, Dr. Kent will be returning home. Morning lessons will be in the Aquaponics Dome. This evening—"

"Thank you, PAM," Nola said, cutting the computer off. She didn't care what was happening in the domes that evening. Her mind couldn't move past the medical storage unit three stories underground.

Nola went to the shower, turned the water on as hot as she could stand and scrubbed the filth and stench of the city off her skin.

Does Kieran have hot water or soap?

Nola shut off the water, pressing her face to the cool ceramic wall. The shower, the warm fluffy towel. It all suddenly felt too extravagant to be allowed.

"You can't save everyone. Just get the medicine."

She turned the water back on and rinsed her hair. Normal. She had to look normal. Like this was any other day.

Mr. Pillion droned on, his voice dulled by the moss and heavy tank glass in the Aquaponics Dome. He spoke in a soothing, calm tone about the effects of algae blooms on fish populations.

Nola hated the Aquaponics Dome. The class was seated in the dug-down section of the dome, eye-level with the tanks of fish.

Mr. Pillion coughed loudly.

Nola sat up straighter, aware of his eyes on her.

"As the fish waste feeds the plants, the plant waste feeds the fish," Mr. Pillion continued. "What we really need to think about is what plants and fish mesh best together in this type of symbiosis, and which plants and fish can best contribute to the dietary, medicinal, and preservation goals of the domes."

The fish smelled terrible, but it was dark and warm by the tanks—a nice place to sleep. The fish swam in slow circles under the roots of the plants.

Nola didn't feel herself slipping into sleep, but her eyes flew open at a sharp kick in the shins from Jeremy.

"Magnolia," Mr. Pillion said, his eyebrows furrowed in concern, "are you feeling quite well?"

Nola sat up straight and smiled. "I'm fine. Just tired. Sorry, Mr. Pillion, it won't happen again."

"Perhaps we should send you to the clinic." Mr. Pillion frowned. "Just in case."

Nola chewed the inside of her lips. Being sent to the clinic would take hours. And if they thought she was sick, they would place her in isolation. She would never be allowed to visit her mother in her lab if the doctors thought there was any chance of her being contagious.

"Really," Nola said. "I just couldn't sleep last night." Her mind raced for an answer. "I don't like being by myself in the house."

Mr. Pillion gave her a sympathetic look. "Of course." He nodded and turned back to the screen where he was working through a list of extinct ocean species.

Some of the students still stared at Nola. She kept her eyes on the board. She never would have been left alone before her father was killed. Before Kieran and Dr. Wynne were banished. She could feel their sympathy radiating toward her. Nola bit the inside of her lip hard, blinking back the tears stinging the corners of her eyes.

"Unfortunately, some species such as Blue Whales were too large for an attempt at their preservation even to be made," Mr. Pillion said.

The whales had been left out in the ocean to fend for themselves. The tiniest algae killed the largest mammal. The injustice of it burned hot in Nola's chest.

But where could we have put a whale?

The end of lesson chimes sounded in the hall. Nola threw her things into her bag and was first to the door. Her mother should be here by now. If her mother behaved as she always had, she would already be in her lab, carefully checking each specimen and experiment to be sure everything was perfect.

"Nola." Jeremy caught up to her and took her hand, easily matching her quick pace. "Are you sure you're okay?"

Jeremy twined his fingers through hers. Nola's heart caught in her throat. Last night she had been walking with Kieran through the dark in a place she should never have been. And now she was going to steal from the domes. She looked up into Jeremy's eyes. Brown eyes as dark as Eden's.

"I'm fine." Nola pulled her hand away, pretending she didn't see the hurt in Jeremy's eyes as she stepped back. "I'm going to go say hi to my mom. Will you let Mrs. Pearson know where I am if I'm late?"

"Sure."

Nola turned and walked down the hall before Jeremy could say anything else.

Her mother's lab was located three floors below the normal tunnels. The research labs were some of the most important parts of the domes, so they were buried deep underground, far out of reach of storms or riots.

Nola went down the first flight of stairs. Offices branched off in either direction, all lit by sun-mimicking bulbs to make sure no one suffered from lack of light while they worked through the day.

There were no lights like this in the vampire tunnels.

Are sun-lights enough like the real sun to make Raina suffer?

Nola shook her head, banishing thoughts of places she should never have seen. But the clearer her thoughts became, the more the pressure of the earth weighed down upon her.

She descended another flight of stairs to where the food and supplies were stored and where those deemed fit for only menial tasks labored.

Then down the final flight of stairs. Nola's chest tightened, even worse than it had breathing the outside air the night before. Guards stood at either end of the hall, protecting the researchers behind their shiny white doors.

One of the guards nodded at her, not bothering to ask the reason for Nola's visit. She came down to the labs often. If she was going into botany, she needed to know as much as possible, even if the depth of the labs made her ill. She had almost begged to go into transportation just so she would never need to descend the steps to the laboratory. But choosing a path outside botany would have killed her mother. Nola would study plants and how to save the world. It was the only path her mother could accept.

Her mother's figure moved on the other side of the frosted glass of the laboratory door. Nola knocked lightly.

"Yes." Her mother's brusque voice cut through the glass.

Nola peeked her head into the lab. "Hey, Mom."

"Magnolia," her mother said after pausing for a moment, as though trying to figure out who would be calling her *Mom*. "What do you need?"

"I just wanted to say hi, see how the conference was." Nola stepped into the room as her mother began typing away on the computer.

"The conference was fine." Her mother moved toward a tray of cooled samples on the table. "We agreed to institute a new policy that will double food production."

"That's amazing," Nola said. "With that much food, we could actually bring produce to the Charity Center."

"Don't be foolish," her mother said. "The excess space in the greenhouses will be used for further plant species preservation. Just because you can't eat a plant doesn't mean we should allow it to be wiped off the face of the earth."

"I'm sorry," Nola murmured.

"No." Her mother sighed, running her hands through her short hair. "I didn't mean to snap. The conference was good." She sank down into her office chair, massaging her temples. "We're going to be converting one of the domes for tropical preservation this year. We're bringing in a new batch of rain forest species, which is truly exciting. Something I've been fighting for since I got this job."

"Then, what's the matter?" Nola perched on her mother's desk.

"Something went wrong with the seed samples while I was gone." Her mother waved a hand at the tray.

Nola leaned over, examining the dishes of seeds. The outsides had cracked where tiny stems had tried to break through, but the green had faded, replaced by withered brown.

"I was trying to see how short the cold simulation could be," her mother said. "The heat at the end of the cycle was too high and fried the seedlings. And I have no idea what went wrong with the program."

"I'm sorry." Nola pulled her mother into a hug.

"It's fine, I just need to—"

"Get back to work," Nola finished for her mother. "I'll see you at home."

Nola walked back out the door and into the hallway. The guards didn't even look to see who had come out of the lab.

Sweat slicked Nola's palms, her heart pounded in her chest.

I won't even make it to the door before they know something is wrong.

Two doors down. All she had to do was enter two doors down. She exhaled and willed her shoulders to relax.

She wiped her palms on her pants and pushed the seed storage door open.

She glanced at the guards, but their backs were still toward her. She slipped inside, shutting the door silently behind her.

Nola's breath rose in a cloud in front of her. Even with the adrenalin pumping through her veins, she began to shiver. The room had been built to keep the rows upon rows of seeds hibernating. Saving thousands of species from extinction.

It had always seemed strange to Nola that the Dome Council didn't place more guards on seed storage. To the Kents, this was the greatest wealth of the domes.

Someday, years from now, when the water had begun to clear and the air was pure again, people would leave the domes. They would spread out around the world to begin again. And these were the seeds they would take with them.

Nola wanted to stay, read every name on every tray and picture what the plants would look like when they had grown. But this room was not where the answers for Eden lay. Blowing heat onto her hands, Nola walked to the end of the room before turning and heading to the back corner.

There it was, just where Julian had said it would be; a grate at the base of the wall, as high as Nola's waist and just as wide. It was bigger than she had thought it would be, and the faint light of the medical storage room filtered through from the other side. It was only three feet. Less than that really.

Nola knelt and pulled out a thin strip of metal, sliding it into the crack at the edge of the grate, gently prying it away from the wall. She stopped every few seconds, listening for footsteps or the *whoosh* of the door swinging open. But as the grate slid into her hands, no sound of panic came—no running feet, no alarm. Taking a deep breath, Nola crawled into the wall. Her hands trembled. She could leave the other side of the grate off. Leave an exit from the cramped darkness. But if someone came in, they would spot the hole in the wall.

Nola grasped the slats of the grate, feeling them cut into her skin as she pulled the metal into place. Her breath came in shallow gasps. The airshaft opened above her, leading to the next floor. Cold air blew on her, coming from stories above, going through filter after filter to get down to her. Nola turned to the other grate, her whole body shaking from cold and panic. She pushed against the metal, but it didn't budge. She leaned her body into the grate, but it refused to move.

"Please, please just open," Nola whispered, twisting to push on the grate with her feet. A whine of metal on metal echoed around the vent as the grate moved a fraction of an inch. Nola froze, waiting for one of the guards to come running into the room, searching for what had made the noise. But the hum of the air system was the only sound.

"Open dammit." She gave the grate two kicks, and it popped out, hitting the floor of the medical storage room with a clatter.

Nola dragged herself into the room and lay on the ground, gasping at the dim ceiling lights overhead. Again, she waited for the pounding of guards' boots as they ran to arrest her. To throw her out into the world. But there was nothing.

She pushed herself to her knees, searching the room. Where there were rows of shelves in seed storage, here there were glass-fronted cabinets, each labeled with its contents. Nola pictured where Julian had pointed on the map. She pushed herself up onto her shaking legs and walked along the back wall. The vials were classified by type. Names Nola didn't understand.

It should be Kieran down here, climbing through airshafts and stealing medicine.

He would know what all the names meant and be brave enough not to fear the guards.

She reached the cabinet in the far corner. Nola didn't hesitate as she opened the glass door. Fog blossomed on the glass at the heat of her hand.

Pataeris. Sitting right on the shelf. Nola picked up the vial. She expected an alarm to sound. Or for PAM to reprimand her loudly. But there was no noise. No hint of danger.

Nola slipped the vial into her pocket and sprinted back to the grate. Back through the darkness and into seed storage. She could be aboveground in ten minutes. She would see the sun. Nola crawled into the shaft and jammed the grate shut behind her, ignoring the sting as the metal dug into her fingers. With a grind and a tiny *thunk*, the grate was back in place. Nola twisted to the other grate as a familiar voice said, "What the hell was that?"

12

Nola froze as footsteps came closer to the grate.

"It sounded like the ventilation unit," a man's voice said.

There was an angry murmur before Nola's mother's voice came loud and clear. "I lost an entire tray because the computer mishandled the climate settings on my experiment. That same computer also monitors the climate settings in this room. Correct?"

Nola could picture her mother's face. Eyebrows raised, nostrils flared.

"Yes," the man said. "PAM monitors both systems."

"And PAM is malfunctioning," Nola's mother growled. "So go get every climate control and computer tech down here and get this fixed before we lose every seed we have!"

Angry footsteps pounded away toward the door. Nola could see a pair of thick black boots through the slats of the grate. She held her breath. If he bent down, he would see her.

After a few seconds, the man walked away. Straining her ears, Nola heard the door *whoosh* shut behind him. He would be back. Back with people who needed to inspect the vents. Nola looked at the other grate. She could go hide in medical storage, but for how long? They would need to check the temperature in there, too.

I'm trapped.

Nola leaned against the metal inside the shaft. She could crawl out now, tell them what she had done, and beg for mercy. They would want to know who the medicine was for.

What if they trace it back to Kieran? And Eden. Wide-eyed little Eden.

Nola opened her eyes. There was another way.

She looked up into the darkness above her. How far up was it to the next floor? Ten feet, maybe twelve? And how long before the man came back?

Nola swallowed and took a deep breath. It was no different than climbing onto her roof. Except for the darkness, metal walls, and tight space. Not to mention the possibility of being banished from her home.

She placed her hands on either wall. Her sweaty palms slipped on the smooth metal. But the walls were close. Close enough for her to balance her weight as she lifted one foot and then the other onto the walls. Although the metal of the airshaft moved with a heavy clunking sound as she pressed against it, Nola didn't stop. It didn't matter if a guard heard. If she stopped, she would be caught. Her pulse thundered in her ears as she climbed, gaining mere inches in height with each step. Her arms shook, her legs cramped, but she couldn't stop.

Kieran.

She took a step.

Kieran will come tonight, and he'll take the medicine to Eden.

Another step.

Once Eden is well, she can grow up strong.

Another step.

Then she'll take ReVamp.

Nola's grip faltered, and she slid down an inch. She jammed her arms into the walls as hard as she could.

Shadows moved above. A foot higher, and she would be to the next level. Nola inched up to the grate. Through the latticed metal, she could see rows of bunks. The guards' housing. And on the other side an office, with the only visible chair empty.

Her fingers shaking, Nola dragged herself onto the ledge by the office, and with the last ounce of energy her legs could muster, kicked the grate away. Gasping and shaking, she threw herself onto the office floor.

Nola lay on the carpet, her eyes closed, trying to convince her heart it should try to keep beating. She waited for a voice to yell—someone to scream at the girl lying on the floor. But there was nothing.

After a minute, Nola opened her eyes. The office was small and empty. A desk and a chair sat in front of a tower of drawers. A faint humming filled the room. Still shaking, Nola pushed herself to her feet, searching for the source of the sound. It couldn't be an alarm. Not with a noise that steady.

A picture of Captain Ridgeway with Gentry and Jeremy perched on one corner of the desk. The Captain wore civilian clothes, and all three of them smiled broadly. Jeremy was shorter than Gentry, so the picture must have been a few years old at least. Nola reached for the picture, wanting to study the normality of it.

The humming stopped her. It came from the drawers. Nola placed her hand on the metal tower. It was cold, like the cabinets below.

Glancing at the office door, Nola quietly fitted the grate back into the wall and opened the buzzing cabinet.

Tiny vials lined the cold drawer. Like the one in her pocket but filled with deep black fluid.

"I don't think it's the vents." The voice traveled up the shaft.

Nola snapped the drawer shut, tearing toward the door. She turned the handle and pulled the door open just a crack. There was no one in sight, though she could hear voices in the distance. Nola ran her hands over her hair in a hopeless attempt to smooth down her curls, and stepped into the hall.

She walked slowly and deliberately, hoping no one would notice the dust on her clothes.

Two men came out of the barracks. They looked Nola over before one elbowed the other and winked at her. The two men laughed softly as they went down the hall.

Nola blushed. They thought she was down here with a guard.

At least they haven't arrested me. Yet.

Half-running, she sped down the hall and up the stairs. She turned a corner and slammed into a group of terrified looking people.

"Sorry." Nola reached for the vial in her pocket before she could stop herself.

If the three she'd run into noticed anything strange, it didn't show as they murmured their apologies and continued toward seed storage. All three wore maintenance uniforms and anxious looks on their faces. They should be worried if Lenora blamed them for the lost seedlings. Nola waited until the workers were out of sight then sprinted the rest of the way up to the atrium.

Nola staggered at the bright light and fresh clean air of the atrium. She wanted to sit on the floor and cry. She was out of the dark and aboveground. The bright green leaves on the trees rustled as the vent blew out air. They were running harder than usual, probably testing the system. That was good. Nola nodded to herself. The more air through the vents, the less likely anyone would notice sweaty handprints.

"Nola!" a voice called across the atrium.

Nola froze, unsure whether to run or not, then finally settled on turning to see who had shouted for her.

"Nola!" Jeremy said again as he ran toward her.

The people who had been enjoying the calm of the atrium scowled at him as he passed.

"Where have you been?" he said as he reached her. He wasn't even out of breath. All of his preparation for guard training was paying off.

"Nola?" he said again, this time with concern in his voice as he took her shoulders.

"Yes?" Nola said.

"You missed our time in the greenhouse," Jeremy said.

She had been gone longer than just lunch. Mrs. Pearson would want to know where she had been.

"I went to see my mom," Nola said. "One of her experiments went wrong, she was upset..."

"And you ran for it?"

That was right. More or less.

Nola nodded.

"I'm sorry," Jeremy said, brushing the sweaty hair from Nola's face. "It must have been some run."

Nola tried to smile at his joke.

Jeremy took her hand and led her down a side path, away from the still glaring bystanders. He stopped under the low-hanging branches of a tree, out of sight of the rest of the atrium.

"Are you sure that's all that's wrong?" Jeremy said softly. "Because you could tell me. Whatever's wrong, whatever's bothering you, you can trust me. You know that, right?"

"I do."

"It's just," Jeremy began, looking down at Nola's hand clasped in his, "I'm here for you. If you were worried about being alone when your mom was away, I could've, I mean, we could've spent time together. Because I want... I want to be with you, Nola. All the time."

Jeremy's hand stroked her hair, then rested on the back of her neck. And he was kissing her. Gently, he pulled her in close, lifting her up so she stood on her toes. His heart pounded so hard the beats resonated through her chest. Nola froze as something in her pocket pressed against Jeremy's hip.

She gasped and took a step back.

"Nola." Jeremy reached toward her.

She pulled her hand away from him without knowing she had moved.

"I'm sorry," Jeremy said, his face red and his eyes filled with hurt. "I thought, I thought you felt the same as me."

Nola's mind raced as she tried to think of feelings beyond fear. The vial in her pocket burned her leg as though it were on fire. Surely Jeremy could see the flaming vial, the proof of her betrayal.

He knows what I did.

"Just forget it," Jeremy said. "Forget I ever... It won't happen again. But I meant what I said. If you need me, I'm here." He turned and walked down the path.

She should let him go, get the vial back home, and wait there for Kieran. Jeremy was disappearing through the branches.

"No." Nola ran after him, taking his hand.

He turned to look at her, his eyes bright and brow furrowed.

"Forget this happened," Nola said. Her mouth had gone dry. She didn't know what she was saying as the words came tumbling out. "Forget you kissed me and I was a sweaty mess who can't manage to think right now."

Jeremy nodded. Pain still filled his face.

"But try it again," Nola said. "Not today. But sometime."

Nola turned and ran through the atrium. She needed to get away before Jeremy asked questions she couldn't answer.

Back through the tunnel and into Bright Dome. She had already missed class. There was no point in going back. There would be no more trouble for missing evening lessons. Up the walk and into her home, Nola shut the door behind her, leaning against it and panting.

She closed her eyes. She had the medicine. She'd finished her job. Now all she had to do was wait for tonight and Kieran would come for the vial. But Jeremy had kissed her. Nola slid down to sit on the floor, trying hard not to think of Jeremy kissing her. Of his warm arms around her.

There were more important things to worry about than if she wanted to be kissing Jeremy in the atrium right now. She slipped her fingers into her pocket and pulled out the tiny vial. She held it up, and the light shone through the orange liquid. There was so little in the tube.

Is this really all it takes to save a little girl's life?

Nola pushed herself to her feet and climbed the steps to her room, absent-mindedly grabbing a bowl full of fruit along the way.

Setting the vial on her desk, Nola popped a sweet grape into her mouth. How desperate would you have to be to take Vamp and give up food like this? Nola pulled her drawer out from her desk and set it on her bed. Vial in hand, she reached all the way to a tiny recess at the very back. Carefully, she slid the drawer back into place. It was as though the vial had never existed.

Nola curled up in bed, staring at the drawer. The sun hadn't set yet. It would be hours before Kieran came. Her arms and legs burned. Fatigue muddied her brain. Slowly, her eyes drifted shut.

Darkness filled her room when she woke up. The sun had gone down, and the house was quiet.

The dim clock in the wall read well after eleven. Her mother must have been home for a while. Nola moved to sit up but froze as a shadow shifted.

"It's me," Kieran whispered, taking a step into the pale strip of light that came through the window. "I didn't want to startle you."

"It's okay," Nola whispered, pushing herself to her feet. "I got the vial."

Kieran took a deep breath, catching Nola's hands as she reached for the drawer and pulling her to his chest.

"I thought they'd caught you." Kieran pressed his lips to her forehead. "I was watching the domes. People were coming in and out, looking at the air vents."

"There was something wrong with the climate control." Nola rested her cheek on Kieran's chest. "I had to climb up the vent. I ended up in the Guard barracks."

Kieran pulled away to look into her eyes. "I'm so sorry, Nola. I never should have let Emanuel get you involved."

"He wants to save his daughter." Nola shrugged. "He needs the medicine."

"*Eden* needs the medicine." Wrinkles formed on his forehead. "I won't let Emanuel ask you to do something like that again. It's too dangerous."

"It's fine." Nola laid her fingers on his lips. They were soft, and his breath was warm.

"Nola." He took a step forward. And he was kissing her.

Her knees went weak, but his arms locked around her, holding her tight. Her heart raced as he gently parted her lips with his own.

"Kieran," she murmured, lacing her fingers through his hair.

Kieran froze and backed away, leaving Nola swaying on the spot.

"I have to go," Kieran said, his voice hoarse.

"Now?" Nola stepped in front of the door.

"I live on the outside," Kieran said. "You live in here. What are we supposed to do?"

"I don't know." The rush of heat drained from Nola's body, leaving a cold numbness in its wake.

Kieran took her hands in his. "The hardest part about leaving the domes was losing you." He ran his fingers over her cheek. "But I can't have you. I can't come in here. And I won't"—he cut Nola off before she could speak—"let you leave the domes to find me."

"I miss you." Tears spilled from her eyes, leaving warm tracks running down her cheeks.

Kieran brushed her tears away with his thumb. "I have to go. You know I'm right."

"Stay," Nola whispered. "Just for a little while." She lay down on the bed, pulling Kieran down with her.

She curled up next to him, resting her head on his chest. His heart beat slowly under her ear.

"When will I see you again?" Nola murmured.

Kieran tightened his arms around her, and she knew his answer.

Never.

Nola clung to his shirt, willing time to stop passing so he would never leave.

"Sleep, Nola," he whispered. "Just sleep."

Soon, she had drifted away to the slow rhythm of his heartbeat.

The sun streaming through the windows woke Nola with a gasp the next morning. She sat up, looking for Kieran, but her room was empty. There was no mark on the bed where he had been—if he had even been there at all.

"Kieran," Nola whispered, opening her closet. Her clothes hung in an undisturbed row. She turned back to her room. The fruit bowl sat empty on her desk.

Nola yanked the drawer free, letting it clatter to the floor. She felt into the back corner. The vial was gone. But something small had taken its place.

A slip of paper wrapped around something hard. Nola unfurled the paper and found a little charm. A tiny tree, delicately carved out of wood. Nola held the charm up to the light. A barren tree with a split on one side, a perfect copy of the tree that hid the forest entrance to Nightland.

Nola looked down at the paper. At the note in Kieran's untidy scrawl.

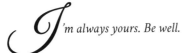

I'm always yours. Be well.

*N*ola sank to the floor. He was gone. Kieran Wynne had left the domes. Again.

13

"Nola," her mother's voice came through the door. "Are you awake?"

"Yeah," Nola said, forcing her voice to sound normal, like she hadn't just lost her best friend.

Again.

Nola's mother poked her head through the door. "Good. I was worried when I came home last night and you were already asleep."

"I'm fine," Nola said. "Just tired, really tired."

"Well, come on down. I brought some treats from Green Leaf." Her mother winked and left.

The attendees of Green Leaf always brought food with them—rare fruits that were only grown in their own domes. Nola's stomach rolled in disgust.

Kieran had stolen a bowl of grapes. She could picture him, Dr. Wynne, and Eden sharing the fruit. They were probably the only people in Nightland who could eat it. And they would sit in the kitchen, savoring every bite. While she ate papayas and pomegranate seeds.

Nola went to the bathroom and looked in the mirror. Her curls surrounded her face like a tangled lion's mane. The dark circles under her eyes made her look as ill as an outsider.

Her hands shook as she splashed cold water onto her face.

She swallowed the scream the smell of the soft, clean towel sent to her throat.

Gripping the edge of the sink, she stared into the mirror. "You've done your part, Magnolia. It's over."

She picked up the comb and tore it through her hair on her way to the kitchen. She didn't care about the pain as she brushed away the last of the filth from the vents. Had it not been for the tiny tree in her pocket, it would have been as though it had never happened at all.

Nola ate her breakfast silently as her mother griped about the subpar maintenance of the cooling system.

"It's pathetic really." Lenora sipped her tea. "We're trying to preserve the resources the world has given us, and they look at me like I'm overreacting when they endanger our seed supplies. Like I'm worried *I* might overheat."

"Right." Nola nodded.

Has Eden taken the medicine yet?

"And I'll be busy enough as it is without having to worry about faulty cooling systems." Lenora took the empty plates from the table and set them in the sink. "We're going to have to start working on the greenhouse consolidation within the next few days if we're going to get the rainforest dome prepped for planting by the end of the month."

"Right."

How long will it take for the Pataeris to take effect?

"Well, I'll see you tonight." Lenora walked out the door without looking back.

"Have a good day, Mom," Nola murmured to the empty house. "I kissed two boys yesterday and stole dome medicine to save a vampire's kid. See you tonight."

Nola grabbed her tablet and headed out of the house. Dark clouds loomed over the horizon. A deep green tint shaded the sky. Acid rain would be falling on the city in a few hours, burning anyone who strayed outside. Destroying any hope for unprotected crops.

"First acid rain of the year," a voice came from over Nola's shoulder. Gentry Ridgeway limped toward her. "It'll make things worse in the city. A few people had managed to grow a bit of food but—" she shrugged.

The growers would have to start over again.

"How are you?" Nola asked, looking from the cut on Gentry's forehead to the brace on her leg.

"I'll be fine." Gentry blew a bit of her short, blond hair away from her eyes. "Busted leg and a cut-up head. Dad just likes to overreact and tell everyone in the domes I got banged up."

"He worries about you."

"And I worry about Jeremy." Gentry limped a step closer to Nola. "Look, I try not to get involved in my baby brother's life. He's a good kid. He'll be a great guard. And for some reason, he's decided he's head over heels for you."

Heat leapt into Nola's cheeks.

"I don't know what happened between you two yesterday, and quite frankly I don't care," Gentry pressed on, "but I think we can both agree Jeremy is the nicest guy you're going to be able to find in this place. Right?"

"Jeremy's great," Nola said.

"Add that to the fact that he actually likes you, and I see you as one really lucky girl." Gentry pulled herself up to her full height, seeming to tower over Nola. "So, whatever you said that got him all confused yesterday, fix it. I don't care what you have to figure out, or how you have to do it. That boy would walk through fire for you."

"I didn't—I never," Nola pressed her fists to her temples, trying to squeeze all her thoughts together into something that made sense.

"I know you never tried to get him to go all crazy for you, but it happened," Gentry said. "And I don't want to see him hurt. So, make a choice and stick to it. You're a nice girl, Nola. You should get a nice guy. This isn't Romeo and Juliet. This is the domes. You pick someone, and you build a life."

"I'm seventeen," Nola said. "Jeremy is wonderful, but I just—"

"Don't explain anything to me. If you don't want Jeremy, that's your deal. But tell him. And don't wait forever to do it."

Nola nodded, tears stinging the corners of her eyes.

"Now get to class before Jeremy freaks out and thinks you're avoiding him."

Nola nodded and walked down the stone path.

Jeremy would be waiting for her in class. Waiting to make her laugh. Wanting to hold her hand. Offering a world of safety and sunlight, far away from the darkness of Nightland.

It had taken nearly three weeks to rearrange the plants in the Amber Dome to make more room for the crops from the Leaf Dome. Classes had been cancelled since all the students were needed to help transfer the fragile plants. If something went wrong and the crops were lost, the food supplies of the domes would disappear with them. All nonessential workers had been assigned to the delicate task.

The days were a blur of work—digging, sorting, and planting until the light became too dim. The domes had become a frenzy of chaos, perfect for avoiding all the Ridgeways.

Nola's mother had begun work on modifying the Leaf Dome two days before, preparing for the shipment of trees and animals that would arrive from the south domes later in the month. The soil content needed to be altered. Different fertilizers, different acidity. Everything the new rainforest would need to grow.

Sweat beaded on Nola's forehead as she hauled another bag of soil up the stairs to the dome. The air hung heavy with the scent of perspiration and fertilizer. The temperature had been turned up to mimic a tropical climate. The only one who seemed to be enjoying the heat was Nola's mother, standing in the middle of the Leaf Dome, new schematics in hand, shouting orders as plant and seed trays were loaded out of the dome.

"You know," Jeremy grunted, sending Nola stumbling as he lifted the bag she'd been dragging up the last few stairs, "there are, what, ten thousand people living in the city? Don't you think we could pay them to haul the dirt? I mean, we could do the planting, but I'm supposed to be going through the training material before I start guard training. Instead, I'm hauling glorified cow poop."

"We can't have outsiders in the domes." Nola searched for a clean place on her sleeve to wipe her forehead.

"Not even once?" Jeremy smiled cautiously.

"No," Nola said, more forcefully than she had meant to. She took a breath. "It wouldn't be fair to show them everything we have and then kick them right back out into the city." She reached up to the little tree charm that hung around her neck. It would be wrong to show Eden the clean air and bright lights of the domes. Her father couldn't live in the light anyway.

"I'm sorry." Jeremy's brow wrinkled. "It was a joke."

Nola arranged her face into a smile. "I know." She pushed out a laugh, but it sounded tinny in the humid air.

"Do you want to get some water?" Jeremy asked, holding out his dirt-covered hand, reaching for Nola's equally filthy one.

"Sure." Her stomach fluttered as she took his hand.

Water stations had been set up along the sides of the dome. Nola's mother's eyes flicked to them every few minutes, making sure no one dared slack off during the planting.

Dew clung to the outside of the water vat, and dirt from the planters' hands had turned to mud on its surface. Jeremy poured two cold glasses and, holding them both, walked away from the others in line for water.

"Here," Jeremy said, passing the glass to Nola. His fingers closed around hers. A shiver ran up Nola's arm.

She didn't know if it was from the cold of the glass or Jeremy's touch. Nola pulled away, taking a drink and turning to watch the planters.

"Are we okay?" Jeremy asked after a long pause.

"What?"

"I kissed you," Jeremy said.

Nola's breath caught in her chest as she remembered Jeremy holding her tight. The warmth of his body flooding into hers.

"And for the past three weeks you've barely spoken to me."

"I'm sorry." Nola shook her head, not knowing what else to say. She couldn't explain she hadn't been talking to anyone because all she wanted to do was scream. And she couldn't stop obsessing over not knowing if the medicine had saved Eden or if the whole thing had been pointless. And she most definitely couldn't tell Jeremy she was terrified of talking to him because if she said something wrong, Gentry might murder her.

"It's all right. I know," Jeremy whispered, taking Nola's hand in his.

"Know what?" A buzz of panic started at the back of Nola's mind.

He turned her hand over, running his thumb along the lines on her palm. "It's Kieran."

"Kieran?"

He knows. He saw Kieran come through the glass. He saw him come into my house.

"You love him." Jeremy let go of Nola's hand.

"I—what?" The buzzing vanished, leaving Nola blinking at Jeremy.

"You two were together. He got banished. You still love him," Jeremy said. His face was set, not with anger, but determination.

"We were friends," Nola said.

"You dated."

"Only for a few months."

"When they made him leave," Jeremy said, "it was like you broke."

Nola remembered. Crying in her room for days. Barely eating. Not speaking to anyone. Until Jeremy made her, forcing her everyday to become a little more human again. Making her laugh when she thought it was impossible.

And they were back there again.

"He was my best friend," Nola said, "and they took him away. But he, we, it's not like we were going to get married." But was that true? If he had stayed, would they still be together? Would they have been together for years, or for their whole lives?

A life in the sunlight with Kieran by my side.

"He was my friend, too," Jeremy said. "And I don't expect you to forget him."

"He's not dead," Nola snapped.

The workers standing by the cooler glared at her.

"He's not dead," Nola whispered. He was just outside the domes. Through the tree. She gripped the charm at her throat without thought.

"He's gone," Jeremy said. "And he's never coming back." He stepped forward, raising a hand to caress Nola's cheek. "But I'm here. I'm right here, Nola. And I'm not going anywhere."

"Jeremy," Nola whispered.

His hand smelled like soil and life. Like the domes and everything they protected.

"I think we could be something wonderful," Jeremy murmured. "I think we could be happy."

Nola looked into his eyes, and the fear that had clung to her heart for weeks faded away. She raised her hand to hold his as it rested on her cheek. "I think so, too."

Standing up on her toes, she leaned forward and brushed her lips gently against his. Her heart fluttered, and her stomach danced. But the world stayed upright. There was no rabbit hole for her to tumble through like with Kieran.

"Magnolia," an angry voice came from behind her.

Jeremy looked over Nola's head and jumped away from her as though burned.

Nola spun around to see her mother's rigidly angry face.

"Magnolia," Lenora said. "I would have expected you to show a little more respect for work that is so important to the domes. And Jeremy"—she rounded on Jeremy, who suddenly looked smaller than Lenora—"if you expect to join the Outer Guard like your father and your sister, you will have to learn some discipline. Priorities need to be respected. Especially where my daughter is concerned."

Lenora grabbed Nola by the arm and dragged her away. Past the water station, where the people now openly gawked at the Kents, through the planting lines, and to an empty section of the dome.

"Mother," Nola said as the men carrying the planting trays stopped to stare, "I can walk on my own."

"And I can see exactly what you walked into," Lenora spat.

"I'm seventeen," Nola said, yanking her arm away. "I kissed a boy. I shouldn't have stopped working, I'm sorry. But you like Jeremy."

Lenora stopped and glared at her daughter. Nola could read the battle raging in her mother's mind, warring between what she wanted to say and what she knew would be most effective.

"Jeremy has his path, and you have yours," Lenora said, her tone clipped. "You have an obligation to the domes. Above all other things, the domes come first. And *we* believe the best way to preserve the domes is by preserving the plants and people within them. Nothing more, nothing less. Jeremy Ridgeway does not fit into that plan."

Lenora took her daughter's shoulders and steered her to the far corner of the dome. A line of trays lay next to the glass, filled with spinach plants that were past their prime and tomato vines that had stopped bearing fruit for the season.

"Harvest the dirt," Lenora said.

"Dirt?" Nola examined the last few stunted carrots that had been pulled from the soil.

"Get the plants out of the dirt," Lenora said. "Put the plants on the carts for compost. Save the soil in the bins. It's still fertile. It can be used in the new Amber Dome beds once the roots from these plants are gone. When you've done that, you come straight home. You do not speak to anyone. You do not stop anywhere. You are—"

"Grounded," Nola finished for her mother.

"I'm glad you have enough sense left to figure that out." Lenora turned and stalked away, leaving Nola alone with the aging plants.

---

*D*arkness had fallen before Nola finally limped up the steps up to Bright Dome. Her back throbbed from spending hours stooped over the plants. Choosing each bit of edible food and sorting it from the dead plants to be composted, laying the food neatly on trays to be sent down to be distributed to the residents of the domes.

The lights blazed in her house as Nola walked up the worn stone path. Nola flicked her eyes up to the stars, giving a silent plea her mother wouldn't want to talk about Jeremy again.

She rubbed the dirt from her hands onto her pants before opening the kitchen door. Holding her breath she counted three seconds of silence. Maybe Lenora had fallen asleep, or better yet, was still locked in her office down in the tunnels.

"Magnolia," Lenora's voice came from the corner, "how long can it possibly take to finish a simple task?"

Nola chewed the inside of her cheek, her fatigue telling her to argue with her mother, her common sense telling her to keep quiet and hope it ended soon. Nola stepped into the bright kitchen and closed the door behind her.

"I asked you a question," Lenora said, stepping in front of Nola and blocking her path up the stairs. "Why has it taken you so long to get home?"

"I came home as soon as I was finished." Nola took a step forward, watching the dirt fall from her clothes onto the polished kitchen floor.

"Why on earth did it take you five hours to sort the trays?" Lenora snapped. "It would have taken a ten-year-old two."

"Then you should have asked a ten-year-old to do it," Nola growled, knowing it was a mistake to have spoken as soon as she saw the lines form around her mother's pursed lips.

"I asked you," Lenora said. "Did you stop to see Jeremy?"

"No." Nola dug her filthy nails into her palms. "I sorted the edibles from the scraps. Got rid of the compost, prepped the food for distribution, and labeled the soil trays for transfer. And yes, that was a lot of work, and yes, I just finished."

Lenora raised an eyebrow. "I never told you to salvage any food. Those plants were past their prime."

"There was still good food," Nola said.

"And it will do just fine as compost." Lenora waved a hand. "If I had wanted it for distribution—"

"You're just going to throw that food away?" Nola asked.

"No, we're going to compost it," Lenora said.

"But it could be eaten." Nola's mind scrambled to grasp her mother's meaning.

"We don't need it," Lenora said, walking back to her computer at the table.

"But the people in the city do," Nola said. "We could send it to them."

"There isn't enough to feed the whole city. It isn't even enough for an afternoon at the Charity Center. I appreciate your extra effort, and your coming straight home, but next time I suggest you pay closer attention to instructions."

"But the food could go to the city." Nola followed her mother to the table. "There are hungry people who need to eat."

"There isn't enough to go around." Lenora didn't look up from her computer. "Besides, the outsiders can take care of themselves. They aren't our concern. They've invented enough drugs to keep themselves plenty occupied without our getting involved."

"Mom, those people out there are dying." Nola shoved her hands through her hair, feeling the dirt crumble into the dark strands. "Even the little kids, all of them are sick. Those drugs they take are the only way they can survive."

"I know that, Magnolia." Lenora lifted her hands from her computer and folded them in her lap. "The people in the city are suffering. Their lives are filled with hardship, want, and pain, which is why we have a moral obligation to help them however we can. The Charity Center is more than enough—"

"Feeding them, what, a few times a month? Each age group only goes to the Charity Center once a month, and we call that helping? That isn't enough. We have good food here you're going to get rid of. We have clean water. We have medicine that can help them. It could save their lives!"

"We don't have enough for all of them," Lenora said, her voice growing sharp. "I know it is a difficult truth to accept. But we don't have enough resources to feed everyone. The greenhouses can only produce enough uncontaminated food to feed the population of the domes."

"Then grow more." Nola paced the kitchen. "Build another greenhouse, get rid of the new tropical plants, increase food production."

"We're trying." Lenora stood and took her daughter by the shoulders, stopping her mid-step. "What do you think the Green Leaf Conference is about? We are trying to secure the future of the human race. We have to preserve our resources—"

"But what about preserving those people?" Angry tears formed in Nola's eyes.

"We're doing our best. Everyone here is working to find a way to save what's left of our planet."

"But what if the person who could figure out how to save us all is stuck out there? What if there's some kid in the city who's smart enough to figure out how to grow enough food that no one will ever be hungry again?" Tears streamed down Nola's face.

"We'll never know." Lenora picked up her napkin and wiped her daughter's face. "I know it's terrible. I wish we could feed everyone, but we can't. The domes aren't about saving this generation. These domes were built to preserve the human race—to protect our DNA and the ability to produce healthy children. So that when we find a way to get rid of the toxins in the air and the water, there will actually be healthy humans left to carry on."

"And what about the people out there dying right now?" Nola choked through her tears.

"If a life boat isn't big enough to save everyone on a ship, that doesn't mean you let all the passengers die. You save as many as you can, and you head for shore." Lenora stared into her daughter's eyes. "It is the only way."

Nola turned away. She couldn't stand to look at her mother anymore.

"Hate me if you want," Lenora said. "It's a terrible truth. But it's one we have to live with. It's the only way we can survive."

"I don't know if I can do that." Nola didn't wait for her mother to say anything. She walked back out the kitchen door, letting it slam behind her.

Rain pounded down on Bright Dome in fierce sheets, the water tinted brown in the dim light. The rain would burn everything in its wake tonight.

How acidic would rain need to be to leave marks like the ones on Desmond's skin?

Nola wanted to run out into the rain. To scream and cry and let the world burn her for living hidden from its pain for so long. To tell the outsiders there was food and medicine waiting inside the domes.

Nola walked to the gurgling fountain at the center of the dome. Its noise was barely audible over the rain that grew harder by the minute.

Nola stuck her hands into water, washing away the dirt before splashing her face. The cold water gave her goose bumps wherever it touched her skin. It was cleaner than any of the water they had on the outside. She stood and ran to the stairs, not wanting to be near the fountain anymore. It was too lavish, too selfish.

Her feet carried her down into the tunnel before she could even think where she wanted to go.

The Iron Dome was near the very center of the compound, beside the atrium, directly above the barracks. All of the Outer Guard with families lived in that dome with the barracks beneath for unmarried guards. The Iron Dome and the barracks were the only residences where weapons were kept, the only place where metal could shield the glass walls in case of attack.

A guard waited at the top of the stairs to the Iron Dome.

"I'm here to see Jeremy Ridgeway," Nola said before he could ask, hoping the darkness would hide her tear-streaked face.

The guard stared at her for a moment before nodding and letting her pass without another word.

The homes were smaller here. Utilitarian units meant to house soldiers. There were no trees here that could block sight lines. Only low-lying plants were allowed in the Iron Dome. Nola's skin tingled with the feeling of being watched.

Jeremy's house sat on the outskirts of the dome. The only hint that the home belonged to the head of the Outer Guard was its being shaped like a slightly larger shoebox than the others.

Light streamed through the windows of the house, and voices came from the kitchen.

Nola ran a hand over her face as she tried to think. Captain Ridgeway wouldn't like her crying at his door this late at night. Nola crept around to the side of the house, hoping no guards would be lurking in the shadows, ready to shoot her with one of their shiny needles.

Nola knelt, tracing her fingers through the edge of the garden bed, searching for a few pebbles. Carefully, she tossed the handful of stones at Jeremy's window. Nola tensed at the faint clatter of the rocks against the glass. She held her breath, waiting in the dark.

Please don't be in the kitchen, Jeremy.

Jeremy's window slid open and he popped his head out, looking around. He smiled as his gaze found Nola. "Aren't I the one who's supposed to be throwing rocks at your window?"

"I just..." Nola began, but she didn't know why she had needed to see Jeremy, only that she hadn't known where else to go.

"Are you okay?" Jeremy asked, his tone shifting from light to concerned.

Nola shook her head.

She gasped and stumbled back as, in one swift movement, Jeremy vaulted out of his window and landed next to Nola with barely a noise.

"You've been training," Nola said, her voice shaking.

Jeremy didn't answer as he wrapped his arms around her. She laid her head against the hard muscles of his chest. She had never noticed them there before.

He's already becoming one of the elite.

Her breath caught in her throat as she began to cry again.

"*Shh,*" Jeremy hushed, petting her hair. "You're okay. I've got you." He held her for a moment in the darkness. Both of them flinched as a barking voice carried from the kitchen.

"Come on." Jeremy threaded his fingers through Nola's, leading her away from the house to a stand of ferns near the wall of the dome. Jeremy dropped down to his knees, hiding his height in the shadows, and pulled Nola to follow.

"What's wrong?" He pushed Nola's curls away from her face. "Is your mom that upset about us?"

"Yes," Nola said before shaking her head. "She is, but that isn't what's wrong."

"Then what is it?" Jeremy took Nola's hand and pressed her palm to his lips. "You can tell me, Nola. Whatever it is, you can trust me."

Nola's mind raced back. The I-Vent, ReVamp, the break in the glass, Kieran. She could tell Jeremy everything.

You wouldn't have to be alone anymore. You wouldn't have to lie anymore.

Jeremy would understand why she couldn't stand her mother or the idea of only saving the chosen few.

"I do trust you." Nola swallowed, tightening her grip on Jeremy's hand.

Light splashed out of Jeremy's front door as five Outer Guard in full city uniform poured out of the house.

Jeremy dove to the side, pulling Nola out of the light and clamping a hand over her mouth.

They waited, frozen and silent until the group disappeared down the dark path.

Nola pulled Jeremy's hand from her mouth. "Why were there Outer Guard in full city uniform in your house?"

"My dad's their boss," Jeremy said, his voice tight.

"Guards only wear those uniforms when they leave the domes," Nola said. "Why would they be hanging out in your house like that? If they're going on patrol, they should be leaving from the barracks."

Jeremy looked to the house. The kitchen door was closed. "My dad doesn't trust the Dome Guard right now."

"Why?" Nola asked. "The Outer Guard and the Dome Guard are the same. They're just an extension of each other."

"You can't tell anyone," Jeremy said. "My dad wouldn't have told me, except I'll be in training next month. And Gentry has been going out with the patrols lately. I started figuring out something was going on."

Nola nodded.

"The Outer Guard have found a den. It's a bunch of Vampers all living underground together." Jeremy glanced back at the house. "The Dome Guard think it's not our business. That the Vampers should be able to do what they like on their side of the river. But the Outer Guard, they're out there on the street every night. The wolf packs running around are bad enough, but that many Vampers, if they decided to come after the domes..."

"We couldn't stop them."

Raina and Julian breaking through the glass. The people from the club coming in search of blood.

It would be a massacre.

"But why would they want to attack us?" Nola said.

"They don't understand what we're doing in here." Jeremy swept his hands up to the glass of the dome. "We're trying to save the world. We live trapped in here for the good of the species."

Trapped in a lifeboat while the rest of the world drowns.

"It's okay." Jeremy pulled Nola to his chest, pressing his lips to her hair. "They're close to figuring out where the den is. Once they do, the Outer Guard will go in—"

"And what?" Nola's mouth went so dry she could barely form the words.

"Neutralize the threat." Jeremy looked deep into Nola's eyes. "I won't let anyone hurt you."

Eden. Tiny little Eden couldn't hurt anyone if she tried.

"What if they don't want to hurt us," Nola whispered, her voice trembling. "What if all they want is to survive? And they have to live underground to protect themselves?"

Jeremy leaned in, brushing his lips against Nola's. "You always want to believe in the good in the world. I think that's why I love you."

Nola forgot how to breathe as Jeremy kissed her, holding her close to his chest. Nola pushed away, falling back onto the grass, her heart racing as her body remembered she needed air.

"Jeremy—"

"Don't say anything now." He stood and reached down, pulling Nola to her feet. "I know it's a lot. But it's true. I love you, Nola." He took her hand, turning it over to kiss her wrist.

Her knees wobbled as tingles ran up her arm.

"And I can wait." Jeremy smiled. "I can wait till you're ready."

A bubble of pure joy washed away all thought. There was nothing in the world but his brown eyes and his smile meant only for her.

The lights in Jeremy's living room flicked off.

Jeremy cursed. "I have to go." He kissed Nola on the top of the head. "I'll see you in the morning."

He ran toward the house and vaulted through his window before Nola could remember why she had come to the Iron Dome.

The food.

She was angry with her mother for not wanting to share the domes' food with the people the Outer Guard were going to attack.

Nola's hands trembled as she reached for the tree pendant at her throat.

Kieran.

If the guards went into the tunnels, they would find Kieran. Nola looked up at the sky. Rain still pounded down on the glass. Did the guards already know about 5th and Nightland? How long would it take them to get there?

Keeping her eyes front, Nola walked back to the guard at the stairs. His helmet and coat hung on the wall next to him.

"Captain Ridgeway wants you at his house," Nola said. Her voice sounded far away as though someone else were speaking. "He heard someone prowling around."

The guard nodded stiffly before running toward the Ridgeway house. Grabbing the coat and helmet from the wall, Nola bolted down the stairs, not bothering to wonder what the guard would think when Captain Ridgeway told him there had been no prowler.

16

The oversize coat hung down over Nola's hands. But she would need the protection from the rain. She'd already tucked the inner glass to the side. Nola's fingers slid across the outer glass, slipping on the condensation.

"Please just move," Nola whispered. What had been such a simple plan when she took the guard's jacket now seemed impossible.

What if I can't find the tree in the rain? What if the door is locked from the other side?

Gripping the glass, she pulled with all her might, not letting up as she felt a jagged edge slice into her fingers. Finally, the glass moved and she pushed it aside, sucking on the cut. She would have to be more careful putting it back when she came home.

Nola shoved the helmet onto her head. The stench of someone else's sweat flooded her nose, overpowering the acrid scent of the night. Wrapping her hands tightly in the coat, she crawled out into the rain, twisting carefully to replace the glass before standing up and running down the hill.

She didn't bother searching for guards. She wouldn't be able to see them coming through the rain, which pounded down on her coat. She could feel the weight of each drop as it struck the fabric. She had never dreamed rain could have such weight—that each drop would have individual definition.

The sound of her breathing and the rain striking the helmet matched the pounding of her heart as she ran down the hill toward the forest.

Her heel slipped out from underneath her, and before she could try to right herself, she slid down the hill. She screamed as something struck her spine. Digging her bare hands into the mud, she finally stopped, lying on her back. The helmet had somehow stayed on. Rain and mud smeared the visor.

Nola pushed herself up. Tears flowed from her eyes as pain shot from her spine. The skin on her hands burned from the rain. Nola wiped them on her pants, but it was no good. Her hands still stung. She looked back over her shoulder. The dim lights of the domes were barely visible.

Her bed and her shower were at the top of the hill. A doctor who could make the pain in her hands stop was at the top of the hill.

She turned back to the trees, scrambling to her feet. Her ankle throbbed as she walked into the forest. She searched the darkness for a barren tree with a slit she could climb through. But in the rain, all the trees looked the same. Nola glanced back at the domes. She had been able to see Bright Dome when she came out of the tree with Kieran. Squinting through the visor, she tried to make out which dim light was Bright Dome. It was hidden behind the Amber Dome with its wide stance and low ceiling. Nola walked left, closer to the bridge into the city, studying each tree as she went.

A shadow passed in front of her. Nola dove behind the nearest tree, pressing herself into its shadow. Her breath came in quick gasps. The Outer Guard. If they had found the tree, they would find Nightland.

If they find me...

Nola peered around the side of the tree, searching for the moving shadow. And there it was, fifty feet in front of her. The tree that hid the entrance to Nightland. Nola waited for a moment, holding her breath, searching for an Outer Guard in the night. Nothing moved.

Run, Nola, you need to run! the voice inside her head shouted, but her feet wouldn't move.

Ten seconds, Nola. Her father's voice echoed in her memory. *You get ten seconds to panic. Then you're done. That's all you're allowed.*

Nola nodded.

Ten, nine, eight, seven...

What if the Outer Guard were already through the door?

Six, five...

What if they had already found Dr. Wynne's Laboratory?

Four, three...

Kieran.

Nola ran toward the tree, ignoring the pain that shot through her back and the grip of the mud as it tried to steal her shoes. Her fingers closed around the edge of the bark as she pulled herself through the opening.

Crack!

Pain shot through her head before burning cut through her ribs. Blackness overtook her before the scream left her mouth.

17

Her mouth tasted like dirty cotton. She tried to lick her lips, but her tongue cracked with the movement. She tried to take a breath, but pain shot through her lungs, and a cough caught in her sandpaper-like throat.

She opened her eyes. Spots danced in her vision, blocking out the scene around her. The lights in the room were bright—much, much too bright.

The medical wing. I must be in the medical wing.

But the skin on her hands still burned.

Nola tried to lift her hands to look at them; it felt like sand had filled her arms, making them too heavy to move properly. The skin on her hands was red against the white light.

"Nola," a voice breathed.

Footsteps pounded across the floor, and Dr. Wynne and Kieran hovered over her, their faces blurred.

"Nola." Kieran knelt, taking Nola's hand. The cold of his fingers soothed her skin.

"What—"

"Don't try to speak." Dr. Wynne disappeared from view, coming back with a cup in his hand. "You need to drink."

Kieran lifted Nola's head. She gasped as pain shot through her skull. "Sorry," he whispered before tipping cool liquid into Nola's mouth. It tasted metallic and stale, but it coated her throat and made it easier to breathe. Kieran sat on the bed, lifting Nola to lean against his chest before giving her more of the foul fluid.

"Where am I?" Nola asked after a few sips.

"Nightland," Kieran said.

Nola's mind raced. Back to the tree. To the pain. "But the Outer Guard. They found me."

Dr. Wynne looked at Kieran before speaking. "It wasn't the Outer Guard. It was our guard."

"Why in Hell were you wandering through the woods in a guard's uniform at night?" Kieran said, anger creeping past the concern in his voice. "They thought you were trying to break in. They almost killed you. If they hadn't recognized you, they would have."

"I had to tell you," Nola said, remembering her urgency and coughing in her haste.

Kieran lifted more water to her mouth.

"There's no time." Nola pushed the cup away. "I only have a few hours."

Kieran glanced to his father. "Nola, you've been here for two days."

The bed swayed. Her head spun, blurring the room around her.

Two days. Nola tried to reason through the words. *I've been here for two days.*

"That can't be right." Nola shook her head and the world danced in bright spots.

"Careful." Kieran steadied her as she tipped toward the edge of the bed. "We patched you up as best we could, but you need to be careful."

"They'll know I'm gone." Nola pictured her mother calling for her when she didn't come out of her room in the morning. Did she think Nola had snuck out to be with Jeremy? And Jeremy. What did he think when Nola's mother came searching for her? How long did it take them to figure out she was gone? Had she already been banished in absentia?

"Why on earth did you come out in the rain?" Dr. Wynne pressed something cold and metallic against Nola's forehead. "You could have gotten lost in the storm, or sick from the rain, you aren't used to the toxicity. And then being stabbed on top of it all."

"Stabbed?" Nola asked, remembering a searing pain in her back.

"They thought you were trying to infiltrate Nightland," Kieran said. "They didn't mean to hurt you."

"The Outer Guard." Nola pushed away from Kieran to seize Dr. Wynne's hands. "I have to talk to Emanuel. I have to see him right now."

"Why?" Dr. Wynne said. "I know it must be frightening to be away from the domes for so long, but you're safe here."

"No one is safe here." Nola twisted to throw her legs off the bed. Every muscle in her body ached. "The Outer Guard. They know about Nightland. They're trying to find a way in. They might already know how. You have to get everyone out."

Dr. Wynne and Kieran exchanged silent glances.

"I'll go," Kieran said, lifting Nola and laying her back on the bed. "Stay. Let him take care of you. I'll be right back." He disappeared behind the head of the bed, and the slam of a door shook the room a moment later.

"Well," Dr. Wynne said, sitting next to Nola's bed, "you have a concussion. But you're awake, so a good rest is all we can do for that. The knife didn't go too deep, and thankfully it missed all the really important bits or you would have bled to death before they got you to me. You've been stitched up, and I've given you everything I can to make sure you don't get an infection."

"There's a hole in me?" Nola said, bile burning her throat at the thought.

"Yes, and no." Dr. Wynne took off his glasses and cleaned them on his shirt. "I may have tried something a little… experimental."

"Experimental?"

"I needed to heal the wound as quickly as possible, and we have such limited resources." Dr. Wynne's hands fluttered through the air.

"What did you do?"

"Well, after doing as much as I could"—Dr. Wynne looked at the ceiling—"I gave you a few tiny injections of ReVamp."

Nola's heart raced as though trying to prove its lack of humanity.

"It was all very localized," Dr. Wynne added quickly. "You should have no long term effects. Your body temperature and heart rate are still very normal. And I must say the wound has healed exquisitely. Once you're rehydrated and can get up and moving, I would say you should be just fine in a few days. Maybe less. As I said, it was an experiment. And the rate of healing has been extraordinary."

"So, you didn't make me a…" Nola couldn't bring herself to say the word.

"Vampire?" Dr. Wynne shook his head. "No. Though if you hadn't woken up soon, a full injection may have been the only choice. But it seemed, under the circumstances, that your return to the domes would be infinitely more difficult if you had become a vampire."

"I don't think they'll take me back." Nola stared at her red hands. "I left. I went outside, without permission, to help vampires. I don't think that's the sort of thing the domes will take me back from."

"Don't give up hope yet," Emanuel's voice came from behind the bed.

Nola struggled to sit up, and in a moment Kieran sat beside her, supporting her weight.

"Emanuel," Nola began, the words tumbling out, "the Outer Guard. They know about Nightland. They know there's a huge group of vampires living together underground. They think you're all working together, planning to attack the domes. And they're looking for you. They want to destroy you. And they're getting closer to finding you. They could be at 5th and Nightland right now, trying to break in. You have to get everyone out of here. It's not safe anymore."

Emanuel considered Nola for a moment, his black eyes narrowed. "How do they know about Nightland?"

"I have no idea," Nola said. "But they do."

"How do you know?" Emanuel asked.

"Jeremy Ridgeway." Nola's face flushed.

Emanuel's eyes flicked to her cheeks, and more heat flooded her face.

"His father is the head of the Outer Guard," Nola said. "I saw guards coming out of his house in full uniform. I asked why, and Jeremy told me."

"Why?" Emanuel asked. "Is it common knowledge in the domes?"

"No." Nola shook her head. "Jeremy's father told him about Nightland because Jeremy is joining the Outer Guard next month. And Jeremy told me because"—Nola thought of Jeremy sitting with her in the dark—"because he trusts me."

Kieran stiffened by her side.

"And why did you come to tell us?" Emanuel turned his gaze to the ceiling. "Why did you place warning us over the trust of Jeremy?"

"Because," Nola said, balling her red, scarred hands into fists, "you are good people. It's not your fault you have to live out here. You're doing the best you can. You aren't going to attack the domes, so how could I let the guards attack you? It would be a slaughter. They have weapons—"

"We are well guarded." Emanuel knelt in front of Nola, taking her hands in his own. "We have more protection than the guards can comprehend. But knowing they are coming, we can ensure that when they arrive we can turn them away without unnecessary violence. You have saved lives in coming here, Nola. You were incredibly brave."

"Thank you." The words caught in Nola's throat.

"I will make sure you are not punished for your bravery," Emanuel said. "We will find a way to get you home."

"They won't want me."

"There may be a way. A way that will get you home and save lives in Nightland." Emanuel stood to leave. "Kieran, please see that she has food and fresh clothing. I'll go speak to the others and see what we can think up to save our hero." He nodded to Nola and left.

"I'll be right back," Kieran said, gently squeezing Nola's hand before following Emanuel.

"Well," Dr. Wynne said after a long moment. "Let's check your bandages, shall we?" He pushed his glasses up on his nose. "Lean forward."

It wasn't until that moment Nola realized she wasn't wearing her own clothes. She had been changed into an old hospital gown. It was worn, soft, and tattered around the edges.

Nola winced as Dr. Wynne pulled the sticky bandage from her skin.

"Hmmm," Dr. Wynne murmured as he ran his fingers across her back.

"What?" Nola asked. "Is it infected? Am I becoming a vampire?"

"Not a bit," Dr. Wynne said. "It's even better than I expected."

Nola pushed herself to her feet, tottering for a moment before stumbling to the cracked mirror in the corner of the room. Pulling the robe down over her shoulder, she twisted to see her back in the mirror.

"Careful," Dr. Wynne warned. "You don't want to tear anything that's newly mended."

Then her eyes found it. A red, raised, jagged mark three inches long right under her left shoulder blade.

"You're very lucky you were wearing the guard's coat. Otherwise the knife would have penetrated your lungs. And that"—Dr. Wynne spread his hands —"would have been a very different story."

"It looks like it happened months ago," Nola said, trying to touch the mark.

"She shouldn't be standing," Kieran said as he came back through the door, balancing a plate on top of a pile of clothes.

"I feel better standing." Nola studied her face in the mirror. She looked pale, like she hadn't slept for days, but otherwise healthy. The only marks on her were the scar on her back and the red of her hands.

"You should feel better the more you move." Dr. Wynne smiled. "I gave you another tiny bit of ReVamp this morning." He waved away the frightened look on Nola's face. "You needed it to heal. And as I said, no lasting effects. And the more the drug is circulated, the better you'll recover."

"That's remarkable." Nola rubbed her fingers over the tight red skin on her hands.

"It seemed a bit much," Dr. Wynne said, his brows furrowed, "to give you localized ReVamp injections in your hands just to fix the inflamed skin. The chance for infection is so small, it's really only cosmetic damage, and they can mend that in the domes."

If I ever get back into the domes.

"Thank you." She pushed her face into a smile. "Thank you for saving my life. ReVamp...what it can do is amazing. We don't have anything that can do this in the domes."

"You need to eat," Kieran said, pulling out the desk chair and setting down the plate of food.

"Right." Nola swallowed the lump in her throat. Her stomach rumbled at the sight of food. She hadn't eaten since the domes.

She looked down at the food on the plate. Some sort of chopped vegetables she had never seen before lay next to a hunk of bread and a small bit of meat.

"I know it's not what you're used to," Kieran said, handing Nola a fork as she sat down at the desk, "but it's not bad."

"But will," Nola said, glancing between Kieran and Dr. Wynne, "will it make me sick?"

"This is good food," Dr. Wynne said. "It's the best we have."

"I'm sorry," Nola said. "I didn't mean—"

"It would take years for you to get sick from this," Kieran said. "It may not be dome-pure, but Nightland spends a lot of time finding the best soil we can. We work hard to keep the irrigation water clean. This is better than anything you'll get on the streets."

"Thank you," Nola said. "For sharing." She took a bite of the vegetables, trying not to wrinkle her nose at the metallic taste of the food.

"That's the ReVamp." Dr. Wynne perched on the edge of the desk. "The unfortunate taste should dissipate as you metabolize more food. The meals here really aren't that bad."

"Why do vampires grow food?" Nola choked down another bite.

"For the kids," Kieran said. "For the people in the city who don't have anything to eat."

"Vampires feed people?"

"The ones in Nightland do," Kieran said. "Emanuel doesn't want to keep everyone in Nightland forever."

Dr. Wynne stood, clapping his hands together. "I'm sure Emanuel will be back any minute with a plan to get Nola out of here, and she should be dressed." He walked out of the room, holding the door open for Kieran to follow.

"I'll be right back," Kieran said.

The door shut behind them, leaving Nola alone. She took a bite of the bread, hoping the tinny taste would be different. It wasn't.

She picked up the clothes that had been left for her. Thick black pants and a stitched-together black leather top. Both were worn and patched in places.

Nola dug the heel of her hand into her forehead. She was alive, that was good. They wanted to get her back to the domes, also good. Dr. Wynne was hiding something from her. Badly. Not so good.

18

She pulled on the clothes without letting herself consider the rough texture of the leather against her bare skin. They had been made for someone larger than her, with muscle and curves Nola lacked.

A knock sounded on the door.

"Are you dressed yet?" Kieran called.

"Yes?" Nola said tentatively, staring at her pale face and leather-clad body in the mirror.

I look like I belong in Nightland.

Kieran came in, not bothering to suppress his laugh as he saw her.

"Thanks." Nola grimaced, taking another bite of the bread and instantly regretting it as the metallic taste flooded her mouth.

"You look great." Kieran ran a hand through his hair. "Just not like you. It's going to take them a while to figure things out. Emanuel has a grand plan, but they still have to iron out the details."

"What kind of grand plan?" Nola pushed the food around her plate, searching for an appetizing bite.

"Emanuel doesn't usually share his plans with me," Kieran said, his face darkening for a moment, "but I trust him."

"What were you saying before, about Emanuel wanting to get people out of Nightland?" Nola looked into Kieran's eyes, seeking a real answer.

"Nothing."

"Then why did your father make you leave?"

Kieran grinned. "You know him so well."

Nola waited in silence.

"There's a lot of land, other places away from the domes," Kieran whispered, his words flowing more quickly as he spoke. "There are places where the soil isn't as bad. Where there isn't a polluted river in the backyard. The domes were built here because they needed the city for laborers. But they abandoned the city as soon as the domes were ready. Why should we sit here waiting to die if there's something better out there?" He stretched his arms to the sky through the dirt above them.

"Why didn't your father want me to know?"

"Emanuel doesn't want the domes to know." Anger crept into his voice. "He's worried they won't want us to build a good place of our own."

"Aboveground?"

"For Eden," Kieran said. "The vampires can't stay in the light."

"But the food," Nola asked. "Do you grow it underground?"

"I was sort of hoping you'd ask." Kieran's eyes gleamed with excitement. "I think you'll be amazed with what we've done." He stood, walking toward the door before reaching a hand back to Nola. "Come with me?"

Nola stood and took his hand, not caring where he led her.

They were in the same part of Nightland where she had seen Eden. They passed the kitchen, but the little girl with the big brown eyes was nowhere to be seen.

"Eden," Nola asked as they slipped into the gallery, "is she—"

"She's fine." Kieran beamed. "The medicine helped. She can breathe now. I actually had to chase her this morning. We had a hard time keeping her out of your room."

"Why?"

He led her out into the tunnel and in the direction of 5th and Nightland.

"You're her hero, Nola," Kieran said, stopping and turning to face Nola so quickly she ran into him. "Literally. You saved her life." He ran a finger over her cheek. "You are braver than even I imagined." He turned and continued walking down the hall. "And now you've come to save all of us."

"The Outer Guard," Nola said as Kieran pushed through a heavy metal door and into a narrower tunnel. The low ceiling left only a few inches of clearance over Kieran's head. "Emanuel may think they can't get into Nightland, but they could. They're..." She searched for a less cowardly word than *terrifying*. "You know them. They aren't like everyone else in the domes. If they decide to come in here, they won't stop because they're destroying your home."

"Or killing people," Kieran growled. "I know. *We* know. But they don't know us. And when they try to come after us, they'll see. This isn't their city. It's ours."

They walked in silence for a moment, the tunnel becoming narrower and the lights dimmer. Sweat beaded on Nola's palms, burning the raw skin. She could feel the anger radiating from Kieran, overpowering her panic at being in the tunnel. He stopped at a dead end. Crumbling concrete and dirt had caved in the wall in front of them.

"What happened?" Nola asked. "Did a cave-in cover the garden?"

"We found our own way up." Kieran pointed at the ceiling above him to a narrow hole and a thin metal ladder. "You first."

Nola reached above her head to the ladder, but this was more than climbing out her window or even up the vent. Her fingers only grazed the bottom of the first rung.

Kieran's hands closed around her waist, and he lifted her up over his head. Nola grabbed for the ladder, gasping. "Thanks." Her arms shook, and the skin on her palms stung as she began to climb.

With a ringing *thunk* that shook the ladder, she felt Kieran launch himself onto the bottom rung. She closed her eyes for a moment, taking a breath before continuing to climb. Soon, even the dim light from the tunnel had disappeared. Nola groped the air in front of her, feeling for each rung to pull herself up.

"How far up are we going?" she asked after a few minutes when her muscles burned in protest.

"About 124 rungs," Kieran answered.

"Was I supposed to be counting?" Nola puffed.

"Nope," Kieran said, adding slowly, "but you should start watching your head… now."

Nola froze, waiting for something to swoop out of the blackness at her face.

"Reach up," Kieran's voice drifted through the darkness.

Hesitantly, Nola reached one hand overhead. Cold, flat metal blocked the path above her. She pushed, and the metal lifted easily, letting in a flood of outside air and the faint glow of the moon through the haze of the city. Giving the door a heave, she flipped it open with a loud *clang*, then climbed out into the night and onto a roof high above the city.

Rows of plants stretched out in front of her. Scraps of every kind had been used to make raised beds for the garden. A row of beans was surrounded by planks of an old painted sign for *The Freshest Oxygen Bar in Town*. An apple tree grew in the broken bed of a truck. Rows of melons sprouted from the base of an old shipping container.

"How?" Nola breathed, running her fingers along the leaves of a plant. The texture was perfect. No damage from the acid rain, no signs of blight.

"It takes a lot." Kieran leapt onto the edge of the old truck and pulled a red apple down from the tree. "We had to get miles away to find soil that wasn't contaminated by the old factories. It took a few months to find the right spot. By then, we had found enough planting containers, though getting them up here was a chore. We had to make sure none of the Outer Guard saw us hauling old truck beds up the side of the building."

"But they could have helped." Nola leaned in close to the apple tree and smelled the earth. The scent was different from the dirt in the domes, less pungent in its fertility, but still clean and fruitful. Free from the chemicals that flowed through the river.

"I don't think they want to help vampires." Kieran tossed the apple to Nola. "Even if the vampires are growing food for starving kids."

Nola ran her thumb along the smooth red skin of the apple. "But the forest, the trees there are dying from the rain. The chemicals burn them."

"These plants aren't watered with rain. Stay here." Kieran ran down the rows of strange planters.

Nola held the apple up to the moonlight. The fruit didn't match the size of those grown inside the glass, and the skin lacked the luscious, vibrant color expected of Lenora Kent's crops. It couldn't match the perfection of the domes.

This food can still save people's lives.

Nola looked out over the city. Only one building stood taller than the garden, blocking the light of the domes from view as though her home didn't exist at all.

The *buzz* of a rope being pulled quickly came from the direction where Kieran had disappeared. An odd flapping sound pounded all around the roof as long sheets of fabric unfurled from the sides of the plant beds. Hung from wires so dark Nola hadn't noticed them before, the cloth rose up high, floating into the sky like sails before, with a shuddering *whine*, they all turned at once, making a patchwork of fabric that covered the whole roof.

Before Nola could really begin to think through what she had just seen, Kieran had returned to her side.

Nola moved her mouth for a moment, searching for the right words.

"I designed it." Kieran beamed. "It took Desmond and Bryant a long time to find the material, but it works."

"How?" Nola gaped.

"The material is waterproof and coated against the rain. It's what the old triage tents were made of, back when there were doctors on the outside. They scavenged all of this, and then we built the pulley system. We put the fabric up to keep off the midday sun and any rain, but the rest of the time, we leave it open."

"But the water?" Nola climbed up onto the truck bed to feel the fabric. It was light and thin, but coated in something that felt rubbery, like the Outer Guard's jackets.

"The rain runs off of the tent and into a filtration system." Kieran shoved his hands into his pockets, looking every bit the proud genius Nola had known him to be. "It's rudimentary, but it gets the water for Nightland and for the plants clean enough to be used. And this is just one rooftop. If we could find the materials to farm on other roofs, we could feed the city. And if we could take all this with us, we could build a home somewhere without the smog of the factories and the stink from the river." Kieran grabbed Nola around the waist, sweeping her into his arms. "We could help people, really help them."

His dark eyes stared into hers, his gaze so intense she flushed and looked away.

"It's brilliant." Nola tucked her hair behind her ears and took a step away from Kieran.

"And it's all because of you," Kieran said. "All that studying in botanicals your mother was always making you do. It gave me the idea. I came up with the plan and built the pulley system. My dad did the chemical testing and pretty much everyone else in Nightland helped with the rest."

"And the guards never noticed?"

"We're still here." Kieran shrugged. He lifted Nola's hand that held the apple up in front of her. "Take a bite."

Carefully, Nola bit into the apple. Her teeth pierced the skin, and juice flowed into her mouth. Through the bitter metal tinge of the ReVamp, she could taste the sweetness of the fruit. "It's amazing," she whispered. "It's real food."

Kieran smiled. "I know."

Nola held out the apple for Kieran to take a bite.

"No, it's for you." Kieran shook his head, his gaze fixed on the juice dripping onto Nola's finger.

"But it's wonderful." Nola took a step toward him. "You should enjoy the fruits of your labor."

"No." The light of the moon caught the corner of his eyes. No color broke through the shadows. Only black where emerald green should have been.

Pain ripped through Nola's chest as the apple tumbled from her hand. "Kieran, you're a vampire."

19

"Nola," Kieran said, reaching toward her.

Nola took a step back. Pain shot though her leg as something sharp cut into her calf. She didn't dare look away from Kieran as warm blood trickled down her ankle.

"Nola, you're hurt." Kieran stepped forward.

"Don't touch me." Nola felt for the truck bed behind her. She stepped sideways, gasping in pain as she put weight on her leg.

"Let me help you." Pain flooded Kieran's eyes. "Nola, I would never hurt you."

"You're a vampire," Nola spat.

"So, is Emanuel—"

"That's different."

"And Raina, and Desmond. You came out here to save vampires."

"But not you!" Nola shouted. "You weren't supposed to be like them." Tears streamed down her face.

"Why?" Kieran asked. "Why does it matter?"

"You drink blood?" Nola's voice quaked.

"Yes."

Nola choked on a sob.

"But not human blood, never human blood." Kieran took a step forward.

Nola tried to run, but her leg gave out under her, sending her tumbling to her knees.

"Nola," Kieran whispered.

She could hear his heart breaking as he said her name.

"I've never attacked a human," he said, his voice cold and dead. "I only drink animal blood."

Images of Kieran sucking the life from a poor animal's neck seized Nola's mind.

"We have a farm for the animals," Kieran said. "It's no different from eating meat."

"Yes it is." Nola tried to stand, but her leg couldn't bear any weight. "I thought you were trying to save the vampires. Find a way to make them human."

"You can't go back," Kieran said. "Once you're a vampire, the change is permanent. Either inject the Vamp or die. It's a one-way trip, Nola."

Nola sobbed on the ground. Kieran's green eyes were gone.

I'll never see them again.

"I had no choice," Kieran said. "I was running out of time."

"What?"

"After three months out here, I got sick," Kieran said. "I had been giving out food, there was a cough going around. It didn't do anything that bad to most people. But I didn't have the same immunities. After a few days, I couldn't breathe. My dad didn't know what to do. He had been working on a new kind of Vamp. One that didn't change people's personalities. It wasn't ready, but he didn't have a choice. I was drowning. Drowning in my own body. I was terrified. I was dying."

He knelt next to Nola, and she didn't back away.

"He gave me a small injection of ReVamp like he did for you, trying to get the disease out of me, but it didn't work. He had to give me a full dose. It felt like my lungs were on fire. I thought I would boil in my own skin. Then my lungs filled with ice. And then my whole body was filled with ice. I was sure I would freeze to death. But eventually, I stopped shaking, and I got used to the cold. It took a few days, but I woke up." Kieran looked into Nola's eyes. "I'm the first of the new vampires."

Nola looked down at Kieran's hand in hers. She hadn't realized she had reached for him. His cold skin sent chills up her arm.

"Does it feel different? Touching me?" Nola said.

"I can feel the blood flowing through your veins like lava," Kieran said. "But the heat doesn't hurt."

"They said in the domes that vampires hunt people, that they attack them and drink their blood."

"The ones on the streets do," Kieran said. "But not in Nightland. They only take blood they pay for."

"Pay for?"

"There are desperate people in the city," Kieran said. "They sell their blood to vampires. But most of us take the blood from the farm animals."

"So, even though—" Nola glanced down at her bloody leg, her wanting to know warring with her fear of Kieran.

"I can smell your blood," Kieran said before she could speak. "It smells sweet."

"I smell like candy?"

"A little. But I'm still me. And you know me, Nola. You know I would never hurt you. I would do anything to protect you."

Nola nodded, not trusting her voice.

Kieran placed his hand on Nola's cheek. A tingle ran down her spine, leaving goose bumps in its wake.

"We should get you back to my dad," Kieran said. "I think you need stitches."

"I don't know about that ladder," Nola said. "I can't even walk."

"Do you trust me?" Kieran grinned mischievously.

He looked like the old Kieran. Her Kieran, who she knew better than anyone, planning something that would scare and excite her. The Kieran who had taught her to climb onto her roof. The Kieran who would save a city with a garden.

"Absolutely."

In one swift movement, Kieran lifted Nola onto his back. "Hold on tight." He ran to the open trap door.

"You can't carry me all the way down," Nola said as Kieran twisted onto the ladder, taking two steps down and shutting them into the darkness.

"Just trust me, Nola," Kieran said before taking both hands off the ladder and launching them into the void.

The air rushing past them stole the scream from Nola's throat. Kieran laughed as they sped through the darkness.

Nola tightened her grip, holding onto Kieran with every bit of strength she had. And just when she began to fear the ground, Kieran landed as light as a cat on the tunnel floor.

Gently, he pried Nola's arms from his neck, pulling her around to cradle her as though she weighed nothing.

"I told you to trust me." Kieran smiled.

"Mmmmhmmm," was the only noise Nola could manage as she pulled herself closer to Kieran's chest.

Kieran pressed his cheek to her hair, rocking her gently for a moment.

328 | MEGAN O'RUSSELL

"I didn't mean to scare you," he said.

"Of course you did. You always liked to scare me." Nola let go of his neck and smacked him on the chest. "But I'm not mad. It's nice to know—" Nola paused for a moment, searching for the right words. His heartbeat pounded through his chest and into her hand. Its rhythm beat slower than hers, pumping the cold blood through his body in a rhythm she didn't recognize. "It's nice to know your sense of humor hasn't changed."

Kieran beamed down at her. "Never. I'm still me, Nola. Just me with super strength… and a different appetite."

His smile disappeared, and his eyes begged her to understand.

"You're Kieran," Nola said. "You're still my Kieran."

He leaned down and brushed his lips against hers. The cold of his touch tingled her skin.

"I will always be yours," he whispered.

A door rasped open down the hall. Kieran cursed under his breath. "We need to get you back to my dad."

"It's not bleeding that badly." She didn't want to go back to the others. Back to the worn hospital gown and cold tools. If she could just stay here with Kieran for a few minutes.

"It's bad enough." Kieran walked down the tunnel.

Nola felt his muscles tensing as though he were preparing for a fight.

"I don't want to freak you out, but the other vampires will scent your blood."

"Scent my blood?" Nola looked down at her red-stained leg.

"You smell like fresh baked brownies," Kieran said, his voice tight.

"Do you need to leave me here?" Nola's voice came out as a squeak.

"I told you before, I would never bite a human." Kieran rounded the corner.

A dark shape waited for them in front of the door to the main corridor.

"But some of our people are recovering human biters," Kieran said. "We don't want them to relapse."

"What happened to her?" a deep voice called from the shadow.

"Cut her leg," Kieran said, his voice steady and calming as though he were trying to soothe a frightened animal. "I'm taking her up to my father now." Kieran took a step forward. "You know my father. Dr. Wynne."

"ReVamp." The man leaned out of the shadows. The scars covering his face twisted as he frowned. "He made ReVamp."

"Yes," Kieran said. "Have you had ReVamp?"

"I turned long before the good doctor decided to save us all." The long white scars cut through his skin as though something had clawed his face over and over again.

"Then you are one of the strongest to have joined Nightland," Kieran said, still walking forward. "It takes a special vampire to understand how we must change to survive."

"I did change to survive." The man tossed his bald head back, displaying more scars coating his neck. "I changed because my lungs were rotting. I came down here to be safe from the Outer Guard."

"Nightland is about more than being safe from the guards," Kieran said. "Nightland is about hope. It's about creating a better future."

"Nightland is about rules." The man took a step forward. "It's about protecting one man's vision while the rest of us hide underground."

"We aren't hiding," Kieran said.

Nola clung tighter to Kieran's neck as he shifted her weight in his arms.

"Every night we are working to make things better," Kieran said.

"Better for the ones who haven't been turned."

"Better for all of us." Kieran had stopped moving forward.

"Then why won't you let us eat?" the man roared.

Nola flew from Kieran's arms, landing on the ground behind him, knocking the wind from her. The thumping of fists on flesh came from behind her. The sharp crack of breaking bones and muffled yells echoed through the tunnel. Pain shot through her as she gasped, forcing air back into her lungs.

She rolled onto her side, trying to see who had been hit, but they were moving too quickly for her to know if either was hurt. The man lifted Kieran, tossing him into the wall with a sickening *crunch*. Dust from the ceiling fell into Nola's eyes as the walls trembled.

The man took Kieran's head, slamming it back into the wall.

"No!" Nola screamed.

The man turned to her. His eyes were pitch black. He opened his mouth, hissing and showing two long, bright white fangs.

20

The vampire ran his tongue along the sharp tip of his left fang, coloring its point with his own blood.

Nola watched in horror as the vampire's blood dripped down his chin, making him look more animal than human.

"Leave her alone." Kieran launched himself onto the man's neck, sending him face first into the dirt. He grabbed the man's head, slamming it into the ground again and again until the man's screams of rage stopped.

Kieran let go of the man, standing up and jumping over the blood pooling on the dirt floor.

He reached down to Nola. Red coated his palms.

Nola tried to reach for him, but she couldn't make her arms move. The crimson pool seeped toward her.

"Nola," Kieran whispered. "He was going to kill you."

The man's bloody fangs flashed through Nola's mind as tears ran down her cheeks.

"He'll wake up in a few hours," Kieran said. "But I'll make sure Raina's found him before then."

"He's dead." Nola's voice cracked.

"He's a vampire. He'll heal. But I won't let him hurt you. Not ever." Kieran reached down for Nola again. "Can I touch you?"

Nola nodded, clinging to Kieran as soon as she was in his arms. She buried her face in his chest, squeezing her eyes shut as Kieran leapt over the man's body. She could feel the uneven pounding of the floor under Kieran's feet and the air flying past them and knew he was running. She wanted to look, to watch the tunnels fly by, seeing them as Kieran did. But she kept her eyes closed, afraid if she opened them, another pair of bloody fangs would be waiting.

Soon, Kieran slowed to a walk.

A door *clicked* open in front of them.

"What happened?" a voice with a lilting accent said.

Nola opened her eyes, and Julian was staring at her, his face tense. They were in the gallery. Julian held an open book in his hand.

"She cut her leg in the garden," Kieran said, not stopping his stride as Julian joined them. "I was trying to get her back here, and we were attacked."

"Someone thought she was a dinner bell, eh?" Julian said. "Did you kill them?"

Kieran shook his head. "Just smashed his head in. He'll wake up in a bit. He's in the last tunnel on the way to the garden."

"I'll get Raina." Julian held open the door to Emanuel's home before leaving them and walking back out through the gallery.

"What's Raina going to do to him?" Nola asked.

"Nothing more than he deserves," Kieran said.

The old woman in the kitchen looked up as they passed but didn't try to follow.

"What's going to happen?" Panic clenched Nola's chest.

"Raina will execute him," Kieran said. "We all make the deal when we choose to live in Nightland. No violence within these walls. No attacking humans. No attacking each other. That man is a monster. We can't keep him here. We can't let him out in the world, or he'll leave a string of bodies behind him, and we can't give him to the Outer Guard—"

"Or he'll tell them exactly where to find us," Nola said as Kieran swung open the door to Dr. Wynne's lab.

"What on Earth?" Dr. Wynne said, pushing up his glasses as he stared at Nola. "Was she stabbed again?"

"No, she cut her leg." Kieran lay Nola down on the cold metal table. "The apple tree truck."

"And your hand," Dr. Wynne said, glancing at Kieran as he cut away the bottom of Nola's pants, exposing the jagged gash.

Nola's stomach turned at the sight of her own ragged flesh.

"Broken," Kieran said. "Foot, too."

"What?" Nola tried to sit up on the table to look at Kieran, but he grabbed her shoulder, holding her down.

"Do you need it set?" Dr. Wynne asked, seemingly unconcerned by his son's broken bones.

Kieran flexed his hand and stomped his foot a few times. "Just the hand."

"Pardon me, Nola," Dr. Wynne said, disappearing behind Nola's head. There was silence for a moment, and then a sharp *crack* and a muffled groan.

"Thanks," Kieran said, coming around to Nola's side, keeping his right hand by his chest and gripping Nola's hand with the left.

"Are you all right?" Nola asked.

Dr. Wynne fluttered around the laboratory, gathering tools.

"Fine." Kieran smiled down at Nola, only the corners of his eyes betraying any pain. "It'll be healed in an hour or so. One of the vampire perks."

"Speaking of vampire perks," Dr. Wynne said, placing a tray of tools next to Nola, "I'm afraid your food is going to be distasteful for longer than anticipated. I can stitch you back together, but you've lost a fair bit of blood, and with the rust and filth on that truck bed, the risk for infection is too significant. I'm going to stitch you back together and give you another localized dose of ReVamp."

Dr. Wynne raised a hand as Kieran began to protest. "She will be at no risk of being changed, but I don't think her mother would like her returned to the domes sans a leg."

"You're sure it won't change her?" Kieran asked. "Dad, you have to be sure."

"I am quite sure." Dr. Wynne picked up a threaded needle. "ReVamp will only affect the brain and circulatory system if it is injected directly into the blood stream. Think of this as a localized anesthetic."

Kieran opened his mouth to argue again, but Dr. Wynne waved him away. "You must trust me, Kieran. I did invent the stuff after all." He turned to Nola. "You might want to take a deep breath, dear, I have nothing to numb you with."

Nola squeezed Kieran's hand, shutting her eyes tight as the needle pierced her leg.

Her stomach seized at the tugging of the thread pulling through her skin.

"Prison," Nola said through gritted teeth, searching for something to distract her from the nauseating sensation of her flesh being violated by a needle and thread. "The man who attacked us, why can't he go to vampire prison?"

"There's no such thing as vampire prison," Kieran said with a touch of laughter in his voice.

The needle pierced Nola's leg again, and she redoubled her grip on Kieran's hand. "But we're underground. With all the tunnels, why can't you make a prison? Then you could lock him up instead of just killing him."

"We barely have the resources to keep Nightland safe from the outside," Dr.

Wynne said, his voice low and slow as he continued to work on Nola's leg. "And if the Outer Guard really are going to try to break in, well, we can't afford to have people guarding someone who attempted to kill a Nightland guest."

"Put him in a steel room and deliver him meals," Nola said, trying hard not to think of the fact that *she* had nearly been the vampire's meal.

"He's a vampire, Nola," Kieran said, stroking her hair as she bit her lip, trying not to pull away from the pain.

There was the *tink* of metal on metal and the sound of footsteps walking away.

"If we left him alone, he could try and dig his way out or tear through the stone," Kieran said. "There aren't many things an angry vampire can't break through given enough time. And we only have enough of that kind of metal for the door to the outside. There isn't a way for us to lock him up."

"Silver doors all around?" Nola said.

Kieran chuckled. "Vampires can touch silver."

"So, it's not like the sun allergy *going to get lots of blisters and die* type thing?" Nola asked as Dr. Wynne's footsteps returned.

"Well," Dr. Wynne said, "I wouldn't recommend wearing silver as some irritation can occur. A bit of discoloration and some nasty swelling in rare cases, but if you're afraid of a vampire, I wouldn't suggest trying to kill them with a silver cross. It could take hours for him to be bothered with it at all. This will sting a bit."

A needle pierced Nola's skin again. Pure ice poured into her flesh, freezing the wound on her leg. Nola groaned as cold unlike anything she'd ever felt before seared her skin.

Keep breathing. You have to keep breathing.

Opening her eyes, she glanced down at her leg. The skin around the wound had become stark white, while the cut itself turned a violent red.

"Don't watch it," Kieran said, taking Nola's face in his hands and turning her to look into his eyes. "It's better if you don't watch it."

Nola let out a deep, shuddering breath. "What about stakes through the heart? Is that true? Should there be a ban on wood in Nightland?"

"If you destroy a vampire's heart, he will die," Dr. Wynne said.

The sound of metal instruments being laid on a metal tray came from the end of the table, but Nola didn't look away from Kieran.

The ice in her leg had changed now, from something stagnant to something squirming as though worms crawled under her skin.

"It's about the only thing a vampire can't heal from," Dr. Wynne continued. "Well that," he paused, "and decapitation. But I see hardly any of that in here. It is very hard to cut an entire head off without meaning to. And if you meant to cut a person's head off, I don't know why you'd bother bringing them to me for help. At that point, it's really a matter of hiding the body where it won't smell too terribly and the Outer Guard won't find it. I suppose that's what makes the river so popular for those things. But there must be lots of other choices—"

"Thanks, Dad." Kieran cut his father off just as Nola began to wonder how many bodies had been dumped in the river and if there were any bones left or if the toxicity was so high everything had been eaten away.

"You can sit up now," Dr. Wynne said, pushing himself backwards on his rolling stool.

Nola opened her eyes a crack to look at her leg. The squirming had stopped. Now it felt like someone was holding a bag of particularly cold ice on her calf. The skin around the cut was still pale, but the cut itself was what made Nola sit up to examine her leg more closely.

There were twelve stitches in her leg, holding together a cut that looked to be at least a few days old. Shiny new skin had bridged the gap between the two ragged sides.

"The stitches will make sure everything heals in the right place, and the scarring should be minimal," Dr. Wynne said, his brow furrowed and lips pinched as though afraid Nola might not approve of his handiwork.

"That's incredible." Nola poked the cut before Kieran lifted her hand away. "If they had this in the domes—"

"They'd never use it," Dr. Wynne said. "ReVamp alters you at a genetic level. Not badly for you. In a week, you won't notice you were ever injected. Still, the whole point of the domes is to preserve a genetically healthy human race. ReVamp changes the way DNA works. It alters your body at the most basic level. Why do you think they despise the vampires so much?"

"Because all the ones they deal with are violent." Nola's voice rose in excitement. "If you could show them this—"

"Then they'd still kill us all if they had the chance," Raina said as she slunk into the room. "A drug is a drug, impure genes are impure genes, and a vampire is a vampire. They don't see differences. It's all black and white, and they don't give a shit how many of us die out here."

Nola opened her mouth to argue, but Raina held up a finger.

"Please don't fight me on things you don't understand, little girl. You'll make me sorry I didn't manage to stab you through the heart."

"You're the one that stabbed me?" Nola said, looking at the knife tucked into Raina's belt.

Raina followed her gaze. "Did you expect me to throw my knife away in remorse? You were sneaking around."

Nola opened her mouth to explain, but Raina cut her off with the wave of a hand.

"I know you were coming to save us from the big, bad guards. And I do appreciate the sentiment. But the way I see it, it wasn't my fault you were in a very bad place at the wrong time, and I did lend you some of my very fine old clothes. And since you'll apparently be needing to borrow yet another pair of pants, as you can't seem to keep from bleeding all over the place even if I didn't cause it, I would say we're pretty even."

"Pants versus stab wound," Kieran said, one dark eyebrow raised. "That's a rough trade to call."

"It's a cold, cruel world. You take what you can get." Raina glared at Nola. "We're good, right?"

Nola nodded. "We're good."

"Excellent." Raina flashed a smile that made Nola more nervous than the knife had. "Because we've figured out a way to get you home. And any trust issues could definitely get a few people killed."

Nola looked to Kieran who gave the slightest shrug.

"Emanuel wants us all to meet in the gallery." Raina turned back toward the door.

"It must be a grand plan if he wants us in the gallery," Dr. Wynne said, moving over to a sink in the corner to wash his hands. "He always likes to make big announcements in there."

Kieran took Nola's hand and helped her off the table. Her leg still felt shaky as she put pressure on it, but the unbearable pain and terrible weakness had gone.

"Thank you, Dr. Wynne," she said, taking his hand in hers as he moved for the door. His skin was warm to the touch.

"Of course, dear." Dr. Wynne smiled. "You are family. And, well, it is my job, I suppose."

"I'll help her." Kieran wrapped an arm around Nola's waist. "You go on ahead."

"Your dad," Nola whispered as soon as Dr. Wynne was in the hall, "he hasn't taken ReVamp, has he?"

"No. He hasn't needed it yet. He had more immunities than I did from sneaking in and out so much, and he doesn't think people should take it unless they have no other choice. How did you know?"

"His hands are still warm," Nola said, sinking into the cold of Kieran's hand cutting through the leather that separated their skin. "And his eyes are still green, like yours used to be."

"Very observant," Kieran said as they walked into the hall, him supporting most of Nola's weight. "He'll have to take it soon, though."

"What wrong with him?"

"He's started losing weight. He can't focus. He goes on tangents even worse than usual."

"Maybe being underground is getting to him," Nola said. "Maybe, if he got out—"

"He's too valuable," Kieran said. "They won't let him go where they can't protect him."

"Even if he wants to?" Nola stopped walking and nearly toppled over as Kieran continued forward.

"This is about saving people, thousands of people. He understands that," Kieran said. "He's starting to show signs of toxicity poisoning. If he takes ReVamp, he'll get better. And when we get out of Nightland, he'll get all the fresh air he wants."

Kieran pushed through the heavy, wooden door into the gallery.

Bryant and Desmond sat stone-faced on one of the large couches. Raina sat next to Dr. Wynne while Julian leaned on a bookshelf, and all of their eyes were fixed on Emanuel who stood in the center of it all.

"Nola." Emanuel spread his arms to her. "I see you've recovered nicely from your accident."

"Yes," Nola said, suddenly aware that everyone's attention had shifted to her. "Dr. Wynne is brilliant, and the garden was amazing."

"I'm glad you appreciate what we are trying to accomplish here"—Emanuel's brief smile vanished—"as I am afraid we need to ask for your help once again."

21

"What kind of help?" Nola asked, resisting as Kieran tried to guide her to a chair.

Emanuel paced across the carpet. "The only way to get you home is for the domes to believe you were brought here against your will. If we are operating under the guise that vampires broke into the domes and kidnapped you, then, and I mean no offense, we must also maintain that we wish to give you back. I am sure we can all agree it would be a very unlikely story that we in Nightland kidnapped sweet Nola and she managed to escape us and arrive home undamaged."

The group in the room nodded.

After a reluctant moment, Nola nodded, too. "I don't think I could escape a few hundred vampires in an underground lair alive."

"Good." Emanuel's shoulders relaxed. "We've contacted the domes and informed them of your kidnapping and made our ransom demand."

"What did you ask for?" Nola's said.

If the domes have to give something vital, it could put the whole system in danger. The life boat could sink, and it would be my fault.

"We asked for things that will be very valuable to us and can be easily replaced by the domes," Emanuel said. "Common seeds of plants that no longer grow on the outside. A few doses of medicine for the children. Nothing the domes will even miss."

Nola nodded.

"We've asked them to meet us on the bridge tomorrow, an hour before dawn," Emanuel continued. "That should make them feel secure while giving us ample time to get back underground. By daybreak, you'll be cozy in the domes, and Kieran will have some new seeds for the garden."

"But if they think you broke in and kidnapped me, won't that give the Outer Guard a reason to come after you?" Nola asked.

"They don't need a reason to come after us," Desmond said. "They'll come no matter what we do."

"And you have to be back in the domes when the Outer Guard bang on our door." Raina's hand rested on the hilt of her knife as though expecting the Outer Guard to run into the gallery as they spoke.

Nola reached for Kieran's hand. "But what will I tell them when they ask me what happened?"

"That's where I come in," Julian said. "We've worked it all out so you can give them enough details to be believable without telling them anything that could endanger Nightland. I'll coach you on all of it. Dr. Wynne and Kieran won't be involved. As far as the Outer Guard will know, we broke through the glass in Bright Dome to get you."

"They'll seal it," Nola said. The squirming knot of fear in her stomach disappeared, leaving her hollow. "I won't be able to get back out."

"I think," Dr. Wynne said, looking down at his hands, "that will probably be for the best."

"You almost died out here, Nola," Kieran said, turning to face her. "Next time, you might not make it through the woods."

"So, I'll just never see you again?" Nola's voice was tight, higher than usual. "I'll just go back to the domes—"

"And live the life you're meant to have," Dr. Wynne said. "You can't keep going back and forth, and you can't stay out here."

"Why?" Tears crept into Nola's eyes. "Why can't I stay? You need me. I could help with the garden. I know more about agriculture than any of you."

"You'd get sick," Kieran said, his voice barely a whisper as he brushed the tears from Nola's cheek. "You'd get hurt. I won't let you die out here."

"What about ReVamp?" Nola said, remembering the bitter taste of metal in her mouth. "It saved you."

"You could never go home." Pain filled Kieran's eyes. "You would never see your mother again. I want to keep you more than anything, but I won't take the sun away from you, Nola."

He pulled Nola into his arms, and she buried her face in his shoulder. "How many times are we going to have to say goodbye?"

GIRL OF GLASS | 339

"Not to be completely insensitive," Raina said, "but a few of us still have to risk our lives to get the princess back to the castle. So, rather than focus on true love lost to circumstance and the bad luck of her going back to Jeremy my-father-wants-to-destroy-Nightland for comfort—"

"Raina, don't," Kieran muttered.

"Don't tell the truth? I think we all know why Jeremy gave Nola the info that sent her here. And we can be sure the Domer will take care of her once we make the trade."

Nola's cheeks flushed in anger and embarrassment.

"Let's stop pretending this is *Romeo and Juliet* unless you both want to end up dead. Why don't we give Nola to Julian to make sure she doesn't get herself caught for being a traitor, and once they're done, you two can go feel each other up in a dark corner."

The room froze for a long moment.

Bryant moved first. "Gonna go make sure we have enough vamps on board for the swap."

Desmond followed him out into the tunnels.

"I'll take you to the kitchen to work on your story," Julian said, awkwardly patting his hands on the sides of his legs. "I think we have something that resembles tea for you to drink."

"Anyone want to help me bury the guy who tried to kill Nola?" Raina asked, looking at Kieran.

"Just go, Raina," Kieran said, his face stony and impossible for Nola to read.

"All the dirty work for me. How kind." Raina stepped forward, baring her teeth.

Julian's hand closed around Nola's arm, and he led her from the gallery.

The door muffled Kieran's shouted response.

 "Does it all make sense?" Julian asked as Nola finished her third cup of what was not really tea.

"Yes." Nola traced a jagged line that had been carved into the wooden kitchen table with her fingertip.

"It's about more than being able to repeat the details to me." Julian sipped from his dark mug.

Nola had closed her eyes when he had poured something from the refrigerator into it. *Knowing* he was probably drinking blood and actually *seeing* him do it were two very different things.

"You have to understand the story you're telling," Julian said.

"I get it." Nola kneaded the point of pain that pierced her forehead. "You kidnapped me to find out whatever you could about what my mother had learned at the Green Leaf Conference. I got hit on the head and stabbed a bit. Told you what you wanted to know since it didn't really matter anyway. You made the trade."

"Good girl." Julian tapped his knuckles on the table.

Nola dug her fingers into the wood, watching the white of her knuckles blossom through the red scars on her hands. "What if I don't want to?"

"Want to what?" Julian cocked his head to the side.

"What if I don't want you to make the trade?" Nola said. "What if I want to stay in Nightland? Help with your work."

"Kieran's already explained." Sympathy crept into Julian's voice. "If you stay here, you'll end up a vampire. Perhaps not right away, but eventually it would be either ReVamp or death."

"But being a vampire doesn't seem so bad."

"It's not," Julian said. "It took me a few years to get off the human blood and a decade more to forgive myself for all I'd done. But once you get used to blood and darkness, it's not such a bad life."

"Then let me stay," Nola said. "I want to be here. I want to help you save people."

I want to be with Kieran.

Julian studied his pale hands for a long moment. "I'm afraid that's impossible."

"But you just said—"

"I said being a vampire wasn't that bad. I didn't say you could be allowed to stay in Nightland."

"But—"

"They know you're here, Nola," Julian said. "We've told the domes we kidnapped you. If we don't give you back to them, it could start a war. And if the domes decided to fight the vampires in earnest, I don't even want to begin to imagine how terrible the damage to both sides would be. You have to go back. There is nothing else to be done."

"I could tell them it was me. That I ran away. Then they'll banish me."

"Think, Nola. Between the story we've written for you and the truth, which do you think they're most likely to believe?"

"But if I only tell them the truth, your story won't matter."

"They know the beginning of our kidnapping tale," Julian said. "That will be enough. They'll claim brainwashing or coercion. We have to give you back in the trade. It's the only way."

"The only solution is a lie," Nola said.

"A lie, yes." Julian patted Nola's hand. "And a hope you might eventually forget how wonderful the truth you lost could have been."

Nola closed her eyes, hating the sympathy on Julian's face.

"We can work on your story again tonight," Julian said, taking Nola's cup to the sink. "It's late. You should get some sleep."

"By late you mean early?" Nola's head spun from fatigue and trying to keep everything straight in her mind. What had happened since she left the domes, what she had to say had happened, and what could never happen.

"The morning is rather new." Julian washed both of their cups.

"Do vampires sleep?"

"Yes." Julian gave a half-shrug. "Most sleep at least an hour or two a day, mostly out of habit. We can go for a week or more without really feeling the physical need to sleep. But when days don't end, it takes a toll on the mind."

A door in the back of the kitchen opened, and a tiny girl emerged, her curly hair still rumpled from sleep.

"Eden." Julian swept the little girl into his arms.

Eden's face split into a grin, and she giggled as Julian rocked her back and forth.

"How are you this fine morning?" Julian said.

Eden bit her lips together, her brown eyes on Nola.

"Don't be afraid," Julian said, following Eden's gaze. "You know Nola. She's the one who got you your medicine. Can you say *thank you, Nola?*"

"Thank you, Nola," Eden said in a voice barely loud enough to be heard before burying her face in Julian's neck.

"Why don't we take Nola someplace she can get a bit of sleep, and then you and I can go find your father?" Julian asked.

Eden nodded.

Julian led Nola into the hallway and toward the room lined with bunks. Nola expected him to lead her to one of the metal bunk beds, but instead, he walked farther down the hall than Nola had been before.

"I'm sure no one will mind." Julian stopped at an unmarked door and gave it a cursory knock before swinging it open. "Sleep well."

Nola stepped into the room, not turning as the door closed behind her.

It was Kieran's room. She could tell without him even being there. He and his father had barely been able to take anything with them when they left the domes. A few pictures hung on the wall. Kieran with his parents all smiling at a party. Kieran and Nola high up in the willow tree in Bright Dome.

There were sketches of plants and animals. And Nola. She stared back at herself from the wall.

But the drawing was a perfected version of herself. The shape of the face was right, and so were the eyes. The pale freckles that dotted her nose and the tiny mark near her eye were all there. Still, she looked different. Calm, beautiful, and angelic.

A version of me I could never hope to be.

Nola reached up for the picture, wanting to study it, to see what Kieran's idea of her could teach her, but the door opened again.

"Julian said he was done for the morning," Kieran said, glancing from Nola to the sketch of 'perfect Nola.'

Heat rose in Nola's cheeks. "We're done."

"Sorry," Kieran said, running a hand through his hair, "if that's weird." He swept a hand toward the sketch. "You weren't supposed to see that."

"It's beautiful," Nola said.

"Not as beautiful as the original."

His words hung in the air for a moment.

"I haven't seen you draw anything since—" Nola paused.

Why am I making this worse?

"Since my mom died." Kieran picked up a pad of paper from the desk. His mother's face gazed up at them, a smile caught on her lips. "It took a while."

Nola took Kieran's hand, squeezing it tightly.

"You should get some sleep." Kieran lifted a small pile of clothes from the bed and tossed it onto the ground.

Nola laughed.

"I know," Kieran said. "Even down here where I hardly own anything I still can't keep my room clean. Dad comes in here every day to stare at the mess."

"Some things don't change."

"Maybe," Kieran said, his eyes locking with Nola's for a moment before flicking away.

"Kieran, Jeremy and I," Nola said, willing herself to get the words out before she lost her chance, "we're not together."

"Yet."

"No."

"You've kissed him," Kieran said. It wasn't a question. "You've kissed him. And even if you're not together yet, even if you're not in love with him yet, you will be."

"No, I won't."

"He's a good guy, Nola." Pain etched Kieran's words. "Hell, he's probably a better guy than I ever could have been even if I'd stayed in the domes. He's steady and strong. When you get home, he'll take care of you. He'll be with you every day while you try to forget what you saw down here. And then one day you'll realize he's the best thing you've got. And in a few years the Marriage Board will tell you it's time to pick someone as your pair, and you'll pick him. You'll get married, have kids, and forget all about Nightland—"

Nola cut off his words with a smack. Her hand throbbed from hitting Kieran's face, but she couldn't see more than his blurred outline through her tears.

"How dare you," Nola said. "How dare you decide what my life will be, what Jeremy's life will be?"

"I didn't decide. The domes did."

"What if that's not what I want?" Nola yelled. "I don't want to be with Jeremy just because—"

"Because it's the way things work for Domers."

"Because I can't have you." Nola sank down to her knees. "You say I have to go back to the domes to survive, but what kind of life will I have?"

Kieran knelt, wrapping his arms around her. He smelled like he always had, the scent she had known for years.

Are vampires supposed to smell so human?

"That's the problem with trying to save the human race," Kieran whispered. "You lose humanity."

Nola swiped her tears away with trembling hands.

Kieran lifted her onto the bed. "Sleep, Nola."

Nola shook her head as more tears streamed down her face. "I can't. If this is it, if I never get to see you again, I want to be with you. I don't want to sleep. I don't want to miss it."

"You aren't going to miss anything," Kieran murmured. "I'll be right here. I'll hold you close. And when you wake up, you'll still be in my arms. Won't that be a thing to remember?"

He lay down next to Nola, and she put her head on his shoulder in the place where she fit so perfectly.

"Goodnight, Nola," Kieran whispered. "I love you."

His words ran through her, filling her up before shattering her.

"I love you, too."

22

Ice surrounded her. But something deep in the back of her mind told her to hold the ice closer even as she shivered. That the cold she was feeling was precious and not to be let go.

"Nola," a voice whispered as the cold began to move away. "Nola, you're shaking." Lips brushed her forehead.

Nola's eyes fluttered open, and Kieran was gazing down at her. She pulled herself closer to his chest, not looking away from his eyes. Their black was still rimmed in a thin band of gold-speckled green.

"I don't mind the cold." Nola traced her fingers along Kieran's chin. A strong chin. A man's chin. Bits of stubble caught on her fingers.

When did we become grownups? Did it happen before the world got this dark or after?

Kieran wrapped both arms around her, pulling her to his chest. Nola closed her eyes, relishing the feeling of being held so tight he could not possibly let go.

"It's time to get up anyway," Kieran said, again pressing his lips to her forehead. "Bea will have breakfast waiting for you, and Julian will want to talk through your story again."

"Can't they wait?" Nola gripped Kieran's t-shirt with her fingers.

"Probably not."

Nola's stomach squirmed at the regret in his voice.

"How long before it's time?"

"Eight hours until you leave Nightland. Nine until the exchange."

Nola's ribcage turned to stone. She couldn't breathe. Her lungs had no space to expand. "That's not much time."

"Let's not waste any of it." Kieran tipped Nola's chin up. Softly, gently, he kissed her.

Nola's heart raced. She pressed herself against him, memorizing the feeling of his body next to hers.

With a creak, the bedroom door swung open.

Nola gasped as Dr. Wynne stared down at them, his face a mix between confusion and disappointment.

"Nola, you're needed in the kitchen." Dr. Wynne's voice was brusque and businesslike, something Nola had rarely heard from him.

Nola awkwardly struggled to climb over Kieran without looking him or Dr. Wynne in the face.

The bed springs creaked as Kieran stood.

"Nola, to the kitchen," Dr. Wynne said. "Kieran, stay here."

Nola walked out into the hall without looking back.

The door slammed behind her. She squeezed her eyes shut and took a shuddering breath.

They'll let me say goodbye to Kieran.

They would have to or…

Or what?

She would refuse to go back to the domes in the exchange and let the Outer Guard destroy Nightland?

A laugh shook Nola's chest. A high hysterical laugh she wouldn't have recognized as her own if she hadn't felt it ripping from her throat.

"I like it." Raina's voice pulled Nola from her frenzy. "A little insanity. It'll help sell the kidnapping story to the Domers."

"A *little* insanity perhaps." Julian peered over Raina's shoulder, his dark cup already in his hand. "But if she really has lost her mind, she might not be able to remember what to tell them, and then where would we be?"

"I remember," Nola said. "I remember all of it. I know the coat and trying to escape. I know I was dropped and there were lots of voices. I know all of it." Nola tugged a hand through her knotted hair. "I'm a quick learner. Just let me go back to Kieran."

"Really? You've already been in there all night," Raina said.

"And I'd really like for you to shut up!" Nola growled.

Raina smiled and tossed her purple and scarlet hair over her shoulder. "Is that what you want?"

"I think Raina should go back to practicing killing things," Julian said, stepping around Raina, "and Nola should come and brush up her details with me. Raina will get to stab things, which always makes her more cheerful, and the sooner Nola and I are done, the sooner she can be swept back into young love's tender throes."

"Fine." Raina turned and sauntered back toward to gallery. "See you in a few."

Julian gave Nola a tight smile. "After you."

The old woman was already standing over the stove in the kitchen, poking at something in a pan with a wooden spoon.

Nola sat down in the same seat she had taken the night before, willing herself not to start tracing the scratch with her finger again.

The *clink* of a plate being pulled from the cupboard brought Nola's attention back to the present as Bea shuffled over with breakfast—grilled vegetables and a little hunk of meat.

"Thank you," Nola murmured, deciding not to ask what sort of meat it was. She sniffed the plate, her mouth beginning to water. Carefully, she speared a green vegetable onto her fork. It tasted earthy and pungent, but like food.

"No more tinny taste?" Julian asked.

"It's gone," Nola said. She watched as Julian took a sip from his cup. "Do you miss food?"

"Me?" Julian chuckled. "No." He paused for a moment. "No, I really don't miss eating. But then, I was so ill before I became a vampire, eating had ceased to be a real option for me, so I suppose I am a terrible judge."

"Right."

"Now, down to business." Julian rubbed his hands together. "Who moved the glass?"

The next few hours passed slowly, Julian asking Nola the same questions in slightly different ways until her head spun.

"Well," Julian said when Nola had explained how she had gotten out of the Iron Dome for the twelfth time, "I think that's as good as we're going to get. And just remember, if you get confused, tell them you hit your head and all you remember is darkness and fear. Hopefully they'll feel sorry enough for you to leave you alone until you can sort out what you're supposed to say."

"You know the Outer Guard," Nola said as real fear clawed at her stomach. "They aren't known for their kindness and compassion."

"Careful, Nola," Julian said, "you're starting to sound like a Nightlander. I think our time here is done." Julian looked over Nola's shoulder.

Nola turned to find Kieran leaning against the doorframe. His dark hair stuck out at odd angles, and anger marked his face.

"I tried to keep things as swift as possible."

"Thanks, Julian," Kieran said, stepping into the kitchen and taking Nola's hand.

"Get our Cinderella back here by three. We don't want her to be late for the party being held in her honor." Julian nodded to them both and left the room, still holding his cup.

"How did it go?" Kieran asked after a long moment.

"Good," Nola said. "At least I think it went well. I've never been prepped to tell a giant lie before. What did your dad say?"

"Nothing." Kieran pressed his palm to his forehead. "Everything I already knew and had decided to forget. Dad's great at that."

Nola took Kieran's hands in her own, tracing the calluses that marked his palms with her finger.

"What do we do now?" Nola asked, studying Kieran's face, trying to memorize every line, even those formed by anger.

"If we were in the domes," Kieran said, twisting his hands so their fingers laced perfectly together, "I would say we should climb onto your roof and look at the stars."

"Or go lay under the willow tree," Nola said. "How many hours do you think we spent under that tree? Not talking or doing anything really. Just being together."

"Not nearly enough."

Nola laid her head on his shoulder. "We could go back to the garden."

"It's raining again," Kieran said. "Besides, I don't think Emanuel will let me take you aboveground until it's time. It's too risky."

"I can't just sit here." Nola stepped away from Kieran, her body telling her to run from the room. To keep running and running so the world couldn't catch her. "I can't just sit and count down the time. I need to do something."

"You've never been good at waiting." Kieran caught Nola around the waist, pulling her back into his arms.

"Never." Nola wound her arms around him. Her stomach purred.

If Dr. Wynne hadn't walked in, where would we be right now?

"I have an idea." Kieran swayed side to side with Nola as though they were dancing. "Let's go to Nightland."

"We're in Nightland." Nola laughed in spite of herself as Kieran twirled her under his arm.

"5th and Nightland. Let's go dance. We'll forget morning is ever coming."

Nola leaned in and kissed him. "Promise you'll hold me?"

"Until the sun comes up."

Kieran took her hand and led her out to the gallery.

Nola expected there to be someone at the door to make them stay in Emanuel's house, but Kieran led her into the tunnel without interruption. Whatever Dr. Wynne had said, he wasn't keeping Kieran from 5th and Nightland.

They didn't talk as they walked. What was there to say?

The closer they got to the club, the more Nola worried she wouldn't fit in with the other revelers.

I'm wearing Raina's old clothes. I can't get much more vampire than that without ReVamp.

Every few hundred yards, a vampire stood against the wall. They didn't wear any sort of uniform, but something about their posture, the way their gaze followed her and Kieran, made Nola certain they were guards.

"Did Emanuel put the extra guards on watch?" Nola whispered as they passed another guard, this one a boy not much older than herself with flaming red hair. "Because of the Outer Guard?" The red-haired boy's neck stiffened at the mention of the Outer Guard.

"Yes," Kieran said. "The housing tunnel is under strict watch. The club can defend itself, and so can the working areas. But this tunnel is where the kids are. The ones who can't fight. It's where Eden would be if Emanuel weren't her father."

The hairs on Nola's neck prickled at the thought of Eden hiding from the Outer Guard.

"Don't worry." Kieran kissed Nola's hand. "We're safe down here. You warned us, and we're better protected than we have ever been before."

A thumping noise echoed in the distance. A low, rhythmic buzz that shook the floor under Nola's feet.

Nola's heart began to race as they grew closer to the music of Nightland. Two tall guards stood, arms crossed, knives in their belts, in front of the metal door.

One of them lifted his head as Nola approached as though sniffing the air.

"That her?" he said to Kieran who nodded.

The other guard turned and swung open the door. The music flooded into the hall so loudly Nola could barely hear herself call "thank you" as the guards ushered her past.

Flashes bounced down from the ceiling, throwing lights so bright into Nola's eyes, she was blinded when she tried to look into the shadows.

Vampires filled every corner of the club. The music thumped into her very bones. Each vibration shook her lungs, making it impossible for her to get a deep breath.

Kieran laced his fingers through hers, leading her out into the mass of surging bodies to find a place on the dance floor. Every time they passed a group of revelers, their eyes locked onto Nola.

"They're all staring at me," Nola whispered.

"Huh?" Kieran shouted above the music.

"They're all staring at me." Nola pressed her lips to Kieran's ear.

Kieran looked around the crowd, giving a nod to a group of vampires with dark red and black tattoos etched into their skin. "No one here will hurt you." He wrapped his arm around Nola's waist.

"Because they're all nice vampires who don't believe in eating Domers?" The question caught in Nola's throat.

"Because you're with me." Kieran smiled and swayed with the music. "Because they know you're the Domer who came here to help us."

The people around them began to dance again, surging as one massive unit. Kieran held Nola tightly, swaying gently. "Ignore them," he said. "Let it just be us."

Nola looked into Kieran's eyes. The green was almost gone now, replaced with black. But the darkness didn't frighten her. In his eyes she could see his soul pouring out to her with every glance.

Kieran smiled and took her by the hand, spinning her under his arm. Nola tossed her head back and laughed. The music swallowed the sound of her laughter, but it didn't matter. Kieran was laughing with her. He pulled her back into his chest, one arm wrapped around her waist, holding her tight.

He brushed the loose hair from the sweat on her forehead. He ran his fingers over her curls as though hoping to memorize each strand. The music changed, and the crowd around them cheered. This song was faster, with shouted words Nola couldn't understand.

Kieran didn't sway with this song. He only gazed at Nola, sadness filling his eyes.

"Nola…" his mouth formed the word, but Nola couldn't hear the sound. She laced her fingers together around his neck, leaning up until their lips met.

She tightened her fingers in his hair, pulling him even closer. His heartbeat thudded through her chest, overpowering the music until there was nothing left but him. His hands traced the skin from her waist to her ribs. She gasped at the ice of his fingers.

Their eyes met for a moment before he was kissing her again, wrapping his arms around her so her feet left ground. She disappeared, lost in a haze. There was nothing left in the world but her and Kieran. Cheers and shouts glided past, but she cared for nothing except Kieran and her hunger for him. She teased his lips, reveling in his taste.

A loud *clang* shook the air, and Nola looked up. Her feet still hovered above the ground as Kieran held her, but they were in a tunnel away from the crowds of 5th and Nightland. The thick stone walls muffled the thumping of the music. Lamps dotted the corridor, leading off into the darkness, but no shapes moved in the shadows. They were alone.

23

"Nola," Kieran breathed, pressing his lips to hers gently at first, then with growing desperation.

This is it. All we'll ever have.

Kieran lifted her against the wall and pressed himself to her as his hands explored the bare skin of her back. Nola pulled herself closer to him, as though they could melt into one and the bridge would never come. She moaned as Kieran's fingers grazed her ribs, sending pulses of pleasure trembling through her.

"Kieran," she breathed, wrapping herself around him.

This is perfect. This is right.

"No." Kieran stepped away.

Nola crumpled to the ground, hitting her head on the stone wall.

"What?" Nola said, blinking to see Kieran past the stars that danced in front of her eyes.

"I want you, Nola," Kieran said, his voice desperate and sad. "I want to keep you here. I want to make you mine."

"Then do it." Nola swallowed the lump of fear in her throat as her words hung in the air. "I'm not afraid."

Kieran stepped forward, taking Nola's hands and helping her to her feet. She swayed as pain shot through her head, but the ache did nothing to shadow the longing that filled her. Kieran traced her lips with his finger, then placed his hand over her heart.

"You have to get to the bridge." Kieran turned and walked down the tunnel.

"Kieran," Nola said, forcing her feet to move as she ran after him. "We have time."

"A few hours," Kieran said, not slowing his stride.

"One night. You said we could have one night. I thought—"

"I want you, Nola." Kieran turned to face her. He took both her arms, holding her tight. "More than anything, I want you. But the whole point in giving you back to the domes is to make sure you have a life."

"I can have a life tomorrow."

"And what would you tell Jeremy?" Kieran said. "Would you lie? Never mention it happened? Or would you admit you gave yourself to a Vamper in a filthy tunnel?"

"It's none of Jeremy's business."

"You belong with him!" Kieran pulled away from Nola and paced the tunnel, tearing his hands through his hair. "I lost my chance with you when I got banished from the domes."

"That wasn't your fault—"

"It doesn't matter." Kieran punched his fist into the wall. Tiny bits of rock clattered to the ground.

Nola ran to him, taking his hand in hers, expecting to see blood and broken bones. But his hand was perfect. The skin unharmed.

"See," Kieran panted. "I'm not who I used to be." He took Nola's face in his hands. "I love you, Magnolia Kent. I will always love you."

"Kieran, please don't." Pain dug into her chest.

"But I love you too much to let you stay down here in the dark." Kieran kissed her cheek. "And I love you too much to give you one night in a tunnel and send you away. You deserve the world, Nola."

He took her hand and turned down the tunnel, but Nola couldn't make her feet move.

"Kieran," she whispered, not waiting for him to turn back to her. "I love you, too. And I should have a choice."

His fingers tightened around hers, and together they walked down the tunnel toward 5th and Nightland.

Say something. There has to be something you can say to stay here. To stay with him.

They had nearly reached the metal door when a loud *thunk* echoed through the hall.

Nola stepped away from the door, expecting a burly guard to walk through. But the metal door stayed shut.

There was another *thunk*, and the noise from the club changed. The music silenced, replaced by frightened voices.

Thump.

The ceiling shook, sending a rain of dust down onto Nola and Kieran. More *thumps* came, breaking over the screams of the crowd. The door to 5th and Nightland swung open, and people poured out into the tunnel just before—

Bang!

The sound pounded into Nola's ears, blocking out the cries of the people around her.

Kieran grabbed her, shoving her against the wall and covering her with his own body as chunks of the ceiling came tumbling down.

There was more shouting and the sound of people running away down the tunnel.

Soon the shouts of fear vanished, replaced by roars of anger.

"Shit," Kieran muttered.

Nola looked up in time to see red beams of light darting through the dust of the ruined club.

Faint *pops* echoed through the air, and Nola watched the shadow of a vampire fall before Kieran knocked her over, pinning her to the ground.

"Get out of our home!" a voice roared.

The screech of metal on metal wailed through the hall, followed by the sound of splintering wood and howls of pain.

The vampires were fighting back.

"Nola, I need you to run," Kieran said just loudly enough for Nola to hear his deadly calm voice. "I need you to run down this hall and not stop until you find where it meets up with the big tunnel. Go left from there, and you can find your way back to Emanuel's."

"You want me to get help?"

Another series of *pops* punctuated the shouts, but the vampires had armed themselves. This time, a guard fell to the floor. Another figure in a black uniform leapt into view, bringing down a heavy baton onto a vampire's neck.

"Help is already coming, but they can't see you here."

A *bang* shook the floor.

Nola watched in horror as the wall between the tunnel and Nightland began to collapse. Before Nola could gasp, Kieran had lifted her and was sprinting down the hall, carrying her in his arms.

He rounded the corner and held Nola to the side as a dozen vampires armed with swords, knives, and weapons Nola didn't recognize, ran past.

"Go," Kieran said. "Get where it's safe."

"Come with me!" Nola clung to Kieran's hand.

"They're invading my home, Nola," Kieran said. "I have to fight."

"I'll fight with you," Nola said, searching the floor for a rock, anything to defend herself.

"There are vampires in there," Kieran said, cupping Nola's face in his hands. "If you bleed, they could attack you. The guards can't see you. Just go. I'll meet you in the gallery when it's over." He kissed Nola, quickly, urgently as shouts and the grinding of metal on metal came from the fight. "I love you, Nola. Now go!" he shouted over his shoulder as he disappeared into the dust.

Nola wanted to run after him. To shout at the guards to stop. These were people, too, and they had a right to protect their home. But if they saw her, they'd know she was a traitor, and the war with the domes would begin.

She stifled a sob and ran down the hall, half-blinded by her tears. Another group of vampires tore down the passage, knocking Nola off her feet. Pain shot through her wrist and ribs as she hit the ground. Spitting dirt from her mouth, Nola pushed herself to her feet, staring down at the hot sticky blood that covered her palm.

"Shit." She glanced up and down the tunnel. There was no one in sight, but a vampire would come soon. A vampire that could smell her fresh blood. Pulling with all her might, Nola tore the sleeve from her shirt. Grabbing a handful of dirt in her bleeding hand, she wrapped the leather around the soil, hoping it would be enough to cover the scent of her blood.

Nola ran down the hall, but the sounds of the fighting didn't seem to get any farther away. The guards had gained ground, delving deeper into Nightland.

How many guards had they sent that the vampires still hadn't—Nola couldn't stop herself from thinking—*killed them?*

Finally, she reached a door. It was metal but thankfully light enough for her to move on her own. Pain seared through her palm as she gripped the handle with both hands, forcing the dirt deeper into her wound.

As soon as she was through the door, she shoved it closed behind her. There was a lock on the inside of the door, a heavy metal bar that could be slid into place. It could block the Outer Guard from the hall—maybe only for a minute, but it would be something. But it would lock the vampires in with the guards. Shouts came through the metal door.

"Stay in formation. We don't leave without the girl."

Nola slammed the metal bar into the lock and stared at the door.

They were searching for her. If she let them find her, maybe they would leave. The fighting would be over. They had fought their way this deep into Nightland. The Outer Guard were stronger than Emanuel had thought.

But if they found out Emanuel had lied, they could destroy everything.

You can't be seen! Kieran's words pounded through her mind as the door shook.

Nola ran left down the corridor.

Please let me be right. If Kieran is hurt...

She pushed the thought out of her mind. He was a vampire. He only needed to protect his heart.

A woman stood in a doorway, clutching a sweater to her chest as she looked up and down the tunnel.

"Get inside," Nola shouted as she ran past. "The Outer Guard are here."

The slam of a door sounded behind Nola.

Her legs burned. How much farther until she reached Emanuel's house. Would she even be safe there? A group of vampires running in ranks, dressed all in black, charged past. Nola recognized Desmond's scarred, bald head as he ran in the lead.

Nola raced farther down the tunnel, where vampires still stood in the hall with no apparent concern for the attack.

"What's got the guards riled?" a man asked, stepping out in front of Nola. His long white fangs peeked over his bottom lip.

A human drinker.

"The Outer Guard," Nola panted, keeping her wounded hand clamped tight at her side. "They got into 5th and Nightland. They're coming."

The lights overhead flickered as though confirming her words.

"And the human runs," the vampire sneered. "Bloody and weak." His eyes moved from Nola's panicked face to her injured hand. "I could protect you. The little girl lost in the dark."

He stepped closer, and the vampires around him shifted, forming a ring around Nola.

"Beautiful, weak, and so sweet," the vampire said, his black eyes gleeful. "You need protection. I could protect you. Make you mine." He leaned close to Nola, his fangs mere inches from her neck. The stench of sweat and stale blood wafted off his skin. He leaned closer, his nose brushing her neck. "You smell so pure, so clean."

"I am a guest of Emanuel," Nola said. "I am here under Emanuel's protection. And if you so much as touch me, Raina will have your head." Nola stepped back and stared unflinching into the vampire's black eyes.

"Raina." The vampire straightened.

"She owes me," Nola said. "Now get out of my way before the Outer Guard come."

The vampires stood frozen for a moment before, as a unit, they stepped back and out of her way.

Nola sprinted down the hall, the scent of the vampire still caught in her nose.

Soon, the doors became nicer, and she found the carved wooden door that led to Emanuel's home. Five guards stood flanking the entrance to the gallery.

"Nola." Bryant stepped forward as Nola skidded to a stop. "Where's Kieran?"

"At 5th and Nightland," Nola said as quickly as her panting would allow. "He stayed to fight. The Outer Guard made it through the doors. They're in the corridor."

"We know." Bryant opened the door to the gallery. "Get inside. They'll take you someplace safe."

Nola stepped into the gallery, and a cold hand closed around Nola's arm.

"And here I thought you might have run into the waiting arms of the guards," Julian said, dragging Nola through the gallery and to the living quarters.

"I thought about it," Nola said, her breath still coming in short gasps, "but I didn't know if it would make them stop. And Kieran said to stay out of sight."

"Kieran is a very smart lad." Julian led her through the kitchen and the narrow door in the back. There was a wooden door on the right and a heavy, metal door straight ahead.

Julian pounded on the metal door with his palm. "Dr. Wynne, I have Nola."

A shadow flitted behind a tiny piece of thick glass in the door. A creaking came from the other side before the door, even thicker than the entrance to 5th and Nightland, ground slowly open.

"Oh, thank God," Dr. Wynne said, beckoning Nola into the room.

"Reseal the door." Julian turned and ran away.

Dr. Wynne put his shoulder into the door and slid it shut before turning a thick metal wheel in the center that closed the lock with a heavy *clunk*.

"Where's Kieran?" Dr. Wynne asked as soon as the door had been secured.

"He's fighting," Nola said. A horrible stone of guilt settled in her stomach. "He told me to run. But there are others there. He'll be fine. He has to be."

"Nola dear," Dr. Wynne said, his voice unusually tired, "I gave up on my son being safe the moment I turned him into a vampire. It was my fault we were banished from the domes and my drug that turned him."

"To save his life."

"I saved his life by making him a part of a very dangerous community." Dr. Wynne took off his glasses and kept his gaze down as he slowly cleaned the lenses on his shirt.

Nola didn't miss the glimmer of tears in his eyes.

"Every day I have with him is an extra gift I don't deserve. Kieran is a brave man. He would never sit idly by while others are in danger. Of course he's fighting. And he won't stop until everyone is safe."

"But he'll be okay," Nola said, unable to keep a trace of question from her voice.

"He's a vampire, Nola," Dr. Wynne said. "And a strong one at that. That is the best assurance we have that he'll be back in a few hours. Beaten, bloody, maybe missing a few fingers. But he'll still be Kieran, and he'll heal."

"Because you made him that way." Nola turned to the door, wondering how long it would be until someone came for them.

"Because I made him that way."

Nola scanned the room where she'd been trapped.

No. Protected. They're keeping you safe.

She had expected concrete, weapon-lined walls. But instead, a pattern of bright blue clouds decorated the eggshell-white walls. Along one side sat a small bed with a soft pink comforter, and in the corner Bea rested in a rocking chair, apparently unfazed by the commotion around her. Eden huddled at Bea's feet, clutching a ragdoll.

Of course Eden sleeps in the safest room in Nightland. Emanuel wouldn't have it any other way.

He's keeping me safe, too.

"How are you?" Nola asked, sitting on the floor.

"Good," Eden muttered, crawling over and planting herself firmly in Nola's lap. "Did you get a booboo?"

"A little one," Nola said, shaking her head at Dr. Wynne's startled look. "I fell and cut myself. It's not that bad. I just wanted to hide the smell."

Dr. Wynne pulled a wash basin and jug down from the dresser in the corner and sat on the floor next to Nola.

The walls shook, and Eden clung to Nola's neck. "It's okay," Eden whispered into Nola's ear. "My daddy made this place safe for me, and he'll come get us when he gets rid of the bad men."

"He sure will." Nola pushed Eden's curls behind her ears with her good hand, trying not to flinch as Dr. Wynne began washing the dirt from her other palm.

The walls shook again, and Nola swallowed hard, trying not to show Eden her panic. Trapped underground. What if the tunnel collapsed? They would be buried forever.

Nola tried to picture herself in the domes, full of light and air.

Far away from Kieran.

"Why did the bad men come?" Eden asked, standing up so she was eye to eye with Nola.

"They aren't bad men," Nola said. "You know how you're afraid of them? They're afraid of you, too. And sometimes when people are very afraid, they do things they shouldn't, and they hurt people."

"Why are they scared of me?" Eden tipped her head to the side and scrunched up her forehead.

"Because they don't understand how wonderful and precious you are," Nola said. "They don't understand your daddy is just trying to make a safe home for lots of people."

"If they did, would they go away?"

"I think so."

"When I get big, I will teach them we are nice, and my daddy is nice," Eden said, lifting her pudgy chin in determination.

"I'm sure you will."

"All done," Dr. Wynne said, tucking a bandage around Nola's palm. "While I admire the ingenuity of using dirt to try and cover the blood odor, I wouldn't recommend using tunnel dirt for that purpose in the future. It's not really sanitary. Although if it's either that or be considered a snack, I suppose the chance of infection is worth it."

"Right, desperate times only." Nola stood and sat on Eden's bed. The mattress springs creaked under her weight.

Eden followed her, curling up and tucking her head on Nola's lap. Another *boom* echoed through the walls, this one more distant than the last.

Were the guards being driven back, or simply coming at them from another direction?

Eden whimpered and covered her face with her doll.

"Hush," Nola said, stroking the girl's silky, black curls. "We're safe here. Just close your eyes and relax."

Nola hummed a song her father had sung to her when she was very little. She couldn't remember the words anymore. Only that she had liked the tune—the song had made her feel happy, safe, and sure her father would always be there to fight the demons away.

Nola kept humming as Eden's breathing became slow and steady, hoping Eden would fare better than she had. And Eden's father would come home.

---

*L*oud banging on the door shook Nola from her stupor. Eden clamped her hands over her ears. Dr. Wynne ran to peer through the glass slit in the door. Even Bea sat up straight in her rocking chair, the first sign she had given that she had noticed anything strange.

"Emanuel," Dr. Wynne said, opening the door and tripping over Eden as she streaked past him into her father's waiting arms.

Emanuel swept Eden up, holding her to his chest. "It's all right," he murmured. "You're safe, Eden. Daddy would never let anyone hurt you."

He had been in the fight. A long cut marred his cheek and blood matted his hair. The cut already appeared days old.

"Kieran?" Dr. Wynne said, before Nola could form the word.

"He's alive," Julian said from behind Emanuel's shoulder.

"Alive?" Nola clung to the door.

"He was hurt," Emanuel said. "Badly. But he'll heal."

"They didn't get his heart?" Dr. Wynne lifted a trembling hand to his glasses.

"No," Julian said, "though they tried their damndest. He's unconscious now, but I think if you give him another dose of ReVamp—"

"He shouldn't need anymore. Not for weeks." Dr. Wynne's voice sounded thin, like there wasn't enough of him left to contemplate the injuries of his only son.

"He needs to heal more quickly," Emanuel said. "Stitch him up, and give him an injection. Then we can wake him and get him to the bridge."

"Bridge?" Nola said. "What happened to Kieran that he needs more ReVamp? He's supposed to be able to heal."

"He will," Julian said.

"But—"

"Kieran needs to be fit for the exchange," Emanuel said. "We're moving forward."

"But they attacked us!" Nola said so loudly Eden covered her ears again. "They came in here and ruined everything, and you think they'll go through with the deal?"

"They'll have to," Emanuel said. "They won't leave you standing on the bridge."

"And you're just letting them take me?"

"They only sent in a handful of guards." Julian spread his hands in a helpless gesture. "If we tried to keep you here, it would be a rallying cry to start an all-out war."

"We can't protect Nightland if they decide to do that," Emanuel said, handing Eden to a waiting Bea who shuffled past them into the kitchen. "They could blast down from the city."

"It would be catastrophic, and not just for Nightland. For the humans who are still trying to survive aboveground," Julian said. "But after tonight, I can't find it in myself to believe the Outer Guard wouldn't do it."

"So, we go to the bridge." Nola's voice sounded far away as she said the words.

"I'll try and wake Kieran," Dr. Wynne said.

"Don't." Nola gripped his sleeve. "Let him sleep. He needs to heal."

"He would want to be there," Julian said.

Nola shook her head, wincing as the pain of heartbreak cracked in her chest. "I don't know if I have the strength to walk away from him." Her voice came out barely louder than a breath.

"Is there anything you want me to tell him?" Dr. Wynne asked, squeezing Nola's hand.

"Nothing that will make it hurt less."

The tunnels had collapsed in places. Bits of stone and piles of dirt littered the corridor. Some of the light bulbs had blown out, and those that remained flickered feebly.

Raina maintained a viselike grip on Nola's arm as she steered her though the halls, half-lifting her over the ruble.

"I'm not going to try and run," Nola said as Raina's fingers dug painfully into Nola's arm when they passed a vampire lying in a pool of his own blood. The man's breath rattled though his wounded chest. "Should we help him?"

"He'll heal," Raina said. "And I'm not worried about you running. We have a lot of pissed off vampires who don't know if the Outer Guard are going to try and attack again. I'm supposed to get you to the bridge, and I'll be damned if I let someone snatch you before trade time. Sorry, you'll just have to live with the bruises."

Sour bile rose in Nola's throat as Raina led her past a woman mumbling and crying as she clasped her bloody stump of an arm.

They reached 5th and Nightland, but if Nola hadn't known their destination, she wouldn't have recognized the club at all.

No music pounded through the air. No dancers writhed to the pulsing beat. The bright flashing lights had been replaced by pale moonbeams creeping in through the giant hole that led to the streets above. Lined up along one wall lay five vampires, their hands crossed gently on their chests. Nola tried not to look at the horrible wounds that covered their bodies. One woman had a hole larger than a fist in her chest. One man's head was barely attached to his neck. All were too far gone to heal.

Under the hole where the trap door to the street had been lay six guards, their bodies torn and beaten, their faces still hidden by helmets. The body of a tall, broad shouldered male lay farthest down the line. His boots were shiny and new, his uniform hardly worn aside from the tears from the fight.

"Jeremy." Nola wrenched her arm away from Raina and ran to the end of the line. She knelt next to the body and cradled his head, trying take off the helmet. Her hands shook too badly to manage even its slight weight.

"Let me," Raina said, lifting away Nola's trembling hands.

Raina pulled off the helmet, and tears streamed from Nola's eyes as a head of bright blond hair emerged.

Nola had seen this man before. He was just old enough to have always been in the class above her. Lying in the dirt, he looked like a child.

A surge of guilt flooded through Nola.

Not Jeremy. It's not Jeremy.

He hadn't been lost to Nightland. But someone would mourn when the blond boy didn't come home.

"Not him?" Raina asked after a moment.

"Not him." Nola pushed herself back up to her feet. "What are you going to do with them? They're Domers. They should be burned and scattered to the wind."

"After we get you traded back, we'll figure that out," Raina said, taking Nola by the waist and lifting her high into the air, passing her to hands that waited at street level. "If they play nice and give us what we asked for, we might give the remains back as a peace offering."

Desmond set Nola down on the cracked pavement.

"And if not?" Nola asked, giving a nod of thanks to Desmond.

"We put them in the river," Raina said. "It's where all the death around here comes from anyway."

"It's time," Bryant said from his place at the head of the pack of vampires that had assembled as Nola's escort.

Nola nodded, feeling more like she was being led to the gallows than sent home.

Bryant led them through the city. A haunting *clang* echoed down the empty streets every time he struck his pipe on his open palm.

The journey to the bridge seemed much shorter than the first time Nola had made the trek alone in the darkness.

As the bridge rose in the distance, a lone figure in a long, black coat emerged from the shadows. A silver sword peeked out from under the coat's trim.

"Nice of you to join us," Raina said.

"I was scouting the bridge, if you must know," Julian said as he matched step with Nola. "And they do seem to be playing nicely."

A strangled cough came from Raina. "We'll see."

The first gray of dawn peered up over the hill.

The shadow of the Outer Guard caravan waited across the river.

Nola stood flanked by vampires. Julian and Raina each held one of her arms.

"Just stay calm," Julian said in a low voice. "They want to get you home safe, and so do we. If we all stay calm, we'll be in the tunnels before daylight and you can have a nice breakfast with your loving mother."

Nola nodded, not trusting her voice.

"Don't play the victim just yet," Raina said. "Keep your big girl panties on until you get back to the domes. Then you can curl up in a ball and tell them how badly we abused you."

"I won't lie," Nola said. "You're not monsters. You never hurt me."

"They have to believe we kidnapped you," Julian said. "Don't worry about our image. Keep the story believable, just like we practiced."

"Besides, I stabbed you," Raina said, a glint of laughter in her eyes. "Use that for your inspiration."

"Right," Nola said. "That *did* really hurt."

"It's time," Desmond called from his perch on the side of the bridge.

"Forward ho," Julian said, pushing Nola in front of him and Raina as though using her as a human shield.

"Can't I walk next to you?" Nola said, fighting her instinct to run as guards piled out of the trucks.

"I want to get you home safe, dear," Julian said, "but I'd like to get home, too. And they're much less likely to shoot you than me. So, you first."

"Right." Nola put one foot in front of the other. But somehow the distance between her and the trucks never seemed to lessen.

I'll have to walk until dawn. We'll still be walking across this bridge when the sun rises and burns the vampires.

With a bright flash, all of the trucks turned their lights on as one, shining them directly at Nola. The hiss of the vampires echoed behind her. She tried to lift a hand to cover her eyes, but Julian and Raina kept her arms pinned to her sides. She squinted, trying to see past the lights. Spokes of bright white emanated from the sides of the glow that blinded her.

Shadows moved in front of the lights, and red beams joined the white ones.

"Lower your weapons," Desmond's deep voice boomed from far behind her. "Lower your weapons, Domers, or Magnolia Kent goes into the river."

The flashes of red lowered toward the ground.

"Magnolia, are you all right?" A magnified voice came from the far end of the bridge.

"Yes," Nola said, her voice stuck in her throat. She swallowed. "Yes!" She shouted.

"Bring the package to the middle of the bridge," Desmond called. "Once we confirm you've given us what we asked for, we'll give you the girl."

Lights bounced across the bridge as three guards ran forward, two with rifles pointed at the vampires, one with a box in his hands.

"That's it?" Nola asked. "That's all you wanted?"

"It's a lot." Julian let go of Nola's arm and took a step forward. "I'm coming to inspect the package."

Nola held her breath as Julian ran toward the rifles all alone.

"He shouldn't be out there by himself," Nola said. "What if something goes wrong?"

"Careful, Domer," Raina said, "you almost sound like you care."

The guards placed the package in the middle of the bridge and took three steps back.

Julian bowed to them as he reached the box before kneeling over it.

A minute ticked past and then another as Julian examined the package.

"It's all here," he finally called over his shoulder.

"Here we go." Raina pushed Nola forward. "Try not to end up in Nightland again."

"In case you stab me a little too well next time?" Nola asked, trying to sound cavalier as her knees wobbled with each step.

"If you hadn't been wearing an oversize protective guard coat, I would've gotten you in the heart. And then what would we have to trade?" Raina said.

Nola turned to see a smirk on Raina's face.

"Hooray for oversized coats," Nola whispered, unsure if any sound had really come out.

Julian stood, hands behind his back as he faced the guards.

"I'll pick up the box," Julian said. "Then Magnolia walks to you."

"The girl comes to us first," the guard said.

"Funny how I know our prisoner's name, and you call your citizen *the girl*."

"Julian," Raina hissed.

"Anyway," Julian said, "I pick up the box, then you get *the girl* whilst we run away. If you don't agree"—Julian pointed over his shoulder, and instantly cold hands wrapped around Nola's neck—"one flick of my dear friend's wrists, and Magnolia is no more."

Silence hung over the bridge. Raina's fingers around Nola's neck drained the warmth from her body, leaving her shivering.

"I like that," Raina murmured. "Keep it up."

"Take the box," the guard said.

"Thank you." Julian lifted the box that seemed to weigh hardly anything, at least to a vampire.

"Now the girl," the guard called.

"Good luck," Raina said, shoving Nola forward.

Nola stumbled before her legs remembered how to walk. The bridge echoed with each step under the heavy boots Raina had given her. In two steps, she was past Julian. A moment later, a guard lifted her into his arms and sprinted back across the bridge, carrying her like a child.

Roars spilt the night as the Outer Guard's trucks started.

Nola twisted, trying to look back at the other end of the bridge to see if the vampires had made it to safety. In the glare of the truck lights, she could almost make out two figures running away across the bridge.

"You're safe now," the guard who carried her said.

"Is she hurt?" Lenora jumped out of the back of a truck and ran toward them. Someone pushing a gurney sprinted forward.

Lenora grabbed her daughter's hand as the guard lowered Nola onto the gurney. Nola gagged as the smell of medicine and cleaner surrounded her.

Lenora gasped, looking horror-struck at Nola's red, scarred hands. "What did they do to you?"

"Out of the way, ma'am," a doctor said as two guards lifted the gurney into a truck. Lenora clambered in after, and the truck sped up the hill.

A guard waited in the corner of the truck. He reached out, placing a hand on Nola's shoulder before taking off his helmet.

Sweat covered Jeremy's forehead, and tears welled in the corners of his eyes.

"You're alive," he whispered, lifting Nola's hand to his lips. "Thank God you're alive."

The slow, steady beeping marked the minutes they forced Nola to lay in bed. After the Outer Guard raced her back to the domes, the doctors had made Lenora and Jeremy leave. They ran tests and scans, drawing her blood and searching her entire body for signs of harm.

"I'm fine," Nola said, so many times the words seemed to lose all meaning.

They put a mask over her face and made her breathe in medicine that smelled like soured fruit, then stuck needles into her arm to pump in antibiotics. Each of her bruises had to be recorded. Kieran's finger marks showed purple on her arms. The doctors all spoke in low voices about the horrible abuse she had suffered.

Nola bit her lips until they bled, fighting the need to scream that Kieran had been saving her life when he bruised her—he would never ever hurt her. But then they would know where Kieran was, and they would never believe her anyway.

Finally, when the sun had fully risen, the doctors left.

Before Nola could take a breath, more people invaded the bright white cell. Jeremy's father walked stoically into the room followed by a man with a bald head and thick black eyebrows, wearing a Dome Guard uniform. The embroidered rectangle on his chest read *Captain Stokes*. Lenora and Jeremy followed close behind, Lenora leaning on Jeremy's arm for support.

"How are you, Magnolia?" Captain Ridgeway asked in the softest tone Nola had ever heard him use.

"I'm fine," Nola said for the hundredth time that hour.

Captain Ridgeway nodded to Lenora and Jeremy, and they parted ways, taking up posts on either side of the head of Nola's bed as though guarding her.

Jeremy reached out to take Nola's hand, but it was heavily bandaged in thick foam. They had to heal the imperfections the rain had left on her skin.

Nola wanted to tear off the bandages and throw them to the floor.

Why does it matter if I'm not dome perfect?

"Magnolia," Lenora said, "did you hear him?"

Nola looked to Captain Ridgeway. He stared down at her with mixed concern and anger on his face. Nola hoped the anger wasn't for her.

"No," Nola said. "Sorry."

"I need to ask you what happened when they took you," Captain Ridgeway said. "The more we know, the sooner we can act."

"Act?" Nola tried to sit up in bed, but Jeremy's hand on her shoulder held her down.

"We need to know how they got in and what happened to you," Captain Ridgeway said, his eyes boring into Nola's as though he hoped to watch the events unfold within them. "The more we know, the better we can protect the domes and make sure the Vampers don't get in here again."

"All right," Nola said.

"They've said we can stay, if it'll make it easier for you. If you'll feel more comfortable," Lenora said, brushing a hair from Nola's face. She hadn't done that since Nola was very little.

"But if you would rather speak to us alone," Captain Stokes said, his glare darting from Lenora to Jeremy, "then I am sure they can wait outside and see you when we've finished."

Will it be easier to lie with them in here, or to say it all again later?

Jeremy's hand warmed Nola's shoulder. He was there, protecting her from his father and Captain Stokes.

"They can stay," Nola said.

"Fine." Captain Ridgeway nodded. "Now, start from the beginning."

"The beginning..." Nola's mind raced back to kissing Jeremy under the bushes. "I had a fight with my mother."

Lenora gave a sharp exhale. Nola looked up and found tears welling in her mother's eyes.

"I was upset, so I went to see Jeremy," Nola said. "I know it was late, and I shouldn't have been there—"

"I should have walked you home," Jeremy said, his voice a low growl.

"No." Nola laid a mittened hand on Jeremy's. She should have made them leave. She had only thought of making it easier on herself, not protecting them. "They wanted me. If you had been there, they would have hurt you."

"What happened when you left Jeremy?" Captain Stokes stepped forward.

"I was leaving, and then two people came out of the dark," Nola said, remembering the words Julian had taught her. "A man and a woman. The woman had a knife. She told me to send the guard at the stairs to Jeremy's house. She said she would kill me if I didn't. Her eyes were black. I knew she was a vampire and I wouldn't be able to run away, so I did it."

"What happened next?" Captain Stokes asked.

For the first time Nola noticed the recorder sitting in his palm.

"They made me put on the guard's hat and coat. We went back to Bright Dome, and in the back there was a loose section of glass. We crawled through it and into the rain."

"Did you move the glass or did they?" Captain Stokes asked.

Fingerprints. Julian had warned her once she told the guards how she had gotten out, they would check for fingerprints.

"I did," Nola said, "mostly. The woman told me to, and I tried, but it was heavy. The man ended up moving it in the end."

"What then?"

"We went outside. Down the hill toward the bridge. The rain was so thick, I could barely see. I got scared. I didn't know where they were taking me. So I ran. I barely made it ten feet. Something sliced into my back, and I fell. I think that's how I hurt my hands." Nola glanced down at the thick bandages that hid the red scars. "My head hurt, and when I woke up I was locked in a room. There was a doctor who took care of me. Then he came to ask me questions."

"Who's *he*?" Captain Ridgeway asked, a fire brewing in his eyes.

"Emanuel." Nola whispered the word. Julian had told her to say it, said to give the name, that the Outer Guard already knew who commanded Nightland, but the hatred in Captain Ridgeway's eyes frightened Nola.

Jeremy's hand tightened on Nola's shoulder. Had he heard of Emanuel, too?

"What did Emanuel want to know?" Stokes asked.

"About Green Leaf," Nola said, her stomach throbbing as her mother gave a tiny sob. "They wanted to know what seed groups you had brought back and if we were expanding the domes to accommodate planting the new crops. I was scared, and it didn't seem important, so I told him."

"Good girl," Lenora said. "Why on earth would they think you knew anything worth all of this?"

"I don't think they really cared," Nola said, keeping her words steady. "I answered Emanuel's questions, and he left. I didn't see anyone again until they came to tell me they had given you a ransom demand and you had agreed to the swap. A few times, they gave me food. But the next time Emanuel came to see me was for the trade. They put a bag over my head and took me to the bridge. I didn't see anything until the bridge was in sight." Nola looked to Stokes. "I'm sorry I can't be more helpful."

"You've done very well, Magnolia," Captain Ridgeway said.

"Dr. Kent, Jeremy, why don't you give us a few minutes?" Captain Stokes said, his tone brusque and hard.

"Why?" Jeremy tightened his grip on Nola's shoulder. "You've asked your questions. She needs to rest."

"I'm afraid there are a few things left unanswered," Captain Stokes said, "and I think perhaps it's better to leave Magnolia on her own to answer them."

"I'm not leaving my daughter," Lenora said. "Ask your questions."

"As you wish." Stokes nodded. "The doctors found traces of drugs in your system. A version of Vamp."

Lenora gasped and seized Nola's face in her hands, staring into her eyes.

"I'm fine, Mom." Nola sat up, trying to push her mother away with her mittened hand. "The doctor gave it to me. Just a tiny bit. He was saving my life."

"By trying to make you a Vamper?" Jeremy sat on the bed next to Nola, examining her eyes as though searching for a monster behind the blue.

"Vamp helps you heal faster," Nola said, touching Jeremy's cheek with her bandaged hand. "They don't have a hospital like we do in here. I was stabbed in the shoulder. I would have died. And I'm fine. I can eat food and everything."

"And your leg?" Stokes asked.

"I don't know how that happened," Nola said. "But the doctor said he did the same thing as with my shoulder. Is that all?"

Nola stared at Stokes who glanced at Captain Ridgeway before responding. "No. There are bruises on your arms."

"And they matter more than me being stabbed?" Nola said.

"They're hand prints," Captain Ridgeway said. "Marks like that, someone pinned you down."

Lenora grabbed Nola's arm with shaking hands and pushed back her sleeve. "Oh God."

Jeremy wrapped his arm around Nola, pulling her close to him. His angry breaths rattled against her cheek.

"What's your question?" Nola didn't let herself flinch as she met Captain Ridgeway's gaze. She had been pinned down. Kieran was trying to protect her from the Outer Guard's attack, but that had been after Julian had taught her the lie.

"How did you get those marks, Magnolia?" Captain Ridgeway asked. "We need to know who pinned you down. Did someone hurt you?"

"Did one of the Vampers attack you?" Stokes asked, stepping in front of Captain Ridgeway. "Did Emanuel force himself on you?"

"What?" Nola screeched. "No, why would you think that? I told you they kept me in a room."

"Where Emanuel visited you," Captain Ridgeway said. "It's not your fault, Magnolia. No one would blame you."

"Emanuel never hurt me," Nola spat. "He would never lay a hand on me."

"You were stabbed." Jeremy's face was ice white, pain wrinkled the corners of his eyes where laughter should have lived. "They *did* hurt you."

"Yes," Nola said. "No. Yes, I was stabbed. No, Emanuel never raised a hand to me. He never would. You talk about him like he's some kind of monster—"

"He's a Vamper."

"He's a leader!" Nola shouted, shoving her mother and Jeremy away. "He is a leader of a lot of very desperate people. Emanuel doesn't want to hurt anybody. He's just trying to help his people survive!"

"Then where did you get the bruises?" Captain Ridgeway asked, the angry lines between his brows the only sign he had noticed Nola's outburst.

"When your guards tried to destroy Nightland," Nola said. "When you decided to blow your way into the tunnels when you had already agreed to a deal. Emanuel had come to get me. There was an explosion nearby, and part of the ceiling in my room fell. Emanuel saved me. He knocked me down and pinned me to the ground, out of the way of the falling rocks. He didn't want me to get hurt."

No one spoke as all four stared at Nola.

"Magnolia," Lenora said when the silence had begun to pound in Nola's ears, "you should rest. I'm sure any other questions they have can wait until later."

"Yes, Dr. Kent," Captain Stokes said, "I'm sure we can speak more after Magnolia has regained her composure."

Nola laughed. "I'm sure we can."

"Come on." Jeremy took her elbow, guiding Nola to lie back on the bed.

"Dr. Kent, if I could have a word," Captain Stokes said, still not pocketing his recorder. "In my office."

Lenora looked down at Nola.

"Go, Mom. Get it over with so they can leave us alone."

"I'll be back soon," Lenora said, tucking the sheets in around Nola before following Captain Stokes from the room.

"You'll be safe here," Jeremy said. "I won't let anyone hurt you. Not ever again." He leaned down and kissed the top of Nola's head.

"There are guards in the hall," Captain Ridgeway said, his face softening. "You can sleep. The domes are secure."

"Thanks," Nola said.

Captain Ridgeway turned to leave, but Jeremy sat down next to Nola.

"Can I stay with you?" he whispered.

His father had stopped outside the door, standing guard, feet planted apart, one hand on his weapon.

"To see if I drool?" Nola asked. Her eyelids weighed as heavy as lead as she laid her head down on the pillow.

"To see that you're safe," Jeremy said, taking Nola's bandaged hand in his. "I almost lost you, Nola. I could have lost you forever." He kissed the inside of Nola's wrist. "I can't risk that again."

"I'm not going anywhere." Pain tore at the edges of Nola's heart as she said the words.

I have nowhere to go.

She couldn't leave the domes. Her future lay inside the glass prison. But as she drifted off to sleep, her mind flew to Kieran, lying in a hospital bed deep underground. And she knew he would be thinking of her, too.

Hurried whispers lured Nola back out of sleep. It took her a moment to realize the voices came from the shadows beyond her door.

"This is my fault, Dad." Jeremy dragged a hand over his short hair. "I should have protected her. I should have made sure she got home safe."

"You should have." Captain Ridgeway took his son by the shoulders. "You *should* have walked her home. You *should* have made sure she wasn't alone in the dark. Every day for the rest of your life you'll wish you had walked that girl back to her mother."

Jeremy clutched his chest as though someone had punched a hole straight through him.

"But it's still not your fault. There was no reason you should have thought Vampers would have found a way into the domes, let alone targeted Lenora Kent's daughter. Just because you *should* have walked her home," Captain Ridgeway said, still gripping Jeremy's shoulders, "that doesn't make what those monsters did your fault. That's on them, not you."

"It *is* on me," Jeremy said. "I could have stopped it. All of those scars are my fault. If one of those monsters raped her—"

"She says they didn't."

"She says they would never hurt her." Jeremy turned away from his father, and light fell across his face. His eyes were wide with madness and pain. "She thinks they're good people, Dad. What if they brainwashed her?"

"They didn't," Captain Ridgeway said. He turned to look in at Nola, and she clamped her eyes shut. "She's confused, but she's still her. It happens sometimes. Kidnap victims start to sympathize with their kidnappers."

"So, what do I do?" Jeremy said.

"Let her heal," Captain Ridgeway said. "Give her time to sort out everything those monsters put her through."

There was a long pause.

"And keep a close eye on her, in case she sorts things out the wrong way."

"Thanks, Dad."

"I always thought you'd be a good Outer Guard, Son," Captain Ridgeway said. There were two soft thumps of Jeremy being patted on the shoulder. "Between your mother's blood and mine, I knew you'd have what it takes. But now, I'll be damned if you don't turn out to be the best guard we've ever seen."

"Why?" Jeremy asked. His voice sounded closer, and his shadow fell across Nola's eyelids as he stood next to her bed.

"Because you've got that girl to fight for."

---

*T*he doctors swarmed Nola as soon as she woke up. More blood to be drawn, more drugs to be administered. Lenora sat by her daughter's bed the whole time, asking questions about everything they were doing until Nola asked her to stop. She didn't want to know what the needles were for. She just wanted them to finish their work and leave her alone.

She hadn't seen Jeremy since she woke up. Every time she thought of him, the guilt rushed back. He blamed himself for her being kidnapped, but that wasn't what had happened at all.

"Where's Jeremy?" Nola finally asked her mother when they took the horrible breathing mask off after a half-hour treatment.

"I sent him away." Lenora pinched the bridge of her nose. "He didn't sleep last night. He stayed awake, watching you. He's terrified you'll disappear again. I am, too."

"Mom—"

"I'm sorry we fought." Tears shone in the corners of Lenora's eyes. "You are a good and kind girl. You have a bigger heart than I am capable of, and if I had lost you—"

"You didn't."

"I know. And I am so very grateful for that." Lenora patted Nola's hand. The thick mittens had been replaced by green silicone gloves filled with goo that didn't seem to warm up no matter how long it touched her skin.

"And Jeremy," Lenora said. "He's a good boy. It's difficult for me to admit, but I was wrong about him. And his father. I don't think either of them slept while you were gone. If it hadn't been for Captain Ridgeway and the Outer Guard, I don't know if we would have gotten you back alive."

"Right. You're right."

Julian had taught her the lie.

He didn't teach me how to live with it.

"How's Sleeping Beauty?" Jeremy appeared at the door.

"I'm fine," Nola said.

I'm never going to get to stop answering that question.

"I thought *you* were sleeping," Nola said.

"I did." Jeremy smiled. "I'm bright as a daisy."

"If you're going to sit with her for a while…" Lenora said, standing.

"Go to your lab, Mom." Nola shooed her mother away.

"I'll check in later." Lenora gave a quick wave and slipped out the door.

"Wow," Nola said. "For her, that was downright clingy."

"She was worried about you." Jeremy sat down on Nola's bed, holding out a cup of foamy green sludge. "Terrified actually. We all were."

"So, now you want to poison me for scaring you so badly?" Nola sniffed the cup. It smelled like a mix between fungus, chlorophyll, and fertilizer.

"It's a detox shake." Jeremy grinned. "It's what the guards who go outside the domes regularly drink to help purify their systems."

Nola took a sip, and gagged on the thick froth.

"I never saw my dad with this." She tried to push the cup away, but Jeremy lifted it back to her mouth.

"He would have had it in the barracks, not at home. Drink up."

Grimacing, Nola took another sip.

"You'll be having this for meals for a few days."

"Lucky me." Nola took a gulp and regretted it instantly.

"You *are* very lucky." Jeremy took her face in his hands, leaning in so his forehead touched hers. "And I am very lucky to have you home."

"Jeremy."

"I thought, when the raid didn't get you"—Jeremy's hands shook—"I thought we'd lost you for sure."

"The Outer Guard," Nola said, freezing with the cup halfway to her mouth, "were they sent down to the tunnels to get me? Only to get me? Emanuel had already made a deal."

"We didn't think they'd show at the bridge, and we couldn't leave you with the blood suckers."

"But the guards. Six guards died." The air vanished from the room. From the domes. "And vampires. Vampires died, too. Because of me."

Her glass shattered as it hit the floor.

"No. Because of the Vampers that took you," Jeremy said. "They took a citizen of the domes. We had to get you back. Those guards knew what they were getting into."

"Dead." The line of guards, their bodies torn and twisted, flashed through Nola's mind. "Bloody and dead because of me."

Sobs broke over her words. Gasping breaths racked her lungs, sending pain shooting into her heart. She had tried to help, and now there was blood on her hands.

Jeremy bundled her into his arms. Hushing softly, he lay back on the bed, cradling her to his chest. "It's all right, Nola. It's over now. I'll keep you safe. I love you."

It took two days for the doctors to allow Nola to go home. Two days of smiling sweetly and hoping no one looked too close. Jeremy stayed with her all the time, only leaving when Lenora came by for a few hours here and there.

Three times the doctors had retested her blood, making sure the level of Vamp had decreased. Making sure she hadn't been turned.

A full set of guards came to escort Nola home. Lenora held onto Nola's arm the whole way to Bright Dome, as though terrified Nola might crumble and fall. What Lenora should have been afraid of was the voice in the back of Nola's mind screaming, *Run!*

But how could Nola run when she was flanked by guards?

Nola could sense Jeremy's eyes on her back as they walked. He hadn't said anything about her breakdown in the hospital. Only sat with her as she stared at the ceiling, wondering if the bodies of the guards had been returned to the domes or dumped into the river. He'd made small talk about the planting and had given regards from classmates. But mostly he had just held Nola tight as though he feared she would shatter into a thousand irreparable pieces. He didn't know how right he was.

"Here we are," Lenora said when they approached the house, as though Nola might have forgotten what her home looked like in a week.

"Thanks for walking me," Nola said to the guards, looking at their boots instead of their faces.

"You're welcome, Miss Kent," one of the guards said.

Nola glanced up to the man's face. He was broadly built with a square jaw and bright blond hair.

"Your brother," Nola forced the question out. "He was at Nightland?"

"He was a brave man, miss," the guard said, the sudden crease between his eyes his only show of grief. "He died a hero's death."

"He did," Lenora said, taking the guard's hand. "And we are so very thankful."

The guard nodded to Lenora and looked back to Nola. "Welcome home."

Lenora kept her hand on Nola's back as she guided her into the house.

"Well," Lenora said as soon as she had closed the kitchen door, leaving only herself, Nola, and Jeremy in the house, "I guess I should make dinner. A nice welcome home meal."

"You don't have to," Nola said. "You can go back to the lab."

"No." Lenora shook her head, straightening Nola's braid over her shoulder. "I want to make you a welcome home dinner. Jeremy, you'll stay of course."

"Thank you, ma'am," Jeremy said.

"I think I'll go to my room for awhile," Nola said.

The clanging of the pots and pans drilled into her ears as she climbed the steps.

Nothing should be this normal. This calm.

Jeremy's footsteps followed her up the stairs.

"I'm fine," Nola said as she opened the door to her room. "I can find my..." but her words trailed off as she stared at her desk. A beautiful orchid waited for her.

"Do you like it?" Jeremy asked. "It's an old tradition. To bring your girl flowers."

"Where did you get it?"

Bright purple speckled the white petals.

"I have an in with the head of Plant Preservation," Jeremy said.

"It's beautiful." Nola turned to face Jeremy, feeling a genuine smile flicker across her face.

"Not as beautiful as you." Jeremy pressed his lips to the top of Nola's head. "I love you."

He had said it a dozen times since Nola came back. She still didn't know how to answer.

"Jeremy, I—" How could she begin to break his heart?

"Don't," Jeremy said, wrapping his arms around Nola. "I don't need you to say it back. I don't need you to tell me you want to spend the rest of your life with me."

Nola's heart stopped as Jeremy tipped her chin up to meet his gaze.

"But I need you to know that I love you. I've loved you for years, Nola, and if I hadn't told you before they took you, if you hadn't come back..."

"But I did," Nola whispered.

"And now I have the chance to tell you every day," Jeremy said. "I won't lose that."

Nola pulled her gaze away, looking back at the flower. The bloom seemed so strong, so sturdy, but a fierce wind could break its stem. Damage it beyond repair.

"I know you need time," Jeremy said. "You need time to sort through everything that happened. But I'll be here. I'll help you any way I can. I love you. I want to spend the rest of my life with you."

Nola's heart skipped. For a moment, she wasn't sure it would start beating again. For a moment, she didn't want it to.

"I'll wait for you, Nola. As long as it takes."

"But what if I'm not here?" Nola said.

Better to make a break. A clean break.

Jeremy froze his arms still around Nola's waist. "What you do mean *not here?*"

"I can't stay here. I can't stay in the domes." Now that she'd begun, the words tumbled out. "Eleven people died because of me. I can't stay locked in here and pretend it didn't happen. If I go out there, I could help people. There are gardens, ways to grow food out there. I could help people have food to eat. I could save lives. And then maybe those eleven deaths would mean something."

"They do mean something," Jeremy said. "Those guards who went down after you were trained. They were doing their jobs."

"They should have left me!" Nola clamped her hands over her mouth. "But they didn't. I'm here, and they're dead. And the only way I can live with that is to make my life worth it."

"You can do that here," Jeremy said, taking Nola's hands in his larger ones, making her newly healed skin disappear beneath his grasp. "You are brilliant, like your mother. You can join botany, help with the work of the domes."

"That's not good enough." Tears stung her eyes. "There are people dying out there right now, and I can't just pretend it isn't happening. I've seen it. I can't ignore it."

Jeremy studied Nola for a minute as though searching for a crack. "Fine. We'll leave the domes."

"We'll? Jeremy, no you don't understand."

"I lost you out there once. I won't do it again. I love you, Nola, and love means finding a way to stay together. You go out there, I go, too."

"Jere—"

"But not yet. You say you want to help people, and I understand that. But you haven't even finished school yet. You finish school and do your apprenticeship, then we'll go."

"An apprenticeship takes a couple of years. I can't stay here that long. There are people out there who need help now."

"There will always be people who need help, Nola. But how much more good will you be able to do when you're fully trained?"

Nola buried her face in Jeremy's shirt, shutting her eyes as tightly as she could bear.

"Once your training's done, we'll ask to be released from the domes." Jeremy held her tight, his broad shoulders surrounding her, blocking out everything else in the world. "I'll have a few years as a guard by then. I'll be able to protect you."

"Jeremy," Nola said, not taking her face from his chest. "I can't let you do that."

"You're not *letting* me do anything," Jeremy said.

"And when we get sick?"

Jeremy stepped back so Nola had to look at him. "I won't let that happen."

He meant it.

He would leave the domes for me. Leave everything he knows to follow me.

"I should go down," Jeremy said. "I don't want your mother to get worried about my being up here. She made a whole list of rules for me."

"She did?"

"Yep," Jeremy said. "And I'll follow them to a T. I don't want to lose my 'Nola privileges.'"

Nola took Jeremy's hand before he could leave. "How are you so good?"

"Because"—Jeremy leaned down, brushing his lips against Nola's—"I've spent a long time trying to become the kind of man you deserve." He smiled and disappeared through the door.

Nola went to the head of her bed, sinking down onto the floor. She took deep breaths, staring down at her perfect hands, trying not to let panic take her.

Jeremy loved her. He was perfect and good. He would do anything to keep her safe.

Kieran.

They had said their goodbyes. She should leave him alone. He didn't want her to be a part of Nightland, didn't want to make her a vampire.

Nola dug her fists into her eyes. Being a citizen of the domes meant making sacrifices to build a better world.

The figures of the dead eleven swam into her mind. The people who would morn for them, the days they would never get to live.

Nola reached into the desk drawer for a piece of paper. Her fingers closed around the tiny wooden tree Kieran had left for her.

Her hand shook as she found a pen and began to write.

D ear Jeremy,

I'm sorry. I'm sorry I'm not the girl you need me to be. I have to go now. I can't wait. I can't survive it. Please don't try to find me. More people will get hurt, and I can't survive that either.

Thank you. Thank you for being there even before I knew it was you holding me up. Please find another girl to love. Someone who can give you the life you deserve.

I love you, Jeremy. You are good, and brave, and everything wonderful. I will always love you.

Please forgive me,

Nola

S he folded up the paper and tucked it under the orchid. He would find it first. He would tear apart the domes searching for her. Nola tugged on her work boots and pulled her thick coat from the closet, hiding the tree charm in her pocket. She could sneak out now while they thought she was resting. She would go to the atrium. Sneak onto a truck and find a way out from there.

Nola's mother's laugh rang up the stairs. She hadn't heard her mother laugh like that in years. The urge to run to her mother and hold her close froze Nola in place. But if she went down the stairs, she might never find the courage to leave.

Nola slipped the note back out from under the flower pot.

Please explain to my mother. And tell her I'm sorry.

She scrawled the words quickly and tucked the note back in place.

Taking the I-Vent from her drawer, she slipped it into her pocket. Eden might need it. Sitting on the windowsill, she swung one leg out the window.

BANG!

29

The sound shook the glass of the dome as brilliant orange flames lit the night. Nola tumbled backwards into the room, hitting her head on the floor. The ceiling spun as shouts shot up from the kitchen.

"Nola!" Jeremy shouted.

"What's happening?" Lenora screamed.

Jeremy threw open Nola's door.

"Are you hurt?" he knelt by her side.

"I fell," Nola said, shaking her head and sending her vision spinning again, "but I'm fine."

Flashing red light poured through Nola's window as the emergency siren blared to life.

"Is she all right?" Lenora ran into the room.

A piercing *beep, beep, beep* cut in between the siren's wails.

"We're under attack." The color drained from Lenora's face. "The domes are under attack. I have to secure the seedlings." Lenora looked down at Nola.

"I'll get her to the bunker," Jeremy said, yanking Nola to her feet. "You go."

Lenora nodded and ran out the door.

"Who's attacking us?" Nola screamed as another explosion shook the house. A fresh burst of orange lit the night, coming from the direction of the atrium.

"I don't know," Jeremy said, pulling Nola's arm. "But we have to go."

He ran down the stairs and out into the night, half-carrying Nola as she struggled to keep up.

Other figures dashed through the dark, heading for the tunnel. Nola couldn't recognize the people in the flickering shadows of the fire that blazed in front of the atrium. There were two bunkers for catastrophes in the domes. Nola had always thought they were for natural disasters—a hurricane strong enough to destroy their home—but now the Domers ran from monsters in the dark.

Tiny *pops* and *bangs* pounded through the glass as the guards added their weapons to the cacophony. At the base of the stairs Jeremy turned right, away from the atrium. The entrance to A bunker was there, under the vehicle site. But all the Domers ran away from the fighting, fleeing to the same hope of safety: the B bunker under the seed storage area.

Nola sprinted next to Jeremy, her feet pounding as quickly as they could. She stepped on something soft and tumbled to the ground.

"Nola!" Jeremy screamed, lifting her to her feet before she could see what she had tripped over. A man lay face down on the ground, blood pooling around him.

Jeremy pushed Nola against the wall as another group came running by, barely missing trampling the man.

"He's breathing." Jeremy hoisted the man over his shoulder. "We can't leave him here."

A *pop* sounded in the hall behind them.

"Go!" Jeremy pushed Nola in front of him.

Down more stairs and past the Dome Guard's quarters. The doors to the empty barracks sat open. All of them had gone to the atrium.

Nola ran flat-out, Jeremy keeping up even with the added weight of the man.

They sprinted down another hall. A knot of people ran toward them. Nola moved to the side, letting them pass on their way to the atrium. The red lights flashed overhead, lighting the corridor and glinting off a head of scarlet and purple hair sliding out from under a hat.

"Raina!" Nola screamed.

Raina glanced back then picked up speed, running to the head of the knot of vampires, each wearing a heavily sagging pack.

"Stop!" Nola turned and tore back up the hall after the vampires.

"Nola, no!"

She heard Jeremy's shout but didn't slow down.

She sprinted up the stairs, ignoring the pain in her lungs, reaching the top just in time to see the last of the vampire pack round a corner toward the atrium. Nola pounded after them. People fled from the fight up ahead. Wounded guards were being carried into the hall, but there were still sounds of fighting coming from the atrium.

"Stop them!" Nola shouted to a group of guards that ran past her down to the tunnels Nola had just run out of, but the guards kept moving, their eyes focused front. Just before the atrium, the vampires turned left into the entrance for the small Grassland Dome.

Nola followed, barely hearing the shout of "Nola!" behind her.

The Grassland Dome had always been quiet and peaceful, filled with the rustling of grass. But tonight, screams rent the air. The explosion that had shattered the atrium had broken apart the glass here as well. A wide swath of the dome wall had shattered.

The vampires ran toward the break in the glass. In a moment, they would be outside. Nola couldn't catch them.

A group of guards ran in from the night, weapons raised high, blocking the way out.

Something hit Nola hard in the back, knocking her to the ground before a series of pops blasted over the bedlam.

"Stay down." Jeremy pinned Nola to the ground.

"Their bags." Nola shoved Jeremy off of her, trying to stand. "Their bags are full. They stole from us!"

Nola looked around wildly, half-expecting Emanuel to appear out of the dark and explain what was happening.

"I'll warn the guards." Jeremy leapt to his feet and charged toward the fight.

The guards battled hand-to-hand with the vampires now. Knifes and clubs flashed in the night.

"Jeremy!" Nola screamed after him. The vampires would tear him apart. "Jeremy."

Nola ran after him, ignoring the sting as the tall grass tore at her legs. More vampires and guards had joined the fight, with more appearing from the darkness every moment. Jeremy charged toward the middle of it.

Nola ducked as a pipe flew from the hand of a fighter, whizzing only a breath away from her skull. A cold hand grabbed Nola's wrist, jerking her back.

Before Nola could look at the face of the man who had grabbed her, he knocked her to the ground, planting a knee in her stomach. The man smiled and bared his glistening white fangs that were already stained red with blood.

"Help!" Nola screamed.

The man laughed. No one could hear her over the chaos.

He leaned down, pinning Nola's arms to the ground. She screamed as his fangs pierced her skin.

"Get off of her," a woman shouted, and the man was torn from Nola and tossed aside like a ragdoll.

Nola grabbed the place on her neck where the man's fangs had been ripped from her flesh. Hot blood streamed down her collar bone.

Raina stood over her in the dark.

"That one is to be left alone!" Raina shouted at the man. "It's his orders."

But the man had already reached for his knife. Holding it high in the air, he threw the blade at Nola, bloodlust glinting in his eyes.

Nola saw the knife. Watched it flying end over end toward her heart. There was nowhere to run, nothing to do.

Raina leapt to the side, and the sharp point of the knife disappeared into her chest.

"No!" Nola shouted as Raina collapsed to the ground.

The man looked down at Raina's body and ran, cutting through the fight and out into the night.

"Raina." Nola crawled over to her.

The knife stuck out of Raina's chest, moving as she fumbled for the hilt. Raina coughed, and blood trickled out of her mouth.

"You're okay." Nola lifted Raina's head into her lap, pushing the scarlet and purple hair away from her face.

A trail of blood dripped from Raina's lips to her chin. She coughed again, and a horrible gurgling sound came from the wound.

"You can heal from this." Nola pushed her hands down around the blade, trying to stop the bleeding. "Should I leave the knife in or take it out?"

A shrill whistle came from outside the domes.

"It's too late for me, kid," Raina said, her voice crackling as she spoke. She coughed a laugh and smiled. "Funny that a knife stopped me."

"I'll get help," Nola said, laying Raina's head gently down. She stood, searching for a vampire who would know what to do. But all the vampires were running out through the glass. The guards who were left standing were still trying to fight, but there were too many vampires.

"Stop please!" Nola shouted. "She needs help! Raina needs help."

Only one of the fleeing pack turned to face her. He wore a dark hood, but as the red light hit his face, she saw him.

Kieran.

His eyes were coal black, no hint of green or gold left at all. He carried a heavy box in his arms and was surrounded by vampires holding weapons.

"Go!" a voice shouted. Bryant lifted his pipe and charged at the guards.

Kieran looked at her for only a moment longer before racing after him.

"Kieran," Nola whispered, sinking to the ground. There were more shouts of pain and a visceral scream.

"Jeremy!" Nola shouted.

He was in the center of the fight, trying to stop the vampires.

Nola turned back to Raina. Her eyes were closed, but she would heal. She had to. Nola wrenched the knife from Raina's chest and ran into the fight.

Jeremy's left arm hung limp and bloody at his side. In his right hand, he held a guard's club, which he swung at a boy with brilliant red hair.

Nola had seen the red haired boy in Nightland. He had looked so young and helpless in the tunnels beneath the city. Now he bared his teeth, violent hatred twisting his face. He swung his broken sword at Jeremy's neck. Jeremy jumped backwards, dodging the jagged strip of metal, and swayed sideways. He had stepped on a guard who lay face up on the ground, her eyes wide open and blank.

The red-haired boy lunged again, taking advantage of Jeremy's stumble. Jeremy tried to duck, but his wounds slowed his reflexes.

Jeremy!

Nola couldn't make her mouth form the word. She raised Raina's knife high in the air and sank the blade into the boy's back. The sword fell from his hand as he screamed in rage and pain before dropping to the ground.

He lay still next to the fallen guard, his eyes as blank as hers.

"Nola." Jeremy scrambled toward her.

"I know where the heart is," Nola said.

"Nola," Jeremy said, "are you hurt?"

"I know where the heart is." Nola turned away from the red-haired boy. He wouldn't wake up.

"We have to go," Jeremy said, pushing Nola to move with his good hand that still clutched the club.

They ran back out of the Grassland Dome. Blood slicked the corridor floor.

"We need to get you to the bunker." Jeremy turned toward the corridor that led to seed storage and safety.

Nola ran to the atrium instead, grateful that Jeremy's heavy footfalls followed her.

Most of the glass on the city side of the atrium had been shattered. Shards of it covered the ground. The vampires had fled into the night. Guards stood at the break in the glass, trying to secure their ruined wall, shooting at the vampires that fell behind the rest of Nightland's retreat. Bodies lay twisted and broken on the ground. A blond girl lay by the door.

"Nikki." Nola knelt next to her, not caring as the glass sliced her knees.

She placed a hand on Nikki's chest. Blood coated her pale pink shirt. Her throat had been torn out, and terror filled her unmoving face.

Nola kept her hand pressed to Nikki's chest, waiting for a heartbeat she knew wouldn't come.

"She must have tried to come to the atrium bunker." Jeremy lifted Nola's hand away.

The sounds of the fighting had ended, replaced by cries of fear and pain mixing with shouted orders.

"Guards on the break, keep watch!" a voice bellowed in the darkness.

"Dad." Relief flooded Jeremy's face.

"All others to the armory." Captain Ridgeway stood in the middle of the rubble. Blood covered half of his face, a gash still dripping on his brow. The stoic man who defended the domes had disappeared; a raging warrior now commanded the Outer Guard. "We're going after the Vamper scum."

Jeremy nodded and stood.

"What are you doing?" Nola grabbed his good arm as he moved to follow the others.

"Going with the guards."

"But you can't." Nola held tight to his hand. "You're hurt."

"I have to, Nola." Jeremy's voice was low, filled with an anger she had never seen in him before.

Nola wrapped her arms around him as he tried again to walk away. "You said we had to get to the bunker, so let's go. We'll go together."

"Gentry and my dad will both be out there," Jeremy said.

"They're both Outer Guard."

"So am I. I was sworn in the day they took you," Jeremy said. "It was the only way I could help find you. Nola, I have to go."

"What if you're hurt? What if—"

Jeremy leaned down, silencing her protests with a kiss. Nola wrapped her arms around his neck, pulling herself closer to him, desperate to keep him there with her.

"I can't lose you," Nola whispered as he pulled away.

"Never." Jeremy smiled. "I love you, Nola. I'll be home soon." He was gone before Nola could stop him.

30

Nola stood frozen in the sea of chaos, unsure of what to do. The guards would be going to Nightland soon. She knew more about the tunnels than any of them.

I can't let anything happen to Jeremy.

Nola ran to the front of the atrium. The shattered glass crunched beneath her feet with every step. Blood pooled on the floor in places. Boot prints smeared the red, leaving designs of death in the battle's wake.

Had the blood spilled from Domer or vampire veins? Was there even a way to tell?

The engines of the guard trucks had already rumbled to life.

"Wait!" Nola shouted as the guards loaded into the back. "I have to go with you!"

"Not a chance," one of the guards said, blocking her at the break in the glass.

"But I've been in Nightland. I can help." Nola watched the stream of uniforms filing out of the domes, wishing she could catch a glimpse of Jeremy.

"Miss, you're injured. You need medical attention."

Nola's hand flew to her neck, sticking to the blood that covered her skin.

"The guards," Nola said. "Some of them are hurt, and they're going."

Gentry ran past, jamming on her helmet.

"Gentry!" Nola sprinted after her, catching Gentry's arm as she climbed into the truck. "I have to go with you."

"No citizens are to leave the domes, no exceptions," Gentry said. "Get to the bunker. Your mother will be there."

Nola took a breath, trying not to scream. Her mother waited below, guarding the seeds. But Jeremy would be in the tunnels.

Jeremy fighting Kieran.

"I can help. I know about Nightland!" Nola shouted desperately as Gentry turned away.

"If you think you have important information," Gentry said, "go to the Com Room. The operation is going to be controlled from there. Maybe they'll talk to you."

"Thank you," Nola shouted, already running for the far end of the atrium.

In the back of the atrium stood the tower, the only concrete structure to rise above the domes. Two guards flanked the doors to the staircase.

"I have to get up there," Nola panted, trying the push past the guards, who easily shoved her away.

"I'm afraid not, miss," the guard said. "Go to the medical unit. They can help you there."

"I'm Magnolia Kent. I was held in Nightland, and I have information that can help them. Please, you have to let me help."

One guard nodded to the other before raising his wrist to his mouth. "Magnolia Kent is here. She says she has information that can help."

There was a pause before a voice crackled out of the man's wrist. "Send her up."

"Thank you." Nola slid through the door before it had fully opened. She sprinted up the staircase.

This area hadn't been touched by the attack. The vampires hadn't bothered to break into the Communications Center.

Nola pounded up the flights of stairs, adrenaline pushing her to run faster.

How long until Jeremy reaches Nightland?

A guard waited at the top of the stairs, punching the code in to open the door only when Nola stopped, gasping for air, on the top landing.

"In here." The guard ushered Nola into the wide room.

She had been in the Com Room only once before. Years ago. Her entire class had been brought up here to see how communication with the other domes and the rest of the outside world worked. That day, the room had been a place filled with wonder, where she could see the face of a person on the other side of the world as they spoke. That day the world had seemed infinite and wonderful.

Today, chaos filled the tower.

Happy faces weren't smiling back from the screen. Instead, a live feed of the guards on their way to Nightland took up the whole wall. The Outer Guard poured out of their trucks onto the street at 5th and Nightland.

"Magnolia." Captain Stokes limped toward her. "They said you have information."

Nola's mind flickered back to her lessons with Julian. Sitting at the table, learning the things she was allowed to say.

The lie doesn't matter anymore. Nightland destroyed my home.

"I know where in Nightland Emanuel lives," Nola said. "I can tell your men how to get there."

Stokes stared at her for a moment. "Do it."

"But there's a little girl," Nola said as a man strapped a headset on her. "You have to promise me you won't hurt the little girl."

"We aren't the monsters here," Stokes said. "We don't hurt children."

The Outer Guard were in Nightland now.

"Tell them which way." Stokes fixed his gaze on the screen.

Nola squinted at the picture, trying to make sense of the shadows. "The second tunnel on the left, the one with the door blown off. Go that way."

The guards all moved in formation, slowly and methodically sweeping their lights in the tunnel. As the beams flashed over the rubble, Nola remembered the last time the guards had been in Nightland. Kieran had protected her, and now she was sending the guards after him.

"How far down?" Stokes asked.

Nola swallowed and looked out over the atrium. Smoke still billowed from the fire below. Through it she could barely see the dome helicopters taking flight. The helicopters had no sides. No defense against attack. But the brave pilots would fly over the city to try and aid their compatriots. They were going to help Jeremy.

"They'll hit a bigger tunnel. Follow that left until they find the wooden door," Nola said, her voice a harsh whisper. "It's old, and the wood has carvings in it. Go through there to the gallery. It's like an old library." Nola waited, watching the screen.

Screams carried through the feed.

"Behind you!" a man's voice shouted.

"I've got him!" a woman answered.

A *pop* and a scream of rage flooded Nola's ears as the screen flashed and went black.

"There are more behind him!" a voice shouted. "Keep going. We'll cover you."

The sounds of labored breathing and more shouting pounded into Nola's ears.

"I think I found it," the voice said after a moment. "Yep, this is it."

"We're clear," a different voice said.

"Where now?"

"Go through the door at the end," Nola said. "There's a kitchen on the right. In the back, there's another door. Through there is a heavy metal door. It's the safe room. That's where Emanuel will be."

"How do you know?" Stokes turned to Nola, his eyes sharp even though blood dripped from his leg.

"That's where his daughter will be," Nola said. "He wants to keep her safe."

"We're in the kitchen," the voice came through the headset. "The room is empty. The room with the metal door is open."

"Emanuel left." The words felt hollow in Nola's mouth.

"What?" Stokes said.

"Emanuel left," Nola said. "If Eden is gone, he will be too."

"How do you know?" Stokes asked, his forehead so furrowed his eyebrows had become one angry strip of black.

"The garden." Nola pointed out the window to the skyline of the city. "On the roof above Nightland, the second tallest building in the city, there should be a garden on the roof." Just because Emanuel left didn't mean all of Nightland was gone. Maybe Kieran had stayed behind in the city, saving the poor and the hungry.

The guard barked orders for a helicopter to circle the building.

Nola watched the light of the helicopter circling in the air. It looked like a fairy, far away over the city. Barely even a speck in the distance.

"There's a bunch of trash on the roof, sir," the pilot's voiced crackled in her ears. "It looks like there was something here, but whatever it was, it's gone now."

Nola's heart crumpled. The static of the screen swayed in front of her. "They're gone."

The garden, Dr. Wynne, Kieran.

"He's gone."

Nola's knees buckled. Arms steadied her and lifted her to a chair. But she couldn't think, couldn't move beyond Kieran.

Gone.

They sat her in a chair in the back of the Com Room. A doctor came up and cleaned and wrapped the wound on her neck.

"You're a lucky girl," the doctor said. "If you'd torn your jugular, there's nothing we could have done."

"Raina saved me." Nola stared at the dried blood that still covered her hands.

Mine, Raina's, the red-haired boy I killed, Nikki's. Who else's?

She couldn't even remember.

"Magnolia." Stokes came over from the giant screen. He had been shouting into the com a few minutes ago. Vampires had been hiding in the tunnels, waiting to ambush the guards. The guards kept talking about Emanuel leaving traps. But Emanuel would be out of the city by now, finding cover before dawn.

"Magnolia," Stokes said. "I need to ask you some questions."

"She needs to rest," the doctor said, planting himself in front of Nola.

She wanted to thank him, but Stokes had already pushed the doctor out of the way.

"I have guards risking their lives in the city," Stokes said. "She can rest when they do."

The doctor looked as though he might argue for a moment before shaking his head and walking through the metal door to the stairs.

Nola wanted to follow him. But where would she go? Had her mother made it home yet? Was her house even still standing? Had Bright Dome been destroyed?

"How did you know the path through the tunnels?" Stokes asked.

"He walked me from 5th and Nightland, from the Club to the gallery," Nola said. "He wanted me to see where he lived."

"And the garden on the roof?"

"He took me up." Tears burned in the corners of Nola's eyes. "He wanted to show me what they had built. He said they were finding a way to feed the city."

"Why didn't you tell us?"

"He said not to," Nola said. The burning had moved to her throat. "He said you would destroy the food, and people would starve. I thought they only wanted the ransom. I thought it was over and I would never see him again. He said they wanted to be left alone. I didn't want more fighting." Tears streamed down Nola's face.

"Sir," a man shouted from the front of the room. "We have a problem. The convoy's been attacked at 10th and Main."

Stokes cursed and ran back to the screen.

"We have wounded!" a voice echoed over the com. "We need emergency medical assistance."

Guards tore around the room, calling everyone they could for help. Nola pushed herself to her feet and stumbled to the door, running from the room before anyone tried to call her back.

Guards sprinted up and down the stairs. What had happened on the street? Sour rose into Nola's throat.

Wolves. There are still werewolves on the streets.

Back in the atrium, guard trucks drove in and out of the break in the glass, ignoring the place where the ruined door had been. Doctors rushed to the injured.

Nola watched as uniforms ran past, searching for Jeremy in the throng.

She shoved her shaking hands into her coat pockets. Her fingers closed around the tiny tree.

A truck rolled in, and gurneys were pulled from the back, but the doctors walked straight past. Those guards had been covered in white sheets. The doctors couldn't do anything for the dead.

Nola stood still as the chaos moved around her, her eyes constantly searching for Jeremy in the crowd. Every time a gurney passed, her heart stopped.

Not Jeremy. Please, not Jeremy.

Her nails dug into her palm as she gripped the tree. The wood cracked in her grasp. She pulled her hand from her pocket to stare at the broken and blood-

394 | MEGAN O'RUSSELL

covered charm. Tipping her palm, she let the tree tumble to the floor. The wood disappeared in the sea of shattered glass and blood.

The sky had turned from gray to pale orange as the sun began to rise, then back to gray as dark clouds coated the horizon. Trucks scrambled back out to the city. They had to get the rest of the guards inside before the rains began.

Lighting split the sky in the distance. The rumble of thunder shook the broken glass.

Another truck pulled into the dome. There were no gurneys this time. Only guards carrying their injured fellows.

"That's the last one!" the driver called just as the rain began to patter against the dome.

Nola ran toward the truck. Jeremy had to be in there. He had to be in the back of the truck. Nola scrambled into the truck bed. Blood stained the empty seats. "Jeremy."

She jumped down from the truck, stumbling before running through the crowd. "Jeremy! Jeremy!"

The bodies draped in white had been lined up against the wall, waiting for the families to be notified and the grieving to begin.

"Miss, you can't be over here," a guard said as Nola swayed staring at the bodies.

"Jeremy Ridgeway." Her mouth was dry. She could barely form the words. "Is he—"

"Nola," a voice called from behind her.

Nola turned to see Jeremy running toward her.

"Jeremy." Before she could remember how to move she was in his arms. She wrapped her arms around his neck so her toes barely touched the ground, pressing her cheek to his, feeling his warmth pass into her.

Tears streamed down her face as she sobbed, the exhaustion and pain of the horrible night finally flooding through her.

"Shh," Jeremy whispered. "I'm here."

"I thought," Nola coughed, "I thought I'd lost you. I waited, and I looked for you, but you didn't come back in the trucks. I thought you were gone."

Jeremy pulled away, looking down into Nola's eyes. "I would never leave you, Nola."

She leaned in, pressing herself to him as she kissed him. The world spun, but he held her close, keeping all she had been from slipping away.

Thunder shook the air again.

The rain pounded down on the dome, pouring through the break in the glass in solid sheets.

"What are we going to do?" Nola asked.

The guards backed away from the break, watching helplessly as contamination violated their home. But there was no way to fight the rain.

"We salvage what we can," Jeremy said, still holding Nola close. "Then we rebuild, we move on."

"We move on."

Jeremy took Nola's hand, and she didn't argue as he led her away from the atrium. Through the broken dome and past the broken bodies. Down the corridor to Bright Dome. Back home. There was nowhere else to go now.

Nola's journey continues in Boy of Blood.
Read on for a sneak preview.

NOLA'S JOURNEY CONTINUES IN BOY OF
BLOOD

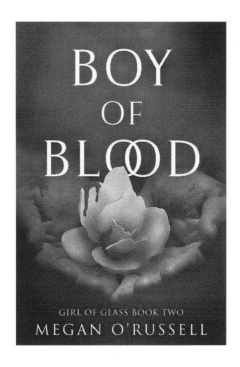

Continue reading for a sneak peek of *Boy of Blood*.

1

Drops of bright red streaming and swirling into nothingness. Deep red from someone.

Someone's veins had been split open. Were they dead or still clinging to life?

The blood didn't care as it was washed away. Swept down the drain by the pure water of the domes.

Nola's sobs echoed off the shower walls, blocking out the sounds of the outside world. She knelt on the floor, watching the blood turn from crimson to pink as the burning water removed all traces of the battle. Someone knelt beside her, washing her, murmuring comforting things she couldn't hear. They combed their fingers through her tangled curls, removing bits of glass and dirt.

She should look. See who was taking care of her. But what did it matter? As soon as they knew what she had done, they would disappear. Or she would. They would learn the truth. Then Nola Kent would vanish.

Strong arms wrapped her in a towel and carried her to her bed. Outside the window she caught a glimpse of the rain pounding down on the dome. But the storm wouldn't taint Bright Dome. Nola's home hadn't been harmed. They had destroyed her world but left her home. A poor attempt at pity.

Something sharp pierced her arm.

"Hush," Jeremy whispered. "It'll help you sleep."

Before Nola could say she didn't deserve sleep, darkness took her.

*H*er mouth tasted of cotton and blood when she woke. Her arms and legs were heavy, like someone had buried her alive. But they hadn't. She lay in her bed as though nothing had happened. A beautiful orchid sat on her desk. Jeremy had brought it for her.

A flower for his girl.

It might have been a century ago.

Nola bit the inside of her mouth, willing herself not to scream. Footsteps on the stairs finally made her sit up in bed. Someone had dressed her in her mother's robe. It smelled like Lenora Kent. Fresh flowers, earth, and strong cleaner.

She rubbed her hands over her face. Her fingers found the bandage on her neck as her bedroom door swung open.

Jeremy walked in, balancing a tray of food. A smile lit his tired face when he saw Nola.

"You're awake." Jeremy set the tray down and sat next to her on the bed. "I wasn't sure you would be yet."

"You gave me something to sleep?"

"The doctor did." Jeremy brushed a dark brown curl from her cheek.

"Doctor?" Nola thought back, trying to find where in the blood and tears a doctor had come near her. "I don't remember a doctor being here."

"Two days ago," Jeremy said. "He put the patch on your neck, too. He said you should be okay now. No permanent damage."

She kicked free of the covers and stood, tipping sideways and knocking into her desk.

Jeremy grabbed her around the waist before she could take another step toward the mirror. "Careful."

"I want to see it." Her fingers trembled as she pulled off the pale-pink patch on her neck. Two thin, white marks showed on her skin. Shaped like teardrops and barely raised at all, they were the only trace that a Vamper had bitten her, tried to kill her only two days ago.

"The doctor can work on it some more," Jeremy said, his deep brown eyes meeting Nola's in the mirror. "He'll get rid of the scars."

Nola studied her reflection. The dark curls belonged to her, but the face had changed. Paler and harder. She looked more like someone from the outside than a girl who'd spent her life in the safety of the domes.

"I don't want him to fix the scars." Nola turned away from her reflection and didn't fight as Jeremy drew her into his chest. He was so tall, and his well-muscled shoulders so broad, it felt as though he could fold her into his body and protect her from the sun itself.

Safety is just another myth.

"It happened," Nola said. "The domes were attacked, I got bit, and people died. We can't make it not true, and I don't want to pretend we can."

"Okay." Jeremy kissed the top of her head. "If that's what you want, we'll make the doctor leave the marks alone."

She stood in Jeremy's arms, waiting for something to happen. For a siren to sound or fire to rip through the Kents' tiny house. But no crashing danger came. No screams, no flames. Just Jeremy. His smell of fresh earth that matched the domes mixed with the starch in his new guard's uniform. Jeremy, warm and steady, holding her up even when she couldn't find the strength to hold him.

"What's happened?" Nola asked, when the silence grew too loud to bear. "Since...since I fell asleep."

"Not much." Jeremy guided her back to the bed. "The rain stopped for an hour that first night, and we scrambled to get the places where the domes were shattered fitted with temporary covers. But that's about all. The wounded are all out of the medical wing and back home except for the worst few. And the dead—"

"They can't be burned until the rain stops." Nola's empty stomach churned at the thought of the line of dome dead waiting their turn.

"With this much acid rain, we haven't been able to go into the city to see if any of the Vamper scum who did this to us are still there, but on the plus side—"

"They'll be stuck wherever they are, too." She tried not to picture Kieran hiding underground with the others from Nightland, packed into dark holes, desperate not to get burned. But Kieran had betrayed her, had betrayed the domes. He had led the Vampers into her home and stolen from the domes. Innocent people died because of him.

Because I trusted him.

Her hands shook, and her breath came in ragged gasps.

"Nola, we're safe here." Jeremy kissed her palm. "No one is going to get back in here to hurt you. I won't let them."

"Jeremy," Nola said, fighting to keep her voice steady enough for her words to be understood. The time had come to tell the truth, to rip open the terrible wounds before they had more time to heal. "When I was with the Vampers from Nightland—"

"Jeremy," a voice called from downstairs. "Is Sleeping Beauty still out?"

Jeremy smiled at the sound of his sister's voice. "Nope, but you would've just woken her up anyway."

Footsteps sped up the stairs, and Gentry Ridgeway stepped into Nola's bedroom. Her eyes lingered on the robe Nola wore for a moment before she spoke. "All people able to move and not on guard duty are to report to the Aquaponics Dome in twenty minutes. There's a meeting about the plan for moving forward with..." Gentry gestured to the walls around her as though to say *our existence.*

"I'll be there soon," Jeremy said.

"Nope." Gentry shook her head. Her dark blonde hair she wore barely longer than Jeremy's ruffled around her face, making her, for a moment at least, appear softer than the fierce Outer Guard she was. "You *and* Nola will come now." Gentry held up a hand when Jeremy began to argue. "She's awake and can move, she has to come to the meeting."

"It's fine," Nola cut Jeremy off when he opened his mouth to argue again. "I'm fine. I'll come to the meeting."

"Good," Gentry said. "We need everyone who's left to work their asses off to get this place put back together. Every single one of us will have to give our all for the domes to survive." Gentry said the last words to her brother, giving him a hard look before walking out of the room.

Nola waited for the sound of the kitchen door closing before looking back to Jeremy. "Does Gentry not think you're doing your part? I mean, you're not even eighteen yet, and you're already an Outer Guard. Why would she—"

"That's not what she said." Jeremy took her hand, carefully helping Nola to her feet. "And that's not what she thinks. We lost a lot of people and a lot of supplies. The domes have to be repaired, and now there are a bunch of rogue Vampers who've declared an all-out war on us. The domes were built to help us survive in this broken world, and now the world is trying to break us. But there is no way in hell I'm going to let them." Jeremy leaned down, brushing his lips against Nola's. "I promise."

It took Nola longer than normal to pull on clothes. Every muscle ached as she dragged her shirt over her head. Her fingers burned as she tied the laces on her work boots. She didn't have the will to force her curls into a tight braid, so she let her hair hang wildly around her shoulders. Just another thing knocked out of place in the strict order that preserved the domes.

She let Jeremy lead her down the stone paths that cut through the grass and wildflowers, weaving past the willow trees and tall maples that made up the green spaces of Bright Dome. Even the roofs of the houses had been planted with thick moss. Every detail had been planned to make the most of the precious space within the glass.

Dome perfect.

But not anymore. Bright Dome had changed since she stumbled through it after the attack. Sleeping bags and boxes of food hid beneath the dangling tendrils of the largest willows. Neat piles of clothes nestled next to the bubbling fountain.

"Some glass in Low Dome and Canal Dome got cracked." Jeremy followed Nola's gaze. "The rain isn't getting in, but the Council doesn't want people sleeping in there. We moved most of the singles into the Guard barracks, but the families had to find other places."

"So, they're sleeping on the ground?" A knot formed in Nola's throat. "They're sleeping in the dirt like the homeless in the city."

"Not like in the city." Jeremy led her away from the makeshift camp, down the stairs and into the tunnels that were the paths between domes. "In the city, the people who sleep outside aren't safe. Here, they are. They're fed and guarded, and it's only for a few days. As soon as the rain stops, we can get Low Dome and Canal Dome fixed, and everyone can go home."

She nodded, not trusting herself to speak.

The cleaning crews had been busy in the tunnels. There was no glass from shattered lights left to crunch beneath their feet. All traces of blood had been scrubbed from the floor. The normality of it, the cleanness, was worse than the blood had been. Horrible things had happened. Mopping the floor wouldn't make it go away. It would have been easier to see the horror. To point to it and scream *this is why I am broken!* But the halls were scoured to perfection.

People packed the Aquaponics Dome by the time Nola and Jeremy arrived. Half-buried with the fish tanks sitting below ground-level, the dome was dark at the best of times. With the storm raging outside, it was impossible to tell if it was night or day down by the meeting, where the department heads stood in a line in front of the fish.

Hundreds of people crowded together. Some in work uniforms, others in normal clothes. The sight of them all jammed together like animals set Nola's nerves on edge. But worse was the fact that they all fit. There should have been more of them. Enough people to spill up onto the stairs. There should have been chatter and laughter bouncing off the glass. But the only sound was the dull hum of the fish tank pumps. The people stood silently as if the funerals had already begun.

"People of the domes," Captain Ridgeway, Jeremy's father and the head of the Outer Guard, addressed the crowd, "we have come upon a dark and terrible time. Our mission has always been, will always be, to protect the people, plants, and animals that are in these domes. We do not do this for our own survival but for the survival of the human race. To protect our children's children. Since the domes were founded, those who live on the outside have coveted the resources we hold, right down to the clean air we breathe. But never before has a group maliciously tried to destroy mankind's best chance for survival." Captain Ridgeway paused, surveying the crowd. "They tried to destroy us, but what they don't understand is that we learn. We have learned where we were weak, we have learned the depths to which they will sink to annihilate us, and we will never allow them the opportunity to attack the domes or its people again."

The crowd clapped and cheered. Shouts of "For the domes!" and "Destroy the Vampers!" carried over the din.

Captain Ridgeway held up a hand, and the moment of celebration faded. "We have a lot of hard work ahead of us. Sacrifices must be made to push forward for a better, stronger future than the domes have ever dreamed of before. Together we will stand strong. Together we will push forward. Together we will become the future the world needs us to be!"

The shouts of the crowd echoed off the glass, drowning out the sound of the thunder beyond.

2

"I just want to help," Nola said for the hundredth time as she followed her mother through the seed cold-storage room.

"Magnolia, I don't have time for this," Lenora snapped, moving to the next row to check the temperature of the seed trays.

"You would have more time if you let me help you!" Nola let her voice ring off the walls.

Lenora stopped moving and pinched the bridge of her nose. "I know you want to help. You are a wonderful girl who wants to help the domes, and I appreciate that more than you will ever know. But right now, the most important thing is to protect these seeds. Without these seeds, the people in the domes could starve, and even if we managed to survive on corn, we would leave nothing for future generations to bring back out into the world. The Vamper scum stole three boxes of my seeds, and now with the dome repair, I can't trust the air system to be reliable. I'm sorry, Nola, but the most helpful thing you can do is leave me to my work."

Nola stood for a moment, teetering on the verge of shouting again. "Right. Sorry, Mom."

She turned without giving her mother a chance to say another word and stalked past the shelves upon shelves of seeds, not stopping until the cold-storage door *whooshed* closed behind her. Nola leaned against the concrete wall of the hall, letting the panic of being three stories underground take her. Her vision swam and her heart raced. Every nerve in her body told her she would be crushed to death at any moment. The panic at being so far below the surface was better than the terrible fear and self-loathing that filled her aboveground, surrounded by the blatant signs of attack.

The seeds were stored deep under the earth in the safest place the domes had to offer, but still the attackers from Nightland had gotten into seed storage and medical storage right next door. More than thirty feet of hard-packed earth above and the Vampers had gotten in and out. They had known where they were going and exactly how to get past the guards. Nola's hands shook. She dug her nails into her arms, willing herself not to scream.

Footsteps came toward the door of medical storage. Nola pushed away from the wall and hurried down the hall, past the guards, and up the stairs.

"Miss Kent," the sharp voice sounded as soon as she reached the landing on the next level.

She froze for a moment before dashing up the next flight of stairs.

"Miss Kent, I need to speak with you immediately."

Nola turned slowly, not needing to see his face to know Captain Stokes was the one calling her, his black eyebrows pinched at the center as he glared at her.

Captain Stokes was the head of the Dome Guard, the ones who protected the domes themselves. Just as Captain Ridgeway was the head of the Outer Guard, the elite unit that patrolled the streets of the city across the river, fighting on the front lines when riots overtook the decaying slums.

It was Captain Stokes' men who should have stopped the attack from ever happening. His Guard who had failed five days ago.

"How are you, Captain Stokes?" Nola's voice wavered as the powerfully built man approached her.

He limped, still favoring his right leg after the battle, but that didn't make him any less intimidating.

"My fallen guards are up next for burning, the ones who are still alive are protecting the shattered side of the domes, and the damned doctors can't set my leg properly," Stokes said. "How well do you think I'm doing, Miss Kent?"

"About as well as the rest of us," Nola said. "Everyone's lost something, Captain Stokes."

"But was everyone surprised by the loss?" Stokes narrowed his eyes. "I need to talk to you about your time as a prisoner in Nightland."

Though she had been expecting his words, her heart began to race.

"You told us you had only seen the inside of your cell when you first came home, but when the attack came, you became a fount of information." Stokes leaned closer, backing her into the wall.

The knowledge that Captain Stokes had every right to glare at her like he knew each horrible thing she had done didn't make it any easier to not run away.

"How to navigate the tunnels of Nightland, how to find their leader's home, even where they had been storing things aboveground. I'd like for you to explain to me how you knew all those things if you never left your cell, Miss Kent." Stokes' face was only inches from hers, but something in the foul stench of his stale breath emboldened her.

"What happened to me in Nightland was outside the domes," Nola said. "What happens outside the domes is Captain Ridgeway's concern, not yours. If Captain Ridgeway wants to talk to me, he knows where to find me. In the meantime, why don't you go check on your guards? Make sure no more of them end up in line for burning."

She sidestepped Stokes and darted up the stairs, not breathing until she had reached the lights of the dome two stories above. Sunlight touched her face as she gasped for air. Even through the glass of the dome the sun warmed her skin.

Her feet carried her toward Amber Dome, away from the workers with their heavy boots and noisy tools that toiled frantically to fix the side of the atrium before the rains returned. Back down a flight of stairs and into a short tunnel. Heavy panes of glass leaned against the wall, waiting to be used in the atrium. But the steel had to be fixed first. It would take days for the wall to be in place, and no one knew how long for decontamination to be complete.

The steps leading up into the Amber Dome were empty, and the few people tending the crops in the low, wide dome didn't pay Nola any mind. The vents blew in clean air, and the fans lifted the scent of fresh, moist earth and vibrant leaves. Rows of leafy green vegetables ran along the outer edge of the dome, closest to the glass, but she headed straight for the center, to the middle of the wheat field that swayed in the breeze. She ducked her head low as she walked so no one could see her path, and when all the walls were out of sight, she lay down on the warm soil, letting the green and amber stalks surround her.

Thick, gray smoke cut through the dazzling blue sky above. Ten would be burned today. Ten of the seventy-two fallen Domers. A list had been read over the com that morning. PAM had displayed their faces on all the computer screens for ten minutes, one last memorial to those who had died. This was the third day of burning, and they hadn't even made it to the fallen guards yet. They would be burned last, their sacrifice in protecting the domes given the highest point of honor.

Twenty-seven guards had been lost.

Nola rolled onto her side, covering her head with her arms. Twenty-seven guards who wouldn't be there to defend the domes if Nightland attacked again.

But the Vampers from Nightland had fled the city. Taken everything they had and vanished. They could be hundreds of miles away by now. Or only a few. Kieran had never told her where it was Emanuel, the leader of Nightland, wanted to take his people.

She took a shuddering breath. Pain shot through her, but there were no tears. How could she cry for herself when she knew what was to come?

She had thought before that Nightland would never attack the domes. She had been delusional enough to believe she knew Emanuel and Kieran. That they were good people who would never harm her or her home.

Seventy-two dead.

Her home had been shattered. She had to pay the price, but she would be damned if she was going to wait for Stokes to come for her. Nola looked back up to the bright sky. The smoke had started to fade. Another body gone. Scrunching her eyes, she tried to memorize the bright blue. She might never see the noon sky again. But the blue held no thrall. No lightness or joy. All that was left for her was justice and darkness. She stood and, walking tall, headed straight for the Iron Dome.

Order your copy of Boy of Blood *to continue the story.*

THE TETHERING

THE TETHERING, BOOK ONE

Love stronger than magic.

PROLOGUE

Seven Years Ago

Jacob Evans sat in the front row, looking back whenever he could at the new girl two rows behind him. He didn't want her to catch him staring, but he couldn't help himself. A few times her eyes met his, but Jacob didn't care. None of the other kids in school had ever liked him anyway. What did it matter if the new girl thought he was rude?

He glanced at her again. She stared back at him and smiled. A beautiful smile that made him like the new girl.

Jacob never sat in the cafeteria to eat lunch. He would hide in the bathroom or find an empty classroom to eat in when the weather was bad. But today was beautiful, one of the first nice days of spring, so he found a big shady tree far away from the other students.

He had half a peanut butter sandwich for lunch today. Money was running low, and he couldn't even guess when his father would be back. Jacob huddled around his sandwich possessively, like a squirrel protecting a nut. People always stared at his meager lunch. Not to steal, but to judge, which felt much worse.

The new girl walked out of the cafeteria and onto the lawn with her shoulders hunched. Jacob couldn't tell if she was upset or just weighed down by the enormous lunch bag she carried. She looked at him and strode straight over, blowing her long black hair out of her eyes.

"Can I sit?" she asked.

Jacob nodded.

She let her giant lunch bag fall to the ground. "I'm Emilia." She held out her hand for Jacob to shake. "I'm in your class."

Jacob didn't move. He stared into Emilia's grey eyes. Why was she speaking to him? What did she want?

Emilia smiled before sitting and unpacking her lunch bag. She pulled out two sandwiches, carrots, apples, cookies, juice, milk, and what looked like an entire tray of brownies.

Jacob swallowed hard, willing his stomach not to growl. That was more food than he usually got to eat in a week.

"I told Molly not to pack me so much," Emilia said. "I think she was worried nobody would like me. Or maybe that I would starve to death my first day of school."

"Who's Molly?" Jacob asked. "Is she your sister?"

"No, she's the housekeeper and cook. And she takes care of me sometimes, when there's no one else around."

Jacob nodded, wishing he had a Molly to feed him when there was no one else around.

"She packed more than I could ever eat." Emilia held out a sandwich to Jacob. "She'll be heartbroken if I bring anything home."

Jacob looked at Emilia and knew she wasn't there to be mean or make fun. "I'm Jacob," he said quietly. And for the first time he could remember, he ate until his stomach was full, and he sat with a friend.

Six Years Ago

*E*milia knew Jacob hated lightning storms, though she had never asked him why. Maybe it was because no one had ever comforted him during storms when he was very small. She could picture exactly where she would find him once she managed to climb onto the roof of the porch. Sitting at the head of his bed by his pillow, crushed up in the corner of the walls.

The porch lattice was slippery in the rain, so she took her time climbing up to his window. She tapped lightly before slipping her fingers into the crack and sliding the window open. She didn't bother to look around the room as she took off her raincoat and shoes, leaving them to drip on the stone-cold radiator without any hope they might actually dry. Finally, she peered through the darkness at the bed in the corner.

There sat Jacob, smiling through his fear because she had come for him.

She crept across the worn carpet, the boards beneath creaking with each step, then picked up his pillow, held it to her chest, and sat beside him. The next time lightning struck, he didn't flinch.

Five Years Ago

The cafeteria at Fairfield Middle School was particularly noisy that day. Jacob liked the noise. People were less likely to notice him.

He headed straight to a table in the far corner. No one ever went over there. No one but Emilia. Eating with her was the best part of his day. He sat and waited for her to come to him.

"Hi," Emilia said as she emerged from the crowd. She sat across from him and started organizing her lunch tray. She looked at Jacob and the empty table in front of him where his lunch should have been. "Your dad's still not back." It wasn't a question.

Jacob traced the graffiti on the table with his finger. He didn't like to talk about his father with Emilia. It ruined his time with her. He didn't like to think about bad things when she was around.

"Did you run out of money?" Emilia asked.

Jacob didn't answer. Whenever Jim left town for a job, he left behind some money. Jacob had learned over the years to be careful with it, to stretch it as far as he could. But occasionally he ran out anyway.

"Here." She cut her burger in half, passing him the larger of the two pieces.

"I'm fine." Jacob shook his head.

Emilia's right eyebrow arched as she stared him down. "There's no point in going hungry." She gave him her milk, too. "Come over after school, and we'll make up some grocery bags for you. Molly is making pizza tonight. You can stay for dinner."

Jacob looked away. Tears burned in his eyes. He hated pity.

Emilia reached over and grabbed his hand. "Jacob, don't. I was lucky when I got Aunt Iz. It's only right I share her with you."

Four Years Ago

*I*t was hot. That horrible kind of hot that seemed to make even Jacob's bones sweat. He lay on the floor of the living room underneath the ceiling fan. He watched as it swirled around. It didn't make the room cooler, but it kept the air moving, making it easier to breathe.

School would be starting again soon. Usually, Jacob dreaded the start of school, but it had been so hot all summer, he had been daydreaming about sitting in an air-conditioned classroom.

This hadn't been his best summer on any account. Jim had left five days after school let out, and he hadn't been back since. Luckily, Jacob had gotten old enough he could find odd jobs around the neighborhood. He weeded for twenty dollars, mowed for fifteen. It wasn't much, but he had managed to keep himself fed.

The only good part of the summer was Emilia. Most days she would come over to get him, and they would go somewhere. Anywhere. To her house, to the park. He didn't care where they went as long as she was there.

Jacob closed his eyes and waited for the knock on the door. He loved that knock. It meant good things were about to happen.

He only had to wait a minute before the porch step squeaked.

Knock, knock, knock.

---

*T*he water was wonderful and cool. Emilia ran through the trees, grabbed the long rope, and swung out over the deepest part of the water before letting go. The air shot from her lungs as she pushed herself up to the surface, laughing.

"Come on, Jacob!" she called.

But Jacob sat in the shallow water, shaking his head. "Emi, I don't think we should use the rope."

Emilia scrambled out of the water and ran back through the trees, the pine needles pricking her feet as she prepared to charge back to the rope.

"I don't think it's safe," Jacob shouted.

Emilia had already started running toward the water. She glanced back at Jacob, sticking out her tongue as she grabbed the rope. She soared out over the glistening water and knew something was wrong. The rope swung in an arc back over the rocky bank.

Emilia screamed as the rope slipped from her grasp. She felt her wrist snap, and something sharp pierced the top of her forehead when she hit the ground.

"Emi!"

There was splashing behind her.

"Emilia." Jacob knelt next to her.

She tried to sit up. The trees swam in front of her eyes, but everything looked red. Somehow strangely red.

"It's okay." Jacob wiped something from her face. A smear of red streaked his palm, and she knew it was blood. Her blood. "Everything is going to be okay."

Emilia forced her eyes to focus on Jacob. He was pale, and his eyes were wide.

"You're going to be fine," Jacob whispered.

Suddenly, a warmth moved up her fingers into her arm. Heat burned in the top of her head. She gasped at the pain shooting down through her skull.

And then it was gone. All the pain had vanished.

Tears glistened in Jacob's eyes and something else she had never seen before. Her lungs turned to lead.

"I'm fine, Jacob," Emilia said, trying not to choke on the fear that was drowning her. "I'm fine."

"*I* have to go."

"Please, Emilia, you can't do this." Jacob grabbed her hand, pulling her away from the window. "You can't leave me."

"I have to." Tears streamed down her face. "I'm sorry I can't explain, but I have to go."

"Then take me with you."

"I can't."

"Emi, please," Jacob begged, but Emilia pulled her hand away.

"No." Her voice broke. She needed to go now, while she could still make herself do it. She slipped her necklace over her head and pressed it into his hand. "I'll come back for you, I promise." She climbed out the window and onto the porch roof. "I'll come back for you as soon as I can. Don't forget me."

1

WINDOWS

Jacob rolled over, unwilling to let the sound of his alarm tear him from his dream. He tried to hold on to the image of her, but it was already drifting away into memory. He reached out and turned off the alarm.

He hadn't dreamt about her in months. Not that he hadn't thought about Emilia. He did that every day. The memory of the day he had first met Emilia Gray, seven years ago now, was one of the best he had.

He rolled out of bed and stumbled to his dresser. He had changed a lot from the little boy hiding under a tree. Now sixteen, Jacob was one of the tallest boys in his class, though he still had the thin look of someone who had grown quickly in a short time. His hair was as blond and shaggy as ever, and he had developed a golden tan from working outside all spring.

"She's gone," he told himself. "Get used to it."

He dressed quickly, throwing on whatever smelled clean, and stopped on his way out the door to check in his father's room. Jim had been gone for a few months now, and since the bed was still made, Jacob assumed he hadn't come home last night.

"Great," he muttered, slamming the front door behind him on his way to another day at Fairfield High.

Fairfield, New York was a nice place. At least in Jacob's opinion. Of course, he had never actually been anywhere else. The town was small and picturesque, and the streets were always clean. With summer's approach, the only scent in town came from the iris blossoms that coated the town square. Planted in color-

420 | MEGAN O'RUSSELL

coordinated beds, they surrounded the gazebo that was regularly used to host town events. Signs rising above the blooms proudly stated the irises were a gift of the Ladies' Library League, the group of women who kept the town pristine and perfect.

The schools were excellent, the stores locally owned, and the houses well painted. Except for Jacob's house, which hadn't been painted in his lifetime. He tried to keep up the house as much as he could, but Jim didn't care enough to help. The Ladies' Library League always noticed, but what was Jacob supposed to do?

Jim had drifted from job to job ever since Jacob was two. That was the year his mother died. When Jacob was eight, Jim had started taking work away from Fairfield. He was hardly ever in town anymore. It was normal for him to disappear for months at a time, working...somewhere. He usually left some cash behind, but Jacob didn't care about Jim's money so much anymore. He'd been doing odd jobs for years, and now that he was older, people around town were willing to give him larger jobs with better paychecks. Thanks to a profitable spring, he'd had enough money not only to eat since the last time Jim had skipped town, but to keep the electricity and water on, too. Jacob laughed to himself. That had been a feat.

No one greeted him when he walked into Fairfield High, but he didn't mind. Anonymity suited him. School was a means to an end, and Jacob wanted out. Out of Jim's house, out of Fairfield. But most of all, he wanted to be good enough for her.

Jacob had made up his mind freshman year that he was going to be the best in the whole school. He was going to get a scholarship, go to college, and make something worthwhile of himself. Days at school flew by. Teachers loved him. Students ignored him. It was perfect.

Jacob sat in chemistry class, allowing his mind to wander. He had already read through the entire book, and the lectures were useless since his teacher insisted on reading from the book verbatim every day.

There was a cough at the door.

Jacob looked over with the rest of his classmates, hoping something would break the monotony.

Principal McManis stood in the doorway, his hands flitting between his watch and glasses. He seemed like a decent guy, and Jacob liked him, so he gave an encouraging smile.

The principal did not smile back. "Jacob Evans, I need to see you in my office."

Sweat beaded on Jacob's palms. He could feel the eyes of his classmates burning holes into his face. He got up to follow the principal.

"Bring your bag."

That wasn't a good sign. Bring your bag meant he was in so much trouble he wouldn't be returning to class, or maybe even to school, for quite a while. But Jacob was always very careful to stay out of trouble. If the school wanted to talk to his father about his behavior, they would find out how often Jim was gone. Then Social Services would be all over him.

Jacob picked up his bag and carefully repacked his chemistry book before starting toward the door. Every time he passed a desk, its occupant started to whisper. By the time he reached the principal, the room sounded like a balloon slowly letting out its air.

Jacob's worn sneakers squeaked as he walked down the hall, and McManis's loafers clacked like they were made of the same worn tile as the floor. The sound of their shoes echoed through the corridor like a siren, telling every room they passed that someone was being led to the principal's office. Not once did McManis look over at Jacob.

McManis ushered Jacob into his office and shut the door. Windows surrounded the room, looking out at the secretary's office and the locker-lined hallways. The secretary kept glancing through the window at Jacob. When he caught her eye, she quickly began shuffling papers on her desk.

"Please sit down." Principal McManis took a seat behind his desk, still avoiding Jacob's eyes. He took a drink from his *#1 Educator* mug, set it down, and rubbed his thumb along the rim, wiping away something Jacob couldn't see.

Was McManis waiting for him to speak or just buying himself time?

"Look," Jacob said, "whatever you think I did, it must have been someone else. You know I would never—"

"This isn't..." McManis paused. "I'm—there was an accident."

Jacob stared at his principal. If there was an accident, why was he in trouble?

"I'm afraid I have some bad news," the principal said, studying his hands. "Your father was found in a hotel room. They aren't sure yet how it happened." He finally met Jacob's eyes. "I'm afraid he's gone."

Jacob's heart stopped. His brain started to scream. All of the bones in his body burned. McManis was still talking, but Jacob couldn't make out the words over the screaming in his head.

A sharp *snap* slammed into his ears right before the windows in the office exploded, sending shards of glass everywhere. The shrieking in his mind was punctured by more glass breaking, more windows flying apart. He stared down at the bits of glass shimmering on the floor.

He gasped as the principal knocked him to the ground, covering Jacob with his own body. Other screams echoed in the distance. It took Jacob a moment to figure out the panicked screaming wasn't in his head. As the fire alarms started wailing, Jacob tried to push himself up to see what was happening, but Principal McManis forced him back down.

Voices cut through the mayhem as teachers tried to calm their students. Students shouted for help, not knowing what to do.

The principal cursed. "Stay here, Jacob. Do not leave this room until a fireman or I tell you to. Got it?" McManis didn't wait for an answer as he shoved Jacob under the desk.

The shattered pieces of the *#1 Educator* mug cut into Jacob's palms, and the smell of spilled coffee filled the air. The coffee puddle was warm, and he watched with fascination as his red blood mixed with the brown liquid.

Jacob listened to Principal McManis order a school lockdown. The *thud* of doors slamming shut echoed down the hall. A few moments later, McManis's voice came back over the speakers, saying to evacuate as quickly as possible. A school with broken windows couldn't be locked down.

Jacob waited in the office for McManis. A few minutes passed before the principal returned for Jacob and led him outside to the rest of his class. Jacob was almost grateful for the confusion when the fire trucks arrived. No one stopped him or asked if he was all right. He blended perfectly into the chaos.

The emergency workers set up triage sites for the injured, but no one had been badly hurt. A few students needed stitches, and some were so panicked they had to be sedated, but there were no real injuries.

The police bomb squad swept through the building but found nothing. They checked for a gas leak, but the lines all seemed to be in good working order. The rumblings in the crowd said the police were at a loss to explain how every piece of glass in the building had shattered. No one was allowed to leave.

At what should have been dinnertime, all of the students' parents who had rushed to the school brought them food. But Jacob had no one who cared that his school had apparently been *attacked by terrorists*. At least that's what the news reporter nearest him told her viewers at home. A woman from a church group gave Jacob water, food, and a blanket at about nine o'clock in the evening, and he was too tired to refuse.

Finally, the police said they'd gathered all the information they needed, which was none at all, and that they would be in touch with updates.

Jacob started to walk home. Principal McManis's booming voice carried over the crowd, calling Jacob back, but he kept walking. Social Services would come for him soon enough.

The lights were off in the house, but Jacob was used to that. He was used to being alone. He opened the creaky door and sat down on the couch. This may not have been a happy home, but it was the only one he knew. He looked around the living room. The dingy wallpaper peeled away at the corners. A faint scent of dust and damp hung in the air. Jacob kept the house clean, but Jim never gave him the money to fix anything. The couch he sat on was older than he was. The stained fabric glistened in places where the springs were beginning to wear through.

He should be doing something. Like planning a funeral. But he didn't even know where Jim's body was. Not that he had the money to pay for a funeral anyway. Sleep. He needed sleep. Everything else could be handled tomorrow.

Jacob climbed the stairs to his room. Out of habit, he looked into Jim's room. It was the same as it had been that morning with the bed still untouched. For some reason, Jacob had expected it to look different, as though permanent absence would leave a visible mark. He pulled Jim's door closed and went to his own bed.

He didn't even remember closing his eyes, but a steady tapping that echoed through the empty house pulled him back out of sleep. He dragged the blanket the woman from the church group had given him over his head. He wanted sleep, not social workers.

But the tapping continued. It sounded closer than the front door. Maybe it was hail. No, the sound was too regular for hail.

Jacob sat up and looked blearily around his room. The sound came from the window. A figure crouched outside, tapping lightly to wake him up.

2

THE MANSION HOUSE

Jacob tossed off the blanket, ran to the window, and threw it open.

And there she was. Emilia Gray.

She pushed herself through the window and threw her arms around Jacob's neck. "Jacob," she said, her voice full of pain and concern. "I'm so sorry."

Jacob froze for a moment, unsure if he was actually awake, until the cool night air whispered through Emilia's hair, carrying with it the soft scent of lilacs. "Emi?" he whispered, wrapping his arms around her. She felt warm and incredibly real.

She pulled away to look him in the eye. "I came as soon as I heard everything that happened. Are you all right?"

"I'm—" Jacob reached up and touched Emilia's face, brushing a strand of long black hair from her forehead. "You're here?" His voice sounded raw. "Are you really here?"

"I'm really here," Emilia said. "I came back for you. I promised I would. Jacob, I'm sorry."

He pulled her into his arms and buried his face in her hair, trying hard to remember how to breathe. She hadn't changed that much. Her hair was long and black, and her eyes were misty grey. She was taller now but still her. Still perfect.

"Are you okay?" Emilia whispered.

"I'm fine." Jacob pulled away and ran a hand through his hair, trying to stop his head from spinning. "I think I might be in shock or something. I'm so used to Jim being gone. I guess I just don't understand that he isn't coming back. Is that weird?"

"I don't think so."

"How did you know?" Jacob asked. "How did you know about Jim so fast? I mean, I only found out this morning."

"I know, and I know this is an awful time. But I had to come now before it was too late."

"He's dead. I don't think there's really a time crunch," Jacob said with a hoarse laugh. The laugh caught in his throat and turned unexpectedly into a sob. He tried to breathe, but it only made the sobs louder.

Emilia pulled him over to the bed and curled up in the corner, putting Jacob's head on her shoulder.

Jacob didn't know how long he had cried, but he hurt everywhere. He hurt like he had run a marathon. His throat was dry, and his eyes stung. He stayed sitting next to Emilia on the bed. She had held him as he cried for losing the father who was never there. As Emilia reached up to wipe a tear from his cheek, he vowed he would never cry for Jim again. It was over. Jim was gone.

Jacob took a deep breath. "Thank you." He looked down at Emilia's hand holding his.

"I'm so sorry, but we can't stay here." She silenced Jacob's protest. "I didn't come here because of your father. I came to get you. Just like I promised I would. It's time now," she said slowly. "I am so sorry about Jim, but I need you to come with me."

Something wasn't right. Emilia was here in his room. They were together, but she looked worried. Almost frightened.

"I came because of what happened at your school. What you did to your school."

Jacob shook his head as her words sank in. "Is that what the police are saying? I was with Principal McManis when it happened. It wasn't me." Panic crept into his chest. He looked around his bedroom, sure the police were going to break in at any moment to arrest him.

"The police think it was some sort of terrorist attack. I love how they can invent logical explanations for just about anything." Emilia pulled Jacob back when he started toward the window to look for police cars. "They don't suspect you at all."

Jacob searched Emilia's eyes, unsure if he should be relieved or more afraid. Who else but the police would come for him?

"But we know you did it," Emilia said. "You broke all those windows. Well, every piece of glass in the building actually."

"What do you mean I broke the windows?"

"Jacob. You are special. Different, like me. You have abilities you don't under-stand, but when you're upset—"

"What are you talking about?"

"Magic, Jacob. Wizardry, sorcery, *maleficium*, whatever you want to call it. I'm a witch, you're a wizard, and we need to get out of here."

Jacob stared at Emilia. He ran his hand over her cheek.

She grabbed his hand. "Jacob, I'm real. And this is real. There is a whole world out there. A magical world. But you have to decide right now if you want to be a part of it. There are things in my world that are beyond your imagina-tion, but if you come with me, you can never go back to being normal. You can never come back here."

"Emi." Jacob shook his head. "This is crazy."

She brought his hand between them. It was covered in small cuts from shards of McManis's mug. His hand warmed in her grasp. Not unpleasantly so, but as though it were submerged in warm water. Then his skin tingled and stung. The places where the skin had been broken became almost iridescent. Finally, the glow subsided, and the cuts started to fade. After a few seconds, his hand had completely healed.

"It is real." Emilia stared into Jacob's eyes. "Will you come with me?"

Jacob couldn't think beyond Emilia's return. He was tired, and his brain felt fuzzy. His school was wrecked. His father was dead.

He wanted to be angry with Emilia. To shake her for making him even more confused, to yell at her for disappearing for four years, and for clearly having left out some very important details in the course of their friendship. He didn't understand what was happening.

Emilia's hands were so delicate in his. He would do anything to keep her from disappearing again. He would follow Emilia Gray to the ends of the earth.

"Do I need to pack anything?" he asked.

"Only if you want to." Emilia gave him a hard, serious look. "Jacob, are you sure this is what you want?"

"Yes."

Emilia offered to help him pack, but there wasn't very much Jacob wanted to take with him. He already had everything important packed in a box under his bed. Pictures of his parents. A book his mother had written her name in. All of the notes his father had left on the kitchen table every time he went out of town. Jacob kept the box packed in case a social worker came for him. All he had to do was throw some clothes into a bag, and he was ready to go.

He turned off the lights and walked out the front door. He hesitated with the key in his hand for a moment before leaving it in the lock. Under the streetlight, a very shiny black car waited for them.

Jacob didn't look back as he walked to the car. He didn't need to. There was nothing left for him there.

Emilia opened the car door for him.

"Nice to see you, Jacob," Samuel, the Grays' driver and gardener, spoke from the front seat. "I am very sorry for your loss."

Jacob nodded, studying Samuel's reflection in the rearview mirror. Samuel had dust-brown hair and laugh lines that never faded. But there were new, harsh lines around his eyes and forehead Jacob had never seen before. Lines that hadn't come from Samuel's constant knowing smile.

Emilia climbed into the car. "If we hurry, we might make it before everyone wakes up."

"Somehow I think there'll still be trouble," Samuel said as they drove away from Fairfield.

"Where are we going?" Jacob asked when Samuel turned the car onto the highway. Since Emilia had left, he had only been on the highway twice for school trips. It was strange to see the night whisking by at sixty-five miles per hour.

"To the Mansion House. It's about two hours away." Emilia chewed her bottom lip. Jacob recognized that worried look. "Aunt Iz might be awake when we get back. She didn't want me to come with Samuel, but I convinced him I had to come. I wanted to get you myself."

"Two hours away." Jacob shook his head. "Two hours away and you never once came to see me?" His head started to spin again. As the minutes ticked past, things made less and less sense.

Emilia looked at him with pain in her eyes. "It wasn't my choice. It's so complicated, and it's not supposed to be me who explains. There are rules that can never be broken. At the house, you believed me when I told you you're a wizard. Now you have to believe me when I tell you there are rules and responsibilities that come with those powers."

"Powers." Jacob rubbed the skin on his palm that had been healed less than an hour ago. "Powers?"

Emilia shook her head. "Not now. You should sleep."

He didn't want to close his eyes and risk her being gone again when he opened them. The first rays of light crept over the mountains. He had a hundred questions. Where had she been? What was he capable of? But really, he was too tired to push for answers. So he sat with his fingers laced through hers and watched the sunrise.

They crossed the border into Massachusetts and drove through a small town. A paperboy pedaled past on his morning route, the sole inhabitant moving down the sleepy streets on his bicycle. Would Jacob's school or his father's death be in the newspaper?

They drove past the town and onto a smaller road lined so thickly with trees it was impossible to see more than a few feet on either side of the car. Samuel turned the car left onto a driveway no one would notice if they didn't know exactly where to look. A hundred feet down the drive, they came to a tall stone wall surrounding the property. A set of iron gates etched with strange symbols swung open. The car shuddered as it passed through the gates.

Emilia squeezed his hand. "Don't worry. It's just the *fortaceria*. A spell to turn outsiders away."

Jacob nodded, amazed he hadn't been rejected by the gate.

The driveway was so long and the trees so large, at first he couldn't see the house at all. When the building finally came into view, Jacob had to agree with its name. It was a mansion. Not anything hugely luxurious, but delicate and stately. Definitely larger than any of the houses in Fairfield, but somehow it still seemed homey.

As they stopped in front of the house, several people came running through the front door at once. They called to the car, but Jacob couldn't make out their words over the *crunch* of the gravel. First out of the door was a dark-haired boy, tall and muscled, who seemed to be the same age as Jacob. Then a small, blond girl of maybe eleven or twelve, still wearing her pink pajamas. A red-haired boy came next, dragging Molly, the Grays' cook. Last came an older man, small and toady, wearing a maroon bathrobe. He had Aunt Iz on his arm. She was, of course, smiling her wry smile as the car stopped.

The dark-haired boy ran to open Emilia's door. Jacob thought he heard Emilia whimper as the boy reached in and pulled her from the car.

The boy crushed her to his chest. "What the hell were you thinking? Do you have any idea—"

"Dex, I'm sorry," Emilia said, "but I had to go—"

"Go running into the epicenter of an incident like this? Do you know what could have happened to you?"

"Yes, Dexter, I do. That's why I had to go." Emilia pulled herself away. She glanced at Jacob in the car. "Please, Dex," she whispered in a voice almost too quiet for Jacob to hear.

Dexter brushed Emilia's hair off her face and kissed her before pulling her back into his arms.

3

ON THE BRINK

All of the air had been sucked out of the world. There was no air in Jacob's lungs and no air left for him to inhale.

Emilia broke away from Dexter and took Jacob's hand. She smiled at him as though nothing were strange or wrong. She drew Jacob out of the car and led him to the steps, where the rest of the welcoming committee waited.

"Everyone, this is Jacob. Jacob, this is Claire Wren." She indicated the little blond girl. "And Connor Wright, Molly's nephew." The red-headed boy waved. "Professor Eames." The man next to Aunt Iz bowed. "And Dexter Wayland," she said, looking back at the boy who had just kissed her.

Dexter walked up to Jacob and shook his hand. "It's a pleasure to finally meet you." As they let go, Dexter wrapped his arm around Emilia's waist, inserting himself firmly between her and Jacob.

Jacob thought he saw a gleam in Dexter's eye before Molly pulled him into a back-breaking hug.

"It's so good to see you again, Jacob. Let me see." Molly held Jacob at arm's length and tutted noisily. "Well, you need to be fed up a bit, and your hair needs cutting."

Then Aunt Iz was upon him. She held his face in her hands and looked straight into his eyes, as though she were seeing everything that had happened in the last few years just by staring at him with that deep, penetrating gaze.

Iz smiled sadly and nodded before turning back to the rest of the group. "A strong cup of tea and some food in my study, Molly. Connor, please take his things to the green room. And yes, Claire, you may see to the closet."

Claire squealed with delight and grabbed Jacob's backpack from Connor before darting into the house.

"Samuel," Iz called to the driver, "get some sleep before you go, and try to keep her under control."

Samuel nodded.

As the car pulled away, Iz turned back to Jacob. "Come to my study. There are quite a few things we need to discuss." Iz held up a finger, stopping Emilia when she tried to follow them into the house. "No, Emilia, I will speak to Jacob alone. You and I shall have a little chat later."

Iz didn't yell, but her tone left no doubt Emilia was in serious trouble.

Jacob glanced back as he followed Iz into the house, his stomach disappearing as Dexter kissed Emilia again.

The inside of the Mansion House was as lovely as the outside. Early morning light poured in from every direction. A grand cherry staircase cut through the center of the house. The air smelled like wood and cooking. Very good home cooking.

Iz led him down the hall to a large cherry door. A barren tree with branches that reached to the sky and roots that dug deep into the ground had been carved into the wood.

Jacob touched the symbol.

"It's the crest of the Gray Clan," Iz said as she opened the door to her study. She gestured for Jacob to sit.

"I've seen it before," he said. "On the ring Emilia always wore."

"Very good." Iz smiled. "I gave that ring to Emilia on her seventh birthday, and she still wears it all the time."

Molly came in with food. While she sorted the tray, Jacob looked around Iz's study. He sat on a plush green chair. Iz's desk and the table with the food were both carved of the same rich cherry wood that adorned the rest of the house. Books of all sizes lined the walls, and a large mirror had been set into a recess in the corner next to a shining black piano.

Finally, Molly left, and Iz handed him a cup of tea and a fresh biscuit. "Molly is right. You could do with some feeding up." Iz sat behind her desk.

The room was as different as could be, but Jacob still felt like he was back in Principal McManis's office.

"Eat." Iz sipped her own tea.

Jacob just nodded. He didn't know what to say. "Thank you for breakfast," was all he could manage a few mouthfuls later.

"I am sorry for all you have been through," Iz said. "And I deeply regret my family was not there to help you through the last few years. We all care for you very much. Leaving you behind in Fairfield was not an easy decision. Although, I am sure you can now see that we did have a very good reason for our abrupt departure."

"'Cause I'm a wizard?" Jacob asked.

"Because you are indeed a wizard."

"What does that even mean?"

"It means you have the ability to do things far outside the realm of possibility for humans," Iz said.

"You have the ability to affect the world around you with your mind and your energy," said a voice from behind him.

Iz's voice. It was Iz's voice Jacob had heard behind him, but she was still sitting at her desk.

He glanced over his shoulder to see where the sound had come from, and Iz was there, standing by the door. He whipped his head back toward the desk, but Iz's seat was now empty. Jacob turned slowly to look behind him again.

Iz smiled. "A party trick I know."

"But," Jacob sputtered, shaking his head. "But you were sitting. I was looking at you. How?"

Iz walked back to her seat at the desk. "Some might call it telekinesis. Some call us mutants, as the new popular media is inclined. But I prefer the terms *witch* and *wizard*. It is what we have been called historically, and it makes it seem far less likely that we will end up in a freak show. Or be captured by government agents and put into white rooms. Though, I'm not saying that isn't a possibility these days."

Jacob nodded again. White rooms, energy from inside him. It was too much.

"You can still go home, Jacob. I didn't want Emilia to retrieve you because I know how"—Iz stared into Jacob's eyes— "persuasive she has always been to you. If you stay here, we will shape you into a wonderful wizard. You will be able to do and see things that most can't even begin to imagine. But there are things you need to know. You're walking into a world on the brink of war, and unfortunately, the incident at Fairfield High may have made things worse."

"Incident? You mean what I did?"

"Yes." Iz nodded. "The *terrorist attack*."

"But it wasn't an attack. I didn't mean to do it. If it was even really me. Which I'm really not sure it was." Jacob started to feel fuzzy again.

"The human news says terrorist, and some members of Magickind seem to agree."

"What? It was an accident. I swear."

"I know, Jacob, but people see things the way they want to see them, not necessarily the way they are. There has been some"—Aunt Iz paused—"conflict of late within Magickind, particularly among wizards. Unfortunately, as the normal human population expands, it leaves less room for the magical world to exist undetected. Some of us have started purchasing large tracts of land, adding to what was already owned by Magickind. You see, some of our people cannot co-exist with humans. Centaurs, fawns, fairies, mermen, griffins, dragons—"

Jacob leaned forward. "Are you serious? Dragons?"

"Jacob, dear"—Iz smiled—"if you can accept that you're a wizard, you need to accept that other legends are, in fact, real."

Jacob nodded slowly.

"Other wizards have started integrating more into society. Recent generations have even started to attend public schools. But there are also those who have taken a more radical approach." Iz paused, taking a slow sip of tea. "Attacking any humans who come near their homes and, in some cases, even killing them.

"Some wizards have recently gone so far as to attack humans who have in no way encroached on their territory. And I'm afraid your actions at your school yesterday"—she raised her hands as Jacob started to protest again—"however accidental they may have been, might be viewed along those lines. As a rebel act of terrorism, and the largest one we have seen in quite some time."

"But it was an accident," Jacob said. "I would never hurt anyone."

"And hopefully the rebels will understand that. But if they do view it as an attack, it may be the rallying point they have been waiting for. In which case, things could go very badly, very quickly. Ours is a delicate peace."

"So, what can I do?" Jacob asked, setting down his teacup harder than he had meant to. "How can I fix this?"

"There is nothing you can do to fix it, Jacob, but you could go back to Fairfield and never have to hear about any of this again. We would bind your powers. You could be normal."

Jacob thought for a moment. "And Emilia?"

"You would never see any of us again."

Jacob stared at Iz, trying to make sense of everything she was saying, but all he could see was a dragon and fire in his mind. But then Emilia's face replaced the horrible dragon.

"I'm staying. I want to stay. I want to be a wizard." Jacob stood, his gaze darting around the room as though a sign would appear that read *Being a wizard and staying with Emilia starts here.*

"All right." Iz held out a hand to stop his frantic search of the room.

"Is that why Emilia came to get me, because some"—Jacob swallowed, trying to say the word—"witches think I'm a terrorist?"

"No, we came to get you so quickly because we feared what other wizards might make of you if they got to you first." Iz stood, ending the conversation. "You don't need to be around people right now. You need time. Go rest. When you're ready, find Molly. She'll feed you."

Iz directed Jacob to his room. Up the main staircase, down a hall, and up a smaller staircase that led to the old servants' quarters, which had been declared the *Boys' Wing* by Connor.

Jacob shut himself into his assigned room on the top floor. The room was green, but not outrageously so. A large four-poster bed took up the center of the space with a green comforter that matched the green curtains and the green carpet. Small windows placed high in the walls peeked out through the sloped roof, looking out onto the trees that surrounded the house.

Someone had set a vase of fresh lilacs by the bed. The flowers filled the room with the subtle scent of a late afternoon. Jacob smiled. Emilia had left them for him. She knew he liked lilacs best, though he doubted she knew it was because the flowers reminded him of her.

Jacob wandered around his new bedroom. The carpet felt soft, even with his shoes on. He went into the bathroom. It was large, but manly. The shower was black granite from floor to ceiling with a sliding glass door. It was the sort of bathroom he had only ever seen in photographs.

He looked at himself in the mirror. He was pale. His eyes were red and swollen. And somewhere in this house, the girl he loved was either being yelled at by Iz or kissed by Dexter. His hands started to shake. Suddenly a hot shower seemed like the best idea in the world.

4

MADE TO BE BROKEN

The sun was high in the sky when Jacob woke later that morning. He had put his dirty clothes back on after his shower since he couldn't find his bag. His brain ached, and he was starving. No one had told him where the kitchen was, so he wandered downstairs to look around.

The house was huge. Every surface had been polished to perfection. A crystal chandelier shone over the dining room table and large couches made room for a dozen people to sit in the living room.

Jacob wandered outside onto a stone veranda overlooking a sprawling garden filled with flowers and trees. Finally, he smelled something wonderful and found the kitchen.

He knocked.

"Come in, silly boy, and get your lunch. You look like a half-starved rat," Molly fussed as she examined him, clearly judging his lack of nutrition. A rather plump woman, Molly had the same bright red hair as her nephew and more freckles than anyone could ever count. "Eat, eat." She steered Jacob to sit down at her worktable where a plate waited for him.

Jacob started with the thick stew and a roll before he even bothered to look at his salad.

"That's a boy after my own heart." Molly laughed as she began to peel vegetables for the evening's dinner.

Jacob watched her for a few moments. "Molly, couldn't you just do that with magic?"

"Oh sure," she said. "*Pelloris.*" The carrot that had been in her hand ripped its skin off and placed itself on the cutting board. "But if you use magic all the time, it ruins the fun."

"Could I do that?" Jacob asked.

"Sure," Molly said with a smile, "but you'll need a few lessons first. We don't want you peeling yourself by accident. That would be a nasty one to fix."

"Could Emilia do that?" Jacob pointed to the perfectly peeled carrot and tried not to shudder at the thought of peeling himself. Would Aunt Iz be able to reattach his skin?

"She helps most days. But I'm afraid she's in a spot of trouble and will be in her room the rest of the day doing some rather difficult spell translations. Iz was not pleased with her running off in the middle of the night. Samuel would have been perfectly fine on his own." Molly moved on to the potatoes. "That girl is a strong-willed one. More stubborn than a pigheaded mule."

They sat in silence for a moment. Jacob's bread turned brown as it soaked up the juices from his stew.

"I should have known there was something different about her." Jacob shook his head. "She always seemed so much more, I don't know, real than the rest of us. So much more alive or connected." He pushed his plate away and grabbed a peeler to help Molly. "I should have noticed, or she should have told me."

"Don't you be judging her." Molly shook her knife at Jacob's nose. "It's not as though she didn't want to tell you. We have laws, you see. Magickind has been hiding for hundreds of years, and it hasn't been easy, mind. We've had to come up with rules and laws to govern us all. And one of the very first rules is keep the secret. Tell no one. If Emilia had told you, she would have been in for a world of trouble. Especially with the possibility of you joining us one day. That would have made it worse."

"What do you mean?"

"The minute someone displays any potential, if they are not a magical child already being raised by a magical family, all ties with anyone in the community must be immediately severed."

"But I never displayed any potential," Jacob said. "I never did any magic until yesterday."

"Do you remember the day we left?" Molly asked.

Jacob nodded. Nothing could make him forget that day.

"When Emilia fell, she broke her wrist. And you, Jacob"—Molly tossed him a potato to peel—"healed her. As soon as that happened, our laws forced us to leave Fairfield, and you, at once."

"But why?" Jacob asked angrily. "Wouldn't it have made more sense to teach me before I destroyed an entire school?"

Molly left her work to sit next to him. "My guess is the day you healed Emilia, you were terrified. Your blood was pumping, and you probably had a fair bit of adrenaline going, too. You did something beyond normal human capacity in an extremely stressful situation. That wouldn't necessarily make you a wizard. If Emilia had told you then and there all about witches and wizards and the rest, and you never showed another lick of magic after that, she would have broken the rules. That is why all contact had to be severed."

Jacob laughed and shook his head. "That's easy for you to say. But being left behind was—"

"Terrible," Molly finished for him, patting his arm. "I know. But don't go blaming anyone but the Council." Molly got up and returned to her pile of vegetables. "Iz said for you to go to her study as soon as you're ready. She'd like to get a start with you as quickly as possible."

Jacob got up to leave but stopped in the doorway. "What would they have done to her? If she had told me?"

"Stripped her of her powers," Molly said to the rhythm of her chopping. "And banished her from all contact with Magickind...forever. Makes you as good as dead if you ask me."

Jacob nodded slowly. "Thanks, Molly."

He drifted out of the kitchen, lost in thought. He took a wrong turn on his way to Iz's study and found himself in a large library. The walls were lined floor to ceiling with shelves of books. Desks were scattered around the room, each in a different state of disarray.

Connor and Dexter sat at their desks, engrossed in their work. Claire hummed loudly, rolling herself along on the ladder that allowed access to the higher shelves. There were empty desks in the library, too, and Jacob could tell which one was Emilia's, even though she wasn't there. Hers was the one with a vase of fresh flowers on it. He wondered if Dexter had brought them to her. Jacob shook his head and slipped away.

When he found Iz's study, her door waited open.

"Welcome to your first lesson." Aunt Iz clapped her hands delightedly as she rose from her armchair. "And let me say, Jacob, I am thrilled to be your teacher." She patted his cheek the same way she had when he was young. "Now, help an old lady to the garden. We're going to be practicing outside today. The weather is lovely, and I really don't want all the furniture bashed up again." She laughed merrily as they moved out into the hall and toward the veranda. Iz was not feeble in any way. In fact, she was more agile than most people half her age, but

Jacob offered his arm anyway. "You would be amazed how often I have to redecorate."

"Couldn't you just fix the furniture with magic?" Jacob asked.

"If I did, I would still be stuck with the same furniture I had forty years ago." She smiled up at Jacob, her eyes twinkling. "And what fun would that be?"

They strolled past the stone veranda and down the path onto the lush lawn. Iz was right. It was a lovely day. Cherry blossoms dripped down from the trees, and the flowers balanced on the edge of full summer bloom. The garden was filled with so many trees, it looked more like a forest than any lawn Jacob had ever seen. There were beech trees and willows, giant evergreens and tiny saplings. But the most remarkable thing to Jacob was how alive everything felt.

The moisture in the air shot vitality through Jacob's veins. He could almost hear things growing within the earth. The green of the grass and trees was more vibrant than any he had ever seen. The flowers didn't look yellow or red or blue. They embodied what those colors were meant to be. And the smell…a thousand scents rolled into one that filled his lungs and made him feel thoroughly alive.

Aunt Iz stopped by a stone bench far enough down the path to hide the house from view. The bench sat in the center of a small clearing surrounded by trees and carpeted with wildflowers. She sat silently.

Jacob glanced up and down the path, searching for someone else who might be coming. "Why?" He brushed his fingers along the deep violet of a blooming iris. "Why is everything in this garden so much more alive than anything I've ever seen?"

"Because we sing to it," Aunt Iz answered simply.

Jacob didn't like singing. Music had never been an area in which he excelled. His music teacher in elementary school had written in his report card that he was lacking in musical ability and had difficulty matching pitch, but had a good work ethic. Trying and failing was not a quality he wanted to display on his first day with Iz.

"Even if the magic done on these grounds isn't specifically aimed at the flowers," Iz said, "they still come up to listen. This garden is wild and wonderful because as the earth feeds us the energy to do our magic, we also feed the earth."

"So, basically you make the flowers bloom?"

Aunt Iz looked up into the canopy of trees. "We don't make them. We supply the energy, and they do the growing. We nurture them and give them the strength they need to grow on their own. I suppose that's why I love my garden. It reminds me of my students."

Jacob followed Iz's gaze up to the treetops. The sunlight peered back at him through the leaves. As beautiful as the glittering emerald light was, he didn't see any magic.

"Now," Iz pondered aloud, "where to begin?" She leaned down and picked up a fallen leaf. She closed it in her hand and held it for a moment before blowing the leaf away.

The leaf didn't fall to the ground. It had folded itself like a paper airplane, and Iz's breath carried the plane up through the trees. The leaf slowly floated out of sight. "Magic is not some cosmic explosion. It is merely a manipulation of the world around you. There are some rules. Most are for safety's sake. And all have been broken at some point."

Jacob nodded his head. That sounded like physics. And physics he could do.

Aunt Iz continued, "The first thing we need to teach you is how to focus your mind. There is no point in teaching you spells if you are not focused enough to perform them without injuring yourself or others. Do you see this tree?" She stood and crossed to a tree Jacob hadn't noticed before.

Amidst the abundance of life in the garden, this one small sapling struggled to survive. It didn't have very many leaves and grew too crooked to be strong. Something so weak and deformed didn't belong in this place.

"Make it healthy." Aunt Iz patted Jacob's shoulder and headed back down the path to the house.

"What?" Jacob started after her.

She turned him around and pushed him back to the clearing.

"But how?" he said. "I'm really sorry, Aunt Iz, but I think that tree is doomed."

"Tell me when it's green," Aunt Iz called over her shoulder.

Jacob looked at the sad little tree. "You have got to be kidding me."

5

SOUNDS IN THE NIGHT

He closed his eyes and took a deep breath. "All right," Jacob said to himself with much more confidence than he felt. "I can totally do this. She wouldn't assign me an impossible task." But he couldn't quite figure out how to go about saving the tree.

It needed to make chlorophyll, which required light, water, and air. Maybe he could find a watering can and some fertilizer. He had done plenty of yard work back home whenever money ran out.

Samuel had actually been the one who taught him how to take care of plants when the Grays still lived in Fairfield. Samuel had never used magic for gardening. At least Jacob didn't think so. Jacob pushed his palms into his eyes and rubbed hard.

"I need to rethink my entire childhood. There must have been magic in Emilia's house. I was just too stupid to notice."

Maybe the tree had a bug problem. But he doubted the answer was so dull. He searched the clearing for a clue, a sign of some sort, but found nothing. Finally, after several minutes of fruitless scouring of the grass, he sat cross-legged on the ground and stared at the poor tree.

Hours passed. Jacob tried asking the tree for suggestions. The tree was unhelpful. Jacob's limbs ached from sitting for so long, so he started pacing in wide circles around the tree. When his feet got tired, Jacob tried closing his eyes and picturing the tree strong and healthy. Again he tried asking the tree what would make it feel better. But it was no good. He had no idea how to heal a tree by magic.

In an act of sheer desperation, he tried singing to the tree. His off-key rendition of *I've Been Working on the Railroad* did nothing.

Finally, when the sun had begun making its way back down, a voice carried up the path calling him in for the night.

Claire waited for him on the veranda, smiling mischievously. "Good first day?" she asked as she led Jacob back into the house.

"Yeah." Jacob tried to sound at least a little cheerful.

"Liar." Claire's extremely blond left eyebrow climbed very high on her forehead. "Don't worry. I did tons of magic by accident before I came here, and it still took me forever to be able to do anything I actually wanted to do. You're not stupid. It's just hard."

"Thanks, Claire," Jacob said, feeling a little better. Voices drifted from the dining room, and he stopped Claire right before they walked in. "But could you do me a favor?"

"Don't tell Dexter you're having trouble?" Claire smirked. "Sure." She walked into the dining room, giggling.

"Jacob." Professor Eames stood up at one end of the table. "Please choose a seat."

Jacob looked around the table. There was an open seat next to Samuel and one next to Dexter.

Dexter looked at Jacob and nodded.

Jacob clenched his fists and took a breath before sitting next to Samuel, where he would be less likely to cause a major incident. Like a falling chandelier.

The entire household was at the table, except for Emilia. She was probably still stuck in her room.

"Greens first," Aunt Iz said to Connor from her seat at the head of the table.

"Yes, ma'am." Connor reluctantly replaced the dish of cheese-smothered potatoes.

"Professor Eames," Dexter said after placing a large portion of salad onto his plate, "I read an article on the Siren Theory and its implications in the ability of wizards to impose paradoxical travel on those around them, as well as its possible connection to the 1892 smugglers' brigade disappearance. I was wondering if you might have any insight."

The conversation flowed like dry mud during dinner. Professor Eames and Dexter engaged in a lively discussion, with Aunt Iz inserting important concepts

Jacob didn't understand. Molly and Samuel joined in occasionally, and Claire and Connor both seemed to follow along, nodding in all the right places. Jacob felt lost and in way over his head. As dinner came to an end, everyone helped bring the dishes to the kitchen before going to the living room.

Jacob took a seat on a comfy couch off to the side, and Dexter followed him.

"Did you enjoy dinner?" Dexter sat on the arm of the couch Jacob had chosen. "I always look forward to our dinner discussions. They are so enlightening. Did you enjoy the subject tonight?"

"Sure." Jacob forced a smile. "But I'm really wiped, so I'm gonna go."

He stood and walked out of the room, barely pausing to wave to Aunt Iz and Samuel, who were deep in conversation at a small table in the corner.

Dexter must have known he didn't understand a damn thing they'd said at dinner. Jacob climbed the stairs to his room, trying not to give in to the temptation to give one of the stairs a good kick. A broken toe wouldn't make him feel much better. He was too tired to be social anyway. Emilia was still banished to her room, and she was the only one he really wanted to talk to.

Jacob found his room and slammed the door. He winced at the sound, hoping no one downstairs had heard. Jacob tried lying on his bed, but he couldn't seem to breathe. This was too much, far too much to deal with in one day. His father was dead, he had left the only home he had ever known, and he was a wizard.

He rolled onto his back and rubbed his face with both hands. Emilia was back. She was a witch. She had come back because he was a wizard. He knew he should be grieving. He should be scared. He had essentially dropped out of high school. He didn't know when he would be going back to Fairfield High. Or if.

Jacob pressed the heels of his hands hard into his eyes. He needed air.

High school dropout, orphan, incompetent wizard.

Jacob's bedroom windows were open, wafting in the cool evening breeze. He followed the fresh air to the window and squeezed himself through onto the slanting shingles of the roof. He sat, breathing deeply and trying to muddle through the last thirty-six hours of his life. Stars emerged from the darkness. Even though Fairfield was a small city, it still didn't have as many stars as Jacob could see from here. The trees rustled as unseen creatures prowled through the night. He closed his eyes, trying to imagine centaurs pacing through the woods.

The centaurs screamed at him, calling him a terrorist. Jacob's eyes snapped open when one of the centaurs threw a spear at him. He shook the fantasy from his mind and tried to focus on the real world around him. His mind was too jumbled right now to let it wander. He listened again to the sounds of the night.

There was a new noise, a strange noise, and it was on the roof. A scraping sound, like claws pulling across the shingles, moving closer. He looked over and froze. Someone was coming toward him, not clawing the roof, but walking on the air.

6

THE ORPHANED GRAY

For a moment, panic flooded Jacob's chest, but even in the pale moonlight he recognized Emilia. She wore a nightgown and walked very slowly.

Jacob rubbed his eyes to be sure he wasn't hallucinating. But when he opened them, Emilia was still moving toward him. It looked like she was walking on stones trying to cross a creek without getting wet. A *scrape* punctuated each step as shingles pulled themselves off the roof and floated in the air for Emilia to walk on. As she passed, they would *rasp* themselves back into place, leaving no sign they had ever moved at all. Jacob shook his head in amazement.

"Kind of cool, huh?" Emilia stood on two shingles that hovered in the air, waiting for her to take the next step.

Jacob nodded, trying not to look shocked by her entrance.

"How are you?" Emilia stepped onto the roof and sat down beside him as though she hadn't done anything abnormal. The two shingles she had been standing on scraped themselves back into their usual place.

"It's been a little crazy."

They sat in silence for a moment.

"Oh, here." Jacob reached into his pocket and pulled out a little pouch. Just a bit of fabric and some string. He'd made it himself to hold the necklace Emilia had left with him. Jacob always carried the pouch with him. He had every day since she'd left. He took Emilia's hand and slid the necklace from the pouch onto her palm.

Emilia's eyes lit up. "You still have it." She turned the sapphire pendant over in her hand before sliding the long chain around her neck. "Thank you, Jacob. Thank you for keeping it safe for me."

Her smile stole his breath away.

"No problem." He stared at his worn shoes. Silence overtook them again. A thousand things Jacob had wanted to say to her over the last four years raced through his mind. Things about his life and school and wanting to go to college. But now, with Emilia sitting right next to him, only one question came out. "Why did you leave it with me anyway?" Jacob asked, his voice sounding gruffer than he had meant it to.

"So you would know I was coming back," Emilia said. "You knew this was the only thing I had from my mother. You knew I would never abandon it, just like I would never abandon you. Leaving you like that was a horrible thing to do, but I didn't have a choice. I couldn't explain. I wasn't allowed to. I wasn't even supposed to say goodbye. But I wanted you to know I was coming back, even if you didn't know why I had to leave."

She paused, but he couldn't think of anything to say.

"Jacob, it was the best promise I could make."

"Why does the necklace matter to you?" Jacob looked Emilia in the eye, searching for a truth he could actually understand. "Was it even your mother's?"

"I think it was," she said. "I really don't know."

"How can you not know?"

"I always told you my mother died when I was little, and Aunt Iz was my only relative," Emilia said. "That's not really the truth. Someone left me on the doorstep here with a note and this necklace when I was only a few days old." Emilia looked down at the sapphire pendant. Delicate veins of silver held the deep blue teardrop stone in place. "Aunt Iz decided she might as well keep me since someone had left me specifically for her, especially since it seemed I would turn out to be a witch.

"There was no point in trying to find me a normal family if she would just have to come take me back in a few years anyway. I guess the necklace must have been my mother's since she left it with me. At least I assume my mother left me. I don't know who else could have." Emilia spun the pendant between her fingers. The sapphire caught the moonlight and sparkled brighter than it had during the four years Jacob had kept it for her.

"Aunt Iz didn't mind someone leaving a baby on her doorstep?" Jacob asked.

"Iz would never turn anyone away. Especially not a cute little baby."

It was odd to Jacob that Emilia didn't seem bothered by this. That it was all right her mother had abandoned her on someone's doorstep.

"It's okay." Jacob took Emilia's hand in his. His heart caught in his chest, and he quickly let go. "I get why you wouldn't want to tell me your mom left you."

"I'm sorry I never told you. It just seemed too strange. If you didn't know my mother was a witch, it wouldn't make sense for her to leave me with Aunt Iz."

Jacob shook his head. "I know what it's like to have family stuff you don't want to talk about."

"Jacob, it's not like that. I would tell you anything. I trust you more than anyone else. *Dead* is easier than *missing witch*, that's all." She laughed a little.

Jacob couldn't really understand why.

"Did you ever try to find her?" he asked.

"She could find me if she wanted to. I'm still here."

"I'm sorry."

"Don't be," Emilia said. "I got lucky. I got Iz."

"Why were you allowed to stay?" He didn't want to find a hole in her story. Didn't want another reason to be angry.

"The note Aunt Iz found with me said *Care for my Emilia. She will be one of us.*"

"But if proof is necessary—"

"Exactly. Proof of ancestry wasn't possible, so Aunt Iz called a Council meeting. She cared for me in the week before the gathering could take place. Of course, she just had to decorate a nursery, and she bought me a mobile with stars on it. Apparently, I didn't like when the mobile stopped turning, because I started turning the stars myself with magic. Aunt Iz wrote to the Council of Elders and told them they didn't need to bother with the meeting. And that was it. I had shown I was a witch, so it was completely within the rules for her to keep me."

Emilia smiled at Jacob. Leaves and twigs from the roof rose above their heads and slowly started to circle around them like a solar system. All the objects rotated perfectly along their orbits with Emilia as their sun. "Still one of my favorite tricks."

"How does it work?" He waved his hand at the swirling leaves.

"You're not supposed to cheat." Emilia hugged her knees closer to her chest. "And my helping you would definitely qualify as cheating."

"But I don't understand. Half-dead trees don't just get better." Jacob yanked a hand through his hair. "That's not how things work."

Emilia reached up and took his hand. She pulled a leaf from the air and placed it in his palm.

"Yes," she said. "That is exactly how it works." She smiled and the leaf turned a vibrant shade of green, as bright as any other in the garden. "That is how it works for me and for you, Jacob. You have to leave behind all of the rules you thought existed. Because this"—she looked up at her halo of leaves—"is real, and you can be a part of this world. I know you can. You belong here with us."

Jacob wondered if *us* included Dexter. "Would you have come back for me if I couldn't do magic? Would it have bothered you to never see me again?"

"Of course." Tears glistened in the corners of her eyes. "Of course I would have come back for you. I had to wait. There are rules—"

"Who cares about the rules?" Jacob snapped, anger creeping back into his voice. "You were my best friend. I needed you, and you weren't there."

"I know." Tears streamed freely down her face. "I've tried a million times to think of another way, but the Council would never allow it. I'm sorry. I'm so sorry I left you all alone."

"I always wondered why Iz didn't take me. I mean, if your mother died and she took you. But she never offered to take me. She fed me, bought me shoes, took me to the doctor, but never wanted me to live with you."

"I asked her." Emilia stared out over the trees. "I wanted her to take you, too. You would have been happy with us. But she said no. It wouldn't have been safe if you lived with us. Eventually, you would have figured out we were witches, and then we would all have been in trouble. So I started wishing for you to be a wizard. Then I finally got my wish, and we had to leave you behind completely."

Jacob brushed her tears away with his thumb. It didn't matter how much he hurt. He never wanted to see Emilia cry. "But you came back," he said. "I'm here now, and you won't have to leave me behind again."

"I told them I had to come and get you myself." Emilia turned away from Jacob and looked back out into the night. "Because if I didn't, you would never have forgiven me."

Jacob lay back on the roof and gazed at the stars as Emilia's solar system circled around them.

7

THE LIFE OF A TREE

Jacob woke up early the next morning. The sun peered through his window, shining into his eyes. But he didn't open them. If he hadn't dreamt the last forty-eight hours of his life, then he was at Aunt Iz's house, he was a wizard brought here to be trained, Emilia had come back for him because his father was dead, he had destroyed his school, and he was suspected of being a terrorist. And Emilia had a boyfriend who had no problem kissing her in front of the entire family. Jacob's new family.

Jacob lay in bed, trying not to think about real or not real. As his mind started to clear, he realized the bedsprings weren't poking him. He moved his foot and his toes brushed along soft sheets made of some kind of fabric he had definitely never slept in before.

He opened his eyes and found himself in the green room. He couldn't have slept for more than a few hours, and yet he was wide awake. Rolling quickly out of bed, Jacob strode to the bathroom and studied himself in the mirror. He still looked the same as he always had. More tired maybe, but the same.

"I am a wizard," Jacob said firmly to himself. "I am Jacob Evans, and I am a wizard." It still didn't sound right. "Hi, I'm Jacob, and I'm a wizard. I've been a wizard for two days now." Jacob laughed. The sound bounced around the room.

He stepped into the shower, turned the water on as hot as he could stand, and pressed his forehead to the cold granite wall. This new life was going to take some getting used to.

When he finished showering, Jacob went to the closet to look for his bag, assuming it must have made it to his room by now. But the closet was filled with clothes Jacob had never seen before. A note was stuck on the front of the clothes that read *Compliments of Claire.*

Everything in the closet was clearly brand new, but all of the tags had been removed. The clothes were very stylish and expensive looking. Suddenly Claire's excitement at his arrival made perfect sense. She had wanted the excuse to go shopping. As he dug for his bag in the bottom of the closet, he found another note.

Took your clothes, so you'll have to wear these.

Kisses,

Claire

Jacob scrunched the note in his hand and chose the least expensive-looking thing he could find: a pair of jeans and a soft red T-shirt. The outfit probably cost more money than he usually spent on food in a month. It fit him perfectly. Had Claire somehow measured him magically, or was she just that good at shopping? As soon as he stepped into the hall, he was greeted by the smell of Molly's delicious cooking wafting up the stairs.

He paused on the landing. For the first time in a very long time, he had a roof with no leaks, clothes that fit, and a hot breakfast waiting for him downstairs. His life may have been turned upside down, but things were definitely looking up.

Jacob was surprised to find Claire and Connor already in the living room.

"Breakfast will be ready in a bit." Connor glanced up from his book. "You can sit with us to wait if you'd like."

Jacob sat on the massive, rust-colored couch in the center of the room. Connor smiled at him but apparently didn't feel the need to fill the silence. Claire, however, muttered under her breath while staring very intently at her feet.

Jacob watched for a few moments until his curiosity got the better of him. "What are you doing?"

Claire didn't respond, so Connor answered for her. "She obsesses over her nails."

Jacob leaned forward to look.

"I am thinking very deep and important thoughts," Claire retorted while changing the shade of pink polish on her toes to be slightly pinker with a few muttered words.

"Right." Jacob leaned back on the couch.

"So, big day for you, huh?" Claire said, seemingly satisfied with her pedicure.

"Claire," Connor said.

"What?" Claire cocked her head to one side with the look of a confused puppy. "He just got thrown into the magical crazy pot. You grew up being a wizard. You don't get it. I know what it's like to figure out this freak stuff is for real." She turned to Jacob. "When they took me from my home when I was seven, they told me fairies were real and I was destined to be something more, and not to screw up because MAGI would come after me. That sort of thing really messes with your head."

"MAGI?" Jacob asked.

"Magical Agency for the Gathering of Intelligence," Connor said. "The Council of Elders created MAGI to deal with safety, secrecy, and law enforcement issues. They run everything. Even Spellnet." At the confused look on Jacob's face, Connor added, "Spellnet is a computer program. Magic leaves very distinctive energy waves, and MAGI set up a system to monitor those energy waves by satellite. It's a huge organization. And the satellites' nets cover the entire globe."

"Wizards use computers?" Jacob asked.

Connor nodded. "Keeping tabs on all the wizards in the United States got a lot easier when MAGI switched from paper files to a computer database."

"Right."

"Only problem is you can't do too much magic near electronics. One too many spells with your cellphone in your pocket, and the phone gets fried. It happens to Dexter all the time. He always has his phone on him. MAGI agents have crazy rules for what they can do in headquarters. They use human locks on the doors and firewalls on the computers."

"There is nothing wrong with a little human hacking," Claire snapped.

Connor hid his face in his book.

"And," Claire continued, "all the MAGI databases and Spellnet are funded by normal people who buy MAGI inventions. MAGI takes magical concepts and converts them into technology. Which is why Iz has such nice things. But she shares the wealth. She bought the Graylock Preserve so the centaurs could have more land. And she sends money wherever it's needed. She just bought a bunch of land in Africa, but she won't let me visit." Claire sulked, picking up her polish bottle and starting on her fingernails.

"Why Africa?" Jacob asked.

"Dragons. They only live in Africa. We don't keep them in America anymore," Claire said.

"Why?"

"They're lizards. They like the desert," said a sarcastic voice from behind Jacob's shoulder.

Jacob turned to see Dexter leaning against the doorframe, grinning as if dragons being in the desert should have been common sense to a kindergartener.

"They were hunted to near extinction in New Mexico and Texas," Dexter said. "They used to love Death Valley, but now there are too many tourists. So the remaining dragons were sent to Africa. There's more space there. The dragons were pushed out of their rightful territory by humans. That's why the rebels have named themselves the Dragons. In honor of the true kings of nature that were forced into hiding."

Connor shot Dexter a look that clearly said *shut up*.

The room fell silent for a moment.

"And these Dragons are saying I attacked my school?" Jacob tried to put the pieces together. "How did you guys know what happened at the school was caused by me?"

"MAGI Trackers." Connor turned back to Jacob. "The Council has a team that monitors large spikes in magic on Spellnet. They have a grid system of the whole world, and if anything spikes it, they go investigate. Luckily, Ms. Gray has friends on the tracker team. They tipped her off so we could get to you first. She told them your area was of special interest to her."

"What would've happened if you hadn't gotten to me?"

"We think the Dragons have someone inside the tracker team, too, because lately they've been getting to some of the new ones first," Claire said.

"Then what?"

"We don't really hear about anyone once they're with the rebels," Dexter said. "Some say they kill them. But in my opinion, they train them."

"For what?"

"Who knows?" Connor cut in with another hard look at Dexter. "But I'm sure it's not good for us." The room turned to ice as Dexter and Connor glared at each other. "We watch, and they watch. It's just a matter of who gets there first."

"How about werewolves?" Jacob asked, more to break the tension than because he actually wanted an answer.

"Werewolfism is a rabies-like disease," Professor Eames said as he entered the living room. "The last known case was in 1954. It is believed the disease has been eradicated, but there are frequent rumors of the existence of werewolf colonies."

"In my research, werewolfism is spread through insect bites." Claire picked up her bright pink computer from the floor.

"Have you been conducting research, Claire?" the professor asked, smiling.

"Yes. The werewolf disease is actually spread through the bite and subsequent attachment of lunaticks." Claire looked around. "Get it? Luna-ticks, like the moon, and crazy people. No? Emilia thought it was funny."

"I believe breakfast is ready." The professor chuckled as he led the way to the dining room.

8

WHERE TO BEGIN?

Breakfast was wonderful. Eggs, bacon, sausage, and fruit. Molly kept loading double portions of everything onto Jacob's plate, while keeping up a running commentary on how thin he was and how a growing boy needed a sturdy breakfast. Jacob was so full he thought he might not need to eat for days. Molly, however, was still trying to put more food on his plate when the professor stood up and said, "Jacob, I believe it is time for our lesson."

The professor led Jacob down the hall to his private study. Jacob had expected the room to look exciting, filled with cauldrons or strange gadgets, but it looked like a normal elderly gentleman's library. He was surprised to find many of the book titles were familiar to him and seemed not at all magical. The professor had *The Complete Works of William Shakespeare* and several volumes of Charles Dickens. There was *Walden* by Thoreau, as well as large sections on physics and astronomy.

There were, however, several unusual-looking volumes on the desk. One rather old and exceedingly large volume lay open. The book wasn't ancient, but more like a well-worn textbook. There were notes in the margins and creases in the binding where some pages had been turned too many times.

"Now, Jacob, where to begin?" Professor Eames asked as he seated himself behind his desk.

Jacob stared at the professor, hoping he wasn't expected to answer. His mind was still half wondering if a woodland fairy was going to be given the breakfast leftovers by Molly.

The professor leafed through a file on his desk. "Magic is a very complicated and dangerous endeavor. Isadora will teach you how to find the power within yourself. I will teach you how not to harm yourself or others. And I am afraid my lessons will be rather more tedious. You must learn the history of our kind, the language of magic, and the current status of Magickind around the world. Although"—Professor Eames ran his finger down a sheet of paper and tapped the bottom. He smiled at Jacob, his face creasing in well-worn wrinkles—"according to the school records MAGI pulled for you, you are an exemplary student. Fairfield High School, by the way, thinks you have transferred to a private learning institution, which is as close to the truth as is necessary."

Jacob nodded, unsure what the appropriate response would be.

Professor Eames reached under his desk and pulled out three books, the largest of which was an identical but less worn copy of the open volume on the desk. "These three books hold the majority of our magical knowledge. The *Compendium* is a written account of our history and laws, and it defines the lines between good and bad magic." Professor Eames placed a black leather book on the table. "*ATLAS*, or *Acknowledged Territories, Lands, and Societies*, maps out which groups live where, what the defined boundaries are between territories, and contains a breakdown of Wizarding Clans and magical species." *ATLAS* was a large, flat book with a green cover.

"*Lingua Veneficium* is a record of spells, complete with instructions on how to perform the incantations." This was the large red book like the one lying open on the desk. "These books are only owned by wizards, and the penalty for allowing any of these volumes to fall into non-wizard hands is very steep. The most important thing is to keep the secret."

Jacob picked up *Lingua Veneficium*, opened it, and scanned the text. "These spells are based in Latin. I recognize the roots."

"I see your academic prowess has not been overestimated." A smile lit Professor Eames' face. "The spells are based in Latin. Latin is a common language that is rarely spoken. It is useful to us for the same reason it is useful to scientists. We call the language used in spells the *Lingua Magnifica*."

"So, is there something special about Latin?" Jacob flipped through his new textbook. His magical textbook. "Did magic originate with that language?"

"You don't need words for magic. Words simply make it easier for you to focus your energy. You can think *fire* and the candle may light, but so might the curtains, or the cat. And I am rather fond of that poor little cat." Eames chuckled at his own joke.

Jacob laughed feebly.

"Some words that have been used for hundreds or even thousands of years are now magical," Professor Eames said, "but only because of the magic wizards have poured into them."

As the professor spoke, Jacob pictured each of the words floating out of his mouth as a spell bursting with light.

"So if I say"—Jacob paused, looking for a word in his book—"*umbrafere*, I'll turn into a shadow?"

The professor grinned. "If you were focusing your magic behind it, yes, but since you have yet to master that, no. Nothing would happen. The power comes from the mind itself. Exacting your will on the world around you. We can change objects because deep down they are all matter. The universe doesn't care what form the matter takes. As long as you do not try to create or destroy matter, really it's all the same. All of the spoken spells and wands or talismans are just ways of focusing your energy. It's not the talisman that is important. It is the power of the wizard behind the talisman."

"Talisman?" Jacob's brows knit together. He pictured himself trying to heal the tree with a life-sized crystal skull.

The professor rested his chin on his hands. "Think of magic as electricity. The human body can conduct small amounts of electricity without sustaining physical damage. But if you send enough volts through the body, a human will die. A wizard can conduct a small amount of magic, but if the energy is too great, death is the inevitable result. The purpose of a talisman is to help you focus the energy away from your body and into a chosen external object to avoid overloading your system.

"A talisman isn't necessary for minor spells, but any major spell attempted without a talisman could very easily prove fatal. And a talisman can be anything, but it is better if you feel a connection to it. It can be something you find, create, or inherit. And it will have no magical significance until you start to use it. Eventually, as you send more magic through your chosen object, it will begin to retain some of your magic. It will remember how magic works and will eventually increase your strength and power."

"So," Jacob said, picking up a pen that was sitting next to him, "basically what you're saying is I could use this as a talisman?"

"In theory, yes. But it probably won't work very well. To use the electricity metaphor, it may not be the right conductor for you. And if you use it once and afterward leave it behind, and then use a stick once and leave it behind, you'll never build any power in your talisman or become truly comfortable with it."

"How do you know what talisman is right for you?"

"You will know when it comes to you. I fashioned my wand from a broken fence post on my family's farm the day I decided I needed to leave them a very long time ago. Emilia was given a ring on her seventh birthday that she uses. She used her necklace until she left it behind with you. Samuel has a staff. He's always loved being outdoors, and he says a good sturdy staff is more useful than just about anything else. And, if worse comes to worst, he can always bash someone on the head with it."

"Hmm," was all Jacob could manage. He imagined himself in the grocery store carrying a giant staff, king of the frozen food section.

Professor Eames didn't seem to notice Jacob's mind wandering. "Dexter has two talismans actually, which, while still functional, is not really necessary, but his wrist cuffs were heirlooms. You should set your mind to finding a talisman as quickly as possible. I am afraid you must be on the educational fast track, if you'll forgive the term."

"Why?"

The professor examined his wrinkled hands for a moment. "Isadora informed you of the rebel situation, did she not? If the Council does view you as a threat to Magickind, either because you are in league with these self-styled Dragons or because you are uncontrollable, then you may not be allowed to stay with us. The Council would either bind your powers or send you to the Academy."

"The Academy?"

"Most magical families either pass down the knowledge themselves, or in a case where a parent wants a higher magical education for their child, they are sent to professors, such as myself, for an apprenticeship. That is why Dexter is here. He and Emilia have both been my apprentices for a few years now.

"Some children born into families where no one else has magical abilities are also sent to professors for education, like Claire. In the case of students who do not have a family to foster them as we have fostered Claire, or who are too difficult to control, they are sent to the Academy, the only formal magical school in America. It is not the most pleasant place, and I can assure you, you will receive a much better education here."

"Right." Jacob pictured cold, grey walls and lines of cots in vast dormitories. He definitely did not want to be sent to some institution, and he would not leave Emilia. "Fast track it is."

"Then let us begin!" Professor Eames exclaimed.

Jacob spent the rest of the day in the study with the professor, though Professor Eames never asked him to do any magic. They spent most of the time working on spell phrasing.

The professor insisted Jacob not try any magic until he had succeeded in completing Aunt Iz's task. As the hours passed, Jacob wanted to scream that if he wasn't to do magic until the tree was healthy, he might as well go pack his bag for the Academy now. But would the Academy even take him? Still, Professor Eames seemed perfectly content to work on pronunciation.

When there was only a half hour until dinner, the professor sent Jacob away, instructing him to read some of *Lingua Veneficium* that night.

Jacob dropped his books in his room and went to find Emilia, wanting to tell her everything Professor Eames had told him. He went down the old servants' staircase into the main body of the house, where the bedrooms had taller ceilings and bigger closets. Emilia, Claire, Iz, and Molly all lived on the second floor of the house in the Ladies' Wing. Down here, portraits lined the hall, hanging between oversized windows. Jacob preferred his cozy attic room. Sleeping with a chandelier would have felt too much like living in a museum.

Jacob wandered down the wide and carpeted hallway. He didn't know where to find Emilia's room. He was about to call out for her when he heard raised voices down the corridor. He crept forward, not wanting to disturb anyone, before realizing the voices belonged to Dexter and Emilia.

"You went to see him last night, didn't you?" Dexter's voice slipped through the crack under the door.

"Yes," Emilia answered in a very matter-of-fact tone.

"What were you doing?" Dexter demanded.

"Talking, Dex. Just talking." Jacob could tell from the tone of her voice she was tense. Dexter was treading on thin ice. "I used to go over to his house every night, and we would talk, just like last night. His life has fallen apart. He lost his father, found out he's a wizard…he's my best friend, and he needs me."

Dexter snorted.

"What?" Emilia asked. "What is your problem with him? He's my friend. Can't you at least try to be nice to him?"

"No," Dexter said flatly, "because he shouldn't be here."

Angry footsteps pounded toward Jacob.

"Em, wait. Look, I know he's been through a lot. But he should go to the Academy."

Jacob heard Emilia growl. He knew that growl. It meant Dexter was screwed. Apparently, Dexter sensed the danger as well.

"No, listen to me," Dexter said. "He shouldn't be here. Not after what he did to that school. He should be someplace more controlled."

More footsteps resonated through the door as Emilia tried again to leave. Dexter's heavier footfalls shook the floor as he chased after her.

"He should be with more people like us. See what our world is really like."

"But he's my friend," Emilia said.

THE TETHERING | 457

"That's not all he wants."

There was silence. Jacob's heart pounded so hard he could hear it.

Dexter spoke again. "You know I'm right."

Seconds ticked past as Jacob held his breath, waiting for her response.

"I love you, Emilia," Dexter said. "And I trust you. But don't expect me to be happy he's here. I hope he knows I will fight to keep you."

For a moment, everything was quiet, as though the entire world were waiting for Emilia to say something. Suddenly, heavy footsteps moved toward him. Jacob barely had time to dart through an open door across the hall and hide before Dexter stalked past. Jacob pressed himself against the wall and waited to be sure Dexter was gone.

So Emilia knew. She knew he was in love with her. But she hadn't told Dexter she would never be interested in Jacob, hadn't said he could never be anything more than a childhood friend.

Jacob smiled to himself. He might have a chance.

He listened carefully as a minute ticked past, then peered around the corner to make sure the hall was empty before creeping down to the dining room. He could talk to Emilia later. The last thing he wanted to do right now was distract her from how pissed off she was at Dexter. He sat down to dinner, determined to be as nice to Dexter as humanly, or rather, wizardly possible. Let Emilia decide who was the better man.

9

GREEN

Jacob propped all his pillows at the head of his bed and settled in to do his reading in *Lingua Veneficium*. The professor had only told him to familiarize himself with the format of the spells, not assigned specific chapters for reading. The book didn't seem to have chapters anyway. Nor was it in alphabetical order, at least not by spell wording or English translation. Rather, the book seemed to be categorized by desired spell results. Though there were no section headings.

Jacob flipped to a page where each of the spells seemed to involve lifting. *Elevare* was a levitation spell designed to lift physical objects. And *cantus relovare* was used to lift simple curses.

All of the spells included their wording, or for more complex spells, the necessary incantation, but none actually said how the magic part was supposed to work.

Inluminaquio included a note about only being able to be performed under a full moon. *Spessenatura* was done by drawing out the essence of the object the wizard desired to copy, thus the talisman had to be in contact with said object.

Jacob slammed the book shut and was sorely tempted to chuck it across the room. He needed to be on the fast track. To prove he should be here. To prove he was good enough for Emilia. And reading through a bunch of spells wasn't helping.

He rubbed his eyes, trying to push the temptation of sleep from his mind, and looked out the window. The treetops swayed in the gentle breeze, shifting the stars in and out of view. The tree was the key.

Jacob got out of bed and picked up his *Lingua Veneficium*. He opened his door quietly and crept into the hall. He paused to listen but didn't hear anyone moving about the house. No one had said he had to stay inside at night, but he assumed Iz wouldn't appreciate his going out to the garden at one in the morning.

Nothing stirred but the swaying trees as he slipped out the veranda doors and onto the garden path. The moon was bright, and he easily found his way to the frail little tree.

Again he tried sitting in front of the tree, willing it to be healthy. He tried asking the tree nicely. He even tried saying a few of the spells he'd found in his book. *"Adfirmare. Sanavire. Alescere!"* He was sure he had the pronunciation right, but nothing worked.

Jacob was about to go back to the house and look through the shelves of books in the library to find a clue. Those books had to have something in them about dying plants.

He was tired, so tired, but determined to finish this.

Trying to decide what to look up when he got back to the house, he closed his eyes and laid his hand on the thin trunk of the tree. Suddenly, a flash of something strange flared before him, like a feeble light flickering from the center of the tree. Jacob yanked his hand away. He opened his eyes and examined the sapling.

The tiny trunk remained bent, and the leaves withering and frail. Jacob carefully placed his hand back on the tree and closed his eyes. There it was, the light in the center of the tree again, but he was prepared this time and didn't shy away.

Ever so slowly, he became aware of another light, an energy within himself, but it burned brighter and stronger than the light in the tree. He took a breath and felt the core of energy burn hotter with the flow of air, as though a bed of hot embers were living under his lungs, feeding on the oxygen they pulled in. Tentatively, almost instinctively, Jacob pushed a little energy out into his hand.

In an instant, the light connected with the tree, as if the spark within his body and within the tree were magnets drawn together. The energy flowed out of his body, but it didn't feel like he was losing anything. There seemed to be a source inside him so vast the amount of energy he poured into the tree was insignificant. Or else he had a limitless supply.

The light in the tree became stronger and brighter. Then gently, very gently, he released the connection. For a moment, he was afraid the tree would fade. He didn't want to open his eyes and find the tree was still sickly, or worse, dead.

But when he opened his eyes, the tree had bloomed. It was still small, but the branches were covered in new green leaves. The tree emanated life, just like the rest of the garden. Jacob stared, amazed at what he had done.

Magic. He had done magic.

Exhaustion took over his body, weighing down his arm. He couldn't help laughing as he lay back on the grass.

"Yet another redefinition of impossible."

There was a snap from the tree above him, and a single branch fell, smacking him hard on the face. Jacob sat up, rubbing the sore spot on his nose. A stick lay in the grass next to him, about a foot long and almost perfectly straight. He stared for a moment. Had the tree meant to hit him? Maybe the tree was angry because it hadn't wanted to be healed. Was there such a thing as a suicidal tree?

He held the stick up to the tree. "You want this back?" he asked, only half joking.

Then the moonlight peeked through the trees, shining down on Jacob. The stick in his hand shimmered in the pale light. It was thick on one end and slowly tapered to a point on the other. The thicker end seemed to fit perfectly in his hand, with a slight groove for his first finger to nestle in. There were no knots or imperfections, and the wood was so smooth it looked almost polished.

It was a wand. His wand. His talisman.

Jacob patted the tree as he got up to go to bed. "Thank you." And proudly carrying his wand, he followed the moonlit path back to the house.

---

*B*right stars filled the night, and a cool spring breeze whispered through the trees. Emilia shivered, and Dexter wrapped his arm around her, leading her deeper into the woods. Into the wilder part of the garden where no one would be able to see them from the path.

Emilia peered through the dense shadows. She could have sworn she'd heard footsteps on the path a minute ago. A rustling shook the bushes. Emilia gasped as a red fox darted past them.

"Shh," Dexter whispered. "He won't hurt you. You're with me." He smiled and kissed her on the forehead.

"Dexter, what are we doing out here?" Emilia pulled away.

"I wanted some time alone with you." Dexter drew Emilia farther into the trees.

"Dex—"

"No arguing, Emilia," Dexter cut her off, kissing her hair. "I wanted to tell you I'm sorry for our fight this afternoon."

"Thank you." She rested her head on his shoulder, enjoying the softness of his shirt on her face. "But we aren't allowed to be out here like this. If Aunt Iz finds out, she'll kill us. Possibly literally."

Dexter lifted her face and looked into her eyes. "You were on the roof with Jacob last night." He tucked her hair behind her ear.

"Dex, that's different."

Dexter kissed her. His mouth soft but possessive. "Yes," he said, wrapping his arms around her. "It's very different."

10

WIZARD'S WAND

The next morning, Jacob sprung out of bed, eager to tell Aunt Iz about his success and to show everyone his wand.

"My wand," he said to himself as he picked it up off the bedside table. "Guess I really am a wizard now."

He went to the mirror and posed with the wand, wanting to make sure he looked impressive. He started dueling imaginary opponents, darting across the room, defending a dark-haired, grey-eyed maiden from a thousand foes. He dove and rolled across his bed, impressing himself with his catlike landing.

Jacob cringed as giggles carried through his open window, sure he had been caught dueling with the air. He walked sheepishly over and looked out, but no one was watching him.

Emilia and Claire didn't even look up from their yoga practice on the lawn. Claire had fallen and was enjoying lying in the grass more than performing her exercises. Emilia reached down, trying to convince her to get back up, but Claire yanked Emilia to the ground. The two girls wrestled on their mats, Emilia scolding through her giggles. The pink of Claire's mat screamed against the green of the grass, while Emilia's pale purple blended in with the soothing morning.

Jacob smiled. The colors suited them both perfectly.

He ran from his room and bounded through the house to the yard, where Emilia was still trying to pull Claire off the grass.

Claire finally scrambled to her feet when she saw Jacob running toward them. "Morning," she said. "Would you like to *ohmmmm* with us?" Claire danced around Jacob, flapping her arms. "The psycho bird dance is good for the soul."

"No." Emilia dragged Claire back to her mat. "Yoga is good for focusing your energy so you stop turning all of my things pink, including my cat."

"But don't you think it's an improvement?" At the fiery look on Emilia's face, Claire fled for the house.

"You forgot your mat!" Emilia called after her, but Claire's bright blond hair had already disappeared through the veranda doors. Emilia shook her head and started rolling up the mats. "I really think that girl is worse than I ever was." She looked at Jacob for an answer, but instead of saying anything, Jacob held his wand out to her. She studied the stick for a long moment. "You did it. You healed the tree."

"Yep, and this was its thank you gift." He twirled the wand between his fingers like a baton.

"That's amazing!" Emilia squealed as she flung herself at him. Jacob staggered from the impact before wrapping his arms around her. "You did it so quickly. Now they'll have to let you stay! Does Iz know? She'll be thrilled! Everyone will be." She kissed him on the cheek.

"Careful," Jacob said, even though his stomach purred at her level of enthusiasm. "Don't want to upset anyone."

"What, Dexter?"

"I don't think he'll be too happy about me staying," Jacob said, secretly hoping Dexter had seen the whole thing through the windows.

"Of course he wants you to stay with us." Emilia bent to roll her mat, no longer looking him in the eye. "Don't judge Dexter, Jacob. He really is a great guy."

Jacob tensed. "Mmm-hmm" was the only noise he could make.

Emilia whacked him playfully in the stomach with her mat. "Really, don't. Just try to get to know him. Please."

A week later, Jacob could not have been happier with his life at the Mansion House. He had yoga on the lawn with Claire and Emilia in the mornings, three wonderful meals at the huge family table, and lessons with Aunt Iz and Professor Eames. Jacob had been told by everyone that he was doing exceptionally well, and the lessons were increasingly interesting.

Iz spent her time teaching him to channel his power through his wand, and Professor Eames focused on teaching him specific spells. He spent time in the student library reading other books on magic besides the *Big Three*, as Connor liked to call *ATLAS*, *Lingua Veneficium*, and the *Compendium*. And every evening, Emilia would help him make sense of the day's work, tutoring him on particularly difficult spells and concepts. Or sometimes just sitting on the veranda talking, Emilia telling him about the magical world and all its strangeness, and Jacob, in turn, telling her about all the people they had known back in Fairfield.

Jacob sat in Iz's office, enjoying the warmth of the midday sun as it poured through the open window, daydreaming about asking Emilia for help with his spell pronunciation that evening. Not that he needed it, but that was beside the point. He liked being helped, because he had to sit close to Emilia so they could read from the same book.

"Jacob," Iz said, gently calling his attention back to her. "A very important part of learning to effectively use magic is control and concentration. Once you learn to truly focus your mind, you will be able to do amazing things."

Aunt Iz walked over to her shelf and retrieved not a book, as Jacob had expected, but a round fish bowl. She set the bowl on the desk in front of him. Apart from being filled with water, the bowl was empty. There weren't even any marbles at the bottom.

"What I want you to do is create a water vortex. *Vertunda.*"

The water at the top of the bowl began to swirl. Within seconds, the swirling had reached the bottom of the bowl, creating a perfect miniature tornado.

"The principle of creating a vortex is the same at any level, though the energy required does increase with size. The point of this exercise is not only to create the vortex, but also to maintain it for a prolonged period of time."

"How long?" Jacob asked.

"Let's try creating a vortex first. After that, you can work your way up. Your first goal will be five minutes. Now, focus on the water. The incantation is *vertunda*," she said slowly, emphasizing each syllable. "Now speak clearly and picture the water beginning to swirl."

"*Vertunda.*"

---

*I*t was a bright and beautiful Sunday morning. Jacob hadn't set his alarm since yoga didn't happen on Sundays. Aunt Iz believed in taking a day of rest. She and the professor didn't teach, Molly didn't cook, and Samuel let the grounds grow wild. The students all caught up on their work or just took a nice relaxing day.

Jacob crawled lazily out of bed at half past ten, and even though he knew at least Aunt Iz and the professor must have been awake for hours, the house held the staggering stillness of sleep. Jacob didn't even bother changing out of his pajamas before starting down to the kitchen. Only on Sundays were any of them allowed to eat without dressing for the day first.

Voices and rich peals of laughter lured him toward the kitchen before Jacob had even reached the first floor. He recognized that laugh. It was Emilia, and something was making her very happy. He thought of Dexter making her laugh like that, and his stomach tightened.

Jacob reached the kitchen and popped his head through the door, hoping Dexter was still in bed. He didn't even have time to see who was in the kitchen before he was hit square in the face with a fist-full of flour. He sputtered and brushed his eyelids clean.

Emilia leaned on the counter grinning, and Claire rolled on the floor in fits of laughter, her face red from the lack of air.

"Morning to you too, Claire." Jacob shook his head like a wet dog. Flour formed a cloud around him, sending Claire into a fresh fit of hysterics.

Claire shook her head and gasped. "No," she said, struggling to form words. "No." She pointed to Emilia.

Jacob turned to Emilia, but before he could say anything, he was hit in the chest with a fresh clump of flour.

Emilia laughed at Jacob's shocked face, her glee daring him to retaliate.

"Oh, it's on," Jacob said, taking two long strides to the counter.

Emilia had already darted across the kitchen.

Jacob seized the bag of flour and chased Emilia in circles around the room, tossing flour at her like a maniacal flower girl. Jacob leaped over Claire, who lay on the floor threatening to suffocate at any moment. Finally, Jacob caught Emilia with one arm and, pinning her to his side, emptied the rest of the bag on her head as she shrieked. They tumbled to the floor, gasping and laughing.

There was a cough at the kitchen door. The laughter died instantly as they looked over to find Dexter standing in the doorway.

"Dex," Emilia said breathlessly as she pushed herself off Jacob and stood. "We were going to make pancakes, but, well, I'm not very good at cooking."

"My father is here to see Isadora, and he wanted to say hello to you. I'll tell him you are indisposed." Dexter turned to leave.

"I can get cleaned up." Emilia followed him to the door.

"Don't bother," Dexter said. The door thumped shut behind him.

"*Ablutere*," Emilia muttered, and all of the flour collected itself nicely into the trash can.

"Emi." Jacob put his hand on her shoulder.

"I'm not hungry anymore. I think I'll go shower." She walked out of the room without looking back, but it didn't matter. Jacob could hear the tears in her voice.

"Come on, Claire." Jacob turned back to the kitchen. "I make great pancakes."

As Jacob searched in the pantry for a fresh batch of flour, an unfamiliar voice spoke in the hallway. "Thank you for your time, Isadora. I will contact you again soon. Dexter, shouldn't you be studying? I believe that is, after all, what you are here for."

"Yes, Father."

Dexter's words were followed by the sound of footsteps and the front door closing.

"Ooh, burn," Claire muttered from behind her mixing bowl, which had turned an interesting shade of fuchsia.

11

OUTFOXED

Knock, knock, knock.

Jacob rolled over in bed and looked out the window. Moonlight poured in, but there was no Emilia outside.

Knock, knock, knock.

The sound came from behind him. From his bedroom door. Jacob glanced at the clock. 1:30 a.m. Everyone should be in bed by now.

Knock, knock, knock.

It was louder this time, more insistent. Jacob threw off his green comforter and went to the door.

Dexter leaned against the doorframe, looking perfectly well dressed, even in pajamas.

"Dexter?" Jacob asked, still feeling stupid from sleep.

"Sorry to wake you, Jacob, but I'm afraid this couldn't wait." Dexter shouldered past Jacob into the room. Jacob's door closed without him touching it. "First off, I want to apologize. I haven't been as welcoming to you as I should. Emilia means everything to me. She's why I'm here. I want to be with her."

"Right," Jacob said, not really sure how to respond. *I'm here because I want to be with her, too* didn't seem like the best choice.

"You're important to her. She was a wreck when she left you. I even bought her that stupid cat the professor is so in love with to cheer her up. But nothing worked. She always missed you. Now you're here, and she is the happiest I've ever seen her."

Jacob nodded.

"We both care about her. So why should we fight when all we want is what's best for Emilia?" Dexter held out a hand. "Welcome to the Mansion House."

"Thanks."

They shook, and Dexter smiled. "Good, down to business. We have a tradition here at the Mansion House. An initiation of sorts. Emilia doesn't want you to do it. She's too worried about you, thinks you can't do it. But Connor, Claire, and I have all agreed you're ready." Dexter pulled a pink piece of paper from his pajama pocket. "Claire made this up for you. She was going to be the one to tell you about it. But since I wanted to apologize, I thought I should do it instead."

"What is this initiation?" He took the piece of paper from Dexter. It was a typed list of spells.

"Simple. Go into the woods, catch a moon fox, and put it in this." Dexter waved his hand, and a silver cage appeared at Jacob's feet. "Bring it to breakfast tomorrow. The list of spells contains helpful suggestions, in case you need a few ideas."

"Moon fox?" Jacob eyed the cage.

"They really are harmless. I would say you could talk to Emilia about it tomorrow. But tonight is the last night of the full moon, and that's the only time the moon fox comes out."

"Right." Jacob had read about things that only came out during the full moon.

"It's easy. Claire did it when she got here, and she was only seven. If you don't think you're up to it, that's fine." With another wave of Dexter's hand the cage disappeared. "I just thought you might want to show off a bit after all your work."

A war raged in Jacob's mind as he studied Dexter's calm face. Dexter was trying to be nice, so he should go. Dexter was never nice, so he shouldn't trust him.

"Emilia will be happy you didn't go," Dexter said. "I'll say goodnight."

Dexter walked past Jacob and had his hand on the door before Jacob stopped him.

"So, how do I find this moon fox?"

Dexter smiled.

---

*T*wenty minutes later, Jacob was trudging through the woods, alone and slightly cold. "*Inluesco.*" He held the orb of light out in front of him, trying to pick his way carefully through the trees. He was off the path now, far beyond his little tree. When the house was no longer in sight, he extinguished the light in his hand and waited in the dark.

He stood still, peering into the night. The cold of the ground numbed his feet. He clenched his fists. If Dexter had sent him out here for nothing...

Then he saw it. A light hovering through the trees. Jacob stalked forward slowly, easing his feet onto the ground, careful to make no noise.

Floating not twelve feet in front of him was a silver fox. The animal glowed the soft white of the full moon and glided through the air like a ghost.

Jacob took another step forward. A twig snapped under his foot.

The fox spun around, growling.

Jacob fumbled for the pink paper, drawing his wand.

"*Inluminaquio*," he read in the silver glow. Instantly, a light shone down on Jacob. A light so bright he could barely see the fox. But the growling moved toward him.

He shielded his eyes and tried to read the next spell. "*Procellita.*" The wind whipped around him. Leaves and dirt pelted his face, but through it all gleamed the shining white teeth of the moon fox coming closer.

Jacob cursed and took off, darting through the trees. The bright beam followed like a searchlight emanating from the sky itself. He ran like a fugitive, the wind and branches ripping his clothes. He tried to find a spell on the list that could stop all of this, but before he could read anything, the wind grabbed the pink paper and yanked it away. A growling close to his ear pushed him to run even faster.

His mind raced, fumbling for words. A spell, any spell. "*Crevexo!*" he shouted, aiming his wand behind him. The ground shook beneath his feet, but the growling came closer.

"*Viperelos!*" Something hard and damp coiled around his ankle. He fell face first into the dirt as a tree root snaked around his leg.

"*Mesalvo!*" he screamed, trying to free himself. But nothing happened. In front of him, the fox glowed brightly, only inches away, baring its teeth.

"*Perago canticum!*" a voice called from behind him.

The wind stopped, the light went out, and a red fox fell to the ground with a whimper and ran away.

"Jacob." Emilia ran toward him. "Are you all right?"

"I'm fine." Jacob gasped for air.

"What the hell are you doing out here?" She knelt by his trapped ankle. "*Everto.*"

The root snapped, and Jacob flexed his ankle, trying to get blood back into his foot. "You don't know?"

"I was asleep until that crazy light woke me up. Why were you trying to capture moonlight?" She pulled Jacob to his feet.

"To catch a moon fox," a voice answered from behind them. Dexter walked out through the trees, smiling.

Emilia cast a death glare at Dexter, and for the first time, Jacob was glad she wasn't looking at him.

"Moon fox, Dex? There is no such thing as a moon fox," she snarled.

"I know that. It was just a silly prank. We were bonding, right?" Dexter's smile faltered.

"Bonding in the middle of the night? Were you watching the whole time? Did you see the spell he was trying to use? And you." She rounded on Jacob, who suddenly missed the growling fox. "Why would you come out here looking for a moon fox? Were you going to try and find a leprechaun, too? I've heard Aunt Iz wants to keep them in the yard now. And don't forget the dragon in the garage. Claire really loves her new pet! And where on earth did you get those spells? Do you have any idea how dangerous a maelstrom spell can be?"

"I got them off the paper—" Jacob glanced at Dexter, whose face paled in the moonlight. Claire had nothing to do with that paper.

"Em," Dexter murmured.

"Just go," Emilia said. "I'll talk to you tomorrow."

Jacob waited for Dexter to argue, but he turned and walked away.

Emilia stayed silent until Dexter disappeared from view. "Are you sure you're not hurt?"

"I'm fine," Jacob said. "I'll know better than to listen to him again."

Emilia started walking down the path, leaving space for Jacob to walk beside her. "The thing is, after Fairfield, I sort of fell apart. He was there for me. He might not be the easiest to deal with all the time, but he loves me, Jacob." She shook her head. Her hair floated down and covered her face.

Jacob wanted to push the hair away. To tell her he loved her. That he would be there for her always.

She stopped and looked into Jacob's eyes. "And I love him. Even if he is a jerk sometimes. Even if I may have to murder him tomorrow. I'm sorry about all of this. I'll make sure he stops. He won't bother you again."

Pain cracked in Jacob's chest as though his heart had been ripped out. She loved him. She had just said it. Emilia loved Dexter.

"Emilia?" a voice whispered from the back door.

"Great," Emilia murmured.

They jogged up to the veranda doors where Claire waited in her pink pajamas.

"What are you doing out here?" Claire asked, smirking as she glanced from Emilia to Jacob. "I woke up, and there was a weird light, so I went to your room and you were gone."

"Did you wake anyone else up?" Emilia asked.

"No," Claire answered defensively. "I came to see what the fun was."

"Don't worry about it, Claire," Jacob said as he slipped inside. "I was just out hunting."

THE TABOO MAGIC

Jacob tried to avoid the library the next day. Dexter was in there, and he didn't want to deal with him. Jacob kept picturing himself throwing things at Dexter's head, and the temptation was becoming almost too strong to resist. But he needed to get some work done, and Emilia was off in the woods somewhere anyway.

So Jacob entered the library, sat at his desk, and pulled out his copy of *Lingua Venificium*, trying to concentrate on his book instead of all the things he wanted to scream at Dexter. How could Emilia love someone like that? He opened the book and began to read.

Shielding Spells

A Personal Shield Spell is most effective when being used to guard the spellcaster only. A P.S.S. may also be used to cover others, but all persons to be covered by the shield must maintain physical contact with the spellcaster at all times. The P.S.S. incantation is Primurgo.

Group Shield Spells are spells that are meant to shield a place rather than a specific person. While G.S.S. are possible, a group or casting circle is needed to maintain a strong shield. Many groups choose to create their own shielding spells to prevent their shield from being easily penetrated by attackers. The most common incantation for a G.S.S. is Primionis.

Jacob shoved the book away. Shield spells weren't holding his attention.

Dexter closed his book and placed it into his desk drawer. The lock clicked loudly. Dexter smiled at Jacob and sauntered out of the room, whistling.

Jacob wanted to chase Dexter down the hall and tackle him. Or at least throw something hard and heavy at the back of his head. Like a desk. Or a fist.

The front door slammed. He looked at Dexter's desk. What had he been so obnoxiously snooty about? It was just a book, and Jacob was allowed to read all the books in the house.

He got up quietly and took his *Lingua Veneficium* over to Dexter's desk. He glanced back through the open door before flipping to the page for unlocking. *"Compuere."* The lock clicked. Jacob pulled out a little brown book entitled *The Taboo Magic*. It seemed like an odd book for Dexter to be treating so possessively. *"Proprioris,"* Jacob said, and the book flipped itself to the last page it had been opened to. He turned back a few pages to find the beginning of the section.

Tethering

The magical binding of two people. Historically, tethering was an integral part of a wizarding wedding. After a tethering ceremony, the coniunx, *or tethered couple, would gain the ability to sense one another and would develop a greatly increased emotional attachment.*

In today's wizarding society, tethering is rarely included in wedding ceremonies. It is generally considered archaic and makes divorce much more difficult, as a tethering can only be severed by the death of one of the coniunx. *The demise of half of the pair is incredibly painful for the remaining party and often results in their subsequent death.*

Jacob tossed the book back into the drawer as though it were poisonous and continued contact would contaminate him. He locked the drawer and hurried back to his desk. No wonder Dexter hadn't wanted him to see the book. If Dexter thought Emilia would ever tether herself to someone like him, to anyone—

Jacob's water glass exploded. As he bent to pick up the pieces, all he could picture was Dexter's head exploding instead.

13

FULGURATUS

"*Aperestra ab externum. Arcanestra ab externum.*" The shutters in Jacob's room swung open and closed as he paced and nervously repeated the spells to himself. He had been at the Mansion House for a month now, and the professor had decided it was time for his first formal test. Not that the grades could be reported to anyone, but Jacob still wanted to do well.

Emilia had stayed up late into the night helping him study. She had even snuck back to her room by walking on the roof shingles so Dexter wouldn't know how late she'd stayed.

Jacob checked the clock. 8:56 a.m. Time to head down for his lesson.

"*Elevare,*" Jacob muttered under his breath, levitating the pencil in his hand as he walked down the stairs.

He arrived at the professor's office, but the door was shut. Jacob raised his hand to knock before realizing there were voices on the other side of the door. One voice belonged to Professor Eames, but there was another deep, rumbling voice Jacob didn't recognize.

"Are you quite sure Willow was taken?" Professor Eames asked. "I know it may be difficult for you to consider, but is there a possibility she left on her own? She is nearly an adult, after all."

The other voice answered, but Jacob couldn't make out the words.

"If MAGI is looking for her," the professor said, "I'm sure she will soon be found. I'll contact Larkin and make sure she takes a look at Willow's file. And

Proteus, my friend, I promise to do what"—there was a pause—"poking about I can."

The low voice rumbled again.

"Yes, he's probably outside right now. It's nearly time for his lesson. Jacob," the professor called, "please come in."

Jacob entered the study and looked around for the owner of the low voice, but the professor was alone.

"Good morning, Jacob," the professor greeted him, smiling. "I would like you to meet my friend, Proteus." He indicated a mirror on his desk.

Jacob crossed around the desk to look into the mirror. Staring back at him was the most strangely fascinating man Jacob had ever seen.

His eyes held a fierce and wild look that was both intimidating and worthy of hero worship. Grey streaked his long, curly black hair, which flowed past his bare, well-muscled shoulders. His chiseled face was tan and weathered, and his eyes an unnaturally bright shade of blue.

The man in the mirror surveyed Jacob. "Jacob, it is very nice to meet you. I hope someday soon we shall meet in person." He nodded to the professor, and with that the mirror became a reflection of the room.

"How did you do that?" Jacob asked, examining the seemingly normal mirror.

"That was skrying. Magical people learned long ago how to communicate with each other through mirrors." The professor's eyes twinkled. "You don't think humans came up with Skype on their own, do you?"

Jacob shook his head in amazement. "So that other wizard just called your mirror?"

"Well, normal skrying works rather like a telephone. One party will attempt to contact another. The second party has the ability to accept or decline the communication. There is a form of skrying that can be done without the acceptance of the second party, but it is, shall we say, frowned upon." The professor moved the mirror onto the shelf and started rearranging his desk to prepare for the morning lesson. "And incidentally, Proteus isn't a wizard. He's a centaur."

Jacob tried to picture the man he had just seen in the mirror. "He looked so...human."

"Centaurs generally do from the waist up," the professor said as he picked up his wand. "Now, let us begin your examination with a few basics. Please demonstrate three different ways to form a magical light in this room."

*I*t took more than three hours for Jacob to finish the professor's test. He lit the room, made water froth, changed the color of the professor's clothing, and created a shield spell strong enough to block the pennies the professor tossed at him. He finished the test hungry and tired, but proud of himself.

"Well done, Jacob." Professor Eames clapped as Jacob levitated a pencil from the desk into his hand. "Well done, indeed! I must say I am very impressed. Isadora will be pleased. Why don't we go and brag about your progress over lunch, and then we can spend the afternoon working outside. I have quite the treat planned for you."

Everyone had already started eating when they took their seats at the large dining room table.

"Well, everyone," the professor said jovially, helping himself to a large portion of pasta salad, "Jacob has just done very well on his first test."

"That is wonderful, Jacob," Iz said.

Emilia smiled at Jacob from across the table, while Connor, who sat next to him, reached over and patted him on the back.

"I knew you weren't going to be completely useless," Connor said with a grin.

The only people who didn't seem happy about Jacob's success were Dexter, which was to be expected, and Claire, who was uncharacteristically silent and dressed in black. Jacob had never before seen Claire without some shade of pink in her clothing.

Emilia followed Jacob's gaze. "Don't mind her." She fixed Claire with a disapproving stare. "She's pouting."

"I am not pouting," Claire replied, her voice clipped and her nose in the air. "I am in mourning."

"Claire lost her computer privileges for the next month," Iz said, passing the cranberry juice. "Her computer is locked in my office, and she is not to borrow anyone else's."

"But I need my laptop," Claire groaned. "I'm not whole without it." She tipped her head all the way back and stared at the ceiling, crossing her arms tightly.

"Then you should stop trying to hack into other people's computer files and learn to mind your own business." Dexter shook his fork at Claire.

Claire pounded both fists on the table. "I didn't try to hack into anything. I succeeded. And maybe I was doing something really nice and important."

Dexter laughed. "Of course you were. What were you trying to do, find a way to buy next month's clothes today? That is very important."

Tears glistened in the corners of Claire's eyes. "What would you know about doing something nice?"

"Children," Iz said, a quiet warning in her voice.

"I didn't start it. Wonder Woman over there did." Claire crossed her arms in front of her face and sang the Wonder Woman theme song.

Jacob grinned, and Emilia dipped her head toward her plate to hide her smile. Dexter fumed in his seat, twisting the cuffs on his wrists. Somehow his anger made the Wonder Woman cracks twice as funny.

"I think I've finished eating now." Dexter stood. "Thank you for lunch, Molly." He strode quickly from the room.

Everyone else finished eating in silence.

"We should go outside for our afternoon lesson now, Jacob." The professor rubbed his hands together as Molly cleared away the plates. "I do think you will enjoy it."

They went outside onto the sun kissed lawn.

Dexter lay in the grass next to, what appeared to be, a giant, floating dartboard.

"Ah, Dexter," Professor Eames said as Dexter sat up lazily, "thank you for joining us." He went over to the dartboard and rapped on it. "Good, feels nice and sturdy." He turned to Jacob with a smile. "Today we are going to work on Lightning Darts, or Shards as some call them. It is a very simple offensive device, and this"—he patted the dartboard—"will help with your aim. No talisman, for now. We don't want the darts to get too powerful."

Dexter pulled off his cuffs and laid them carefully on the grass next to his phone. He grinned at Jacob before standing up and facing the dartboard. "*Fulguratus.*" A small, silver lightning bolt appeared in his hand. It crackled and sparked like real lightning, but it didn't burn Dexter as he rolled it through his fingers. Then, in one fluid motion, he threw the lightning at the board. It struck the very center, leaving a tiny singe mark. "Bull's eye."

"Very good, Dexter." The professor beamed. "I thought it might be nice for you to have someone to practice with, Jacob, and Dexter is fond of this game."

"Great." Jacob tried to sound enthusiastic.

The professor nodded fervently. "Now, the spell to create the bolt is *fulguratus*. And to formulate the energy, I want you to picture a lightning bolt in your hand. You must picture the shape of the bolt very clearly, then fill it in with your energy. Go on, have a try."

Jacob flexed his right hand and tried to picture a lightning bolt. He imagined the zigzag edges and the bright light it would emanate. "*Fulguratus.*" For a moment, the center of his hand shone with a white light. Jacob jumped, so shocked by his success his concentration faltered, and the light faded.

"Very good," the professor said.

Dexter, however, looked unimpressed.

"Try again, try again," the professor said.

Trying again would have been a lot easier without Dexter standing there judging him. Jacob shook his hand and tried to focus. He pictured the lightning bolt crackling with energy in his palm. *"Fulguratus."*

This time the bolt stayed, and as he watched, it turned into a real, tangible object that was both cool and smooth in his hand. Jacob ran his thumb along its edge, the energy of the shard humming through his skin.

The professor clapped and cheered. "Now throw it at the board!"

Jacob took careful aim and threw the sparking, shimmering bolt at the target, missing the center by inches.

"Haha! Wonderful." Professor Eames laughed. "It looks like you might have some competition, Dexter."

Dexter glowered. He placed his hand in the air, palm up, and a bolt appeared without incantation. "I always enjoy competition."

They spent the next hour practicing with the dartboard. Jacob improved rapidly. Gym class had finally come in handy. All those years of dodgeball had taught him something about hand-eye coordination.

"Excellent!" the professor exclaimed as Jacob hit his first perfect bull's eye. "Now all you need is to work on formulating the bolt more quickly."

"Thank you, Professor," Jacob said, wishing the library window faced the garden. Then Emilia would have been able to watch his success.

"Joseph," Molly called from the veranda. It took Jacob a moment to realize she meant Professor Eames. "Joseph, I would like to speak to you inside, please." Molly hurried toward them. She was pale, and her forehead was lined with creases.

"Is everyone all right?" Jacob asked. With so much magic in the house, it was always possible for someone to get struck by a badly aimed spell.

"Yes, yes everyone is fine, boys. Professor, now please." Molly took Professor Eames by the arm and led him back to the house.

Jacob moved to follow them inside, but Dexter stepped in front of him, blocking his path.

"Done already?" Dexter asked. "We could keep playing. We could even spar."

"Spar?" Jacob asked, his hackles rising at the tone in Dexter's voice.

"The board is only for target practice, and you seem to be doing well enough with that. So we might as well spar."

"I don't think Professor Eames would like that." Jacob pushed past him toward the house.

"That was the plan for today anyway. He had me come out here so we could spar. Unless you feel uncomfortable without the babysitter." Dexter sneered.

Heat rose in his chest as he turned to face Dexter. "Fine. We'll spar. What do we do?"

"Stay." Dexter pointed to Jacob as though he were a badly behaved dog before striding twenty feet away. Then, without any warning, he turned back to Jacob and shot a lightning bolt straight into his stomach.

Jacob fell to the ground with a grunt as if he'd been kicked by an angry centaur. All of the air had been knocked out of his lungs.

Dexter paced in front of the target. "Now it's your turn." Dexter watched as Jacob struggled to his feet. "Really, you should go immediately after me, but that's all right. I don't mind waiting."

Jacob formed a shard in his hand. He focused and threw it straight at Dexter, but Dexter threw a bolt of his own, which knocked Jacob's to the ground, singeing a patch of grass.

Dexter laughed. "Blocking is fundamental. I'm sure you'll pick it up." He threw a bolt into Jacob's knee, which buckled and sent him back to the ground. "Eventually," Dexter added with a grin.

Jacob didn't bother standing up before forming a bolt of his own, which grazed Dexter's shoulder but didn't stop his laughing.

"Emilia will be proud." Dexter brushed the embers off his shoulder.

"You must really hate that I turned out to be a wizard after all," Jacob said as he heaved himself up off the ground. "Bet you thought I would never show up."

"On the contrary," Dexter said, casually throwing a lightning shard from hand to hand, "if she had never seen you again, Emilia would have spent the rest of her life hating herself for leaving you. Now you're here, and the guilt is gone. There are no more *what ifs*. Emilia can truly be mine."

Jacob didn't reply, but Dexter correctly interpreted his silence.

"Oh, I know you'll fight for her." Dexter laughed as he sent another lightning shard into Jacob's stomach. "But I'll win."

"Dexter!" a voice shouted from the patio. Connor ran toward them. "What the hell?" He stopped next to Jacob, who was doubled over from the last blow. "You all right?"

"Fine," Jacob grunted. "Dexter was just teaching me about sparring."

"Well, if Aunt Iz finds out about this, Dexter will be in it so deep he won't be sparring for a long time." Connor glared at Dexter.

"It was all in good fun," Dexter said with an easy smile. "Not my fault he doesn't know how to play. And you had best watch your mouth. *Lavlui*." Soap bubbles appeared in Dexter's hand, and he threw them at Connor before striding to the house, whistling.

"Are you sure you're all right?" Connor asked as soon as Dexter was out of earshot. "Emilia will fry him for this. I don't know what his problem is. He's always been a—" He used a word that made Jacob laugh.

"Don't let Molly hear you saying that," Jacob warned.

Connor shrugged. "But Dexter's never been like this."

"Don't tell Emilia," Jacob said. "I can manage Dexter myself."

"Okay, but why don't you spar with me for a while? I won't go easy on you, but at least I'm not a psycho."

1 4

WHAT TOMORROW MAY BRING

That night, after most of the house was asleep, Jacob lay awake in his room, searching the *Compendium* for information on famous duels. He was too worked up from the day to sleep, and pain still shot through his knee from Dexter's well-aimed blow. The knee wasn't too swollen, just stiff and sore. Jacob wanted to ice it, but getting ice might mean running into Molly, and he was sure she would want to know exactly what he had done.

Jacob sighed and lay back on his pillow. A book dug into his spine. He pulled *Lingua Veneficium* out from under himself and stared at the spell book for a moment. Surely there must be an ice-making spell in it somewhere. The professor had warned him not to try new spells alone, and the stupid fox incident had gone badly. But if he did one, tiny spell, no one would ever need to know. He glanced around the room, half expecting Professor Eames to jump out of a shadow wagging one of his wrinkly fingers.

He flipped through the book until he came across an entry: *To Freeze*—Strigo motus. *Aim the talisman at the desired target and voice spell.*

That was easier than any of the other spells Jacob had tried with Professor Eames.

Jacob read the words out loud a few times to make sure he had the pronunciation right, then picked up his wand and aimed at his hurt knee. "*Strigo motus.*" His knee shimmered for a moment. Jacob sighed as the pain vanished.

He went to stand up to put his books away, but when he put his legs over the side of the bed, his right leg stayed straight as a board. Jacob tried to bend it, but it wouldn't move. He touched his knee but couldn't feel anything. His knee didn't feel cold. It didn't feel at all. Jacob cursed.

He tried again to bend his knee, but it had frozen in place. He flipped *Lingua Veneficium* back to the Freeze spell. There was no counter spell written next to it. Or cross reference. Or alternate translation.

Jacob cursed again. He didn't want to risk piling another spell on top of this one, and he might need to be able to bend his knee again at some point in his life. He needed help.

There was no way he could go to Iz. She would want to know why he was hurt. The professor would be angry Jacob had tried the spell. Molly would worry. He would rather cut his leg off than ask Dexter for help. He was sure Emilia could fix it, but she would ask too many questions. And he didn't want to tell her about what had happened with the sparring. Connor and Claire he didn't trust with the safety of his leg.

The only one left was Samuel. Samuel didn't seem like the type who would ask too many questions.

Jacob pushed himself off the bed and wobbled out of the room to find Samuel, dragging his useless leg behind him. He managed all right until he got to the stairs and almost fell a few times trying to move quietly in the dark. But eventually, he made it to the ground floor by sitting on his butt and scooting along one stair at a time, pausing every few seconds to check that no one was coming. The thought of being found like that was too humiliating to contemplate.

Samuel lived right off the kitchen in a small stable that used to house animals. It had been renovated so he could have a door that opened to the gardens instead of a hallway.

When Jacob arrived at the stable, he found Samuel sitting outside in a rocking chair, gazing at the stars. Samuel didn't seem to notice Jacob's ungainly approach.

"Um, Samuel?" Jacob said as he reached the rocking chair. "Do you have a minute?"

Samuel blinked and turned toward Jacob. "Sure. What do you need?"

How could he ask for help without mentioning how he had gotten hurt? Was there another logical explanation for freezing his own leg? "Well, it's nothing really. I...ah, well, I didn't know who else to go to, and I really, really don't want anyone else to know."

Samuel leaned forward, frowning. "Right."

"So, I was hoping maybe you could help me but not tell anyone," Jacob said. "Especially not Aunt Iz or Emilia."

"All right. I'll do what I can to help, and I won't tell. Unless it's something Isadora really needs to know."

Jacob stood silent for a moment. Was this the sort of thing Aunt Iz would *really* need to know? But Jacob couldn't see another solution to his problem. "I froze my knee," he mumbled. Jacob braced himself for Samuel to yell at him. But instead, Samuel laughed.

"Is that all?" He shook his head and pinched the bridge of his nose. "I have to admit, from the way you were talking. Whew!"

"What did you think I meant?" Jacob asked.

"Nothing, it's just, with the way kids are these days…" Samuel raised his eyebrows. "Knees, I can fix." He pulled up another chair. "Sit, let me see."

Jacob sat with his right leg sticking straight out in front of him and pulled up his pant leg.

Samuel examined Jacob's knee. "What spell did you use?"

"*Strigo motus.*"

"Right. Easy fix." Standing, Samuel grabbed his staff, placed one end on the ground, and said, "*Cantus relovare.*"

Painful sensation flooded back into Jacob's knee. A thousand hot needles pricked his leg, all searching for the spot that would hurt him the worst. Jacob breathed in through his teeth.

"It'll hurt for a bit, but there'll be no lasting damage. You should sit still till the pain stops. It'll be a few minutes." Samuel sat back down.

"Thanks," Jacob said through gritted teeth.

"Mind telling me why you decided to try a spell on yourself?"

"I thought it would be like icing it," Jacob answered. "My knee was bothering me."

"From your little bout with Dexter?"

"How did you know?" Jacob asked.

"Connor told me. And don't be angry with him for doing it. He wanted to know if he should tell Isadora or the professor about it. Connor was worried about you. He's a good kid."

"What did you tell him?" Jacob asked.

"That what's between you and Dexter should stay that way. Connor was right to stop Dexter this morning. But I have known Dexter Wayland for some time, and whatever you did to make him angry, it's best you two sort it out on your own." Samuel looked at Jacob. "Unless, of course, you want help?"

"No." Jacob shook his head. "I want to deal with him on my own."

"That's what I thought. Sometimes we have to fight for what we want. And if you want something enough, the fight will be worth it."

"Yeah," Jacob said. Did Samuel know more than he let on about why he and Dexter were really fighting? It sounded like Samuel wanted Jacob to win. He knew he had always liked Samuel for a reason.

They sat in silence for a few minutes.

"Why are you still awake?" Jacob asked. "If you don't mind my asking," he added quickly.

"We all have fights ahead of us. Some are coming sooner than you'd think. And sometimes you need to decide what you're willing to give to win before you go into a fight."

"You're talking about the Dragons, aren't you?" Jacob asked, already sure of the answer.

Samuel nodded.

"Is it getting that bad?"

"Isadora and Professor Eames don't want to worry all of you. But yes, it is getting that bad. And the word is, tomorrow it'll get worse."

"If the rebels are so set on humans finding out about wizards, why don't they just tell them?" Jacob massaged the blood back into his knee.

Samuel didn't answer right away. He stared up at the stars, as though waiting for them to answer for him.

"It's easy, really. Let's say a month ago I met you on the street and told you I was a wizard," Samuel said. "You would have thought I was crazy. Suppose I tried to prove it by showing you my powers. You would have said it was an optical illusion or some new technology. So instead I go to a news station or a government official and make a public announcement. The government would assume I was seeking publicity, or I was insane and possibly dangerous, in which case I would be imprisoned and have to go through the trouble of escaping and going on some wanted list."

Samuel shook his head, tracing shapes in the dirt with his staff. Jacob wished he knew what or who crept through Samuel's thoughts. A breeze flowed from the base of Samuel's staff, scattering the dust of the drawings away.

"The only way to convince the general population of the existence of magic is by a show of force involving so many wizards the truth would become undeniable," Samuel said. "But a demonstration of that size is a very hard thing to organize without the Council or MAGI noticing. Whatever the rebels are planning must be big. The only way to gain from a public display like that is to scare humans into submission.

"We can only assume it will be grisly enough to scare the general population into allowing Magickind some form of power. People won't automatically assume wizards are behind the attack. They're more likely to jump to militarized terrorists of the human variety, or, in some places, the work of the devil. But they won't be able to deny something is happening. That a new kind of power is rising. Terrifying thought, isn't it?"

"What sort of thing would the Dragons do to scare people?" Jacob asked.

"Don't know. But the Dragons have let the word spread they're planning something big. We don't know what, but they want us to be watching when it happens. So we wait for what tomorrow may bring."

"Then what?"

"The fight begins. Never be afraid to fight for what you believe in, Jacob. Or for what you love." Samuel stood up. "Your leg should be better by now. Best to get some sleep."

"Goodnight," Jacob said as Samuel closed his door.

---

*J*acob lay in bed, staring at the ceiling, thinking of Emilia. How many times she had climbed through his window. How many days it had been just the two of them at school. And it had never mattered how bad things were as long as he had her. Emilia smiling. Emilia laughing.

He was in love with her.

The thought of Dexter kissing her, protecting her, made a snake curl in his stomach. He had always been in love with Emilia, and now he was going to do something about it. He would fight for her with everything he had.

And the Dragons? He pictured the vague threat the Grays all feared. It didn't feel like his fight. A few people he had never met were missing. Some settlements he had never even heard of were being threatened. The Council was only a faraway authority to him.

But Emilia.

He took a breath, and for a moment he could smell her scent as though she were lying next to him. If it was her fight, then it would have to be his, too. There was nothing he wouldn't give to protect her. He didn't know what was coming, but Samuel was right. All he could do was wait for what tomorrow may bring.

As Jacob slid into sleep, visions of fire and floods pulled him into darkness.

15

THE BREAKING POINT

"Claire, put the computer away. You know you're still grounded," Emilia said, her voice hinting at a warning. She didn't need to look over her shoulder to know whose computer keys were clacking away behind her. Emilia went back to her reading.

The ability to align oneself with the cardinal directions is a fundamental skill that is often overlooked.

Click, click, click.

"Put the computer away, Claire. You're going to get in trouble again if Aunt Iz catches you."

"I can't." Claire's voice was strange, dull.

Emilia turned.

Tears streamed down Claire's face. Her lips trembled.

"What's wrong?" Emilia asked.

Claire stood and tore from the room.

"Claire!" Emilia followed her, ready to run outside and take care of whatever horrible drama had gripped her today. But Claire stood in the living room, eyes fixed on the big TV, the remote hanging forgotten in her hand.

Water raced everywhere. People screamed as a fire blazed in the distance.

"Requests for aid are being sent out all over the country, but the explosion at the Neversink Dam was catastrophic. There are simply not enough first responders. Homes and businesses have already flooded, and the waters continue to rise. Tragically, the

force of the water was so intense that those caught unaware had very little chance for survival.

"Emergency crews are currently focusing on evacuating the outlying areas to prevent further casualties. The number of missing is still unknown, and confirmed deaths are already in the hundreds. Authorities have said that, at this point, it is impossible to determine what the death toll may ultimately be."

The reporter continued with information about evacuation sites and numbers to call for help locating loved ones. A government official warned civilians to stay away. The roads near the dam were too hazardous to risk travel. There was nothing to do but let the emergency crews try to evacuate as many people as possible. At least two towns would be lost before the flood could be stopped.

An arm wrapped around Emilia's waist.

"What happened, Dex?" she asked.

"It was the Dragons," Samuel answered from the hall before Dexter could respond. "I just got a call from Larkin. I need to head out."

"But how do they know?" Connor asked, not looking away from the horrors on the screen.

"They track everything." Tears streamed down Claire's face. "Something like this...Spellnet would see it."

Samuel left without another word.

Dexter threaded his fingers through Emilia's and led her to the couch. She buried herself in his warmth, wanting to wake up in her bed. Safe, without flooding, without death.

"What's wrong?" Jacob asked, and Emilia turned toward his voice. He stood in the hall, pink-faced and smiling.

"Jacob." She scrambled over the back of the couch and threw her arms around him. He was warm from the sun. She breathed in his scent of grass and life.

"There's been an attack," Dexter said. He held his hand out to Emilia, drawing her back to the reality of attacks and death. "The Dragons destroyed a dam."

"How do you know it was the Dragons?" Jacob asked.

The television now showed live footage from a helicopter flying over the water as it raced into another panic-swept town. Emilia couldn't tear her gaze from the devastation on the screen. Her stomach rolled at the idea that this massacre had been manufactured.

Dexter's arm closed around her again, and she let him lead her back to the couch. But she held onto Jacob's hand, pulling him along with her. She couldn't let go of him. It was too hard to find air. Wizards had done this. Wizards had killed all those people.

"Maybe it was an accident. I blew up a school," Jacob said.

"This was too deliberate," Dexter said. "Too perfect. The way the dam cracked, and how many towns the water is going to reach. The Dragons are making a statement to Magickind. They can attack. They can kill en masse, and the humans won't even know how it happened. They killed those people on purpose." Dexter stroked Emilia's hair, tucking it behind her ear. "The game just changed, Em. There's no point in hiding from it."

They waited for hours, grouped in the living room, staring at the television in numb horror. Watching helplessly as limp children were carried by hysterical mothers. Students stood on the roof of their school, calling desperately for help. Soaked emergency workers fought to pull just one more survivor from the racing waters. A man in a suit stood on a podium to make the announcement: the dam's collapse had been deliberate. This was an attack. The entire country had been placed on high alert.

Molly kept pacing to and from the kitchen with tears in her eyes. Iz and Professor Eames had locked themselves in Iz's study. Finally, Iz came out looking, for the first time in Emilia's memory, old. The living room group moved to the door to meet her.

"The Council has called an emergency meeting," Aunt Iz said.

Everyone nodded. This was expected under the circumstances.

"Jacob," Aunt Iz said, "they have requested your presence."

"What?" Jacob asked.

Professor Eames stepped forward and looked Jacob in the eye. "In light of this morning's events, the Council now feels an immediate inquiry into the incident at Fairfield High School is required." The professor addressed the rest of the family. "Jacob is to present himself to the Council at noon tomorrow. He will be tried by the Council for the destruction of Fairfield High School and questioned about the events at the Neversink Dam."

"He had nothing to do with this." Emilia stepped in front of Jacob, protecting him from an unseen danger. "They can't use him as a scapegoat. He's been here with us."

"And we will convince them of that." The professor held up a hand to halt Emilia's protests. "He has no choice but to attend the meeting. Now, go and pack your bag, Jacob. You will be leaving for the airport as soon as possible." The professor turned to Dexter. "Your father is going to the Council meeting, of course, and he would like you to stay with your family in New York. He has sent a helicopter for you, which should be arriving shortly."

"I'm going to New York, too." Emilia slipped her hand into Jacob's. "He's not going without me."

"Of course," Aunt Iz said. "I expected as much."

"I'll make arrangements for you two with Molly," the professor said, patting Claire and Connor on the shoulders before leaving for the kitchen.

"I'll pack for you." Claire's voice shook. "You wouldn't do it right anyway." As Claire ran up the stairs, Emilia thought she heard a stifled sob.

"I'll be right back," Emilia said before racing to her room to throw things into a suitcase.

Dexter followed without a word.

Emilia closed her eyes and tried to breathe. The panic in her chest didn't subside.

She pulled her suitcase from under the bed and tried to pack calmly, but her hands refused to stop shaking. Her dresser drawers opened before she could reach them. All her clothes were a mess. Shirts or sweaters? And pants, she needed pants. One sweater seemed determined not to fold. Emilia threw it onto the bed with a frustrated shriek.

Arms slipped around her waist. Emilia sank into the warmth of the body behind her. "Dex, I…" She couldn't finish explaining why she needed to go to New York.

Dexter turned her around, comforting her with a kiss. He stepped around her and folded the offending sweater.

"Thanks," Emilia said as he slid the sweater into her suitcase.

"Emilia," Dexter said, zipping her bag, "I just spoke to my father. The helicopter has an open seat. Come with me."

"Dex."

"The ride will be shorter, and you can meet Iz at the house in New York." Dexter lifted Emilia's bag.

She placed her hand on top, pressing the case to the bed. "I have to stay with Jacob. Help brief him for the meeting."

"I'm sure Iz can do that."

"But I want to help," Emilia said, hating the look of disappointment in his eyes. "I'm sorry, Dex." She kissed him lightly. "I'll call you when we land."

Emilia took her suitcase from Dexter and headed downstairs. When she got to the living room, everyone had already gathered. Aunt Iz had booked the tickets, and Professor Eames was bringing around the Cadillac since Samuel had already left with the BMW. Molly had prepared bags of traveling snacks, and Claire had packed Jacob's suitcase, which was larger than Emilia's.

The family slowly trickled outside, like mourners congregating for a funeral.

Connor carried the suitcases to the car before slipping back into the house. Emilia wanted to say goodbye to Dexter, but he was already waiting in the clearing for his father's helicopter.

"Emilia," Aunt Iz said from the driver's seat.

Emilia slipped into the back of the car. Molly clung to Jacob for a moment before bustling back to the kitchen. Jacob climbed in next to Emilia. Claire waved as Professor Eames led her inside.

As Aunt Iz drove away from the Mansion House, Jacob looked back. Emilia prayed he would be with them when they returned.

16

DRAGON'S FLIGHT

They arrived just in time to check in and get through security. Even through his fear, Jacob found the airport fascinating. What would it look like from high above in the plane? Tiny ants piling into a big bug that could fly? The whole process seemed absurd.

"Shoes," Emilia said as they loaded their belongings onto the conveyor belt that fed the x-ray machine.

"Huh?" Jacob asked, still focused on a man who had been pulled aside after the metal detector declared him a threat.

"You have to put your shoes through the x-ray." Emilia rolled her eyes and leaned in to whisper. "And these people would think traveling by magic was crazy."

"So you could really fly on a broom or a carpet?" Jacob asked in a hushed tone.

"Sure." Emilia prepared her bag for the x-ray machine.

"So why are we here?" Jacob asked.

"The wind chill is awful, there's a huge risk of being sighted, and you can't pack very many shoes," Emilia whispered back. "Some people choose brooms, but I'll fly in a climate-controlled plane any day."

"Claire would hate brooms. No shoes? How ever would she survive the lack of outfit coordination?" Jacob tried to laugh but stopped immediately. The laugh sounded cold and wrong somehow. He watched people being shuttled through the body scanners as he waited for his backpack and shoes.

What would it be like to fly on a broom? He could fly wherever he wanted. No roads or tickets to worry about. He could fly away from the Council. He wouldn't have to stand trial. He could take Emilia and just go. Find someplace sunny and warm neither of them had ever been.

Aunt Iz led them quickly through the airport. They arrived at their gate just as first class passengers were being called to board.

As soon as they were seated, Aunt Iz handed Jacob a golden folder embossed with the lettering *C.O.E.: Persons, Procedures, and Potential Problems.* "This has everything you need to know, and don't worry too much about the details. The most important thing is to be respectful."

Jacob opened the file and began reading. The first few sheets were filled with pictures of Council members and brief biographies outlining personal accomplishments, family histories, and notable attributes of the land they controlled. Next to each Council member was a picture of their Clan crest. Jacob touched the tree of life symbol by Aunt Iz's picture before moving on to the others. He counted thirteen Council members in all.

"Do they represent all the territories in America?" Jacob whispered to Emilia.

"Some of the territories are much larger than others," Emilia said. "It depends on what the population of the area was when the Council was formed. The territories in the east are much smaller in terms of land than the ones in the west."

Jacob nodded. The plane raced down the runway, gaining speed. The front wheels lifted off the ground, pushing Jacob back against his seat. He didn't like the feeling it gave him in his stomach. It felt too much like the dread that had already taken up residence there.

He read for a few minutes, moving on to the *Procedures* section. "What does *Hosting Authority* mean?"

"There used to be a problem with the different Clan heads trying to take more power than was rightfully theirs," Emilia said. "One of the problems was who should be in charge of Council meetings, and who should get to host the meetings. Some people would try to host meetings in the most ridiculous places, hoping some Council members wouldn't be able to find the meeting to vote. The best solution was to always have the meetings in an easy-to-reach place, so they chose New York City."

"But isn't that a bit conspicuous? I mean, wizards gathering with so many humans around?"

Emilia shook her head. "New York is packed with so many kinds of people, no one ever notices anything. The next problem was finding a place. One Elder bought a home in Manhattan and said all the meetings could be held at his house, but no one would agree since his Clan would always have home field advantage.

"So all thirteen Elders now have New York houses, and the meetings rotate between them. Helps to ensure none of the neighbors notice a bunch of wizards meeting. And whoever's house the meeting is in gets to conduct the meeting, and the scribe is also provided from the ranks of that Clan, which helps distribute power more evenly. No one but the thirteen Clan Elders and the scribe are allowed into meetings, not unless they're part of a trial."

Jacob went back to his folder. Iz snored quietly in the seat next to him while Emilia read over his shoulder.

The rules for the trial seemed simple enough. Don't speak unless spoken to. Answer all questions honestly. No human is ever allowed into a Council Meeting. Not even as a witness. Not even if their child is on trial.

"What happens if someone is found guilty by the Council?" Jacob whispered.

"Jacob, that won't happen." Emilia slipped her hand into his.

"But if it does, what could they do to me?"

Emilia shifted in her seat, leaning closer to Jacob's ear. "For minor offenses, the Council can give fines or, in some cases, forced services for the benefit of Magickind. Helping to clean preserves, things like that. For more serious things, they can bind your powers. Make you a *Demadais* and banish you from magical society. No witch or wizard is allowed to speak to anyone who has been stripped of their powers. *Demadaies* have to live as humans for the remainder of their lives. It's different for creatures. The sentient ones rule themselves."

"But what if you're accused of something really serious?"

"Then they give you a choice of life imprisonment or death. There are two dungeons in the United States, but only the Council knows where they are. Honestly, most people just choose death."

"How do they kill you?"

Emilia sat quietly for a moment. "They don't. They make you do it yourself."

Jacob's stomach jolted. For a moment, he thought it was the shock of the idea of the Council offering him life imprisonment or suicide. Then he realized Emilia had reacted to the jolt, too.

The plane rumbled.

Emilia squeezed his hand. "Turbulence. Don't worry, this happens all the time."

Jacob squeezed Emilia's hand back. Maybe it was worth being on a shaky plane if he could hold Emilia's hand this tight.

With a *ding*, the fasten seatbelt light came on. The rumbling worsened.

Anxious chatter filled the cabin. A small child near the back of the plane began to cry.

Aunt Iz woke with a start.

"It's ok—" Emilia began.

"No." Iz unbuckled her seatbelt to get up.

"Aunt Iz, the fasten seatbelt light's on because of the turbulence." Emilia tried to coax her back into her seat.

"This isn't an air pocket, Emilia. This is magic. Someone on the plane is causing this."

Panic froze Jacob's veins. "Is it me?"

What if he did it again? What if he broke all the windows? He would kill everyone on the plane. Everyone around him would be sucked out into the abyss.

"It's not you." Iz stepped into the aisle. "Someone is doing this on purpose."

"Ma'am," a harassed flight attendant drawled as she bustled up the aisle, "you're gonna need to sit down. The pilot has turned on the fasten seatbelt sign."

"I am afraid this cannot wait. Please get out of my way." Aunt Iz tried to move past the woman.

The flight attendant planted herself directly in front of Iz, refusing to budge. "Federal Aviation Regulation states—"

"I need my medication." Iz pushed past the woman toward the cockpit.

With a gasp, Iz grabbed the seatback in front of her and collapsed to the floor. Jacob tried to squeeze past Emilia to help Iz, but Emilia wouldn't let him through. The attendant rushed to Iz, calling for the other flight attendants to help.

As soon as the last attendant was focused on Iz, Emilia grabbed Jacob's arm and whispered, "Stay here and make sure they don't leave her."

Jacob didn't want to stay, standing helplessly hunched over his seat with his head banging on the low ceiling every time the plane dropped. He wanted to help Iz, who apparently couldn't breathe, or find whoever wanted to take down the plane, but Emilia was already gone.

17

THE NAMELESS MARTYR

Emilia tried to think as she moved up the aisle. Iz never took medication. She had lied to give Emilia a chance to save the plane. But how could she find a magic user without doing a location spell people would notice?

She stopped in the aisle next to a man who barked, "The fasten seatbelts light is on for a reason, girlie!" when she bumped into him. But Emilia ignored him and closed her eyes.

She took a breath, willing herself to focus on the flow of energy around her. The engine pulsed electricity into the plane, which shook violently. There was magic in the air, but it was too scattered to follow.

The people she passed tried to calm one another in panicked voices. The plane bounced so badly now no one noticed her grabbing roughly onto their seats as she made her way up the aisle. She kept moving, scanning every face she passed, looking for signs of a spell.

She had almost reached the back of the plane when she felt a burst of energy. Her eyes darted between the passengers surrounding her. It had to be one of them.

On one side, an elderly man grumbled at his pale and wrinkled wife, who looked as though she might be ill. Behind them, a young couple were entwined, kissing one another. None of them could be performing the spell. None of them were concentrating on the plane.

All the other passengers near her were glancing around nervously, talking to their companions, and tightening their seatbelts.

The plane lurched harder than ever, throwing Emilia headfirst into an armrest. Something hot trickled down her nose. Emilia pushed herself up, struggling back to her feet as she wiped blood away from her eyes. The armrest she had hit her head on was slicked with red. The plane shook again. She stumbled and grabbed the shoulder of the armrest's owner, coating him in her blood.

"I'm so sorry," Emilia said.

The man hadn't seemed to notice the blood she'd smeared on his bare arm. He smiled as he listened to music through his headphones, swaying to a rhythm only he could hear. A dragon tattoo wrapped down the man's neck from his cheek to his chest. Emilia stumbled backward, fighting the urge to run away.

"I love you, baby. From now till the end of forever, I'll love you." The couple behind the man professed their undying love for each other, but Emilia concentrated on the man's voice.

"*Navista obitum. Rexhibeo omnis grexa.*"

He was chanting a spell. Speaking calmly, with a smile on his face.

The plane shook violently, sending luggage tumbling into the aisle and oxygen masks falling from the ceiling. Lights flickered overhead. In the front of the plane, someone started to shout the *Lord's Prayer*.

"*Fulguratus!*" Emilia shouted, no longer caring if anyone noticed her magic. She threw the lightning shard into the phone in his hands, then watched as the energy from her strike streaked up the wires, through the headphones, and into the man's ears.

He screamed and scraped at his ears, but his headphones were melting down his face like lava, burning a path through the dragon tattoo.

"Oh God!" someone shouted from behind her. People had turned to stare at her and the man. The smell of burning flesh and plastic mixed with the scent of Emilia's blood. The elderly man's wife vomited onto his lap.

"I think lightning struck the plane," Emilia said, trying to avoid the eyes of everyone around her. "He needs help."

Emilia ran back up the aisle, leaving the man screaming in agony behind her. Her legs shook so badly she didn't notice the plane was flying normally again. As she slid into her seat, one of the passengers in the back of the plane called for someone to help the man with the dragon tattoo, screaming about lightning striking the plane, but no one shouted to bring back the girl who had hurt him. No one understood what they had seen. Emilia turned her face to Jacob, trying to hide the gash on her head from her fellow passengers without leaving blood on Jacob's chest.

"Emi." Jacob tilted her chin up so he could see where she had been hurt.

"I'm fine." She put her head back down just in time as the flight attendant helped Iz back into her seat.

The pilot came over the loud speaker as Iz fastened her seatbelt. "Ladies and gentlemen, I apologize for the unexpected turbulence, but we seem to be all right now. You may remove your masks. We have requested to be moved up in the landing order and should be setting down in New York in just a few minutes."

Emilia tried to staunch the bleeding, hoping it looked like she was covering her face to cry. But as Iz thanked the flight attendant for her help, a drop of blood fell from Emilia's hands onto her unfortunately pale pink shirt.

The flight attendant reached for Emilia and tugged at her hand. "Miss, are you injured?"

Emilia kept her face turned away, but her palm was slicked with blood.

"Miss, you require first ai—" The flight attendant stopped as Iz gently touched her wrist.

"*Immemoris*," murmured Aunt Iz.

The flight attendant relaxed, and her eyes glazed over.

"Nonsense." Iz patted the flight attendant's hand. "This girl is perfectly fine. She just spilled her drink. However, I would appreciate your giving us several moist towelettes."

The flight attendant turned slowly and walked away.

"Let me see, Emilia," Iz said.

Emilia turned, still trying to keep her face out of view of the other passengers.

"*Pelluere*," Iz whispered.

Emilia gasped through her teeth as the spell took effect.

She turned back to Jacob when the attendant returned with the moist towelettes.

"Here you go, and don't forget to keep your seatbelt fastened. We're gonna be landing soon," the woman said with a huge smile.

"Is she okay?" Jacob asked.

"She'll be fine." Iz unwrapped a towelette for Emilia.

Emilia took the sweet smelling cloth, trying to clean her hands. "Memory spells can have a few undesirable, temporary side effects."

Iz reached into her purse and pulled out a small, silver-backed mirror. "All this excitement. I think I need to powder my nose."

"*Skry*," Emilia murmured as Jacob stared after Aunt Iz. "MAGI would be my guess."

No one stopped Iz when she left for the toilet. The flight attendants were too busy looking after the man with the dragon tattoo, except for the one Iz had used a spell on. She was sound asleep in her seat at the front of the plane.

"Here." Jacob opened a packet and began to clean Emilia's face.

She touched the place where the cut had been. The skin on her forehead had knit perfectly back together. The problem was her shirt. More blood had trickled onto it, leaving stains too big to hide.

Jacob took all of the bloody wipes and put them in his waxy paper airsick bag before struggling out of his sweater. "Cover the blood."

"Thanks." Emilia slid into the sweater. It felt warm and cozy, two things that didn't mesh with the last few minutes of her life.

"Thanks for keeping us alive." Jacob squeezed her hand.

Fire trucks and ambulances surrounded the runway where the airplane landed. The first passenger off the plane was the man with the dragon tattoo. He was moaning, barely conscious as the paramedics wheeled him down the aisle.

"I don't feel guilty," Emilia said, hanging on to Jacob's hand, fighting the fear that someone would try to tear her away. "Is that bad? I just destroyed a man's ears. There's only so much magic can heal. Spell damage like that, I don't think he'll ever be able to hear again. And I don't regret it."

"You saved us, Emi. You shouldn't feel guilty for doing what you had to."

Emilia held her breath and tried not to be sick at the sight of the plastic still melted to the man's neck.

"The real pity," Iz said, "is that the police will never arrest him. Even if they knew he was responsible, they could never prove it. MAGI is sending representatives over to the hospital. We can only hope they get there before the Dragons try to rescue their comrade. Although I'm not sure it should really be called a rescue. Going back to a group like that after a failed mission must be very unpleasant."

As they made their way through the crowds to baggage claim, Emilia couldn't help scanning the faces of everyone passing by. Would the Dragons send someone else after them? Jacob's arm brushed Emilia's as they walked, and somehow feeling him next to her eased her panic.

"But if he had taken down the plane, wouldn't he have died, too?" Jacob whispered while they waited for their bags. "Could a spell save you from that?"

"No," Iz said. "The leader of the Dragons must be a very persuasive person to convince him he should be a martyr and not even be allowed the credit."

"Huh?" Jacob asked.

Iz's phone buzzed. "Ah, Samuel is here. We can finish our conversation in private." She led them out the doors to where Samuel waited with the black BMW.

"Nice to see you all," he said, and though he seemed at ease, Emilia followed his gaze as it roamed over each of them in turn, searching them for signs of damage.

Once they had all climbed into the car and Samuel had pulled out into traffic, Iz resumed her explanation. "You see, Jacob, it is too much of a coincidence that a Dragon tried to crash the plane we, or much more importantly you, were on. If that man had been successful, the Council of Elders and MAGI would have blamed you. They would have had no way of knowing there were, in fact, four wizards on the plane. You would have been branded a killer and made an honored martyr for the Dragons, which means the man who actually destroyed the plane would never have been discovered by MAGI or celebrated by the Dragons."

"But how did they know which plane we were on?" Emilia asked. "You only booked the tickets a few hours ago."

"Someone told them," Samuel said from the front seat. "Someone with access to that sort of information. It could be a Council member, or a MAGI agent, or a friend someone in the family spoke to."

"So really all we know is that we can't trust anyone. Great." Emilia pulled off Jacob's sweater. She started a cleaning spell, removing the blood from her shirt.

"There are people we can and must trust," Iz said. "If we stop communicating with our allies, we will be alone and more vulnerable than we have ever been before. We simply need to be much more selective. The most important thing is to get Jacob through his trial tomorrow. After that, we will turn our attention to these terrorists."

Terrorists. That sounded right.

"For now, Samuel and I will leave you two to enjoy yourselves for the rest of the day. Please be home by ten o'clock. Jacob has a very long day tomorrow."

"What? Is that safe?" Emilia asked. "If there are people trying to get Jacob, they need to do it before tomorrow. Shouldn't we stay with you?"

"No. Samuel and I are going to the house to redo all the safety enchantments and make sure no one has been there who should not have been. Then I will meet with some friends from MAGI. I have also instructed the professor to bring the rest of the household here. It would be best if we were all together."

Emilia started to protest again.

"But not," Iz interrupted, "until the house is secure. I don't want either of you there until everything is ready, and since we don't know who else to trust, there is no other safe house for you to go to. The safest thing for you to do is disappear into the crowds of the city. Do not use any magic, and no one will be able to find you. No one knows you are going to be roaming the city except Samuel and me."

Emilia nodded. "What about you?"

"Samuel and I will take care of each other," Iz said as Samuel pulled over on 5th Avenue in front of a large department store. "Stay together, and try to enjoy the day. In times as uncertain as these, we must find joy and freedom whenever we can."

Emilia pulled Jacob out of the car.

Iz pressed a clip of bills into Emilia's hand.

"Thanks, Aunt Iz," Emilia said.

"Call if you need me," Samuel said.

And with that, Jacob and Emilia were alone in the Big Apple.

18

CITY THAT NEVER SLEEPS

Nothing had prepared Jacob for New York City.

Chaos of a kind he had never seen before surrounded him. Thousands of people passed each other on the streets, going about their different lives. The lilt of so many different languages touched his ears Jacob lost count, but two words were on almost everyone's lips.

Airplane. Dam.

The police on the corner were talking about it, sitting high above the crowd on their horses, trading theories on what they thought had happened to the dam. But none of them looked at Jacob. No one suspected he had flown on the ill-fated plane to New York to stand trial for the deaths at the Neversink Dam. Or that the malfunctioning airplane that had landed so close to the city had been his fault as well.

Emilia steered him through the crowds to show him the best of the city. She took him to the park and for frozen hot chocolate. He watched her coo as she gazed into windows whose displays danced with diamonds.

A pain burned in Jacob's chest. She was trying to give him a perfect day. In case it was their last.

Aunt Iz's New York home was a brick townhouse on the Upper West Side. The lights inside blazed bright, and Samuel met them at the cab when they arrived.

"How do you like New York, Jacob?" A strained look filled Samuel's eyes as he led them up the front steps.

"It was great." A sense of dread settled into Jacob's stomach.

"Samuel, are you all right?" Emilia asked.

"I'm fine, Emilia. Larkin and Stone are here. We've been discussing recent events." Samuel ushered them into the house.

Recent events seemed like a strange way of saying *that time when a band of vicious killers tried to frame you for crashing a plane, and oh right, they tried to kill you, your best friend, and the closest thing to a parent you have.* Jacob laughed to himself, and Emilia arched her eyebrow quizzically.

"Don't worry about it," Jacob muttered.

The house wasn't as big as the Mansion House, but it was by no means small. It had the same homey, yet elegant feel Iz seemed to favor.

Emilia started down the long, carpeted hall beside the staircase.

"Where are you going?" Samuel stepped in front of Emilia.

"To the dining room to see Larkin."

"You can't go in there, Emilia. They're having an important meeting, and it can't be interrupted," Samuel said. "Why don't you show Jacob where he'll be sleeping? Molly hasn't arrived with the others yet, so he can have first pick of the guest rooms."

"What sort of important meeting can't we go to?" Emilia scowled. "The trial tomorrow is for Jacob. He has a right to know what they're saying, and I want to go with him."

"Sorry." Samuel shook his head. "Iz told me that if you said that, I had to tell you there are some things Jacob can't know tomorrow. If he knew them and some of the Council members found out, it would only make things much worse for him. Jacob is safer not knowing, which means you can't know either."

Emilia glared at Samuel, her fists clenched

Jacob almost expected to see steam blossom from her ears.

"Fine," she sighed finally.

Emilia turned without another word and stalked up the stairs.

Jacob gave Samuel an apologetic smile before following her.

Emilia walked up two flights of stairs and into a bedroom that had to be hers. It smelled like lilacs and had a wonderful view of the old brick houses across the street. Both of their suitcases waited on her bed.

"You can choose whichever room you want." She handed Jacob his suitcase.

Jacob took his bag to the room next door and dropped it onto the bed without even turning on the lights. He really didn't care where he slept. He just wanted to get back to Emilia. He was in her room again in less than thirty seconds. Even that short time away had made it hard to breathe. She was like an anti-anxiety pill.

Emilia handed him the golden folder from the plane. Jacob settled into a comfortable chair in the corner to reread all the information he could apparently be allowed.

"How are you doing it?" Emilia asked.

Jacob set the folder on the floor. She had curled up on the windowsill. She looked almost like the Emilia he used to know. The small one who used to sit beside him as they gazed at stars for hours.

"How are you calm? You've only known about all of this for a few weeks. But you're fine. We were attacked and almost killed on a plane. And you're fine." Her voice cracked. She hid her face behind the thick black veil of her hair.

Jacob walked over and sat beside her. He thought for a moment, gazing at the New York skyline. "I'm not fine." He pushed the hair away from Emilia's face, tucking the strands behind her ear. "I'm terrified. But I am going to go in front of that Council tomorrow, because if that's what it takes to be a part of your"—he stopped himself—"this world, it's worth it."

Emilia smiled and pressed his palm to her cheek. "Always worth it."

*J*acob and Emilia studied the C.O.E. file together late into the night. They heard Molly arrive with Claire and Connor, but no one interrupted them or came to tell them to go to sleep. Emilia's phone buzzed several times before she turned it off and put it out of sight under her pillow. Dexter would not like being ignored.

Jacob didn't know what time they finally fell asleep, Emilia curled at the head of her bed while Jacob slumbered in the comfy chair. When morning came, Molly knocked on the door, summoning them both down to breakfast. Emilia led Jacob to the dining room, where Aunt Iz was already eating. There was no sign of the MAGI agents.

"Where's Larkin?" Emilia asked as she sat down at the table.

"She and Stone left late last night." Aunt Iz passed Emilia a plate of eggs. "The man from the plane disappeared from the hospital before MAGI arrived. They joined the group looking for him this morning. She wanted me to tell you she is very sorry she didn't get to see you this time, but she will call you this week and visit as soon as she can."

Jacob's stomach tightened. The man who had tried to kill them was out there again. As easy as that. And Jacob was the one standing trial.

"I am sorry I was not able to talk you through more of the information in the file last night," Iz said, wrinkles forming between her silver eyebrows.

"I'm fine. Emilia and I spent hours going over everything."

"Good." Iz smiled. "Eat quickly and go get dressed. We have to leave in one hour. The Proctor House is all the way across town, and traffic will be a nightmare."

"I'm coming, too." Emilia looked at Iz sideways as she ate her eggs, as though daring her to say no.

"Normally, I would say no, but as that would only result in your taking a cab across town by yourself and attempting to sneak into the Proctor House, I suppose you may come. You will not be allowed into the meeting, of course." Iz stood. "And remember, you must hold your tongue and be polite, for Jacob's sake as well as your own."

"I will be the sweetest angel!" Emilia called after her.

19

THE COUNCIL OF ELDERS

An hour later, Jacob found himself in a car making its way across Manhattan. He wore charcoal grey slacks and a deep blue shirt. Claire had pinned a pink note to the shirt.

The blue will make you look grown up and responsible. It also complements your eyes. Don't argue, just get dressed.

You can do this.

Kisses,

Claire

They drove past stately stone homes and massive buildings. The number of people the city contained still amazed Jacob.

Samuel navigated the car onto a road that cut through Central Park.

The strangeness of driving past groves of trees with skyscrapers peeping over the tops sent Jacob's head spinning.

They arrived at the Proctor House on the Upper East Side where a tall man in a dark suit waited outside.

"Ms. Gray." He nodded as Aunt Iz led them into the house.

There were still a few minutes left until Jacob's appointment time, but the buzzing of voices already drifted down the hall.

"Ah, Isadora!" An elderly man bustled toward them. Rather cheerful looking, the man had a large belly and a red face. He had no hair on top, but out of both sides of his head grew long white curls.

"Orem," Iz said with a smile, "it is lovely to see you again."

Orem kissed Iz on the cheek. "Emilia, you have grown!" He laughed, taking both of Emilia's hands and holding them out to the sides so he could get a better look at her. "Sometimes I cannot believe how quickly the years pass."

"Mr. Proctor, this is Jacob," Emilia said.

Mr. Proctor's smile faded when he turned to Jacob. "Yes, well, I can't really say it is a pleasure to meet you. Not under these circumstances, at any rate. You should go wait in the study. They'll call you when it's time."

"I'll go with you." Emilia slipped her arm through Jacob's elbow and began to lead him away.

Mr. Proctor made a faint grumbling noise.

"Just for the wait, not the meeting," Emilia reassured him with her most winning smile as she walked Jacob down the hall to the study.

It wasn't like Aunt Iz's or Professor Eames's studies at all. This study had books, but they were only on one wall. The other walls were covered in glass cases. One of the cases displayed a sword with a sign that said it had been used by one of the greatest dragon hunters of the sixteenth century. There was a manifest from the prison in Salem where accused witches awaiting trial had been kept, a wand that had been the talisman of the first head of the Proctor Clan, and dozens of other magical artifacts.

In the center of the room rested a large and ornately carved desk. The placard on the front read *Marshal Orem Proctor, C.O.E.*

Emilia pushed the placard aside and perched on the desk's embossed leather surface. "Mr. Proctor doesn't care so much about actual magic as he does seeming important. His family was almost removed from the Council altogether when I was little. Ever since, he's been desperate to hold on to his Council seat."

Jacob gazed up at a large painting of Merlin hovering majestically over a mist-covered lake. "What happened to get him removed? I thought the Council was a forever thing." He peered into a case that held a silver knife with a tag that read *Sacrificial knife used by Aztec wizards. Note: Generally the sacrifices were of Magickind, as their blood was thought to be more potent and pleasing to the gods.*

Jacob swallowed hard, trying to push air past the knot in his throat. He didn't want to think about wizard sacrifices. Panic surged through him again. He sat by Emilia, clenching his fists so she wouldn't notice his trembling hands.

Emilia glanced at the open doorway. "He was grooming his nephew as his heir, but the stupid kid got greedy. He went to the Hag for help."

"Hag?" Jacob asked.

"All you need to know is Iz doesn't really like him," Emilia said, "and he doesn't always like her from what she says. But he always pretends they're the best of friends whenever they see each other."

"Why doesn't Iz like him?"

"She says he has no morals. He'll do whatever it takes to hold on to his seat on the Council. It doesn't matter if it's right or wrong as long as it keeps him in power." Emilia took Jacob's hand. "Don't think he'll be friendly in there. He'll treat you however he thinks will please the majority of the people in the room."

Jacob nodded. His mouth had suddenly gone too dry to speak.

A woman cleared her throat loudly behind them. "Please follow me, Mr. Evans. Ms. Gray, if you wish to have lunch, there is food available in the kitchen."

"I just ate," Emilia said.

"There is food in the kitchen. You may eat or not, but you will wait there." The woman left the room, and Jacob followed her, waving lamely at Emilia as he went.

"Sit." The woman pointed to a wooden chair opposite a large set of double doors. The doors were carved wood, but unlike those at the Mansion House, these seemed heavy. Everything at the Mansion House breathed life, but walking through these doors could lead Jacob to a dungeon. Or death. The woman swung one of the dark doors open and entered the room, leaving him alone in the hall.

Jacob waited outside the meeting room. He didn't want to sit. He wanted to run for his life, or at the very least, pace the long hallway. But he sat, too afraid his legs might give out if he tried to stand.

He kept going over key phrases in his head. Points Emilia had told him he needed to make to the Council, if they gave him the chance, which she said wasn't very likely.

Finally, the door opened and an elderly man beckoned him in. He suddenly felt as though the wait had been too short and he needed more time to prepare. But it was no good. The old man waited for him to follow.

Somehow his legs carried him into the room. If he hadn't been so nervous, he might have appreciated the beauty of the large dining room, adorned with rich red and gold wallpaper. Three elegant crystal chandeliers hung from the ceiling, and a long mahogany dining room table stood in the center of the room.

The witches and wizards at the table were all seated facing him. Jacob felt like he had walked into a painting of The Last Supper.

He looked up and down the table. Iz sat to the far left. She gave Jacob a small smile. There were ten other wizards in all, eleven counting the elderly gentleman wheezing behind him. This was wrong. The C.O.E. folder had specifically said thirteen Clan Heads and one scribe. There should be fourteen people sitting at the table waiting to judge him. Two Clan heads were missing.

The elderly gentleman who had shown him into the room shuffled back to his place at one end of the long table where a laptop sat open, waiting for him. Mr. Proctor sat at the other end of the table. According to Council rules, the representative of the Clan whose house they were meeting in had the right to preside over the Council meeting, which meant Mr. Proctor would be in charge of his trial.

"Jacob Evans, you have been summoned before the Council to discuss the incident that took place at Fairfield High School." Mr. Proctor studied a sheet of paper on the table. "You have been accused of rebel behavior. Namely, performing magic in front of non-magic people and causing property damage in excess of thirty-seven thousand dollars and injury to over one hundred people. These charges are very serious. Please explain your actions."

Jacob opened his mouth to speak, but words wouldn't come. "Umm...wha... I." He looked to Aunt Iz, who raised her shoulders and took a deep, exaggerated breath. Jacob nodded and followed suit.

"I was at school when the principal called me to his office. He—" Jacob didn't want to relive this in front of these people, but there was no other choice. "He came to tell me my father had died. Then before I knew it, all the windows exploded."

"As simple as that?" a dark-haired man to Jacob's left asked. "Are you denying you caused the damage?"

"No," Jacob said quickly. "It was me, but I didn't know it at the time. I didn't know what I was capable of."

"Can you describe how you felt when it happened?" asked a woman with dyed black hair and far too much makeup. Jacob almost didn't answer he was so fascinated by her overly arched, painted-on eyebrows.

"I felt," Jacob said, pulling his gaze away from the woman's face, "like everything inside shut down for a second. I couldn't breathe or think. There was this anger and pain that started to swell in the back of my brain—and then it happened."

"Why anger?" a little man asked.

"My father and I didn't really get along. He was gone all the time, and I felt like he didn't care. When the principal told me he was dead, I guess I knew he was gone for good, and my father still probably wouldn't have cared."

"I think that is a very understandable reaction," the black-haired, too-much-makeup woman said. "Though I could never condone destruction, I can easily believe it was accidental."

A few of the other Council members nodded in assent.

"But that was not the first time you did magic, was it, Mr. Evans?" the dark-haired man asked.

"Mr. Wayland," Aunt Iz said with a hint of warning in her tone.

The man's dark hair and chiseled face left no doubt in Jacob's mind that he was Dexter's father.

"The other incident to which you are referring was reported to the Council immediately after it happened, and that was years ago," Iz said. "No one was harmed, and Mr. Evans had no idea what had happened."

"But Mr. Evans seems to be very clever. How do we know he didn't realize he had extraordinary abilities then?" Mr. Wayland asked.

"I didn't," Jacob rushed to say. He could feel the tide in the room turning, and not in his favor. "I didn't know anything."

"Emilia Gray didn't tell you anything?" the pointy-looking witch who had sent Emilia to the kitchen asked.

"Let me answer that, Mr. Evans," Aunt Iz said. "Emilia Gray is my ward. She came to me immediately following the incident. Council procedure was thereafter followed to the letter. As with all first manifestations of magic, communication was severed until after the second incident at Fairfield High School."

"It is not your place to answer questions for the person standing trial," Mr. Wayland snapped.

"Nor is it the purpose of this Council meeting to question the conduct of my ward," Aunt Iz said without even looking at Mr. Wayland. "It is common for two displays of magic to occur before a wizard is accepted as a member of Magickind. Are we here because Jacob's display was one of extraordinary power, or because the Dragons, whom he has never had contact with, are trying to twist a young boy's grief into something sinister?"

"Mr. Evans," Mr. Proctor's voice rose unnecessarily as though he were yelling over a fight, "will you attest that you were unaware of any magic involving Emilia Gray, that you were unaware of any of your magical capabilities at the time of the Fairfield High School incident, and that the Fairfield High School incident was in fact unintentional and the result of extreme emotional distress?"

"Yes," Jacob said, amazed he could actually make a sound.

"Then I think it is time for a vote."

"What about the incident on the plane yesterday?" a skeletal man to his left asked, staring at a paper in front of him. "MAGI states that all one hundred seven people aboard were in danger. Including you, Ms. Gray. Certainly, yesterday you were aware you are a wizard, Mr. Evans."

Mr. Proctor riffled through the sheets of paper in front of him. "I have no listing of such an incident being under consideration for this trial."

"That is because it is not a part of this trial," Iz said. "But I thank you, Mr. Chandler, for being so careful to ensure the Council has full awareness of all pending issues." She nodded to Mr. Chandler. "I myself was planning to bring the matter to the Council's attention at a more appropriate time."

"If this boy almost caused a plane to crash, it should most certainly be part of this trial, which is primarily about the use of destructive magic in front of humans." Mr. Wayland pounded his fist on the table.

"Yes, of course. But Jacob was not the cause of the incident on the plane. He was very nearly the victim of it."

Murmurs spread around the table.

"I have a full file of evidence from MAGI that proves it was not Jacob who endangered the plane, but rather a Dragon assassin," Aunt Iz said. "MAGI has pulled security footage from several cameras in the airport that clearly show the man being wheeled into an ambulance."

"An ambulance?" Mr. Proctor mopped the beads of sweat from his forehead with a silk handkerchief. "But if he was the one doing the attacking—"

"Emilia and I were on the plane as well."

"Emilia who?" said the man at the laptop.

"You know very well I mean Emilia Gray, Mr. Ogden," Iz snapped. "When we became aware the plane was, in fact, being attacked by magic, we stopped the attacker. It was quite gruesome. Emilia melted the man's headphones right into his ears. The smell was repugnant."

"If Emilia did magic in front of humans, she should stand trial as well." The bony man tapped the table with his withered finger.

"Emilia who?" Mr. Ogden asked again.

"For God's sake, Emilia Gray, you idiot," Mr. Wayland shouted.

"Emilia Gray should not stand trial for saving over a hundred people!" a very wrinkled woman said. "Did the humans notice anything?"

"Yes," Iz said. "But as they were all fearing for their lives at that moment, I'm sure none of the other passengers will be reporting anything unusual. After all, who would believe them?"

"They could report it," Mr. Chandler spat. "Just because it was your ward who performed the magic—"

Iz's knuckles turned white as she clutched the edge of the table. "MAGI is monitoring the passengers closely to be sure none of them talk. If they do, memory spells can and will be performed to mitigate any damaging memories."

"And how is it that you alone have all this information from MAGI?" Mr. Wayland asked, standing up and pointing at Iz.

Jacob wanted to stop Mr. Wayland and defend Iz. But his body seemed to have forgotten how to move.

"Are the Gray pockets that deep?" Mr. Wayland asked. "Do you own MAGI?"

"I have information you do not because I am willing to ask. Because I am willing to listen to what MAGI has to say instead of getting my information from far less reputable sources that do not have the best interests of Magickind in mind." Iz pulled a file from her bag and slapped it down on the table. "I have evidence proving the incident was but a small part of a plot by the Dragons, and that the plot goes much deeper than one plane crash."

"That sort of information should not be bandied about in front of a person standing trial, Isadora," Mr. Proctor sputtered.

"Precisely, Mr. Proctor. So let us take a vote on Mr. Evans's case and move on to matters of real significance concerning the safety not only of Magickind but of humans as well."

Jacob wasn't sure if Iz was right to push for a vote so soon. So many of the Council members were glaring at him. He didn't know if he could win. And Mr. Wayland would definitely send him to a dungeon if he got the chance.

"Fine," Mr. Proctor growled. "I hereby ask the Council to vote on the matter of Jacob Evans. All those who think Mr. Evans is guilty of rebellious acts endangering Magickind, raise your hand and say *aye*."

Mr. Chandler and the woman who had brought Jacob to wait outside both raised their hands instantly, along with Mr. Wayland. "Aye," their voices chorused.

A pudgy witch in the corner also raised her hand. "Aye"

Mr. Proctor looked around.

Jacob was sure if one more Council member raised their hand, Mr. Proctor would, too. Emilia had been right. He wanted to be on the winning side, no matter whose life would be destroyed as a result.

The room had gone quiet. Mr. Proctor's left eye started to twitch. "Is that all for the ayes?" he asked, sounding like a child who'd had his toy taken away. "Those who think Mr. Evans is not guilty, raise your hand and say *nay*."

Aunt Iz's hand was first in the air, followed quickly by five others.

Mr. Proctor raised his hand last. "The nays have it. Jacob Evans, you are hereby cleared of all charges. Please leave the room. The Council has important matters to discuss." He flapped his hand dramatically at the door, shooing Jacob out.

Jacob pushed himself to his feet, hardly believing it could be over so quickly.

"Thank you," he said as he half-ran to the door. He had almost made it into the hall when he heard a voice behind him.

"Mr. Evans." Mr. Wayland's voice dripped with malice. "In the future, I suggest you try to avoid any actions that might bring you back in front of the Council. Remember where exactly you stand within Magickind and don't cross your boundaries and meddle in things in which you have no rightful part. Should you ever be brought in front of the Council again, I doubt you will find us so generous."

"Right," Jacob said. "I do appreciate your generosity, Mr. Wayland." He slipped into the hallway, pulling the door shut behind him.

Immediately, pounding footsteps raced toward him. He turned just in time to see a blur of black hair before Emilia threw herself at him. Jacob wrapped his arms around her. He wasn't going to the dungeons.

Emilia shook in his arms. Her tears fell on Jacob's shoulder.

"Shh. It's okay, Emi." He pressed his cheek to her hair. "They voted not guilty."

"I know." Emilia hiccupped. "But they were being so awful, I thought…" A new wave of tears sent her back to Jacob's shoulder.

"How do you know what they said?"

"Come on." Emilia wiped her cheeks and dragged him down the hallway.

"Where are we going?" Jacob asked.

"To listen to the meeting."

"But I just managed to not get sent to the dungeons, and they sent me out here so I wouldn't hear what they're talking about."

"Jacob, someone is trying to kill us, or more particularly, you. Don't you want to know why?"

Jacob didn't answer. He had been so happy about the trial being over he had almost forgotten the whole attempted murder thing.

"Come on, and be quiet."

20

THE TIPPING POINT

Emilia pulled Jacob through the crisp, white kitchen, which had either never been used, or was cleaned with a liberal amount of bleach several times a day. She pushed through a narrow door in the corner of the room into a small pantry.

Emilia turned sideways and pulled Jacob in behind her. "Close the door," she whispered.

The door clicked quietly shut. The only light came from a small air vent at the very bottom of the back wall. "What are we doing in here?"

Emilia reached into her back pocket and pulled out a tiny mirror. "Not getting caught. *Volavertus.*" The mirror shimmered for a moment, casting strange shadows onto the pantry walls, before voices sounded from the depths of its glowing surface.

"The time has come for action."

"I think that's Mr. Chandler," Emilia murmured, holding the mirror up close to her ear.

"We can no longer be driven from our homes and forced into hiding. Now is when we must act. It is time to show the humans who they are stealing from. To show them the consequences of their actions and prove we will take retribution."

"What are you doing?" Jacob asked, his eyes flicking from Emilia to the mirror.

"I snuck a mirror into Iz's purse on our way in." Emilia smiled. "You don't think Claire's the only trouble maker in the family?"

"But Iz never accepted—"

"Shh," Emilia hushed him. "My mirror to my mirror. No acceptance needed. Now listen."

"Are you mad, Mr. Chandler? Or perhaps I misunderstood." Aunt Iz spoke calmly, but Emilia recognized the danger in her tone. "Are you actually suggesting we reveal ourselves to the world? That we should attack the general population outright?"

"Do you—" Mr. Chandler tried to interrupt, but Iz continued, her voice still calm but louder now.

"If humans discover the existence of our kind, they hunt us."

"Let them try," growled a voice, too softly for Emilia to identify.

"They may not be able to find any real witches, but humans are violent," Iz said, each of her words striking like arrows. "Do you want another massacre like the one at Salem? Those people never found a real witch, but they killed each other. Innocent humans who knew nothing about magic. Some wizards think it doesn't matter. A few human deaths don't bother them. But I believe a human life is just as sacred as a magical one, and I will grieve the loss of either, equally."

"Then you are a fool, Isadora Gray." It was Mr. Wayland who spoke this time. "You would sacrifice the progress of our kind to protect humans, who have proven themselves to be vicious murderers, horrible bigots, and incapable of protecting the planet we have been forced to share with them. We must ensure our own survival, whether or not that is conducive to the survival of humans."

"Mr. Wayland hates humans," Emilia whispered, answering the confused look on Jacob's face. "His territory is crowded, and MAGI says it's too dangerous for him to expand his land. Dex says his dad thinks the humans have taken too much."

"Are you proposing the Council condone the killing of humans?" a woman's voice asked.

"No," Mr. Wayland said. "I am proposing we let the Dragons follow their course and thank them when they're done. I would never expect this Council to have the courage to do anything significant for the advancement of Magickind."

"The rebels aren't just some fringe group anymore. They are gaining power, and quickly. If they reveal us to the public—" said a woman's frail voice.

"Ms. Sable, please," a male voice said. "There have always been problems controlling some of the more rebellious young wizards and travelers, but as long as the Clans remain in alliance—"

"The Clans haven't been *in alliance* for a long time," Emilia whispered in Jacob's ear. "If he thinks—"

Iz's voice spoke clearly and firmly through the mirror. "The reports from MAGI have suggested the recent atrocities are not the acts of disgruntled youths, but systematic attacks by a rebel group strong enough to be called an army. These Dragons are a real threat and must be treated as such. Already there have been disappearances. Proteus's daughter Willow disappeared weeks ago."

"What does that have to do with us?" Mr. Wayland snapped.

"Centaurs don't just go missing. There are so few places for them to go. Proteus has heard rumors of wizards on the preserve. Wizards traveling together."

"A group of travelers taking up residence on a preserve is not unheard of," Mr. Proctor said. "And even if there are a few rebellious sorts in the woods somewhere, does that really need to cause this kind of concern?"

"Some of the resources the rebels have—the numbers, the money—are unprecedented for a mere group of travelers," Iz said, her voice steady as the murmurs in the room grew. "They are receiving help from within the Clans. Aiding any group whose aim is to expose our existence is against the very principles upon which this Council was founded, as well as against the laws that govern our kind. Any wizard or Clan found aiding the rebels would be committing an act of war against the rest of the Clans and the Council of Elders.

"Should the situation progress to that point, the international community may also consider involving themselves for the protection of Magickind the world over. If this conflict escalates to an international level, the freedoms we have long enjoyed in America could be lost to us forever."

"Is that true?" Jacob glanced up from the mirror and bumped heads with Emilia.

"Yes," Emilia said, aware for the first time of how close she was to Jacob. Of his hip pressing against hers.

"If the international community sees American wizards standing up and taking their rightful place at the head of society," Mr. Wayland said, his voice rising in excitement, "they will see the Dragons are right in demanding that Magickind be given their due. They will hail the Dragons as leaders and heroes."

"What the Dragons are doing is wrong." Iz's voice rang loud and clear over the angry chatter in the room. "And not all wizards will agree to stand idly by. This could turn into a war between factions of Magickind, as well as a war with the humans. What will this Council do when the human government decides we are a threat and bombs one of the preserves? Whose hands will that blood be on?"

"Humans could destroy us. They would lock us up." The mirror shook in Emilia's hand. "They'd do tests on us. Does Mr. Wayland want Dexter to end up in a padded room?"

Jacob wrapped his hand around hers, helping her hold the mirror steady.

"If the humans are naïve enough to threaten us, then we shall destroy their government," Mr. Chandler spat.

"It is not for us to decide what path their government takes," Iz said.

"But it could be!" Mr. Wayland shouted.

There was silence.

Emilia held her breath.

"I am afraid that is not something my family will ever be a part of, Mr. Wayland," Iz said softly.

"Until such a time as trust can be restored within the Council, I suggest we end this meeting," a man's low rumbling voice said.

"Or until such a time as a new Council has been formed," Mr. Wayland snapped without even a note of apprehension in his voice.

Mr. Proctor sputtered. "That is a treasonous statement. That could constitute a declaration of war."

"So be it," Mr. Wayland said.

The *clomp* of footsteps and the *crash* of a door being flung open carried through the glass.

The relief Emilia had felt at Jacob being declared innocent vanished.

War. They were facing an all-out magical war. Dexter's father wanted it to happen. And she had just heard the beginning of it.

"Jacob," Emilia whispered as she silently pushed Jacob toward the pantry door, "we have to get out of here. Aunt Iz will be looking for us."

Jacob reached for the door, but Emilia stopped him, putting her hand on his chest. His heart raced beneath her palm.

"No one can know what we heard," Emilia said. "Not even Iz."

They emerged into the bright whiteness of the kitchen. Emilia pushed herself up to sit on one of the sparkling counters. Her breath caught in her throat. Tears burned in her eyes. She forced the air from her lungs as a laugh, trying to smile. Trying to look as though the world weren't falling apart.

"You did it, Jacob. You get to come home." Emilia took his hand, holding on to it like a lifeline.

Jacob slid onto the counter next to Emilia. A smile hitched onto his face. Their eyes met. So much had changed since the first time they had sat together at Fairfield Elementary.

At least he's safe, Emilia thought. She squeezed Jacob's hand, and for a moment, his smile became almost real.

Aunt Iz found them in the kitchen and rushed them out the front door and into the waiting car. Samuel's face fell at the sight of Iz's grim expression and Jacob and Emilia's plastered on smiles.

"Oh, Jacob," Samuel said, worry spreading into his eyes. "What did they say?"

"Not guilty," Jacob said.

"Wonderful." Samuel pulled out into traffic. "They had no other choice. No way they could've convicted you."

"Funny," Jacob muttered. "You seemed to think they had convicted me a second ago."

"They'll be glad to hear the good news at the house. Claire and Connor have been calling me all morning wanting to know what's happening." Samuel looked at Jacob through the rear view mirror. "Everything's going to be fine now."

Samuel gave them a smile. A smile Emilia couldn't help noticing didn't quite reach his eyes.

21

BEYOND THE BARRICADE

As soon as the car stopped, Claire burst out the front door, followed closely by Connor. Jacob plastered a smile on his face and climbed out of the car.

"Jacob!" Claire shouted as she launched herself at him with such force he fell back into the car and onto Emilia. "Did they let you off?" she squealed, still locked around him.

"Yep," Jacob choked, barely able to breathe.

Emilia laughed as Claire tried to squirm her way backwards out of the car.

Connor reached in and grasped Jacob's hand. "I knew you'd be okay," Connor said, giving him a back-thumping hug.

"Thanks," Jacob said, distracted by the sight of Molly running down the stairs with tears streaming down her face. She gave him a big kiss on the cheek.

"Everything all right then?" she asked.

"Yep," Jacob said.

"Good." Molly wiped her tears on a kitchen towel. "We'll have a celebration feast in the kitchen."

The three of them marched Jacob into the house, chatting excitedly. Emilia followed closely behind. The professor met them in the hall and gave him a "well done," but never made it to the kitchen. Jacob suspected Iz had pulled Professor Eames and Samuel away to tell them about the Council meeting.

Jacob sat at the table while Claire dished him ice cream and sang silly victory songs she made up on the spot.

You can have chocolate or vanilla because you're a lucky fella.

I'll even add Nutella and a little hot fudge!

Molly bustled about the kitchen baking treats, and Connor asked for a blow-by-blow. Everyone seemed so happy he was safe.

This must be what having a family felt like. A whole house full of people who genuinely cared about what happened to him. And he cared about all of them, too.

Emilia sang along with Claire. She smiled and laughed, but when her eyes met Jacob's, he could sense the fear she couldn't quite hide. He had finally found a family, and now they were all in danger. The knot in his stomach tightened unbearably.

After an hour, Aunt Iz showed up in the kitchen, looking tired but happy. Samuel and Professor Eames were nowhere to be seen. Jacob suspected they were already out doing something for Iz, but the victory celebration continued.

Finally, after Claire curled up under the table, clenching her stomach and declaring her imminent demise from too much ice cream, Molly cleared away the feast, and Jacob escaped to his room to change. He needed quiet to process everything that had happened. He had started unbuttoning his shirt when a quiet knock sounded on the door.

"Jacob," Emilia called from the hallway.

"Come in."

Emilia walked straight over to him and buried her face on his chest. "We can do this, right?"

He held her close. "You and me, we can do anything, Emi."

Emilia laughed a little and stepped away, brushing a tear from her eye. "Iz says to get dressed. She's taking the two of us to see a show to celebrate. It's her New York City tradition. Claire says she packed a theatre outfit, and she doesn't want to hear any arguments."

Emilia had almost reached the door when Jacob had to ask, "And Dexter? Did you get ahold of him? Is he coming?" He hadn't wanted to bring Dexter up, but what sort of a friend would he be if he didn't?

"I tried to call, but he won't answer. I understand he's mad at me, and that's fine. But I wish he were here instead of with his horrible father." Emilia scrubbed her face with her hands. "I just want to find him and tell him the awful things his father said." She took a deep breath and pushed her hair away from her face.

"He'll turn up."

"I know." Emilia gave a halfhearted smile. "You'd better get dressed before Aunt Iz has a fit. Molly's got more food for you in the kitchen when you're ready." The door closed behind her.

As much of a jerk as Dexter had always been to him, Emilia was right. If Mr. Wayland was going to try and break apart the Council of Elders, Dexter should be warned. He had been living with the Grays since the family left Fairfield. Dexter was just as much a Gray as he was a Wayland. If lines were going to be drawn, he should have the chance to choose which side he wanted to be on. And Jacob had no doubt Dexter would choose whichever side of the line kept him with Emilia.

Jacob opened his suitcase and sifted through the clothing for something labeled *theatre*. Sure enough, there was an outfit waiting for him, neatly folded and sealed in a bag. He shook his head. Leave it to Claire to think of packing something like this when he was on his way to a trial. But then, who could have foreseen an assassination attempt on the plane? Or Council members who actually supported the Dragons?

Jacob didn't particularly want to go to the theatre. He wanted to run. Take Emilia and run as far away from the broken Council as possible. Get her away from whatever danger lurked in the shadows. Go someplace nice and quiet where not even magic could reach them.

The outfit Claire had chosen for him didn't make him feel any better. The pants were dark, and the light shirt had a mandarin collar. Jacob didn't care what Claire thought. This was overkill. He sat on the kitchen counter eating a sandwich and feeling ridiculous. He looked like he should be in a magazine. Well, except for the sandwich part.

"Are you ready?" Emilia asked as she walked into the kitchen. She stole a piece of chicken that had fallen out of Jacob's sandwich and onto his plate, oblivious to his enamored stares. She had pinned up her hair to display her delicate, dangling silver earrings. She wore a light blue chiffon dress that whispered every time she moved. She pulled on a cream sweater that matched the color of his shirt perfectly.

Jacob made a mental note to stop arguing when Claire dressed him. The girl obviously knew what she was doing.

*J*acob had never seen a musical before, let alone a Broadway show. His school had done shows every year, but when finding food required constant work, the school play had never seemed important.

Iz insisted that being introduced to Broadway was a delicate procedure. A person only had one chance to see their first Broadway show, so it had to be a good one. Preferably a classic.

As they sped downtown in a bright yellow cab, Iz's face beamed while she explained the intricacies of musical theatre, but Jacob was too busy wondering where Samuel was. Where had he gone to make riding in a cab necessary? Jacob smiled and nodded but didn't really catch much of Iz's explanation of the important meaning in this particular show.

They climbed out of the cab next to the theatre and joined the lines of people waiting to be directed to their seats.

The theatre was as close to a fairyland as Jacob could imagine any building outside Aunt Iz's domain to be. Chandeliers cast their glistening light onto the patrons below. Red velvet curtains draped the stage, hiding the promise of the story within. Emilia pulled Jacob into his seat as the orchestra began tuning their instruments, searching for the perfect pitch to create their music.

Jacob's mind was still racing when the lights in the theatre dimmed. Then the show began, and it touched everything he felt inside.

The mother who sent her child away, hoping she would find a better life. The evil policeman bent on upholding the law, regardless of why the crimes were committed. The young people willing to fight and die to create a new world, a better world filled with the hope of equality for all people. A heart-broken girl dying for a man who couldn't even see how much she cared. Young lovers who wanted nothing more than to stay with each other but had to risk eternal separation to fight for a new life.

As the young fighters built a barricade, trying to find a way to survive the coming battle, Jacob couldn't help but wonder who in the story he would be. If a battle did come, which side of the barricade would he be on? Which side was the right side? Was he the heartbroken lover destined to never be loved in return, or was he the hero risking everything to protect the girl he loved? And most importantly, was protecting a secret worth all this blood? Was salvaging the Council worth being a part of the fight for a better future? Would it be better to wait it out someplace quiet and see who was left standing when the whole thing was over?

The young men on stage fell on the barricade, dying for their cause. Trying to create a new world they would never see. What did it look like when wizards killed each other? Did a dead wizard look different from a dead human?

As a small boy was killed onstage, Emilia reached over to hold his hand. She laced her fingers through his. Tears streamed silently down her cheeks.

Yes. Samuel was right. The fight would be worth it. If there were a way to protect Emilia, he would do it. Because he loved her. And as afraid as he might be of the fight to come, it was nothing compared to the fear of losing her. He would do whatever he could to keep Magickind from being discovered. He would fight the rebels. He really had no choice.

Jacob squeezed Emilia's hand and she squeezed back, and for that moment in a darkened theatre, she was his.

The show ended, and Jacob stood to clap with the rest of the audience. The crowd exited the theatre in a pack, all happily chattering about the wonderful performance.

"I have always loved that show," Aunt Iz said as they waded through the throng.

"What did you think?" Emilia slipped her arm through Jacob's, keeping him close as people pushed their way onto the sidewalk. Large cars with dark windows lined the streets, waiting to whisk the stars away from their adoring fans.

"It was great," Jacob said, trying to maneuver through the crowd. People had lined up, cramming themselves against the ropes that barred them from the stage door.

Emilia laughed as he furrowed his brow in concentration, searching for a path through the human maze in front of them. Jacob saw the gleam in her eye and started to laugh, too. She took his hand and led him toward the street and away from the worst of the crowd, following Iz's bright white hair a few people ahead of them.

It happened in an instant.

Two large men threw open the door of a black SUV and grabbed Emilia, wrenching her hand from his. Before Jacob even knew what was happening, the door of the car slammed shut, dulling Emilia's screams. Jacob leaped toward the door, but the black car sped down the street before he could reach the handle.

"Emilia!" Jacob screamed.

Aunt Iz shouted a spell he didn't recognize, but the car didn't stop. A grate exploded, spewing noxious steam all over the street and allowing the car to disappear around the corner. The crowd panicked, and thousands of people started pushing in every direction, scrambling to find a way out of the sewer haze.

Jacob shoved his way through the panic-stricken crowd, screaming for Emilia, trying to catch a glimpse of the car. But his screams were lost in the sea of chaos, and by the time he fought his way to the street corner, there was no sign of the car or Emilia.

She was gone.

22

BREATHE

Sirens echoed in the distance. Someone must have called the police about the grate exploding, but they wouldn't be able to help. Whoever had taken Emilia was beyond the power of the police.

"Emilia! Jacob!" Iz's shouts carried through the crowd. "Jacob," she gasped, grabbing his arm. "Jacob!"

"They're gone." Dazed, Jacob stared up and down Eighth Avenue.

"We have to get home." Iz tried to move Jacob away from the crowd. "Jacob, we have to go home. We can't help her here."

Aunt Iz gripped Jacob's arm and led him through the crowd and into a cab. She was already on the phone with Samuel. Though she said nothing that would arouse the cab driver's suspicion, Jacob knew Samuel would understand exactly what had happened.

Emilia had been taken.

Jacob felt like he would explode sitting in that cab. Every time they stopped at a light, his chest began to constrict. He tried to breathe, but his lungs wouldn't work properly. He dug his nails into the seat, willing the streets to clear so they could get to the house. The black town car in front of them veered suddenly to the left, as though pushed by some invisible giant. The cab driver didn't seem to notice anything strange had happened as he sped into the vacated spot and continued to weave through the midtown traffic.

"Breathe, Jacob." Iz put her hand on his shoulder and stared straight into his eyes, the cell phone still pressed to her ear with the other hand. "*Viridesca*," she muttered, and the light in front of them turned green. "*Sivexi vaiectus.*" The driver did not pause again until they reached the town house.

A flurry of activity had seized the house by the time the cab finally brought Jacob and Iz to the door. Samuel paced the hall, phone pressed to his ear, speaking in a low, urgent tone. There were some other wizards Jacob didn't know by name, but whose faces he recognized from the Council meeting earlier that day. Had it really only been that morning? It seemed like years had passed since he'd sat with Emilia in that sterile, white kitchen.

The small elderly gentleman walked swiftly to Aunt Iz and clasped her hands. "Isadora, we came as soon as we received Samuel's call."

A redheaded witch joined the conversation. "Did you recognize the men?"

"No," Iz said, accepting a hug from the grey-haired black woman who had sat next to her at the meeting. "I've never seen those men, and they weren't bearing any specific signs of allegiance."

"No dragon tattoo?" the grey-haired woman asked.

"No," Jacob said.

Samuel hung up the phone. "I've notified MAGI and called all our friends in the area. MAGI is sweeping the city for unusual magical activity. I've sent people to the Washington Bridge, Lincoln Tunnel, and the rest of the main arteries, but if they leave by water...there's just too much area to cover."

"Have there been any threats? Any indication?" the elderly gentleman asked, his voice quivering.

Iz shook her head. "Nothing that had anything to do with Emilia."

"But after the Council meeting today—" The redheaded witch glanced at Jacob. "Perhaps we should speak in private."

"No," Jacob growled. "Whatever's happening, I want to be involved."

Samuel put his hand on Jacob's shoulder, but Jacob shook it off.

"I don't care what secrets you think you have to keep," Jacob said. "The only thing that matters is finding Emilia, and I can help."

He looked around at the other wizards in the hall. All of them were older than he was. All of them knew more magic than he did. But he loved Emilia, and surely that had to be worth something. If he was locked out of a room while others discussed where she could be, or what might be happening to her, he would go crazy. Jacob turned to Samuel, willing him to understand.

"He's right." Samuel sighed. "We're in no place to reject help from anyone. Especially someone so invested in finding Emilia." He turned to Iz. "We need to call Dexter. I already tried to contact Mr. Wayland, but he didn't answer his phone or my skry."

Iz took out her phone and handed it to Jacob. "Call Dexter. Tell him what happened, and let him know he may come help with the search. Then join us in the dining room. We need to organize. With any luck, we'll receive a ransom demand."

"Would that be a good thing?" Jacob asked.

"It would mean they were interested in my money and not in Emilia's powers," Iz said with a grim twist of her mouth. "That would be a very good thing."

Jacob remembered what Emilia had said when they were in the pantry that morning. Humans locking wizards up. Jacob pictured Emilia in a white room. Trapped. Experimented on.

Emilia's worst nightmare.

A sour taste flooded his mouth.

Aunt Iz led the others into the dining room, leaving Jacob staring at the cell phone in his hand.

He found the number in the phone and called. Jacob paced the hall as Dexter's phone rang.

Ten seconds passed. Jacob wanted Dexter to answer so he could get this horrible conversation over with.

Twenty seconds.

How could he tell someone he hated the girl they both loved was in terrible danger, and that he'd been there but failed to protect her?

The ringing stopped, and Dexter's voice spoke. *You have reached the phone of Dexter Wayland. If you would like me to return your call, please leave a message at the tone. If you do not leave a message, your call will not be returned.*

"Dexter, it's Jacob. Something's happened"—he paused, trying to find the words—"Emilia's been taken. You should be here."

And he hung up. There was nothing more to say.

23

MAGI

Hours passed. MAGI agents were on their way. Aunt Iz had tried to skry Emilia, but there was no sign of her.

Aunt Iz tried calling and skrying Mr. Wayland again, but he didn't answer. No one had heard from Dexter either.

A shadow of suspicion fell over the house. Council members were supposed to be reachable at all times, especially after such an explosive meeting.

As soon as the MAGI agents arrived, Aunt Iz pulled them into a side room. Jacob made no attempt to eavesdrop, but he was sure she was saying what no one else in the group dared. The Wayland family was missing. Either they had been kidnapped as well, or they were somehow connected to Emilia being taken.

Finally, Aunt Iz brought the MAGI agents back into the dining room. There were two of them, a man and a woman. The woman, who didn't appear to be much older than Jacob, was petite with a rosy face and blond hair. She didn't seem authoritative or imposing at all. But the man looked like exactly what they needed. He was a very tall, dark-skinned man with huge muscles and a shaved head. He looked, frankly...terrifying.

Aunt Iz introduced the newcomers. "These are MAGI Agents Larkin Gardner and Jeremy Stone."

"We've hacked into the New York Police Department's traffic camera system," MAGI Gardner said. "Unfortunately, the video doesn't show her being pulled into the car. But based on timing and the description of the vehicle, we have narrowed down possible license plate numbers and are currently trying to find out if any of those vehicles have left the city. We are also checking the license plate numbers to see if any of the owners have magical connections. Does anyone have any other information?" She scanned each face in the room.

Jacob was about to say something about Dexter when Samuel caught his eye and gave an almost imperceptible shake of his head. The urge to scream that Dexter must be involved somehow boiled in Jacob, but he held his tongue. He wasn't supposed to know what had happened in the Council meeting after his acquittal earlier that afternoon. And if Samuel thought he shouldn't mention his suspicions, he would have to trust him.

It was a horrible night of waiting. Every hour seemed to last an eternity, and every passing second tightened the knot of fear in Jacob's chest. He thought the night would never end. He would be trapped waiting for the rest of time.

As the sun began to rise, there had still been no news. Gardner and Stone had gone back to headquarters. MAGI Gardner said she needed some information from the Spellnet system. Jacob had a feeling she didn't want to ask another agent to search the computers for whatever it was she needed.

Aunt Iz had installed the Council members into guest rooms. But she herself sat on the couch in the living room, staring into the fire. Samuel had left an hour ago with the usual lack of explanation as to where he was going.

Jacob paced in the dining room. He wanted to explode, to break everything in the house, to scream until his lungs ripped out of his body. But destroying the house would only distract the people who were trying to save Emilia. So he paced.

Where was Dexter? As much as he hated Dexter, Dexter did love Emilia. He must have gotten the message by now. Dexter was usually glued to his phone. But if he had gotten the message, why hadn't he come?

There was only one explanation. Dexter must already know where Emilia was. Even if he hadn't been the one who kidnapped her, he must know who had. On the plus side, Dexter would never let any harm come to Emilia. Dexter might be a jerk, but he would protect her. But what Dexter thought best and what Emilia wanted were not necessarily the same thing.

It didn't matter if Dexter loved her. There was no excuse for taking Emilia away from her family.

Sunlight filled the empty streets. New York City felt like a lie. This city did sleep. It was only he and Iz who didn't.

Claire lay curled up like a kitten, her head on Connor's lap, who was slumped and drooling against the arm of the couch. Neither of them had stirred when each of the three Council members were woken by urgent phone calls dragging them away to deal with crises in their own territories.

Ms. Olivia was the first. A fire on a preserve called her away. A human found dead, burned from the inside out, causing the police to ask unfortunate questions, woke the elderly gentleman less than an hour later. The redheaded woman had to leave when the water from the lake next to her home vanished.

All of them gave their apologies as they left, but there was nothing else to be done. Mayhem had broken out in every territory whose leader had sided with Iz at the Council meeting.

How long would it be before something happened in the Gray lands? Was taking Emilia Iz's punishment for speaking out against the Dragons? Jacob wanted to ask Iz, but how could he explain his theory without telling her he and Emilia had heard everything said after he left the meeting? Was taking Emilia enough, or would the Dragons attack again?

Not that it mattered if the Dragons were planning some other horror. They couldn't stop it, so they would just have to wait. Jacob stared out the window, watching the city come back to life.

He didn't have to wait long for an answer. Molly hadn't even managed to chivvy everyone to breakfast when the professor came stumbling out of his study, white as a sheet. He hung onto the living room doorframe for support. Molly rushed over to him, wrapping an arm around his waist to keep him from collapsing.

"I've just heard from Proteus," the professor said. "There's been an attack at the Graylock Preserve. A group of wizards, some with Dragon tattoos, attacked a hermit wizarding settlement. The hermits called the centaurs for help, but by the time they arrived, the settlement had been slaughtered. The centaurs were ambushed. Proteus and a few others managed to escape, but the rest..." The professor sagged farther into Molly's arms.

"Has MAGI been notified?" Aunt Iz's voice trembled.

Molly led the professor to a chair. "Proteus tried to skry, but all the mirrors showed an empty MAGI office. It looked like it had been ransacked."

"Someone broke into MAGI?" Claire asked, looking around as though hoping someone would tell her it wasn't true. "But it's so well protected. If the MAGI are gone, who's going to help the centaurs? Where's Larkin? She can fix it."

No one answered. No one wanted to tell Claire there was no other help. No one mentioned where Larkin might be.

"There's more," Professor Eames said. "The Dragons at the Graylock Preserve...Proteus thought he recognized their leader. It was Mr. Wayland."

Jacob started shaking. The Council was in shambles. MAGI was gone. The Grays were alone. The people in this room were all they had left.

"We have to go," Jacob said. "If Mr. Wayland is there, Emilia could be there, too. We have to go!"

"I'll arrange transport and leave as soon as possible." Samuel turned to leave the room.

"Me, too." Jacob moved to follow Samuel. "I'm going, too."

"Jacob." Samuel shook his head and laid a hand on Jacob's shoulder. "It's too dangerous for you to go." He stifled Jacob's objection. "I'll go, Jacob, and see if there is any sign of Emilia."

"Samuel," Aunt Iz said quietly. "It's too dangerous to go alone."

"I will go, Isadora," the professor said as he struggled to push himself out of his chair.

"No, Joseph." Iz shook her head.

"I'll go with him," Molly said.

Jacob had heard stories about Molly fighting before, but it was hard for him to picture.

"You need to stay with the children," Iz said. "Someone needs to protect them, and I have to go to MAGI. We need to find out what has happened to them. And I need to find Larkin."

"Then let me go!" Jacob marched over to Iz. "I'll stay out of the way. I'll be careful. But I can't just sit here and wait when we might actually have a shot at rescuing Emilia. Please, Aunt Iz. I have to go."

Iz looked deep into Jacob's eyes. He stared back, hoping he could pass whatever test her mind was putting him through.

Seconds slid past. Iz broke eye contact and squared her shoulders. "Claire, hack the Spellnet system and crash it. If MAGI is out of commission, we can't let the Dragons get ahold of that information. Connor, give her whatever assistance she needs. Molly, help the professor inform our friends of the situation. Be careful not to tell them anything that could endanger Emilia if she is being held at the Graylock Preserve. And try to find a reason the Dragons would choose Graylock to attack.

"Samuel, take Jacob. Try to locate Emilia. Do not attack the Dragons. Get in and out quickly. If you can rescue Emilia without a fight, do it. If not, come back here. I will try to find some trustworthy wizards who may be willing to help." Aunt Iz took Jacob's hands. "Do exactly as Samuel tells you. Stay hidden. You are only going as the lookout, nothing more. I know you want to bring Emilia home, but think of what she would want. She would never forgive herself if anything happened to you. And neither would I."

Jacob wanted to say he would be careful, but he couldn't form the words. Without meeting her eyes, he squeezed her hands and walked away.

The family separated, each of them going to their appointed tasks. Jacob barely had time to change out of his theatre clothes before Samuel had a car waiting for them outside. The driver whisked them away to a tall building at the very tip of Manhattan. They went up an elevator that made Jacob's ears pop and out onto the roof where a helicopter waited for them.

Jacob didn't know how Samuel had arranged it so quickly, but at this point those types of questions seemed irrelevant. The air from the helicopter's whirling blades beat them back as though it were a living creature determined to keep them from sheltering themselves within its bowels. Samuel put his hand on the back of Jacob's head, forcing him to double over. He didn't let the pressure off until Jacob was safely inside. Even after Samuel had slid the door shut behind him, Jacob could still feel the noise of the churning air vibrating in his chest.

The pilot never spoke. He sat stonily silent until they were ready to take off. Did he know he was flying two wizards to rescue a witch who was being held on land that had been taken in a bloody battle between wizards and centaurs?

Without a word, they flew over the New York skyline as it glistened in the early morning light. The helicopter ride would have been terrifying even if Jacob weren't going into a deadly situation trying to figure out if the girl he loved was still alive. And despite what Aunt Iz wanted, he had no intention of leaving without Emilia.

FLESH AND BLOOD

Emilia was spinning. Her eyes too heavy to open. She felt buried in sand.

Something was very wrong. Her head felt sloshy, and her skin felt dead, as though every inch of her were wrapped in rubber.

But her wrists...there was something strange. She tried to lift her hand to brush the hair away from her face, but her arm was too heavy to move. She breathed deeply and tried to assess her body.

She was sore. Both arms hurt. But why? Why would her arms hurt? It felt like a vice had squeezed them. Or someone had grabbed them.

Men. Big men had grabbed both her arms hard. Very hard. They'd pulled her. But why?

She took a breath and tried to think. Big men had pulled her into a car.

She wrenched her eyes open, panic bringing her back to her senses. Everything still spun, but she forced herself to sit up.

There were iron cuffs on both of her wrists. They looked like manacles, but there was no chain between them. An inscription in a language Emilia had never seen before had been carved into the cuffs. She tried to focus, to figure out what the writing said, but everything seemed so foggy. It wasn't English. It wasn't Latin. It wasn't even real letters. It looked like runes, but not any she had ever seen. Whatever the cuffs were for, she didn't want to wear them. She tried to pry them off but couldn't find a closure, and they were too tight to slip over her hands.

"*Prolaxio*," she said, trying to make to cuffs large enough to slip off, but nothing happened. "*Prolaxio*," she said again, focusing more this time, but still nothing. There wasn't even the tingle that usually came when she did a spell. "*Prolaxio. Prolaxio.*" More and more panic crept into her voice. "*Prolaxio!*"

Her powers were gone. The bracelets had bound her magic. She was as helpless as a human.

Emilia jerked her gaze up. Her prison wasn't what she'd expected. This wasn't a cell or a white padded room. There were no bars or two-way mirrors. The windowless walls were roughly hewn stone. Other than that, it looked like a bedroom. She sat on a bed with an old-fashioned iron frame. A bookcase lined one wall. Clothes had been laid out on an armchair beside the bookcase, with food on the table next to it.

If her powers had been bound, she must have been captured by wizards. A momentary relief flooded her. Wizards wouldn't perform tests on her. Wizards wouldn't cage her up like an animal for experiments.

Her heart raced as fear rushed through her veins.

The Dragons.

"Help!" she screamed, struggling to push herself off the bed. "Somebody help me!"

She stumbled to the wall and tried to bang on it with her fists, but her hands glanced harmlessly away. Again and again, she threw her fists at the wall. A scream of frustration and panic tore from her throat. No matter how hard she swung, she couldn't reach the stone. She *was* in a padded room. It was just padded with magic.

She searched frantically for an exit, but the only door in the room led to the bathroom.

Emilia was trapped.

She went back to the bed and sat down to wait. Someone had gone to the trouble of making her this prison. They clearly wanted her alive...for now. She could only wait for them to turn up. She ignored her hunger. Never touch food from a magical source you don't trust. Every young wizard knew that. She listened to her stomach growl and stared at the blank wall opposite her bed.

Minutes ticked by, but Emilia didn't move. Tears burned in the corners of her eyes.

Jacob. She had been with Jacob. Did they catch him, too?

Emilia jumped to her feet as a horrible scraping sound echoed through the room. A door appeared in the far wall and crept slowly open. She thought about hiding, then pushed her shoulders back, deciding to meet whoever was coming head on. They already knew she was there anyway.

As soon as the door opened completely, a man stepped through, smiling. Tall and handsome with dark curly hair and tanned skin, he couldn't have been even forty, but he had an air of authority about him. He wore an old-fashioned, black military jacket with a red and gold dragon emblazoned across the front.

"Emilia, I heard you were finally awake," the man said as the door swung slowly shut behind him. "I am so pleased to finally meet you." He scrutinized Emilia from her bare feet to the top of her disheveled head, as though searching for something.

"Where am I?" Emilia asked.

"You are at the Graylock Preserve, which is now the headquarters of the Dragons," the man answered.

Emilia had assumed it was the Dragons who'd kidnapped her, but the man's confirmation only made her more nervous. She dug her nails into her palms, trying to keep the tears from forming in her eyes. "What do the Dragons want with me?"

"Nothing." The man spread his hands. "The Dragons have no interest in you, even though you were Isadora Gray's ward. And Isadora does tend to cause trouble." He shook his head. "I am afraid it is I who has an interest in you, Emilia, and it was I who ordered my men to bring you here."

Emilia grabbed the lamp from the nightstand, ready to defend herself. But the man only laughed.

"Please, Emilia, do not upset yourself. I would never dream of harming you in any way. In fact, I was very displeased to find how bruised you were from my men rescuing you. I assure you they have been punished. I will not allow anyone here to hurt you. You are under my protection, and as it is only by my pleasure the Dragons live, my protection is infallible."

"Then why did you bring me here?" Emilia asked, not relaxing her grip on the lamp.

"Please don't be afraid. I know taking you like that must have been quite a shock, but I promise no harm will come to you here. I regret the anxiety I must have caused you, but it was the only way. Isadora would never have let me see you otherwise."

"Why would you want to see me?" Emilia asked.

"Because I am your father," the man answered simply.

The lamp slipped in her hands. "You're lying," she said through gritted teeth, retightening her grip. "You are not my father."

"How could you possibly know? You've never met your father. Well, here I am!" The man laughed and held out his hand. "My followers call me the

Pendragon, but my name is Emile LeFay. I must say I am so very pleased your mother named you after me."

He waited for Emilia to take his hand, but she backed away as far as she could, leaning into the wall behind her.

"I am sorry to only be meeting you now. Your mother never told me." The Pendragon lowered his hand, looking unsure of himself for the first time. "She never told me she was expecting you. But I knew as soon as I saw a picture of you with that necklace. You look so much like her, and I gave that necklace to your mother when she came to this very preserve with me many years ago. You are my child, Emilia. There is absolutely no doubt about that. *Darthera undolfa ebghodt.*"

A bright glow surrounded the Pendragon, forming red tendrils that seemed to taste the air around him. Slowly, the light reached for Emilia, wrapping around her arms and neck. "You see, my child, blood knows blood."

Emilia felt the world shift. The spell had pulled all the air from the room. The lamp slipped from her hands, and the *crash* as it hit the floor echoed as though from far away.

The Pendragon rushed over to Emilia and tried to lead her away from the broken glass to sit at the table. Emilia shook him off.

"No! Aunt Iz is my family. I don't know you." She stepped away from him. Glass sliced painfully into her foot. The Pendragon caught her arm and lifted her effortlessly over to the chair. Before she could say anything, he had crouched on the floor to pull the glass from her foot.

"Isadora Gray is not your family. I am sorry I was not able to raise you, but you are my child." He muttered a healing spell, and Emilia winced at the sting of her skin knitting back together.

"You kidnapped me." Emilia yanked her foot away from him.

"I took my daughter back. I don't think there is anything wrong with that."

"I'm not your daughter."

He stared into Emilia's eyes. "I know it will take you some time to trust me, but I want to get to know you. Is that so wrong?"

"It's wrong to take a person prisoner, especially when you bring them to the base for a group of murderers."

"You are not a prisoner. You are my guest. My hope, Emilia, is to convince you of how wrong you are about me. About all of us. I am the leader of the Dragons, but we are not murderers. We are freedom fighters determined to create a better world. Just imagine, Emilia." The Pendragon sat opposite her, a manic gleam in his eyes. "A new world with no more war or hunger or pollution. The humans need to be governed. They have made a mess of this world, but I will fix it. I will create a new world in which magic reigns. Where the laws I make will be obeyed. And I will do it with my daughter at my side."

"I am not your daughter," Emilia said again, trying not to show fear as she glared into the Pendragon's eyes.

Grey eyes that looked so much like her own.

25

GRAYLOCK

The helicopter landed in a clearing ten miles away from the preserve. The only time the pilot spoke was when he shouted, "You're on your own to get back," right before he took off.

A black jeep waited for them near a dirt road, which was the only break in the line of trees. Samuel had planned well. The jeep was fueled, and keys waited for them in the ignition.

They climbed in quickly, and Samuel drove down the bumpy road at top speed. "We can't approach from any of the main roads. The Dragons will be watching those. The best we can do is drive most of the way up the mountain on the far side. There are enough back roads to get us there. Once we get near the top, we leave the car and hike two miles down to the opening of the hermit's cave systems, which, according to our sources, is where the Dragons should be." Samuel took a sharp left turn, and Jacob banged his head into the window. "We'll get as close as we can to the entrance without running into any shield spells they might have working for them. Then, we watch."

Samuel braked suddenly, and Jacob grunted as his seatbelt pulled him painfully back. Samuel turned to him. "I know how badly you want her back. I've known Emilia her whole life. I want to get her back, too, but getting captured or killed won't help her. It will only leave fewer people on the outside trying to save her. Got it?" After Jacob nodded, Samuel continued. "If I choose to go in, you have to stay behind. It's the only way Iz can stay informed, and you can contact her if we need help. Do you understand?"

"Yes," Jacob said, comforted that Samuel was willing to go in after Emilia, even if it wasn't what Iz had instructed. It made Jacob feel less guilty about disobeying Iz.

"We will get her back, Jacob." Samuel grabbed Jacob's shoulder before turning back to the road and continuing his race through the woods.

They met no one on their ride up Mount Graylock. But Jacob could feel something dark surrounding the mountain. The air felt alive with energy, an energy intent on malice.

Samuel swung the jeep off the road and through a clump of brush before stopping and hopping out. He pulled two packs and his staff from the back of the jeep. "We might be here awhile." He strapped his pack on then handed Jacob a pocket mirror.

The mirror was small and distinctly feminine. Jacob ran his thumb over the red enamel roses covering the back.

"The professor taught you how to skry?"

Jacob nodded.

"Good. If we get separated, contact me immediately." Without waiting for a response, Samuel walked to the brush he had flattened with the jeep. He planted the end of his staff on the ground, and the stems and branches snapped back to attention. No one would be able to spot the jeep now. Avoiding the road, Samuel started hiking up the mountain.

"Stay close to me, and keep quiet," Samuel said in a hushed tone. "We need to go unnoticed, so we can't use magic to move. They could sense a spell that big."

Jacob struggled to keep up. He had never done any hiking, and though he was athletic, it was hard for him to find his footing. He did all right climbing to the top of the mountain. It was down that was difficult. There didn't seem to be a solid place to step. Whenever he slid or broke a branch, Samuel narrowed his eyes reproachfully but said nothing. They couldn't afford to make noise.

The heat of the day had begun to break through the trees when Samuel veered left, away from their former course. He stopped behind a tree and waited for Jacob to catch up.

"The entrance to the caverns should be just under that rise," Samuel whispered, pointing to what seemed like no more than a mound of rocks carelessly piled onto a misplaced hill. "But I haven't seen any guards yet. We're going to go in low and slow." Samuel pointed to a fallen tree a hundred yards downhill from them. "We should be able to see the entrance from there."

Samuel got down on his stomach and crawled forward. Jacob followed, the downed branches tearing at his forearms and stomach. Samuel stopped every few feet to listen. But there was only silence. Finally, they reached the tree, and both of them peered carefully over its vast trunk.

Samuel's sources had been right. They had indeed found the Dragons.

A man stood at either side of the cave's entrance, dressed in identical black uniforms with blood red dragons emblazoned across their chests. Both guards had shaved heads, which allowed full view of the dragon tattoo etched into each man's skin, beginning at their left ears and winding down their necks. In front of the entrance to the cave, seven witches and wizards sat holding hands. Their mouths moved as one, chanting a spell Jacob couldn't hear. There were only nine guards. Nine against two weren't horrible odds.

"We could go in," he whispered to Samuel, "if we take them by surprise. We have cover. They don't."

"Wait," Samuel said. "*Admeo amisculum.*" Samuel kept his eyes closed.

Jacob scanned from the green tops of the trees to the dead and decaying leaves on the ground, trying to see what effect Samuel's spell might have had.

After a few moments, there was a faint scurrying in the bushes. A small mouse appeared and ran straight into Samuel's waiting hands. "I am sorry, my friend," he said, petting the mouse. "Thank you." He placed the mouse on the ground, and it hurried off toward the cave entrance.

Jacob tracked the mouse by the telltale shaking of the fallen leaves. The mouse was getting close to the cave entrance. It was only a hundred feet away when a bright flash lit the sky as a brilliantly glowing dome appeared around the entrance to the cave. A bolt of lightning ran down the side of the dome. A *crack* of energy and a horrid *squeal* from the mouse rent the silence as the bolt struck the ground.

A moment later, the dome had disappeared, and the sky returned to a perfect pale blue. Jacob rubbed his eyes, trying to rid them of the spots the sudden flash had caused.

By the time he could see clearly, the guards were already moving cautiously forward to where the lighting had hit. One guard held out his wand and the other his right fist, where a gold ring glinted in the sunlight. They seemed satisfied the field mouse had been the only intruder. The men laughed at the poor dead creature, but still, Jacob could hear nothing. As the men returned to their posts, the stench of burning flesh reached Jacob's nostrils, stinging them with the scent of death.

"The circle is making a shield, and a good one at that," Samuel whispered as they crouched behind the tree.

"They're blocking noise, too?"

"Yep, but we don't know if it's only a one-way block. They may still be able to hear us. Whoever is running this place has it very well guarded. As long as that circle is intact, no one can get in."

"Can we send a spell in to distract the people in the circle?" Jacob asked.

"It's not worth the risk. With a shield like that, it could take several tries to see if any spell could break through. And as soon as one spell failed, we would have given away our position."

Samuel drew a half circle with his staff, enclosing them with the downed tree. Then he chanted slowly under his breath. Jacob picked out a few words here and there, but it was definitely not a spell the professor had covered.

"It's a rough chameleon spell," Samuel said when he finished his chant almost a minute later. "We can't risk anything stronger. They can't see or hear us as long as we stay within the line. But if they try to come through..." Samuel shrugged.

"No deadly lightning. Got it." Jacob peered over the tree. "So what do we do now?"

"We wait for someone to enter or exit the shield. That will show us how they get through and give us a better idea of what sort of spell it is."

They took turns watching all day and through the night. The packs had food, water, and blankets, but it was still a long, cold night on the mountain. Jacob had forgotten he hadn't slept in more than a day. When it was Samuel's turn to watch, his body took over, forcing him into sleep even though his anxious mind refused to relax.

Daybreak brought the changing of the guards outside the cave. Seven people came to replace the spell casters, but the seated circle didn't stop chanting. The replacements stepped over their joined hands and formed their own circle in the center. As soon as they were all settled, the new circle joined hands and began to chant.

The new dome formed exactly where Jacob had seen the old one flash. As its walls blossomed downward, it shimmered in the pink sunlight of dawn and was, for a moment, almost beautiful. As soon as the new dome was complete, the outer circle stood up stiffly and stumbled their way into the cave, some helping one another, others chatting tiredly.

"There won't be a chance to get through at a shift change," Samuel said. "They have that covered."

Hours passed, and nothing happened outside the cave. Jacob's foot twitched to an awkward rhythm and his nails dug pits into the dirt. The urge to leap out of hiding and run for the cave entrance grew every minute.

Emilia could be under this hill. Somewhere under these rocks, she could be trapped, scared, or hurt. What if someone were hurting her right now? Anger and panic rose in his chest. He wanted to run, to scream, to attack. Jacob had to force himself to breathe. If he let his magic get out of control now, they could very easily be found.

The sun had climbed high in the sky when something finally happened. Three men emerged from the cave, all of them big, burly, and bald. Two of the men talked to the guards, while the third stood away from the conversation.

The third man looked familiar. An angry red streak broke through his dragon tattoo.

Jacob pointed him out to Samuel. "It's the man from the plane. His ears. Emilia melted his earphones into his ears."

"That's my girl." Samuel chuckled. "He should've gotten worse, if you ask me."

The men moved toward the shield. Samuel and Jacob both tensed, waiting for the shield to drop. Even if Jacob and Samuel weren't going to try to get to the cave, hearing a part of the incantation might give them an idea of how to break through it. But the chanting never stopped. The men passed straight through the shield, which shimmered slightly but didn't strike them down.

"I bet that brat was surprised. He didn't expect to have her locked up. Thought he would get her all to himself," one of the men said, laughing as the sun gleamed off of his closely shaven head.

"I guess his daddy didn't do enough to buy him his girlfriend. Money doesn't matter much to the Pendragon, does it?" the second man answered.

Both guffawed loudly. The man from the plane put his hands to the side, clearly asking what the other two were laughing about.

"Money!" The first man shouted. "The Pendragon doesn't need the Waylands' damn money!"

The airplane man still shook his head.

"Forget it," the second man said. "That pretty little thing had better be grateful Laurent here hasn't gotten his hands on her yet. Won't be so pretty after that." He pantomimed to the airplane man what he thought he should do to Emilia. The airplane man laughed, and the Dragons walked down the hill, the first two talking carelessly as they went.

Samuel grabbed Jacob's shoulder and forced him back down. Jacob hadn't even noticed he had stood, ready to fight the men. He put his head in his hands, pulling his hair, desperately trying to put his thoughts into some workable order.

Emilia was here. They knew that now. Someone called the Pendragon had her. She was locked up somewhere under the mountain. Bile rose into Jacob's throat.

Dexter was here. His father was working with this Pendragon, and they had helped to bring Emilia here. Laurent wanted to hurt Emilia, and it sounded like he might soon be given the chance.

26

FIRST BLOOD

Samuel turned Jacob around to face him, pulling him out of his horrible thoughts. "We have to tell Iz what we know," Samuel said. "If Emilia really is in there, we need to get her out as soon as possible. We also need to call off the search for the Waylands. It's a waste of resources now that we know where they are."

Jacob expressed his opinion of the Waylands with a string of choice expletives.

"I agree," Samuel said. "First, we get Emilia out, and then we get the Wayland scum."

"How did they get out of the barrier?" Jacob studied the cave entrance, more determined than ever to get in.

"I think it might be the dragon tattoos." Samuel pointed at the guards. "Those two have tattoos, and so did the three who left. But none of the chanters do. If I were in charge, I'd make sure the only people who could get through the shield were the people I expected to charge through it to protect the compound from danger. I think the tattoo is like a password."

Jacob nodded, the beginnings of a plan forming is his mind.

"I can't skry Iz from inside the shield," Samuel said. "I'm going up the hill and out of sight. I should be back within a half hour. Stay here and watch the entrance. See what else you can learn."

Jacob nodded, and Samuel silently disappeared up the mountain. Jacob studied the circle casting the invisible shield, waiting for the three men to return. But there was no movement at all. The chanters continued their muted spell, and the guards stood like statues at the entrance to the cave. There weren't even any birds flying overhead. Silence filled the forest.

More than an hour later, Samuel still had not returned. Jacob tried to convince himself Samuel was busy planning a rescue mission with Iz. Maybe Iz had found some MAGI agents and was sending them here. Then Samuel would have to wait for them.

But after another silent hour, Jacob's gnawing dread had grown into an absolute certainty that something had gone wrong.

He pulled out the little red mirror. He would have to leave the shield to contact Samuel. But would he be able to get back into it? *Lingua Venificium* hadn't mentioned reentry into someone else's spell. He would have to risk it.

Jacob slid on his pack and quietly crawled out of the shield. There was a cluster of trees up ahead. If he could make it there, he could stand up and move more quickly. He did just as Samuel had done, stopping to check for sounds every few feet, but he heard nothing.

Finally, he reached the trees and was hidden from the entrance. He stood up and crept noiselessly through the woods. He traveled sideways across the face of the mountain, hoping that even if someone had found Samuel's trail, he would be too far away to be noticed on the same search.

Jacob scanned the area, satisfied no one else would be able to hear him. "*Volavertus* Samuel," he whispered into the red mirror. The mirror glowed brightly in his hand. He waited for Samuel to accept his skry. But instead of Samuel's image appearing, the glow of his mirror slowly dulled, leaving only the reflection of the sky peering through the branches above him.

Wherever Samuel was, he was unable to talk. Jacob had just decided to try contacting Iz himself when the sharp *crack* of a branch breaking sounded behind him. He ducked behind a tree and cautiously peered around the side.

It was the airplane man, but this time he traveled alone. He mumbled to himself, but it was much louder than most people mumble. He seemed unsure if he was actually making noise. "Scratch her face off, and then maybe I'll see what the rest of her sweet little body has to offer." The man cackled to himself. "The Pendragon owes me that much. I was willing to die. Least he can do is give me that damn girl."

Jacob's blood boiled. All thoughts of magic forgotten, he reached down and grabbed a large stick. Not even bothering to be quiet, he ran up behind the man and hit him hard on the head. The airplane man never heard him coming.

Jacob gaped at the unconscious, bleeding man. Blood shone on the end of his stick.

He dropped it, his hands shaking. He had never hurt someone on purpose before. The man on the ground was still breathing, but Jacob had definitely done some damage. His mind raced, flitting between a dozen half-formed plans.

He didn't care what Iz wanted anymore. He didn't care what happened to himself. From what the man currently lying unconscious at Jacob's feet in a growing pool of blood had said, Emilia was going to be given to one of these thugs.

"*Strigo motus.*" Now the man couldn't wake up and resist.

Even though Jacob was strong from years of hard work, he struggled to heave the unconscious man onto his shoulders. The man's warm blood dripped onto Jacob's neck. Jacob's legs shook as he started slowly up the mountain, careful to stay out of sight.

The shield reached to the top of the rock mound above the cave, and that was where Jacob approached, behind the rocks so no one could see. He slowed when he neared the shield and shifted his passenger onto his back like a cape. Making sure the man's shoulders covered his head, he stepped into the barrier.

A cool breeze tickled Jacob's bare skin, but no bolt came from above to strike him down. He had made it through the shield. He was inside the camp. Now he needed to get inside the cave. The chanting was audible now, and even in the bright sunlight, the eerie sound sent a shiver down Jacob's spine.

He slid the airplane man off his back and laid him quietly in the leaves, resisting the urge to land a sharp kick in his ribs. Jacob carefully climbed the rocks in front of him, hoping to see the cave entrance from above. From his perch, he saw the circle chanting and heard them clearly, but it wasn't a spell he recognized. The guards were hidden from view by the outcropping of rocks under his feet.

Jacob cursed to himself. He could either come at the guards head on or jump down from the top of the cave entrance and hope to surprise them. Neither option seemed to hold much hope for success.

He slid down the rocks and tried to think. There had to be a way to get into the cave. He must have learned some spell that could help him.

Jacob reviewed each spell he knew. He went through them alphabetically, just as he would have if he had been studying for a school exam, but it was too hard to concentrate. He would never find the right spell. All the words from the chant kept mixing with the spells in his mind. He should have thought on the other side of the shield when he had silence.

Then Jacob found the answer. He needed to figure out which chant they were using to create the shield charm. He could memorize the chant, use the airplane man to get back out of the shield, skry Iz, and ask for backup. After that, they would be able to break through the shield, rescue Emilia, and find Samuel.

Crawling carefully, Jacob climbed back up the rocks, listening for the exact enunciation of the spell. He closed his eyes, focusing on the chant until he could repeat it with the circle. He smiled, confident he could remember the wording exactly.

He turned to climb back down the rocks, and everything went black.

2 7

TRAPPED IN STONE

It was dark and cold. Jacob was curled up on the floor. He tried to sit up but smacked his head painfully on the ceiling. He reached above his head and met a solid stone wall. He tried to stretch out his legs, but after a few inches they hit stone as well. He kicked down with his feet, but the wall wouldn't move.

Jacob's heart raced, his pulse thudding in his ears. He was trapped in a stone box. He had never been claustrophobic, but this was too much. Jacob groped around for his wand, hoping against hope he might find it trapped with him.

It wasn't.

His breath came in quick gasps. He was trapped and helpless.

Jacob tried to calm his breathing, wanting to preserve his precious and dwindling supply of air. How had he gotten here?

He'd been outside. It was bright, and there was lots of air—

No, Jacob warned himself, *don't focus on the air.*

He had memorized the chant, he was going to leave the shield, and then… maybe he fell into this hole.

You can't fall into a place that has a solid stone ceiling.

He must have been ambushed. He'd been so focused on the chant he hadn't kept proper watch. He hadn't gotten Iz the information, Samuel didn't know where he was, and Emilia was still in trouble.

He needed to get out of this tomb. No. Box, it was only a box. Jacob couldn't let himself think the word *tomb.*

Jacob ran his fingers along the edges of his prison, hoping to find a way to pry the box open. He felt his way blindly in the dark, reaching as far as he could toward his feet, but he didn't have enough room to switch where his shoulders and hips were. He started to work his way back up—maybe he had missed something—when the top of the box moved.

Jacob pushed his fingers harder into a corner, trying desperately to pry the lid off his stone coffin, but the crack shifted away from him. The box was expanding. The ceiling was getting higher. Jacob pushed himself onto his knees and continued searching the walls. If he had made his prison expand, maybe he could find a way out, too.

The box was the size of a small room now and emitted a horrible noise as it grew. The stone screamed as its surfaces raked across each other. It sounded like a hundred nails scraping across shrieking blackboards. Jacob resisted the urge to cover his ears, which felt as though they might explode.

The scraping finally stopped, and the walls ceased their growth. A torch flared to life inches in front of his face. He tried to blink the blinding spots out of his eyes. The scraping started again, but this time it was only coming from the wall behind him. Jacob turned and faced the opening door.

A woman entered the room. She smiled, and just from that usually friendly facial expression Jacob knew she was definitely not the sort of person he wanted to be trapped in this room with. The woman was tall with flowing, white-blond hair. Dressed in tight black pants, with spike-heeled boots, and a tight leather top with a red dragon embossed across her chest, for a moment, Jacob thought he had been captured by Catwoman.

"Hello, Jacob," the woman said as she pressed the door closed behind her. "You have been a very bad boy, sneaking into our camp. Although"—the woman smiled again—"I am very impressed at how you did it. Poor Laurent will be severely punished, which means more fun for me. Though I do hate to play with broken toys."

"Who are you?" Jacob asked, somewhat pleased that, if he was going to be killed, at least the airplane man was going down, too. Emilia would not be a treat for him.

"Domina." She held out her hand as though expecting Jacob to kiss it. When he didn't, she continued. "I am the Pendragon's special helper, among other things. And the Pendragon is very pleased you are here. In fact, he would have much preferred you to walk up to the shield and ask to be let in. Then, you would have been greeted as an honored guest. But with all of your sneaking around, the Pendragon has decided you can't be trusted. Which means you're all mine." She reached out and caressed Jacob's cheek. She slid her ice cold fingers down his neck and dug her black nails into his chest.

Jacob tried to ignore the pain. "Who is this Pendragon?"

"The Pendragon is your lord and master. He controls all that happens here, and soon, very soon, he will control everything. *Subnicio.*"

Something hit Jacob hard in the back of the knees, sending him to the ground. "Where's Emilia?" He stood, unwilling to kneel at this woman's feet, suddenly afraid she might do worse to Emilia than the doomed airplane man.

Domina raised her eyebrows and grinned. "If you knew what I could do to you, you wouldn't be so worried about Emilia. After all, the Pendragon would never let anyone hurt his precious little baby girl. Especially after he went to all the trouble of having her kidnapped. That was quite a bother."

"What? The leader of the Dragons is pretending Emilia is his daughter?"

"Not pretending, my pet," Domina said, almost purring at Jacob's shock.

"That's not true," Jacob spluttered. "That's impossible."

"Give me one good reason."

Jacob wracked his brain, rushing through everything Emilia had told him about her past. But he couldn't think of any real reason it couldn't be true. Emilia had never known anything about her father or mother. How could he prove who her father wasn't?

"Emilia is going to be the princess when the new world order is complete. Sitting at the left hand of her beloved daddy. The right hand is all mine. The real question is will you be alive to hear the wonderful tales of the Pendragon's ascension? I do tell very good stories." Domina pulled a wand from her waistband. "*Tendicanis.*" She gave a lazy flick of her wand.

Jacob flew through the air. His back slammed into the wall behind him, knocking the breath from his body, but instead of falling to the ground, he remained pinned, his arms splayed at his sides. Pressure like gravity itself held Jacob to the wall. He couldn't turn his head or even flex a finger. He tried fruitlessly to free himself, struggling against his invisible bonds as Domina slunk forward.

Domina blew a long, slow breath on her wand. The tip glowed a bright red, and the air around it crackled. She gazed at the tip of her wand lovingly, like it was a work of art she had created. Then she moved it toward Jacob's face. Even with the wand still more than a foot away, it radiated an intense heat. She trailed her wand carefully through the air, as though deciding which part of his face she wanted to brand.

Jacob wanted more than anything to pull away from the heat and inevitable pain.

Domina smiled as she put her cheek on his, her breath caressing his neck as she whispered, "You will never see the outside of this room again. It is either your prison or your tomb. Do as I say, and you may live long enough to call this place home."

For a moment, pain seared Jacob's cheek, and then he knew no more.

SCREAMS IN THE DARK

Emilia sat with her legs curled beneath her in the armchair, reading a book entitled *The Master Race*. All of the books on her shelf were like that. Every one of them expounded upon the superiority of Magickind.

Every gardener knows the lives of the weeds must be sacrificed to ensure the growth of the flower. Evolution cries for a rise of Magickind. Perpetuating the lives of the weak and non-magical is a detrimental practice that must cease.

Cleansing the world. Genocide. The writings made Emilia sick. But she had been locked in that room for God only knew how long, and at least hating the books gave her something to do.

The door began to scrape open and Emilia assumed it was someone bringing her food again. It should be dinner next. That was the only way she knew what time of day it was. Eggs in the morning, sandwich in the afternoon, and a hot meal for dinner.

But the person who came through the door was not carrying a tray.

"Dexter." Emilia leaped to her feet and ran toward the door as it began to scrape shut behind him. "Don't let it close," she cried, but he caught her around the waist and held her back as the door joined seamlessly with the solid wall. "Dex, we have to get out of here!"

"Em, you're all right." Dexter pulled her against his chest and buried his face in her hair.

Emilia tried to push him away so he could see how dire their situation was. But instead, he kissed her. Not a panicked kiss, but a kiss of relief. A wonder-

THE TETHERING | 551

fully, blissfully normal kiss. Dexter was warm and there, and so familiar. Emilia sagged into his arms, letting his kiss wash away all her worry and fear if only for a moment.

Finally, she pulled away. "Dexter, we're locked in, and they bound my magic. But maybe you can still get us through the door. Or get these cuffs off so we can both fight."

Dexter just stared.

"We have to get out of here. I don't know how much time we have until someone figures out you've come for me." Emilia took his hand and pulled him toward the wall. She ran her hands over where the door had been, but her fingers slid over the magical barrier that would not let her reach the stone.

"No, Em," Dexter said, pulling her hands from the wall, "you can't leave."

Emilia stared at Dexter's calm, almost relieved, face, not understanding what he could possibly mean.

"I'm sorry, but you have to stay in here."

Emilia yanked her hands away from his.

"I know you're angry right now, and I'm sure I would be, too."

Backing away, she met the wall and crept sideways, putting distance between herself and this fake Dexter. Imposter Dexter. Dexter, the real Dexter, her boyfriend, would never want to keep her locked up.

"All right." Dexter raised his hands and stayed very still. "Look, I won't touch you, but please listen to me. You have to stay in this room. We might be attacked—"

"We?" Emilia spat at him.

"Fine, the Dragons. The Dragons could be attacked at any time, and the safest place for you is right here in this room."

"The safest place for me is at home with my family. Not locked up underground."

"Emilia, your family is here. I'm here. Your father is here." Dexter took a step forward.

"You knew? You knew, and you didn't tell me?" Emilia grabbed the first book within reach and threw it at Dexter's head.

The corner hit him hard in the mouth. He wiped away the blood with his thumb. "I deserved that."

"You deserve a hell of a lot worse."

"For protecting you? There is a war coming. And who knows how big it's going to be? The Pendragon is right. Things have to change in order for us to survive. The Dragons are more powerful than we ever thought. I love you, Em.

Your father loves you. Is it so terrible for us to want you to be on the winning side of this mess? And trust me, we will win."

"At what cost?" Emilia snatched another, bigger book off the shelf. "How much blood are you willing to spill in order to win? And don't you dare tell me that freak LeFay loves me. One of his men tried to bring down the plane I was on!" Emilia was screaming now. She pitched the second book at Dexter, who swatted it away with his bloody hand. "And you knew, didn't you? You tried to keep me off the plane, but you were perfectly willing to let Iz and Jacob die!"

"I didn't know there was an attack planned," Dexter said, his face paling a shade. "My father only said there was room on the helicopter for you."

Dexter moved forward and reached for Emilia's hand, but she shook him away, disgusted at the very sight of him.

"You have to know, Emilia, I would never hurt you. I would never let anyone hurt you."

"And Aunt Iz and Jacob? Do you think their deaths wouldn't hurt me? And the hundred other people on the plane? What about them? They don't matter to you, do they, Dexter? You wouldn't mind if they died."

"No! I never said that. I told you I didn't know. I didn't know what the Dragons were planning. I didn't even know the Pendragon was your father until I got here." He took a slow step forward, approaching her with both arms outstretched, as though she were a wounded animal. "All I know is I love you, and together we can figure out what or who is wrong in all this mess."

Emilia shook her head. "Oh, Dex. How can you even question who's wrong?"

"Don't you see? This is our chance. To break free from all the hiding, all the secrets. We could show the world who we are. What we can do," Dexter said, his eyes fierce with determination. "The centaurs and fawns could walk the streets. No more hiding on preserves."

"How?" Emilia asked. "How can you possibly think this could work? Humans will never accept us."

"Then we make them. We attack. We show them who the dominant species is. We take back our land. They can't compete with magic."

"Then you'll kill people. Innocent people. And once their blood is on your hands, they'll come after us with bombs and guns." Emilia's voice rose with her anger. "Dexter, you're starting a war. A real war. And it could be a massacre for Magickind. We're outnumbered."

"But a shield spell can stop bullets, and even bombs."

"What? How do you—"

"The Dragons have done tests. There are bases and plans." Dexter captured

Emilia's face in his hands. "This isn't a misplaced rebellion. It's an army ready for war."

"You really don't care then?" Her voice cracked with choked back tears. "You don't care how many humans die?"

"No." Dexter shook his head. "And neither will you once we take our rightful place at the head of this world's society."

"If you really think that, Dexter, you don't know me." She pulled his hands away from her face. "And I certainly don't know you."

"Em…"

"Get out," Emilia whispered. "Get out!"

Dexter fled for the door, which scraped shut right as Emilia's lamp crashed into the stone.

---

milia walked across the dunes. A chill breeze whispered through the night air, but the sand still held the warmth of the day. She paused at the peak of the highest dune, watching the moon play on the waves as they gently lapped up to the shore. A woman stood with her feet in the water. Emilia couldn't see the woman's face, but it was her. It had to be.

She ran toward the woman, wanting more than anything to see her, to speak with her. She had so many questions. She had to reach her. But the sand kept shifting, and try as she might, Emilia could get no closer to the shore.

Emilia searched the dunes for another path to the beautiful woman at the water's edge, but she found none.

She turned back to the woman, ready to call out for help. A wave surged up to the shore dragging the woman under the water and out of sight.

---

*other!" Emilia woke up screaming, her bed drenched with sweat. "Don't be afraid, my Emilia."

Emilia squinted at the figure sitting at the foot of her bed.

"Did you have a bad dream?" LeFay reached for her, but she pulled away. He smiled grimly and stood up. "It is such a pity I wasn't there when you were a child. If you had been with me, I would have made sure you were never afraid of anything. But alas, we cannot change the past." He sat down at the table, which was laden with a much fancier breakfast than Emilia had been given on the other mornings she had spent locked in the stone room. "Please join me. We must do something to celebrate this special day."

"Special?" Emilia asked, her lips pressed flat as she joined LeFay at the table. "The only thing I want to celebrate is you letting me out of here."

"Not possible. I know you are a very determined and strong-willed young woman, which pleases me immensely. But in this case, Father knows best." LeFay poured them both orange juice. "A toast to the protection of my only child."

Emilia didn't raise her glass.

LeFay put his glass back down and folded his hands under his chin, leaning on the table. "You see, Emilia dear, I have formed such a clever plan. It will ensure you remain safely in the protection of the Dragons. It will solidify the allegiance of a very important family, and it will eventually bring you much joy."

Emilia already didn't like the sound of his plan. Not at all. "What would bring me much joy would be going home." She stood up, no longer hungry enough to stay at a table with him.

"That is not a possibility right now. However, if you sit down and eat with me, we will discuss your being allowed out of this room. I am prepared to offer you free rein of the compound."

The Pendragon's gaze didn't falter as Emilia stared him down. He seemed to be telling the truth.

"All I am asking is to eat a meal with my daughter. After we eat, we will discuss how best to maintain your security while giving you a chance to see more of your father's home."

Emilia sat down grudgingly. Getting out of the room would get her one step closer to escaping and getting home.

LeFay raised his glass to toast Emilia again. "To my growing family."

Emilia toasted and took a sip. She was unconscious before her glass shattered on the floor.

WORSE THAN PAIN

Jacob trembled. He hadn't had anything to eat or drink since he had been captured. His right cheek throbbed from Domina's burn.

The room had shrunk to an even smaller size than his original box when Domina left. Now, it was too short for him to straighten his back. Every muscle in his body had seized up and beat its protest with every breath he drew. He wanted to sleep, to fade from consciousness until he didn't hurt anymore.

He had heard someone screaming before. He hadn't recognized the voice, but pain could easily contort a person beyond recognition. At least it wasn't Emilia. Her father wouldn't allow her to be tortured.

The darkness had gone quiet now. The screaming had stopped, maybe ten minutes before, perhaps a few hours. If only his stomach were full, he could sleep.

Food and water would come soon. Dehydrating to death would be too quick and quiet for Domina. She would want to play with him more before he died.

So he waited, thinking of Emilia. Hoping she would find a way out without his help. He had tried to form an escape plan, but since he didn't know where he was, how many guards there might be, or if anyone was trying to rescue him, hoping for an opportunity was really all he could do.

He had almost slipped into a fitful sleep when a horrible scraping sound pierced his brain. The room rumbled as the walls expanded.

Jacob pushed himself to his knees and tried to straighten his spine, biting his cheeks to keep himself from screaming in pain. He crawled to the wall and forced himself up, refusing to be found hunched in a ball in his cell, defeated.

A torch burst into flames. Jacob focused on the wall opposite the torch, trying to get his eyes to adjust to the first light he'd seen since Domina had left.

A chink of light formed on the wall to his left as Domina opened the stone door and entered his cell. She tossed a jar to Jacob. His arms were so stiff and heavy he barely caught it.

"Broth." Domina smiled as she closed the door behind her. "We need to keep your strength up."

Jacob opened the jar and sniffed carefully before taking a small sip. It was cold, but better than nothing.

Domina leaned casually against the wall, smiling at him like a lioness that had cornered her prey.

Then Jacob noticed her belt. His wand stuck out beneath the leather. She was so arrogant she had brought his wand into his cell, assuming he could never take it from her, or perhaps hoping he would try.

Domina caught Jacob staring at the wand, and her smile broadened. "I think it matches my outfit. Don't you? I like to collect things. Talismans from my..." She searched for the words for a moment, twisting a ring inscribed with a tiny bird she wore on her left hand. "Expired playmates. I know you're still alive, but since you won't be needing it any longer, I thought you wouldn't mind if I started to play with it a bit early."

The fury in Jacob's stomach threatened to expel his broth.

"Now, little Jakey-poo," Domina crooned, "don't be angry with me." She scooped her finger through the air as though scooping frosting off a cake.

Jacob watched in horror as the air around her finger started to glow, forming a purple, crackling ball of light. He didn't have time to breathe before she threw the ball hard into his right shoulder. Jacob gasped when his head cracked into the wall behind him. The jar slid from his hand and shattered, but he couldn't see anything through the bright spots of light dancing before his eyes.

Domina laughed. A high, gleeful, girlish laugh, more suited to a child chasing butterflies than a woman bent on torture.

Jacob pushed away from the wall, taking deep breaths to steady himself. But before the room had stopped spinning, Domina hurled another crackling ball at his left knee, which buckled beneath him. He tried to catch himself but was too weak from the lack of food and water. His hands slid uselessly away from him, leaving him face down on the cold floor.

Pain ripped through his thigh as a piece of the broken jar cut deep into his leg. The warmth of his blood spread around the wound. Before he could push himself back up, another buzzing shock of energy hit him in the back, knocking all the air from his lungs.

Jacob gulped at the air, but his lungs seemed paralyzed. Domina's boots crunched the broken glass. The toe of her boot slid under his ribs and she kicked him onto his back.

"Don't you like playing with me?" Domina raised her foot in the dim torchlight. One of her stiletto heels glowed red like a hot iron. She pressed the glowing heel of her boot into Jacob's sternum. His lungs jolted back to life, only taking in enough air for him to scream.

Domina pulled her boot away and paced the room.

Jacob coughed on the acrid stench of his own burning flesh.

She smiled at him with a twinkle in her eye and said, *"Alescere."*

For a moment, Jacob felt nothing. Then the floor beneath him began digging sharply into his flesh. The ground transformed into a bed of razor sharp nails, a thousand talons piercing his skin.

He rolled onto the smooth floor to his right, the nails biting his flesh and tearing the entire right side of his body open. Blood oozed down Jacob's back as he lay panting on the floor, watching the spikes continue to grow. He forced himself onto his knees when Domina started laughing again.

Domina reached down and grabbed Jacob's chin. "Don't be angry with me, love. I've done nowhere near my worst yet." She knelt in front of Jacob and gazed at him lovingly. "All I have to do to break you is tell you Emilia is being taken to her tethering ceremony right now."

Jacob shook his head, trying to make sense of Domina's words.

"She's all dressed up in her pretty white dress. And soon she'll be marched down the aisle." Domina started singing the wedding march. *"Flagrosa."* She pulled flower petals from the air and tossed them onto Jacob. He barely registered the pain as they sizzled on his skin like boiling water.

"You're lying," Jacob growled, fighting to push himself off the ground. "Emilia would never agree to tether herself to anyone."

"Shh." Domina placed a finger over his lips. "I never said she agreed to anything. In a few minutes, she'll be joined eternally to Dexter Wayland. She will never be yours, my love. You will never save your sweet Emilia."

Rage flooded through Jacob. He screamed and grabbed Domina's neck. She laughed and batted his hands away, but angry red burns marked where his fingers had been.

"I suppose you have some magic in you after all." Domina stood, running her fingers over the marks on her neck. "You may be my new favorite plaything."

"Fulguratus!" Jacob screamed, sending a bolt straight toward Domina's heart.

Domina gasped, her smile growing as Jacob's bolt hit her in the chest. "You'll have to try harder. But I can teach you. We'll have plenty of time. *Fulguratus.*"

Jacob fell back when her bolt hit him in the neck. He choked, struggling to pull in air. He tried to push himself up, but his arms shook, unable to hold his weight.

Domina's laugh filled the room as she tipped Jacob's head back and knelt on his chest. "We all have our destinies, Jacob. Yours is with me. And Emilia's is with him."

"No!" Jacob shouted. Fear and anger burned within him as magic began racing through his veins.

Domina's smile flickered for a moment before the room filled with a light so bright it blinded Jacob. Fire seemed to burst through his skin, and Domina's weight lifted from his chest. A horrible *crack* shook the room. Then everything went black.

Jacob lay gasping on the floor. "*Inluesco.*"

In the shadows cast by the dim light of his spell lay Domina, sprawled on the stone, blood pooling around her head.

Jacob pushed himself up, not taking his eyes off of her, waiting for her to spring back up laughing and trying to hurt him again. But she didn't move.

He crawled over, ignoring the pain and the blood dripping from his own wounds.

She lay still. Her eyes wide open and empty.

Jacob swallowed hard and tried not to move her as he pulled his wand from her belt. He pointed the wand at her chest and pulled the triangle of glass from his thigh, ready to use it as another weapon. Still she did not move. Blood pounded in his ears.

Domina was dead. He had killed her.

Jacob shook. He pulled off his shirt and wrapped it around his thigh to staunch the blood flowing freely from his wound. He almost stood before deciding to take Domina's ring as well. Bile rose in his throat when he touched her still-warm hand.

Jacob stumbled to the wall where Domina had entered not even ten minutes before. He ran his hands along the rough stone wall, searching for a knob or button, anything to let him out of this room. The tip of his wand grazed the wall in his search, and instantly the door appeared and began to open. Jacob steadied himself, hoping there were no guards and praying he could find Emilia in time.

30

THE TETHERING

The hallway had been carved of roughly hewn rock. Unlike Jacob's cell, caged light bulbs lit the passage.

Jacob peered carefully out of his cell door. There were no guards in sight. He didn't know if Domina had sent them away for privacy, or if he simply wasn't considered a threat.

He looked up and down the hallway. The passage curved, its path only visible for about thirty feet in either direction. Even if he had been conscious when he was brought in, it wouldn't necessarily be the same path that would lead him to Emilia.

He swore under his breath and headed right. His leg wasn't working very well. His ankle wouldn't flex, and each time he put weight on his leg, more blood pulsed out through his wounds. He was leaving a trail of blood, but he hadn't learned any healing spells yet. That seemed like a really stupid thing not to have covered in his lessons.

After about fifty yards, Jacob came to another corridor crossing the one he was traveling. They both looked the same, but the branch to his left had more wires running along the ceiling than the others. If the Pendragon were going to have a tethering ceremony for Emilia, it would be in the grandest room these tunnels had to offer.

Jacob followed the wires. He turned left, right, right again, then left. But still, he met no one in the halls. The lack of obstacles pinged his nerves. Was he heading farther into the compound? Did they know where he was and just not care? Jacob pushed himself to move faster, pain and panic making him dizzy. How large was this place?

He was about to go back and try a different path when he turned the next corner and voices echoed down the hall. Lots of them. He slowed and moved closer to the wall, preparing for an ambush. But the voices were laughing and chatting.

Jacob glanced around the corner, expecting to see another corridor, but instead discovered a large chamber. This room had been left in its natural state. Stalactites hung from the ceiling, and stalagmites grew from the floor, creating large spikes and columns all around the room. Jacob scanned the chamber. It was the size of a small cathedral and just as grand. Over the centuries, the cave had made itself as beautiful as any man-made creation.

At least fifty people had congregated in the room. Jacob had definitely found the right place.

Dexter stood next to a chair in the center of the chamber.

Jacob lowered himself painfully to his knees and crawled behind a mound that had formed at the base of a grouping of stalagmites. He inched around, finding an angle where his body was hidden from the door, but he was still able to peer over the slippery stone at Dexter.

A horrible scream echoed from an entrance in the far wall of the chamber. Jacob recognized the scream at once.

Emilia, but she didn't sound hurt. She sounded furious.

Dexter turned and stared at the entrance, all of the blood draining from his face. Two men entered carrying Emilia, who was dressed in a long, gauzy white gown.

Her wedding gown.

Emilia's mouth was gagged, and her wrists were bound. One of the men carrying her bled badly from a bite on his ear. The other had claw marks on his face. She had done some damage before they tied her up.

Jacob's heart leaped into his throat at the sight of Emilia, alive and well enough to put up a fight.

A man followed Emilia and her captors into the hall, tall and wearing a jacket with a golden dragon emblazoned across the front. Everyone in the hall bowed as he entered.

So this is the Pendragon.

The Pendragon held up his hand, silencing the hall with a look. The two men carried Emilia over to a chair and forced her to sit. The one with the bloody ear said, "*Saxoris alescere.*" The stone floor surrounding Emilia's chair shifted. It was like watching a sped-up film of a flower's growth, only it was the stone that was growing, forming tall, thin tendrils that wrapped around Emilia, binding her to the chair. She screamed louder, struggling against the stone ropes, but they wouldn't budge.

"Friends," the Pendragon said, raising his voice only enough to be heard over Emilia's screams. He turned to Emilia. "*Oblitus.*"

Emilia still struggled, but her voice had vanished.

The Pendragon smiled and continued in a conversational tone. "Friends, we are here to witness the joining of my daughter, Emilia LeFay, to Dexter Wayland." He paused, and the crowd cheered.

Dexter stared at the still-struggling Emilia, his eyes wide and unblinking.

"Dexter," the Pendragon said, walking over to him, "I am entrusting you with my only child. It is for her safety and protection that I tether her to you. Are you willing to die to protect her?"

"Yes." Dexter looked Emilia in the eyes. "I would gladly die to protect her, Pendragon."

"Very well, my son," the Pendragon said. He touched Emilia's wrists, and the heavy iron cuffs fell into his hands and disappeared. Then he reached into his jacket and pulled out a golden cord, which he gave to Dexter. "Give one end to your *coniunx.*"

Dexter took the cord and knelt in front of Emilia. "Please, Em. I know this seems like too much right now. But you have to know I would never do anything to hurt you. I love you." He pressed one end of the cord into Emilia's hand.

She threw it on the floor and continued to strain against her bonds.

Dexter winced as though Emilia had struck him. Sweat beaded on his forehead, glistening in the light.

"I am not cruel," the Pendragon said. "I know joining so young will be terrifying. Sixteen is such a tender age. But it cannot be helped, Emilia." He brushed her cheek. "My daughter, I do this for your protection. My friends, please proceed to the reception in the gallery. For two such tender children, a solemn tethering would be best."

Jacob lowered himself to the ground. The crowd's footsteps traveled away from him through the entrance in the far wall. When the footsteps were gone, Jacob pushed himself back up. The only people left in the room were Emilia, Dexter, and the Pendragon.

The Pendragon waved his wand, and the end of the cord snapped back into Emilia's hand. The stone ropes binding her to the chair slithered around her fingers, trapping the cord in her hand. Dexter still gripped his end.

"Care for my daughter, and I will gladly accept you as my son," the

Pendragon said. Then, with his head tipped back and his arms outstretched, he began the incantation. Light shone from the golden cord, and the Pendragon seemed to glow as well, oblivious to Emilia's silent cries.

Jacob slid out from behind the rock and limped as quietly as he could toward Emilia.

Dexter stared into Emilia's eyes.

Tears streamed down her face, the angry lines in her forehead screaming all the words she could not say.

"I love you," Dexter said, his voice thick with his own tears. "Emilia, this is the only way."

Jacob stumbled, and Dexter's head snapped toward him.

The Pendragon seemed entranced by the spell and unaware of what was happening around him, but Dexter was going to warn him. Without any thought of magic, Jacob wrenched the cord from Dexter's grasp and punched him hard in the face. Dexter fell, but Jacob suddenly felt as though he couldn't move.

Warmth flowed up his arm and into his chest. Heat surrounded Jacob's heart and spread through his veins. But it wasn't unpleasant. More like his blood had never flowed properly before. Like his body had never had enough oxygen to process.

He took a deep breath, his lungs expanding and pushing the magic through his blood more quickly. The golden glow from the cord radiated up from his hand and surrounded his body. Then the light pulled away from him, snapping back so only his hand glowed.

The Pendragon stopped chanting. Smiling, he lowered his arms and head. He opened his eyes and saw Jacob.

Before he had time to think about what he was doing, Jacob shouted, "*Alevitum!*" The Pendragon grunted as an invisible force hit him, throwing him into the unyielding cavern wall.

Jacob rushed to Emilia. "*Everto.*" The stone ropes that bound her shattered.

She reached up and pulled the gag from her mouth. "Jacob," she said, her eyes dazed as he pulled her to her feet. But Dexter had begun to stir.

"Here." Jacob pressed Domina's ring into Emilia's hand. "We have to go." He pulled Emilia out the door he'd snuck in through minutes before.

They ran down the hall, Emilia slipping the ring onto her finger. Even in her long dress, she could run faster than Jacob. The longer he stayed on his injured leg, the worse the damage from the glass and nails seemed to get. Blood drenched his leg, and his right foot had gone cold.

Emilia tugged Jacob into a small and dimly lit corridor. "You need to be healed." She turned Jacob's back to her.

"Emi." He tried to turn around to look at her. Something was different. Something felt strange, and he knew deep down in his soul that seeing her face would fix everything. But she pushed him back against the wall.

"*Pelluere*. Who did this to you?" Emilia asked as she tried to mend his shredded calf. "How did you get here?"

"Domina. But I really don't think it's as bad as it looks," Jacob lied. It was definitely as bad as it looked, maybe worse. He could feel his calf mending itself, but since some of his muscle was missing, the process of pulling the remaining parts together was excruciating. His thigh suddenly felt as though Domina's red-hot wand were piercing his wound. "They captured me while I was trying to rescue you," he said through gritted teeth.

"Iz sent you alone?" Emilia asked as she spun him around and started working on the burn on his chest.

"Samuel came, too," he answered, his voice tight from the pain of his healing wounds. He gasped as the burn on his chest stung like someone had pressed dry ice to it.

"Do they have him, too?" Emilia asked.

Jacob swore as his cheek started healing. "I don't know. He disappeared before I was captured, and that was at least two days ago. Domina never mentioned finding someone else."

Jacob's stomach sank. If they were very lucky, no one had realized they had escaped yet. But soon everyone would be looking for them. If they stopped to figure out if Samuel had been captured, they wouldn't have enough time to escape. The best they could do was hope Samuel was waiting for them outside.

"Do you know how to get out of here?" Emilia looked around as though searching for an exit sign.

"No, I was knocked out when they brought me in," Jacob said, trying to push past the other thoughts racing through his mind. "I followed the wiring to find you. The biggest wires went to that chamber you were in. The power has to come from somewhere. Maybe if we follow the wires, they'll lead us to the generator."

"And the generator should be near the exit so it can be easily fueled," Emilia finished for him. She frowned at Jacob's wounds. "This is the best I can do for now. Samuel can heal the rest."

They moved back out into the main corridor and continued to follow the wires. They had still seen no one. Emilia took the lead, peering around every curve.

A voice boomed through the halls, and Jacob pinned Emilia to the wall, covering her with his own body. The magnified voice of the Pendragon echoed, banging into their eardrums.

"The prisoner and traitor Jacob Evans has kidnapped my child. Guards, proceed to the compound entrance. All others search the caverns. Emilia is to be rescued unharmed. Anyone who damages her in any way shall answer directly to me. Jacob Evans may be killed on sight. The person who succeeds in destroying him will be generously rewarded."

Emilia looked at Jacob with terror in her eyes. She grasped his hand and pulled him down the corridor. Jacob limped behind as quickly as his leg would allow.

Their only hope was to make it to the entrance before the guards. The tunnel climbed steeply upward. Jacob was sure they had to be nearing the surface. They rounded a corner and almost ran right into the generator, but there was no opening to the outside world. They had hit a dead end.

Voices called in the distance. There was no chance of going back the way they had come.

"I'm sorry," he whispered.

They were trapped. There was no way out.

He hadn't saved her.

KILL ON SIGHT

Emilia met Jacob's eyes.

Kill on sight. They had been ordered to kill him on sight.

"No," Emilia said, "we're getting out." She was not going to let Jacob die boxed in like an animal. Emilia surveyed the room. Maybe if they could find someplace to hide, they could wait for the searchers to go far enough back down the corridor that she and Jacob could find another way out.

Emilia scanned the room for a big enough hiding place. She froze when she spotted a pipe running up through the ceiling. The pipe had *diesel only* painted on it.

"Jacob, I need you to trust me." She moved in front of him and wrapped his arms around her waist like they were posing for prom pictures. "Do not move. *Primurgo.*" The air around them shimmered, and the shouts down the hall became strangely muffled.

Emilia placed her hand on the shield she had created and gently pressed through, careful not to tear the barrier. "Don't move." She aimed at the ceiling. "*Magneverto!*" She said the word and yanked her hand back through the shield just as the gas pipe exploded.

The blast tore through the room. The floor shook as orange flames encased their safe haven. Warmth flared over her skin, but even though the raging flames were mere inches from them, they did not get burned.

A dull *crack* pounded overhead as the ceiling around the pipe splintered like broken ice.

Jacob hunched over her, trying to protect her from the falling rocks. For a moment, the whole world shook. And then there was only dust.

"*Inluesco.*"

A light shone inside the spell's dome. Dust fell gently around them like a snow globe. Only the shaking snow was on the outside, and they were on the inside watching.

She lowered the shield and coughed, covering her mouth and nose with her hand to block some of the dust.

Rubble surrounded them. People screamed in the distance. The cave-in had affected more than just the generator room.

How many people did I hurt? Emilia wondered as another scream reached her ears.

"I think we can climb out." Jacob pointed to a dim light overhead. He started clambering up the rocks.

Emilia climbed after him. She slipped on her dress, and Jacob reached down and caught her hand without looking. The instant their hands met, Emilia's heart began to race, and at the same moment, her fear disappeared. Emilia pulled her hand away quickly and kept climbing.

"It's the sun," Jacob said. "I can see the sunset." Carefully, he shifted a few rocks and made the hole large enough for them to climb through. He pulled himself out and reached back for Emilia.

As her head broke through the dust and rocks, she took deep, gulping breaths of the fresh, clean air. The light from the setting sun burst through the trees. They were on a pile of rocks above a clearing. Chanting carried from below them, but through the trees, there was a way out.

"Come on," Emilia whispered and began to run for the forest.

"No!" Jacob shouted.

Emilia spun around, certain someone was attacking Jacob. He ran over to her and knocked her to the ground, hiding behind the rocks.

But the damage had been done. The guards had heard Jacob's shout.

"We have to run!" Emilia said, desperately trying to pull Jacob to his feet.

Jacob yanked Emilia back to the ground. "There's a shield. It'll fry you. There are chanters keeping it up." Jacob pointed past the rise. The sound of sliding rocks reached them as the guards struggled up the hill.

Emilia scrambled toward the top of the rocks, and Jacob followed. She looked at the circle. All she needed was one good spell to distract them.

But the guards were up the hill and closing in behind them. She screamed as one of them aimed a spell at Jacob that missed by mere inches. She pushed Jacob behind her using her own body as a shield.

"Stop!" one of the guards yelled. "Hand over the girl."

"I will not be handed to anyone," Emilia growled.

"The Pendragon is waiting for you inside. Come with us now."

They were surrounded with guards in front and a ledge behind. Jacob's arm slid around her waist. "Jump back on three," he whispered in her ear.

"One."

"Your father will be most displeased if you resist rescue," the guard said.

"Two."

"You are assisting the enemy and dishonoring the Pendragon."

"Three!"

They jumped backward and were in the air for only a moment before they hit the ground hard and fell over. The guards shouted from the rocks above. Only the two guards at the door had been left below.

"*Fulguratus!*" Jacob cried, and one of the guards fell.

"*Sporactus!*" Emilia shouted. The second guard's eyes went blank, and he swayed for a moment before crumpling to the ground.

Spells showered on them from above. Emilia pushed Jacob into the shelter of the cave entrance and ran toward the chanters, hoping the guards wouldn't risk hurting her. She reached the circle and stomped on the nearest pair of clasped hands, effectively breaking the circle and the chanters' attention. For good measure, she kicked the chanter nearest her in the stomach and punched her in the back of the head.

"Jacob, run!" Emilia screamed and sprinted toward the woods.

Jacob's footfalls pounded the ground behind her. "Emi, the shield!" Jacob shouted.

Spells flew at them from behind, and Emilia didn't dare slow down. She had broken the circle. The shield should be gone. It had to be gone. She heard Jacob gasp when they hit the edge of the clearing, but nothing happened as they shot into the trees.

They were foxes being chased by vicious hounds. No matter how fast they ran, they would still be pursued. She didn't know where she was leading Jacob. She just ran.

Their pursuers gained ground. She had tried her best to heal Jacob, but he still couldn't outrun the guards. And she would not leave him to die in the woods.

A *crack* shook the air as a tree was hit by a badly aimed spell. Emilia stopped short, barely avoiding being crushed by a falling limb. That moment was all the guards needed.

"*Inflaresco!*"

The spell hit Jacob square in the back, and he flew forward, screaming in pain. As he hit the ground, his wand rolled away. "Emilia, run," he coughed. "Go!"

But Emilia stood her ground. She would never let them hurt Jacob, not while she had breath to fight.

The guard who had attacked Jacob fell first, his face bursting with boils that swelled over his eyes and blinded him instantly. Another guard pushed him aside and ran toward Emilia.

"*Crusura!*" Emilia shouted.

The guard's legs snapped together, and he toppled headfirst over a fallen tree.

Just as Emilia was about to turn back to Jacob, a rough hand clasped her wrist and yanked her around. The guard opened his mouth to perform a spell.

Emilia aimed Domina's ring at the man's open mouth and cried, "*Sustaura!*"

The man dropped Emilia's hand as he tore at his own throat, gasping for air that wouldn't come.

The remaining guards circled Emilia, prowling like dogs. It didn't matter what she did; she was outnumbered. An arm wrapped around her throat. Emilia tried to kick, but someone else grabbed her feet. There was an agonizing snap in her finger as someone clawed at the ring Jacob had given her.

The guards threw her to the ground.

Fierce anger burned in Emilia's chest, cutting through her fear. A power and a magic that was not her own. "Jacob, no!" she tried to scream, but a knee on her throat blocked her air.

Then there was light. Bright, burning light. The weight from her body vanished. Emilia covered her face, trying to block out the blinding light. Heat pressed against her. The people around her dropped to the ground, screaming in fear and pain, but she remained unharmed. She heard the crackling of trees igniting. Smoke filled her nostrils.

The screaming stopped. She knew she should uncover her eyes, try to find Jacob, but she was too afraid.

He had lost his wand. She had seen it happen. Using that much magic without a talisman was suicide.

Tears welled in her eyes, breaking through eyelids she still held tightly shut. Emilia shook. A sob ripped through her throat. She could taste the ash in the air.

Jacob, her Jacob. Dead. He had made the ultimate sacrifice to protect her.

She sobbed uncontrollably. She didn't care who heard or who might be trying to attack. Opening her eyes meant seeing Jacob dead, and that would be far worse than anything the Dragons could do to her.

A hand brushed hers. "Emilia." Arms wrapped around her. Even through the smoke, she smelled fresh grass and peat.

She opened her eyes, and there was Jacob, alive and unharmed. The only thing that seemed wrong with him was the worried look on his face.

Emilia threw herself into his arms, crying even harder now. Jacob squeezed her tightly. "Emi, we have to go. I don't know if others might show up." He lifted her to her feet.

The tops of the trees were burning, their trunks stained black with soot. Jacob was right, they had to move, but Emilia couldn't let the whole forest burn. She'd been raised to believe in not harming innocents, even if the innocents were only animals. She closed her eyes and tried to calm herself.

"*Stinagro*," she said. The flames wavered for a moment and then flared up, stronger than before.

"*Stinagro!*" she said again. The flames didn't even flicker.

"We have to move." Jacob pulled on Emilia's elbow. But she was frozen, transfixed by the flames in front of her. "Emi, I'm sorry about the trees, but—" Jacob stopped short and stared white-faced at the solid wall of fire that had leaped up in front of them.

A fiery projection of the Pendragon gazed out of the flames.

THE FACE IN THE FLAMES

The flames spoke, spitting embers into the night, and the Pendragon's voice echoed through the burning forest.

"My child. I am sorry for what this vicious brute has done to you. You were destined to be joined with Dexter, and this blasphemer has stolen you for himself. Return to me, and I assure you I will reverse the tethering spell. Please do not let yourself be forever bound to this murderer. And he is a murderer. Look around you, Emilia. Look at what he has done."

Emilia stared into the flames, but Jacob couldn't tear his eyes from the bodies lying at his feet. All burned. All dead.

"Emilia, let me help you. Come home."

"Never!" Emilia screamed at the dancing flames.

"I am the only one who can reverse the spell," the flames hissed. "Right now, you find yourself drawn to this fiend, but it is only because of the tethering. Let me free you."

"The only way to undo a tethering is for one of the pair to die. Do you really think I don't know that?" Emilia spat.

"It must be done," the Pendragon replied without a hint of remorse.

"I will never let you hurt Jacob." Emilia stepped in front of Jacob, shielding him from the wall of fire.

"Then I am afraid I must do the only thing that I can. If you will not be saved, I must release you from your suffering." The flames leaped into the sky and started creeping toward Emilia. "Goodbye, my beloved." The face disappeared, but the flames continued to grow.

Emilia's warm hand closed around Jacob's and she dragged him down the mountain. The fire leaped from tree to tree, hissing and cracking with each new blaze. For a moment, Jacob thought they might outrun the flames, until the fire started licking the trees to his left and right.

They were being herded, penned in by the growing inferno. With every second, the open space in front of them grew smaller.

They ran, sliding and tripping down the mountain. Jacob's breath came in painful gasps as the smoke swam into his lungs.

He nearly fell when his feet hit hard, flat ground. They had found a road. Emilia kept leading him down the smooth pavement, and he ran as fast as he could, still moving awkwardly as pain shot through his wounded leg.

Emilia's grip slackened on his arm. She was bent almost double, choking on the smoke-filled air. Neither of them would make it much farther. Despite the brightness of the fire, the world dimmed in the haze of black smoke.

There was a roar in the distance, and light charged toward them. The fire was coming at them head on. The end had arrived. Jacob pulled Emilia behind him, determined that shielding her would be his final act. He stood ready to face the flames. But the lights were low, too low, and they weren't coming from the burning trees.

Tires squealed, and a black car stopped inches from Jacob. He braced himself, his lungs searing from the smoke. He swayed on his feet, exhaustion threatening to force him to the ground before a more magical enemy had the chance. Emilia moved to stand next to him, widening her stance, preparing to fight to the end.

Jacob choked in as much air as his lungs could bear and tried to steady himself. The only thing that kept him on his feet was Emilia at his side. She would fight to her last breath to protect him, and he would die if it meant even the slightest chance of her making it out of these woods alive.

The driver's door burst open, and Samuel jumped out. "Are you all right?"

"Samuel!" Emilia cried, running into his arms.

Samuel turned to Jacob. "Is there anyone else with you?"

"What?" Jacob shook his head.

Samuel stared into the blazing wall of flames marching steadily toward them. "Go," he said, pulling Emilia's arms from around him.

"Samuel." Emilia reached for Samuel's arm, but he was already running directly into the fire. "Samuel!" He didn't stop.

572 | MEGAN O'RUSSELL

"Drive!" he yelled over his shoulder. "Drive, Jacob, and don't stop, no matter what!"

Emilia started to run after Samuel, but Jacob caught her around the waist and hauled her back to the car.

"No!" she screeched, kicking Jacob hard in the shins with her heel. "No! We have to get him back!"

But Samuel had already disappeared into the flames.

Jacob threw Emilia into the passenger seat and sealed the door with magic. He sprinted to the driver's side and climbed in. He fumbled with the gears for a moment, then took off down the mountain, thanking the fates the car was an automatic.

The smoke was so thick he could barely see the road. The farther down the mountain he drove, the closer the flames crept. No witches or wizards came through the trees, but horrible howls and screams pierced the night.

"The animals," Emilia whispered. "They're trapped."

Jacob slammed on the brakes when a deer ran in front of them. Fire had found the creature. Flames streamed behind it like a cape of fiery death. The poor creature didn't even notice the car in its fear and pain. It just ran. Not realizing more flames waited for it through the trees.

His hands trembled as he pressed on the gas. Emilia turned and retched into the seat behind her.

He did as Samuel had ordered and sped down the mountain. Up ahead, the flames tried to reach across the road to close the circle. They leaped from treetop to treetop like small children trying to grab hands, but the gap between them was too wide. Jacob pushed the car as fast as it would go. Dangerously fast. And right as a flaming maple began to fall across the road, they passed out of the circle of fire.

A moment later, they were on the main road, but still Jacob didn't stop. He raced through the night, hoping against hope to find a highway that would lead home.

Why had Samuel left them? They could have fought together. He would have known the way home. Why would he run into the flames? Emilia sobbed, trembling in the seat next to him. There was no way they would ever know why Samuel went back, because there was no way he could make it out alive. They would never have a chance to ask him.

Jacob's body screamed from Domina's abuse. He wanted nothing more than to lie down and rest. But Emilia wouldn't be safe until they were back at the Mansion House, so he kept driving.

They found a highway Emilia recognized. The Dragons would know where they were going, but where else would they be safe?

When the sun began to kiss the sky, they turned onto the Mansion House drive. The car shuddered as they drove through the *fortaceria*, but they were allowed to pass. The house recognized Emilia. Now Iz would know they were coming.

As they pulled up to the house, the door burst open. Aunt Iz, the professor, Claire, Molly, Connor—everyone was there.

Almost.

Iz wrenched the car door open and wrapped Emilia in her arms. Molly came to Jacob's door and yanked him out, and Claire flung herself at him, oblivious to the sweat, blood, and ash covering him.

Molly peered into the car, but there was no one else to greet. She stifled a cry. "Samuel?"

"I am so sorry, Molly." Emilia reached for Molly, but Iz grabbed her hand. A streak on Emilia's palm still glowed gold.

Iz stared. Understanding dawned on every face except Claire's.

"What?" Claire pulled Emilia's hand from Iz. "What is that?"

"Oh, Emilia," the professor said. "How? Who did this?"

"LeFay. He's the Pendragon. Oh, Iz." Emilia sobbed, her whole body shaking.

Jacob stumbled to Emilia and wrapped his arms around her, wanting to hold her close enough to make everything all right. Emilia swayed, and Jacob scooped her into his arms and limped toward the house. Iz touched his arm to stop him, gasping when she saw his hand was also marked in gold. Tears glistened in her eyes as she nodded, letting him carry Emilia away.

---

*T*he bedspread shifted under Emilia's back as he lowered her onto the bed. It smelled like flowers, soft and familiar. The swirling pattern on the quilt was the same as when she had left it.

But Emilia saw her blood-stained, gold-streaked hand and pushed herself off the bed, stumbled into the bathroom, and slammed the door behind her. She tried to scrub her hands. The sink flooded with red. Jacob's blood mixed with her own as it flowed down the drain. But who else's blood was on her hands? How many people had died because of her?

Sobs echoed in the bathroom, but they seemed too far away to be hers. All she wanted was to wash the evidence of the past five days from her hands. Her wrists were raw and bloody from struggling against her bindings, but the palm of her left hand would never heal. The gold mark was permanent.

She staggered to the shower and turned the water on as high and hot as it would go. She didn't even take off her clothes. Someone pounded on the door, but she didn't answer. She stood under the water, letting it burn her. The tears running down her cheek mixed with the burning water, leaving no trace they had ever existed. They were simply swept away.

Another tear came, and then another. An unending line of salty soldiers that swirled to their deaths in the drain. She wanted nothing more than to slip down the drain and follow her tears into oblivion. She sobbed so hard it felt as though her ribs would crack and her lungs explode. She knelt in the shower and grieved for Samuel. For Dexter, who was lost to her forever. For the mother she'd never known, and for her father, whom she would fight to her last breath to destroy.

Emilia hadn't heard the door *bang* open, hadn't noticed a hand reach in to cool the scalding water. But Jacob's arms were around her. He smoothed her hair and held her to his chest. He didn't try to stop her tears. He just held her and let her mourn for the happy life to which she could never return.

WHAT WAS LOST

Jacob had wrapped her in a robe. It was fuzzy and warm and blue. Emilia knew it was her robe, but it felt foreign to her, like she'd borrowed the memory of owning it from someone else's life. There were too many fresh and horrid memories for the old ones to hold much meaning now.

Jacob handed her a comb. She stared at his hand. The hand that had lost his wand. But the spell—he had done the spell anyway. And he was still here and alive.

"How?" Emilia asked, meeting Jacob's eyes. "How did you do it?"

"Emilia—"

"How did you do that spell?"

Jacob didn't answer her. Emilia wanted to scream, to run, to know why. Why had this happened to her? To them?

"Jacob," she whispered, "tell me." Tears crept into the corners of her eyes again. She needed an answer to something. And there was no one else to ask any of her other questions. Emilia pulled away from him.

"I don't know," Jacob said as he grabbed her shoulder. "Emilia, I really don't. Please."

Emilia refused to turn around.

"The Dragons had you, and I knew there was no way out. I heard you scream, and I had to protect you. So I did the spell without the wand. I knew I would die without a talisman, and I didn't even really formulate a spell, I just wanted to protect you. And I felt the energy surge, and I thought I was dead. But then everyone was gone but you and me." He paused and walked around to face her. He tilted her chin up and brushed her damp hair away. "I don't know how I did it. But I don't care. You're safe."

Emilia didn't want to meet his eyes. The gold streak glowed on his palm. There was an angry red scar over his heart. Another mark no spell could heal.

She had almost lost him.

Emilia touched the burn on his cheek. "We're safe." And she tucked her head onto his shoulder.

*J*acob lay in bed. Emilia had finally fallen asleep, her head curled on Jacob's chest. He brushed the hair off her cheek. He wanted to stay with her and sleep himself away from the pain.

But the danger wasn't over. Aunt Iz needed to know everything. The more information she had, the safer they would all be.

He slid Emilia's head onto her pillow and crept into the hall. Voices drifted from the kitchen, but he continued to Iz's study. She needed to know first.

Iz's door waited open. Dim light spilled into the hall. He didn't knock. He couldn't bear the thought of asking permission to enter the study to deliver this sort of news.

Iz sat behind her desk, staring at her wrinkled hands, apparently waiting for Jacob. An untouched sandwich and full cup of tea sat on the desk.

"How is she?" Iz asked without looking up.

"Asleep." Jacob sat in the chair across from the desk. The same chair he had sat in the day Iz asked him if he wanted to be a wizard. It hadn't even been two months. It felt like a lifetime. Lives had changed, and lives had ended.

Jacob didn't know where to begin, so he sat in silence, waiting for Iz to look at him.

Finally, she did. "Where is Samuel?"

Jacob explained about the shield and Samuel leaving to call for help. He told her about the tattoo and using the airplane man to sneak into the compound, and about Samuel finding them and running back into the circle.

"He is a very brave man," Iz said. "He may still be alive. Samuel is an excellent warrior. I will not give up hope."

Jacob didn't say anything. He couldn't imagine anyone surviving that fire and fighting the Dragons.

"Jacob?" Iz asked after a few moments. "How did the tethering happen?"

The chamber in the caves flashed in his thoughts. All the wizards watching Emilia being tied down. Dexter holding a golden cord. His hands started to shake, and one was streaked in gold. He clenched it into a tight fist to hide the mark, forcing himself to breathe. He didn't want his fear to wake Emilia. "The Pendragon tried to tether Emilia to Dexter."

"Dexter is with the Dragons?"

Jacob nodded.

Iz stood and paced.

"I tried to stop the ceremony," Jacob said, "and ended up becoming a part of the spell."

"Why would the Pendragon want to tether Emilia and Dexter? Did Dexter request the ceremony? Was Emilia a reward for him?"

"I don't think he wanted to do it. The Pendragon arranged it."

"Why?" Iz waited as Jacob struggled with the words.

"The Pendragon. He's Emilia's father."

Iz stopped mid-stride.

"He said he was doing what was best for Emilia. That he was trying to protect her."

Iz walked over, took Jacob's left hand in hers, and turned his palm to examine it. "How are you? Tethering is—"

"I'm fine." Jacob pulled his hand away.

"Tethering can change how you feel," Iz said quietly, "and it can never be undone."

"I don't feel any different. My world has been centered around Emilia for a long time. The only difference is now it feels physical." He rubbed his ribs just above his heart, ignoring the pain from Domina's burn. "I feel a pull in my chest toward her. And I know she's still asleep because I can feel how calm she is. But I still love her, just like always."

Jacob stood. He needed to rest, to drift away from all the questions. To be closer to Emilia.

But he turned back in the doorway. "The problem is, she was never in love with me. And now, even if she does want to be with me someday, I'll never know if she really loves me or if it's just part of some spell. They took her choice away from her, but I made mine a long time ago."

Jacob turned and walked down the hall.

The banister glowed in the afternoon sun as he climbed the stairs. He walked down the girls' wing and into Claire's room, picked up her fluffy pink chair, and set it outside Emilia's door. He lay back in the chair and closed his eyes.

They needed rest, but he would be there when she woke up.

Jacob and Emilia's journey continues in The Siren's Realm.
Read on for a sneak preview.

JACOB AND EMILIA'S JOURNEY CONTINUES
IN THE SIREN'S REALM

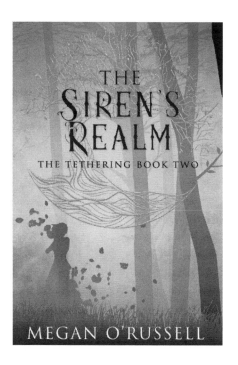

Continue reading for a sneak peek of *The Siren's Realm*.

BOUND

The cool autumn air crept through the house. The trees in the garden had not yet begun to change their leaves, but they seemed to know their time was coming.

Inside the house was silence. As the afternoon sun peered through the window, all it saw was stillness. Emilia sat at her desk in the big library, staring at a page in a little brown book.

TETHERING

The magical binding of two people. Historically, tethering was an integral part of a wizarding wedding. After a tethering ceremony, the coniunx, *or tethered couple, would gain the ability to sense one another and would develop a greatly increased emotional attachment.*

In today's wizarding society, tethering is rarely included in wedding ceremonies. It is generally considered archaic and makes divorce much more difficult, as a tethering can only be severed by the death of one of the coniunx. *The demise of half of the pair is incredibly painful for the remaining party and often results in their subsequent death.*

Throughout wizarding history, some have used tethering as a weapon. By forcing a slave, captive, or unwilling bride to be tethered to a new master, the spellcaster would ensure the forcibly tethered party would be unlikely to attempt escape, and should an escape occur, tracking the coniunx *would be simple. Forced tethering was made illegal in 1813 as a part of the International Wizarding Agreement and is punishable by the severest penalty allowable in the nation in which the offense occurs.*

Captive. Unable to escape. How many times had she read that page in the few months since Graylock? Five hundred, maybe six? Reading the passage never made it any better. Still, she began the page again, hoping the words would somehow be different.

Tethering—The magical binding of two—

The front door crashed open, and an excited shout of "Emilia!" carried down the hall followed closely by, "Claire, don't break the door!"

Emilia slipped the book into the desk drawer before Claire tore around the corner and into the library.

"Emilia!" she squealed, her bright blond hair falling from her ponytail, and her cheeks red from excitement and the wind. "You missed the best thing ever! I helped Jacob with his shield spells, and I sparred with Connor and won!"

Claire began an energetic victory dance as Jacob and Connor entered the library. Connor limped in with a grimace on his face, and Jacob failed to suppress a smile.

"Yes, Claire," Connor said through clenched teeth as he lowered himself into his desk chair, "you did a great job."

"What's that you say?" Claire leaned in toward Connor, her hand cupped around her ear. "You just got beat by a twelve-year-old?"

Emilia smiled, knowing it was what Claire wanted to see. Aunt Iz had always believed that all witches and wizards should know how to defend themselves. Sparring had been a part of the education received at the Mansion House for as long as Emilia could remember, but daily practice hadn't begun until after Graylock. That's how life felt now, split into two pieces—before Graylock, and after.

Emilia noticed Claire's mouth moving. She bounced around, giving a blow by blow of how she had beaten Connor. Claire stood on the back of the couch before launching herself onto Connor.

Emilia forced herself to laugh as cheerfully as she could manage. "That's great, Claire." She hoped her voice didn't sound too unnaturally high.

"Let's go get some dinner," Jacob said, lifting Claire off Connor, taking her by the shoulders and steering her toward the hall.

"But I want to talk to Emilia." Claire twisted away from Jacob's grasp.

"Later," Jacob said firmly. He jerked his head for Connor to follow and led Claire out of the library.

Emilia laid her forehead on her desk. The wood felt cool on her face. She should follow them. It was time for dinner. Molly would be waiting, but other faces would be missing. Everywhere she went in the house, someone was missing.

Emilia's heart started to race. She took a deep breath, but in her mind all she could see was flames. And Samuel and Dexter. They should be here. But Samuel was gone, and Dexter was a traitor.

"Emi." Jacob touched her back, sending her heart racing again, but in such a different way. She sat up and looked into Jacob's bright blue eyes.

"They're waiting for you," Jacob said, pulling his hand back as Emilia shrugged away from his touch.

"Sure." Emilia stood and started for the kitchen, but as she passed the dining room, a chorus of voices shouted, "Happy birthday!"

Aunt Iz, Molly, Professor Eames, Connor, and Claire all stood around the table looking at her. Emilia stared at them.

"You didn't think we would forget your birthday?" Aunt Iz asked, walking over to Emilia and pulling her into a warm hug.

"No, of course not." Emilia blinked away her confusion. She didn't think they had forgotten her birthday, but she hadn't remembered it herself.

"Come sit!" Claire dragged Emilia away from Iz and pushed her into her seat at the table.

"Our little girl is seventeen already." Molly bustled out of the room, dabbing her face on her apron, and returned moments later with large plates of food hovering in front of her. As though held by invisible butlers, the plates all laid themselves down on the table with perfect synchronization. She hadn't cooked a meal like this since before Graylock.

"Claire worked all morning on the decorations," Connor said, pointing over Emilia's head and rolling his eyes as he began to eat.

Emilia twisted in her seat. A pink sign that had *Happy Birthday Emilia!!!!!!!!* written in glitter hung over the door. Pink confetti swirled through the air like snow, and three foot wide pink balloons bounced along the ceiling. The only concession to the fact that pink was not, in fact, Emilia's favorite color was the sole lavender balloon tied to the back of her chair.

Emilia looked around the room. Iz smiled back at her from the end of the table. Her grey hair was tied back in an elegant twist as always, but she looked older than she should. Her face was weathered with lines that had not been there a few months ago. Next to her sat Molly, covered with a light dusting of flour, her greying red hair falling out of its bun.

Next to Molly was Connor, her nephew, with bright red hair to match hers. Molly piled heaps of food onto his plate, continuously tutting about him growing too quickly, and she was right. He was fourteen and tall for his age. He had grown another two inches this month.

On Emilia's other side sat Claire, shaking her head at Professor Eames. The professor was shorter than everyone but Claire. His shrunken frame betrayed his age, but his toady little face was split in a wide grin as he chuckled and Claire giggled.

And Jacob. His dark blond hair needed cutting again. His bright blue eyes twinkled as he listened to Claire trying to explain something to the professor through her laughter.

Emilia knew they were all trying. They were being cheerful for her sake, giving her a happy birthday. But Emilia couldn't look away from the empty places at the table.

Claire had carried Dexter's chair to the yard and set fire to it months ago, as soon as she found out what Dexter had done. But Samuel's seat was still waiting for him at the table, like he was running late to her party and would come bounding in from the garden any minute.

Emilia talked with the family while they ate. Lessons they had done lately. Stories from when Molly was young. Perfectly normal conversation.

Molly brought out a huge cake covered with tiny flowers. In the center of each blossom was a candle burning with a vivid blue flame. As Emilia blew out the candles, each of the flowers floated into the air, joining the confetti that soared endlessly around the room, weaving in and out of the glistening chandelier.

"It's beautiful, Molly," Emilia said.

"Open your presents!" Claire shoved a box into Emilia's hands.

The box was small and covered in pale blue velvet. As Emilia opened it, her breath caught in her throat. Inside was a delicate silver ring with a tree of life, the crest of the Gray Clan, carved into the front.

"To replace the one that was lost," Iz said quietly. "I had it made by the same jeweler."

"Thank you, Aunt Iz." Emilia pushed her face into a smile.

"Now you can use it as your talisman again," Claire said, taking the ring out of the box and shoving it onto Emilia's finger.

"Maybe." Emilia touched the sapphire pendant around her neck. "I think I might try out my necklace a while longer."

Claire wrinkled her forehead.

"I love the ring, Aunt Iz. Thank you." Emilia stood and went over to Aunt Iz. She hugged her tight, trying to put so many things she hadn't been able to say into her arms.

"Jacob has a present for you, too," Claire said, handing Emilia a bigger box as soon as she broke away from Iz.

"Thank you, Jacob," Emilia said as she tore the white, sparkling paper off the box.

Inside was a mobile made of the brightest green leaves. As she pulled it out of the box, the leaves began to spin slowly as though blown by a gentle breeze. A sprig of lilac, Emilia's favorite flower, sat still at the very center as everything else rotated around.

Emilia remembered a night when Jacob had first come to the Mansion House, when he had first learned he was a wizard.

"Making the leaves fly was the first piece of magic you showed me here," Jacob said, pink creeping into his cheeks. "I put a *viriduro* spell on it so the flowers will always stay fresh."

"Well done." The professor leaned in to inspect the mobile.

"Thank you," Emilia said, touching Jacob's arm. His eyes met hers, and she pulled her hand away, sliding the mobile back into the box.

After an hour of dinner, Emilia's face ached from smiling. She hadn't spent that much time with anyone in months. Her brain felt heavy and tired from so much talking.

Molly had given her a new dress and a box of peanut brittle, and the professor had given her a new book on early African Wizards. When Molly finally started clearing the table, Emilia slipped away, running up the stairs to her room before anyone could call her back.

Emilia opened her bedroom window, letting the cold air fill the room. Thousands of stars peered back at her. The trees rustled in the breeze.

She lay down, gazing up at the canopy of her bed, trying to ignore the pull in her chest that told her to go and find Jacob. If she were with him, her heart said, everything would be all right. If she were with him, she would be safe.

Emilia gazed at the silver ring on her finger. She twisted her hand, watching the etched tree of life glint in the light. Where was her other ring, the one Iz had given her when she was seven? Had it been tossed aside in some cave? Was someone else using it as a talisman now? Using her ring to hurt people?

Jacob had given her a different ring to defend herself. One that felt almost exactly like this one. The same smooth band, the same feel on her hand.

Leaping off the bed, Emilia yanked open her dresser drawer and dug into the back corner where she had hidden the other silver ring. That ring had been contaminated, something found in an evil place. She had tossed it into the drawer without looking at it, wanting desperately to get it out of her sight.

Emilia's fingers closed on the cold metal, and she pulled the ring from the stacks of clothes. A silver ring, identical to hers except for the carving. Where hers had a tree, this ring had a tiny bird. A fist closed around her heart.

"Emilia!"

Footsteps thundered up the stairs. Cries of "Emilia!" and "Jacob, what's wrong?" echoed through the house.

Emilia's door burst open, and Jacob raced through, followed closely by Claire and Connor.

Jacob knelt next to Emilia, taking her face in his hands. She hadn't even noticed she was crying until he brushed the tears off her cheek.

"What's wrong?" he whispered.

"What's happening?" Aunt Iz asked as she and Molly panted into the room. The professor wheezed as he shuffled up next to them.

"I never looked at it." Emilia shook her head. Blond hair and a smiling rosy face swam through her mind. She held the ring out to Iz. "I put it away so I wouldn't have to see it. And now it's been so long." Emilia's voice cracked.

Iz took the ring and gasped.

"What?" Claire snatched the ring from Iz. Her eyes widened as they fell on the little bird. "Larkin. This is Larkin's ring. Why do you have Larkin's ring? She's missing. Did she leave it for you here? Is it a message from her?" Claire began tearing through Emilia's drawers. "She might have left something else. Larkin would leave us a clue so we could find her."

"She didn't leave it," Jacob said, wrapping an arm around Claire and pulling her away from the dresser. "I found that ring at Graylock."

"She was there," Emilia whispered. "That's why Samuel asked if we were alone. That's why he went back. To find her."

Larkin had been like a big sister to her, her protector. The Gray student who had become one of the elite MAGI Agents who protected order in the magical world.

Emilia yanked her hands through her hair. "He was going to save her, and we left both of them behind. Jacob, we left them."

"Emi." Jacob reached for her.

"We left them!" Emilia screamed, backing away from all of them. They didn't understand. It was her fault. Larkin was supposed to be indestructible. But MAGI had been ransacked by the Dragons, and Larkin taken at Graylock. Emilia had left them there. Samuel and Larkin, trapped in the dark. Her heart pounded in her chest, and sweat slicked her palms.

"Emilia, breathe," Aunt Iz said softly, just as she had when Emilia was little and lost control of her magic. But it wasn't Emilia who was spinning out of control. It was all of them. It was the world.

The mirror over Emilia's dresser shattered. Connor grabbed Claire and knocked her to the floor. Iz covered her head, the professor yelped, and Molly screamed. Jacob didn't flinch as he stared at Emilia.

"*Reparactus,*" Jacob murmured, and the pieces of glass flew through the air back into their frame. Within seconds, the cracks in the mirror disappeared as if it had never been broken.

Emilia looked into the mirror at an unfamiliar face. The long black hair was hers, but the grey eyes were wild and afraid.

"We will find a way to get Samuel and Larkin back," Aunt Iz said, walking to Emilia and wrapping her arms around her.

"They've been in there for months. If you couldn't find a way to get Samuel out, how are you going to get two people out? It's my fault," Emilia choked.

Molly and the professor herded Claire and Connor out of the room. Jacob slipped out behind them.

"None of this would have happened," Emilia struggled to speak but couldn't get the words out through her gasping tears.

The sheets folded back as Aunt Iz guided her to bed, tucking her in as she had done when Emilia was little. But warm blankets couldn't keep the monsters away. Not anymore.

CLAIRE'S GIFT

Emilia couldn't sleep. She could feel Jacob upstairs, waiting to be sure she was all right. The voices that traveled through the hall were hushed, as though Emilia were a patient with a fatal illness.

Hours passed.

The stars traveled outside her window. Emilia forced herself to breathe, willing herself to remain calm. She didn't want Jacob to come running.

The floorboard outside Emilia's room squeaked.

There was a light tap on the door, and Claire called softly, "Emilia, can I come in?"

Emilia pulled her covers up over her head. She was warm, and it was quiet. Her desire to be left alone warred against how hurt Claire's feelings would be if she ignored her.

"Emilia, are you awake?" Claire's voice came again.

Emilia forced herself to sit up, turned on the light, and arranged her face into a smile. "Come on in."

Claire poked her blond head around the door. Her forehead was furrowed, and her mouth set in a scowl.

"What's up?" Emilia asked.

Claire sat down next to Emilia on the pale purple comforter, clutching her pink laptop to her chest.

"Are you okay?" Claire asked, examining Emilia's face.

"I'm fine." Emilia hoped it sounded true.

"I have a birthday present for you, but I need to make sure you won't freak out and break anything," Claire said in an unusually businesslike tone.

"I promise not to hurt your computer," Emilia said.

Claire nodded, apparently satisfied, and loosened her grip on the pink laptop. "Good, but nobody can know about this. If Iz found out, I'd be dead or sent away in a second."

Emilia's face fell. "Claire, what did you do?"

"I didn't really *do* anything. I'm just not actually supposed to have it." Claire's voice dripped with guilt.

"Did you steal something from Iz?" Emilia asked.

"Not from Iz."

"Claire!"

"Shhh!" Claire clapped a hand over Emilia's mouth. "And it wasn't stealing as much as salvaging. When you were…away, and MAGI was attacked, Aunt Iz asked me to crash the Spellnet database. With no one in the MAGI offices to make sure the system was secure, anyone could have hacked into the files, taken whatever information they wanted, and no one would have known."

"You crashed Spellnet?" Emilia asked, impressed despite herself at Claire's computer skills.

"Absolutely. Really, it was a piece of cake. MAGI wasn't as up on their security as they should have been, so crashing Spellnet wasn't that hard. I deleted their information and then ran a virus that fried the system," Claire said.

"Well, if that's what Iz wanted you to do, she can't be mad at you for doing it. I'm sure you'll be fine," Emilia said, rubbing Claire's back.

"That's not the part where I get sent home." Claire opened her vividly pink laptop and started the process of opening her encrypted files. "Before I deleted the files, I may have reallocated some of them to my computer."

"Reallocated?" Emilia raised her left eyebrow.

"You know you look a lot like Aunt Iz when you do that?"

Emilia's eyebrow climbed even higher.

"Fine, I stole some information. It seemed a pity to throw *all* of it out when we could use it to do some actual good in this cold, hard world."

"What exactly did you take, Claire?" Emilia tried to keep her tone level.

"A few things. The information on Wizard-owned patents, the Spellnet Satellite codes, and the registered Witch and Wizard database."

"Claire, that information is confidential."

"I'm not going to go flashing it around if that's what you're worried about. And besides, you should be grateful. I found something I think will interest you. Unless, of course, you don't want your present?" She paused. When Emilia didn't respond, Claire continued. "I didn't think so. I went through the files of registered Witches and Wizards. I found your father's file." Claire clicked on a folder labeled *Emile LeFay*. "And I think"—Claire took a deep breath—"I found your mother."

Emilia froze. "Claire, LeFay didn't tell me her name. Iz doesn't know who she was. She tried to find her. She asked MAGI for help."

"Iz didn't have free range over the files. And they weren't completely computerized then. All I had to do was enter disappearances around your birthday. It was a lot easier than I thought it would be. I had plans for all kinds of ways to search for her. She was one of only five reported missing around that time, and she was the only girl." Claire clicked open a file.

A photo labeled *Rosalie Wilde* stared out from the screen. The girl in the picture had long, black hair that hung in heavy curls. Her features were smaller than Emilia's, and her eyes were blue instead of grey, but Emilia knew in an instant that Claire was right. Rosalie Wilde was her mother.

"What does it say about her?" Emilia brushed the tears away from her eyes so they wouldn't blur her view of the screen.

"She was a runaway. She and LeFay were apprenticed in the same house. He graduated, and she ran away three weeks later. Her family asked MAGI to help find her. It looks like MAGI put out a few inquiries." Claire scrolled down to a scanned document with dates and contacts, a record of MAGI's failed attempts to locate Rosalie. "They didn't do much until after there were a few murders reported near the Graylock Preserve."

Dark mountains and flames flooded Emilia's mind.

"Over the course of five months, two of the wizards who were listed as missing at the same time as your mother were found dead, along with five humans. A couple matching LeFay's and Rosalie's descriptions were seen in the area. That's when MAGI really started looking for her."

"Because they thought she was a murderer," Emilia said dryly.

"There's no evidence I can find that ties her to any of the deaths, and both of the wizards' deaths were ruled accidental."

"LeFay is a murderer, and if Rosalie was there, she must have been helping him." Emilia pushed herself off the bed and started pacing. She never should have let Claire come in. Being alone was better than this.

"But she left, Em."

Emilia's neck tensed. "Please don't call me that."

That was what Dexter had called her. She hated the sound of it now.

"Okay, Emilia. I won't," Claire said quietly. She was silent for a minute while Emilia continued to pace the room. "These records say Rosalie left Graylock right after the first bodies were found. MAGI started looking for LeFay and Rosalie. LeFay never surfaced, but there were sightings of Rosalie.

"She was seen in a small town in Massachusetts two months after she disappeared from the preserve. Then nothing for about six months. After that, she was seen in California, New York City, and the last sighting was in Maine five months after you were born." Claire closed the laptop and watched Emilia's progress back and forth across the room.

"Thank you, Claire," Emilia said, not looking at her. "Thank you for finding this for me."

"Every time your mom was seen, there was no sign of LeFay. And they were looking for him, too. I think she really did leave him. Emilia, if her birthday on file is right, she was only eighteen when she had you. But she left LeFay. She ran away, alone and pregnant." Claire stood and hugged Emilia, stopping her from moving. "I think she got scared of him and ran. I think she was trying to protect you. If she thought what he was doing was right, she would have stayed with him. It would have been easier. I really think she loved you. I wanted you to know."

Emilia wrapped her arms around Claire. "Thanks, Claire. It's nice to know her name."

"No problem," Claire said, brushing the tears from Emilia's cheek, "and I made a whole file about her. It kind of made me feel like a creeper, but when you want it, let me know." Claire picked up her laptop and started for the door.

"What happened to her?" Emilia asked, not sure she wanted an answer.

"The MAGI trail ends in Maine. But I can work on finding out more if you want."

"That would be great." Emilia nodded. "But don't tell anyone."

"Our secret." Claire smiled and slipped into the dark hall, closing the door silently behind her.

Emilia flopped down onto the bed. Rosalie Wilde. Scared, eighteen, mother? Or evil, wizard supremacist, murderer? She pulled her pillow over her face. All she could see was the smiling, blue-eyed girl, only a year older than herself. But LeFay was eighteen once, too.

Order your copy of The Siren's Realm *to continue the story.*

THE GIRL WITHOUT MAGIC

THE CHRONICLES OF MAGGIE TRENT, BOOK ONE

Adventures that reach new realms.

Death wasn't all that bad. Living had been harder. Dying hadn't even been painful. Every pain from the battle had stopped as soon as the world had gone black. Now there was nothing left but darkness and quiet.

The screams of her friends echoed in her mind with nothing in the silence to block out the unending wails. Were they lying in the dark, too? Free from pain and fear? Were they still fighting, alive and in danger?

Maybe they'd won. Maybe there was someone left to know she had died.

Did they leave her in the woods? Had there been a funeral? A hearse and a casket? Flowers with bright blooms? Did it matter?

She knew only darkness. Unrelenting black.

It did seem a little unfair that death should be so boring. If this was how it was going to be, perhaps existing wasn't worth it. Being alone with nothing but her own thoughts forever? Maggie had never expected much from death, but oblivion would have been better than knowledgeable nothingness.

Days passed in the darkness, or perhaps it was centuries. There was no way to know without anything to measure the passing of time.

The blackness was maddening. It wasn't until Maggie clenched her fist in frustration at the absolute endlessness of it all that she realized she had a hand. Two hands actually. And a back, which was pressed into a hard floor.

Slowly unclenching her hands, Maggie ran her fingers across the ground. It was cool. How had she not noticed how cold the floor was? Carefully, Maggie rolled onto her stomach, feeling the darkness in all directions, stretching her toes out to see if the ground encased her or if she was lying on the precipice of a deeper blackness.

But there were no walls to run into or holes to tumble through. Pushing herself onto her knees, Maggie crawled a little ways forward, expecting to find something to tell her the size of her dark prison.

But still, there was nothing. Only endless darkness she could crawl around.

"Why?" Maggie asked the darkness, finding her voice as she pushed herself to her feet. "Why should I be able to move if there is nothing to see!" She had expected an echo, but her voice drifted away as though her cage were endless.

Recklessness surged through her. She was already dead—what was the worst that could happen?

Maggie took off at a run. Sprinting through the darkness. After a few minutes, her legs burned, and her breathing came in quick gasps.

"Couldn't get a nice breeze for the running dead girl, huh?" Maggie shouted.

Before the words had fully left her lips, a breeze whispered past her, cooling the back of her neck, kissing her face, and pushing her to run faster. The air even had a scent, like the ocean right before a rainstorm. The tang of salt filled her lungs. She could be running on a beach, an endless beach, but the floor was hard and maddeningly flat. And there was no sound of crashing waves.

"I wish I could see," Maggie whispered.

With a scream, she dropped to her knees, covering her face with her hands. Her heart racing in her chest, Maggie slowly opened her eyes, blinking at the dazzling light that surrounded her.

It was as bright as the sun but didn't come from a fixed point in the sky. Rather, it was like the air itself contained light.

The ground wasn't the hard stone Maggie had imagined. The floor shone a bright, pale color, like it was made of pure platinum.

"It's better than darkness," Maggie muttered.

Now that there was light to see by, the idea that this place went on forever seemed absurd. The floor had to lead somewhere. There had to be an end to it.

"Right." Maggie ran her hands through her hair. It was gritty with dirt and ashes and caked with blood at her temple. "Gross." Maggie moved to wipe her hands on her jeans, but they too were covered with dirt and blood. "I couldn't have clean clothes for eternity? All I want is a hot bath."

As though the air had heard her words, the light around her began to shimmer, twisting and folding into a hundred different colors. Coming closer, and growing solid, until, as quickly as it began, the air stopped moving.

Maggie swallowed the bile that had risen into her throat as the world twisted, blinking to adjust her eyes to the dim light of the tent. Her arms tingled like she had just tried to do a very long spell. Maggie gripped her hands together, willing the feeling to stop as she looked around the tent. And she *was* standing in a tent. It was small, only large enough for the little cot that stood at one end and the tub at the other.

The tent was made of deep blue fabric, which colored the light that streamed in from outside.

"Spiced Ale for sale!" a voice bellowed right outside Maggie's tent. She covered her mouth to keep from screaming. Slowly, she crept toward the flap of the tent.

Voices answered the ale seller's call. Bargaining and shouting came from off in the distance, too.

She pulled back the flap of the tent just far enough to be able to peer outside with one eye.

In the bright sunlight outside her tent, a street teemed with people. And not just wizards. There was a centaur at the end of the road, laughing with a group of witches. A troll sat not fifteen feet away, drinking from a mug the size of Maggie's head.

Maggie took a breath. Centaurs and trolls existed—she had known that for years. If she were dead, then why shouldn't she be with other members of Magickind? She gripped the tent flap, willing herself to walk onto the street and ask someone what was going on. How had death shifted from eternal darkness to a crowded street?

But everyone on the street looked whole and healthy, happy even. She was covered in blood and dirt. She glanced back at the tub in the corner. Thin wisps of steam rose from the water. If she was going to spend the rest of eternity here, she shouldn't scare the locals looking like she had just come from a blood bath.

The dried blood on her shirt crackled as she fumbled the mud-caked plastic buttons. The water burned as she slipped into the tub.

"At least a dead girl can still get a bath." Maggie sighed, leaning back into the water, running her fingers through her hair.

Her blood was in her hair—that much she knew for sure—and coating her sleeve, along with the blood of one of the wizard boys she had been fighting with. If he had died, maybe he would be here, too. But there was more blood.

She tried to think back through the fight, to remember what had happened before she had fallen into darkness. But the more she thought, the more disgusted she became. There could be dozens of people's blood on her.

"I wish I had some soap." No sooner had she said it than a bar of soap was floating in the tub, right next to her hand. A tingle in her chest made her pause as she reached for the soap. It felt like she had done magic. Like a little bit of her power had drained away.

That part was normal, but the tiny little space the magic had left behind wasn't refilling itself. It was just…empty.

Maggie scrubbed her hair and under her nails, washing her arms so hard they were bright red by the time she finally felt clean.

A soft towel waited for her next to the tub. It smelled of flowers and fresh air. Maggie breathed in the scent. Her clothes wouldn't smell like that. They would never be clean again.

"I wish," Maggie began, looking around the tent to see if anyone was even there to listen, "I wish for a clean set of clothes." Her stomach rumbled. "And some food."

Instantly, clothes appeared at the foot of the cot, and a platter of food sat on the table, filling the tent with the scent of roasted meat.

A sharp tingling shot through Maggie's fingers for the briefest moment. If she hadn't been thinking about it, she might not have noticed the tiny drain on the magic inside her. Her magic had always felt like a bottomless well before. She could feel it leaving when she did a spell, could feel her body channeling the energy, but it never seemed as though she might run out—as though there were a finite amount of magic she could access.

The scent of the food was enough to lure her from the warmth of the bath. Maggie took a shuddering breath and stood, wobbling on her shaking legs for a moment before stepping out of the tub. Maybe she wasn't using up her magic. Maybe she was just hungry.

Dripping on the grass that was the floor of the tent, Maggie sat in the spindly chair at the wooden table to eat.

She had always assumed, wrongly it seemed, that once you died you didn't have to bother with things like feeling like you hadn't eaten in a month. She had died only a little while ago. Or maybe it had been a hundred years. She wasn't sure it mattered.

A fresh loaf of bread sat on the carved wooden tray along with a hunk of roasted meat and a bowl of fruit. There was fruit that looked like an apple-sized blueberry that had grown spikes, bright orange berries, and a lavender thing the size of her fist that had a peel like an orange.

Maggie tore off a hunk of bread and stared at the bowl of fruit. Those weren't normal. They weren't real. But then maybe she wasn't real anymore either. Her head started to spin. Not knowing what was happening was beginning to feel worse than being trapped in the darkness. Her stomach turned, and she pushed the tray of food away.

"A trip toward the sea." A woman spoke outside the tent.

With a squeak, Maggie tipped out of her chair and fell to the ground.

"I'm tired of the streets," the woman continued, sounding so close Maggie could have reached out and touched her if the canvas hadn't been in the way.

"It's too crowded. I want to see the Endless Sea!"

Another woman giggled something Maggie couldn't understand, and then the two voices faded into the clatter.

Maggie lay on the ground, staring up at the blue fabric above her.

"Maggie Trent, you cannot lay here for the rest of your afterlife." She dug the heels of her hands into her eyes so hard spots danced in front of them. "You are going to go out there and ask someone what's going on." She let her arms fall to her sides. "Because talking to a troll isn't nearly as bad as lying naked in a tent talking to yourself. At least the grass is soft." Maggie laughed. It started as a chuckle then turned quickly into a tearful laugh as panic crept into her.

She had charged into the woods knowing she might die. She had fought and killed. And then her life had ended. But being in a tent where food magically appeared was somehow more terrifying than fighting.

Maggie lifted her right hand, looking at the bracelet that wrapped around her wrist. It was only a bit of leather cord attached to a silver pendant. A crescent moon and three stars, the crest of the Virginia Clan. The last thing that tied her to her family. Funny it should follow her into death.

Reaching up onto the cot, she pulled down the new clothes. A loose-fitting pale top, dark pants, and a wide, sapphire-colored belt were all she had been given. Maggie pulled the clothes on, feeling a little like she was playing dress up. Not that she really remembered playing dress up. That had stopped when she was five.

Twelve years before I died.

Maggie ran her fingers through her short hair and, squaring her shoulders, pulled back the flap of the tent.

The light outside the tent was brighter than Maggie had expected it to be. The sun beat down on her, and she swayed as a centaur brushed past her. This wasn't Earth—it definitely wasn't. There was a wizard juggling balls of bright blue flames and a woman selling pastries shaped like dragon claws. There was nowhere like this on Earth.

Maggie took a deep, shuddering breath. The air smelled like spices, carried on a wind chased by a storm. She scanned the crowd, searching for a person she could talk to. Someone who might be willing to tell her why it felt like her magic was disappearing.

The troll was still sitting on her own at a table in front of a large red tent. Her table was laden with food, and she ate with abandon. Everyone else on the street seemed busy, either meandering to someplace or talking to the people around them.

Pushing her shoulders back, Maggie headed toward the troll. The red tent behind the troll seemed to be a restaurant of some sort. Empty tables sat in the shade inside the tent. There was only one man lurking deep in the shadows—a large man who looked angry as he held a cloth over his nose.

Three feet away from the troll, Maggie opened her mouth to speak, but before she could say, "Excuse me, ma'am," a foul stench filled her nose and flooded her mouth. Gagging, Maggie turned away, hoping the troll hadn't noticed her.

"Watch yourself," a man said when Maggie nearly backed into him.

"I'm sorry," Maggie said. "Actually, could you—"

The man walked away without listening to Maggie's question.

"Excuse me." Maggie stepped in front of a passing woman.

The woman was one of the most beautiful people Maggie had ever seen. She had silvery blond hair that hung down to her waist, lips the color of raspberries, and bright green eyes.

The woman looked at Maggie, her gaze drifting from Maggie's short brown hair to her plain boots. A coy smile floated across the woman's face before she spoke. "Whatever you are looking for, little girl, you aren't ready for me." She turned to walk away, but Maggie caught the woman's arm.

"Please," Maggie said, "I just need some answers. I don't even know where I am."

The woman laughed a slow, deep laugh.

"And I am not a little girl." Maggie let go of the woman's arm, fighting the urge to ball her hands into fists. "I'm seventeen. Or I was before I died. And it doesn't matter what I'm ready for. I'm here."

"You died?" the woman said with a fresh peal of laughter. "Poor child. Bertrand," the woman called over Maggie's shoulder.

Maggie spun to see who the beautiful woman might be calling. The street was full of people, none of whom seemed to be responding.

"Please just help me." Maggie turned back toward the woman.

The woman stood staring at her for a long moment before a man appeared over her shoulder.

"Did I interrupt something, Bertrand?" the woman asked, not bothering to look at the man.

"You are never an interruption, Lena." Bertrand gave a bow Lena didn't turn to see.

"This one *died*," Lena said.

"It's really not funny," Maggie said, wishing she had stayed back in her tent. "I was in a battle, and I got killed. I was fighting for the good guys when I died, so you could be a little nicer about it."

"Fighting for the good guys?" Lena laughed. "She thinks there are good guys. Oh, Bertrand, I just had to call for you."

"I can see why." Bertrand eyed Maggie as though examining a moderately interesting rock. "I shall do my best to help her."

Lena nodded and disappeared into the crowd.

Maggie warred with herself, not sure if she should shout a thank you after Lena or a string of curses.

"May I introduce myself?" Bertrand asked, the wrinkle of his brow showing his awareness that Maggie was considering saying no.

There was something about the man. He didn't seem to be much older than herself, probably only a little over twenty. But something in his eyes made Maggie wonder if he was two-hundred instead.

His long, dark hair was pulled back in a ponytail, and instead of the light clothing most of the others on the street wore, he sported a finely-made coat and vest, which matched his deep blue knickers, long white socks, and silver buckled shoes. Maggie had only ever seen clothing like that in old paintings. But she was dead, and if he had died a long time before she had ever been born, maybe those clothes were normal to him.

"Please do." Maggie's words came out a little angrier than she had meant them to.

"Very well." Bertrand smiled. "I am Bertrand Wayland."

"Wayland?" Maggie asked, her hands balling instinctively into fists.

"Yes. Wayland." Bertrand bowed. "Have you heard of my family?"

"I knew a Wayland." Maggie nodded. "Before I…well, you know…died."

"In battle?" Bertrand asked.

Maggie nodded.

Bertrand tented his fingers under his chin. "How very interesting, Miss?"

"Maggie Trent." Manners told her to reach out and shake his hand. Experience told her not to.

"Well, Miss Trent," Bertrand said, "I have the happy pleasure of telling you you are not, in fact, dead."

"What?" Relief flooded Maggie for only a moment before confusion washed it away.

"You are very much alive," Bertrand said, "but judging from your firm belief in your demise, I now have the unhappy duty of telling you that you are far from home. Very far from home, Miss Trent, and you are in a place I doubt you've ever heard of."

"So where are we?"

"The Siren's Realm." Bertrand spread his arms wide. "Welcome. It's not often we have arrivals who haven't meant to end up here, so I suppose you'll be more confused than most."

"Do people arrive here often?"

"I'm not really sure. If you'll follow me." Bertrand bowed before turning and striding down the street. "You see, time here is a bit funny. A day can feel like an hour or a year. It is all done by the will of the Siren."

"And you're the welcoming committee?" Maggie asked, having to run a few steps to catch up to Bertrand. The sights around her were enough to make her forget to wonder where he was leading her. A centaur smoking a pipe that puffed purple haze stood beside a woman selling jewels of every color Maggie had ever imagined.

"Oh no." Bertrand laughed. "I have simply been here for a while without losing my love for the outside and those who dwell there."

"So who is the Siren?" Maggie asked. "And what do you mean *outside?*"

They had turned off the street where the red tent was and onto a tiny lane. The tents here were short like the one she had bathed in. There were no food vendors here or nearly as many people. A woman sipping wine sat outside the flap of her tent.

"Afternoon." The woman smiled.

Bertrand nodded to the woman as they passed, whispering to Maggie as soon as they were out of earshot, "Never trust that one. She'll cheat you every time."

"Cheat you at what?" Maggie asked. "Look, can you help me get out of here? If I'm not dead, then I might still be able to get"—Maggie stumbled on the word *home*—"back to where I belong. My friends could still be fighting. They might need me."

"Ah." Bertrand stopped so quickly Maggie ran into him. He took her by both shoulders to steady her. "Leaving the Siren's Realm is possible."

"Then how—"

"But getting back to the battle you left…I am afraid, Miss Trent, that might well be impossible." He strode down the lane, once again leaving Maggie running to catch up.

He led her onto a street so wide, centaurs walked down it four across. A line of people waited outside a vivid green tent trimmed with purple silk and embroidered with golden patterns. It was so beautiful Maggie wanted to stop and take a closer look, but Bertrand was still moving, and she didn't want to risk being left behind.

"Why couldn't I get back to the battle?" Maggie asked when she finally managed to get next to Bertrand. "How did I even get here? Why was I stuck in the dark?"

"All from the beginning." Bertrand turned left into a large square packed with people. "It's the best way forward."

He weaved through the crowd toward a fountain at the center of the square. A woman formed of the same shining metal the bright floor had been made of stood at the center of the fountain, her body draped in thin fabric. Her face was beautiful, but in a terrible way that made Maggie's chest tighten just looking at

604 | MEGAN O'RUSSELL

her. In one hand the woman held a goblet, which rained down bright, golden liquid. The other hand was encrusted with jewels of every color and reached toward the bright sky.

The golden liquid from the goblet filled a pool at the woman's feet, and people swam in the bright water.

"Here you are, Miss Trent." Bertrand bowed, gesturing toward the fountain.

"This is the beginning?" Maggie asked.

"The Siren is the beginning and the end. Knowing her rules is vital to living in her realm." He gestured to the fountain again, and this time Maggie found what he was showing her.

Inscribed in the side of the fountain was a verse.

> *In the Siren's Realm a wish need only be made.*
> *Her desire to please shall never be swayed.*
> *But should those around you wish you ill,*
> *the Siren's love shall protect you still.*
> *No two blessings shall contradict,*
> *so be sure your requests are carefully picked.*
> *Wish for joyful pleasure to be shared by all*
> *of the good and the brave who have risked the fall.*
> *But a warning to you once the wish is made,*
> *the Siren's price must always be paid.*

Maggie read through the verse three times without stopping. "What is that?" she asked when her eyes moved up to read a fourth time. "Some kind of demented nursery rhyme?"

"It is the Siren's Decree," Bertrand said, his tone giving a gentle reprimand for Maggie's remark. "It is the most basic rule we live under within her realm. Whether you meant to or not, Maggie Trent, you have become one of the brave who chanced the fall. You have arrived in the Siren's Realm where her greatest wish is for us all to live lives of pleasure and joy. You have, in short, arrived in paradise."

3

Maggie blinked for a moment. "But you said I'm not dead."

"You aren't. Though as you fell into the Siren's Realm without meaning to, I can understand the confusion."

"So who is the Siren?" Maggie asked. "Can I talk to her, ask to get sent home?"

"Miss Trent, I am afraid that is not possible," Bertrand said. "It would be like allowing you to fly a broom before you've learned to levitate. There would be no hope for success."

"But I need—"

"A witch of your caliber should be able to navigate the Siren's Realm quickly enough, and then you will be able to request whatever you like."

"I'm not a witch," Maggie lied, the words falling from her mouth before she knew she had meant to say them. "I'm not a witch. I'm human."

"Yet you know a Wayland and fought in a wizard's battle?" Bertrand's eyebrows knit together as he examined Maggie.

"I have friends who do magic," Maggie said, hoping her excuse would be good enough.

"Then your path to an audience with the Siren will be long indeed." For the first time, Bertrand sounded as though he might actually feel sorry for Not Dead Maggie.

"Why should it be long?" Maggie asked, her temper flaring at the sympathy on Bertrand's face. "I just got here. Why can't I go back?"

"The Siren gives us a land of peace and beauty." Bertrand spread his arms wide. "She gives us the light from above, wonderful food, and loving companionship. But all things must come with a price."

"What price?"

"To be transported back from the Siren's Realm to a particular place requires a lot of magic—"

"But then how did I get here?"

"—and you will need to pay a significant amount of magic if you want to be placed back at the right time and place. And even with all the magic in the Siren's Realm, it still might not be possible. The Siren's ways are as indiscernible as a figure shrouded in mist."

"How"—Maggie cut across Bertrand as he opened his mouth to continue —"did I get here? If I'm not dead, then what happened to me?"

"The Siren's Realm is a world between worlds. It is above and below, hidden in the cracks, just out of sight. Her realm is stitched to ours and a hundred others, holding them fast together. But where those stitches are, there are holes between places. If you did not come here intentionally, then my truest guess would be that you stumbled through one of those stitches."

"Then if I find where the connection is here, I can go home." Maggie searched over the heads of the crowd, looking for anything that might lead her away.

"I'm afraid that might not be as easy as you would like, Miss Trent."

Maggie clenched her teeth, biting back the words the pity in his tone made her long to scream.

"I'm afraid the only way to get back where you want to go is with the blessing and aid of the Siren. And to get that, you'll need magic, quite a bit of it. But please don't despair, Miss Trent. Magic may be the currency in the Siren's Realm, but even a human can make do. The Siren's price must be paid, but it can be done through honest labor. If you are willing to serve wizards who trade in magic, you might eventually be able to find a way home. Not that I would ever recommend abandoning the Siren, but if it remains your will when the possibility arises…"

"People pay in magic here?" The very thought of it turned Maggie's stomach. Her magic was a part of her, as much a part of who she was as her face or her soul. To trade that for what? Food? The bath?

Suddenly, Maggie was very grateful for her lie. She didn't want this man to know she had any magic to trade or have stolen. She wouldn't trade a part of herself to him or anyone else.

"Yes, well, thank you for your help." Maggie backed away from Bertrand. "I think I understand enough to be getting on with now."

"But Miss Trent, you haven't seen the glorious sights the Siren's Realm has to offer."

"I really think I'm fine." Maggie kept walking backward. She stepped on someone's foot and heard them grunt. "Sorry," she said without turning back. "But I really think," she spoke to Bertrand again, "that I'll be fine."

"But a human thrown into a world so magical?" Bertrand bowed. "Miss Trent, it is lucky I was summoned to help you so quickly. Perhaps the golden threads of fate sought to bring us together."

"I really don't think so." Maggie bowed back. "And I have to go."

Without another word, Maggie spun around and sprinted down the nearest street, not stopping until she was thoroughly lost.

She wasn't really sure how far she had run, but somehow she had ended up on a street unlike any she had ever seen. The ground here gleamed like the metal of the fountain with bright, shimmering jewels of every color set into the ornate engravings.

Maggie stared down at the ground. Her Academy-issued boots, given to her as a student of the magical school, were filthy and worn. She glanced around, waiting for someone to yell at her and tell her she shouldn't be standing on such a precious work of art. But the others around her just strolled past, seemingly unconcerned with Maggie's shoes. There weren't many people out on this street, and all those in view wore finely made clothes, fitting in perfectly with their lavish surroundings.

The tents here were made of the same bright fabric as her blue one, but these were coated in jewels to match their colors. The sun had begun to set, and the bright rays made the tents sparkle brilliantly. Maggie walked closer to the tents, pressing away the terrible feeling she wasn't meant to be there.

A bright, white tent, laden with diamonds, stood at the very center of the street. It was taller than a two-story house and wider than a barn. The flaps at the front had been tied open, letting in the evening breeze.

Someone moved inside, their shadow gliding past the opening. Maggie stepped forward, reaching her hand out toward the tent. Inside, she would find peace. A place to rest, comfortable, and safe.

The shadow stopped when Maggie's hand was inches from the gap in front of her. The shadow waited unmoving, willing Maggie forward.

"No!" Maggie shouted. The heads of the passersby turned toward her as she ran back up the street, searching for the path that had brought her to the street of jewels.

The price of peace was too high. How much magic would the shadow want from her?

All of it.

Maggie ran faster, pushing back the tears that threatened to spill over. It would be dark soon. She needed to find the blue tent with the bed and the food.

Perhaps the endless darkness had been better.

"Watch it!" a voice shouted an instant before Maggie screamed and fell to the ground.

She had run smack into an old man pushing a wooden cart. The man smelled like sweat and seaweed. The cart smelled like roasted meat.

"I'm sorry," Maggie said as she pushed herself off the ground. Her wrists ached, and her skinned palms stung.

"You better watch where yer runnin'," the man grumbled, checking his cart for signs of damage. "I'm a nice feller, but not all around here would be so kind about bein' run over. What if you had trampled a dwarf?"

"Sorry," Maggie said again. "I'm just..."

"Lost?" the man said. "Jumped into the Siren's Realm and now you don't know what to do?"

"Apparently I fell in accidentally." Maggie's heart suddenly felt hollow. She had fallen away from the battle where everyone left in the world she cared about could have been killed. And now she was worried about running into the guy with the meat cart.

"You did?" the man said, suddenly seeming much more interested in Maggie. He examined her for a moment, looking from her skinned and bloody palms to her old boots. "Somethin' terrible was happening and then all of a sudden you end up in the dark, eh?"

Maggie nodded.

"And yer not magic at all?"

Maggie shook her head, clinging to the lie though she didn't know why.

"Poor thing. I remember fallin' into this place. I was in a shipwreck, you see. It was awful confusin'. I mean to say, me endin' up here with a bunch of wizards and talking damn half-horses?" The man laughed. "You'll be all right, girl. Find yerself an honest trade, and they'll pay you for it with magic. You can't use it fer spells, but neither can they. Then you'll have a bit of that energy folk here trade like gold, and you'll be able to survive just fine."

"Just find a trade?"

"Aye," the man said. "At least it doesn't get cold here. The storms may be fierce, but they only come up once in a while." He paused, apparently waiting for

Maggie to speak, but she couldn't think of anything to say. "I'm Gabriel." He held out a hand.

Maggie took it, feeling his rough callouses on her skinned palm. "Maggie."

"You got a place to rest for the night?" Gabriel asked. "Some folk round here do some strange things come dark. Wouldn't be right for a girl to be out alone."

"I was in a tent, but I got lost," Maggie said, feeling like a child alone in a shopping mall.

"The Siren has a way of givin' what's needed to point you in the right direction. Try and find yer tent, and you should get there." Gabriel smiled kindly, showing a few missing teeth. "And if you need help, look for me. There aren't many of us folk with no natural magic find our way to the Siren's Realm, and we've got to stick together, those of us that do."

"Thank you, Gabriel."

Gabriel nodded, pushed his cart away, and was soon swallowed by the crowd.

Maggie stood still. Part of her wanted to call after Gabriel and admit that she'd lied, that she was a witch. But what did it matter? There was no part of her that was a witch anymore. No tiny shred of her being that wanted anything to do with magic. Maybe the witch part of her had died in the battle even if she hadn't. She wished Gabriel were still with her, if for no other reason than to have a person to talk to.

Standing in the middle of the street, Maggie closed her eyes, letting the crowd move around her, picturing the blue tent with the tiny cot and the loaf of bread. A place to sleep safely for the night. She waited for a flash of insight or a map to appear in her hands, but nothing happened.

Sighing, Maggie began walking down the street.

My tent. My tent. All I want is to find my tent. My tent.

She repeated the words in her head as she moved down tight alleys of dingy, worn tents and broad streets lined with stalls displaying shining wares.

My tent. My tent.

The sun had dipped low when she came to the fountain square.

Bertrand Wayland stood in the fountain, shirtless and surrounded by giggling women.

Maggie ducked, walking faster to avoid Bertrand's notice. She didn't need pity or patronizing worry. What she needed was her tent.

My tent. My tent!

The stale smell of troll greeted her as she turned onto a street with a ruby red tent whose tables were filled with people drinking and singing along as a centaur played a strange song on a violin.

And at the end of the street was a blue tent. Small and dark in the night.

Maggie ran forward and leapt through the tent flap, grateful to be alone in the darkness.

4

The sea was bright that morning. It had been every morning since Maggie had arrived in the Siren's Realm. The bright sun rose, sparkling on the water, and the breeze carried in fresh, salty air.

Maggie sat in the opening of her tent, her legs spread out on the rock in front of her. Sea birds stared at her as she ate her breakfast. "Get your own bread," she grumbled. But really she was glad for the birds' company. They woke her every morning with their cawing. It was the closest thing to a *good morning* she got.

"Fine." Maggie tossed the last few crumbs to them, smiling as they cawed appreciatively. They probably hadn't meant to end up in the Siren's Realm either. But there they were, at the edge of the Endless Sea, surviving.

She tucked her food for lunch safely away in the tent, tying the flap shut against the birds and breezes. Hers was the only tent on the rock outcropping that jutted out over the sea. She had carried it there herself after that first awful night. Moved everything but the bathtub. She may only have a cot, table and chair, but it was hers. The rock where she lived was hers, and the sea would give her what she needed to survive.

Hoisting her net onto her shoulder, Maggie scrambled barefoot down the ledge, landing in the water with a splash. The sea was cool and wonderful. Maggie smiled as the waves lapped at her waist.

Catch the fish, bring them to the market square for trade, buy what she needed, and come home. It was simple enough. The magic she would be given for the fish was enough for her to survive on. Not since that first night had she touched the stores that lived deep within her. The magic she traded didn't penetrate her as her own did. It floated on the surface. Feeling like a glove as merchants added to it or took away from it with a handshake.

It was barely noon when Maggie dragged her net of fish to the market square. People milled about, buying silk gowns dripping with jewels or perfumes that smelled like faraway lands Maggie had never seen. No one noticed the girl with the fish as she passed by.

There was something in the air that morning. A tone to the chatter that sounded different than Maggie was used to. But gossip had nothing to do with the fish in her net, so she kept moving, only catching bits of conversation as she passed.

"Hoarding," a woman wearing a brilliantly green silk dress spat. "Don't they understand the trade of a finite supply?"

A young-looking man who had the countenance of someone much older stood close to a centaur, muttering, "It's happening again. I can feel it coming on the wind."

Maggie took a deep breath, smelling only fish and perfume on the breeze.

"Find more for me, girl?" Mathilda bustled to the front of her stall. She, like many of the occupants of the Siren's Realm, wore clothes that made her appear to have fallen out of time. Mathilda wore a long, heavy skirt, billowing blouse, and mob cap. "Fish!" Mathilda shouted in Maggie's ear. "Did you bring fish?"

"Yep." Maggie lowered the net onto the ground, letting Mathilda examine her catch.

"You always bring a good catch." Mathilda weighed the fish in her hands. "It's nice to see a new one taking to work so quickly. You know, when I first got here, I lived a life of pleasure. Swimming in the fountains, running about in a scandalous way.

"Ah if the people back home could have seen it! Then one morning I decided not to get out of bed. Didn't seem worth it if all I was going to do was lie around all day anyway. That's when I decided to take up a trade again. Gives the fun meaning if you've worked hard for it."

Mathilda hoisted the net and led Maggie behind the counter to the preparing table. "You'd be amazed what people turn to when they run out of magic. Good to see a pretty thing like you working hard, rather than..." Mathilda gave a disapproving *tsk* as she lopped off the head of a fish.

Maggie nodded silently.

Mathilda decapitated another fish before looking at Maggie. "But then I suppose someone with no natural magic was always going to have to work for the Siren in order to survive. You should be glad she lets fish into her sea."

"There's a whale, too," Maggie said. "I've seen him offshore. I think he might be alone though."

"A whale?" Mathilda asked, one eyebrow climbing high on her forehead. "Wonder how he slipped in through one of the stitches? Funny, the Siren wanting a whale, but perhaps someone missed seeing them in the distance. What a desire to have!"

Maggie rocked on her toes, her most pressing desire to be paid and on her way.

"A whale, I ask you," Mathilda said again before looking back at Maggie. "Time for paying, is it?"

"Please, ma'am."

"When you've been here long enough, you won't be in such a hurry," Mathilda said. "Here we have endless days of sun. You'll never find sickness or hunger. The Siren has given us a land of pleasure. It's a pity to go wasting it by trying so hard to rush through it all." Mathilda reached out and shook Maggie's hand with her own fish-covered one.

Maggie was practiced enough by now she didn't flinch at either the slime coating Mathilda's palm or the tingle that flew in through her hand and up her arm, leaving her skin buzzing.

"Thank you, ma'am," Maggie said politely, turning toward the street.

"See you tomorrow, girl?" Mathilda asked.

"If there are fish in the Endless Sea!" Maggie called back as she walked down the street.

She was used to the streets of the Siren's Realm by now, at least the ones she traveled every day. The streets that led her to the market from the rocks by the sea where she had made her home. Then through the square with the fountain to see Gabriel. There were other familiar faces along the way, too.

Illial, the speckled gray centaur, was in his usual spot on the outskirts of the square, puffing his pipe, his head surrounded by a haze of blue smoke.

"Maggie." The centaur nodded as she passed by. "Does the Endless Sea sparkle this morning?"

"It does every morning." Maggie shook her head, laughing. "You should come and see for yourself. Some fresh air would do you a bit of good."

"When the sights of the square no longer hold my fancy, I will try the sea as a thing to watch."

"Perhaps tomorrow then?" Maggie waved as she moved on, knowing full well that Illial wouldn't be coming to the rocks by the sea the next morning, just as he hadn't for the last few months. At least she thought it was months. By the time Maggie had wanted to keep track, she couldn't be sure how long she had been there anymore. Seventy-two notches marked the pole in her tent. Seventy-two sunrises she could count.

The smell greeted Maggie before Rushna came into view, sitting outside a tent, eating as usual. The female troll wore her usual tablecloth-sized loincloth. A beautiful man who was almost as tall as Rushna sat beside her, gazing lovingly at the troll as she ate.

"Morning, Rushna," Maggie called as she passed.

Rushna nodded but didn't look away from the beautiful man. Maggie walked a little faster, not trusting herself to hide her giggle. There was something to fit every desire in the Siren's Realm.

Maggie turned a corner and cut down a side alley, avoiding the green tent where the minotaur stood guard, then up another lane.

"Fresh roasted meat!" Gabriel's voice carried down the street.

A small crowd had gathered around Gabriel, ready to trade magic for a hot meal.

Watching the people in line ready to give their magic away made Maggie queasier than the stench of fish that incessantly clung to her.

Finally, she was the only one left standing in line.

"Busy today," Gabriel said when he looked up to find her his sole remaining customer.

"Lots of trade."

"You hungry, too?" Gabriel asked, giving her a hard look. "If we were outside the Siren's Realm, I would worry about you starvin' to death or freezin' come winter."

"Then I guess I'm lucky winter never comes." Maggie grinned, holding out her hand. The instant Gabriel took it, a dull sting ached on her palm. The feeling was there for only a moment. As soon as their hands parted, the stinging disappeared. Maybe that's why people were willing to part with their magic so easily. It only hurt for a second.

Gabriel handed Maggie a big leg of fowl before biting into one himself.

"Are you still all right, livin' down there on them rocks?" Gabriel's weathered forehead wrinkled with concern. "I don't know if I like the idea of a young thing like you livin' so far from the others like us."

"I'm fine there. I like the quiet."

"But the others like us," Gabriel said, "we all live together, and we keep each other safe."

"I am safe. It's the Siren's Realm."

"I know, I know." Gabriel shook his head, and Maggie waited patiently for him to continue.

She knew what he was going to say. He had been saying the exact same thing for months. But deep down, Maggie liked Gabriel's dire warnings. Just the same as she liked Illial's blue smoke, Rushna's smell, and Mathilda's chatter. She knew them, and they knew her. If she didn't show up one morning, they would notice. Gabriel might actually miss her. It was a strange sense of belonging, but it was the best she had.

"And when the magic folk get jealous of us earnin' a livin', that's when the trouble will start again," Gabriel was saying in a guarded voice.

Maggie nodded. She had missed the first part of the speech but knew it well enough to know when to nod.

"Then the Siren will get angry, and it'll be a bad day for all of us."

"But why?" Maggie asked, knowing what the answer would be, but willing to let Gabriel enjoy his speech.

"Because when magic folk come to the Siren's Realm, they have only what magic they bring in with them. When it's out, they're done. Nothin' to give to the Siren and nothin' to trade with the lot of us."

"Like a battery that can't recharge."

"Yeah, like a battering." Gabriel nodded solemnly, and Maggie hid her smile. "And when enough of 'em run out, they'll come after us that have worked hard to earn our way, us that didn't never ask to come here." Gabriel's gaze drifted up and down the street before he whispered, "And that times a comin', and it's a comin' soon."

"What?" Maggie said, almost dropping her meat. This was a part of Gabriel's dire warnings she hadn't heard before. "What do you mean?"

"I've seen three in the last few days," Gabriel whispered. "Ragged folks in clothes what looked like they should have been nice before. Hungry look in their eyes just wanderin' around."

"But only three," Maggie said. "That's not very many compared to how many people live here. I mean, how many of us are there anyway?"

"Three is more than there should be," Gabriel said. "The Siren, she hides people who can't give no more. Lets 'em survive out of the way. But she won't trap 'em. She isn't cruel. If a few have decided to come out, more will follow. And it'll be folk like us they'll come for first. Seen it twice before in my time, and it's ripe to happen again." Gabriel took Maggie's hand in his.

"I just don't want to see you hurt, girl. Storm's a comin'. I spent my days on a ship before I ended up here. You might not be able to scent it yet, but I'm tellin' you, girl, one of the Siren's storms is fixin' to blow us all away."

Something in the way Gabriel spoke sent a chill down Maggie's spine. "It'll all be fine. And if things get bad, we just keep our heads down, right?"

"I've got a feelin' you don't know how to keep yer head down, girlie." Gabriel laughed, but the usual glimmer didn't appear in his eyes. "You slipped into the Siren's Realm during a battle. But this is a fight none but the Siren can win."

"It all seems like false advertising," Maggie said, pausing to think while she finished her last bit of meat. "Because if this really were a paradise of joy and pleasure, there would be nothing to worry about. Not ever."

"It's not paradise," Gabriel whispered, leaning in close to Maggie's ear. "It's the Siren's Realm, and she'll do with it what she pleases. And no one knows what the Siren will choose to bring with a storm." Gabriel scanned the street. "Go on, girl. Best to get back to your tent before the sun is down. The Siren's will will be done."

There were still hours until sunset, but something in the way Gabriel spoke made Maggie want to be back in her blue tent on the rocks.

"See you tomorrow," Maggie called as she hurried down the street.

"If the Siren wills it."

Cold settled into Maggie's chest at his words. She spun to look at Gabriel, but he had already disappeared.

5

Her net clutched tightly in her hand, Maggie made her way through the winding streets of tents. She had meant to stop and buy bread before making her way back to the rocks, but Gabriel's words had frightened her. Now the late afternoon sun seemed tainted by something darker than the approaching night. Whispers on the street sounded more urgent than the usual intrigue and gossip that flowed from the open tents.

"Wine for sale," a man in a crimson robe called as he made his way down the lane.

"I'd better not," the man closest to Maggie said to his companion, "best to be cautious at the moment."

Only a few people had moved toward the man with the wine. The rest stayed warily away.

Maggie took off at a run. If they were going after humans, they would come after her. *You were born a witch, you stupid girl!* the voice in Maggie's head shouted. But it didn't matter. She had told everyone she had no magic of her own. And it was a lie she wasn't willing to break.

She rounded the corner to the last short alley she would need to take to reach the shore. Standing right in the center of the narrow road was Bertrand Wayland, his long hair pulled back in a slick ponytail, his shoes shined, and his clothes perfect. He walked calmly down the road alone.

Maggie had often seen him on the streets and always ducked away before he could catch sight of her. It was easy when he was surrounded by his usual gaggle of beautiful women. But he was utterly alone today, not even speaking to the people he passed.

Maggie froze for a moment, her desire to get home warring with the urge to put as much distance between herself and Bertrand Wayland as possible.

She made the decision to hide in the shadows and wait for him to pass a moment too late.

"Miss Trent." Bertrand bowed and walked quickly toward her. "What a pleasure to see you again." There was an urgency in his tone not reflected in his smiling face. "I was actually hoping to run into you this afternoon. I was—"

Maggie turned on the spot and ran, cursing herself as her fishing net slipped from her fingers but not daring to pause to retrieve it.

"Miss Trent," Bertrand shouted after her, "I only wish to speak to you for a moment!"

She had spent every day in the Siren's Realm avoiding Bertrand Wayland. She wouldn't speak to him now. If trouble was coming, the last thing she needed was someone questioning how she had fallen out of a wizard's battle without being a witch.

Maggie turned onto a street she had never seen before, then down a wide lane with flowerbeds on either side. The packed dirt path narrowed so she couldn't avoid stepping on flowers that had left no room for her feet.

Tall tents lined the flowered lane, and centaurs milled about. Maggie glanced over her shoulder. There was no sign of Bertrand, only an elderly centaur who seemed angry at Maggie for crushing the flowers. Still, Maggie kept running, and running. Soon, the tents grew even taller, and the street became wide and hard. The tents changed from bright colors to gray, and then the gray canvas turned to stone.

Great houses with iron bars crisscrossing their windows lined the cobblestone walk. Maggie screamed as she tipped forward, pitching toward the canal that ran between the homes. Gasping, Maggie staggered back, leaning on the cool stone of a building as her head spun and her lungs stung.

The streets were empty though light shone through a few of the windows. Faint music floated down a nearby street. A violin playing a slow song. The first few notes were beautiful and calm. Like lovers would be riding the soft current of the canal in a graceful boat, listening to the peaceful music. But the more Maggie listened, the more wrong she knew she was.

The song wasn't about love. It was about fear. Quiet, penetrating, inescapable fear.

A shadow passed by a window across the canal, and Maggie clapped a hand over her mouth to keep herself from screaming. This wasn't the part of the

Siren's Realm she belonged in. She belonged on the sunny rocks with her tiny tent. The people here, who protected themselves with stone and iron, couldn't possibly want someone with no magic of her own hiding in the shadows of their streets.

The violin music played faster now, making Maggie's heart race more quickly than the running had.

Bertrand Wayland or not, she needed to get home. Back out to the tent on the rocks where she could wait out whatever storm was coming.

"Make it through the night, Maggie." She dug hers nails into her palms as she turned back the way she had come. "Get home and make it through the night. You've made it through worse, so just do it, you silly girl."

Not allowing herself to run, Maggie headed back up the street. The glimmers of light from the windows were disappearing quickly, as though those hiding within the thick stone walls didn't want to give any sign they were there.

"Get to the tent." Maggie pushed away the dread in her chest shouting that if the people in the stone houses were afraid, her canvas tent would be anything but safe.

The gray tents had come into view when she heard the first scream.

"Please, someone! Help me!"

Instinct told Maggie to hide in the shadows, but she ran toward the anguished cry.

"No! No!" the voice called desperately.

Maggie tore down the row of gray tents and turned toward the sound, freezing as the terrible sight came into view.

Four ragged, pale people stood over a man who lay shaking on the ground.

"Please don't." The man screamed as one of the four—a woman with matted hair hanging to her waist—reached down and seized the sides of the man's face.

A pale, silver light glowed under the woman's palms as the man screamed again.

His magic. She was stealing his magic.

"Stop!" Maggie shouted.

The woman's head snapped up to look at Maggie. The magic thief's face had regained its color, and her black hair was no longer matted but shining and sleek.

"Leave him alone." Maggie forced the words past the knot in her throat.

The other three turned their attention to Maggie.

"Please," the man on the ground groaned. "I have to be able to give. Leave me something to give."

The biggest of the ragged group kicked the man hard in the stomach.

"Stop it!" Maggie shouted over the man's scream of pain. "What has he done to you? Why would you hurt him?"

"Not hurt," one of the ragged people said, taking a step toward Maggie. The man was short and missing patches of hair. "We're taking what he shouldn't have in the first place. It only hurts because he doesn't want to give it up."

"Give what up?" Maggie asked, her gaze darting between the four as they crept toward her.

"Magic," the short man said, his tone so loving it made Maggie's skin crawl. "He's been hoarding it. There's only so much to be had, and if some keep it all, the rest of us have nothing to give."

"But you can't just take it." Maggie took a step backward as the man smiled at her.

The four laughed together.

"We can," the woman said, "and it doesn't hurt us at all. No, it feels so good. Let me show you, pretty girl."

The woman launched herself forward, arms outstretched, her nails scraping Maggie's face as she leapt backward and ran.

A screaming cackle followed Maggie as she sprinted back down the row of tents.

"Stop her!" one of the ragged men shouted, and four sets of pounding feet followed Maggie.

Maybe he'll get away. Maybe that poor man will be gone by the time they're done with me.

Maggie raced past the row of gray tents and down another avenue she had never seen. Bright white tents dotted with rainbow colors sat in a long line. She had no idea where she was going. But the screams of the black-haired woman followed her, so she kept running.

Night was coming fast. Soon it would be dark, and she could find a place to hide. Her lungs ached, pain shot up her legs, but she kept running.

The white tents turned back to gray. Whether from the fading light or actual color, Maggie didn't know. The lane twisted, and Maggie's feet hit hard stone, sending her tumbling forward. Pain shot through her hands and head where they struck the cobblestone street.

"Just give us a taste, and we'll let you go!" one of the men shouted.

Maggie leapt to her feet, sprinting between the stone buildings, desperate to find a place to hide. How could people so sickly-looking run so fast? But the doors were locked and barred. If she had been able to use magic, she could have thrown open one of the doors in an instant.

Maggie rounded a tight corner, careful not to tip into the canal that reflected the stars up above. The gaps between the stars caught Maggie's eye as she kept running. Clouds covered the night sky. The storm had arrived.

"A place to hide," Maggie muttered. "I want a place to hide."

A hand shot out of the darkness and closed around her arm, dragging her into the shadows.

6

A hand covered Maggie's mouth before she could scream.

"Do not make a sound, or they will find you, Miss Trent," a voice whispered urgently in Maggie's ear. "I don't fancy fighting four Derelict when the Siren has chosen to bring a storm upon us."

"Mmmhmmnaa," Maggie tried to speak against the hand.

"I will release you, Miss Trent, but I do insist you remain quiet."

Maggie nodded as much as the stranger's grip would allow, turning to see who had grabbed her the moment she was free.

Bertrand Wayland held a finger to his lips.

Maggie swallowed the urge to scream or punch him.

"Why the hell did you grab me like that?" Maggie hissed.

Footsteps and shouts sounded from the corner not ten feet away. This time Maggie didn't fight as Bertrand pulled her farther into the shadows.

"Come out, come out, little one!" the short man called, flecks of spit flying from his mouth. "It won't hurt for more than a minute. And when it's done, it's done."

"We want what's ours!" the woman screamed.

They were coming closer. Shadows or not, they would see her and Bertrand hiding. Maggie took a breath, getting ready to step out into the open to fight.

Bertrand took her hand and pulled her farther back than it seemed the shadows could go.

"Move quickly," he whispered.

Several things happened at once. A *whine* of old metal hinges came from behind Bertrand, a patch of light appeared, the woman screamed, "We've got her!" and a bolt of lightning burst through the sky as thunder shook the building.

Before Maggie had time to decide which thing was the most threatening, she had been yanked off her feet and landed on her back in a dimly lit room. A *slam* shook the floor as another *clap* of thunder rumbled outside.

Maggie lay on the floor, gasping. The sound of a heavy lock being turned made her look toward the door. Thick and wooden with bars across, it looked like the doors at street level. Someone pounded on the door to come in. Maggie scrambled to her feet.

"They won't get through the door," Bertrand said calmly. "I'm quite sure of it. Two of the best things about living on the stone streets—doors that lock and much more privacy." He leaned back against the stone wall.

They weren't trapped in a tomb as Maggie had feared. It was more like a narrow entryway with a much less battle-worthy wooden door at the far end.

"The people here don't tend to be nearly as neighborly," Bertrand said. "There isn't the sense of blissful freedom as in the Textile Town, but it is worth it when the Derelict come."

"Derelict?"

"The ones with no magic left. They've used all they have, and when the drabness of nothing becomes too much, they steal from those who have something left to give." Bertrand moved toward the other wooden door. "It really is a pity to see. I've been here for quite some time, however, and it happens again and again. Would you like to come in, Miss Trent?" Bertrand gestured to the door. "The storm is arriving, and I think it will be quite some time before you will safely be able to travel home."

"I can wait here," Maggie said.

"I would prefer you didn't." Bertrand opened the door, and warm light poured into the entryway. The smell of fresh baked bread and herbs filled the air. "If you were to wait in the dark hall, I would feel obligated, as your host, to wait with you. And since the storm is here, I would much prefer to wait by the fire."

As though to emphasize his words, more thunder shook the stone walls.

"Fine." Maggie moved toward the door. "Thank you," she added grudgingly as she went through the door and up five stairs to enter the main house.

It was unlike any other house Maggie had ever seen. The walls were made of stone, giving the whole place the look of a fortress. The windows were set chest high to be above the eye level of anyone on the street. Rain pounded against the glass, nearly obscuring the thick metal bars on the outside of the windows.

With the sound of another lock scraping shut, Bertrand followed her up the stairs.

"This way please." He turned the corner, and Maggie followed, examining the worn, wooden floor as she went.

The wood was grooved with the wear of uncountable footsteps. How old was this house? Or had Bertrand merely wanted worn floors?

Bertrand stopped in a room that looked like a fancy living room from an old movie. A bookshelf stood against one wall away from the barred windows. A fireplace was nestled in the corner, and after a glance from Bertrand, a fire sprang to life.

Maggie flinched. How much magic had it cost him to start the fire? Would it have been less or more to just ask the Siren for matches?

A large painting of a glade in the woods hung above the crackling fire. White trees surrounded a patch of sunlit grass.

"Please do sit." Bertrand nodded to the large red sofa in front of the fire before moving to a tray in the corner.

Maggie sat, watching him work at the tray. Less than a minute later he pressed a cup of steaming tea into her hand. The scent of lavender made Maggie's shoulders relax before she even knew what was happening.

"It is excellent tea." Bertrand nodded. "There's a lovely woman on the market lane—"

"I don't want tea." Maggie set the cup down on the table beside her. "I'm just going to wait here for the storm to pass, and then I'll go home."

"To the tent on the rocks?" Bertrand asked. "Do you really think your tent will still be there after the storm, Miss Trent?"

"How do you know where I live?" Maggie glanced down at the talisman on her wrist out of habit. But she wouldn't be able to defend herself with magic here. Why had she let him lock her in?

"I've been keeping an eye on you," Bertrand said, apparently not having noticed Maggie searching for an escape. "It seemed to be the kind thing to do after your unexpected arrival. It's not often that we have someone fall into the Siren's Realm by chance. And I think in your case it might not be chance at all."

"I—what?" Maggie asked, Bertrand's words distracting her from planning her escape.

"I simply mean, Miss Trent—and I do hope you'll forgive me for being so forward—for a girl who is clearly a witch to fall into the Siren's Realm and pretend to have no natural magic? That's not a thing one forgets quickly."

"I'm not a witch." Maggie's mouth had gone completely dry. "I'm human."

"Miss Trent, even if you weren't wearing a Clan symbol on your wrist—"

Maggie clapped a hand over her bracelet.

"—I knew the first time I shook your hand you were a witch. And a strong one at that," Bertrand finished.

"How did you know my Clan's crest?" Maggie asked, giving up on the lie.

"I came from your world, Miss Trent." Bertrand smiled gently. "Unlike your friend Gabriel, whose world is far from ours, we may have walked the same streets centuries apart. Still, the Clans of my time are the Clans of your time as well."

"Why didn't you say something?"

"If you were determined to lie about being a witch, I assumed it must be for a good reason." Bertrand sipped his tea. "Though, of course, with a lie as dangerous as that, it was clearly my duty to make sure you remained safe."

"Why is saying I'm human dangerous?" Maggie ran her hands through her hair, wondering if it would be worse to be out in the pouring rain than stuck in a warm sitting room with Bertrand Wayland.

"I would have thought you had reasoned that answer out by now, Miss Trent. In a realm where magic is all important—"

"But you can't even do spells here! If I could—"

"Then I am sure those Derelict would never have been able to chase you. But it isn't the spells that are important in the Siren's Realm." Bertrand stood and began to pace the path of a particularly deep groove in the floor. "Some places, they trade gold, or livestock, even bits of paper. Here, we trade magic. Magic is our currency. Ask the Siren for something, she will take a bit—buy something on the street, the vendor will take a bit.

"Everyone takes until there is nothing left to give. Once a person is Derelict, the Siren in her mercy moves them to the shadows where they can exist without needing anything. But nothingness is boring, and once in a great while they find their way back up onto our streets. Then the fighting begins, and the storm blows. The Siren will rinse her realm of anything that does not fit into the order she has created."

"Wait," Maggie said, leaning forward, "so the people out there, the Derelict, is the Siren going to just blow them away?"

"I would be terribly surprised if they were still in the Siren's Realm come morning."

"Where is she going to send them?" Maggie pictured the terrible blackness that had greeted her in the Siren's Realm. Would that be the fate of the Derelict? Did they really deserve something better?

"One problem at a time, Miss Trent." Bertrand held up a hand. "There is nothing more offensive to a Derelict than someone with no natural magic who manages to survive in the light of the Siren's Realm. Those who have worked hard to earn magic for trade are considered usurpers. Those who came in with magic but have managed to gain more than their original share are hoarders. The Derelict will seek to take it all. And a young girl who seems to have usurped so much so quickly would of course be a target for theft."

"But if I had told them I came in with magic, that I'm a witch," she choked on the word, "they would have left me alone?"

"That is a story many human-born have tried to tell." Bertrand sat on the opposite end of the couch. "So, no, I don't believe it would have saved you."

"Do you do this a lot? Stalk people just in case crazies come up from the shadows and try to steal their magic?"

"No. You are a special circumstance. Generally, I try not to bother with what others are going about. My life is enough of an adventure that others' business is rather mundane."

"But I'm not?" Maggie asked, trying to decide if she should feel offended or not.

"On the surface you most definitely are." Bertrand examined her. "But there is something more to you than a girl with a fishing net. You come from my world, a world I fought desperately to leave long ago when the fate of magic seemed bleak beyond all redemption. Yet Magickind continues. You were born and lived a life grand enough for the Siren to rip you from the grips of a battle and drag you into her realm."

"I wasn't ripped. I fell." Maggie ground her teeth, her desire to be inconsequential warring with the need for abandoning her friends to mean something.

"Are the two so very different? No, Miss Trent, I cannot allow the Derelict to get you before I discover what your fate here is."

"Thanks."

"If you wish to thank me, please drink your tea." Bertrand pointed to her abandoned cup. "The storm has yet to begin, and it would be a pity to waste such a fine cup of tea."

Maggie picked up the cup and took a sip of the hot liquid. The vague sweetness and earthy brightness made her breathe a little easier. "Thanks," she muttered, watching the rain lash against the window as the wind began to howl.

7

Her cup was empty, but Maggie still clutched it in her hands. It wasn't even warming her fingers anymore, but she was afraid if she let go, her hands might tremble, and then Bertrand would know the storm was scaring her. The winds had picked up over the last hour, blowing the pounding rain down in horizontal sheets.

Underneath the wind's howling, the rain striking the window, and the thunder crashing, was another noise. A steady thumping that grew louder with the wind's increasing strength. Maggie took a breath, willing her heart to slow. It wasn't until her sixth deep breath that she realized the sound wasn't her heart.

"What's that noise?" Maggie turned to Bertrand, who had moved to an armchair by the fire, sipping his tea and watching the rain disinterestedly.

"Hmm." He sat up straight and set his tea on the table. "By *noise* you could mean the rain, thunder, or wind, or even my sipping my tea, though I do pride myself on excellent table manners. But judging from your frightened tone—"

"I'm not frightened."

"—I must conclude you're speaking of the waves in the canal pounding at the rocks that hold this house above water." Bertrand regarded Maggie for a moment. "And I hope you don't believe I was implying your fear was out of place. On the contrary, there are many times when fear is a very reasonable reaction. The Siren's storms would definitely qualify as one of those situations."

"Should we be sitting here drinking tea?" Maggie asked, ignoring Bertrand's condescending tone. "If the rocks under this house are being battered by the

628 | MEGAN O'RUSSELL

storm, shouldn't we go to solid ground?" Maggie set her cup on the table harder than she had meant to and stood.

Surely the Derelict had gone. She could get back to...to where? Bertrand had been right—her tent wouldn't be safe in this storm.

"The Siren's will will be done," Bertrand sighed. "If she wanted to be rid of you, she would be. If she wanted to be rid of your tent on the rocks and you happened to be in it, you would be gone with the tent. We are but fleas to the Siren, tiny beings that inhabit her realm."

"So if she wants to be done with this house, then we drown?" Maggie tore her hands through her hair. "I've tried to get used to surviving here—I swear I have—but this is too much. Calling up a storm and getting rid of anything she doesn't like?"

"Miss Trent, I don't think you have ever tried to get used to surviving here. Hiding on the rocks and pretending you have no magic. I'm not casting blame"—he held up a hand, silencing Maggie's protest—"I don't know how often a witch has slipped into the Siren's Realm without wanting to be here, and to be pulled from a battle, leaving your friends to fight without you—"

"Leave that out of this."

"You knew nothing of the Siren when you arrived," Bertrand said. "I chose this path, and I have still found it to be trying. The sacrifices we make to live in the beautiful Siren's Realm are much like the sacrifices made to live anywhere. It is only much easier to see the rules here, and seeing makes accepting so much more difficult."

"So we're just supposed to sit here and hope the Siren doesn't blow us away?" Maggie said, hating the panic that surged through her chest.

"Miss Trent, please." Bertrand took her hand, and Maggie didn't have the will to be bothered to pull it away. "I would not have rescued you from the Derelict only to bring you somewhere unsafe. I have lived through five of the Siren's storms. During the first I was out in the Textile Town—"

"Where?"

"The tents." Bertrand gave a dull laugh. "You really should learn more about your new home. Merely surviving isn't what you are meant for. The Siren's storms are terrible in the Textile Town. After that first dreadful storm, I made the choice to move to the Fortress. These stone walls were standing long before I arrived in the Siren's Realm, and I can assure you they will last through the night."

"Unless the Siren decides to kill us."

"If you wish to speak crudely, then yes."

Maggie watched the storm outside the window. Gabriel would be in his tent. If the Derelict hadn't gotten him...

Bile rose in Maggie's throat.

"Miss Trent," Bertrand said gently, "I know this must all be very disturbing to you. Come down to the kitchen. The noise of the storm won't be as frightening, and I have the feeling you could use a good meal."

"I don't want to eat."

"That's usually the time you need food the most." Bertrand bowed and gestured for her to exit the sitting room the way they had entered.

Maggie bowed back before walking into the hall, half-hoping Bertrand would get angry at her for mocking him, but if he noticed, he showed no sign.

They walked down the stone hall with the worn floor. A streak of lightning sliced through the sky, and Maggie jumped backward, covering her eyes against the bright flash of light, and bumped straight into Bertrand.

He caught her under the arms when she was halfway to the floor and set her easily back up on her feet. Maggie's face burned, and she knew it was red. She hated blushing. It was the curse of being pale.

"Careful, Miss Trent." Bertrand took the lead down the hall. "I pride myself on ensuring the safety of my guests."

He opened a door that led down steps like the ones they had come up from the entryway. But these steps went down farther. By the time they reached the kitchen, the sound of the rain was a dull hum, and the thick layers of rock had muted the thunder. The only hint at the ferocity of the storm was the slapping of the waves against the stone.

The kitchen was simple with no windows to be seen. A metal cauldron hung in a fireplace so large it took up a whole wall. Cabinets sat against the two walls beside it, and in the middle of the room was a scrubbed, wooden table. It looked almost homey.

Images of water pouring in through the rocks swam unbidden into Maggie's mind. She swayed for a moment before realizing Bertrand was staring at her.

"I'm fine," Maggie growled.

"You're not, but I would be more concerned if you were." Bertrand strode to a cupboard in the corner, chose a bowl, and placed it on the table. "I think a hot bowl of hearty soup will do you a world of good." In an instant, steaming, brown, beef stew filled the bowl.

"You could have made the stew," Maggie said, not sitting at the table. "It takes less magic to find the things to make soup than to wish it into being."

"You are a clever girl." Bertrand smiled as he sat at the table with his own bowl of bright orange soup. "It does cost more to ask the Siren's favor in giving you something than to seek what you wish for from the other occupants of her realm. But I assume the markets are closed at the moment. And I've always been a terrible cook besides."

"What about this house?" Maggie stepped toward the table. "How much magic did it take to get this place? How come you aren't living in the shadows with the Derelict?"

"There are ways to enjoy all the pleasures of the Siren's Realm without ending up in the darkness. And I have never stolen magic. I hope, Miss Trent, you would never believe that of me. Though I will admit I have had an unusual amount of good fortune in the Siren's Realm."

"Were you just a really strong wizard back home?" Maggie sat at the table, the smell of the soup and her curiosity overpowering her desire to reject anything Bertrand had to offer.

"I was," Bertrand said, "and remain a very strong and rather clever wizard."

"But you can't do magic here." Maggie took a bite of her stew. The taste made the fear that had clung to her chest melt away.

"No."

"And when you're out of magic, you're out," Maggie said.

"Did someone tell you that, or did you figure it out for yourself?" Bertrand tented his fingers under his chin, leaning across the table to examine Maggie.

"I felt it," Maggie said, "the first time I asked for anything here. I felt the magic go out. And then nothing replaced it."

"Then you are as clever as I hoped you would be."

"But you must be out of magic, then." Maggie looked down at her stew to avoid Bertrand's gaze. "All this? If you haven't stolen magic and aren't a secret silk trader, you can't have much left."

Bertrand was silent for a moment. Maggie looked up to find him staring at her as though trying to read a book in a language he didn't quite understand.

"There is a way to refill the cup of magic," Bertrand began slowly. "The Siren has her rules, and magic that comes here with her travelers is finite."

"But you said—"

"There is no rule against bringing in more magic from the outside."

"What? You like, put in a FedEx order for more magic?"

"I'm not sure what you mean by that." Bertrand shook his head. "But no. You cannot ask to have more magic brought in. You can, however, go and fetch it for yourself."

"You can leave?" Maggie dropped her spoon, not caring when her stew sloshed onto the table. "You can get out of the Siren's Realm?"

"I said as much when we first met, Miss Trent." Bertrand furrowed his brow. "I thought you had been listening."

"I was, but you said it took a lot of magic if the Siren was even willing to send you back home."

"I never said anything about fetching magic from home." He smiled sadly. "To get to one specific world would take the help of the Siren. But going home has never interested me. I have already lived in our world. There are, however, ways to slip through the stitches that join the Siren's Realm to the worlds that surround it."

"Worlds?"

"Miss Trent." Bertrand leaned across the table, staring directly into Maggie's eyes. "There is much more to this pale existence than merely surviving. I have always been one for adventure, and the Siren has provided that to me in abundance."

"But you leave?" Maggie gripped the edge of the table so hard her fingers hurt.

"I do, Miss Trent, but the cost can be terribly high. I saved you from the Derelict and the Siren's storm. It is my hope you will learn to do more than survive here in the Siren's Realm. You are far too interesting to be condemned to the shadows."

His eyes searched Maggie's as though he were seeing into her very soul. Examining every fear that had plagued her since she was trapped in the endless darkness. Or maybe even before. Since the battle. Since birth.

"You are not meant for that kind of danger," Bertrand whispered. "Not all of us can be."

"Wait, what?" Maggie asked, but Bertrand had already stood up and strode to the door.

"You should finish your stew before it gets too cold, Miss Trent. I would offer you the guest room upstairs, but I do feel you would be happier down here away from the storm. I shall see you in the morning, Miss Trent. The sun will rise when the storm has passed."

Without another word, he turned and walked up the steps, leaving Maggie alone in the kitchen.

8

Maggie lay curled up on the floor by the kitchen fire. The floor was hard, but the heat of the fire had warmed the stones. And the crackling of the flames made the pounding of the waves seem less ominous. She closed her eyes, willing sleep to come. Surely it was almost morning. But that wasn't how it worked in the Siren's Realm. The sun would come up when the Siren wished for the storm to be over. It could be weeks.

Maggie pressed the heels of her hands into her eyes.

She wasn't meant for danger?

She gritted her teeth. She had been fighting in a battle when she fell into the damn Siren's Realm to begin with. She had been willing to die. But an adventure was too dangerous for her?

Okay, so maybe she had never been the type to seek out adventure. She had been too busy trying to survive her Clan, and then the Academy. She had probably fought more terrifying things than Bertrand Wayland ever had. Choosing to give up on his world to come live a life of pleasure.

"Quitter," Maggie mumbled. "He quit his whole world, and *I'm* not meant for adventure?"

But maybe that was it. She hadn't wanted to give up her world. She had been fighting to save it. And even here in the Siren's Realm, she didn't want to give up her own magic to pay for pleasure. She had spent her days fishing and living off of bread and meat.

But she was being frugal. Keeping what was hers instead of using it to buy fancy silk dresses and beautiful things.

She hadn't wanted to risk her own magic. Hadn't wanted to give up what she had.

Maybe that's what Bertrand had meant. She didn't want to sacrifice what she had for a chance at something different.

Maggie massaged her cheeks, willing her teeth to unclench.

There was nothing wrong with wanting to keep what you had.

But what if there was a chance at something better?

The circle kept going around in her head as the crashing of the waves grew slower and the dull pounding of the rain disappeared.

Maggie stared at the wooden boards of the ceiling, expecting the storm to start howling again or for Bertrand to come down the stairs.

Minutes slipped by. Part of her wanted Bertrand to come dashing into the kitchen to give her another lecture on what the Siren's Realm was really like. Or maybe explain why she wasn't meant for danger.

But the waves grew calmer still, and Bertrand didn't appear. It took Maggie a while to force herself to roll over and stand up. Fatigue weighed on her limbs, and dread of what she would find up the kitchen stairs didn't help her move any faster. Only the thought that if she left immediately she might avoid seeing Bertrand made her climb the steps. Bright sunlight poured in through the iron barred windows, casting the stone walls in a warm glow.

Tiptoeing across the wooden floor, Maggie crept toward the window, holding her breath as she looked outside.

Bertrand had been right. The stone buildings of the Fortress had made it through the storm. But the buildings looked newer now. Cleaner and brighter. The water in the canal shone a gentle blue in the crisp sunlight.

Glancing up and down the hall to make sure Bertrand was nowhere to be seen, Maggie ran as quickly as she dared for the stairs to the entryway, not realizing she might not be able to get through the door to the streets until her hand was already on the big iron handle. But with a tug, the door to the outside burst open, and Maggie darted out onto the walk, pausing only to shut the door before running down the street.

The canal looked beautiful enough to swim in. The windows behind the iron bars were no longer draped with curtains. The Siren's Realm was bright and new and ready for a glorious day.

Through the stone houses and out into the gray tents, she ran. The tents didn't seem any newer or brighter like the Fortress, but they were still there, unmoved by the storm.

The wide row of centaur tents came next. The flowers seemed to have grown in the night, nourished by the storm, while the weeds had drowned, leaving the gardens pristine.

But the centaurs outside their tents didn't seem to be enamored of the flowers.

"The winds of the Siren can be cruel," a speckled male centaur spoke to a dainty-looking female. It wasn't until Maggie was only ten feet away that she noticed the distress on the female's face.

Maggie slowed her run, trying to look like she wasn't listening as she passed.

"It is a part of the path laid by the Siren." The male's deep, resonating voice chased Maggie down the street. "She grants our wishes, but we live only by hers."

Maggie wanted to turn around and ask if one of the centaurs' camp had been washed away by the storm, but it seemed too cruel.

If they really had lost a friend, the last thing they would want was a stranger intruding.

If one of her friends had been lost...

Maggie's heart skipped a beat as fear surged through her.

Gabriel.

He had no magic of his own. What if the Derelict had gotten him, or the Siren had decided she didn't want him around anymore?

Maggie ran as fast as she could, her legs burning as she tore down the streets.

She passed unfamiliar tents and people. One row of tents was so short, those living in them wouldn't be able to stand up right. A long line of black and red tents sat across from a high grass mound.

Fear lodged itself in Maggie's throat. The prickle of tears in the corners of her eyes made her stop running. She would not cry on the streets of the Siren's Realm. Not because she was afraid or lost.

Not for anything.

Maggie took a deep breath. "I need to find my friends. To find out what I lost."

Her hands tingled as magic was pulled from her fingertips.

Closing her eyes, Maggie spun on the spot. After a few turns she stopped, swaying dizzily.

A tiny part of her hoped to hear Gabriel call from down the street, *"What are you doin'? Have you finally lost yer mind to the Siren?"*

But no one called her name. Maggie opened her eyes. Directly in front of her was a row of tents she hadn't noticed before. Low to the ground and sandy brown, they looked like they were meant to be camouflaged on the beach.

Without pausing, Maggie ran forward, searching every shadow for a sign of

Gabriel, Illial, Rushna, or Mathilda. She was so busy hunting for a familiar face, she didn't know she had reached the edge of the Endless Sea until she was standing on the sand.

Maggie sagged, her hands on her knees, gasping for air. Gabriel didn't live by the sea. He lived in a tent…somewhere. She had never seen it. He lived with others who had fallen into the Siren's Realm. He had asked her to come live with them where she could be safe. If only she had gone with him to see the place, then maybe she could have found it.

Cursing to herself, Maggie looked up and down the beach. There were a few people around, but no one she recognized. Off in the distance was the outcropping of rocks that hid her tent.

"Gabriel will be on the same street at the same time as always." Maggie started down the beach. "Follow the routine, and you'll find the people." Her words sounded much surer than she felt.

A middle-aged woman lay on the sand right before the stone began to take over, turning the beach into a rocky shore. Basking in the warm rays of the sun, she beamed at the bright blue sky.

"Good morning!" she called to Maggie as she passed.

"Morning," Maggie said, not halting her stride.

"And what a fine one it is," the woman cooed. "I haven't felt a morning like this in ages."

A shiver shot through Maggie's spine as she wondered if the woman hadn't felt the sun because she had been hiding in the shadows with the Derelict.

Maggie didn't look back as the woman called, "Enjoy the blessings of the Siren, little one."

The rocks were already warm from the sun. Maggie scrambled up them, using her arms to pull herself onto the high, flat level. The storm had washed away the usual layer of sand, leaving the stone smooth and clean. Maggie crouched, running her hand on the smooth rock. The Siren had cleaned all the filth away.

"No." Maggie squinted into the distance, searching for a sign of her tent. "No, no, no!" She ran full tilt across the rocks. She leapt over cracks, barely giving herself time to find her balance. Before she had even reached the edge of the high rock, she knew her tent was gone. The peak of the blue canvas should have peered up over the edge.

But maybe it had just been blown over. She could set the tent back up—she'd done it before.

She stopped, her toes right at the edge, and looked down at the place that had been her home. The rock was flat and shining with no trace a tent had ever been there.

Maggie covered her face with her hands, willing herself to breathe and not let panic take over.

"It'll be fine," Maggie whispered, not caring if the Siren heard her. "Everything will be fine. You've dealt with worse before."

Slowly, she opened her eyes, blinking at the bright sun.

The tent really was gone. Right along with her cot and table. There was no debris in the water, but why would the Siren have let that survive the storm?

It was gone. All of it.

Everything she owned had been washed away by the Siren's storm. All she had left were the clothes on her back. No net to catch fish, no bed to lie down on while she tried to figure out what was next.

Maggie climbed down to where her tent had been. At least the rock was there. She sat on the very edge, dangling her feet over the shallows.

She knew it was foolish, but the rock felt like her front porch. Her home.

A plume of water shot into the air a hundred yards out to sea.

"Mort!" Maggie called, laughing tiredly as the whale's back breached the surface. "You made it, buddy. I didn't know if the Siren was going to let you stay."

The whale said nothing, but lay lazily in the water.

"Are there still fish out there for you? Well, there will be more since I can't fish now." Maggie dug her nails into her palms. "I don't have a place to live anymore. I lost my net, so I can't earn enough to buy another tent."

Maggie paused, hearing the whales imagined response in her mind. *You're a witch, silly girl. And a good one at that. You've plenty of magic to ask the Siren for a new net and tent.*

"And let my tent be blown away next time a storm comes? If I had been here"—she shivered in the warm morning air at the thought—"I might have been washed away with the tent. No, I don't want to move into the *Textile Town*." She held a hand up to silence the whale's protest. "Who decided to call it the *Textile Town?*" She said the words again. Somehow the name felt right in her mouth, and she hated herself for it.

"I don't want to live crowded in with people," Maggie said. "I like it out here. I like the rocks and the sea. It's home. My home, and I want to stay!"

The whale rolled onto its back, showing his stomach to the sky.

"This is where we live, and we're going to stay here. I just have to find a way to earn enough magic to build a Fortress of my own."

Maggie sprang to her feet, newfound determination flooding through her. She knew what she wanted, and she was plenty strong enough to earn it.

"Thanks, Mort!" she shouted over her shoulder as she climbed the rocks toward the Textile Town. "Good talk!"

9

The market square was her first stop. She had walked quickly through the streets, partially due to her newfound determination, mostly because the streets didn't seem like a good place to linger. The tents were all there—the Siren's cleansing hadn't reached into the town itself—but there was a low rumble in all the conversations she passed. A sense of dread and grief.

"I've never seen it so bad," a beautiful young woman with flowing red hair said to the minotaur who guarded the vivid green tent. The line to get in was longer than usual. "I don't know if it's safe to be here."

Making a split-second decision, Maggie turned and walked back to the girl.

"I'm sorry," Maggie said to the girl, bowing to the minotaur before continuing, "but I'm pretty new here. I've never been through one of the storms before."

The girl stared silently at Maggie with her startling green eyes.

"I just," Maggie began, "I couldn't help but overhear. What have you never seen so bad?"

The girl looked up to the minotaur. He looked down at Maggie, considering her with his jet black eyes before nodding. At the minotaur's approval, the girl spoke.

"The Derelict," the girl said, her voice still as loud as it had been before. Maggie wished the girl would speak more softly so the entire street couldn't hear what she was saying. "There were more of them out last night than I've ever seen before. And not just roaming the lanes looking miserable. They were attacking people."

"The ones with no magic of their own."

"Those," the girl said, "and others. They stole magic some people came here with. But the problem is," the girl spoke even more loudly, shouting so everyone waiting in the line could hear, "there's no way to tell who has stolen magic. So the scum get to walk the streets and come into our tent. Filthy, disgusting thieves."

"Enough," the minotaur said, his low voice shaking the inside of Maggie's chest.

With a nod of her head, the red haired girl turned and walked past the line and into the green tent.

"Take heed," the minotaur said.

Maggie watched his mouth move. He had the head of a bull, and there was something comical in seeing his lips form the dire words.

"The street will be dangerous for some time," the minotaur said.

Maggie bit her lips together to keep from smiling.

"Those who have stolen magic will be eager to lose it. And some will try and steal more before they are forced back into the shadows."

Maggie nodded, not trusting herself to open her mouth without laughing.

"If you need a safe place to stay, or a way to earn, Lena would let you in. She has spoken of you before, Maggie Trent."

Maggie took a step back, startled at the sound of her own name. "Thank you." She turned and walked away as quickly as she dared.

Hurrying through the murmuring crowds, Maggie arrived at the market square. Trade was going on as usual, but the mood was solemn.

Nearly everyone was silent and tense except for a group of young men in front of the tent that sold ale. They were sitting at a fine wooden table that was new to the square, laughing loudly.

One of the men leapt unsteadily onto the table and shouted, "A toast! To the greatness and mercy of the Siren!" He thrust his glass to the sky, slopping ale down the front of his shirt.

His friends laughed as he tried to climb off the table, tripping and falling to the ground. He lay on the dirt road, howling with laughter as two of his drunken friends tried to get him to his feet.

Turning away from the raucous men, Maggie walked toward Mathilda's tent, keeping her head low as the murmurs around her shifted from solemn to angry.

Mathilda's tent came into view, and Maggie held her breath, waiting for Mathilda's bright white mobcap to appear.

Sure enough, as the drunken men burst into song, Mathilda popped her head out of the shadows, glowering at the men.

"Mathilda!" Maggie cried so loudly the people near her spun to glare at the noise. "Sorry," Maggie mouthed before ducking into the shadows of the tent.

Mathilda stood behind her row of goods, deep in the shadows and out of sight. On a normal morning, she would have been standing on the street, greeting everyone who walked past, trying to tempt them into buying something.

But today she stood, arms crossed, as though waiting for something she dreaded to happen.

"Mathilda," Maggie said, much softer than she had the first time, "you're okay."

"Of course I'm okay." Mathilda waved a hand. "I was always going to be okay. I was rather worried about you. Waiting through the storm on that rock you call safe."

"I wasn't"—Maggie began before changing her mind—"I found a safe place to wait out the storm."

"And the Derelict." Mathilda *tsked*. "Coming into town. That lot out there, they'd better be careful." Mathilda waved a finger at the men, one of whom was now lying on the table and serenading the sky. "As if we don't know why they're celebrating. Sitting in the market square, throwing magic at the most absurd things. As if they think we won't know why they have so much magic to spare.

"Give me your fish, and you'd best be on your way. People are fearful this morning, and it won't be long before someone decides the square would be safer without that lot. And I can't say as I disagree."

"I don't have any fish," Maggie said, her stomach suddenly feeling hollow as she again remembered the loss of her net. "My net got lost in the storm. My tent, too. Everything really."

"What? Oh, poor child." Mathilda furrowed her brow. "Are you able to give?"

"Yes, ma'am." Maggie nodded. "I just don't know where to go."

"The Siren is the best way for it," Mathilda said. There was no hint of regret at her words. "As long as you can give to her, she'll be the best for those sorts of things. If you wanted a glass of the finest wine or even a fancy silk dress, I could offer some suggestions for where to go, but for this, the Siren."

Maggie hated the thought of the magic flowing freely from her, not knowing how much it would take to get what she needed, but if Mathilda said it was the best way, there was nothing else for it.

"All right," Maggie said, "I'll ask the Siren for it. Thank you."

"Of course, child," Mathilda said as Maggie walked around the table and back onto the bright square. "Wait." Mathilda picked up a piece of bright purple fruit from the table. "Take this. You need to eat." She smiled kindly. "I'll be expecting fish tomorrow."

"Thank you," Maggie said, warmth spreading through her at Mathilda's kindness. She wasn't used to people being kind without reason. But Mathilda didn't ask for a draw of magic or anything in return. She only shooed Maggie away with a smile.

Maggie cut across the square, making her way toward where Gabriel would be. Her path led her near the pack of men. Their stench of sweat and ale turned her stomach.

"Pretty one!" one of the men shouted as she passed. "Come join us!"

Maggie kept her head down, not acknowledging the man's words.

"Come and have a laugh!" the man shouted, his tone growing more insistent.

Just ten more feet, and she would be level with the table. A few seconds and she would be past them.

"I said join us," the man said. "I'm offering—"

But what he had to offer, Maggie didn't hear. The man reached out and grabbed Maggie's hand as she drew level with the table.

With no thought for wishing she could do a spell, Maggie punched the man hard in the face. Pain shot up her arm, but she kept her fist tight, ready to strike again as she yanked her arm free from the man's grasp.

"Oy!" One of the other men shouted. "What's the matter with you!"

The man she had punched stepped toward her. Maggie dug her heel hard into his toes before running down a side street, diving into the shadows as soon as she could. She waited, huddled behind a barrel, for the men to chase after her.

Shouts carried from the square. Angry shouts from more people than had been in the drunken group. Maggie stayed where she was as the noise from the square grew louder.

Maggie took a bite of the purple fruit. It was sweet, thick, and juicy. She hadn't realized how dry her mouth was until the juices flooded it.

Someone was screaming in the square now. It sounded as though a fight had broken out. Maggie stayed in the shadows until the fruit was gone. She cleaned her hands on the grass before leaning out of her hiding spot to scan the street.

The narrow lane was nearly abandoned. An old woman who looked like she might be deaf toddled down the street, but everyone else had disappeared. Maggie couldn't blame them. She wished she could be hiding far from whatever was happening in the square, too. But there was nowhere for her to hide. Her home was gone.

In one swift motion, Maggie leapt to her feet and began jogging down the street. Illial hadn't been puffing on his blue smoke pipe in the market square. But that didn't mean anything. What with the fighting, he was smart to avoid it.

The smell hit Maggie's nose before she reached where Rushna should have been. The tent was there, but the flaps were tied very decisively shut.

"Rushna," Maggie called softly. "Rushna!" There was no answer. But that didn't mean anything. If the tent wasn't selling food, why would Rushna be there?

Maggie walked swiftly. The noise of the fighting in the square had disappeared, and there were people out on this street. A girl near her own age lay in a hammock by the side of the lane, playing with a cat who sprawled lazily on her stomach. Neither the girl nor the cat seemed to be upset about anything. But then they were both there in the Siren's Realm safe and happy.

Maggie wondered if the cat had been wished into being or slipped through the stitches like she had. But there was no way to know. Maybe one day she could wish a cat into being for herself.

Rounding the corner onto the street where Gabriel sold his roasted meat, Maggie's heart soared into her throat.

Gabriel and his cart were in the middle of the lane, surrounded by hungry people. The crowd wasn't as large as usual. But they were still there, waiting for the legs of meat Gabriel passed around.

"Gabriel!" Maggie called from behind two men who vied for the largest piece of meat.

"What do you know? She's alive!" Gabriel's face split into a wrinkled grin, but his smile didn't hide the fatigue in his voice. "I was afraid you hadn't made it through."

"I did," Maggie said, scooting around the men to get a closer look at Gabriel. "My tent's gone, but I was safe inland. What happened to you?"

Gabriel gave the tiniest shake of his head as he passed meat to the last of his customers. Bickering like old women, the two men walked away.

"The good fer nothin' folk who live in the shadows came up to our part of town last night," Gabriel growled. "Busted into our tents just before the storm was comin'. Drove people out into the rain and then attacked 'em. Stealin' the magic others worked hard for." Gabriel's shoulders sagged, and a shadow passed over his face.

"Did they…" Maggie wasn't sure how to ask, or if it was even right to ask. "Did they get to you?"

"One of 'em tried." Gabriel rubbed a leathery hand over his mouth. "Bunch came into my tent carryin' sticks, chasin' me out into the storm. The wind was howlin' somethin' fierce. One of 'em knocked me face-first to the ground right into the water from the storm.

"I felt the magic rippin' out of me like someone was tryin' to pull my skin all off. Lightnin' was strikin' all around, and the wind was terrible. I think they thought I'd be too scared or confused to fight back. But I spent my life before here on a ship. I'd seen worse storms and fought nastier folk."

"So what happened?" Maggie asked. "How did you get away?"

"Rolled over, knocked the bastard off of me, an' pummeled him till he stopped fightin' back," Gabriel said matter-of-factly. "Left him out in the rain, and he wasn't there when the sun finally come up. Don' know if the Siren took him or if he walked away on his own."

"I'm sorry," Maggie said. "Did they get many of your friends?"

"A few," Gabriel said, "but we managed to fight 'em off. That's the good of bein' one who has no magic of their own. I was in plenty of fights before I ever came here, and I never used magic to win any of 'em. I have enough to earn. I'll make do. I'm just glad they didn't get you."

"Thanks," Maggie said as Gabriel handed her a turkey leg. "When do you think it'll happen again? The Derelict attacking and the Siren making a storm."

"Eh." Gabriel shrugged. "Could be a thousand sunrises, could be tonight."

"And we're just supposed to sit and wait for it to happen again?"

"Aye. It's the best we can do."

Maggie took Gabriel's hand, giving him more of her magic than usual. "Then I guess I had better get ready for the next storm."

Maggie took the long way back to the rocks by the Endless Sea. Getting lost in the maze of streets had made her determined to learn her way to all the hidden places she could find.

She had been existing, moving from one day to the next, enjoying the sun and stability. Always fish in the sea, always food for her stomach. But her life hadn't been stable at all. She had been living at the mercy of the Siren without even realizing it. The only power she had was in the magic she possessed.

She found her way back to the Fortress and considered walking along the canals. But Bertrand Wayland strode by, a look of fierce determination on his face, and Maggie walked quickly in the other direction rather than risk having to explain disappearing from his kitchen.

There were no Derelict on the sun-bathed streets, though wariness and solemnity were everywhere.

When it was only a couple of hours before sundown, Maggie returned to her rocks. They were still there, and there was still no trace of her little home.

Maggie lay down on the rock, imagining the blue of her tent above her. The breeze from the sea would rustle the fabric. The morning sun would peer through to wake her.

But it wasn't safe.

Stone. She needed a stone house. But at what cost?

Maggie laughed to herself, imagining shouting *can I get an estimate on a stone house?* to the sky, but too afraid to say it out loud for fear she might actually get an answer.

"Well," a voice said from above.

Gasping, Maggie rolled backward, hiding in the crevice of the rock.

"It seems you have wiped the slate clean again, sweet Siren."

Maggie recognized the voice. Bertrand Wayland stood on the rocks above her.

"You have smoothed out some of the cracks, and hidden the tiny stitches," Bertrand called out to the sea, "but not all. And I will find more. I suppose you would stop me if you wanted to. But I think we both know better than that.

"I will venture out again and bring back more riches for your realm. But I do ask…" Bertrand paused. "Try not to blow Miss Trent away if there is a storm in my absence. I can see you've ruined her home. She's probably living with those who have no magic of their own now. Dear Siren, don't let the poor girl's lie destroy her. And don't let my journey destroy me."

Maggie held her breath as faint footsteps moved away from her.

Bertrand had come here to make sure she was okay.

Weird.

Bertrand thought living with the others she pretended to be like was going to get her taken by the Siren.

Probably true in the long run.

Bertrand was going to go through one of the stitches and bring back more riches. Since you could only bring the clothes on your back to the Siren's Realm, riches meant magic. Magic to build a stone house on the rock by the sea.

Brilliant.

Rolling back out of the crevice, Maggie sprang to her feet and climbed up onto the high rock. Bertrand was three hundred yards ahead, striding toward the city. Glancing around the deserted cliff to be sure no one was watching, Maggie ran after him.

Half-formed plans rolled through her mind. He had said she wasn't strong enough to go with him to wherever it was he went. But what did he know about her? He had figured out she was a witch. So what? She was braver than he knew. Stronger, too.

She would go out, get some magic, come back and build her little stone house.

But what if he wouldn't let her come with him? What if she didn't know how to get back? What if the whole thing was a trap? Or they died trying to find some great adventure? What if she didn't know how to get more magic to bring back in?

Maggie's steps faltered, and she slowed to a trot, keeping Bertrand in sight but never gaining on him.

He didn't seem to be in a hurry as he walked down the lanes. Past the jewel bright tents and on to the gray ones. Maggie had expected him to turn onto the stone streets of the Fortress. But instead, he pressed onward down more long rows of tents.

Soon, the tents weren't so close together. There were spaces between all of them like little yards. Bertrand nodded at people as he passed in his easy manner. Somehow, his nodding to strangers made Maggie angry. Like he thought he was a local celebrity.

But as Maggie passed the people on the spread out streets, they nodded to her, too. Smiling kindly at her. This was the first place she had been since the storm where no one seemed tense.

If Bertrand was looking for some sort of illicit adventure, surely he had gone the wrong way. But he kept walking. He was only a hundred feet in front of her now, but she had to stay that close to keep him in sight as the grassy yards turned into a forest dotted with tents.

The air here smelled damp with earth. Musky leaves added their scent. A log cabin stood in the distance, its chimney merrily puffing smoke.

"What the hell is this place?" Maggie muttered. How could she have spent so much time in the Siren's Realm, talked to so many people, and no one had bothered to mention a forest?

Not that she would have wanted to live there. To some, the woods might feel liberating, but to her the trees felt like a crushing cave. Maggie took a shuddering breath and pushed down the memories of blood, screams, and a bright green light.

She was so occupied with trying not to think she almost didn't hide in time.

Bertrand stopped in the middle of a stand of bright white birch trees. All of them bent gently toward the earth as though they were trying to listen to its secrets.

Peering out from behind a thick-trunked oak tree, Maggie watched as Bertrand paced inside the circle of white birches. He was saying something in a low voice that Maggie couldn't hear. After a minute or so, he began running his hands along the trunks of the trees, as though searching for some kind of hidden catch.

But he didn't seem to find what he was looking for as he moved from one tree to the next. He made his way back to the center of the circle, tenting his fingers under his chin as he gazed through the white branches up to the sky.

Then, without warning, he walked out of the circle of white trees to a large, barren tree three feet to the left. Maggie hadn't noticed the barren tree before. It was so dark and ordinary next to the clearly magical trees Bertrand had just been examining. Bertrand smiled as he stepped toward the tree, and with a bright flash of green light, he disappeared.

Maggie yelped and leapt back, falling to the ground. Something cut into her palm, but she didn't bother looking at it as she sprang to her feet and ran toward the tree.

Bertrand was gone. There was no trace of him. It was as though the tree had swallowed him whole. With trembling fingers, Maggie reached for the tree. She half-expected it to grow teeth and eat her with a tongue of green light, but nothing happened. She ran her fingers along the bark. The rough surface felt warmer than it should have in the shade of the forest. But there was no knob, or instructions. Nothing to say how to follow Bertrand.

Maggie went to the center of the white trees, following what Bertrand had done—searching the trees with her fingers, muttering inventive curses the whole way. If the trees wanted a spell, she didn't have one to give. She stood in the center of the clearing and looked up through the branches. But there was no hidden password or spell written in their leaves.

Maggie jammed her fingers through her hair, willing her brain to come up with a solution.

But there was nothing. She didn't know how to find a way out of the Siren's Realm, let alone what to do once she did. The best thing she could hope for was for Bertrand to make it back alive and then maybe she could convince him to take her with him the next time he left the Siren's Realm.

Maggie's heart sank. She hadn't even really wanted to go, but now knowing she couldn't...

"Nope," Maggie said to the empty woods. "I'm going. I am figuring this thing out, and I am going."

She strode over to the barren tree. There was something there she hadn't seen before. A dark crack, barely big enough to be noticed. Yet the closer she got, the wider it seemed. Almost large enough for her to slide through.

Maggie reached her hand out toward the darkness inside the tree, wondering if she would find only shadows or something living inside. The instant her fingers grazed the darkness, the world disappeared in a bright flash of green, and she was falling.

Cold crushed her lungs, pushing out her last precious bit of air. Whether she was falling or the world around her was moving, she didn't know.

Death.

This can't be death. It wasn't before.

Maggie's brain felt as though it might burst from lack of air.

Maybe she had done it wrong. She hadn't found a way through one of the stitches that led to a faraway world, and now she would just be trapped in the darkness forever.

She opened her mouth to try and ask for a light, but in the void, speaking was impossible.

Dying in battle would have been better.

Just when Maggie had decided that this was, in fact, the end, bright light shone around her, and she was plunged into cold darkness.

But it wasn't like before. This darkness had texture. Flowing around her. Maggie opened her mouth to try to breathe, but water flooded her lungs, burning worse than the nothing had.

Spots danced in front of her eyes. Up, she needed to find the way up. But the world had gotten twisted around, and she didn't know which way might lead out of the water.

Forcing herself to relax, a gentle wave pushed her up the tiniest bit. Fighting with all the strength she had left in her limbs, Maggie kicked up toward the surface.

Bright light and warmth greeted her as she reached the open air, coughing and retching the water from her lungs. Her arms ached as she fought to keep her head above the water, gasping for breath as her head spun. It took nearly a minute for the world around her to begin making sense.

She was in a lake of some sort. Vast though the water was, she could see land on all sides.

The water wasn't freezing. That was good. It was cool and still, almost comfortable to be in.

The shore was covered in trees so thick it looked like a jungle. Faint rustling and hooting sounded from deep within the shadows. High stone cliffs cut through the water, some reaching around to corners and disappearing, some rising like tree-topped spires isolated in the lake.

Luckily, the shore nearest her sat low at the edge of the water. Trees rose up behind, masking the landscape between Maggie and the cliffs in the distance.

Taking one last deep breath, Maggie swam toward the shore. Something brushed up against her leg, but she didn't dare stop to see what it was. If something wanted to eat her, there wasn't a thing she could do about it anyway. The shore was farther away than it had seemed, and by the time Maggie pulled herself belly first onto land, she was gasping for breath again.

"This," Maggie panted, still face down on the ground, "is bullshit."

"On the contrary, Miss Trent"—a voice came from above—"I think you've done quite well."

Maggie rolled onto her back and looked up at Bertrand Wayland.

He wasn't drenched or puffing. He didn't look like he had just fallen through the rabbit hole of doom into some unknown world with creatures shaking the branches twenty feet away. Bertrand Wayland was bone dry, perfectly clean, and smiling.

Maggie lay on the ground, glaring up at him.

Bertrand didn't seem to notice. "I did think when it took you so long in getting here you might have changed your mind and decided not to follow me, which, of course, would have been quite understandable given the nature of our adventure. And you did make it out of the water remarkably calmly. I was prepared to go in after you, but I supposed you must have lived your whole life near the water since you seem so attached to the Endless Sea now."

"What the hell," Maggie growled, pushing herself shakily to her feet, "makes you think you know anything about me?"

"Well, Miss Trent"—Bertrand grinned—"I understand you well enough to know you would be following me today. Well, yesterday for me. I have been here since last night."

"What?" Maggie wrung the water out of her hair. "I was only ten minutes behind you."

"But that is the rub in leaving the Siren's Realm," Bertrand said. "I have never known if the Siren doesn't understand time as we do or if she simply doesn't care to bother with it. But time inside and outside of the Siren's Realm never do seem to line up."

Maggie's mind raced, trying to think of how long she had been in the Siren's Realm. "So ten minutes in the Siren's Realm means a day outside?" She had been in the Siren's Realm for months. The battle at Graylock would be long over by now. Everyone she knew could already be dead.

"Oh no." Bertrand shook his head. "Nothing nearly so simple. Sometimes it will be only a few moments' difference. I was gone from the Siren's Realm for nearly a year once. I came back, and it was only just after lunch.

"There is no way I have ever seen to calculate how much time has passed within the realm when I'm without. It is never less on the outside. Sometimes much more. It is the way of the Siren, and we poor mortals must accept it is her will. Though I did truly hope I wouldn't have to spend a month waiting for you to come after me."

"What made you think I would come after you?" Maggie took off her boots and dumped the water out of them.

"I made sure you knew the lure of what I was adventuring toward and even visited your home so you would know to follow me."

"You wanted me to come!" Maggie screeched, sending something in the woods scurrying for cover. "You're the one who told me it was too dangerous! You're the one who said I should make do in the Siren's Realm!"

"I gave you very practical advice. I only hoped you wouldn't follow it. Now put on your shoes, and let us move along. Adventure is waiting somewhere in this forest, and I intend to find it."

"What do you mean?" Maggie hopped after Bertrand, jamming on her boots. "You *hope* to find adventure?"

"Well, we cannot simply wait by the shore and expect something worth seeing to find us." Bertrand didn't turn to face Maggie as he spoke. He plowed into the jungle, not even checking to see if Maggie would follow.

"You don't know what's here?" Maggie pushed her way through the brush to follow Bertrand.

"No."

"Then how did you know we'd land in water?"

"I didn't."

"But what if we had fallen onto rocks?"

"It would have hurt significantly more."

"I've just followed a madman into a world neither of us knows anything about," Maggie muttered.

"And you don't know the way home, so keep up!" Bertrand shouted back from forty feet ahead. The trees had become so thick she could barely see him.

Branches and brambles tore at Maggie's clothes, ripping the thin fabric and scratching her skin. The air inside the trees was thick and humid. Within minutes, Maggie was puffing and covered in sweat.

Bertrand led them in a straight line, but toward what, Maggie couldn't tell. She wanted to lay down on the ground and rest, but the shaking of the tiny leaves near her feet made her sure bugs of some sort waited for her down there.

Soon, Bertrand began leading them steeply uphill. Maggie scrambled after him. He gradually slowed his pace as the climb became more difficult and finding purchase for their feet took more time. Maggie was ruefully grateful he had stopped climbing so quickly. Her breath came in shallow gasps, and her head pounded from heat and exertion.

She tried to take her mind away from her pain by examining the trees they passed. They were thick and tall with leaves that sprouted high over her head. They were definitely different from the trees she had been around growing up. But there was nothing otherworldly or innately magical-looking about them.

The leaves overhead were large, thick, and a deep green. Maggie gazed longingly at them, wondering if there might be clean rainwater nestled in their crevices she could drink.

With a hoot and a squeak, something launched itself from one tree to another, soaring high in the sky right above Maggie's head. Maggie squealed and dropped to the ground, covering her head for protection.

"What?" Bertrand asked, sounding mildly curious. "Is something wrong, Miss Trent?"

"There are animals up there," Maggie said, keeping one arm over her head as she pointed to where the beast had disappeared. "One jumped through the trees."

"Oh good." Bertrand beamed. "Always comforting to know living things are about. It means something has managed to survive. Now come along, Miss Trent, we have a ways to go before night catches us."

He turned to keep climbing. The way in front of them was steeper than the hill they had already climbed. She would have to use her arms to pull herself up.

"No," Maggie said. "I am not going any farther."

"Really?" Bertrand furrowed his brow. "You run so frequently through the Siren's Realm, I didn't think you would have a problem with our climb."

"It's not boiling hot in the Siren's Realm. There's water in the Siren's Realm. I'm not going any farther until you tell me where the hell we're going."

"Ah." Bertrand nodded, pulling a thin, silver bracelet off his wrist. "It is a bit hotter here than the comfortable climate the Siren so lovingly provides. I can understand how you would become thirsty." He pinched one side of the loop between the fingers of both hands. The silver of the loop grew as he pulled his hands apart, forming a silver tube. When the tube was about seven inches long, he stopped pulling, set it open-side down on his right palm, and tapped it with his left finger. With a sympathetic smile, he held the silver thing out to Maggie.

Pushing herself laboriously to her feet, Maggie examined the smooth silver sides. "A cup?" she asked, looking inside at the solid, silver bottom.

"A very fine cup." Bertrand nodded. "It cost a dear amount of magic to get something of this nature from the Siren that I could slip through the stitches with. But it has proven invaluable." He handed the empty cup to Maggie.

"Do you have any water?" she asked, her throat suddenly dryer than it had been before, now that water was so nearly within her grasp.

"You did say you were a witch, didn't you?" Bertrand asked, bemused. "I assume you know how to create water?"

Rolling her eyes at Bertrand's smug smile, Maggie said, "*Parunda.*" The tingle of magic flew through her body, and the cup was filled with fresh, clean water. But she was filled with magic as well. Filling the cup hadn't drained her of anything. Maggie smiled down at the cup. "I can use my magic here. And I won't lose all of it?"

She looked hopefully at Bertrand as she took a long drink of the cool water in the cup, reveling in the chill as it flowed down past her lungs, making it easier to breathe in the heavy air.

"Yes and no." Bertrand frowned. "Now come along. We have a long way yet to go."

"But you haven't said where we're going," Maggie said, starting to follow. "*Parunda.*" She filled the cup again.

"I don't know where we're going," Bertrand said, choosing a path that would allow Maggie to climb beside him, "but the best way to find adventure is to find the people of this strange world. And to find the people, we must see the landscape."

"So we get up high and see what there is to see."

"Correct, Miss Trent." Bertrand smiled, apparently pleased she had caught on. He began climbing the boulders that led up the side of the mountain. "Keep up!"

Maggie took another long drink of water before pressing lightly on the rim of the cup and hiding her smile as it collapsed back into a bracelet. "Neat."

The water had helped. Her head was no longer pounding so badly she couldn't see straight. But she was still drenched in sweat, and in a few minutes her arms ached in protest at the constant work of pulling herself uphill.

With a burst of rustling branches, another one of the things flew through the trees overhead. It was close enough that she could see a little more of the animal this time. It looked rather like a monkey.

Another tree rustled, and Maggie searched the treetops. She felt her fingers slip from the rock she clung to, teetered for a moment, and fell backward.

A sharp pain shot through her shoulder. With a cry, she fell sideways, rolling off the next boulder. Jamming her fingers into a crack in the stone, she caught herself and, with a horrible jerk on her shoulder, broke her fall.

"Oww, oww," Maggie groaned, pulling herself to sit on the rock. She flexed her fingers and wiggled her toes to make sure nothing was broken.

"Are you all right, Miss Trent?" Bertrand jumped down to where she sat, looking genuinely concerned.

"I'm great," Maggie said through clenched teeth. She raised her arm, and pain shot from her shoulder.

"What made you fall?"

"I saw a monkey." Maggie rolled her eyes at her own stupidity.

"I have seen a few little furry things flying through the trees." Bertrand knelt to examine Maggie's shoulder. "But you really should be more careful." He took Maggie's arm and began twisting it around.

"What the—Gah!" Maggie yelped as her shoulder popped back into the socket.

"We'll have to climb a bit more slowly now, as you'll need to be kind to that arm, Miss Trent."

"Be kind to my arm?" Spots danced in front of Maggie's eyes from the pain.

"It will take a while to heal," Bertrand said, already ten feet above her on the rocks.

"Why can't I just use magic to heal it?" Maggie growled as she climbed painfully to her feet. "In fact, why don't we use a little magic and get ourselves up this mountain in half the time?"

"It won't work," Bertrand said in such a matter of fact tone, Maggie had to take a deep breath before she dared to speak.

"Why won't it work? I made water in the cup." She jiggled the silver bracelet on her wrist at him. "We have magic here. Wasn't that the point of coming?"

"My dear Miss Trent, I think you are a bit new at this to be deciding the point of anything." Bertrand smiled sympathetically. "And water is one of the constants. So you can easily form a cup of water."

"Constant whats?" Maggie moved to run her hands through her hair and instantly regretted it as a dull ache throbbed in her shoulder.

"In every world, there are three things that remain constant." Bertrand beckoned for Maggie to keep climbing.

Grudgingly and painfully, she did.

"In every world I have visited that is, which is not to say these rules will always apply. I would never assume myself to be that grand."

"Really?" Maggie's voice dripped with sarcasm. "You, not grand?"

"I said not *that* grand, Miss Trent," Bertrand corrected, apparently unaffected by her tone. "There are three constants. Water, shelter, and fire. Which means to say the spells I know for each from my time in our former world—"

"You mean Earth?"

"Those spells that I am familiar with from my early training work wherever I go. *Parunda* will consolidate water into a glass. *Primurgo*, or *primionis*, will create a shield, which becomes your shelter. And *inexuro* will light an acceptable fire. Everything you need to survive."

"But food. You need food to survive, but there's never a spell for that," Maggie said, now climbing right next to Bertrand despite the pain in her arm.

"But it is helpful to be able to cook whatever you can find," Bertrand said. "*Inexuro* creates a reasonable flame you can cook over."

"But you're on your own to figure out what's edible? Awesome."

"It is as you say, Miss Trent, awesome." Bertrand grinned. "Or as I prefer to call it— *adventure*."

They climbed without speaking for a while, listening to the hooting and the cawing in the forest as Maggie's mind raced through what she could do with water, fire, and a shield spell.

"But how do you know?" Maggie asked. "How do you know a levitation spell won't work?"

"I don't. But it is a fairly good assumption based on previous experience."

"Then shouldn't we try it?" A bubble of excitement grew in Maggie's chest. "I mean, what if *adsurgo* works here? What if it works better here?"

"By all means, please try it, Miss Trent." Bertrand sat on a rock facing her, an ill-concealed smile on his face.

"You're setting me up." Maggie narrowed her eyes. "It won't work, and you want to laugh at me."

"It doesn't matter if I am setting you up or not, Miss Trent. You are bound to try it for yourself anyway."

Maggie opened her mouth to argue, but he was right. So with a shrug she said, "*Adsurgo.*" It was as though someone had knocked her feet out from under her with a stick. She was airborne for only a split second before she tumbled face-first to the ground.

"And now I hope you see why I didn't try to heal your arm with magic." Bertrand stood and brushed himself off, ready to climb again. "As you can see, the results might have been disastrous. I might have accidentally removed your arm entirely."

"Right." Every muscle Maggie had ever felt, and several she hadn't, ached as she followed Bertrand up the mountain.

"And we really must work on your sword play, Miss Trent," Bertrand called back. "I do beg your pardon if I am making any false assumptions concerning your aptitude, but having skill with a sword can be vital if you cannot use magic to fend off an attacker."

"Nope." Maggie grimaced. "They definitely didn't teach us swords at the Academy."

Maggie had gone numb by the time they neared the top of the mountain. There was nothing but moving forward one more step. Then another. Then another. She had long since stopped looking up to see how close they were to the top. There was no point. They would get there when they got there.

She didn't even look anymore as things rustled in the bushes nearby.

"If you want to eat me, just do it," Maggie growled at the trees.

"I'm sorry, what was that, Miss Trent?"

"I said—" Maggie looked toward Bertrand, but he wasn't climbing a few feet ahead of her. He was standing on the top of the mountain ten feet above her. "We're here?" Maggie's words came out as a whimper. "We're done climbing?"

"For now, Miss Trent." Bertrand lay on his stomach and reached down, catching the hand of Maggie's good arm as soon as she was near enough and dragging her to the top. "And for the evening."

Maggie rolled onto her back, panting and staring up at the darkening sky.

"We do have an excellent vantage point. Though I don't see any people at the moment," Bertrand said.

"Mmmhmm." Maggie closed her eyes and let the breeze play across her face.

"There is a decent ridgeline we can follow tomorrow if we still can't see anything from here."

"A ridgeline sounds great." She raised her hand and gave Bertrand a thumbs up.

"I must say—" Bertrand bustled around, breaking sticks.

Maggie unwillingly opened her eyes.

"—you have done better than I thought you would, Miss Trent." He piled the sticks on top of a flat rock. "I was afraid you might not make it up the mountain, or you might decide to turn around and head right back to the safety of the Siren."

"I don't know how to get back." Maggie sat up and watched as Bertrand built a fire. It had gotten so dark Maggie blinked at the sudden light of the flames. "And I came here to bring more magic into the Siren's Realm. I'm not leaving without it."

"But you've already, shall we say, refilled your magic stores." Bertrand took off his jacket and began pulling things out of his pockets. "So you could go back whenever you like."

"I what?" Maggie said, watching quasi-disgusted as Bertrand pulled two large fish from his pockets.

"You have what you came for," Bertrand repeated as, with a horrible squelching noise, he casually shoved a stick lengthwise through the first dead fish. "You can go back whenever you like."

"Next you're going to tell me to click my heels three times and I'll be back by the Endless Sea."

"I know nothing of clicking heels, Miss Trent," Bertrand said, looking at Maggie as though afraid the heat had done something to her brain, "but you could slip back through the stitch and take what magic you've gained with you."

"Then why the hell did we just climb up a freakin' mountain!" Maggie screamed, her voice bouncing out into the darkening air.

"Because, Miss Trent, I hope for more from you than simply sneaking into a world, stealing a bit of magic, and returning home a little richer but none the wiser. You are in a world neither you nor I have ever seen. Magic connected the Siren's Realm to this place. Only something fiercely magical could have made an opening we can travel through. I mean to find that magic and discover what secrets it holds.

"We would not have fallen into this place if there were no reason for us to be here, Miss Trent. Magic has called us to this world, and I intend to discover why. And if you are the person I believe you to be, I have no doubt you will be following me around this maze of a lake come morning."

Maggie buried her head in her hands, taking a few shuddering breaths before speaking. "I really have no idea who the hell this person you think I'm supposed to be is, but I'm pretty sure I'm not her."

"Self-deprecation is hardly a virtue, Miss Trent. You are important enough to have been drawn into the Siren's Realm, smart enough to respectably make your way in the Textile Town, caring enough to befriend the misfits you meet, and brave enough to defend a stranger against the Derelict. Really, I am beginning to suspect I know you better than you know yourself."

Maggie squeezed her eyes shut against the night as she pictured herself throwing Bertrand from the top of the mountain.

"Would you like some fish?" Bertrand asked. "You will need your strength come morning. Unless, of course, you want to run back to the Siren's Realm simply to prove me wrong."

Pain shot through Maggie's jaw as she clenched her teeth. She slid the bracelet from her wrist, and turned it back into a cup. *"Parunda."* The cup filled with water. "Cheers to adventure."

"Brilliant, Miss Trent." Bertrand beamed, spreading his arms wide as though embracing the dusk. "And what a wonderful place we have found for an adventure!"

Maggie looked out over the edge for the first time. Barely visible in the shadows were more cliffs and spires she hadn't been able to see before. The lake wasn't round, but built like a true maze with canals and offshoots going in every direction and disappearing into the darkness.

"Wow," Maggie breathed. There was a remarkable beauty in the brokenness of the lake.

Impossible to navigate. Water and rock surrounded by thick forest filled with unknown things. For the first time in a very long time, Maggie felt small. Small enough to curl up in the back of a closet and hide until the darkness was gone.

"How are we going to find anything in that maze besides water?" Maggie asked.

"We wait for daylight, Miss Trent." Bertrand slid the first roasted fish from its spear and handed it to Maggie. *"Primionis."*

The air shimmered as the shield blossomed around them.

Maggie took a bite of the fish, her stomach rumbling its appreciation of the food.

"Eat and sleep well, Miss Trent. For tomorrow morning, the true adventure begins."

S leeping in the jungle was not nearly as simple as Maggie had imagined. As night fell, the animals that hid in the trees seemed to decide it was time to come out. Leaves rustled, and unseen things growled and snorted. The fire still burned between Bertrand and Maggie, keeping away the chill that had crept over the mountaintop.

Maggie inched closer to the embers. It seemed wrong that a few hours ago she had been sweating to death and now she was too cold to sleep. A simple spell could have fixed it. But it could have melted her skin off, too.

Maggie stared up at the sky, blocking the haze of the firelight with one hand. Stars peered out from the black, but they weren't stars she had ever seen before. There were no constellations she recognized. Seven stars seemed to be brighter than the rest. Maggie wrapped her arms around herself, trying to squeeze out the thumping in her chest that shouted she was too far from home and the horrible notion that the Siren's Realm had somehow become home. She fell asleep, trying to remember what constellations she had been able to see out her window at the Academy.

"Miss Trent," a voice pulled her from sleep. "Miss Trent, the sun has begun to rise."

Maggie's eyes fluttered open. Bertrand knelt next to her.

"We must begin our watch of the lake." Bertrand's face beamed with excitement. "I have a distinct feeling people are moving about the lake. We need only spot them."

"What?" Maggie rubbed her face. "Why do you feel like there are people moving around?"

"There." Bertrand pointed to a distant patch of low-lying trees. Their leaves were a bright red that was nearly swallowed up by the deep green of the taller trees around them.

Just as Maggie began to wonder what sort of trees could be so red, a flock of birds burst from the branches, cawing their fear before settling into another patch of trees down the lake.

"So there's a predator out there." Maggie shrugged. "It could be jungle cat or bear or whatever they have around here."

"I have discovered in my many travels that whenever one suspects the presence of a predator, it is best to assume the threat is a person until you discover otherwise. People are the most dangerous thing to have creep up on you unexpectedly. And the thing you least want to find you in the dark is usually what is lurking in the shadows."

"Thanks for that." Maggie walked to the edge of the cliff and sat, her feet dangling over the side as she scanned the trees, searching for more patches of red. "You really made me feel better about this whole *finding adventure* thing."

"Miss Trent," Bertrand said from his post facing the other side of the lake, "it will never be my intention to make you *feel better*. It will always be my intention to keep you alive."

"Well, I guess there's something in that."

The morning sun glistened on the lake, showing more of it than Maggie had been able to see the night before. The sight was not comforting. The maze of cliffs and islands reached out to towering mountains in the distance. Once the twists and turns of land covered the water, there was no way to know how much longer the lake went on for.

"We need a map," Maggie said. "Even if we see someone, there'll be no way to follow them without a map. We'll get lost in the maze."

"That is a problem," Bertrand said, "but first we must see where we want to go. Then we will worry about the details of getting there."

Trees stirred on the other side of the lake. Maggie sat up straight and squinted into the distance. Nothing as large as a person appeared. Small brownish things moved along the edge of the water, grazing on something.

"How deep do you think the water is?" Maggie asked. From the top of the mountain, there was no sign of shallows near the shore. The lake simply began in a deep blue, becoming ever darker toward the middle.

"Knowing how magic works in most parts, I would say extremely deep. Deep enough to hide something terrifying in its depths. Or, alternatively, about four-and-a-half feet."

"When I fell in, I went more than four-and-a-half feet down."

"Then we must assume terrifyingly deep is the correct assessment."

They settled back into silence. Maggie's mind wandered as she stared out over the unmoving lake. A bird flew nearby, pale blue, his wings tipped with bright purple. It circled lazily overhead, spiraling higher and higher into the sky before diving into the trees.

A squawk of terror and squeak of pain were followed by silence. Maggie shuddered and turned back toward the lake.

Dead ahead, a boat glided smoothly across the lake's surface.

"Bertrand. I see people!"

Bertrand was by her side in two long strides.

"Should we shout for them?" Maggie asked.

The boat was gliding past them. One person at either end held a long paddle, steering the boat quickly toward a clump of spires.

"They wouldn't be able to hear us from all the way up here," Bertrand said. "We shall watch them as long as we can and do our best to mimic their path."

"But we don't have a boat," Maggie said, feeling minimally guilty at pointing out the obvious flaw in Bertrand's plan.

"Luckily," Bertrand said as the boat slid out of sight, "our slice of land will bring us far enough to be even with where they disappeared, and then it's only a matter of crossing to the spires and seeing what we find."

"So swimming in the terrifyingly deep water that might have something awful in it?"

"Precisely. Now come along, Miss Trent, we have a ridge waiting for us to walk it." He pointed to the rocky ridgeline that led parallel to where the boat had disappeared.

"At least it's not climbing straight up." Maggie sighed as she followed him.

13

The mid-afternoon sun was beating down upon them when Bertrand finally decided it was time to head back down to the water. Maggie's momentary relief at being out of the sun was drowned by the staggering weight of the humid air in the trees.

Rocks tore at her hands as they struggled back down the steep slope, and once she no longer needed her hands to keep balance, she kept the cup constantly filled, passing it back and forth to Bertrand.

"You know," Maggie puffed, "it's good to know you're human."

"I am not human," Bertrand said in a moderately offended tone. "I am a wizard. But wizards still need water."

"And food," Maggie added. "Food would be great."

"If you insist, Miss Trent." Bertrand looked up, searching the trees.

Maggie stood next to him, trying to see what he was looking for. All she saw were trees.

"There." Bertrand pointed after a moment.

The leaves rustled, and one of the monkey-looking things burst into view.

"There is your food."

"You want to eat a baby monkey?" Maggie asked.

"No, Miss Trent," Bertrand said, "I want to take whatever the monkey is eating."

He walked through the trees to where the monkey had appeared.

"But how do we get it?" Maggie asked. "We can't levitate, and we can't use a summoning charm."

"Climb." Bertrand took off his jacket and handed it to Maggie.

"You're going to shimmy up that tree like a *wizard*-sized koala and steal food from monkeys?" Maggie asked as Bertrand ran and leapt at the tree, wrapping his arms around it and beginning to climb the tall trunk.

"That is exactly what I intend to do, Miss Trent."

"What if you fall?" Maggie said. "The monkey was really high up. I can't heal you here!"

"Then I shall not fall, Miss Trent."

"This is great," Maggie muttered. "Really freakin' great. He's going to die, and I have no idea how the hell to get back to the Siren's Realm."

A branch broke not ten feet behind her.

Maggie spun to see who was there, but before she could make sense of it, something thick and dark had covered her head.

Maggie screamed as arms wrapped tightly around her. "Bertrand! Help!"

"Hold her still," a voice growled.

"No. Please!" Maggie yelled as something cut into her wrists, binding them together.

There was a bellow and a *crash*.

"Unhand her at once!" Bertrand shouted.

A muffled grunt of pain was followed by the smack of flesh hitting flesh.

Something hard knocked into Maggie, sending her tumbling sideways.

"We are not here to hurt—"

With a horrible *crack*, Bertrand fell silent.

"Bertrand!" Maggie tried to find her footing and shake off whatever was covering her head. "Bertrand! Leave him alone!"

"Shut her up," a woman ordered. A hand touched Maggie's neck. She crumpled to the ground before she could scream.

---

*P*ain climbed Maggie's wrists. Not a mind-numbing pain or a hateful pain. Just an ache, which seemed to assure her that if she tried to move, something much worse would follow. She was tied up, her back pressed against something hard and straight. Her face was still covered, and the heat of every breath made it more difficult to breathe.

She listened closely in the darkness. The sound of water lapping came from beneath her. The rhythm of steady breathing came from behind her. Movement in the corner. Not constant. Like someone was shifting their weight, uncomfortable from sitting in one place for so long.

"You know," Maggie said as carelessly as she could, "I have to stop waking up like this. Darkness, not knowing where I am. Last time was bad enough. Eternal darkness with nothing to mark time. But this. This is almost worse. Being tied up, my head covered. The person who's keeping me here listening to me rant and not saying anything." She paused for a moment.

"I suppose it would be too much to ask for kidnappers to be polite. That's fine. But, it would be *nice* of you to tell me where I am, you know. I really don't know that. I assume I'm still by the lake, because I can hear the water and"— Maggie paused again—"yep, I can feel the floor moving. So I'm going to say boat or raft."

Maggie leaned her head back, resting it on the surface behind her. "I know you can understand me. Because I could understand you when you decided to attack my friend and me and knocked me out. I assume my friend is the one passed out behind me. It's probably good he's sleeping. I don't think he'll take being kidnapped very well, and I would hate for him to hurt you.

"Of course, it's probably rude of me to assume you're the asshole who decided to use magic on me to bring me here. Especially since I've been lecturing you on manners. But it's hard to have a nice conversation with someone who won't let you see them and won't even answer your questions. I don't even know what it is you think we've done that gives you the right to hold us like this. It must have been something bad—"

A sharp guttural noise sounded from the corner.

"Oh," Maggie said. "You think we've done something *very* bad. You're mad at us."

Something moved in the corner.

Maggie held her breath for a moment, wondering if she had gone too far, waiting for another touch of a hand to knock her out. But nothing happened.

"Whatever it is you think we've done, you're wrong," Maggie said. "We didn't mean to end up here. We don't even really know where *here* is. My friend caught a few fish, we climbed a mountain, slept there, came down, and then you caught us. Are any of those things why you're mad? Are the fish sacred or something? Because we really didn't know."

The person in the corner stayed silent.

"So it wasn't any of that," Maggie said. "Then whatever you're mad at us for, we didn't do it. And if I have to wait here until you believe me, so be it. I doubt your plan is for me to die of starvation and dehydration if wherever we are requires us to be guarded. I mean, that would be a terrible waste of time and resources. So, since you're planning to keep me alive, could I please have some water? Food would be great, too."

Nothing.

"Okay fine," Maggie said, "I'll wait here until the guards change or your leader wants to talk to us or whatever. But I promise you, I'll be much nicer about all of this than my friend. So you'd be better off explaining why you've kidnapped us before he wakes up, because after...well, ropes and bags on our heads or not, you'll be in huge trouble."

The floor in the corner creaked, and footsteps moved around the room.

"My name is Maggie, by the way," she said as the footsteps got farther away. "Maggie Trent. I'm from Virginia in the United States of America on a world called Earth where our stars are very different from yours. I fell into the Siren's Realm in a flash of green light. That's where I met my friend Bertrand Wayland. He told me there were ways to fall back out of the Siren's Realm into worlds I had never seen before. We did slip back out of the Siren's Realm, and we landed here.

"I don't know what this world is called, or why you're so afraid of us. We're only adventurers. We want to explore, not to hurt anyone. But if you try to hurt us, we will fight back. You may not believe me now, but you don't want to fight me. Because I will win, and I will hurt you if you make me. So whoever it is you're going to tell about the prisoner who won't stop talking, make sure you mention that. We managed to find a way out of the Siren's Realm. We can find a way out of this."

The footsteps moved away. The tone of them changed after a door closed. The ground where the person had gone was hollower, like a ramp. A ramp between rafts.

"Bertrand," Maggie whispered. "Bertrand Wayland, wake up."

The sound of steady breathing continued behind her.

Maggie closed her eyes, listening carefully to everything around her, waiting for some new sound to tell her more about where she might be. Far away there were sounds of people. Faint conversations she had no hope of hearing. The bindings on her arms were warm. Warmer than her skin. Maggie twisted her hand so she could feel the rope. A faint tingle hummed in her fingers as soon as she touched it. The rope was laced with magic.

"Bertrand," Maggie whispered, knowing full well he couldn't hear her, "does this seem like a good time to risk a spell from home and hope it doesn't go too badly wrong, or are we not that desperate yet? Didn't think so."

Maggie sat waiting.

"I really hate waiting. It's the worst part of bad things happening. Because there isn't anything you can do, you know? You just have to sit and wait for the world to come crashing down."

Footsteps echoed on the thin walk outside, more footsteps than had left before. Three different voices were conversing softly as they drew nearer.

"Abeyla," a man's voice said, "if you had heard her, you wouldn't doubt me. I don't think they are Enlightened."

"Then how did they get here?" a woman asked.

"She says they fell with a green flash of light," the man said.

"An Enlightened wouldn't know about the Land Beneath," a second man said.

The door creaked open, and the sounds of the footsteps stopped right in front of Maggie.

A hand grazed the top of her head as the bag was pulled away.

Maggie gulped in fresh air, blinking in the dim light before looking at the people who stood above her. Two men flanked a gray-haired woman. All three of them glared down at her.

"She isn't old enough to have been sent out by Jax," the first man said. He was young, not much older than Maggie. Too young for the lines of worry etched around his eyes. His tan face was framed by light blond hair so pale it made his bright blue eyes look even more dazzling.

"Wow," Maggie breathed.

The woman stepped forward. She was older with the same bright blue eyes as the boy and a terrifying scowl. "If Jax was assuming his spies would be killed, then it would only make sense to send someone he hadn't wasted training on."

"But if they weren't meant to survive, then why send them at all?" the second man said. He appeared nearly as old as the woman, but his hair was still solidly black. "How would they report back?"

"He could be assuming that if they don't, we've killed them," the woman said. "Then he would find us by default."

"That seems like a wasteful plan," the first man said. "They could have been killed by animals as easily as by us. It's a waste of life."

"Jax Cayde has never been concerned with the loss of life," the second man said.

"If it helps," Maggie said, "I don't actually know who this Jax dude is and have a strong resentment to being called cannon fodder."

The three of them stared at her for a moment.

"Cannon fodder?" Maggie repeated. "You don't have cannons? It means I don't like the idea of being sacrificed...basically."

"Who are you?" the woman asked.

"I already told the person who was in here." Maggie looked at the younger man, whose neck tensed. "I told you."

"Maggie," the man said. "She said her name was Maggie Trent."

"And what's your name?" Maggie asked.

"We will be the ones asking questions," the woman said, shooting a withering glare at the young man.

"Sure." Maggie shrugged. "I have nothing to hide, but I am hungry and thirsty, and my friend is probably dehydrated as hell. So how about we compromise? You give me some food and water, have someone check on my friend, and then I will happily tell you whatever you want to know."

The woman locked eyes with Maggie for a moment, appraising her.

"Very well." The woman turned to the young man. "Tammond, get the prisoners food and water. Lamil, take a look at the other one."

The blond boy, Tammond, gave a quick bow before opening the door and slipping outside. Through the dazzling sunlight, Maggie caught a glimpse of the lake outside before Abeyla closed the door.

"Bertrand Wayland," Maggie said as Lamil, the black-haired man, moved behind her. She twisted, but the bindings around her middle were too tight for her to see where he had gone. "My friend's name is Bertrand Wayland."

"I thought you weren't speaking until you were fed," the woman said.

"Call it a show of good faith," Maggie said. "But if you want information about this Jax person, you'll be disappointed, because I've never even heard of her."

"Jax Cayde is a him," the woman said. "And we all wish we had never heard his name. Perhaps you truly have been that fortunate."

The woman turned and walked out of the room, closing the door firmly behind her.

Maggie examined her prison. It was made of roughly hewn wood with bamboo braced across the walls like rungs of a ladder. A tiny window sat atop each of the walls, filtering in dim light under the thatched roof. The thick wooden pole Maggie was tied to was the only thing in the room.

Sounds of Lamil moving slowly came from behind Maggie, but she couldn't see what he was doing.

"Is he okay?" Maggie asked when Lamil had stopped moving for nearly a minute.

"He'll be fine," Lamil said.

"Thank you." Maggie sagged back against the pole. "You might not believe me, but we really didn't come here to spy on you."

"I'm not the one you should be worried about," Lamil said. "Even spies whose

668 | MEGAN O'RUSSELL

masters don't care if they die aren't likely to keep a fire burning on a mountaintop in the middle of the night."

"You saw the fire," Maggie said, feeling stupid for not having figured it out sooner. "That's how you found us. How long were you following us in the woods?"

"Long enough to know that, sent by the Enlightened or not, you and this Wayland could be a danger to us all."

"In that case, thank you even more for helping him."

"I do as Abeyla commands," Lamil said before walking out the door.

A brief view of the sparkling lake outside was all Maggie saw before the door slammed shut behind him.

14

"Bertrand," Maggie whispered. "Bertrand, wake up. Bertrand!" Maggie shouted.

"For the goodness of the Siren, Miss Trent, please do not scream at me," Bertrand muttered from his side of the pole.

"You're awake?" Maggie twisted fruitlessly, trying to see him.

"Apparently so," Bertrand said. "Have we been captured?"

"No. I just thought getting tied up in a raft hut would be a great thing to add to our adventure."

"Sarcasm is unbecoming when the person you're speaking to has a terrible headache."

"I'm sorry your head hurts." Maggie took a deep breath, willing herself not to scream just to make Bertrand's head pound. "But we've been kidnapped. They think we're spies from some guy named Jax. I told them we aren't even from this world so I don't know what they're talking about."

"And how did they take that bit of information?"

"They didn't kill us, and I made them agree to feed us before we'd answer more questions."

"Interesting," Bertrand said. Maggie could almost hear his forehead wrinkling as he thought. "That would definitely give the impression that we have, in fact, been captured by the good guys."

"Why? 'Cause they used magic rope to tie us to a pole instead of just beating the answers out of us?"

"Because hunger is an excellent tool when trying to persuade someone to give up their secrets. It implies they really don't want to hurt us." Bertrand paused. "Or they intend to hurt us so badly hunger will no longer matter."

"You're right," Maggie said through clenched teeth. "We're definitely being held by the good guys. Is this a normal part of what you do?"

"I mean, I cannot say it hasn't happened before," Bertrand said in a tone so calm Maggie wanted nothing more than to reach around the pole and shake him, "but every world is different. I've been declared a god twice, king four times. Imprisonment is sometimes easier than being declared ruler. It's so much harder to slip away when people are trying to protect you."

"You have got to be kidding me."

"Oh no. There were statues and everything."

Before Maggie could contemplate the horror of people worshiping a statue of Bertrand Wayland, the door had swung back open.

The man called Tammond entered, carrying a bucket of water with one hand and balancing a tray of food with the other.

"Who's come in?" Bertrand asked.

"Tammond," Maggie sighed, only realizing her tone once the word was said and instantly hating herself for it. "Tammond," Maggie said again, this time hiding the fact that his dazzling blue eyes were making it hard for her to breathe, "is the one who agreed to bring us food before we answer questions."

"Ah good," Bertrand said. "Wonderful to meet you, Tammond. My name is Bertrand Wayland. As I assume Maggie has told you, whether or not the disclosure was wise we have yet to see, we are not of your world. We slipped here from a different realm. The Siren's Realm. Perhaps your people have a legend about such a place. Pure delight and endless joy?"

"I am here to bring you food," Tammond said, "not to discuss the Land Beneath."

"The Land Beneath?" Bertrand said. "Ah, fascinating."

"Thank you for the food," Maggie said, leaning forward to look at the tray as Tammond set it on the ground. Neither of the men seemed to notice.

"And who is it you're fighting here?" Bertrand asked.

"I already told you," Maggie said. "Some guy named Jax."

"Abeyla will speak to you once you've eaten," Tammond said.

"Is Abelya in charge here?" Bertrand asked.

"Abeyla is the leader of the Wanderers."

Tammond set a carved, wooden plate of food down on Maggie's lap just within reach of her fingers.

Maggie managed to get a piece of pink fruit covered in soft spikes in her hands.

"The Wanderers," Bertrand repeated as Tammond made his way to the other side of the pole. "That's you. And Jax's people are?"

"Are you sure you don't already know?"

"Oh yes, quite sure," Bertrand said. "But I do think it wise to stay abreast of local politics when one is being held prisoner."

Bending her head as far down as she could, Maggie raised the fruit to her mouth. The skin was thick and didn't have a real taste. But the meat inside the fruit was amazing. Juicy and sweet, lighter than air in her mouth. She let out a little moan.

"Miss Trent, are you all right?" Bertrand said sharply as Tammond's head poked around her side of the pole.

"I'm fine." Maggie wiped the juice from her chin. "It's just really good food, and I was really hungry."

Tammond smiled, and for a moment Maggie forgot to breathe.

"I'm glad you enjoy it," Tammond said, lifting the bucket of water for Maggie to drink.

His fingers grazed her face, and he froze, a faint bit of pink creeping into his perfect cheeks. "You should drink, Maggie."

The water was cool and had a faint hint of earth. This water had not been created by magic.

"What's the fruit called?" Maggie asked.

"Fire fruit." Tammond moved to the other side of the pole with the bucket.

"Why fire fruit?" Maggie asked, hoping he would look back around to her side of the pole.

He did, giving Maggie an intrigued look.

"You really don't have it where you come from?"

"Nope." Maggie shook her head before taking another heavenly bite.

"The trees the fruit grow on, the leaves turn red. When they are as bright as fire, the fruit is ripe."

"Fascinating," Bertrand said in a tone that clearly said fruit was the least of his concerns, "but I think knowing who we are accused of spying for would be a much more interesting topic of discussion."

"I'll tell Abeyla you're ready for her," Tammond said, giving Maggie one last drink of water before leaving the hut.

"Well, Miss Trent, I suppose I should be grateful."

"That I convinced them to feed us instead of kill us? Yep, I'll take that gratitude." Maggie stared at the door, willing Tammond to come back in and look at her with his unnaturally bright blue eyes. It was at the same moment that she realized she was willing her sexy captor to come back that self-loathing set in and Bertrand spoke.

"No, I doubt they would have killed us. Having brought us all the way here, they would have wanted to speak to us both before resorting to murder. I am speaking of your affinity for the blond boy. I must admit when deciding to allow you to travel with me, I was concerned you might decide you had feelings for me, and I'm afraid that would be impossible."

"What?" Maggie coughed through her mouthful of thick, seedy bread.

"I'm not one to be tied down, Miss Trent. Not to a place, nor to a person. Adding to that the fact you are several centuries younger than me in experience if not in appearance, I hope you can see how impossible an arrangement that would become. And I am glad you moved on so quickly."

"You're right," Maggie said. "I'm really good at moving on."

"I'm so glad," Bertrand said. "But do be careful not to become too attached to the locals. It becomes difficult upon departure, and you can never be too sure what their local laws of modesty might be."

"Girls trying to marry you in all the realms, huh?"

"You haven't any idea, Miss Trent. I am so glad I don't have to worry about that with you."

"Happy to help."

They sat in silence. The longer Maggie listened, the farther away some of the sounds seemed to be. Voices that had shouted to each other earlier were now barely loud enough for her to hear.

Footsteps came up the thin ramp, and Abeyla murmured to someone.

Lamil was the first in the door, then Abeyla. Maggie's heart sank when Tammond didn't reappear. She rolled her eyes at her own stupidity as Abeyla began to speak.

"You've been fed. Now tell us what Jax is planning."

"Ah, you must be Abeyla," Bertrand said pleasantly, "the woman in charge. I am thrilled you came to question us yourself."

Abeyla moved to the side of the pole so she could see both Bertrand and Maggie at the same time.

"You know my name?" she asked, her eyes narrowed.

"Well, the nice blond boy, Tammond, said Abeyla was in charge, and I assume that is you," Bertrand said. "It really is an honor to be questioned by the leader of a group. Things tend to stay so much more reasonable."

"If you would like me to remain reasonable," Abeyla said in a low and dangerous tone, "then tell me what Jax is planning."

"We don't know," Maggie said. "Sincerely, we don't."

"Even if you are not one of the Enlightened—" Abeyla began.

"So, that's what his people are called," Bertrand cut across.

"Everyone in Malina knows Jax Cayde is the Master of the Enlightened," Lamil said.

"And here we have found the answer," Bertrand said. "We are not from Malina. We are from another world far from here."

"The Siren's Realm." Abeyla glared at Maggie.

"Yes, Ma'am. Tammond said you call it the Land Beneath."

"It seems Tammond said a lot of things." Abeyla's face was set so tightly, Maggie couldn't tell if she was starting to believe them or not. "What is this world you come from called?"

"The planet?" Maggie said. "Earth."

"What land?"

Maggie swallowed the urge to say Disney as Bertrand answered, "It was the British Colonies when I left, but Ms. Trent came to the Siren's Realm quite a bit after my time."

"The United States of America," Maggie said, an unexpected pang hitting her chest. "I was born in Virginia. My family was of the Virginia Clan, but I grew up farther north at the Academy. It's a school. Well, prison-slash-school. It's where they put kids with magic who don't have anywhere else to go. That was in Delaware. But I guess you don't know where that is, so I don't suppose it matters."

Abeyla knelt down, her face not a foot away from Maggie's, and stared directly into her eyes. "Why did no one want you? How did you get sent to this Academy?"

"I lost my family." Maggie pushed the words past the lump in her throat. "There's always been disputes about who should be in charge of the Virginia Clan. My family had a blood feud with another family, so there was always fighting.

"My father wanted control of the entire Clan. He attacked the people who were in charge, but the others from the feud, the ones who had always hated us, they joined with the people my father was fighting. My mother sent me to the Academy right after the attack. Within five days of my getting sent away, my whole family was dead. And who wants to take care of a kid from the wrong side of a blood feud?"

Maggie bit her lips together. The metallic taste of blood flooded her mouth, ridding her of the unbearable urge to cry.

"I'm so sorry, Miss Trent," Bertrand said from the other side of the pole.

"Don't be," Maggie said. "People die all the time. Mine just died all at once."

"I didn't know being a witch in our world had stolen so much from you. I can understand why you wanted no part of magic in the Siren's Realm."

"I don't think that worked out so well," Maggie said.

"That has yet to be seen," Bertrand said.

"And the decision seems to lie with me," Abeyla said. "A lost orphan wound up on the Broken Lake—it has happened before, but what about you?" Abeyla narrowed her eyes at Bertrand.

Maggie wished she could see Bertrand's face as Abeyla stared him down.

"What is your story?"

"I lived in a land where magic was forbidden and we were all meant to live like humans. With no joy or laughter, suppressing our magic until we died of awful mundanity. I refused to live my life in breathless boredom, so I left. I found the Siren's Realm and have been living there quite happily ever since, with the occasional exploration of other lands, of course."

Maggie couldn't shake the feeling there was more to the story than Bertrand let on, and Abeyla seemed to agree.

"A man who runs from his world in search of pleasure?" Abeyla stood. "Even Jax Cayde wouldn't want you."

"I take it I've proven my point?" Bertrand asked. "That we are not, in fact, spies or enemies, only travelers?"

Abeyla looked at Lamil for a moment. He gave a small nod.

"I believe you," Abeyla said, "because if Jax had spies coming for us, the simplest lie for you to tell would have been that you had come here to train with the Wanderers. Jax would have found such an elaborate lie distasteful. And I'm sure even Jax's most dispensable spies wouldn't dare do something to displease him."

"Even to save their lives?" Maggie asked. "Jax sounds like a real asshole."

"A lovely description, Miss Trent."

"Jax is a terrible man," Abeyla said, "and I am afraid you might be in more danger here as travelers than as captured spies. If Jax comes, he will not care if you are a Wanderer or not. He will slaughter every living thing in the Wandering Place."

"Great." Maggie leaned her head against the pole. "Can we get untied? That way we won't die strapped to a pole."

Bertrand gave a low laugh.

"Of course." Abeyla raised her hand slowly through the air, and the ropes lifted away as if they had never been tied at all. "But I am afraid you will have to stay with us until morning. You are far from where we took you, and night is nearly here. You could never find your way through the maze alone, and I won't risk my people escorting you in the dark."

Lamil nodded. "A wise choice."

"You will be our guests until morning, then I offer you transport back to where we found you. I suggest you take it. We have not seen Jax or the Enlightened on the Broken Lake yet, but the waters are too vast for us to see all. And I assure you, Jax is coming."

Maggie's heart raced at the finality of Abeyla's words. "Thank you for your hospitality."

"Tonight we shall celebrate the travelers from the Land Beneath." Abeyla turned toward the door. "Every moment that can be celebrated must be cherished." She walked out of the room. Lamil followed her. This time, they did not shut the door behind them.

15

"The Land Beneath," Maggie said, more to push Abeyla's parting words from her mind than anything else. "It sounds like we crawled up from Hell, doesn't it?"

"It wouldn't be wise to make the Siren's Realm sound too appealing." Bertrand stood up and peered out the door. "I've always suspected that is why there are so many from our world in the Siren's Realm—the stories sound so forbidden and enticing. I don't know how anyone resists."

"She also likes to drag people in, remember?" Maggie got stiffly to her feet, rubbing the sore places on her arms where the ropes had bound her.

Looking through the door, Maggie couldn't have said how far from where they had been they currently were, only that they were someplace different.

Surrounding them were high walls of sheer rock, which came down to the lake with no beach to keep the water from lapping gently at the cliffs. Out in front was a channel that curved slowly until it blocked the view of whatever lay beyond. The sky had turned a dusky blue, and soon, even the nearby cliffs would disappear into the darkness.

"I think it's time for a bit of exploring, Miss Trent." Bertrand stepped out the door and onto the ramp.

Maggie nodded before following. Even knowing Bertrand couldn't see her, the silent affirmation that she was choosing to explore and not being dragged into the darkening night was comforting.

The ramp—well, walkway really—was made out of thin bamboo tied together with the same brownish-green rope that had bound them to the pole.

The gentle sway of the water beneath was just enough that Maggie could feel herself move.

Bertrand was already ten feet down the walkway, striding forward with confidence Maggie was unsure she could match. Four steps out onto the ramp, she looked to her left and gasped.

She stood, staring for a moment, trying to force her brain to register what it was she was seeing.

Houses.

A hundred houses floating on platforms made of the same bamboo planks she was standing on. Walkways led from one house to another, wrapping around the sides, cutting across open water, looping to go over the roofs of the houses.

And people everywhere. Sitting on docks outside their front doors, paddling their boats in for the night. A group of children were swimming in the water with an elderly man keeping watch from the side. A little boy not more than three splashed the old man, who pretended to try and dodge the deluge of water, laughing all the while.

In the center of the houses was a structure larger than the rest and a full story taller. The thatched roof seemed to have been peeled away and lay against the sides of the building. Through the gaps between the houses, more people could be seen, surrounding the large building. Young people, around Maggie's age, but they weren't laughing like the children.

Each of them had a look Maggie knew very well. The look of someone who was preparing to fight and knew that a fight might mean saying goodbye to everything they held dear. Even their own lives.

"We should go there." Maggie jogged on the walkway to catch Bertrand, hating the feeling of the ground bobbing under her feet.

Bertrand didn't even look where she was pointing. "Of course we're going to the center of it all, that's why we're here. The center of the wheel might not be where adventure lies, but it is where one can best see what trouble there is to get into."

"But didn't you hear Abeyla?" Maggie whispered, keeping as close to Bertrand as the narrow walkway would allow. "These people are about to be attacked by a very bad man. This isn't an adventure, it's a battlefield...battle-lake...you know what I mean."

"Adventure often comes in the midst of battle, Miss Trent." Bertrand glanced at her with a gleam in his eyes. "Why do you think there are so many heroes who carry swords?"

"But this isn't an adventure for them. It's their lives." Maggie grabbed

Bertrand's arm, forcing him to stop mid-step.

Slowly, he looked down at her fingers clasped around his arm. Without a word, he peeled her fingers away and placed her hand back at her side.

"My dear Miss Trent, I think we must come to an agreement." Bertrand's tone was so patronizing Maggie wanted nothing more than to shove him into the water and see if he ended up back in the Land Beneath. "We both agree we are here to gain a little magic and have a wondrous adventure if this land will allow it. I believe we are both individuals with enough conscience not to want any harm to befall the good people who call this floating village their home.

"But, and this is a very important *but*, Miss Trent, we do not know this world. We do not know the history of their fight with Jax Cayde. They might very well have been in the wrong and are now criminals forced into hiding for doing unspeakable things."

"But you said—"

"People change." Bertrand held up a hand to silence her. "I hope that will be one of the first lessons you learn, Miss Trent. Hopefully for the good, but some inevitably for the bad, people change. We cannot help people when we don't know whom we are helping. I will not hurt people if there is a chance they might be innocent. We are here to learn and to have an adventure. Not to save people who have embroiled themselves in a war we know nothing about."

He paused, staring so intently at Maggie, it took all her willpower not to look away.

"You're right," she said finally. "Maybe Jax is a real live Robin Hood and the Enlightened are his Merry Men. But then what are we supposed to do?"

"We go to that big building, see what there is to see, learn what we can learn, and hope adventure presents itself."

"But what if these really are the good guys?" Maggie asked. "What if our adventure is helping them survive whatever Jax is sending after them?"

"Then what an adventure it shall be."

16

Stares followed them as they made their way through the town. Children were pulled out of their path by adults, and whispers seemed to move faster than the wind.

They had started moving in the direction of the large building, but the ramps didn't make sense.

Some houses were attached by the ramps to the ones catty-corner to them, but not the ones next door. A high ramp, held aloft by thick staffs of bamboo, looked like it should lead them directly to the roofless building. The thing shook so badly as they crossed its narrow slats, Maggie wasn't sure it was actually meant for people to stand on.

Her nails biting into her palms, she took deep breaths, telling herself this would be the last walkway and then they would be at the big building. But when they reached the ground level, they were on another platform ten feet of open water from where they wanted to be.

"I say we swim." Maggie shrugged. "It's not too cold to get wet."

Maggie moved to sit on the edge of the dock, hoping the water here wouldn't be any colder than the part of the lake she had landed in.

"Maggie!" a voice called from across the water. She pitched forward, swinging her arms wildly to catch her balance.

A strong arm wrapped around her middle and yanked her back, landing her right on her butt.

"Careful, Miss Trent," Bertrand said over her muttered, "Ow."

"Are you all right?" a voice called from across the water.

Tammond. Beautiful Tammond, his hair glowing even in the setting sun, was ten feet away from her, looking terribly concerned.

"Fine!" Maggie said, adding in a whisper, "I'm just going to jump in and drown myself now."

Tammond stood in front of the large building. The people around him stared at Maggie, too. Heat crept into her face as she blushed.

"We got a little turned around trying to find a way there." She pointed at the big building, not knowing its name.

A girl with bright red hair leaned in toward Tammond as she giggled.

"The paths can be complicated." Tammond smiled. "Wait there. I'll come and get you."

"Great!" Maggie's voice squeaked as she spoke. "Thanks."

Tammond cut through the crowd and out of sight.

"Miss Trent," Bertrand said, taking her by the elbow and helping her to her feet, "I think it would be best for us to explore separately this evening as there is so little time to discover if there is an adventure here for us. In fact, we only have one night. One brief night, Miss Trent. If you need me please do come and find me."

"Thanks," Maggie said. "Not sure how I'd do that, but sure."

"And remember, Miss Trent, your virtue is your own, but I do hope you'll protect it."

"I—wha—"

"Maggie." Tammond rounded the corner in the opposite direction of the large building. He beamed at her. Like the sun. Her own personal blond-haired, blue-eyed, muscular sun. "I'm glad to see they've decided you aren't here to betray us."

"Yeah," Maggie said breathlessly. "Not evil traitors makes things good."

"How eloquent, Miss Trent," Bertrand said.

"Are you trying to get to the Fireside?" Tammond asked, not looking away from Maggie.

"Is that the big one?" She pointed stupidly across the water, silently cursing her finger for doing something so mundane as pointing.

"It is, and I would be honored to escort you there."

Maggie blushed and followed as Tammond led them back the way he'd come.

"Is that your primary gathering place?" Bertrand asked, breaking the glorious silence Tammond had left in his wake.

"It is our library, our school, our meeting place, and where we gather in the evenings when the village must go dark. It's where the children ride when we travel."

"A simple *yes* truly would have sufficed, but I appreciate your thoroughness."

"What do you mean *travel*?" Maggie asked as Tammond led them down one dock barely wide enough to walk on and onto another that cut through the center of a shop filled with tools.

"You have much to learn, Maggie." Tammond looked over his shoulder with a charming smile. "The Wanderers' home may be small, but it is a place filled with wonder."

They walked across loosely-tied bamboo that sat barely above the water.

Tammond reached back and took Maggie's hand, steadying her as the bamboo swayed.

A thrill shot up Maggie's arm and filled her chest with a warm and brilliant buzzing. "Thank you," she murmured as her cheeks flushed.

"Here we are." Tammond swept an arm through the air. "Welcome to the Fireside."

It was larger than it had looked from far away—three stories high and made of thicker wood than the other buildings in the village. Up close, Maggie could see ropes tied to the roof, which had been peeled away. Wide doors opened out onto a walkway broad enough to allow people to stand five across.

"Impressive." Bertrand examined the peeled-away roof. "Why the moveable covering?"

"To let the sun in during the day for the school children. We tip them up to cover the firelight at night. For rain and moving, we shut the roof tight. We can't afford to have extra rooms, and this is the simplest way to ensure we can use the Fireside for whatever we need."

"Awesome!" Maggie said, her stomach sagging as Tammond looked at her confusedly.

"Great." Maggie corrected. "It's a really great idea. Having one room that does lots of stuff. Like classes and fires…"

"May we see inside?" Bertrand asked.

For once, Maggie was relieved Bertrand was talking.

"Please." Tammond bowed then led them through the crowd.

People gawked as Maggie and Bertrand passed.

It was strange. There were people near Abeyla's age and people near Tammond's age, but there didn't seem to be anyone in the middle. As though for twenty years no one had joined their village.

Before Maggie could begin to come up with a reason why there were no thirty-year-olds, they had entered the Fireside, and she forgot to think.

The four walls were lined with books and shelves reaching from the floor to the eaves right below where the ceiling would have been. Tables with long benches sat along the walls, waiting patiently for students to take their seats. But the fire was what drew Maggie forward. In the center of the room was a metal disk twelve feet wide, holding a swath of low-lying flames, which danced hypnotically, casting the shelves of books in their warm glow.

"Wow," Maggie whispered. "This is not like school back home."

"Not like school anywhere in Malina," Tammond said. "It was never really meant to be this way. The Wanderers were never meant to live all packed together like this. But this is how we've survived. And for the younglings, it's home."

Twin boys around ten-years-old entered the Fireside, carrying trays of food. Both looked terrified, and after a silent battle, one inched forward and spoke so softly to Tammond, Maggie could barely hear from three feet away.

"Abeyla told us to bring food to the spies." The boy's voice wavered as he spoke.

"They aren't spies," Tammond said kindly. "They are only travelers."

"But they're strangers," the other twin squeaked, looking terrified at his own boldness.

"Child," Bertrand said, bending down to look straight into the boy's eyes, "strangers can often be the best sorts of people. You see all those people?" Bertrand pointed to the Wanderers peering in through the doors. "I assume you've known them your whole life."

Both boys nodded.

"You know their stories, you know their ways. But there is the rest of the world to greet. Many, many worlds to know. If you are terrified of anything you have never seen before, how are you to learn about any of it?

"The secret isn't to be afraid of strangers. It's to love the strangeness. Love the challenges it brings. Once you do that, you'll see the dangers that are real. And how much safer will you be if you spend your time fighting those who mean to bring harm rather than those whom you simply do not know?"

"That was actually really good," Maggie said.

"I am quite aware of my aptitude in dealing with children, Miss Trent."

One of the twins passed his tray smilingly to Bertrand while the second shoved his in Maggie's direction, not even bothering to look away from Bertrand as he did it.

"Children are the ones who will tell the most about what's happening in a place," Bertrand said. "They've been too busy learning to walk and speak to have perfected lying. I really should have found a way to bring you a book to write everything I say in, shouldn't I? I am teaching you invaluable things every minute, and I sincerely doubt you are remembering all of it."

"Thanks?" Maggie followed Bertrand to a table. He sat on one side and Tammond on the other.

"If you don't mind," Bertrand said, "I would love to hear more about Jax. Anyone who can be a threat to a group in such a remote location must be either very smart, or very evil."

Maggie stood looking at the two vacant seats left at the table. If she sat next to Tammond, she could be near him while she ate. But if she sat next to Bertrand, she could look at Tammond while she ate.

"Jax Cayde is a terrible combination of both," Tammond said, his voice lower than before, as though he had aged ten years in saying that short sentence.

If she sat across from Tammond, he would watch her eat. She sat down next to him as he began to speak.

"It all began—"

"I do love a good origin of strife tale," Bertrand said, not touching his food as he leaned forward, intently listening to Tammond.

"It all began," Tammond said again, "long before I was born. In some ways, even before my mother was born. Magic has always been a part of our blood in Malina. The same as has the water and the wind. Some have more magic than others, but the power has always been there, since the first stories of the river carrying our land forward. Magic has always been taught to all. It was a right of birth.

"The Wanderers were the teachers. Those most skilled would be trained at the University. When they had finished their studies, they would go out into Malina, stopping in villages and passing on what they had learned." Tammond dug his fingers into his beautiful blond hair. "It may not seem like the best way to people who have seen the Land Beneath."

"It does seem like there are rather large gaps for students to fall through if teachers are simply wandering through towns, teaching what they like." Bertrand tented his fingers under his chin in his now-familiar thinking gesture.

"Every summer, all the Wanderers would travel back to the University. The greatest among them would teach classes. Maps were drawn up, deciding who would go where and what they would teach," Tammond said. "It was planned to the last detail. All to be sure every person would have the opportunity to learn."

Bertrand nodded, Maggie stared, and Tammond continued.

"Thirty years ago, Jax Cayde took up the position as head of the University. He had been one of the greatest Wanderers. Never afraid to climb high into the mountains if there was one person living in the snow who wanted to learn.

Everyone was thrilled, thinking Jax would bring a new age of enlightenment to Malina." Tammond paused, studying his hands, which were gripped tightly together on the table. "It began slowly at first. Not allocating the senior Wanderers to poor towns. Then not sending them as often.

"In his fifth year, he decided at the summer meet not to send any Wanderers at all. Teachers protested. Who were they to decide who should be able to learn the ways of magic? But Jax was persuasive. He told them the Wanderers were the most valuable resource in Malina and their lives couldn't be risked traveling to remote areas. Children should be brought to learn at the University. Some Wanderers refused to obey, and Jax told them to do as they pleased, but they would receive no help from the University. Over the next year, those Wanderers vanished. Some killed by villagers, others disappearing in the wild. All of it seemed to confirm what Jax had told them. No one suspected he might be behind it."

"Jax killed his own people?" Maggie asked, the rich orange pudding she had been eating suddenly tasting foul.

"He did," Tammond said. "But it took people a long time to see what was happening. Jax started by offering for all children to come to the University to study. But the cost of sending a child far from home and losing their labor was too much for most families to consider. The teachers tried to find ways to help, to make it easier for children to make the journey, offering to collect them themselves. But Jax wouldn't allow it. And when a few poor children finally managed to make it to the gates of the University, Jax turned them away, calling them unworthy of the great legacy of magic.

"The Wanderers revolted, declaring magic a right of all in Malina. Jax gave a speech under the painted window in the great library. He told them magic was meant for greater things than to ease the tilling of fields, and as long as they allowed magic to remain common, none would ever grow to reach his full potential. Magic was not meant to serve Malina, but to rule it. He showed the Wanderers magic like they had never witnessed before."

"And the Wanderers believed him," Bertrand said darkly.

"But how?" Maggie asked. "If it was going against everything they believed in?"

"You would be amazed the insanity one impassioned speaker can turn a reasonable crowd toward," Bertrand said. "But Jax didn't convince them all?"

Tammond shook his head. "Of the four-hundred Wanderers, more than sixty left the University that night, determined to strike out on their own and teach all who wished to learn."

"Only sixty?" Maggie asked, her stomach sinking even further into that terrible sick feeling.

"A powerful man is hard to disbelieve, Miss Trent."

"The sixty organized and began teaching," Tammond continued, "always traveling in pairs now, recruiting new teachers whenever they could. Some expected Jax to make them all disappear as he had with the others who had gone against his wishes. But this time he worked through lies, telling the common folk the Wanderers were dangerous. That they were spreading falsehoods and teaching magic too perilous to be used. He said the Wanderers were thieves, stealing from the people they pretended to help. Making children who showed the potential to be greater than them disappear in the night."

"Did people believe him?" Maggie asked.

"Some, but the Wanderers pushed on. Their duty was to teach, and they were determined to fulfill their promise to the people of Malina."

"Whether the people were grateful for it or not." An angry knowing filled Bertrand's voice.

"For three years, the Wanderers taught, fighting to regain the people's trust. Gaining new members whenever they could. I think that's when Jax realized he wasn't going to be able to make them quietly disappear. He had been building his strength at the University. Demanding to be called *Master*"—Tammond said the word with disgust—"by all who studied under him. Giving the title of *Enlightened* to his followers. The Wanderers knew the Enlightened were strong and held no love for them, but no one thought they would attack. Magic being used in war was not a thing ever seen in Malina. Magic is a gift to be treasured, not abused for the terrible purpose of pain and death."

"If only more thought like you," Bertrand said.

"So they attacked and then what?" Maggie asked, wanting the story to be over as quickly as possible. Not because she didn't want to hear, but because the pain of it beat unbearably in her chest.

"The first attack came in the night during the summer meet," Tammond said. A chill swept through the room as though the night wind knew well the horror of which Tammond spoke. "They came in quietly, aiming to kill everyone without a fight. Maybe they had hoped the people wouldn't notice all the Wanderers were gone. But Jax had underestimated our numbers. A fight broke out, and most of the Wanderers managed to escape.

"Word of the attack brought more supporters to the Wanderers as people began to see Jax for the monster he was. They fought and fought. Innocent people were killed. Marcum, the leader of the Wanderers, didn't want any more unnecessary blood spilled. So he led Jax's army here to the Broken Lake for the final battle. Jax brought everyone he had from the University who could fight. Hundreds of his men came through the water to join the battle, with Jax Cayde himself at the helm."

Maggie pictured a man riding a wave of fire, power crackling at his fingertips as he shouted deadly curses into the night.

"It was too much," Tammond said, grief filling his voice for the first time. "Jax slaughtered the Wanderers. He left the lake glowing red with blood."

"I'm so sorry," Maggie murmured at the same time Bertrand said, "But then how did you end up here?"

"Twelve of the wounded managed to hide in the woods. Weak and beaten, they decided to stay here. They built their homes on rafts so they could move throughout the Broken Lake, finding new places to hide." Tammond smiled sadly. "But some were determined to find them.

"Family members who refused to believe those who they loved had been lost. Even if the ones they loved hadn't survived, when they saw what Abeyla had built here, away from Jax, they stayed. Some who wanted to learn from the fabled battle came. They stayed. Children were born, and our home was made."

"And no one who wanted to hurt you ever found you?" Bertrand asked.

"A few who couldn't be trusted have found their way through the maze to us."

"What did you do with them?" Maggie wondered how many others had been tied up in the little cabin.

"If they were confused or lost and meant us no harm, we pulled all memories of the lake from their minds and moved them to the other side of the mountain. If they were Enlightened, we took them far away and killed them."

Maggie swallowed. "Good thing we aren't Enlightened."

"Very good." Tammond turned his bright blue eyes to meet Maggie's, and for the second time, she forgot how to breathe.

"But why do you think Jax is coming now?" Bertrand asked. "You all seem to believe his invasion is imminent."

"Over the past few years—"

Maggie looked toward the sound of Abeyla's voice. As Abeyla approached the table, everyone she passed bowed their heads. Maggie hadn't noticed how many people were listening to Tammond speak.

"—we've been sending Wanderers back out to teach." Abeyla raised a hand before Maggie could even begin to ask a question. "We are meant to be teachers. What is the point in training a new generation if the knowledge never leaves these waters? It is our purpose, and the longer we hide here and do nothing, the stronger Jax Cayde's hold on Malina becomes."

"And he's found out you are once again trying to educate the masses?" Bertrand asked.

"He captured two of our Wanderers," Abeyla said. "They were good people. But under Jax's torture, most would break in time. Our friends in the world have told us Jax is preparing the Enlightened. He's stopped teaching them normal magic. He now only teaches them to fight."

"So Jax finds out his old enemies have been prospering, hidden safely out of sight, and he decides it's time to come looking for you," Bertrand said.

"And to bring an army," Maggie added.

"Precisely," Tammond said.

"We don't know when Jax is coming," Abeyla said, "but we do know he has left the University with three hundred men and disappeared into the wild. There would be no reason for him to travel in the shadows unless he was coming for us."

"Then you should leave the lake," Maggie said. "Go somewhere he can't find you."

"If Jax can find us here," Tammond said, "there is nowhere in Malina he won't follow us. We move the village to many secret places on the lake. Even the people he captured wouldn't be able to tell him where in the maze to find us. So we keep moving and hope he doesn't catch up."

"And when he does?" Bertrand asked.

Maggie didn't miss the *when*.

"We fight," Abeyla said without a hint of fear in her voice. "He may be strong, but we are much stronger than the first time we met. He will be fighting on our waters. We may win."

"But what about the kids?" Maggie asked. "All the little kids. Where are they going to go?"

"There is a place for them to hide," Abeyla said. "A place where Jax will not follow them."

"Then why can't you all go hide there?" Maggie asked. "Why fight at all? Why not go to The Siren's Realm or the Land Beneath or whatever you want to call it?"

"Miss Trent," Bertrand said gently, "that battle you were taken from, when the Siren pulled you away. Would you have left your friends to fight without you if you had been given a choice?"

A cold fist closed around Maggie's heart. "No. No, I wouldn't."

"And would your friends have abandoned their cause to run away and leave their world a worse place without them to defend it?"

"Never."

"Then you cannot ask the Wanderers to run," Bertrand said so softly the bystanders a few feet from their table wouldn't be able to hear. "We are new to this world. Their war is just a story by firelight to us, but to them it is the truth they breathe. This is the world that gave them life. You cannot ask them to leave it to a man like Jax Cayde."

"I'm glad to know some truths hold fast even outside our land," Abeyla said.

"Some truths remain in every world I have seen." Bertrand bowed. "Abeyla, I will not try and persuade you to give up your fight. The spreading of knowledge is a worthy cause. I understand you wish for us to leave in the morning, and I respect your decision. But I have fought in many battles against many foes. Perhaps I can be of some assistance. If in no other way than giving advice before I leave. It seems to me the Wanderers have been a people of peace. There may be holes in the safety of your village you have not found."

Abeyla considered him for a moment. The flickering of the fire cast shadows into the gentle lines of her face, making her look twice her age. "I would be a fool to turn down help. When you're ready."

"Now is the perfect time." Bertrand stood. "There is never time to waste when battle nips at your heels." Bertrand looked to Maggie. "Stay here, try not to get hurt, and if battle does come, do remember not to use any magic here that might get you killed."

"Right." Maggie nodded, not sure if she should feel grateful for Bertrand's concern or punch him in the face for thinking she couldn't take care of herself.

"Don't worry," Tammond said, "I will make sure Maggie comes to no harm."

"Brilliant," Bertrand said dryly before following Abeyla out of the Fireside and into the night.

17

Maggie sat at the table, not sure where to look. If she looked at Tammond, she might drool. If she looked at the people around her staring at her, she might run. So instead she looked at the books lining the walls.

"How did they all get here?" Maggie pointed to the shelves upon shelves of books.

"We brought them here," the girl with the red hair from outside said as though Maggie didn't understand things could be carried.

"The first Wanderers who came to the lake brought their books with them," Tammond said after glaring at the girl with the red hair, who huffed and stalked away. "Others who came to join brought more. A few times, we've sent people out to find new books, ones that were necessary to learn. All of the books we have in the village reside in this room."

"But," Maggie said, hoping her words wouldn't offend, "wouldn't it be safer not to keep all your written knowledge next to a giant fire?"

Sniggers floated around the crowd.

"The Fireside is safe." Tammond took Maggie's hand in his and led her toward the fire. Heat rushed to her face, and she hoped the warmth of the flames would be a good enough excuse for the redness creeping into her cheeks.

Placing his palm on the back of Maggie's hand, Tammond moved her fingers toward the flames. Fear told her she would be burned, but Tammond stood close behind her, his steady heartbeat thrumming into her back. A foot before her hand reached the flames, her palm touched something soft—an invisible barrier as cool as the water of the lake, even as the heat of the fire passed through it to warm the room.

"Wow," Maggie breathed.

"The fire is safe for all of us," Tammond said.

Maggie turned to face him. His chest pressed into hers. He gazed down into her eyes.

"It's…beautiful."

Tammond smiled. "I have seen many beautiful things, but I had never thought to count the Fireside among them."

Giggles came from behind Tammond's broad shoulders. The group in the Fireside had grown. Teenagers and adults alike stared at Tammond and Maggie by the fire.

"Perhaps we should go." Tammond kept his voice low. "There are other beautiful things to see in our village."

Maggie nodded, not trusting herself to speak, and followed Tammond out into the dark.

The night had grown cool with the breeze across the lake. The surface of the water reflected the stars, and the moon gave depth to the mountains around them, casting their high peaks into silhouette. The roof of the Fireside had been raised up to block the light of the flames within. In the village no lights shone. No lamps peered through windows. No cooking fires crackled.

"Is everyone asleep?" Maggie whispered.

"Some are," Tammond said. "The rest are either at the Fireside or enjoying the darkness."

A thrill shot through Maggie's stomach as she wondered what *enjoying the darkness* might mean.

"Don't worry," Tammond said, taking Maggie's hand in his, "the stars and the moon will give us enough light to make our way through the village."

"I'm not worried." Maggie pulled her gaze from Tammond to watch where she was stepping. "It's just sad that you all have to hide in the dark."

"Only at night." Tammond gave Maggie a shining smile. "And to be free from the Enlightened, to be able to teach and learn, it's worth hiding our fires at night."

"Did you ever go out to teach?" Maggie asked.

He had led her away from the Fireside to a walkway that skirted the very edge of the village. This walkway was longer and more solid than the others she had seen.

"No," Tammond said, a hint of bitterness creeping into his voice. "You aren't to teach until you've reached twenty-one years. They won't let me leave the lake until next year."

"I'm sorry."

"It is as it must be. Besides, my mother has told me many times I am too rebellious to be trusted in the outside world. I would be too likely to fight someone who opposed free teaching, and then where would we all be?"

"Your mother gets to decide if you get to go?"

"If your mother is Abeyla."

"Wait." Maggie tugged on Tammond's hand, forcing him to stop. "Abeyla is your mom?"

"A fact the Wanderers will never let me forget." Tammond grimaced. "It's not easy being the son of your people's savior."

Maggie opened her mouth to say something comforting and brilliant, but, "No, I guess it wouldn't be," was all that came out.

The long path ended, and he led her up onto a high ramp. This one didn't sway as they climbed bamboo slats ten feet above the row of houses they had walked past.

"Why the ramps?" Maggie asked, wishing there was a bit more light to see where she was stepping and trying not to picture herself falling through someone's roof and into their bedroom.

"To see above the village, and hold the village steady when we travel." Tammond sat on the ramp, drawing Maggie down to sit with him.

"How does the village travel?" Maggie asked. Tammond's arm brushed against hers, and her stomach purred.

"If you stay a little longer, perhaps you'll see."

"Hmm." Maggie didn't trust herself to say words.

"It must seem small here to you," Tammond said, gazing at Maggie as though wanting to drink in every bit of her, "between your home and the Land Beneath."

Maggie clamped a hand over her mouth, trying hard not to laugh.

Tammond raised an eyebrow and smiled at her.

"I—" Maggie began, shoving aside the instinct that told her not to talk about anything that mattered, "I mostly grew up in a place about this size, but without the lake and mountains."

"At the Academy." Tammond nodded, taking Maggie's hand in his. "The school cared for you?"

The warmth of his touch made Maggie shiver. The cool night air suddenly seemed too cold to bear. Tammond wrapped an arm around her, pulling her close to his side.

"They didn't." Maggie searched for the words that would cause the least sympathy. "They didn't really care for us. They fed us, taught us, and kept us alive, but that's about it. We weren't allowed to leave the grounds. I didn't see the outside world for twelve years. Twelve years of gray walls."

"No wonder you decided to leave for the Land Beneath."

"I didn't decide." Maggie fought the images of blood and the scent of fire even thinking of the green mist brought flooding back to her. "There is a bad man—our version of Jax, I guess. He's evil and wants to kill a whole bunch of people. Not everyone in our world has magic, and he wants the people that do to be able to control the people that don't.

"Friends—well maybe not friends, but the people who let me out of the Academy—were going to fight the bad guy, and I volunteered to go with them. It was terrible. Fighting in the woods, people dying everywhere. Our people, the bad guy's people. And blood...so much blood."

Tammond pulled her closer, leaning his cheek against the top of her head.

"Then in the middle of it all, there was this green mist, and I saw someone in it, a friend of mine. I ran forward to try and help him, but he wasn't there. There was nothing but darkness in the mist, and then I fell. That's how I ended up in the Land Beneath. I didn't choose it."

"I'm sorry."

The honest sympathy in his voice made it hard for Maggie to breathe. "Don't be. I survived."

"I'm glad you did." Tammond looked down at Maggie. His face was so close to hers. Gently, he pressed his lips to her forehead. "And I'm glad you landed in the Broken Lake as well."

"Me, too." Maggie held her breath, waiting to be kissed again, this time preferably on the lips.

"I've never met someone like you. My whole life I've lived in a beautiful place with wonderful people. Always moving. Always surviving. I never realized..." Tammond brushed the hair from Maggie's face. "Maggie Trent, you are a blazing light in the darkness."

She stared at him for one heartbeat, then another. Forgetting to breathe as her mind raced, imagining what his lips would taste like. "Stars," Maggie gasped when her lungs finally remembered they needed air.

"What?"

"Your stars are different from ours," Maggie said.

You stupid girl, you ruin everything! Every good and beautiful thing! Now he hates you!

"I suppose all worlds have stars as unique as their people." Tammond lay back on the ramp, laying his arm down beside him to make a spot for Maggie.

Okay, maybe he doesn't hate you, but don't mess it up again.

Maggie took a deep breath and lay down, resting her head on Tammond's shoulder.

"I've only been here, the Siren's Realm, and home," Maggie said. "But all the stars have been different. When I was little, my dad told me people made up constellations and stories about the stars so they could feel close to home even when they were really far away. Now I understand why. Not seeing the stars I'm used to, it makes me feel further from home than anything else."

They lay in silence for a moment. The waves gently lapped against the village, which creaked softly with each movement.

"We have stories for our stars, too." Tammond's voice was as soothing as if he were telling a bedtime story. "Maybe if you know our stories, you won't feel so lost."

"I'd like that."

"The seven bright ones," Tammond said, pointing to each of them in turn, "are the captains of the seven ships that brought the first people down the great river to Malina from a land far away where magic only lived in the dark, hidden places. Right there"—he pointed to six stars that were close together, making a diamond with the two extra stars coming out the top—"is the great ship that came before the seven and discovered Malina."

"Imagine," Maggie said, "discovering a whole new world no one has ever seen before."

"You've found a whole new world." Tammond turned to face Maggie. "Do you wish there weren't people here?"

His lips were close to Maggie's...so very close. "Ummm. I..."

His lips brushed hers. Gently, carefully, as though afraid she might push him away. Pulling herself closer, Maggie deepened the kiss. His heartbeat echoed in her chest, racing as she twined her fingers through his hair.

"Maggie," he whispered as he pulled her closer, wrapping both arms around her as though he wanted to be sure she was real.

Maggie gasped, all thoughts of stars and faraway places gone. She was here with Tammond, and nothing else mattered. His hand found her hip, tracing a line up her side through her thin shirt.

"Miss Trent," a voice came from below.

Maggie squeaked and rolled away from Tammond. Her shoulder found the edge of the ramp, and before she could stop herself, her torso was hanging out over thin air.

"Maggie!" Tammond shouted, grabbing Maggie by the ankles to keep her from falling into the water below.

"Miss Trent," Bertrand said calmly, his upside-down face level with Maggie's as he stood on the roof beneath the walkway, "I see you have had a chance to explore the finer sights of the village."

So much blood had already rushed to Maggie's head it was impossible for her to blush. "What do you want?" Maggie snapped as the bamboo cut painfully into her back.

"We need to discuss our departure plans, Miss Trent."

"Now?" Maggie widened her eyes, hoping fruitlessly that Bertrand would understand and walk away.

"Yes, right now, Miss Trent," Bertrand said, "but I think it would be better if you either came down to the roof or went back up on the walkway. It would be rude to ask Tammond to continue holding you by the ankles when our discussion does not require you to be upside-down."

"You," Maggie growled at Bertrand as Tammond pulled her back up onto the walkway and lifted her to her feet in one swift motion.

"Thanks," Maggie gasped.

Tammond caught her around the middle to keep her from falling back over again.

"My pleasure," Tammond said. "I should let you two talk. The sooner you leave, the safer you'll be."

"But—" Maggie began, but Tammond leaned down and was kissing her again. Her knees melted as she leaned into his strong chest. Tammond pulled away, kissed her on the forehead, and walked down the ramp into the darkness.

"Well," Bertrand said.

Maggie spun to find Bertrand standing two feet behind her.

"Don't do that." Maggie grasped her chest. "Do not sneak up on people."

"In general or when they are doing illicit things in the dark?"

"I don't think that's any of your—"

"Whatever you do is my business as I am personally responsible for your safety while outside the Siren's Realm."

"What?"

"I brought you here, Miss Trent, and I intend to bring you back to the Siren' Realm alive. Which brings me to my next point—our departure."

"I think we need to stay—"

"We can't leave in the morning—"

"What?" Maggie said. "You think we should stay, too?"

"Certainly, Miss Trent. I've seen their guards. The sort of magic they use is fascinating and well worth exploring. But from the stories I've been told of this Jax, they are in no way prepared to handle that sort of attack. The Wanderers study magic for magic's sake. Jax studies magic to learn how to control and destroy. I don't think any of them even truly think they can win a battle against Jax. What sort of people would we be if we abandoned our hosts to such a terrible fate?"

"Terrible people," Maggie said more emphatically than she had meant to.

"And why do you wish to stay, Miss Trent?"

"Same reasons as you," Maggie said. "We can't let Jax destroy this place. That would be very bad."

"Good." Bertrand nodded again, apparently not having noticed anything strange. "Then the best thing we can do is rest. Abeyla has informed me the village will be moving in the morning. She will wake us in a few hours to watch the preparations. Once we are in the new position, we will help the Wanderers to train and prepare the village for war."

Bertrand strode down the ramp, not bothering to look back to see if Maggie followed.

18

The room they were given was better than where they had been held prisoner, though nearly as small and made almost entirely of bamboo. The walls, floor, and shutters were all made of bamboo of some kind. Even the bedframe was bamboo. Luckily, the mattress was something soft. Maggie didn't want to know what she was sleeping on badly enough to think of anything beyond gratitude it wasn't bare rock.

She lay staring at the thatched roof, trying to sleep. Bertrand was already breathing in a maddeningly steady rhythm. If only Tammond were here instead of Bertrand. Kissing her, holding her.

Dammit.

Every time she closed her eyes all she could see was Tammond. Smiling. His blue eyes sparkling.

She opened her eyes and looked back up at the crisscrosses of the ceiling.

Way to make out with the guy who kidnapped you earlier today. Good for you, Maggie. Awesome choices.

But then she closed her eyes, and Tammond was pulling her close to his big strong chest. Holding her like he would never ever let her go.

Before she knew if she had actually fallen asleep, there was a knock at the door.

Maggie leapt out of bed and dragged her fingers through her hair.

"I didn't take you for an early riser, Miss Trent," Bertrand said as he pulled on his jacket.

"I'm full of surprises." Maggie yanked open the door to find a person a third of Tammond's size.

A little girl with big brown eyes stared up at Maggie.

"Excuse me," the little girl's voice wavered with fear. "Abeyla told me to come get you. You're to watch the traveling from the Fireside with us." The girl averted her eyes and gave a half-curtsey.

"Ah, perfect," Bertrand said over Maggie's shoulder. "And what is your name, little one?"

"Mina," the little girl said barely loud enough for Maggie to hear.

"Well then, Mina," Bertrand said, "lead on please. I don't want to miss any of this."

Mina smiled and reached through the door, taking Bertrand's hand in her own and pulling him past Maggie.

"They'll start as soon as the sun touches the mountains," Mina said, her voice quiet even in her excitement. "And we can see all of it from the Fireside. When I am big, I will be a rower like my mother. Now I am too small, but I watch with the others so I can learn."

"Watching is a very good way to learn."

Even though the sky was just beginning to turn gray, the village was already bustling with people, all moving silently in patterns that suggested they had done this very thing many times before.

"Mina," Bertrand asked, his voice matching the quiet of the morning, "how often do you move the village?"

"Used to be every six days." Mina led them down a path that cut below the short eaves of a building, making Maggie and Bertrand double over to follow. "But since the grownups have been scared of the bad people coming, we move every three. The runners go to the hills every three days now, too, to tell where we're going."

"Runners?" Maggie asked, but before Mina could answer they had reached the Fireside, and she had turned around to beam at them.

"I know faster ways than the big folks." Mina planted hands on her hips, her chin tipped up with pride. "I'm a good leader."

"You did very well, Mina." Bertrand bowed.

Maggie was glad he didn't mention they got there faster because they had climbed through places too small for *big folks* to fit.

"It's almost time," Mina said, taking Bertrand's hand again. "We can watch the unwrapping and moving from the deck if you like, but we have to stay here."

"That's fine," Maggie said. "Thanks for bringing us."

Mina didn't seem to notice Maggie had spoken. She was too busy staring adoringly at Bertrand.

A whistle sounded from the front of the village. Maggie peered through the houses but couldn't see the source of the sound. A shuddering of the deck below her feet was the first sign of what the signal had meant. Mina grabbed her and pulled her away from the edge of the dock.

"Don't fall in."

Maggie opened her mouth to say she wouldn't, but the words disappeared as the high ramp nearest them started to sink toward the water. Two men were removing the heavy poles that had held the walkway high in the air as a woman pushed another pole against the building opposite her. As the walkway lowered to the water, the houses moved away from each other, unfurling into one long line.

Moving carefully across the deck, Maggie could see the other high walkway being lowered. Low walkways were being tied together to lock the houses into place with the Fireside at the center. The village was transforming from a watery maze into a barge, solid and ready for travel.

There was no shouting of orders or panicked movements. Everything was fluid. From the knots being tied to make sure the ramps were joined, to the great poles being stored.

Soon, boats were being lowered into the water on both sides of the Fireside and tied to the edges of the walk. Maggie leaned out as far as she dared to see more boats being tied all along the village. Rowers climbed into their boats as others climbed onto the roofs.

As soon as the last boatman was in place, each of the people on the roofs raised a hand, and a voice from the front of the village yelled, "Forward!" As one, the rowers began paddling.

At once, the deck surged forward, jarring Maggie and making her stumble, but with the next stroke, the only movement she could feel was the steady momentum of the village.

"Amazing."

Maggie jumped as Bertrand spoke right over her shoulder.

"An entire village moving," Bertrand said. "Without threats or fuss. Just moving on to the next place."

"No!" A man paddled up along the side of the village. "Stop please! We can't leave. We can't!"

The man leapt from his boat and up onto the Fireside walkway. "Please stop this! Abeyla! Please!" The man's face was desperate and pale. Dirt caked his hair, and scratches bled on his cheeks. "Abeyla!"

"Elson." Abeyla appeared around the corner, her voice tense. "We can't stay. You know we can't stay."

"But my wife is still out there!" the man cried. "My wife, Abeyla!"

"I know, Elson," Abeyla said, "but for the good of the village, we must move on."

"My wife was out in the jungle for the good of the village!" Elson shouted. "Searching for resources for the *good of the village.*"

"Lana knew the risks," Abeyla said. "She knew the risks as we all do."

"So we leave her behind? Two days gone, and we consider her lost forever?" Tears streamed down the man's furious face.

"She can find the watchers in the hills," Abeyla said, holding her hands out as she approached Elson. "The watchers always know where we are going. Lana knows to go there. She will find her way. But we can't risk the entire village to wait for one person."

"She's my wife."

"She knows the way to the watchers," Abeyla said, taking Elson's shaking hands in hers. "She can find her way home."

"And if the Enlightened have found her in the woods?"

"Lana is a brave woman," Abeyla said. "She would never betray the Wanderers."

Elson collapsed to the ground, shaking in his tears.

Abeyla knelt beside him. "It is not an easy path we tread. The life of a Wanderer is hard and long. Lana is a brave and strong woman. She holds magic deep within her blood. She will find her way to the watchers, and they will send her home. You must believe that."

"Yes, Abeyla," the man said weakly through his tears.

As if on a silent command, a big man appeared at Abeyla's side and half-lifted Elson to his feet before leading him away down the ramp.

Abeyla watched them for a moment before turning to Bertrand. "It may seem cruel to leave one of our own behind, but the best safety we have is in staying hidden."

"Protecting the many is not an easy task," Bertrand said. "Yours is not a place in which many could stand."

"No," Abeyla said, "but sometimes leaders aren't given a choice. When everyone else is gone, you must stand up and do your best to protect whatever is left." Without another word, Abeyla walked away toward the front of the village.

Through it all, the rowers had never stopped pulling the village forward. The boat Elson had rowed up was tied to the side of the deck, clunking uselessly along as they traveled.

A shuffling and sniffling from the opening to the Fireside caught Maggie's attention. The children were huddled in the doorway, fear on their faces. Mina stood at the front of the pack, her little eyes brimming with tears.

"You all right?" Maggie asked. She had never been good with the little ones at the Academy. They cried too much and worried too much about getting home. Maggie had learned the uselessness of tears years ago.

"I hate the Enlightened." Mina rubbed her nose with her hand. "They ruin everything. They make the runners go more. And make it harder for people to get home. And when they come, they'll put all of us in the dark place to hide."

"That does sound pretty scary." Maggie sat down on the deck as Bertrand gave a warning growl of, "Miss Trent."

"But I think you're pretty brave," Maggie said, "and when you're brave, it's okay to be scared of the dark and the Enlightened. But you don't let your fear stop you. Do you like it when the village moves?"

Mina nodded. "We're almost to the rocks. The rocks are the fun part."

Mina was right. The village had almost reached the rocks that curved a path to the rest of the Broken Lake. Maggie's heart leapt into her throat. They wouldn't be able to fit through the opening. The village would hit the rocks and crumble. They would all drown before the Enlightened even had a chance to reach them.

Maggie took a breath, making sure her voice would be steady. "Why do you like going through the rocks, Mina?"

"I like the rocks because it feels like the lake is hugging the village, like it's promising to protect the Wanderers." Mina gave a wet smile and pointed up at the rocks high overhead. "See? They're so tall they almost block out the whole sky. I bet if we stayed right here, the Enlightened would never find us."

"Why do you move?" Maggie asked. "Why travel the lake?"

"Magic leaves marks," a boy at the back of the pack said, clapping his hand over his mouth in astonishment at his braveness. It took him a moment to recover before he spoke again. "When we stay in a place, we fill it with our magic. And if we stay too long, the marks start to stay, and then it's easy for people to find us. We used to be able to stay longer, but now that we know we're being watched, we have to move more often to stay safe."

"Wow," Maggie said, not letting her gaze stray to the rock outcropping that jutted out over their heads. "Sounds like a great system. What kind of magic do you do here? I've seen the fire inside. How it's protected so no one can get burned, but what kind of magic do you do that makes a mark?"

The boy's face flushed with embarrassment as he made his way to the front of the children.

"I-I can do this." The boy smiled as his feet rose a few inches into the air before he landed back on the deck with a *thud*.

The children behind him giggled, and he turned to them, whispering angrily, "I'd like to see you do better."

"That was quite impressive, young sir." Bertrand nodded.

"Oh watch what I can do!" Mina ran through the other children and returned a moment later, holding a red flower the size of her hand.

Staring at the flower with such concentration her forehead wrinkled, the flower turned from red, to purple, to a bright pink.

Soon all the children were clamoring to show what magic they could do. One girl made herself light enough to climb the wall using only two fingers on each hand. A little boy juggled tiny balls of green fire. Maggie and Bertrand laughed and applauded as one child after another did their best magic to impress the guests.

The mountains slid by, and the rowers kept pulling, moving them to unknown parts of the lake. The people on the roofs directed the rowers with arm signals, slowly turning the village where it needed to go.

The children's display ended with one boy pelting rocks at a girl who would block the pebbles before they could reach her with the wave of a hand.

Maggie and Bertrand applauded along with the other children so enthusiastically the two sparrers bowed deeply before taking their seats.

"I think we have learned a great deal about your magic." Bertrand stood and bowed to the children. "You have given us an excellent demonstration, but now if Miss Mina will show us a place, I would like to get a higher view of our travel."

"Best go fast," one of the older children said urgently, "we'll be to our new spot soon."

"Then time is of the essence," Bertrand said.

Mina took his hand and led him from the other children with a look of great importance on her face.

She led them to the backside of the Fireside and pointed at the closest house. "You can go up there, but don't go farther. We aren't supposed to leave the Fireside while we're traveling."

"I assure you we shall stray no farther," Bertrand said, going into the house and straight up a ladder in the center.

"Thanks," Maggie said to Mina before climbing the ladder, more than a little grateful Mina didn't try to follow.

The ladder led up to a trapdoor, which opened out onto the roof, giving them a view of the lake around them. They were headed toward a narrow entry between two spires. Maggie could see the shore behind the spires—a gentle slope that led from the water to the mountain miles behind.

"I am pleased, Miss Trent," Bertrand said. "I didn't think you would be so good with children, and they have provided us a fount of information by your asking one simple question."

"What fount of information?" Maggie held her breath as the fronts of the boats that dragged the village passed between the spires.

"We now know they do not have a language for their spells," Bertrand began. "We've learned they train their children from a very young age. They use no talisman. We've also learned I was unfortunately correct in my assumption that they are sadly ill-prepared to fight Jax. The oldest of their children can do basic shielding against non-magical objects only."

"But it's still a shield," Maggie said. "I'm sure the adults can do more."

"The adults hide," Bertrand said. "The children can't defend themselves. As soon as the village is settled, I will ask Abeyla to meet with her best fighters. She knows I wish to offer my help, and, given their position, even the fighters should be glad to receive it."

"Okay," Maggie said. "You help them prepare for battle, and what do I do? Please don't say hang out with the kids more."

"You seem to have formed a, shall we say, close attachment to Tammond," Bertrand said, not pausing or even seeming to notice when Maggie blushed bright red. "I will ask Abeyla if he can train you in their ways of magic. Then, when the battle comes, you will be prepared to fight."

"What about you?" Maggie asked as the village reached the inside of the cove and, with a whistle from the front of the village, rowers climbed back up onto the docks. "Won't you need to know how to fight?"

"My dear Miss Trent, I have traveled to many places and am much more adept at picking up different forms of magic than you are. I appreciate your concern, but I assure you when the time comes, I will be more than capable of assisting in the battle. Let Tammond help you. I will learn by teaching the fighters."

"Fine," Maggie said, her stomach already fluttering at the thought of spending more time with Tammond.

"But do remember, Miss Trent, though our stay with the Wanderers may have lengthened, we remain visitors in their lives."

"Yes sir," Maggie said, wondering if Tammond would be able to find a private place to teach her the ways of the Wanderers' magic.

19

"The magic is already in your mind," Tammond said. He stood right behind Maggie, his breath whispering on her neck as he gently covered her eyes. "Magic runs deep in your blood as it does in ours. Feel it pulsing through you."

Maggie took a shuddering breath, trying to focus on Tammond's words instead of how close he was standing.

"Feel the magic in your hands. Find its texture, its warmth."

Maggie's hands trembled in front of her. There was warmth—she could feel it. Like she was holding her hands on either side of a candle. But it didn't feel like magic. There was nothing leaving her body, no energy being lost. Only a pale heat that didn't feel like it had much to do with her at all.

"Find the fire. Nurture it, and allow it to grow. Let its warmth surround you. Let it fill you."

But she didn't want the warmth to surround her. She wanted Tammond.

Heat like embers flew against her palms.

"Ouch." She pulled her hands away.

Giggling sounded around the Fireside. Maggie moved her head to look toward the sound, but Tammond kept her eyes covered.

"It's all right," he said soothingly. "Just try again. Concentrate."

"Wouldn't it be easier to focus if I could see?" Maggie growled to another round of giggles. "Or if I weren't being watched by an entire village worth of kids."

"It's nice to know some grownups aren't very good at magic either," a little voice said from the corner.

"Mina, be nice," another voice squeaked.

"Now try again," Tammond said.

"Are you sure we couldn't go somewhere else?" Maggie asked, knowing it would be no easier to concentrate on magic if she were alone with Tammond.

"We'll stay here for now," Tammond said. "This is the room for learning, so what better place to start? Now concentrate."

The sun had begun to drift down toward the mountains before Maggie managed to hold the light in her hands. It had taken her hours to manage it with her eyes closed, and it wasn't much easier to form the pale light with her eyes open. The sphere didn't have much distinction. It wasn't something that could be thrown or left to hover in the air and provide light. It was only a manifestation of magic.

Maggie wanted to shout that a manifestation of magic wasn't going to do any good when Jax came, but Tammond was determined this was the way she must learn. And he stood so close, staring at her with his bright blue beautiful eyes, she couldn't bring herself to argue.

Finally, when their lesson was done, he let her sit next to the Fireside while he collected food for them. There was a dull murmur from the adults in the gathering place Maggie wouldn't have noticed if she hadn't heard it before. Something had happened. Something the children weren't supposed to know about, and something they didn't want to tell her.

Maggie stared at her hands on the table. In the warm light of the fire, they looked normal. The faint scars from fishing in the Siren's Realm couldn't be seen. There was no mark to show she held any magic. Just two pale hands against the dark wood of the table. Back home, she could have thrown the table across the room. Burned it in an instant. Torn it apart and used the pieces to fight. But here she was helpless. Barely able to cast a basic spell.

And she and Bertrand were supposed to help these people survive. Suddenly their whole plan for adventure seemed the most horribly selfish thing imaginable. They wanted adventure, but the Wanderers wanted to survive. How dare they think they could help?

Maggie had just made up her mind to find Bertrand and tell him it was time to leave when a plate of food was slid in front of her. She looked up to find Tammond smiling down at her.

"You did well today." Tammond took a seat on the bench opposite her.

"I made a bit of light." Maggie ran her hands over her face. "I'm useless. It's a waste of time for you to even be trying to teach me."

Tammond caught her hand in his. "Learning is never a waste." He looked at her palm, tracing the lines that crisscrossed her hand.

A tingle shot up Maggie's arm.

For the love of God, girl, keep it together!

"And you are doing very well. Now eat, Maggie." Tammond pushed her plate closer to her. "There is still much for you to learn. A whole library's worth, in fact."

Maggie examined the shelves of books. They were worn and had strange leather patches in places, like ancient bound books from back home. The books even had titles embossed on their spines.

The Founding of Magic in Malina, A Light Within, The Magic of Others: Tales of Magic within Animals.

"I can read the titles," Maggie said, leaving her food untouched on her plate and moving to the bookshelf. She pulled down *The Magic of Others* and opened to the first page.

Though magic has long been known to flow through the blood of Man in Malina, it is also known that animals who share our land...

"I can read the books." Maggie ran her fingers along the words.

"Reading is a fine skill to have," Tammond said.

"But I can read your words, and I can speak to you." Maggie shook her head, trying to think of her words before she spoke them to make sure it was English that was coming out. "Back home, there are hundreds of languages people speak, and I only know one of them. How is it that I fall from the Siren's Realm into another world and I can speak and read your language?"

Tammond considered for a moment as Maggie read another line in the book.

Old fables suggest in times long ago, animals that possessed magic would align themselves with men, becoming their partners in the creation of magic.

"Magic," Tammond said finally. "The only reason I can think of is magic. The Siren's magic allowed you to come to us. Magic has allowed you to speak to us."

A tingle shook Maggie's shoulders at the idea of the Siren herself watching, twisting the words in her mind so she could understand the Wanderers. Dread dripped into her stomach, forming a layer of trepidation that lurked beneath her fear of Jax Cade.

Slowly, she placed the book back on the shelf. "I'll have to ask Bertrand. He would know better. He's been so many places."

But the next moment all concern for magic controlling the words she spoke was washed away by a scream from the shore.

20

"How dare you!" the voice screamed.

Maggie ran out of the Fireside, pushing past the children crowded by the door.

On the shore not thirty feet away, two of the Wanderers stood opposite a man dressed all in black.

"How dare you come to our village and make threats." The voice belonged to a man from the Wanderers. Rage contorted his face.

"I have not come to make threats," the man in black said. "I am a messenger of Jax Cayde. We have found your watchers in the hills. There is no one left to give you our warning. We have found your home." The man turned to face the village. "I have come upon your patrol without their knowledge. You cannot fight us."

"We will fight you," the second Wanderer on the shore spat. "All of us will fight you."

The man in black turned to the woman and smiled.

Rage filled Maggie's chest. Without thinking beyond wanting to stop the man from smiling as he made threats, Maggie walked to the edge of the docks and slipped silently into the water.

The water was cool and calm.

"Maggie," Tammond hissed, but Maggie didn't wait to hear what he was saying. Taking a deep breath, she dove beneath the surface.

The water was clear enough to see her way as she swam toward the shore, aiming behind the man in black. Months spent fishing in the Siren's Realm had made holding her breath easy, and before her lungs burned from lack of air, she had reached the shore.

Peeking up above the surface, she could see the man still facing the Wanderers.

"You have been given two days to surrender," the man said, his voice loud, clear, and full of confidence that not taking Jax's terms would mean certain death for the Wanderers. "Those not guilty of crimes against the Enlightened will be reeducated and allowed to join society. Those who have fought against the Enlightened will be tried for crimes against the great people of Malina."

The eyes of the male Wanderer caught Maggie's, widening as she raised her head above the water. Maggie pressed a finger to her lips, hoping it was a universal enough sign for him to know to keep quiet.

"You—" the Wanderer began, haltingly "You! How dare you come here and threaten the Wanderers? We are the true teachers of Malina. Our ways are older than yours."

Maggie pulled herself silently onto the bank, feeling the eyes of everyone in the village on her back.

"If you were so wise, old man," the man in black spat, "perhaps you would know when your time had passed."

A spell. One quick spell and the man in black would drop to the ground unconscious. Or a flower would grow. Maggie cursed to herself, wishing any of her sparring training were useful now. But it didn't matter.

"Two days, old man. You have two days to get your people in order."

A branch lay on the ground, smaller and lighter than Maggie would have wished for but she didn't have time to look for anything else.

"When the Enlightened fight, they fight to kill," the man said. "This is the only mercy you will see from us."

Raising her arms high, Maggie sprinted toward the man, bringing the stick down on his head with an almighty *crack* before he could turn to see what the noise was. The man crumpled to the ground, a look of surprise etched on his face.

"I've never liked other people's mercy," Maggie murmured as shouts rose from the village. "It always comes at too high a cost."

"Maggie!" Tammond leapt into the water, swimming quickly to shore.

"Miss Trent," Bertrand called from his spot on the docks, "you must be careful when doing such things."

"I really don't get a *nice aim!* or anything?" Maggie said.

"Oh, your aim was excellent, Miss Trent, and I agree—stopping his incessant threats was a valid choice," Bertrand said as Tammond emerged from the water and ran toward Maggie. "I am merely urging caution."

"Well, thanks for appreciating my valid choice," Maggie said as Tammond took her face in his hands.

"Are you all right, Maggie?" Tammond searched her face for some kind of harm.

"Yeah, I'm fine." Maggie looked toward the man on the ground. "He's the one who might not be okay. Is he still alive?"

The male Wanderer who had been shouting at the man in black knelt down next to him.

"Even if he is dead, you must not blame yourself," Tammond said, taking Maggie's hand as she leaned over the body.

"I wouldn't," Maggie said. "He threatened the village, and he threatened the kids. If I broke his head, it's no more than he deserves."

"He's alive," the Wanderer declared.

"I'll try harder next time." Maggie's voice was so cold, it nearly shocked her for a moment. But the moment was brief. There was no time to cry over a hurt person who wanted to hurt you. Her family had taught her that a long time ago.

"Get him in the boat." Abeyla had arrived onshore in a tiny boat rowed by Bertrand. "We need to get him tied up in the village. He may have information."

Tammond nodded and dragged the Enlightened to the boat, letting his head hit the rocks on the ground along the way.

"Sorry if I bonked him too hard," Maggie said as Abeyla turned her stern gaze to her.

"Don't be," Abeyla said. "You were brave and protected my people. We are not used to violence or conflict. It is not a thing we have resorted to in many years. But it would be impossible to argue the time has come to fight. I will not begrudge you drawing first blood. Perhaps we needed someone from the Land Beneath to show us how very close that time has come."

"So what do we do now?" Maggie asked, following Abeyla back to her boat. "You aren't going to surrender, right?"

"We have been given two days," Abeyla said. "We will move the village to the safest place we have and deliver the children to their refuge. When the Enlightened come, we fight."

"Great," Maggie said as Bertrand rowed Abeyla back to shore, leaving Tammond with Maggie. "I guess I should find myself a bigger stick."

"Maggie, you could have been killed," Tammond said.

"I've never been good at hiding when bad people come knocking at the door." Maggie shrugged. "We could all be dead in two days anyway."

"But I don't want you to be hurt." Tammond took Maggie's hand, pressing it to his chest. "This isn't your fight."

"So you want me to leave?" Maggie asked.

Tammond leaned down and gently brushed his lips against hers. Hoots and cheers sounded from the children on the dock. "I don't want you to leave. You are brave, Maggie. But bravery might not be enough to keep any of us alive."

Maggie smiled and kissed Tammond again, leaning in so his body pressed against hers. This time sounds of disgust were mixed in with the shouts from the children.

"I can take care of myself," Maggie said when she finally figured out how to breathe again, "and if I'm going to be here when the Enlightened come, then I'm going to fight. I'd rather get hurt than watch the people around me suffer."

Tammond smiled sadly. "I suppose it would be too much to ask for you to be so brave *and* willing to hide."

"Way too much."

"Miss Trent," Bertrand shouted from the dock, "could you please come back to the village? Battle is now imminent, and we have more pressing matters to attend to."

Bertrand's words froze the children in place, as though threats from the defeated man in black meant nothing, but Bertrand saying danger was coming had somehow made it real.

"Shit." Maggie let go of Tammond and waded out into the water. After about two feet of shallow shore, the water dropped off into blackness. Maggie stepped off the edge, letting herself fall for a moment.

The cool water surrounded her. No noise. No threat of battle. Only water. The water didn't care if she breathed or cried. The water wouldn't care who won the coming battle. Maggie loved it for its indifference. The water wouldn't even care if she decided not to find her way back to the surface.

"The magic is already in your mind. Magic runs deep in your blood as it does in ours. Feel it pulsing through you."

Maggie closed her eyes against the pressing darkness, ignoring the sting in her lungs. There it was. That hum she had felt her whole life. The essence of magic that flowed through everything she was. But it was different now. Without the crackling brightness that threatened to break her. A gentle part of her now, flowing softly with each beat of her heart. Unable to break her as she let it drift out of her hands, warming the water. A dim light shone around her,

710 | MEGAN O'RUSSELL

and instinct made it clear all she needed to do was let go. Let the light work its will.

With one tiny kick, Maggie flew through the water, bursting out into the fresh air and landing with a gasp on the dock.

Maggie stumbled, and strong arms caught her.

"Miss Trent," Bertrand said, steadying her, "I'm glad to see you haven't given up."

"Me?" Maggie panted, bending over to catch her breath. "Never. Just trying to figure out this whole magic thing before the big bad wolf comes knocking."

"Maggie." Tammond pulled himself from the lake up onto the deck. "That was amazing! I knew you could find your magic."

"It was easier in the water than with a bunch of kids watching." Maggie wrung the water out of her hair as a whistle sounded from the front of the village.

"It's time to move again." Tammond ran toward the raised walkways.

"We won't get where we're going before dark." Maggie followed him, dodging the others who sprinted to their positions. "Can't we wait until morning?"

"We have to get to the safe place," Tammond grunted as he hoisted one of the heavy support poles from under the walkway.

Maggie helped him lay it on the ground before he moved to the next pole.

"What about this safe place is so safe?" Maggie pressed herself against the wall of a house as a group of four men ran past, carrying a boat. "And if it's safe, why haven't you been there this whole time?"

"Safe doesn't mean we can't be attacked," Tammond explained. "It just means there will only be one direction for Jax to attack us from. And the dark place for the children is nearby. We have to leave the children in safety before we can go to the overhang." He moved to the edge of the raised walkway and began untying the ropes that bound it to the top of the dock.

"The overhang?" Maggie moved to the other side and dug her fingers into the ropes. The rope was warm, and the magic that flowed through it pulsed in her fingertips.

"The overhang is the safe place." Tammond leapt aside, pulling Maggie with him as two women pushed a long walkway into the water and bound it to the sides of the houses, making a solid ramp that bordered that section of the village.

Tammond ran toward the front of the village and, without pausing, leapt into a boat that waited in the water.

Seconds after he lifted his paddle, another whistle split the air, and, as one, the rowers began dragging the village.

"So what can I do?" Maggie asked, widening her stance to steady herself as the village surged forward.

"Nothing," Tammond said. "There is nothing any of us can do until the children are safe."

21

Maggie sat with Bertrand in the Fireside. The children weren't running around or playing while the village traveled this time. Even the smallest among them seemed to know something terrible was coming.

"I hate feeling like this." Maggie tore her hunk of bread into tiny little crumbs. "I hate not being able to help. I wish we could at least row."

"We aren't as skilled as they are," Bertrand said. "They will move more quickly and safely without our help."

"Then what exactly are we supposed to help them with?" Maggie banged her fists on the table.

A tiny boy whimpered.

"Sorry," Maggie muttered, "but what exactly are we supposed to be doing to help? I'm just figuring out how to use magic here, we don't know how the Enlightened are going to attack, we can't even help row the damn boats." Maggie rammed her fingers through her hair.

"We help them to see the holes in their defenses," Bertrand said. "They've been planning to hide at the overhang for years. They might not see if it is a flawed plan."

"So we're just going to make sure the walls hold?"

"Miss Trent"—Bertrand leaned across the table, speaking barely above a whisper—"the village was threatened, and it took you with a stick to defend it. Like it or not, we have both seen more fighting than most of the Wanderers."

"I'll just run at Jax with a stick and hope he's caught unawares." Maggie took a bite of fruit, more to have something to do than because she was actually hungry. Something about knowing the time before battle was drifting quickly away made things like food seem irrelevant. But she would need food in her stomach when the battle came, even if she didn't know how she was supposed to fight.

A whistle from the front of the village made all the children freeze.

"I think we may have arrived." Bertrand stood up and strode to the door as Maggie scrambled over the bench she had been sitting on.

The air outside the Fireside had changed. It wasn't only the fear of the people who were scrambling out of the boats and back up onto the raft. There was something palpable in the breeze that drifted slowly by.

They weren't in an outlet of the main lake this time. They were stopped alongside a high and jagged cliff. Trees coated in layers of vines grew from the vertical surface, making it look as though someone had tipped the ground onto its side and forgotten to right it.

Parents of the children from the Fireside had come to the deck that surrounded it, hugging and kissing their children as though they would never see them again. The sun had already sunk low in the sky. Soon it would be too dark to allow the village to move at all.

"Quickly," Abeyla called over the crowds. "Get the children into the boats."

"But Abeyla," a young woman said, holding a crying little girl tightly in her arms, "we will have to stay here overnight. Let us keep the children with us tonight. They can leave in the morning."

"I will never be fool enough to trust Jax Cayde to keep his word," Abeyla said. Every face in the crowd turned toward her. "We cannot trust he will not attack before morning. The children will go to safety tonight. I will not risk their lives on the promise of a murderer."

The woman looked at Abeyla, her face stricken. But she nodded, kissing her little girl on the forehead before moving to the left side of the docks.

The largest of the boats waited along the side. One by one, the children were passed into the waiting arms of the rowers. Some screaming and crying, others resolute, knowing tears would make no difference.

"Maggie," Abeyla said under the noise of the departure, "you are going to the dark place with the children."

"What?" Maggie said. "I'm not going to hide with a bunch of kids."

"Not to hide." Abeyla held up a hand to halt Maggie's protests. "To learn. The dark place has magic hidden deep within its walls. Magic the Wanderers have spent many years exploring and molding. That is why the children will be safe there. The darkness itself will protect the innocent."

"What you did today was brave, Maggie, and you have clearly shown you have magic within you. We normally don't send one who has so much yet to learn into the darkness, but there is no time for you to wait. And you do not seem like one to shy from pain or fear."

"Sounds great," Maggie said.

"Go into the darkness, and you will come out capable of more than we could teach you in years of books and gentle magic."

"Trial by fire." Maggie nodded. "If that's the way it has to be, then Bertrand and I will get through it."

"I won't be joining you, Miss Trent," Bertrand said. "I'll be staying to help in guarding the village."

"But you're not from here either," Maggie said, feeling as though she might be getting the short and painful end of the stick. "Shouldn't you have to go through the fear-and-pain suffering training?"

"As I've said, Miss Trent, I've learned the language of many types of magic." Bertrand held out his palm, and a funnel of dark air formed instantly. Within seconds, lightning blossomed from the storm, lighting the dimming night.

"Nice party trick," Maggie snarked.

"Effective magic in this land," Bertrand said.

"Fine, so you just want me to go into the dark place with the kids and hope I find some suffering I can learn from?" Maggie asked. The boats carrying the children had cast off from the village and were rowing toward the cliffs. "Sorry, my mistake. I'll swim to the dark place and hope I don't drown."

"I'm taking you Maggie," Tammond said, appearing behind his mother's shoulder, his face covered in sweat from rowing. "Surviving the journey into the dark place is impossible without a guide you trust. So"—Tammond paused, his face flushing for a moment—"I thought it should be me."

The idea of being trapped in the darkness with Tammond made all Maggie's anger at being sent away fade.

"Sure," Maggie said, pleased her voice came out stronger than it felt. "Let's go."

"Abeyla," Tammond said, "if the Enlightened come, don't let us stay hidden in the dark. I would rather fight for my home than wake up in the morning to find I have no family."

Abeyla took her son's face in her hands. "If Jax comes for us, it will sound like thunder in the darkness. No matter what I want, you will know when the battle begins."

"Then I'll be waiting for the thunder." Tammond hugged his mother before turning to Maggie. "Let's go."

Maggie followed him to the edge of the deck where one, small wooden boat waited, bobbing in the gentle ebb and flow of the lake. Tammond held his hand out to help Maggie down into the boat.

Maggie paused, turning back to Bertrand. "Do me a favor. Make sure you live until morning, okay?"

"Have you grown attached to me, Miss Trent?" Bertrand asked.

"No." Maggie grinned. "But I don't know the way back to the Siren's Realm."

Maggie climbed down into the boat, and as soon as she sat, Tammond began rowing toward the cliffs not forty feet away.

22

Maggie stared at the sheer rock wall Tammond rowed them quickly toward, his gaze fixed at a point near the base of the cliff. Maggie narrowed her eyes, trying to see what he saw in the shadow.

The darkness at the water's edge had depth, and the blackness seemed much thicker than any shadow she had ever encountered.

"Is that the dark place?" Maggie whispered.

"It is." Tammond held his paddle in the water, slowing them as the tip of their boat entered the darkness.

Maggie only had time for a quick glance behind before the shadow swallowed all the light.

"Tammond," Maggie whispered, grateful to hear her voice could penetrate the veil of blackness. "Tammond?"

"Yes," Tammond said. He was paddling again. The sound of his oar dipping into the water and the boat's movement forward were steady and sure.

"How can you see where we're going?" Maggie asked. "Or better yet the way out?"

"I can't see anything," Tammond said, and Maggie could hear the smile in his voice. "I can feel it. I can feel the magic in the walls that surround us, and I can feel the magic of those waiting for us up ahead."

"So you're just going to leave the kids in the pitch black for a few days while we have a little war outside?" Maggie asked, imagining how frightened little Mina must be. "Doesn't that seem a bit cruel?"

"Is hiding them more cruel than what Jax would do to them?" Tammond asked. "And there will be light for them. It's just in front of us. Close your eyes, Maggie. Try and feel where we're going."

With a sigh, Maggie closed her eyes against the darkness. The only thing she felt was the desire to not be moving toward something she couldn't see. She dug deeper, trying to remember what it had felt like just a while ago in the water. Magic inside her, surrounding her.

Tammond dug his paddle into the water, turning the boat.

"No," Maggie said, discovering the words as she said them. "You were right before. The kids are straight ahead."

"See, it's not so hard to see in here after all."

Maggie opened her eyes to find a tiny spot of light hovering ahead. As small and dim as a candle, flickering feebly in the distance. As they moved forward, the light grew larger and brighter much more quickly than seemed possible. In less than a minute the boat bumped into the edge of a rocky shore where the children sat waiting.

The people who had delivered the children were already getting back into their boats. An older woman stood with two teens not much younger than Maggie at the edge of the water, saying goodbye to the rowers, ready to take charge of the children.

The rowers glanced at Maggie and Tammond as they arrived before continuing to climb wordlessly into their boats.

"Maggie!" Mina burst out of the pack of children and ran toward Maggie as soon as her feet were on the rocky shore. "Maggie, have they sent you to be safe, too? I will take care of you here. I don't know my way around yet, but I can figure it out very quickly so you should stay near me."

"She can't," Tammond said, lifting Mina under the arms and carrying her back to the group. "Maggie has to go deep into the darkness, and you can't follow her there."

"But why does she get to go and not me?" Mina's brow wrinkled. "I have been studying magic in the Fireside much, much longer than she has."

"Because," Maggie said, "I have to learn how to fight. That's my job. Your job is to stay safe here so you can grow up to be much stronger and braver than I'll ever hope to be."

"You think I'm brave?" Mina's eyes widened.

"Very brave." Maggie ruffled the little girl's hair. "Now you wish me luck being brave, because Tammond and I haven't got much time."

Mina threw her pudgy arms around Maggie's middle. "You'll be brave. I know you will be."

"Thanks, Mina."

Tammond took Maggie's hand and led her through the children, away from the water and toward the wall beyond. There were three openings in the cave wall. One was tall and wide with light shimmering in the distance. Another was narrow and pitch black. The third was jagged and had the air of being a place a person should not go. But in that tunnel there was a bit of light as well. Not shining to light the way, but glowing a pale blue that seemed to be more a part of the tunnel than an outside force trying to make it hospitable.

"Which way?" Maggie asked, hoping for the well-lit tunnel and knowing that wouldn't be Tammond's answer.

Without saying anything at all, Tammond led Maggie through the jagged entrance into the blue tunnel. Before they had walked ten feet, the voices of the children vanished.

"Creepy," Maggie muttered.

The light in the tunnel came from the walls themselves. A faint sheen that glimmered on the black surface of the stone, shifting every moment, as though millions of tiny little lights were moving about lives of their own.

"How does it work?" Maggie touched the wall. The instant her finger grazed the stone, the lights around it shone brighter and moved more quickly. Maggie trailed her fingers along the wall, laughing as the lights moved faster and faster.

"I don't know how it works," Tammond said, drawing Maggie away from the wall and guiding her farther down the tunnel. "I don't know if anyone does."

"So it's just magic then?" Maggie grinned. "Little lights that live in stone."

"Exactly." Tammond leaned down, brushing his lips against hers.

Maggie stood on her toes, lacing her fingers through his hair to pull him in closer. His fingers found the small of her back, and tingles raced up her spine. Her lips parted, and he deepened their kiss, holding Maggie so close she wasn't sure she would ever remember how to let go.

"Maggie," Tammond whispered, tipping Maggie's chin up so he could look into her eyes. "Maggie, I don't want to lose you."

"Then don't." Maggie leaned in to kiss him again, but Tammond pressed his fingers to her lips.

"Maggie, traveling through the darkness is frightening and painful—"

"So I've heard."

"You might hate me on the other side."

"No, I won't." Maggie took Tammond's face in her hands, reveling in the faint roughness of the stubble on his chin. "It's going to be terrible, but I'll just have to do it."

"Not if you stay here with the children. You could help guard them, and you wouldn't have to—"

"I'm never going to sit in the background while other people fight." Maggie took Tammond's hand and dragged him down the tunnel, walking more quickly and confidently than he had. "I'm not going to say it isn't nice to have someone who wants to keep me out of harm's way. It is nice, really nice actually. But it's not going to work. I hope you can handle that."

Maggie turned to Tammond, blushing in the dim blue light.

He ran his fingers through her hair. "You can't care for a bird and ask it not to fly." He pressed his lips gently to her forehead. "But please fly carefully, little bird."

"I'll try." Her heart racing, she turned and walked down the tunnel, knowing if Tammond started kissing her again she would forget what they were there to do.

Soon, the tunnel sloped downward. Maggie expected the lights to fade, but the deeper they went, the brighter and more vibrant the lights became. Ten minutes passed, then twenty. The tunnel twisted and turned but always moved downward.

"How much longer?" Maggie asked. It would be dark outside already. They couldn't afford to waste more of their precious night.

"When you're ready, we'll be there," Tammond said.

"Ready for what?" Sweat dripped down her back. "I'm definitely ready to get to where we're going. And if there's going to be lots of pain, I'd just as soon start now."

"Then we should be there soon."

Maggie wiped the sweat from her forehead, wishing the tunnel could at least have the courtesy to be cool. But the farther they walked, the hotter it became.

"You know, if we don't get there soon, we're going to boil to death." No sooner were the words out of her mouth than the lights in the distance began to change.

The dim, shimmering glow was replaced by something vibrant that coated everything in sight. The lights danced through the air, flashing as though their movements had purpose and meaning. Maggie ran forward, wanting to see the lights, to understand what they were saying. Tammond's footsteps pounded behind her, but he didn't call after her to slow down.

A cavern three stories high and large enough to fit half the village waited at the end of the tunnel. Lights danced across the surface of the rocks, speeding through the darkness like shooting stars. What Maggie had thought were lights moving through the open air were really bright reflections of the lights on the walls cast onto the haze that filled the air. The thick steam smelled like fresh summer fields, hot chocolate, and home baked bread.

Maggie gazed around the cavern, trying to find where the steam was coming from. It poured in from every direction, seeming to emanate from the walls themselves.

"Where is the mist coming from?" Maggie turned to Tammond, swaying as her head spun in the heat. Sweat dripped into her eyes, blurring her vision.

"I think it comes from the same place as the light."

Maggie wiped the sweat from her eyes with her shirt, blinking and focusing on Tammond, trying to steady herself. He stared back at her with concern on his face. His perfectly dry face, without a trace of sweat on it.

"You aren't hot?" Maggie's words wavered as she fought to pull in breath.

"No. I can't feel the heat. The steam feels like cool mist to me. Its scent and heat are only for you."

"So—" Maggie panted.

Tammond leapt forward and caught her around the middle as her knees buckled.

"So I'm just supposed to sweat the magic out of me? Well, it shouldn't take very long." The lights danced more quickly now, swimming through the stone overhead like a hundred shooting stars. "A meteor shower just for me. Too bad it's so hot. I don't like hot. I just want the...the stars."

"Let go, Maggie." Tammond's voice sounded far away as his face faded into the darkness. "Follow where the stars are leading you."

"No," Maggie said, a cold hand clasping her heart as she understood. "No, I don't want to go. Don't make me go. Tammond!"

"Tammond?" The man next to her on the patchwork blanket turned to her. "Who's Tammond, sweetheart?"

"Daddy," Maggie breathed, reaching toward him with her pudgy child's arms. "Daddy!" She threw her arms around his neck, burying her nose in the collar of his flannel shirt.

"It's okay, Maggie," her father cooed. "You're okay. I'm here."

Maggie stood and wiped the tears from her eyes with the lacy sleeve of her nightgown. A shooting star flew by and then another. "The shooting stars, Daddy. We came out here to watch the shooting stars?"

"Of course we did, sweetheart." Her father rumpled her hair.

"Daddy, I had the worst nightmare," Maggie hiccupped, a fresh wave of tears streaming down her face. "I was grown up, and you and Mommy were dead. And I had lived someplace awful, and I never got to be with you."

"Maggie, darling." Her father took her by the shoulders, looking at his little girl with sympathetic eyes. "That wasn't a dream, sweetheart, and this isn't one either."

"What?" Maggie asked. The lace on her nightgown faded into nothing. "No, this has to be real. Daddy, I want this to be real. I want to see Mommy!" But before she could beg for her mother, the little girl Maggie had disappeared. Maggie herself sat on the blanket beside her father. Her clothes torn from the jungle. Her boots wet from the lake.

"I'm not going to see Mom, am I?" Maggie asked, her voice low, not meeting her father's eyes for fear of more tears coming.

"You will," her father said. "But not how you want to."

"Is this the pain they were talking about?" Maggie squeezed the sides of her head as though, by sheer force of will, she could push her thoughts into an order where any of this made sense. "I get to see you for a minute and then lose you again? Because that's really low."

"No darling. There is real pain to come. This is just an unfortunate side effect of what has to happen. You have to learn to fight. You have to learn now. And the best way the darkness knows how to do that is through fear. Fight when you're afraid, and the magic will learn how to come pouring out of you."

"What am I supposed to be afraid of?" Maggie looked around. They were in a field bordered by forest. The normal sounds of nighttime drifted through the trees. An owl hooted faintly, the tall grass rustled in the breeze. "Daddy, there's nothing here to fight."

A scream sounded from the corner of the field. Pitched high in terror, it was a voice Maggie would know even if she hadn't heard it for a thousand years.

"Mom." Maggie sprang to her feet. "Mommy!"

Maggie sprinted toward the scream.

"Fight, Maggie." Her father's voice trailed after her. But his footsteps didn't join hers. Maggie glanced behind. The blanket was gone. Her father had disappeared into the night.

"Daddy!" Maggie hesitated for a moment, wanting to run back and find her father. But another scream echoed, and she ran toward her mother.

The house was there. Just where it should have been—at the very edge of the field next to the trees. Strangers were outside the house.

And her mother was there, kneeling in the grass, defending something Maggie couldn't see as the attackers drew closer.

"*Terraminis!*" Maggie shouted the spell, expecting the ground around the feet of the strangers to crumble, but nothing happened.

Her mother screamed spells, shooting balls of fire and shards of lightning at the dark figures.

"*Fulguratus!*" Maggie screamed as her spell rebounded, knocking her back and shooting pain up through her arm and into her chest, streaking into her lungs so she couldn't breathe. "Mommy." Her lips formed the words, but she had no air to scream as the strangers moved in.

Her pulse quickened, her heart pounding against her ribs as her mind raced for an answer. Rolling onto her stomach, she dug her fingers into the grass, letting the anger and fear within her flow into the soil.

The ground shook, and one of the attackers fell over. Gasping for breath, Maggie staggered to her feet.

Her mother had seen her. Their eyes met for a moment.

"Maggie, help!" her mother screamed. "Help us!"

Us.

Her mother knelt hunched over something in the grass.

A body. Her father. Dead.

The men had killed him first. Maggie had known that. The other Clan had murdered her father and then killed her mother as she tried to protect her husband's body.

"No!" Maggie screamed, running full tilt toward the men. "Mommy, no! Run!"

Reaching deep down for the last bit of magic she could find, Maggie willed the energy into her hands, shaping it into magic strong enough to make the bad men go away. But she didn't know how. Didn't know what to make the magic do to stop them.

One of the strangers held his hand high. A spell crackled in his palm, just like the one Maggie was trying to create. But his magic came quickly, and before she could scream, the spell hit her mother.

Eyes wide and terrified, Elle Trent fell to the ground, dead.

"Mommy!" Maggie let the spell that had formed in her hands spill out into the night, burning everything in its wake.

Fire burned through Maggie. She was not immune to her own magic. But with the pain came darkness. Her mother's and father's faces disappeared.

"No." Maggie felt herself saying the word before the world reformed around her. "No!"

But she wasn't at the old farmhouse anymore. Her parents were not there for her to save.

She stood in a hall with gray concrete walls. The Academy. Screams echoed down the corridors, and she knew before she moved what she would find.

Blood smeared on the walls and floor. Panic. Death.

Her feet carried her forward before she made the decision to move. A boy, Mark had been his name, lay dead on the floor. His stomach ripped open by claws.

Maggie took a shuddering breath. She couldn't save him. She wouldn't be able to save any of them. She could only sit and wait. Wait for the screaming to stop, for it all to be over. She knew how this ended. Blood in the night. Students —her friends—dead. The Academy destroyed.

"Help!" a voice called in the distance. She didn't even recognize who it was. But they were crying desperately. Maggie raised her hands to cover her ears.

"Someone please!"

Maggie ran forward, feeling the magic in the air and letting it flow into her. Fighting was better than waiting. Better to let the monsters hurt her than to listen to them hurt someone else.

724 | MEGAN O'RUSSELL

She rounded the corner and found the beasts waiting. A little girl no older than ten—Vera, no, Ellen, that he been her name—was pinned against the wall. A black beast smiled as he drew closer to her, stepping over the bodies of the dead. The monster was only a man, really. A man whose skin had turned into black, shining armor and who had given up his hands for sharp talons that reached for Ellen's throat.

"Stop!" Maggie shouted. The word tore from her throat, bringing magic with it. The air pulsed with her breath, knocking the monster from his feet.

Maggie breathed the magic onto her hand, warming it, filling it with strength she had never known. She ran forward and grabbed the head of the monster, pushing it into the stone ground until, with a dull *crack*, the thing stopped moving.

"We have to go," Maggie said.

Ellen ignored the gore on Maggie's hand as she grabbed it, letting Maggie lead her down the hall.

"We need to get you to the cafeteria," Maggie said. "Everyone will be there."

"I want to stay with you." Ellen's voice shook. "Please don't let more of the monsters come."

At the girl's words, three beasts rounded the corner, their talons clicking as they slunk forward.

"Ellen, stay behind me," Maggie said calmly, not taking her gaze off the glistening, black beasts that approached.

"You fight us?" the closest monster hissed. "You know you cannot win. It is decided."

"Gonna try anyway," Maggie growled, feeling the magic in the floor beneath her. It hummed as though it were alive. A living force waiting for a command. Digging her hands into the air as though the magic beneath her were palpable, Maggie clawed upward. The ground trembled and rose, forming a wall blocking the path of the monsters.

"Ellen, we have to go the other way."

At Maggie's words, the little girl ran back down the hall and into the black talons that waited for her. Shining red poured onto the floor as Maggie screamed, and the scene disappeared.

"I won't."

She knew what was coming. She couldn't change anything that was about to happen. Wouldn't be able to stop any of it.

"Don't make me do this," Maggie whispered, keeping her eyes firmly shut as sounds emerged around her. "I won't do this. You can't make me."

Spells were being shouted. Screams of pain and rage carried through the noise of the battle. The *swoosh* of a sword close to Maggie's head didn't even make her flinch. That wasn't how it had happened. She hadn't been killed by a sword. She hadn't died in the battle at Graylock at all.

"Emilia!" Jacob screamed.

Maggie could picture him—running toward the girl he loved, bent on protecting her from every danger. But had he managed it? She hadn't seen everything that had happened. Hadn't been there to find out who had survived, if any of them.

Maggie opened her eyes. The battle raged all around her, spells shooting through the trees and shattering the rocks around the entrance to a cave. The entrance seemed so small. Such a strange place for power to be lurking.

But the Pendragon was there, fighting with his men. Determined to kill everyone who fought against them and to destroy the world Maggie loved.

Maggie walked slowly toward the cave, not flinching when spells streaked toward her, not stepping aside when a centaur ran past, whip flashing in his hand. She didn't care if they hurt her. It didn't matter anyway. She wanted only to see, to know what had become of them all.

The ground lurched and crumbled, dropping away to form a gaping hole in front of the cave. Green mist blossomed from its depths. Dexter. She had seen him in the shadows. That was why she had run forward, to save Dexter. But this was different, wrong.

Dexter wasn't standing in the mist—the mist was alive in its own right. It reached for Maggie with tangible tendrils, determined to pull her into the darkness. To drag her away so she would never know what had happened.

"Leave me alone!" Maggie turned and bolted through the battle. An arrow whizzed overhead. Maggie ducked but kept running, leaping over bodies, not looking closely enough to know if they were friend or foe. She could feel the mist behind her, drawing her back toward her fate.

A tree cracked in front of her and toppled toward the ground, blocking her path. Pushing the air with all her strength, Maggie shoved the tree out of her way. She ran farther, toward the edge of the battle. There was no one fighting here. Only bodies left to wait for the victor to deal with. A body lay between two trees. Eyes wide and blank as they stared at the sky.

"No!" Maggie paused. Only for a moment, but that moment was enough. The mist wrapped around her, dragging her toward the darkness.

"No!" There was magic in the mist, stronger than any she had felt before. Stronger than anything inside her. "Please don't!" But the mist had no pity for her screams. She reached out, grabbing a tree, trying to halt the terrible pull of the mist, but her hands slid uselessly across the bark.

Her hands dripped blood, which fell through the mist, not tainting its bright green with the deep red. The mist could pull her away, but a drop of blood could pass through. It couldn't hold everything. It wasn't all-powerful. Only magic.

Maggie closed her eyes and felt the magic swirling around her. Without caution, she drew the magic inside her. Letting it fill her until it burned, until there was no Maggie left. Only magic.

With a scream that drowned out the battle, Maggie threw her arms wide, severing the mist as though it had merely been a string trying uselessly to bind her.

She turned to the chasm that led to the Siren's Realm, toward the blackness that led to her fate. Magic crackled from her fingers, sparking brightly as the battle faded.

Scooping her hands through the air, she filled the pit with darkness, blocking her path to the Siren's Realm as the shadows surrounded her.

Maggie lay gasping and shaking on the ground. The heat from the cavern had gone, and she was as numb as though she had been lying in snow.

"Maggie." Tammond knelt next to her.

Maggie blinked, trying to focus on his face in the dim, blue light.

"I'm back," Maggie croaked. Her throat hurt like she had been screaming.

"You never went anywhere." Tammond lifted her from the ground and cradled her to his chest.

He was warm, and Maggie pulled herself closer to him, shivering.

"I did," she said. "I did leave here, and I went to the worst places."

"I heard." Tammond held Maggie tightly. "I heard everything you said."

"And that's how you're supposed to learn?" Maggie asked, anger welling inside her. "You get to go revisit the worst moments of your life and watch helplessly as people die?"

"You go to the moments that will make your magic strongest. What they are varies with each person."

"I hadn't even seen it happen." Maggie crawled away from Tammond, afraid she might be sick on him. "I was hundreds of miles away when my parents were killed. Was that even how it really happened?"

"I don't know. The mist shows you what it must for you to learn. I don't know how much of it is true."

"Great. Torture as a tutor." Maggie rubbed heat back into her hands. "Does this mean we can go back up and fight Jax now? Am I all crazy powerful?"

"The powers you feel in the mist aren't what you'll really have, or I would be able to transform into a wild cat." Tammond smiled tentatively. "But you've felt the magic pour out of you, and now you'll be able to find it again."

"Awesome." Maggie pushed herself unsteadily to her feet. "All that so I can see how something feels. 'Cause I really needed all that pain for some freaking magic!" Maggie's voice echoed around the cavern. "That's great."

Tammond moved to wrap his arms around Maggie, but she stepped back.

"Don't." Her voice caught in her throat. "Thank you, but don't." Tears stung in the corners of her eyes. "I'm not really good with sympathy."

"As you wish." Tammond stepped back. "We can begin the next step of your training."

"Of course there's more. Now what? I walk on hot coals?"

"We go into the darkness and let your magic work."

"Doesn't sound as bad as the last part, so it's probably going to be worse."

"Not worse." Tammond took Maggie's hand and led her toward the back of the cavern. "Just darker."

The mist had cleared, leaving the blue lights still dancing on the ceiling. But their light didn't touch the hole in the back wall. The opening was barely tall enough or wide enough for Tammond to fit through, but he crossed into the pitch black without hesitation, leading Maggie behind him.

"Are there monsters back here or something?" Maggie whispered, grateful to hear her voice sounding off the walls around them, carrying as though they were in a long narrow tunnel. "Or is it going to be more like jumping over molten lava?"

"It's different for everyone," Tammond said.

"But you're going to stay with me?" Maggie asked, tightening her grip on Tammond's hand without meaning to.

"I am," Tammond said. "You found the magic within yourself, but the way magic works in the dark dream is different from the way you can use it in the real world."

"*Dark dream* sounds right," Maggie said. "But real world might be a stretch. No offense but—"

Maggie fell silent and froze where she stood. Her voice had echoed as though she were in a vast place, larger even than the cavern where the mist had been.

"Tammond," Maggie whispered, but still her voice carried around the space, "where are we?"

"I need you to trust me, Maggie." Tammond slipped his hand from Maggie's, leaving her alone in the dark.

"I'm not really great with trust." Maggie stepped forward, but Tammond wasn't there.

"Where you were taught—"

"The Academy," Maggie said, moving to her left where Tammond's voice had come from.

"At the Academy"—he sounded like he was behind her now—"did they teach you to fight?"

"Yes, a bit." Maggie tensed, raising her hands, waiting for Tammond to strike. "I learned some on my own, too. Didn't have much of a choice, really."

"Then attack me." Tammond was back in front of her. It sounded like he was only a few feet away.

"What?" Maggie stepped backward. "I'm not going to attack you."

"I'll defend myself, Maggie." Tammond sounded as though he were mere inches in front of her. "But you have to attack."

Focusing all of her energy into her hand, Maggie pulled the air into her fist, compounding it into a sphere. Without a sound, she threw it as hard as she could at where Tammond's voice had last been.

"The spell was good," Tammond said from far behind her. "But you need to be able to sense where I am. You can feel the magic in you, in the air around you. Now feel the current I am creating."

"Don't you think when Jax attacks, I'll be able to use my eyes to see who's trying to kill me?"

"Jax Cayde can set fire to the water," Tammond began, and Maggie silently knelt, placing her palm against the stone floor. "He can fly without wings…"

Maggie pushed the magic from her palm into the stone, sending a ripple toward Tammond. Maggie pictured it. The rock made soft, moving in a wave, wrapping itself around Tammond's feet. A small grunt of surprise made her sure the spell had worked, but the sharp cracking of rock a moment later meant he had broken free.

"Nicely done," Tammond said. "But using my voice to find me wasn't what I asked you to do."

"Fine," Maggie growled, closing her eyes against the blackness. Sure enough, she could feel the magic moving through the air around her. Could feel it surging through her veins with every beat of her heart. And there was something in the vast swirling power of it all she was sure must be Tammond. Whipping her hand through the air as though grabbing a dart, Maggie hurled the spell at what she thought was Tammond.

A dull *thunk!* echoed through the dark as the spell struck stone.

"Better," Tammond said from the opposite direction.

Maggie ran her hands through her hair. If she only had a bit of light. Without thinking about how to form the light, a pale red orb shimmered into being right above her head. Maggie spun on the spot, looking for Tammond, but the light reached only a few feet in each direction.

"More light," Maggie whispered. Magic surged through her, and in a moment twelve orbs had split from the first, zooming in every direction, filling the cavern with their faint red glow. Tammond stood not twelve feet from her in front of a grouping of stalagmites ten feet wide that reached nearly to the ceiling. All around the cave as far as her lights could reach, stalactites and stalagmites showed the slow passing of time.

"You shouldn't have done that yet," Tammond said, worry filling his voice.

"Why not? It worked." Maggie pushed the air from her hands so it hit Tammond in the stomach. "Tag, you're it."

"But they come toward the light, Maggie." Tammond moved closer to her as a sharp clicking began in the shadows. "And they won't want you to see."

"They?" Maggie searched the shadows. "You never mentioned anything about a *they*."

"I said I would stay with you, and I will." Tammond squared his shoulders as though preparing to fight. "Wanderers never face the shadows until their training is complete. You weren't meant to see them."

"Well, then you should have told me not to turn on a light," Maggie whispered as a pair of pinchers appeared from behind the rock.

The thing was small, no bigger than a housecat. But it wasn't the size that terrified Maggie. The thing looked more like a scorpion than anything else Maggie could think of, and its shining black armor forced bile up into her throat as she pushed away the memory of the monsters that had destroyed the Academy.

"What the hell are those things?" Maggie said as more of the scorpions crept out into the light.

"They live here," Tammond said. "And they don't like visitors."

"Then why the hell are we here?" Maggie grabbed Tammond's arm, dragging him toward the exit just visible in the darkness on the far wall. But their path had already been blocked by more of the creatures.

"Get rid of them," Maggie said. "I don't care what you wanted to do down here. We're leaving."

"I can't get rid of them." Tammond sounded afraid.

Maggie followed his gaze. He wasn't looking down at the floor where the creatures were growing in number, but rather three feet above them where Maggie couldn't see anything at all.

"What are you seeing?" Maggie asked.

Tammond answered with a scream as bright streaks of white light flew from his palms, striking some invisible thing that shrieked. He leapt in front of Maggie, sending another spell at something she couldn't see.

But the black creatures were moving closer.

Drawing the heat from her fear, Maggie let her magic flow. Flames poured from her hands, covering the floor in a sea of fire.

The creatures scuttled away from the flames. Some weren't fast enough, and with *hisses* and *pops*, the fire consumed them.

"Maggie, get down!" Tammond screamed, covering Maggie's head.

A sickening *crunch* sounded as Tammond flung his arm through the air, striking something that left blood dripping from his hand.

"Tammond!" But she didn't have time to see how badly he was hurt. The black creatures had surged forward again. With a shout that shook the air, Maggie slammed her foot onto the ground. The stone rippled like waves in the sea, throwing some of the creatures back.

Something sharp dug into the top of Maggie's head, and she swung her arm up. It connected with something hard, and rubbery wings flapped against her hand as the thing escaped her grip.

"Tammond, duck! *Primionis!*" Maggie screamed, praying the spell would work. The shield blossomed above Maggie's head, forming a shimmering dome around her and Tammond. She pressed her palm through the shield and closed her eyes, letting all the magic she could feel funnel into her.

Eyes shut tight, she let lightning and fire pour out into the cave.

Howls rent the air, but still Maggie didn't look. Soon the only sounds were the whooshing of the fire and the crackling of the lightning. Trembling, Maggie opened her eyes and lowered her arm. The cave's walls were scorched. The things that had been attacking them were gone.

"Maggie, are you all right?" Tammond took her by the shoulders, examining her.

Maggie touched the top of her head where blood coated her hair.

"I'll live," Maggie said, "but this is a really shitty way to train people. Sending monsters after them? I mean, what if we had been eaten alive? Wouldn't have been much good fighting against Jax now would we?"

"You weren't supposed to light the room." Tammond laid his palm on Maggie's head. Heat trickled down her scalp. "You weren't meant to jump right to the end."

"Still, fighting scorpion monsters and invisible things—not really my idea of advancing the learning curve."

Tammond took his hand from Maggie's head, and she felt where the cut had been. Her hair was still sticky with blood, but the cut had healed.

"Thanks," Maggie murmured.

"They don't usually attack like that, not with such force. They belong in the shadows and are creatures of darkness. They appear to everyone, but never in the same way. They'll fight us, but I've never heard of them attacking in such numbers."

"So what?" Maggie sat on the ground, hoping Tammond wouldn't notice her legs shaking. "The shadows just really hate me because I'm not from Malina, because I'm not a Wanderer?" She clenched her fists, digging her nails into her palms as tears welled in her eyes. "As if watching my mom die wasn't bad enough, I had to get attacked just for good measure?"

"We cannot learn to fight from the light or from the good things we know." Tammond knelt beside her. "Peace begets peace, and it is how we hope to live. But when fighting must come, we can't expect to learn to survive it staying only in the sun."

"Is that why I was lucky enough to jump ahead? Because I'm not made of peace and light? Because I know exactly what it is to fight, and hurt, and hate? Because I've seen death, and the shadows can smell it on me?"

"Maggie," Tammond whispered her name. In the dark cave, it didn't sound like a name at all. But like a prayer, rising up to the sun far above the darkness. A wish for something away from shadows and pain.

He kissed her gently, as though afraid she might push him away again. His mouth was warm on hers. He was alive, so very alive. With the burned rocks surrounding them, and unknown horrors ahead, he was there. Pulse racing in time with hers.

Maggie moved in closer so her body pressed against his, forgetting where she ended and he began. It didn't matter. Nothing mattered as long as he was holding her. If he held her tightly enough, nothing horrible would come for them. They would never have to go back up to the lake and everything that waited above.

Tammond's hands ran up her sides as his mouth moved to her throat, making her gasp with pleasure. The lights in the room faded away. But Tammond was there, holding her.

The floor was hard and cold. Maggie lay curled up, her head on Tammond's shoulder, listening to the steady beat of his heart. She wanted to stay there forever. Just the two of them in the darkness. But a forever of peace was meant only for the dead.

"How much longer until dawn?" Maggie finally asked, her voice echoing through the dark.

"Not much longer." Tammond kissed Maggie's forehead.

"Then we should go. I don't even know if I've finished my training."

"I don't think the training was ever going to work for you." Tammond shifted to sit up. "Not the way it's supposed to. The Wanderers found this place to teach other Wanderers. You aren't one of us."

Maggie froze for a moment. "Is that a good thing or a bad thing?"

Tammond leaned down, his lips finding Maggie's. "A very good thing. As Bertrand said—we know everything we know. You know different things. I think you proved you can use your magic here. There's nothing more the dark place can teach you. You did here in hours what most take years to find."

"I did spend years training in a dark place." Maggie pushed herself to her feet. "It just wasn't here."

"I only hope it's enough to keep you safe." Tammond's hand found hers in the dark as though it was the most natural thing that had ever happened.

Maggie smiled, letting him lead her blindly forward.

She didn't speak or ask how long it would take to make it to the blue cavern. She was listening too hard for the *click* of legs scuttling or *whoosh* wings flapping. But the only sound was the soft thudding of their feet as they climbed upward.

In only a few minutes, lights shone dimly in the distance. But it was a different cavern than the one they had been in before. This cave was barely wider than the passage they had been traveling. Green lights sparkled on the walls. Maggie tensed, waiting for the lights to crawl out of the rock and draw her back into the Siren's Realm, away from the battle to come. But she wasn't ready to leave yet.

"Why is it different?" Maggie whispered, leaning in close to Tammond. "We didn't go down this way."

"The way into the darkness can never be the same as the way back out."

"Right," Maggie said, not sure she understood. But it didn't matter as long as he took her back to the surface. The darkness that had felt mysterious and magical now seemed threatening and suffocating.

Her shoulders were tense, ready to fight more monsters from the dark, ready to hear her mother's screams again.

"I think I know why Bertrand couldn't come down here," Maggie said as the tunnel tipped steeply upward. "He wouldn't just have burned the shadows. He would have knocked the whole mountain down."

The children's voices echoed through the tunnel, and Maggie broke into a run, dragging Tammond behind her. Torchlight gleamed in the distance, a small figure silhouetted against the flickering glow.

"Mina, don't!" a voice shouted, but the little shadow was already running down the tunnel toward Maggie.

"Maggie, Tammond!" Mina called as she ran. They had been far enough away that by the time Mina reached them, she was puffing. "I waited up for you all night!" Mina panted proudly. "It was a very long night, too. Though I suppose it will always look like night while we have to wait down here."

"You should have slept, Mina." Maggie didn't argue as Mina took her hand and dragged her up the tunnel.

"But I was worried about you," Mina said. "I wanted to be sure that if you needed help, someone would be able to hear you scream. But I didn't hear anything at all. Was it easy down there? Did you not get to do your training? I've heard stories about the tunnels, and it should have been awful."

"It was pretty bad," Maggie said, "but we survived, and that's what matters."

Mina stopped in her tracks, turning to face Maggie. "You are very brave."

Maggie blushed at Mina's wide eyed admiration.

"Thanks." Maggie took the lead, pulling Tammond and Mina behind her, knowing the shadows were no worse than what waited out on the lake.

The rest of the children huddled around the opening to the tunnel, peering into the dark.

"I told you not to go down there." An older boy grabbed Mina by the shoulders as soon as she was in reach. Apparently he hadn't been brave enough to venture into the tunnel to fetch her.

"I was going to Maggie and Tammond," Mina whined, wriggling away from the boy. "They can keep me safe."

"Don't ever say that," Maggie said, feeling the eyes of the children upon her. "When scary things are coming, you have to take care of yourself. Don't trust other people to protect you from the shadows. They might be willing to try, but at the end of it, you have to take care of you." Maggie's voice rang around the cavern.

A tiny boy behind her sniffed as tears crept down his cheeks.

Tammond looked at her, his brow wrinkled. "Maggie."

"I'm sorry, but it's true," Maggie said, her voice much gentler this time. "We're going to fight to keep all of you safe." She looked around at the frightened faces of the children. "Trust that. Trust that we will do everything we can to make sure none of the Enlightened come anywhere near you. But you can't go running at something dangerous with blind faith that it'll all work out okay, or that someone else will take care of you."

"B-but then what do we d-do?" the crying little boy asked.

"You take care of yourselves." Maggie knelt so she was at eye level with him. "Set up guards so you'll know if anyone is coming. They have to watch all the time."

"We do have guards," one of the older boys said indignantly.

"Good." Venom slipped into Maggie's voice. "Then teach the young ones to stand guard with you. Have a plan for if Jax comes through the dark. Know what you're going to do if we lose this battle."

More of the children were crying now, but it didn't matter. Better to have them afraid than dead.

"You can't count on the Wanderers rowing back in to take you from the dark place. You have to be ready to fight for yourselves." Maggie strode toward the boat waiting at the end of the rocky shore. She didn't look back to see if Tammond was following her. She didn't want to see the faces of the children staring at her with fear in their eyes.

"Get in." Tammond stepped into the tiny boat.

Maggie's hands shook as she gripped the sides of the boat while Tammond rowed them into the darkness. The Wanderers had penned the children into a cage they couldn't escape from. And there was nothing she could do about it.

"Why did you scare them like that?" Tammond asked as their boat was swallowed by the shadows.

"Because leaving them in a cave and hoping for the best is better?" Maggie said. "You think a couple of older kids and one old lady who can barely walk are going to be able to fend off Jax if he comes for them? They need a plan of their own, to be able to fight for themselves."

"They are too young to fight."

"Do you really think Jax is going to care?"

Tammond said nothing for a moment. The only sounds were his paddle dipping into the water and Maggie's angry breathing.

"He won't," Tammond finally admitted. "Jax will kill all of them if he finds his way into the dark place. But the jungle is no safer. The mountains are no safer. There is no safe place in Malina for the children of Wanderers. If he finds his way into the dark place, there will be nothing they can do."

"They can fight!"

"They'll lose."

"But at least they'll die fighting." Maggie's voice cracked. "It may not seem like a big difference to you. But if Jax comes, it'll be better for those kids to die fighting than hiding in the dark. Believe me, I know."

Tammond didn't say anything more as their boat emerged from the cave into the cool morning light.

The village was waiting as it had been the night before, tied up tight, ready to move at a moment's notice. A man stood watching the entrance to the dark place, and as soon as he spotted Maggie and Tammond, he gave a warbling whistle.

Abeyla appeared next to him before they reached the dock, and Bertrand was there a moment later.

Abeyla looked down at her son. "Are you all right?" Her voice sounded tired as though she had spent a sleepless night just like Tammond and Maggie.

"We're fine," Tammond said. "Maggie did very well. She moved much more quickly than I expected her to."

Abeyla turned an eye to Maggie as she climbed up onto the dock. "More quickly?"

"I made the room light up, and there were creepy black scorpions, so I burned them all." Maggie looked to Bertrand. "You were right, though. Shield spell works just the same as home."

"Do you think she is prepared to fight?" Abeyla asked Tammond.

Maggie resisted the urge to say she was right there and could speak for her own damn ability to fight.

"I—" Tammond began before looking at Maggie. "She is able to use magic, she is fearless, and she has seen many dark things before."

Abeyla nodded and gave a high-pitched whistle. "Then it is time for us to go to the safe place."

People emerged from their houses and moved to the docks, lowering boats into the water. Each person's face looked tired and drawn. But it wasn't the normal sleepy feeling of early morning. There was a dark resignation and fatigue that permeated the air. A heavy cloud of dread had settled over the village. They knew something terrible was coming. All that was left was to face it.

27

Tammond jumped back down into the little boat that had carried them out of the dark place, ready to row with the whistle from the front of the village.

"What were you going to say?" Maggie knelt at the edge of the dock, speaking quietly so no one rushing by would hear.

"You know darkness." Tammond's eyes filled with pain. "You know how to work in it better than some who have studied the shadows for years."

"How is that a problem?" Maggie asked. "I'm good at magic here, I can fight, and I'm not scared. Those all sound like really good qualifications to me. I'm not going to be in the way or be a danger to the Wanderers. I can help, and you need all the help you can get."

"I don't think you'll be a danger to the Wanderers." Tammond's voice was dark and low. "I'm worried about you. You know so well the pain that is coming, I'm afraid you'll greet it as an old friend."

The whistle sounded from the front of the boat, and, as one, all the rowers pulled forward, moving the village away from the caves.

"I'm not...I..." But Maggie didn't know what to say.

"Come, Miss Trent," Bertrand said, laying a gentle hand on her shoulder.

Maggie stood and followed him toward the Fireside, grateful for the reason to not have to explain herself to Tammond.

"Don't be mad at the boy," Bertrand said as they entered the Fireside. The room was abandoned. It seemed vast in its emptiness. The sound of the ropes squeaking against the wood carried throughout the space with no voices to cover the noise.

"I'm not mad at him." Maggie sat at a table, grateful for the bread and fruit some kind person had left behind.

"He's worried about you." Bertrand sat opposite her, tenting his fingers under his chin. "A strange and beautiful girl fell into his life. A girl who is more dangerous than any he's ever known, and brave enough to use that danger. It's not his fault he's afraid."

"Is it my fault for coming here?" Maggie dug her fists into her eyes, wishing she could sleep for even five minutes.

"Miss Trent, one of the many things I have learned on my journeys is that blame is rarely significant. There are too many accidents, too many unforeseen consequences. I doubt even the Siren herself knows every possible outcome for all the choices she makes. You meant no harm. In fact, we are trying to help, and our help has been gratefully accepted. Beyond that, it is the fault of no person we can blame, including ourselves."

"I just…"

"Weren't expecting to care so much for the locals?" Bertrand finished for her. "Ah, Miss Trent. We adventure for knowledge and magic. We fight to help a just cause. But it's the people who pull us along when things become dark."

"Right," Maggie said, not sure if she really understood Bertrand and not knowing if she wanted to.

They fell into silence as the village rowed slowly forward. The sun crept up in the sky until it poured in over the high walls of the Fireside. Maggie tipped her head back and let the sun warm her face, trying not to wonder how long it would be until Mina felt the sun on her skin again.

The morning light glowed through Maggie's closed eyes. She could be anywhere. The Siren's Realm. Home. The sun always felt the same.

Then the light was gone. The warmth disappeared. Maggie opened her eyes, ready to fight whatever was blocking out the sun. She didn't wait for Bertrand's murmur of, "What have we here?" before running outside to look.

An overhang, larger than the village itself, jutted out over the lake. The thick stone clung to the side of a cliff with no cracks in its surface, no sign that it might crumble and squash them all.

"Well, that is one way to block an attack." Bertrand squinted at the rock above.

The overhang was made of the same kind of rock as the surrounding cliffs, but there was something about its perfection that made it seem like it didn't belong over the Broken Lake.

The whistle came, and the rowers stopped, digging their paddles into the water so the village came to a shuddering halt.

Maggie stepped onto the dock, facing away from the cliffs. The water beyond the shadow of the rock sparkled in the sun. In the distance, a low bank rose up to the base of the mountains. Cliffs surrounded them on either side, cradling them from behind and stretching out toward the mountains. There was no way to approach the village but from dead ahead. Jax wouldn't be able to catch them unawares.

"They really like penning themselves in," Maggie said softly to Bertrand as he stood next to her, gazing at the distant mountains.

"Like rabbits hiding in a den," Bertrand said. "The principle works as long as the fox can't dig deep enough to reach them."

"And is willing to give up if he fails." Maggie ran her fingers through her hair, picking out flecks of dried blood, trying to push past her fatigue to put her thoughts in order. "They need to have people on the outside who can help if they get penned in. Who can attack from behind and surprise Jax."

"Miss Trent." Bertrand turned to Maggie with a smile. "I think we might have just found how we can best be useful."

"We're going to go play hidey hole and then jump off a cliff into the battle and save the day?"

"I think that is the basic principle." Bertrand walked quickly away toward the front of the village, Maggie following close behind.

The Wanderers stored their boats, but the movements were different this time. It wasn't the same practiced motion Maggie had seen before. Some of the Wanderers knelt at the edges of the docks, pressing their hands into the water, eyes shut tight. Others gazed silently at the face of the rock. Instead of the village unfolding and the bridges being raised, sharply carved bamboo spikes were inserted on the edges of the docks, pointing out menacingly over the water.

Abeyla stood on top of one of the houses, surveying the progress of those working beneath her. Bertrand walked straight into the house and climbed the ladder inside. Maggie was a step behind, and soon they were standing on the roof.

The Wanderers worked on the decks below. The gentle hum of magic touched Maggie's skin as spells radiated from every direction.

Maggie wanted to ask what all the protections were, but Bertrand had already begun speaking.

"But of course if you don't agree, Abeyla, we are willing to serve you in whatever way we can."

Abeyla looked between Bertrand and Maggie. Deep creases and shadows marred her face. She looked older than she had just a few days ago when Maggie had first met her.

"I am not a warrior." Abeyla sounded weary. "I am not a general or a fighter. I am a teacher who has managed to keep her people alive and fed. The Wanderers have never been soldiers. Jax Cayde—"

"Cannot be allowed to win," Bertrand said. "I was never a soldier, either, but our weakness can be an advantage. Let Jax's men advance. And we will be waiting for them."

"Do it," Abeyla said. "Take three with you and go where you think it best. Do not attack until there is no other choice. Once Jax knows where you are, he will come for you, and then we shall have no one left on the outside."

Bertrand nodded and started down the ladder.

"Make sure Tammond is one of the men you take." Abeyla's gaze stayed out toward the sparkling water. "And be careful."

"We will."

Half an hour later, they were in a boat skirting the edge of the cliff.

Tammond stared back at the village as the rower propelled them forward.

"She'll be okay," Maggie said. "Abeyla can take care of herself."

"Better than the rest of us can," Tammond said. "She will stand at the front of the battle and face Jax herself. And now she's sent me away so I can't stand in her place."

Maggie slipped her hand into Tammond's, grateful when he squeezed it tight instead of pushing her away.

The boat gave a dull *thump* as it knocked into the rocks. They had stopped beyond the steep cliffs. Here the rocks were broken, and boulders had piled up, giving them a way to climb. Bertrand was the first out of the boat, quickly scaling the rocks to make way for the next.

Selna, a woman with dark hair and deep brown eyes, followed him. Then Giles, a young man with broad shoulders who looked as though he could row the whole village himself. Tammond took Maggie's hand, helping her balance as she climbed out of the boat.

"Lamil," Tammond turned to the older man who had rowed them past the cliffs. "You go with them. I'll row the boat back to the village."

Lamil smiled sadly and shook his head. "Abeyla has given orders. You are to go with Bertrand. I am to stay behind."

"But you're a good fighter," Tammond said, standing resolute in the boat. "You fought Jax when he set fire to the lake. You should be on the cliffs. You'll be able to see what Jax is doing. You'll know better when to strike."

"Abeyla has given her orders," Lamil repeated. "Abeyla is our leader, and you will follow her commands."

"It is my place to protect her," Tammond said, desperation creeping into his voice.

"Tammond," Maggie said, "we aren't going to the cliffs because we aren't going to fight. We *will* fight. We only need to wait until the time is right."

"But if Jax attacks Abeyla, how will I help her from the top of a cliff?" Tammond rounded on her.

"You won't," Bertrand said. "It will be up to those near her to fight by her side. But we will play our part. We will fight. And I promise you, our chances of death in glorious battle are just as great as those who stay behind."

"And we have the worse job," Maggie said. "We have to be strong enough to watch and wait for the right time." Sickness twisted Maggie's stomach, knowing how terrible that wait would be.

28

The rocks dug into her scabbed palms as they climbed the mountain. The ridge-line, which had sloped gently down to the lake, became steeper the closer they got to the overhang. Boulders were replaced by smaller rocks that slid under their feet with every step, and for the last twenty minutes of the climb, they had needed to use their hands to steady and pull themselves up.

Sweat dripped down Maggie's back by the time she managed to drag herself, panting, up onto the top of the mountain. She rolled onto her back, catching her breath and staring up at the bright blue sky. Everything was peaceful and calm. Not a storm cloud in sight. No hint that danger would find them by dawn.

"It really is beautiful here," Maggie said as Tammond crawled up next to her.

"It is." Tammond rubbed the dirt from his hands onto his pants. "I'm told it's one of the most beautiful places in all of Malina."

"Perhaps when this is all over, you will be sent into Malina as a Wanderer and will be able to see which parts of Malina are most beautiful for yourself." Bertrand was already on his feet, standing thirty feet away, staring over the edge of the overhang.

The cliff was one solid piece of stone without a crack or imperfection, just as they had seen from below. Forty feet behind was a stand of trees whose roots had penetrated the rock, finding a way to survive on top of the mountain. Maggie tried not to think of how deep into the rock the roots might reach as she stood and joined Bertrand, walking carefully toward the edge.

There was no sign of the village below. No hint they were even standing on an overhang. From the top, it looked like a normal cliff leading down toward the water. Maggie's head spun from the height, and she stumbled back.

Tammond wrapped an arm around her waist.

"Careful," he murmured as he, too, looked down toward the village. "We won't be able to see what's happening below, only Jax's approach."

"And you're sure he'll come from the front?" Maggie asked, already knowing the answer as she surveyed the land. The only way to attack the village was from dead ahead.

"We know where he'll come from," Selna said. "We just don't know what he'll bring with him."

"Right." Maggie lowered herself carefully to sit at the edge of the cliff, her feet dangling over the water more than two hundred feet below. "So, we sit here and wait for something to happen."

Tammond sat beside Maggie, pressing his right palm forward. The air in front of them shimmered and thickened, blurring the lake for a moment before the world came back into focus.

"They won't be able to see us then?" Bertrand knelt and poked the air in front of the cliff, which seemed to bow at his touch.

Tammond shook his head.

"We should start watches," Selna said. "They aren't supposed to be here until morning."

"And you trust that?" Giles asked, his hands on his hips and his eyes narrowed.

"Not even a bit," Selna said, "but when they do come, we'll need to be as rested as possible. I'll take first watch. You all go sleep."

"Two at a time." Bertrand settled himself on the cliff. "I'll watch with you."

"Thanks," Maggie said, grateful for Tammond taking her hands as she stood up, her head swimming from fatigue and the height of the cliff.

Tammond led her to a patch of shade under a tree not far from the ledge. Maggie wished for a bed, but shade and hard rocks would have to do.

"I can take first watch, Selna," Giles said, still looking threatening.

"Rest, Giles," Selna said. "When the battle begins, I won't let you miss it."

Giles paused for a moment, looking as though he wanted to argue, before walking twenty feet away and lying down in the sun.

"Selna won't sleep," Tammond said as he stretched out on the rocks next to Maggie. "Not with Mina in the dark place."

"Is Mina her daughter?"

Tammond nodded.

Maggie had known the big brown eyes looked familiar. "What about Giles?"

Giles lay on the ground, facing the open water. Maggie had no doubt he was watching Jax's path.

"His brother was one of the Wanderers who were sent back out into Malina," Tammond whispered so softly Maggie had to move her face right next to his in order to hear. "His brother was one of the ones who didn't make it back to the Broken Lake. We know Jax took some of them. Tortured them for information. But we don't know if Giles's brother was with them. We don't even know if he's alive or dead. Just gone."

Maggie moved her head onto Tammond's shoulder, reveling in its warmth even in the midday heat.

"His brother might still be out there," Maggie whispered. "He could be a prisoner. He might have wandered so far he forgot to come home. He could have a wife and kids and be a farmer."

"I don't know which would make it worse for Giles." Tammond kissed Maggie's forehead. "Having Jax hurt someone he loved, or having the person he cared for forget to come home."

"Well, when we take Jax down, maybe we can get Giles some answers." Maggie closed her eyes, instantly falling into sleep.

"How was I lucky enough to find someone so brave?" Tammond's words followed her into the darkness.

"*I* see them," Bertrand's voice was sharp and firm, all hints of playful adventure gone.

Maggie was blinking and sitting up before Selna rushed over to her and Tammond. "It's time."

The sun hung low in the sky, coloring the horizon a bright, dazzling red.

"This isn't sunrise." Maggie crept toward the edge of the cliff.

"He's come early." Bertrand's face was dark. He looked older, harder, like a person Maggie had never met before. The adventurer was gone, replaced by a warrior with no fear of blood.

"We thought he would." Tammond crouched at the edge of the cliff, peering out into the distance.

"I'm not surprised by it," Bertrand said, "but it does make me dislike him even more."

Maggie knelt beside Tammond, trying to make her tired eyes focus on what the others were seeing. In the fading light, she glimpsed something near the shore on the far side of the lake. From this distance it looked like an animal swimming quickly out into the water. But trees were moving through the lake, too. A vast stand of trees.

"There are hundreds of them," Selna whispered.

Maggie rubbed her eyes with the heels of her hands before looking back out over the water. The trees that had been moving weren't trees at all, but groups of men standing on rafts that rowed across the lake. And the animal who had swum farthest was a man, standing on a raft only a few feet wide. There was no one on that raft rowing it forward. No sign at all of how the craft moved. But the man glided over the water, floating swiftly toward the village.

"Jax," Maggie said, not needing anyone to tell her she was right.

He had left his men far behind, struggling to catch him as they rowed.

When he was near enough for Maggie to make out his jet-black hair and pale skin, Jax spoke.

"Wanderers," his voice boomed, shaking the cliff under Maggie's feet.

She wanted to run from the edge before it came tumbling down, but something in Jax's voice made her stay.

"Too long have I allowed you to be a stain on the greatness of Malina. Too long have I let you spread fairy stories and lies. I will not permit the blight you have created to spread any further."

A shout rose from the village beneath, but unlike Jax's words, these were muddled.

But Jax seemed to have heard and smiled before he responded. "Would waiting until morning change your fate? My men are trained soldiers, and we outnumber you. You are not fighters. How long did you really expect to survive hiding in your hole?"

"Jax Cayde," Abeyla's voice carried up from the water as she appeared beyond the edge of the overhang. She stood on the front of a boat as Lamil rowed her steadily forward. "You think that's what we've been doing on the Broken Lake all these years? Surviving? We've been thriving, Jax. While you built your walls and trained your armies, we had families. We learned. We built a home. Who has spent their time better, Jax?"

"You've built homes." Jax smiled. "Had children. I gave you the opportunity to allow your children to survive. You denied my offer."

"That evil little—" Selna leaned forward as though readying herself to leap over the edge of the cliff to attack Jax herself.

Bertrand grabbed her arm and pulled her back. "Abeyla is running out of time."

Maggie looked back at the lake. The men on the rafts were catching up to Jax. In a few more minutes, they would be at his side.

"I never trusted your offer, Jax," Abeyla said, a hint of sadness touching her ringing voice. "Such a pity you turned against the Wanderers' calling. You would have been a wonderful teacher."

"I am more than a teacher. I am a master!" Jax spread his arms wide and the water rose up to meet them.

For a moment, he looked like an eagle with unbelievably large wings before the water began to churn. A wave raced forward, striking Abeyla and Lamil's boat, but Abeyla stood calmly on the bow as the boat lurched with the wave.

Tammond leaned in close to Maggie, staring down at his mother.

"A master, Jax Cayde?" Abeyla asked.

Tammond tensed, and Maggie took his hand.

"That is not the way. There is no master of magic." Abeyla stood on the very edge of the boat, balanced perfectly on the thin rail.

"If you truly believe that, then I have much to teach you before I allow your departure from this world." Jax threw his arms forward, and again the water surged toward Abeyla and Lamil. But Abeyla was flying through the air, soaring above the water.

With a guttural cry, white-hot light flew from Abeyla's palms. For a moment, Maggie thought she had missed. The lightning hadn't struck Jax. Instead, it had hit the raft that held him above the water. Instantly, the raft gave a terrible *crack*. Jax swayed for a moment, but stayed upright as the raft caught fire.

Abeyla landed on the water not fifteen feet in front of Jax. Maggie expected her to sink, but Abeyla landed catlike on top of one of Jax's waves, which had frozen in place.

"Fire does not fear fire." Jax waved a hand, and the smoke from the fire disappeared. Flames still lapped at his feet, but his view of Abeyla was unobscured. "I am the one who burned the Broken Lake. Are you so anxious for me to do it again?"

The flames from Jax's raft melted down over the sides. The fire didn't extinguish or even falter as it touched the water. The blaze grew, absorbing the blue of the water and spreading quickly with dancing sapphire flames.

"Jax Cayde," Abeyla said calmly as the fire surged toward her. "You never think that anyone else can learn. You've never seen how magic can grow and evolve if you only let it."

Holding her hands below her mouth as though blowing sand into the wind, Abeyla let out a great breath. The fire in its path flickered as it was pushed back, its blue light fading. But in a moment the fire had grown brighter, flames leaping a foot above the lake.

"It's gone wrong." Maggie's mind raced, trying to find a way to save the village from burning.

"Wait," Tammond whispered.

The flames weren't racing toward Abeyla anymore. They had cascaded in the other direction, toward Jax and his men who were now right behind him.

The men shouted in fear as the fire streaked toward them. A few leapt from their rafts, but in a second the flames had engulfed the water around the boats, giving the men no way out.

A handful of the men seemed to be prepared, working magic Maggie could barely see. Shields shimmered around a few of the rafts. One lifted itself out of the lake, hovering out of reach of the flames, while another was now surrounded in a cocoon of water.

But other boats burned. The men on them screaming in fear and pain as the flames surrounded them. Maggie's throat tightened as the smoke scented with burning flesh reached the cliff, but she squinted through the haze to see what Jax was doing.

He wasn't helping his men, hadn't raised a finger to save any of the Enlightened who cried for his aid. He stood, staring at Abeyla.

"You've grown hard in these years," Jax said. "You aren't as squeamish as you once were."

"I will do anything to protect my people." Abeyla's words barely cut over the rush of water as a wave twelve feet high soared toward her.

Maggie bit her lips, tasting blood in her mouth as she fought not to scream.

But a spell leapt forward from behind Abeyla. Lamil had joined the fray. A bright purple streak of what seemed like airborne lava flew toward Jax, touching a point above his head and spreading over him, trapping him in its grip. Abeyla emerged from the water, dripping but apparently unhurt.

Two of the rafts had made their way out of the flames and, with a shout, the Enlightened began casting spells toward Abeyla. It was too much, far too much. There were too many for Abeyla to fight on her own. But spells soared from under the overhang as well. The Wanderers had joined the fight.

One of the rafts was hit, and two of the men were tossed overboard. The water around them hardened, leaving the men screaming as their fellows passed over them on their own raft, crushing them to death.

A flock of creatures that looked like water given life flew toward the Enlightened, scratching their eyes and faces, distracting them from casting more spells.

With a scream from Lamil, the water under one of the rafts sloshed into a spin, churning and twisting, sucking the raft under the water. One of the men knelt down on the raft, placing his hand on the deck.

For a split second, the raft rose from the grip of the funnel, but a shattering sound like a thousand glasses breaking shook the air, and the raft fell back into the vortex, disappearing under the water as Jax emerged from his shining purple cage, his eyes glowing with fury.

Before Maggie could take a breath, Jax was raining down spells upon the Wanderers. The remaining Enlightened had rallied by his side and were now pushing forward, toward Abeyla.

Spells flew from the village, too, the flashes of light and terrible smoke so thick, it was impossible to tell what was happening below. It was as though they were looking down on a lightning cloud, knowing there was destruction underneath but without any way to tell what the chaos was.

"We have to get down there," Tammond said, starting for the ridge that led down to the water. "We can't help from up here."

"And what good will you do down there?" Bertrand blocked his path. "We are to stay here. We are the last measure at the end. And listen to them fighting." Shouts echoed up from below, guttural war cries that seemed impossible on the Broken Lake. "They are still pushing back. It is not yet our time."

"They've lost men," Tammond said, shoving Bertrand aside. "We can come at them from behind."

"How?" Bertrand asked, following Tammond. Maggie stood and chased after them. "You have no boat. How will you fight?"

"How will you know if all our people are dying if you can't see?" A mad fury shone in Tammond's eyes. "I won't wait up here blind until it's too late to save anyone. I am going below the smoke so I can see."

He went to the edge of the cliff and began climbing down.

Bertrand looked to Maggie. "Abeyla wanted us to stay here. To wait until the time is right."

"Abeyla wanted her son to be kept alive," Maggie said.

"Follow if you must, Miss Trent," Bertrand said, "but know I will not be there to save you."

"I can save myself, thanks." Maggie walked past him as Tammond disappeared down the ridge.

"What I meant, Miss Trent," Bertrand said, "is do not go looking for the darkness. It seems to like you, and it might not let you go this time. And Miss Trent, I would hate to lose you so soon."

Maggie nodded, a knot tightening in her throat. "Don't you go looking for darkness either. Just because you're old friends doesn't mean he'll let you live."

Not waiting for Bertrand's reply, Maggie followed Tammond down the mountain.

Going down took much less time than climbing up. In a few minutes they were forty feet above the water, beneath the thick blanket of smoke and able to see the battle below. The time the battle had been out of view had made all the difference. The Enlightened had surged forward, moving past Abeyla and Jax, who fought each other head on now, throwing spells with such force the air crackled with the might of their magic.

The fire had disappeared from the surface of the lake. Magic from spells that had missed their marks remained in the water, dancing as vibrant, shimmering lights across the black. It should have been beautiful. But bodies lay in the lake, dark markers that marred the bright magic.

Maggie wouldn't let herself count the bodies or study their clothes to see if they were Enlighted or Wanderer. Nothing could be done to change the fate of the dead.

A horrible *crack* echoed under the overhang as a spell struck the village, splitting it in half. The docks shook, and Wanderers were tossed into the air, some hitting the water, others hitting the hard, wooden dock. Maggie didn't have time to see how many of the Wanderers struggled to their feet.

With a cry of pain, Abeyla fell backward from her tower of water made solid and disappeared into the lake.

For a moment, everything froze, then Jax gave a triumphant laugh.

Maggie clapped her hand over Tammond's mouth before he could shout.

"Stay quiet," Maggie said. "We have to stay quiet or we can't help." Tammond reached to pull her hand away, but she clung on. "I know she's your mom and you want to help her, but we have to be smart. She wants you to be smart."

Jax drifted toward the village. In a minute, he would catch up to the Enlightened, and what chance would the Wanderers have without Abeyla?

Abeyla dead.

Maggie shook the thought from her mind.

"Do you trust me?" She took Tammond by the shoulders, forcing him to look into her eyes.

"I do."

"Then we're going to swim." She took Tammond's hand and pulled him to the very edge of the ridge, hoping she could jump out far enough to clear the rocks. "On three. One, two—"

Her last word was swallowed by a *crack* that blocked all other sound. But she was already jumping, flying farther out over the water than her legs could have carried her without magic. As she fell into the water, she watched the edge of the overhang shatter and plummet toward the lake far below.

The shockwave found her in the water, striking her in the chest and forcing the precious air from her lungs. She clawed her way to the surface, holding tight to Tammond's hand.

She found the air, gasping for breath as Tammond emerged beside her. The rock had been cleaved off in one giant piece, forming a wall between the village and the Enlightened, crushing the attackers who had been underneath. But there were still sounds of fighting within the village. And on this side of the lake were Jax and Lamil.

Lamil stood tall on what was left of his boat, chunks of wood barely stable enough to balance on. He bled from a gash on his chest, gasping as he took shuddering breaths. And nearby, floating facedown in the water, was Abeyla, her gray hair drifting around her head like a shining crown.

"No," Tammond said.

"Get Abeyla," Maggie said. "Get her to shore. I'll go after Jax."

"Maggie, no," Tammond said. "I won't lose you, too."

"Don't worry about me. I have to help Lamil." Maggie kissed him, hoping it wouldn't be the last time. "Meet you in the village."

She turned back toward Jax in time to see a shadow fall from high up on the cliff. A jacket caught in the wind, making it look for a moment as though Bertrand had wings before he disappeared on the far side of the rock barrier.

Two other shadows followed before Maggie took a breath and dove deep under water.

There was no current in the lake. No more shaking from the fallen rock.

Lights streaked overhead, making the water in front of her flicker in the darkness. But swimming forward was easy. In seconds she lost sight of Tammond. But she pushed herself as far as she could before coming up to take a breath. She was close to Jax now. He was still distracted by Lamil. If she could only reach—

A hand closed tight around Maggie's ankle, dragging her down into the lake.

The scream that flew from her throat was muffled by the water. But it didn't matter. Her air was gone. She twisted to see who was pulling her deeper still into the lake. It was one of the Enlightened, his face shining with victory as Maggie struggled. She lunged toward him before kicking hard. She felt her boot hit his face, but still the man didn't loosen his grip.

Her lungs were already screaming. Rage boiled in her. She needed to get away, needed to stop Jax. But her fury held power. Without thought for hurting herself, Maggie let her burning anger go, felt it fly in a white-hot sheet from her body, boiling the water around her.

The man let go of her ankle, and Maggie kicked toward the surface. The burning water didn't hurt her as she swam through it. Her own rage held no power to harm her.

Maggie's head broke through the surface of the water, and she gulped in smoky air. She blinked away the spots in her eyes, desperate to see what was happening around her. Screams came from the village, but the water near her was silent. Lamil knelt in his boat, his right arm hanging limp and useless at his side.

Jax moved toward him, laughing in a mirthless way, not seeming to care that his men still fought in the village.

Maggie swam as silently and quickly as she could toward Jax.

"You could have joined me, Lamil," Jax cooed. "You would have stood by my side, and the Enlightened would have been stronger for it. But then—" Jax looked toward the overhang "—I guess my Enlightened have grown strong enough without you."

"I never would have joined you, Jax," Lamil coughed. "I've never had it in me. I'm not a traitor."

With a scream, Jax raised his hand, ready to strike.

Maggie dove beneath Jax's shattered raft, flipped over in the water, and kicked the wood with every bit of strength she had left. The wood splintered as the impact sent her deep down into the water. Twisting as quickly as she could, she swam back up.

Jax had fallen into the water. She had seen it. Seen him sink for a moment. But by the time she neared the surface, he was already gone.

Maggie kept her head underwater, scanning the lake for a sign of Jax. But there was no shadow. Bodies and splintered bits of wood floated around her, but nothing moved. With no choice left, Maggie surfaced as quietly as she could, taking in a calm breath and looking around.

Jax was there, right in front of her. She forgot to swim for a moment and sank back down below the surface of the water. She could see him now even with the water clouding her vision. Hovering two feet over the lake, Jax stood on a dark cloud that crackled with light. The cloud drew water from the lake, growing larger every moment as Jax again advanced on the village.

Maggie slipped her head into the open air, pressing her hands to the surface of the lake. She shut her eyes tight, hoping against hope her magic would work.

A scream of pain came from nearby, but Maggie didn't dare look.

With more strength than she knew she had, she forced her magic out into the water, forming a solid sheet of ice that reached in every direction. She shivered as the water around her grew cold. The ice expanded, gaining ground every second, crackling and splintering as it surged toward Maggie. Soon the ice would close around her neck. She wouldn't be able to climb to the surface. Letting go of her magic, Maggie punched the ice, not caring as she felt it tear her skin. Before the ice had time to reform, she pushed herself onto its surface.

The spell had done what she'd hoped. The storm Jax rode couldn't pull any more water from the lake. He was slowing down, but not enough. He would still be able to make it to the fallen rock and then to the village beyond.

Jax raised his hands. Maggie could see magic between them, crackling with such force it bent the air. The village wouldn't survive that spell. It would be gone. Everyone gone. The children left in the dark place.

With a guttural scream, Maggie charged toward Jax, all thoughts of magic gone, her only hope to stop his spell. Jax turned to face her, surprise flickering in his eyes for only a moment before his mouth twisted into a hateful smile.

He swept his hand through the air as though choosing a piece of magic to kill her with, but with a scream, Maggie launched herself at him, grabbing him around the middle and tackling him onto the ice.

Pain shot through her arms as they met the ice, but she held on, pushing Jax into the frozen surface. He screamed as the ice pinned down his arms and legs before growing to surround him. Maggie leapt away as the ice engulfed his body in thick, glassy layers, leaving only his face in the open air.

His screams of rage and pain shook Maggie's bones.

He would break out of her spell. He had already broken free of a magical prison once before.

She didn't know a spell to stop him, didn't know how to bind him.

A *clunk* sounded on the ice nearby as Lamil pulled himself out of the shattered boat and ran limping toward Jax. Something silver shimmered in his hand, and the thing grew with every step, becoming as tall as he was with sharp tips on either end.

Before Maggie had time to think, Lamil drove the end of his shimmering staff through the ice, directly into Jax's heart.

A horrible scream rent the night. Blood filled the ice, coloring it red, and Jax's face became a death mask of his anger.

"He's—" Maggie began, searching for the words in the fog of her mind. "He's dead?"

"He is." Lamil lowered himself onto the ice, setting his staff down beside him and clutching his bad arm.

Jax was dead. The night should have gone silent. There was nothing left to fight for. The Master of the Enlighted was gone. But shouts and cries still came from the village.

"Will you be all right?" Maggie asked. She paused only long enough to see Lamil's tired nod before running toward the village.

The sheet of ice she had created reached all the way to the fallen rock. Maggie sprinted toward the village, grateful for her sturdy boots as she leapt onto the stone without stopping.

The ice hadn't gone past the stone barrier. The water on the other side was still liquid, reflecting the fires that burned in the village. Half of the village had sunk and was nearly out of sight. A corner of it had caught on the rocks in the shallow water and clung hopelessly on. The other half of the village was still floating and shrouded in haze from the smoke trapped under what was left of the overhang.

People were shouting and fighting on the nearest dock, but others had fled to the few clusters of rock by the cliff wall. The shadows of the fighters danced in the firelight.

Bertrand was there, fighting two of the Enlightened, his face calm as the air around him pulsated, sending daggers of broken wood at the men. Selna fought, too. She had her attacker on the run and backed up almost to the edge of the dock. Maggie watched as the man toppled into the lake, and Selna hardened the water around him, leaving him to drown. There was another person fighting, lightning blazing from both hands.

Maggie took a deep breath and shouted as loud as she could, "Jax Cayde is dead! The Master of the Enlightened has fallen."

One of the men fighting Bertrand faltered, and wood struck him through the arms, pinning him to the deck with a howl of pain. But the other fought on.

"There are none of your people left alive on the lake." Maggie's voice was louder this time, echoing off the rocks, drowning out the fighters. "The Enlightened have lost the battle. Leave now!"

The other Enlightened Bertrand had been fighting turned and sent a streak of bright red light toward Maggie. She dove to the side, out of the path of the spell. A shout carried across the water as the Enlightened fell.

There were only two left fighting, both of them moving so quickly they hadn't even paused. It wasn't until a bright white spell flew close to his face that Maggie recognized Tammond.

Maggie dove into the water, quickly swam the hundred feet to the village, and climbed onto the dock.

Tammond had the Enlightened backed against a house, but the man wasn't giving up. Screaming, he threw spell after spell at Tammond, who had formed a barrier around himself and pushed his way forward as the spells slammed into his shimmering shield.

Maggie wanted to shout for Tammond to back away so she could help, but she was afraid to distract him for even a moment. But Tammond's shield was faltering. The Enlightened's magic wasn't sliding harmlessly away anymore.

Tammond shouted in pain as one of the spells struck him.

"No!" Maggie screamed, charging forward, but Bertrand was closer.

With a wave of Bertrand's hand, the slats of the house behind the man reached out and grabbed him like a dozen angry arms before the house burst into flames.

Maggie barely heard the screams of the Enlightened as she ran toward Tammond. He fell to the deck, gasping but alive. Blood covered his hands and dripped down his face. A gash on his right side showed the bones beneath.

"Tammond." Maggie pressed her hands to Tammond's side, trying to stop the freely flowing blood. "He needs help! Please someone help!"

"Maggie," Tammond said, her name trembling in his voice. "Maggie."

"You're okay," Maggie whispered. "We won, you're going to be okay."

"Abeyla is gone," Tammond said. "I couldn't save her."

"But she saved you."

Hands moved Maggie's away from the wound as someone began healing Tammond.

"Abeyla wanted you to survive, and you did. She won. Jax is gone, and we're still here."

A dull light emanated from Tammond's side, and he gasped as his skin knit back together.

"The village was destroyed," Tammond said. "Our home is gone."

"You'll rebuild." Maggie held Tammond's hand.

Bertrand knelt by her side now, helping to lay Lamil down. The old man's eyes were half closed, but he was still breathing.

"First, we'll go get the kids," Maggie said, trying with everything she had to keep pain and fear from touching her voice, "then you'll find a new place to build. And none of you will have to be afraid of Jax Cayde ever again."

Tammond's eyes drifted slowly closed. Maggie looked to the woman who had been healing him.

"Let him sleep," the woman said, her voice weak with fatigue. "The village will still be broken when he wakes."

Maggie lay Tammond's hand gently down on the deck. There were still others moaning in pain, and fire still raged through part of the village. Pushing herself to her feet, Maggie started toward the place where the village had cracked in half, but Bertrand laid a hand on her shoulder.

"The Wanderers will put out the fire," Bertrand said, sounding tired for the first time. "We've done enough."

Maggie looked out toward the lake. Shadows danced on the fallen rock, cast by the dimming light of the fires, and beyond the lake was calm and still. The moon and the stars shone down as though nothing had happened.

"There are bodies out there," Maggie said, not feeling afraid of them or even sick at the death that surrounded them. Too much had happened in the last few hours for her to be able to feel much of anything. "We should collect them."

"We should collect the living first," Selna said. Her brown hair had been burned away in patches, and newly healed cuts marked her neck and chest. "As soon as the sun rises, we should go collect the children."

"Mina will be so happy to see you." Maggie nodded. That small movement made her dizzy. "I'll go with you."

"You'll sleep first," Bertrand said.

"Where am I supposed to sleep when the village is shattered and on fire?" Maggie asked as Bertrand took her by the elbow and led her to the far edge of what was left of the village. Most of the Fireside was still standing. Only one wall of books had crumbled into the water. There were injured lined up along one side. Most were already asleep.

"Dawn is in a few hours," Bertrand said. "Rest until then. Once it's light enough, we'll collect the children."

"I shouldn't be sleeping while others are working," Maggie said as Selna guided her to a bare bit of floor. "I should be up working with you."

"Maggie," Selna said, "you fought Jax. You helped us survive. You went into the water alone. You're allowed to be tired. And you"—she turned to Bertrand

—"you rest as well. When the others can't work anymore, then you'll be awake to continue."

The crackling of the fire had stopped. The patients were no longer screaming. The quiet of the village seemed haunting and unnatural. A faint murmur whispered over the sounds of mourning for those who had been lost.

They carried Tammond in and laid him with the other wounded. Maggie walked over, stumbling on the rough wooden floor. They had cleaned the blood from his skin. He looked as though he were ill, like he was coming through a bad fever, not like he had been through a battle.

Maggie lay on the floor beside him. Not touching him, just listening to his even breathing. Counting each inhale and exhale as another moment they had outlived Jax Cayde. Before she made it to fifty, she was asleep.

Maggie woke with a gasp. Someone had touched her foot. Images of Jax rising out of the water flooded her mind, but before she let her magic loose, her gaze found Selna crouching at her feet, pressing a finger over her lips.

"The sun is rising," Selna mouthed.

Maggie nodded. Gray light peered in through the now open wall of the Fireside. She crawled out from beside Tammond. He didn't move as she crept away.

"I'll be right back," Maggie whispered, though she knew he couldn't hear.

Guards had been stationed on top of the fallen rock. They scanned the lake as the sun turned the sky a pale red.

"What are they looking for?" Maggie whispered to Selna.

"Others who might attack." Selna led Maggie into one of five boats that were manned and ready to be rowed toward the children. "Word from the watchers if any of them survived Jax. Just because Jax is dead doesn't mean there are no more dangers in the world."

Maggie nodded silently. She climbed down into the boat and was grateful when Selna passed her a paddle. Bertrand nodded to her from the boat ahead of them as they joined the line rowing out toward the fallen rock.

Each of the boats stopped and had to be carried one at a time up over the stone before being lowered back down on the lake side.

"Can't we move the rock?" Maggie asked, the boat digging into her hands as they carried it.

"Down is much simpler than up," Selna said. "It wouldn't be safe, and it would take more magic than we can give."

They lowered the wooden boat back down on the other side with a gentle splash.

"But then you'll have to rebuild everything," Maggie said. "You won't be able to salvage any..." Maggie's words faded away as she looked out over the lake.

The ice had melted, leaving broken wood and bodies behind. The bodies of the Enlightened drifted across the surface. Carrion birds circled overhead, ready for their morning feast. A boat was already out in the water, collecting the Wanderers who had fallen.

"What are you going to do with the bodies?" Maggie asked, slipping as she stepped back into the boat. The *thud* of her misstep carried out over the water, making the birds cry even louder.

"The Wanderers shall be sent below," Selna said. "The others will be moved out of sight and left for the animals. It would be wrong for us to deny them fresh meat."

Maggie nodded and paddled forward, trying not to wonder where the Enlightened bodies would be left.

Paddling made her arms burn and her hands ache. But there was something comforting in the movement. Feeling the sting and soreness of the night before made it feel more real. She had fought Jax. There had been a great battle. Abeyla was dead, but her son had survived. The Wanderers had survived, and she, Maggie Trent, had helped to make sure of that.

The back of Maggie's throat hardened as she swallowed the tears that threatened to creep up into her eyes.

Before the sun had risen over the highest mountain, they reached the dark place. Maggie paddled into the blackness, closing her eyes and letting her magic lead her. The walls held the same energy she did. She recognized their power, as they recognized hers. Shouts carried from the darkness as the first boat reached the torchlight.

"It's okay. They aren't attacking!"

Maggie recognized the voice of one of the older boys.

"It's our people!"

"Mama!" a voice shrieked. "Mama!"

"Mina!" Selna shouted from the back of the boat.

Maggie opened her eyes as the torchlight came into view.

"Mina, I'm coming!"

Maggie could hear the tears in Selna's voice. Mina jumped up and down the rocky shore, waving her arms wildly over her head. As soon as she saw Selna,

Mina dove into the water, swimming for her mother as only a child raised on the water could. In seconds, she had reached the boat, and Selna scooped her out of the water, cradling the sopping wet child to her chest.

"Mama!" Mina said. "We were so brave. I stood guard and everything."

"I'm proud of you, Mina." Selna pushed the hair away from her daughter's face. "I love you, little fish."

"Mama, can we go home now? I'm very tired, and I can go sleep in my bed."

"Our home was lost in the battle." Selna kissed her daughter on the forehead. "But we will build a new home, and I promise I will find you a safe place to sleep."

Mina stared solemnly at her mother for a moment. "Were people lost with the house?"

"Yes, Mina."

Maggie turned away, her heart breaking at the grief on Selna's face. Some of these children wouldn't have parents or beds to call their own anymore.

"Mama," Mina whispered so softly Maggie could barely hear, "I'm glad I didn't lose you."

The rippling of water from Selna's paddle told Maggie to row forward. Their boat hit the shore with a grinding bump. The last few children climbed onboard, their faces anxious and afraid.

"Selna," the last boy to climb into their boat said, "have you seen my parents? Do you know if..." The boy's words drifted away as though he were afraid saying them might make them more real.

"I don't know," Selna said. "I didn't see them."

The boy nodded as they rowed back out into the darkness.

The way back to the village seemed longer than the way to the dark place. It might have been that Maggie's arms were burning with fatigue or that anticipation stretched every moment.

Maggie held her breath as they started down the long, watery path to the village. More people were standing on the fallen rock now, waving their arms and shouting greetings to the children. The bodies had been taken out of the water, but two men labored by the side of the lake, building a long raft. And next to the raft floated a large boat whose contents were covered by blankets.

How many people could fit in that boat? How many graves would have to be dug?

"Maggie!" Tammond sat on top of the fallen rock. His face was pale and drawn, but he smiled in relief as he saw her. He struggled to his feet as her boat knocked against the side of the rock and, grimacing in pain, reached down to help her up. She took his hand, careful not to put any weight on it as she stepped out of the boat.

"You're awake," Maggie tried to say, but Tammond was kissing her.

"I thought you'd left," he murmured, keeping his forehead pressed to hers.

"I went with Selna to get the kids back."

Tammond kissed her again. "I know. It's just that, with the battle over, I thought you would disappear."

"I wouldn't leave without saying goodbye," Maggie said.

Fear flickered through Tammond's eyes.

"We just had to get them home." Maggie stepped away to look at the children. Most were in the arms of their parents. But for some, there was no one left to wait for them.

"What's going to happen to the orphans?" Maggie's heart dropped as the older boy who had asked after his parents sat on the rock, tears streaming down his cheeks.

"They'll stay with us," Tammond said, lacing his fingers through Maggie's. "Other families in the village will take them in. This is their home. They will not be sent away."

Maggie looked back at the remnants of the village. It looked worse in the daylight. If everyone crowded together, there might be enough buildings left to have some sort of a roof over everyone's heads.

"Lamil wants to begin rebuilding in the morning," Tammond said. "A new home on the Broken Lake."

"Is Lamil in charge now?" Maggie asked.

"He is." Tammond's eyes shone with unshed tears. "Lamil was the one chosen by Abeyla to be the next leader of the Wanderers. And Lamil has chosen me as his second."

More boats paddled from the village to the rock. It seemed like every person who could move was coming toward the lake.

"Now that Jax is gone, the Enlightened will be weakened," Tammond said. "This is the time for the Wanderers to go back into the world. And Lamil"—Tammond paused, taking Maggie's other hand—"Lamil wants me to lead the others out into Malina while he stays here and protects the Wanderers' home."

"Wow," Maggie breathed. "Wow. Isn't that fast? To be sending people out there or making decisions. I mean, the battle just ended."

"The Wanderers have waited twenty-seven years on the Broken Lake. Abeyla"—Tammond's voice faltered—"my mother wouldn't have wanted us to wait a moment longer. Life is much too short to let grief stop you from moving forward."

Maggie nodded, unsure of what to say.

More men had rowed to the raft. It was finished now. All the knots tied tightly. One by one, the men gently lifted the bodies of the fallen Wanderers onto the raft, laying them out in one long line. Maggie's breath caught in her chest as they lifted out Giles right before Abeyla.

Tammond shuddered and stepped in front of Maggie, turning away from gruesome raft.

"I've never seen Malina," Tammond said, his words coming out in a rush, "but I've heard stories about it and seen a hundred maps. There are mountains and a great sea that stretches out to the east. There are a hundred villages. Places neither of us has ever seen before. Along the northern sea, there is a place where the trees are thicker around than the Fireside. Come with me, Maggie, and we'll find the great trees together."

Maggie froze. Her heart couldn't remember how to beat, and forming words was a foreign thing she might never manage again. Finally, instinct kicked in, sucking air into her lungs. "Go with you?"

"We'll teach magic to those who need us, and we'll see the world." Tammond leaned in and kissed her gently. "With you at my side, Maggie Trent, what couldn't we accomplish?"

"I—" Maggie looked into Tammond's bright blue eyes. He had just lost his mother and his home, but he was still filled with so much hope.

"Miss Trent," Bertrand said.

Maggie spun to face him, her face flushing.

"I believe it is time to return to the Siren's Realm."

"Return?" Maggie repeated.

"The battle is won, the children are safely home, the funeral will commence shortly, and what comes next is rebuilding. Rebuilding is for those who will stay for much longer than we are able."

"But we could help," Maggie said as Tammond's grip on her hand tightened. "We could help them teach, help them build a new village. You said you wanted adventure. Aren't there more adventures to be had here?"

Bertrand took a long look around the lake and the mountains. "There most definitely are, Miss Trent. If you wished to explore all the adventures this world has to offer, I would understand. But if you stayed that long, I fear you would never return to the Siren's Realm, and what adventures would you be missing then?"

"Maggie," Tammond said, "please don't go. Stay with me."

Maggie heard her decision in Tammond's plea before she knew she had made it.

"Actually, I have to go." Pain crept into Maggie's chest as she kissed Tammond on the cheek. "You'll travel. You'll see all of Malina, and it will be wonderful."

"But…" Tammond's face crumpled as Maggie stepped away.

"Malina is your home." Maggie pushed the words past the lump in her throat. "But it isn't mine."

"Maggie," Tammond whispered.

"I'm sorry, Tammond," Maggie said softly as she followed Bertrand off the rock and into a waiting boat.

Maggie didn't allow herself one last look at Tammond before she and Bertrand rowed away. She could never come back to visit, not even if she wanted to. The Siren's time didn't work that way.

The last of the bodies had been laid out on the raft. A thick net with stones tied to the edges was being laid over them.

"We should stay for the funeral," Maggie said.

"It is better to leave quickly, and I never stay for the funerals, Miss Trent," Bertrand said. Only the hint of sadness in Bertrand's voice kept Maggie from shouting at him. "And if we want to leave before nightfall, we'll have to paddle rather quickly."

Maggie took deep, shuddering breaths as she pulled the boat forward, not brave enough to look back at the Wanderers standing on the fallen rock. Not wanting to see Tammond's face as she left him forever. She willed herself not to think about Abeyla or what they would do to the raft. She paddled with all her strength, keeping her eyes forward on the Broken Lake.

"I just left behind a guy whose mom just died," Maggie said an hour later. "Is there some special sort of punishment for that?"

"Or course," Bertrand said from the back of the boat. "It's called *remorse*."

"So I should have stayed?"

"Are you in love with him?"

"No." The word sounded hollow even to Maggie's own ears. "I don't know if I'm sure what that would feel like. Maybe I'm not capable of loving anyone."

"You were raised in a cage, Miss Trent. Perhaps you should give yourself a larger taste of freedom before deciding what you're capable of."

"So, I'm not heartless and irredeemable?"

"Not at all, Miss Trent. I was hoping you'd follow me into this world, because I knew you were too great to live only one adventure. And while I would hold no ill will if you had fallen in love and chosen to stay here, I am very grateful you will be with me the next time an unknown enemy attacks."

"So we're going to do this again?" Maggie's heart lifted at the thought.

"Of course, Miss Trent." Bertrand laughed. "I am always looking toward the next adventure."

The sun kissed the tops of the mountains when Bertrand finally told Maggie to stop paddling. She stared up at the silhouette of the summit where she and Bertrand had spent that first cold night.

They sat quietly for a moment before Maggie spoke. "So how do we get home? And please don't say climb back up that mountain."

"I believe," Bertrand said, "and I have been wrong on occasion, we swim down."

"Swim down? But we fell from up." Maggie leaned over the edge of the boat and stared down into the water. There was no glimmer of green or hint of magic.

"Into and out of the Siren's Realm are not like walking through a door, Miss Trent. In and out are not the same thing."

"Swim down, it is." Maggie stood up in the boat. Without hesitating, she took a deep breath and dove down deep into the water, not waiting for Bertrand.

The way into the darkness can never be the same as the way back out.

The cool water pressed in around her, blocking out the sounds from above. With a few strokes, the light dimmed. The pressure made her ears throb, but she kept swimming down. She waited for her breath to run out or for her arms to get too tired to move. But the water seemed thinner.

She pulled against it so easily, it felt as though she were flying. And even as the world turned to black, she stroked forward again and again, moving so quickly the water became nothing. And all at once, light surrounded her, flashing such a bright green she gasped, filling her lungs with crisp air.

Maggie crumpled to the ground, panting and blinking. The green light faded, leaving only the dull blue of twilight.

She rolled onto her back, staring up at the sky. She was in the center of the circle of bright white trees. A dull *thump* warned her Bertrand had landed next to her before she'd turned her head to look. He was on his feet, looking completely calm without a hair out of place.

"Well done, Miss Trent." Bertrand smiled, giving her a little bow. "I must say for your first time, you did much better than I thought you would."

"Thanks." Maggie got to her feet without waiting for a hand from Bertrand. The pain in her arms from rowing had vanished. So had the cuts on her hands and arms from battle. "It's like it never happened." Disappointment crept into Maggie's chest. "It looks like we never left the Siren's Realm at all."

"That is one of the gifts of the Siren—she likes us to enter her realm healthy."

Bertrand led her out of the circle of trees, past the large dead one, the slit in its trunk completely hidden in the falling shadows.

"But then what was the point?" Maggie clenched her fists as her heart started to race. "If we're just the same as when we left, then why did we go through all that?"

"Well, we did help to save the Wanderers from a massacre. We had our adventure, and don't forget, Miss Trent, we returned with a great deal of magic."

Maggie stopped on the spot, tentatively feeling for the magic inside her. It was dampened again, trapped deep within, but it was stronger than it had been since she had fallen into the Siren's Realm. Stronger perhaps than it had been in her life before the Siren's Realm.

Bertrand beamed at her. "There you are, Miss Trent, you saved lives and received your reward. Now the only question is, how will you use it?"

Maggie smiled, her thoughts flying to the rock by the sea. "I know how to start."

"Well then, Miss Trent," Bertrand said, striding toward the edge of the woods, "all that is left is to enjoy our bounty and decide which adventure shall befall us next."

Maggie's journey continues in The Girl Locked With Gold. *Read on for a sneak preview.*

DISCOVER THE STEAMPUNK WORLD OF
HISTEM IN...

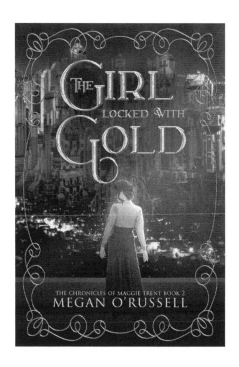

Continue reading for a sneak peek of *The Girl Locked With Gold.*

CHAPTER 1

The weight of the smoke seared her throat as it pressed down into her lungs.

"Ber—" her hacking cough cut off his name. "Bertrand!"

The roar of the flames swallowed her shout.

The world is on fire, and I'll burn with it.

A scream carried down from high above, the voice too shrill to be Bertrand's.

"Hello?" Maggie stumbled toward the sound.

The dense smoke hid the form of whatever landscape burned around her, but the flames danced higher in the direction of the scream, reaching far above Maggie's head with no sign of something she might climb to reach the terrified person.

"I'm coming!" Maggie gagged on a burst of sour smoke. Something in the haze burned her eyes, blurring her vision.

Sparks whirled around her as she swayed, retching black that tore painfully from her throat.

"Bertrand." Her lips formed his name as she fell to her knees.

The heat of the ground burned through her pants, searing her flesh.

"Primurgo." The spell took the last bit of air she had. The shield shimmered to life around her, blocking the waves of smoke, but not the terrible heat of the flames.

Her palms blistered as she pushed herself to her feet, squinting through the smoke.

No figure stumbled toward her. Not Bertrand or even a poor victim of the devastation in this unknown land.

"Bertrand!" Maggie shouted, coughing up more of the black goo. "Bertrand, we have to go!"

A *crack* rent the air, and the ground shook a moment later. Shield or not, they were running out of time.

"Bertrand Wayland, if you've led me to my death—"

"I have not led you to your death, Miss Trent." Bertrand tore out of the darkness, embers licking the tails of his black coat. "Nor have I ever assured your safety."

"Where the hell have you been?" Maggie dropped her shield, and Bertrand grabbed her wrist, dragging her straight toward a tower of fire.

"*Hell* seems a fairly accurate assessment, Miss Trent." Bertrand ducked as a wall of embers collapsed in front of them. Not pausing, he veered around the flames. "It took you so long to arrive, I didn't know if I would be able to wait for you much longer."

"Thanks for not abandoning me." Maggie leapt over a crack in the ground, her toes landing an inch from Bertrand's heels.

"Of course. Now, if you would." With two giant strides, Bertrand plunged into a black pit that consumed the center of the path.

Flat, scorched walls leading to darkness far below were the only details Maggie managed to see before overwhelming nothing consumed her.

The void squeezed every inch of her being. Her lungs couldn't have expanded to pull in air even if there had been any present for her to breathe. A whirling sense like rushing through a vast river tingled her toes, but there was no way to know how fast she moved in the nothing, if she was even moving at all.

As questions she would never get to ask trickled through her mind, a green light flashed into being around her, and pain shot through her knees.

"Ow." Maggie flopped to the side, not caring who might see her lying on the street. "Ow, ow, ow."

"Are you all right, Miss. Trent?" Bertrand hovered over her, silhouetted by the sun.

Maggie took a deep breath, testing her lungs as she rubbed her fingers over her unburnt palms. "No smoke inhalation or third degree burns, so I'd say the Siren worked her magic again."

"Then why are you lying on the ground?"

Maggie shielded her eyes so she could properly see the furrowed lines on Bertrand's brow. His hair was perfectly slicked back in its customary low ponytail. His white shirt and coat tails showed no signs of burns. Even his buckled shoes hadn't been scratched by their brush with fire.

"I'm on the ground because I, unlike perfect you, am not used to jumping back into the Siren's Realm from a land of fiery doom."

"As long as the Siren hasn't decided not to heal all wounds upon entering her realm, I suppose we're all right." Bertrand offered Maggie his hand, helping her to her feet as a gray-speckled centaur rounded the corner.

"How's it going?" Maggie waved, letting an overly-bright smile fill her face.

"As the Siren wills it be done." The centaur nodded and trotted past them without waiting for further conversation.

"Have a nice day." Maggie brushed the dust from the street off her clothes. "So, how long until you find another stitch for us to slip through?"

"Find another stitch?" Bertrand strode down the narrow street, not looking back to see if Maggie followed.

Allowing herself the luxury of rolling her eyes, Maggie trotted after him. "Maybe this time you could find a path out of the Siren's Realm that doesn't lead to Hell."

"The most interesting thing about fire, Miss Trent, is how very temporary it is." Bertrand cut down a wide road lined with tall tents. A gentle wind swayed the colorful fabrics. "Even the worst of blazes will burn out in time. We need only have patience while the flames run their course."

"Wait a second." Maggie dodged around a beautiful woman in red robes to match the tray of wine she carried. "Are you actually saying you want to go back there?"

"Of course, Miss Trent. There are a hundreds, perhaps thousands of tiny stitches joining the Siren's Realm to other worlds. Of all the stitches that exist, the Siren has only allowed us to find a tiny portion. She would not have left a stitch open for us to slip through were there not something interesting and wondrous on the other side. We should not deny ourselves an adventure simply because of a little poor timing."

"You know, that's what I think every time I almost burn to death. As smoke fills my lungs, making it impossible to breathe, *Wow, what a bit of poor timing.*"

"Sarcasm is rarely becoming, Miss Trent."

A wide square opened up in front of them, revealing a platinum fountain flowing in the middle of it all. A statue of a beautiful woman, her nakedness barely concealed by thin fabric, stood at the center of the pool.

A man had climbed up on the edge of the fountain, blocking the crowd from swimming in the sweet liquid. "The Siren's time is shifting away like sand. Her ways are beyond our ken, and times worse than storms are nipping at all of our heels."

"What?" Maggie grabbed Bertrand's sleeve to stop his momentum.

The people in the square were watching the man as he paced the rim of the fountain.

"For in light and peace, there must still come shadows, and it is only the will of the Siren that holds the darkness at bay."

"Let the Siren's will be done," a woman shouted, "and leave us in peace."

A cheer sounded behind the woman, then another.

"Those who do not read the winds shall be eaten by the storm!" the man warned as the crowd surged forward.

"Come along, Miss Trent." Bertrand cut out of the square and down a narrow alley lined with bright red tents.

"Shouldn't we help him?"

A roaring shout sounded from the square.

"Those people could really hurt him," Maggie said.

"A madman who's decided to speak on behalf of the Siren?" Bertrand said. "I don't think there is anything within our power to be done."

A wide lane opened up in front of them. Tables laden with goods from fine silks to fresh baked cakes were open for business. Maggie's stomach turned as a woman shook hands with a silk dealer. Her clothes shimmered for a moment as their colors twisted. Her plain green dress vanished, replaced by a red gown woven through with gold.

Maggie's hands tingled, remembering the feeling of magic zinging through her skin—the shock of it as it left her body in payment for goods, leaving a tiny hole that didn't refill. But if the woman hated the feel of it, her face showed no sign as she gleefully spun in her new gown.

"What do you think they'll do to him?" Maggie averted her eyes as a man paid for a diamond-accented pocket watch.

"I think what the crowd will do to him is the least of that man's concerns." Bertrand kept his voice low as they passed a woman tending a flowerbed filled with bright blue blooms in front of her matching blue tent. "He dares to speak for the Siren. It is never wise to make assumptions of one who provides all that is needed for survival."

"Because you've never tried to tell me how the Siren works?" Maggie whispered.

"I happen to have an uncanny understanding of the Siren and the wisdom to know that sometimes speaking the truth is best done quietly."

The road beneath their feet changed from dirt to cobblestone as they reached the fortress. Weathered and stately houses rose up around them. A lone gondola paddled down the canal, the boatman humming a slow tune. Iron barred windows stared down at them from above, and heavy wooden doors protected against unwanted visitors.

Maggie shuddered at the tingling feeling of dozens of unseen people glaring at her for intruding in this exclusive and intentionally private section of the Siren's Realm.

"I don't think we need waste our time as we wait for the smoke to clear." Bertrand's voice bounced off the stone houses. "You really should work more on your swordplay and hand to hand combat, and this provides an excellent opportunity."

"Remember that time when I was going to live out my days in the Siren's Realm in peace?" Maggie said as Bertrand stopped at a thick wooden door, barely visible beneath the stone overhang of a house. "I was going to fish and live on the rocks by the sea. Enjoy my time not almost dying."

"Let time drift by with nothing to show for it but a bit more wear on your shoes?" Bertrand heaved the wooden door open. The *creak* of the door had become too familiar to startle Maggie. "You would be miserable. If not now, then in a few years."

"Fine." Maggie followed Bertrand into the stone entryway, shoving the wooden door shut behind her and fixing the lock with a dull *clunk*. "But can we both at least agree this morning was not the kind of adventure we want to repeat?"

"But why? Isn't any adventure one survives a worthy undertaking?" Bertrand opened the door at the far end of the tiny, windowless room and strode up the steps to the main house, leaving Maggie barely able to hear his words as she chased him. "We'll give it a few days. By then, the inferno should have died, and slipping into a world of embers should be safe enough. Perhaps we can even discover the source of the blaze."

Bertrand stopped in front of the wide fireplace, lifting a teacup off the mantle and breathing in the sweet steam.

"Unless, of course, you'd like to stay behind and focus on your booming career in the fish trade."

Maggie exhaled, forcing her teeth to unclench. "I'll come with you." She took the second cup from the stone mantle, letting the herbal fragrance melt her frustration. "But only because I don't want you to burn to death."

"How very kind." Bertrand raised his cup to her.

A painting hung above the fireplace. Shadows crept in on either side of the frame with only a dull ray of sunlight peering through at the center. Hints of

THE GIRL WITHOUT MAGIC | 775

texture played in the background, but not enough to decipher what exactly the painting was meant to depict.

"You really should get some new art." Maggie sipped her tea. "Something a bit more cheerful."

"In time." Bertrand nodded. "But I'm still enamored of this piece for now."

Maggie shook her head, not setting her cup down as Bertrand dragged all of the furniture to the bookcase that lined the far wall.

"Would you like to begin with swordplay or boxing?" Bertrand removed his jacket, carefully folding the dark material before draping it on the arm chair.

"Do I want to punch you or try and stab you?" Maggie downed the rest of her tea. "Decisions, decisions."

"Swordplay it is." Bertrand knocked three times on the wall. A panel no more than a foot wide slid aside, revealing two swords and two daggers nestled in red velvet.

"How much magic did the secret compartment cost you?" Maggie asked.

Bertrand grabbed one of the swords, tossing the blade to Maggie.

Maggie caught the hilt and wrapped her fingers around the soft leather.

"I would rather pay the magic to the Siren to keep the blades safe than consider the possibility of weapons ever drifting into the Siren's Realm."

Bertrand lifted the other sword, examining the gleaming blade before bowing to Maggie.

Maggie bowed back, mocking Bertrand, though she knew he wouldn't respond.

"Besides, Miss Trent. We venture out of the Siren's Realm for adventure and riches. What good is bringing more magic into this place if we don't spend it?"

"Touché." Maggie lifted her blade.

"The term is *en garde*." Bertrand lunged, his sword bouncing off Maggie's with a satisfying *ting*.

CHAPTER 2

"Ouch, ouch." Maggie's legs throbbed their fatigue as she scrambled up the rocks by the Endless Sea. "Ouch."

A fine layer of sand coated the rocks, blown up from the stretch of beach where the waves gently lapped at the toes of the residents who preferred to bask in the sun. But the red of evening had begun to take hold of the sky, clearing the beach and leaving Maggie in peace to climb the rocks to her home.

Cracks split the giant stones. Each gap as familiar as the streets she walked every day.

"Learn to fight, Miss Trent," Maggie mumbled as she slid down the edge of an outcropping that hovered over the sea. "It'll be useful, Miss Trent." Blood trickled from the cut on her shoulder. "I'm not just being an ass who wants to jab you with a sword, Miss Trent."

A giant fluke broke through the sparkling water.

"I could just refuse to go with him, Mort," Maggie called to the whale as he lazily rolled in the water. "Tell him I'd rather not jump back into the fiery death world and just wait for the next round."

A plume of water shot into the air.

"I could do it. I could sit this one out. Don't doubt me, Mort. I might prove you wrong."

Maggie turned her back on the Endless Sea and smiled despite the blood on her arm. A tiny, stone house hid nestled on the rock outcropping. There were no seams between the walls and the rocks above and below. Only the thick wooden door and large window with heavy shutters hanging open showed the greatness of the Siren's magic hidden within.

At a touch from her hand, the door swung open. The lamps flickered on before she reached for them, lighting the tiny room with their warm glow. A bed rested in one corner, and a table with one chair in the other. The curving gap where the two rocks that formed the back wall met held her fishing net, a spare fishing net, and three books Bertrand had lent her.

"Home, sweet home."

---

*T*he morning sun hadn't warmed the Endless Sea, but Maggie welcomed the chill on her sore limbs. Catching the fish came easily. The Siren provided plentiful fish in the Endless Sea for anyone who had the will to catch them.

Fill the net, bring the fish to town, sell the fish, purchase supplies, go to Bertrand's, come back home.

Maggie sank under the water, letting the gentle waves lift her hair and sway her limbs.

It had seemed like enough. Before she knew slipping out of the Siren's Realm into other worlds was possible, the routine had seemed like enough. Then having the magic to ask the Siren for her tiny stone house seemed like enough.

Enough is never enough.

Maggie kicked up to the surface, gasping for air.

Fish. That was the first step. Catch the fish, sell the fish...adventure.

Maggie yanked on her boots before her feet had properly dried. Her arms didn't ache as she pulled the net of fish up the rocks. She had done it too many times before.

"You were right, Mort," Maggie turned and shouted to the Endless Sea though the whale was nowhere in sight. "You always are, buddy."

The people on the lanes moved quickly in the mid-morning light, giving Maggie space to haul her net without having to worry about darting around dawdlers.

"Veils for the covering of faces," a woman shouted, her own face draped with a lilac veil. "Worth every drop of magic for a cloth this fine."

"No thanks," Maggie said before the woman took two steps toward her.

"But, my girl—"

Maggie dodged under the woman's arm, knocking her with the net of fish.

A splatter of seawater soaked the front of the woman's gown.

"Sorry." Maggie held one hand up, keeping the other tightly on her net. "I'm so sorry."

"You vagrant, little fish monger." The woman dropped her basket of veils, curling her hands into fists.

"Sorry!" Maggie ran down a narrow alley between two rows of tents.

"I will beat you with your fish, you insolent little Derelict!" The shriek followed Maggie as she weaved through a group of towering trolls and out into the market square.

Heart pounding, Maggie ducked into a sweets stall.

"Do not drip fish on my cakes." The old man who owned the stall wagged a flour-covered finger at her nose.

"No problem." Maggie smiled broadly. "Just looking for a snack. This one is great."

Without truly considering, Maggie lifted a purple circular pastry, holding it in her teeth as she offered her hand to the man for payment. As his flour-covered palm met her sea salt-covered skin, a tingle buzzed in her arm. A shock flew through her, leaving a tiny hole where her magic should have been. The unpleasant feeling lasted only a moment before the man let go.

"Thanks," Maggie murmured through her mouthful of pastry.

The market square was filled with its usual array of shoppers and people watchers. Some moved stall to stall, inspecting the wares though they hardly changed from day to day. Others lounged in the sun, watching the people inspecting the wares that hardly changed from day to day. No one ran into the square looking for the girl who had hit someone with her net of fish, so Maggie headed to the fresh food stalls at the far corner of the square.

The sweet jelly filling of the purple pastry coated Maggie's throat. The taste was something between blueberry and pear, but not quite either. Or maybe both. Good food had never been an expectation at the Academy.

"Mathilda," Maggie called into the shadows behind the counter of her tent. "Mathilda, what sort of fruit is in this?"

Maggie held the pastry out as Mathilda appeared from the shadows, her white mobcap bouncing as she ran toward her.

"It's good, I'm just not sure—"

"Maggie, child, where under the Siren's sun have you been?" Mathilda threw her arms around Maggie, knocking the rest of the pastry to the ground.

"What?" Maggie said as Mathilda took her face in her hands.

"I thought you were dead!" Mathilda grabbed the net from Maggie, tossing the contents on the back table. "Terrible things sweeping through the Siren's Realm, and you decide to just not turn up for a while?"

"What terrible things?"

"I ought to kick you out of my stall and never buy from you again." Mathilda grabbed a knife, lopping the head off a fish.

"Mathilda, what are you talking about?" Maggie leapt aside as Mathilda gutted the fish so enthusiastically, slime spurted from the scales.

"Consistency is important in commerce, and if I can't count on you—"

"Mathilda!" Maggie grabbed Mathilda's knife-wielding hand. "I don't know what you're talking about."

"You don't, do you?" Mathilda looked up to the ceiling of her tent. "Have you been hiding under a rock for the five days you've been gone?"

"Five days?" Maggie balled her hands into fists, tucking them behind her back to hide their shaking.

Five minutes. Maybe ten. That's all we were gone.

"Were you hiding on that rock you call home? Lost track of time?" Mathilda turned back to butchering the fish. "Perhaps it would be better if you lost yourself by the Endless Sea for a while longer."

"Why?"

"I wish I didn't have to be the one to tell you." Mathilda kept her eyes to her task as she spoke. "A sickness has come to the Siren's Realm."

"A sickness?" Maggie rolled the word around in her mouth, searching for a meaning that made sense. "People can't get sick in the Siren's Realm. She keeps all of us healthy."

"She also keeps the sun shining, but that doesn't keep her from bringing the storms."

"What kind of sickness?" Maggie looked out to the shoppers in the square. They were keeping a larger distance between themselves than usual. Diners sat one to a table, not clustered together in groups.

"First heard of it right after the last time I saw you. Man came running into the square, begging for help for his lover who'd taken ill. We all thought he'd gone mad." Mathilda shrugged. "Body was found in the Siren's fountain the next day. Black sores on her skin."

"Someone died? In the Siren's Realm?"

"Stone cold dead." Mathilda accented each word with a chop of her knife. "Folks had quite a time trying to figure out what to do with the body. People have started asking the Siren for protection, but there's no way to know if that's working until it doesn't."

"Have more people gotten sick?" Maggie's mind raced back to all the things she'd touched.

The veil seller, the baker's hand…

"Two more have been buried, but there could be others sick, or dead, and no one's found them."

"That's terrible."

"It is what it is when there's no one in charge to keep things running save the Siren, and she doesn't seem too fussed about it. That's why I thought you were dead. People falling ill, and you just disappearing." Mathilda wiped her forehead with the back of her hand. "Maybe it would be better if you had stayed holed up on your own."

"Is anybody fixing it?" Maggie asked, hating herself for sounding so childish. "I mean, aren't there any doctors in the Siren's Realm?"

"None have come forward." Mathilda wiped her hands before reaching for Maggie. "Do yourself a favor and lie low for a while. I can make do without the fish, and you should have enough magic stored up by now you can ask the Siren to provide for your belly."

"What about you?" Maggie took Mathilda's hand. Her skin itched as Mathilda paid her in magic, but the feeling stayed on her hand like a tight-fitting glove.

"I'll not abandon my shop." Mathilda shook her head. "I don't know if my soul could survive it. I nearly languished to nothing when I lived a life of leisure here, and I don't fancy drooping back into nothing again. I won't risk it. Work is the best way for me."

Maggie took hold of Mathilda's hand again. "Promise you'll be careful and take care of yourself?"

"As the Siren wills it." Mathilda smiled, but the wrinkles around her eyes didn't scrunch up as they should have.

Maggie nodded, her throat too tight to speak.

The weight of the net kept her from tucking her hands behind her back as she walked through the square, carefully avoiding touching anything. A chair pushed out too far into the walkway. A centaur who took up most of the lane.

Heart racing and cheeks flushed, she cut between two tents with their flaps tied tightly shut.

"Don't panic, Maggie Trent, you are fine."

Her heart didn't slow as she weaved deeper into the Textile Town. In a battle, she could defend herself. Even without magic, at least she could see the danger coming toward her and fight for her survival. But with illness…

It could already be on me. It could already be killing me.

"Meat fer sale!" a familiar voice barked in the distance. "Fresh roasted meat fer sale! Don't let yerself get weak with hunger! Good food'll keep the body strong."

"Gabriel!" Maggie shouted from the far end of the street, relief chipping away at her panic.

"I thought you'd still be alive." Gabriel smiled broadly at her, leaning on the side of his cart. "Some I'd think rotting if I didn't see 'em fer a few days when death's come knockin'. But I knew you'd turn up in time."

"I didn't even know anything was happening." Maggie resisted the urge to throw her arms around Gabriel's neck. "I stayed in by the sea for a few days. I only came back into town this morning."

"Probably better if you head back out by the sea." Gabriel handed Maggie a leg of fowl. "I'm not so worried about you gettin' sick, but when people start to panic, it's best to stay out of the way."

"But for how long?" Maggie took Gabriel's hand, still speaking even as he drew magic from her for payment. "A few people have gotten sick, but if whatever this is spreads, it could be a long time before it's over."

"Perhaps. But stayin' safe won't make it move faster or slower. Besides"— Gabriel glanced up and down the empty street—"I think you and I'll come out of this just fine. None of us want to go screamin' about it, but all of them who've fallen with the blackness, they've all had magic. Powerful amounts of it. Maybe they hoarded so much it rotted them from the inside out. But us who come in here with nothing but our boots, none of us has so much as sneezed."

"Is sneezing a symptom?" Maggie asked, a sudden tingle growing in her nose.

"No one knows. Don't think anyone's been found with it who's still able to speak to tell how it started. But us without magic, we'll be just fine. Keep our heads down, keep quiet, and we'll make it to the other side of the Siren's wrath sure as sunrise."

"You think the Siren's killing people because she's mad?" Maggie looked instinctively to the sky as though an angry face would appear to smite her.

"Read that law of the Siren again, girly. No one could wish this hurt on another. It's come from the Siren herself."

"Excuse me," a man with a pink cloth over his mouth spoke from ten feet away. "I'd like to purchase some meat."

"Get on with you. And keep tucked in someplace safe." Gabriel waved Maggie away before speaking to the man. "I've got meat fer you, but yer going to have to touch me to pay me."

Head down, Maggie walked up the lane. A few brave folks still walked through the Textile Town, but the pattern of their movement had a strangeness to it, as though each person were carefully considering who to pass nearest to, checking each face for signs of illness.

That woman looked like she might be ill, or perhaps she'd had too much wine. The young man was hunched over as though fatigue had sapped his will to stand upright.

But I'm hunching, too.

Maggie squared her shoulders, holding her head up high. She wanted to walk home. To curl up in her little stone house and wait for the Siren to end her purge. But if something horrible had found its way into the Siren's Realm, she couldn't just sit back and wait for death to pick people off at will.

"Bertrand Wayland," Maggie whispered to the air. "I want to find Bertrand Wayland."

Tingles flew through Maggie's chest as a little void formed. Closing her eyes, she turned slowly on the spot, tipping her face up to the sky. The sun warmed her skin, beaming its brightness through her eyelids.

How can anything be awful when the sun is shining so brightly?

"Has the blackness taken your mind, child?" a woman snapped.

Maggie gritted her teeth, biting back her retort at being called *child*. "Just looking for someone."

Maggie headed down a wide street, ducking around a woman with a scrap of fabric tied over her face. Tents large enough to house several people sat safely behind long strips of grass. Voices carried through the canvas, but the path was empty.

In the square ahead, groups of people crept past, staring at something Maggie couldn't see, as though unable to look away. Maggie jogged forward, letting her net flop at her side. The Siren's fountain came into view, though Maggie had no idea how the warren of paths had led her there.

The fountain sparkled in the sunlight, but the clusters of people all held back, watching one man who stood on the ledge of the fountain, staring down into the sweet waters. The man turned his face to the side.

Maggie yelped at the awful profile. A long black beak had taken the place of his face, and black gloves covered his hands.

"Bertrand Wayland, what the hell are you doing?"

Order your copy of The Girl Locked with Gold *to continue the story.*

ESCAPE INTO ADVENTURE

Thank you for reading *When Worlds Begin*. If you enjoyed the books, please consider leaving a review to help other readers find Ena's, Nola's, Jacob and Emilia's, and Maggie's stories.

As always, thanks for reading,

Megan O'Russell

Never miss a moment of the magic and romance.

Join the Megan O'Russell readers community to stay up to date on all the action by visiting https://www.meganorussell.com/book-signup.

ABOUT THE AUTHOR

 Megan O'Russell is the author of several Young Adult series that invite readers to escape into worlds of adventure. From *Girl of Glass*, which blends dystopian darkness with the heart-pounding danger of vampires, to *Ena of Ilbrea*, which draws readers into an epic world of magic and assassins.

With the *Girl of Glass* series, *The Tethering* series, *The Chronicles of Maggie Trent*, *The Tale of Bryant Adams*, the *Ena of Ilbrea* series, and several more projects planned for 2020, there are always exciting new books on the horizon. To be the first to hear about new releases, free short stories, and giveaways, sign up for Megan's newsletter by visiting the following:

https://www.meganorussell.com/book-signup.

Originally from Upstate New York, Megan is a professional musical theatre performer whose work has taken her across North America. Her chronic wanderlust has led her from Alaska to Thailand and many places in between. Wanting to travel has fostered Megan's love of books that allow her to visit countless new worlds from her favorite reading nook. Megan is also a lyricist and playwright. Information on her theatrical works can be found at Russell-Compositions.com.

She would be thrilled to chat with you on Facebook or Twitter @Megan-ORussell, elated if you'd visit her website MeganORussell.com, and over the moon if you'd like the pictures of her adventures on Instagram @ORus-sellMegan.

ALSO BY MEGAN O'RUSSELL

Guilds of Ilbrea

Inker and Crown

Made in the USA
Monee, IL
09 December 2020